CADILLAC
PLATOON

A Vietnam War Novel

E. LAWRENCE ADAMS

Hellgate Press   Ashland, Oregon

CADILLAC PLATOON

Published by Hellgate Press
(An imprint of L&R Publishing, LLC)
Hellgate Press
PO Box 3531
Ashland, OR 97520
email: sales@hellgatepress.com

Cover & Interior Design: L. Redding

ISBN: 978-1-55571-984-5

Printed and bound in the United States of America
First edition 10 9 8 7 6 5 4 3 2 1

To my father for his help and encouragement;
to my son, Seth, for his persistence;
to Paul, my boyhood friend, for a thumbs up;
and to Jane for her endless patience.

PART 1
THE SOJOURN

CHAPTER 1

July 1968

HANK KIRBY SHIVERED. A brisk, chill wind cut through his summer khakis and threatened to capture his dark green, overseas cap. A forbidding California fog swirled about him, illuminated in the night by soft blue lights on the runway beyond the waiting Boeing 707.

He and the others had been herded here on the tarmac moments ago. It should have been a straight shot from terminal to plane, but this was the Army, and it required at least one hurry-up-and-wait. He milled around with the other men, glancing over at the plane ever so often. He could feel it staring back at him, its cockpit eyes colder than the wind.

He shivered again with a feeling of uneasy anticipation.

"OK, you guys move out!" barked a major acting like a sergeant. A single line came together and plodded forward.

"Wait! Hold up again," the major shouted, and like a concertina, they bunched up before regaining their distance, and played another chorus of hurry-up-and-wait.

Finally, they were moving again; this time for real as Hank hurried up the step ramp, a part of the procession, knowing he was amid disciplined lemmings, their demise the plane's entryway.

It was not long before they were quietly seated, listening to a stewardess monotoning safety procedures as she fashioned the latest in life jacket apparel. A sign flashed on: "Fasten your seat belts. No smoking."

Hank braced himself.

The huge aircraft taxied to the runway, turned slowly ninety degrees, and stopped. Revving jets whistled to a fever pitch, obliterating all other sounds, disturbing personal thoughts, and then with a sudden lurch the plane accelerated down the tarmac. It angled up and headed into a black void.

From window seat 26A, Hank observed over the heads of his fellow passengers the stewardesses going about their duties. A sandwich snack was hurriedly distributed. Sleep then spread throughout the plane.

After a while, one small reading light came on and kept Hank's section from darkness. His buddy, Dick Kistler, was deeply engrossed in examining the new issue of *Playboy*.

He almost nudged him to turn the light off. But didn't. It wasn't the light that bothered him. It was the silence. Catalytically, it surfaced his thoughts.

Once again, his mind turned to Pam and the moments in time they had been together. He turned to those moments often, choosing different ones to evoke different feelings, like turning to favorite poems in a favorite book of poetry. It was time now to read the first poem again. And later, for he knew he had plenty of time on this flight, he would read the last poem.

He had planned to go home that fall weekend of his senior year at the University of Florida, but he hadn't. No reason to. His home had gone. Three days before, his parents had separated and were planning to divorce. It wasn't too shocking, as he had suspected it for some time. Still, it didn't sit well; so he had decided to stay in Gainesville for the weekend and brood privately by himself.

And so he found himself guzzling Rebel Yell from a soggy Dixie cup, leaning in a corner alone, and observing his frantic fraternity brothers and their dates wildly dancing in celebration of the afternoon's football victory. He didn't really like where he was, but had no place else to go. After all, this house was where he lived, and being near the partying gave him the excuse he wanted to drink his bourbon and get plastered.

The rock band blared on. Amplified guitars stung his ears. Then the band suddenly stopped. Dave Watson entered. Last year's All SEC; and this year's potential All American fullback, Watson was a key provider of the day's victory. A rousing cheer went up, followed by eager clapping and clinched fists slugging the air. It was a great honor of the house to have Dave stop by like a visiting head of state.

His private corner offering him the anonymity he wanted, Hank eschewed participation in the hero worship. Instead his eyes fixed on the girl whose arm wrapped with Dave's. She was quite lovely, about five-six, with delicate features and the long, flowing brownish-blonde hair of a surfer girl. The body of one too. She wore a light, salmon-colored sweater and blue jeans that hugged a shapely buttocks and long legs. Her hair was fresh and clean like fine silk, parted in the middle, and framed a face of defined cheek bones, blue-gray eyes, and spontaneous smile with deep-set dimples.

Hank poured more bourbon. His usual shyness ebbed. Finally, he looked around the room. She stood alone, waiting for Dave's return from a pit stop.

He made his move, plowed through a flood of gyrating bodies, and looked down on blue-gray eyes. They held a mischievous twinkle. And more…He could lose himself in those eyes.

"Would…would you like to dance?" his voice cracked.

She glanced around for some sign of Dave, then looked up. "Sure."

Abruptly, the band stopped. There was an awkward moment as they stared at each other, the reason for their togetherness ending with the music. Then it started in again with "When a Man Loves a Woman." A slow one. They edged out into a mass of slowly swaying bodies. Her hand went into his; her body pressed in. His right arm went behind her, and he realized he still held his soggy Dixie cup. He held it away from her, feeling doltish, but recognizing he owed much thanks to this cup and its contents.

When he met Pam Sadler, he started his book of poetry.

Dick's light was still on.

Hank shifted his position and rearranged his small pillow between his seat and the window. He forced his head, neck bent and crooked, on the pillow. His eyes glanced at the window and he saw his reflection. A wistful smile stretched across his lips.

It had not been the Rebel Yell responsible for calling her the day after, though it had played a role in acquiring her phone number. And then, after subsequent phone calls and quickie meetings between classes and then weekend dates, he and Pam began enjoying one another. More so, they decided in the spring, than anyone else. Something special had magically clicked between them. He had defied all the basic laws of probability theory: he wasn't a football hero, wasn't anything at all important on campus, only a serious civil engineering major specializing in sanitary engineering, with all the attendant ridicule from his fraternity brothers of wanting to make a living out of shit.

It was the spring, too, when she completely stopped dating Dave Watson, and when he met her parents and realized her father hated him as much as his fraternity brothers said Dave hated him. And the reason her father hated him, Pam said, was because her father liked football heroes like Dave Watson.

It was also the spring when he became concerned about the summer and their being apart, and about the fall when she would be starting her senior year, and so would Dave, and they still would be apart.

The Army had come between them, separating them. As a freshman in 1963, thanks to parental prodding, he had enrolled in ROTC. "Better to go in as an officer, then to be drafted as a private," Hank's memory quoted his father. "As an Army officer you'll learn leadership and responsibility that would take ten years to learn in a civilian job," was another one. His father's advice had sounded better in 1963 than it did now.

"Hey Hank, fasten your seat belt," Dick elbowed him while placing his *Playboy* in the seat pocket. "we're landing."

Hank momentarily put his thoughts aside. "Yeah. OK," he responded. He became aware of a jerking vibration as the wing flaps adjusted to slow their progress. "When we get airborne again, better lay off the magazine and get some sleep. It's not going to do any good getting horny where we're headed."

"Oh, yeah? I wouldn't be too sure of that," Dick quipped slyly.

Once on the ground Hank was anxious to take off again. He was exhausted and wanted sleep. He didn't disembark with the others to stretch the legs, work out kinks, and try to glimpse Hawaii from an air terminal. He waited where he was, searching for sleep, though afraid to find it and be awakened minutes later by the commotion of the returning.

Soon they were soaring again. The interior became enshrouded in darkness. Dick had followed his advice and turned out the light.

Hank slept fitfully, his rest marked with constant stirring and shifting and dreaming that he wasn't really on this flight. That he was only dreaming he was.

"Your breakfast, sir."

He gave a startled jump. A honey-haired stewardess was addressing him. She leaned toward him and thrust a tray of sausage and scrambled eggs in front of his face. Hank took it and she strode back up the aisle.

Dick poked him with his elbow. "She must be infantry," he commented.

"Why's that?" Hank muttered as he tried to clear the cobwebs of a sleepy stupor while placing his breakfast on his tray table. He could see that others around him had been served sometime ago. Honey-hair had let him sleep.

"Her hips. Didn't you see them? They said 'follow me.' That's our motto, you know."

Hank laughed. The sharp edge of tension momentarily dulled for the first time since the flight's beginning. "Go ahead," he urged. "All she has is a pair of hips. Evidently, you didn't catch the rest."

"Don't want the rest. Just her ass," Dick chortled. "Those swaying cheeks are two pistons in slow motion."

Hank smiled and bit into a sausage patty.

Dick drained his coffee, picked up his dinner tray, and shoved it across the chest of the staff sergeant on his right and into the path of the passing stewardess. Already overburdened with discards, she stooped low and let him place it on top.

He put up his table and stretched his big, muscular legs. "Damn my ass aches," he complained. "This sittin' is killing it. How did I luck out with this damn middle seat? I bet I've got the biggest ass of anyone on board." He waited for a reply from Hank. None coming, he said: "Stop worrying my friend. Things could be worse."

"How do you know I'm worrying?" Hank asked through a mouthful of eggs.

"I've known you long enough to know."

Hank nodded as he swallowed his last bite and then washed it down with orange juice. "A year ago this month, at Benning, seems long enough. And things could be worse, I guess," Hank conceded. "It's good we're still together. After we wound up at Gordon, I' d thought that would be it."

"We had some good times there, didn't we?"

"Yeah. Kind of crowded in the apartment, though…rooming with the whoremaster of Augusta, who tried to screw anything in a skirt. Oh, as you were on that…not tried…*did*."

While at Fort Gordon they had shared a two bedroom apartment in Augusta, Georgia. It was an old five-story fire trap, but had the hottest swing spot, the Pheasant Inn, in town in its basement. That was where Dick did much of his woman hunting or "beaver-trapping" as he called it.

"Well you should've joined me. Not my fault your girl was still in school. And not my fault you didn't take advantage that she *was* still in school. Besides, you were too caught up in your battalion's social affairs. Right, Edith?"

"Fuck you, Kistler. You know that shit bothered me."

And it still did. His neck pricked as the unsavory episode momentarily clouded his mind. At one instant he' d been getting his ass chewed out by his heel-locking Battalion commander. The lieutenant colonel, an ex-mess sergeant before somehow getting a commission, had pulled one of his classic pop inspections of the company mess hall for which Hank, as mess officer, was responsible. The mess hall had failed; it was in shambles with greasy plates, dirty floor, and cold, weak coffee, sabotaged by two PFC cooks from Harlem who were having morale problems with their white, Alabama mess sergeant. The colonel, in a loud, clipped voice, had asked Hank what he was going to do about the mess in the mess hall. Hank couldn't hold back. He told the colonel his solution: send the mess sergeant to OCS. The colonel had no appreciation of Hank's dry wit and began screaming, his halitosis breath being more than sufficient punishment for Hank's transgressions.

Then suddenly the screaming stopped, and none too soon, because Hank was about to retch. Then in the next breath the colonel became strangely conciliatory and reminded him of the monthly Battalion party, a boorish, sticky affair for which there was no excuse for being absent, except maybe death.

That night at the party, the colonel had greeted him with fulsome warmth, "Well, how is everything, Lieutenant Kirby? Hope you're enjoying yourself." Before he could get out a word, the colonel went on. "By the way, I have my sister-in-law visiting for the weekend and I know she would be delighted to dance with you. Oh, here she is now." Half turning, and as if on cue, there, standing beside him, was the sister-in-law. "Oh Edith, I was just talking about you. Lieutenant Kirby here said that he didn't know any girls here and would love to dance with someone. Would you care to accommodate him?"

So he had to maneuver some dame around the dance floor, who was twice his age, built like a steamroller, and just as hard to steer. Some sister, some law, yet that seemed typical of this man's Army.

The following week he received a written reprimand from the colonel for his remark in the mess hall. The colonel had said his offense had bordered on insubordination and an Article 15, which was one step below a Summary Court Martial. But in light of his recent conciliatory behavior, he was only receiving the reprimand which would be a permanent record in his 201 File. His so-called "conciliatory behavior" Hank took to mean that Edith had enjoyed a favorable moment with him at the party, and had so informed the colonel.

"Maybe the reason we're still together is that we've got the same career pattern." Dick's voice broke through the dark clouds in Hank's head. "If a two-year obligation's a career. The Army being so fucking alphabetical, Kirby followed by Kistler."

"Let's hope it stays that way," Hank said, nodding in agreement, though knowing it wasn't the real reason they were still together. And knowing Dick knew it too. He liked the fact they were together. He hated the reason.

The seed of the reason had started during their Fort Gordon duty. It had begun with an idea of Dick's, and it was taken to a misjudged fruition—*this trip together*—because they had taken the idea to a plan and from there to implementation.

Dick had included Hank in this idea, this plan, because of their unique bond of friendship, born at Fort Benning, Georgia, the so-called home of the infantry, and their home at Infantry Officers Basic Course IOBC. This school for freshman lieutenants consisted of a strange conglomeration of civilian university ROTC gung-ho, give-a-shits, who didn't get a regular commission and get into the more exclusive, RA (Regular Army) infantry course, and of the don't give-a-shits from ROTC military schools such as VMI, The Citadel, Norwich, and Texas A& M who had decided at their particular institution they didn't want to be RA with an additional year obligation, and hence were exiled to IOBC, or some other reserve officers combat arms school.

Dick's classification was of the ROTC military school, don't give-a-shit, VMI class of '67. Hank was a "Gator," University of Florida, class of '67 and he was an anomaly—a Gator out of the swamp. He was *not* a gung ho, give-a-shit. There were other IOBC anomalies too, to be sure, but they were few and none more so than he who held a BS Degree in civil engineering, sanitary option. He knew he belonged in the Army's Medical Service, where he could ensure that troops were supplied with safe drinking water having a high free chlorine residual, and that their slit trenches were well limed at the end of the day.

At the least he belonged in the Army's Corps of Engineers, or so he told his ROTC instructor. The same captain who had read him his reporting orders that spring of his senior year as he was sitting in the auditorium of the military science building. He had been staring out at the tall Washingtonian palms, oblivious to the fact that it was his name they were talking about, the one who had to report in July to the "Home of the Infantry." Later in the captain's office, after Hank had given his side, the captain had impatiently explained that the Army was often like a great big lottery in assigning individuals to slots and that was one reason, said the captain, that he was here at Florida, instructing fuck-heads like Hank, rather than at the Point with the "Cream of the Crop."

Dick was right, though, on one point. The Army *was* alphabetical. And that was the reason they *had* been together, starting that first day at IOBC when Kirby found himself next to Kistler in ranks in the quadrangle of the huge BOQ that reminded Hank of a big Gainesville dorm. The alphabet had been responsible for them rooming together, but it was a meshing of two different personalities like teeth into gears in a precision fit that had led to their unbreakable friendship.

Dick was liberal arts; Hank engineering. Dick was a ladies' man; Hank was a one-lady man. Dick was an extrovert; Hank an introvert. Dick was confident, about six-four, powerful build, and a leader.

Hank was a worrier, about six feet, lean and slight of build, and though not a follower, also not a leader, more of a stand-on-the-sidelines-and-watch-the-others-go-about-their-business type, observing their business, but aloofly not wanting to be part of it. But like magnets of opposite poles, they had attracted, and in Dick the gator had found a swamp.

Again, maybe the alphabet acted. After graduation from IOBC they both received orders to Fort Gordon. Hank had had another duty station in mind, though—Fort Sam Houston, home of the medical service. He had made formal application while at Benning for a branch transfer, giving the Army a second chance to right a wrong, to take full advantage of his specialized education, at one-third the pay if his engineering services were bid on the open job market. But requests in the Army take time, he knew, and so he had been content for the moment to remain with Dick and await his transfer.

With regard to their Fort Gordon duty assignments Dick was lucky; Hank was unlucky. Dick was a rifle range instructor for the M-14 rifle, a rifle whose place in the Army was now limited to rifle ranges. Basic trainees were taught to fire a rifle where the only place it was being used was the rifle range where it was being taught. Dick rose early in the morning, and knocked off in early afternoon, calling it a week on Friday.

Hank was a training officer for a basic training company of raw recruits. He rose early, too, with Dick. And spent his day purportedly pushing troops, but in reality, spent it having his CO, Captain Filbert, watch him watch his master sergeant, Sergeant Lee, watch his drill instructors watch the trainees do calisthenics, airborne shuffle, eat breakfast, fire weapons, choke on tear gas, eat dinner, play the spirit of the bayonet with padded pugil sticks, and eat supper. And sometimes late at night his CO watched him watch Sergeant Lee watch the DIs watch the trainees crawl under barbed wire and live machine gun fire. They watched that one from a distance. They even did their watching every Saturday morning. And Saturday afternoon he had to watch his colonel, his CO, and other training officers of the Battalion fatuously roll dice for drinks at the Officers Club. And when Hank wasn't watching, he was doing his other duties: XO, mess officer, supply officer, and every other kind of company officer except CO, for he was the only other officer in the company.

In doing his training officer duties, he forgot everything he was supposed to learn at IOBC. To make amends for this shortcoming, the Army had recently sent him and Dick and a contingent of other infantry officers to a two-week refresher course in the jungles of the Canal Zone in Panama. There they learned the esoterics of jungle fighting: avoiding venomous snakes, making a hammock sleeping shelter, getting sniped at by some spec-four with a BB gun, eating monkey meat, or, in Hank's case, not eating.

But the real reason they were together now, elbow-to-elbow, on this 707, had begun one night in their apartment in Augusta. Dick's idea had been the reason, and later, because of it, Hank sadly learned that Dick was sometimes unlucky too.

It began at the zenith of Hank's so far dismal Army career, as he and Dick celebrated the glorious victory of the day. It had all started when the colonel selected Hank's company of basic trainees to represent the Battalion in the annual, single elimination flag football tournament. The selection was made by the roll of the dice at the Saturday afternoon mandatory social hour at the Officers Club. On behalf of the company, Captain Filbert graciously accepted this honor to win one for the colonel and the everlasting glory of the 1st Brigade, 2nd Battalion, Basic Training Charlie Company, and he promptly turned to Hank, raised his mug of beer, and appointed Hank to the position of head coach.

For a training company to win just one game was considered a tremendous accomplishment since the competition consisted of veteran units who fielded veteran teams, some having practiced and played together with no more player personnel changes than an established college team. With this experience factor the veteran teams were more like pro teams when up against a basic training team, which in comparison was more like a college team that prohibited athletic scholarships.

But Hank's team did win one. And they won two. And three, four, five. And as an afternoon prelude to the evening of celebration, they won six. And the championship of the entire Post. First time ever for a basic training company. And it was the first time the colonel had praised Hank for a job well done. And Hank had bathed in this praise, a proud peacock with colorful feathers spread for everyone to see. He wished Pam had been there to see him. He wished her dad had been there too, to see his success on the gridiron. Dave Watson couldn't have done better, maybe not even if he had played. For he was only one man and the game of football was not a one-man sport.

And that was the reason Hank didn't want to spread his feathers for very long. For he was only one man, and though he could perhaps consider himself the architect of victory, he wasn't the decisive factor, which had been a combination of things, such as Dick Kistler, an all-Southern Conference linebacker at VMI, who had been the assistant coach and had devised the plays and the drills necessary to execute the plays. And such as having a quarterback who had been a small college All American and who was on the abbreviated, six-month National Guard program to avoid the draft and hence be able to play pro baseball with the Yankees' farm system. And such as having two PFC cooks from Harlem masquerading as basic trainees that didn't let their skirmishes with the bigoted mess sergeant interfere with their ability to run sub-ten hundred-yard dashes and catch passes with hands so sure they could've been soaking them in taffy during their cooking duties. And having big, mean farm boys who had decided that flag or no flag, no one, especially some pansy spec-four, or buck sergeant, was going to get past them to interfere with their quarterback going long to one of the PFC cooks who had given them double servings of the mess sergeant's blueberry pie.

No, it had not been only Hank. He had admitted that fact to Dick over and over in inebriated slurs that evening of celebration in their apartment, as they sat slumped in threadbare armchairs, looking out over a darkened gravel, potholed parking lot and rusted iron fire escape, drinking one can after another of Black Label. Dick had not listened, though. He had been formulating in his head the ill-fated idea. The reason they were still together.

Dick had belched first and then announced how great life was and how much he enjoyed fucking. He spoke quietly to the parking lot and fire escape, his stocking feet propped up on the window sill. A brisk November wind stirred outside lending a sense of coziness to the moment. Hank leaned closer to catch his words. Dick then said he didn't want to go to *that* place. And it was time to do something about it. So far, they had five months in the Army, out of a twenty-four-month total active obligation. In another six months or so they would be going to *that* place unless they did something about it.

Hank considered reminding Dick that he was ahead of him, that he had applied for a branch transfer and if granted would increase his chances of not going to *that* place, or if he went to *that* place, he would be spending his time removing the shit rather than stepping in it if he stayed in infantry. But he decided not to remind Dick. Maybe Dick had something better.

Dick had belched again, pausing for effect; then began a flowing discourse of his idea. It was all very simple. He would merely use his connections at the Pentagon and have orders cut for the two of them for duty in Germany. That was not a bad duty station. They would like it and they would stay together.

Hank began to laugh, but held back. He had a strange feeling Dick was serious.

He was. He explained that his alma mater, VMI, had special status in the Army. More so really than West Point, though few people knew it and even fewer admitted it. And it was because of George C. Marshall, VMI class of '01, the "general's general," the top ranker in WW 2, Ike's boss and Mac's boss. It was his influence, Dick proclaimed, that was still prevalent in the Pentagon, though he had been dead for some time. And this influence and VMI's special camaraderie among fellow alumni—Brother Rats he called them—would allow Dick to call in the chits and get them both to Germany.

Hank had said nothing. He had many times listened to the beer talking for Dick. He had forgotten the conversation until a month later when Dick informed him he had an appointment at the Pentagon with General Druig, VMI class of '39. During their trip up there the following month in Dick's dilapidated Edsel, Hank had become a believer by listening to Dick's constant, infectious banter about how they were pulling it off.

Dick had talked to the general in private and was equally excited and positive on the trip back. Not even the engine block cracking at night outside of Florence, South Carolina, dampened his spirits. Nor when, after abandoning the Edsel along Highway 301, two girls had picked them up and led them on a motorized snipe hunt, dropping them off at midnight on a lonely country road, saying they were going to take them all the way to Augusta after checking in first with their parents, and never returning.

It was an extra day getting back, but they didn't care. Dick had pulled it off. Hank was even more elated and buoyant than Dick and gave his Mona Lisa smile to the colonel who chewed his fanny for reporting back to the Battalion a day late.

They remained floating in a fantasy world for a month. Hank had called Pam at Gainesville, telling her that he would be going to Germany. Would it be possible for her to go too?

At the end of the month their bubble popped, bayoneted by General Druig, VMI class of '39. In a letter to Dick, typed on official Pentagon stationery, the general admonished Dick for making a cowardly attempt to evade his duty to his country. VMI didn't pull strings to weasel out of *that* place. If there was string pulling to do, it was to *go* to *that* place. *that* place needed VMI men and VMI men needed to serve their country in the finest tradition in *that* place. Because of this, and because it was really best for Dick, he was personally seeing to it that Dick would surely go to *that* place. In fact, orders were now in the process of being cut which would assign Dick, after his Fort Gordon tour and two-week refresher course at Jungle School in Panama, to the First Infantry Division, the Big Red One, in *that* place. And by the way, the general had said, since they were fellow VMI men, and hence in the best tradition of the Brother Rat spirit, he was seeing to it that his friend, Lieutenant Kirby, would be going with him to the Big Red One. The general had used his influence; they would be together.

They were devastated. They were going to the Big Red One. They had certainly gotten a big one, all right—right up the ass.

A month later, Hank heard about his transfer request to the Medical Service. In light of his special education, it was being given favorable consideration, but they could not act at this time since orders were being cut for him to go to *that* place in his present MOS (Military Occupation Specialty) of 1542 (Infantry Platoon Leader). Upon his return from *that* place he could re-apply with excellent possibilities of getting his transfer.

But after *that* place it would be two years in the Army, and Hank would be out and available to the civilian world at full market value.

It was almost a month after hearing the status of his transfer that he and Dick got their orders. The last half of June would be Panama. A great many months beyond would be *that* place.

The talking had long since ended. Dick was back to his *Playboy*. He was now in the window seat, Hank in the middle, having switched seats after relieving their bladders.

Hank twisted uncomfortably. Army remembrances gave him an uneasy feeling. Enough of the bullshit, think the good thoughts, he commanded himself.

It was time to read the last poem, the best one. His happiest, saddest moment emerged before his eyes. The short hiatus between Panama and now.

His last night with Pam.

They finished their dinner at a steak house in Cocoa Beach, then a quick eighteen holes at a nearby Putt-Putt, followed by the movie, *The Graduate*. It was Hank's third time seeing it, catching it twice in Augusta, once with Dick, once by himself. This time his mind had not absorbed it. There was something else going on inside his head; the forecasted scenario that would follow the movie.

They drove in his '62 Ford Galaxy to a favorite parking spot, north of Canaveral Pier and up against the beach. There was privacy here.

Hank's car converted to his own secluded beach bungalow as his feet pushed the front seat all the way back. A quarter moon and bright, winking stars looked through the windshield. Surf rolled and crashed, its sound a special music.

They moved to the middle of the front seat and embraced. Then kissed. Their lips full and moist; their tongues taking turns searching and probing;

their eyes closed. And Hank trembled like never before, with nervous anticipation and excitement, realizing that this special night had finally come, their last night together for a year—their first making love, complete love.

It would have surprised Dick to know that Hank had not yet made love to Pam. Dick naturally assumed any couple going together over a week was shacking up. And after his periodic five-day leaves to Gainesville to see Pam in the interim of a new training cycle of raw recruits, Dick would always welcome him back to the apartment with a knowing smile and bemused side glances.

It would have surprised his fraternity brothers, too. They had had the same knowing smile and side glances when he would return to the house after an evening date with Pam. After all, they surely mused, wasn't she a former Dave Watson babe? Didn't girls have trouble keeping off their backs with Dave? Didn't Dave always confirm this trouble they had?

It surprised Hank as well. Because they loved each other. And for the same reason it would have surprised his fraternity brothers. After all, Pam *had* dated Dave for almost a year. It was this knowledge that had eaten at the insides of him like hydrofluoric acid for the one year and eight months he had known Pam. This knowledge and the fact that what Dave may have done, he had not. Though he had tried; though maybe not too assertively. Once her hands became barriers, he became obedient. Disappointed, frustrated, hurt, but still obedient. He would wait for her to want him.

Tonight she would want him.

Their kissing continued. Their bodies clamped tightly together, becoming one. Their passion moved them past previous limits, almost to completion… until she became rigid and started crying.

"What's wrong?" he asked in a voice wanting to sound soft and tender in an effort to hide his disappointment, hurt, and anger.

"Not this way, Hank. It's not the way I want it," she sobbed.

He pulled her hands down and aided by the quarter moon and starlight, looked into her eyes. They were frightened. "I love you," he said.

"I love you, too."

"Then why not?"

"Because it's not the way it should be, though I want it to be."

It made no sense to Hank. "Even though you love me and tomorrow I'm going away. For a year." He wanted to add "maybe a lifetime," the thought of that possibility sticking in his throat. The possibility seemed too unreal, here in this car with the one he cared for more than anything else in the world.

She reached out and pulled him close. Her arms hugged and cuddled his head. Her cheek rubbed his. "When you come back, let's don't wait. Let's get married right away. Maybe a month or two to plan things. Then let's do it. How about an August wedding?"

He was stunned. Sure, they had discussed marriage before. Yet it was always in a nebulous, distant way. The Army and *that* place standing in the way, forcing their plans to be discussed conceptually, excluding any real details. Now, here was a detail, something real and tangible. It was a substitute for making love this evening, a special evening, but it was a worthy one. He would take it.

"Pam, will you marry me in August of 1969?" he asked formally.

"Yes, Hank. I'll marry you in August of 1969."

"Promise?"

She laughed. Her teary eyes smiled. "Yes. I promise."

They began kissing again, more gently than before, with less passion.

Suddenly it occurred to him that Pam was a virgin. Somehow, she had avoided Dave Watson's moves. And this knowledge made his frustrations palatable. And she had promised to marry him in August of next year.

"Hey, Hank, can you believe this?" Dick's loud voice stirred him from his reflections. "They're setting up a screen…looks like we're gonna see a flick." He pulled the shade across the portal to help darken the interior.

"Maybe it's an Army training film," Hank muttered indifferently.

"I'll be…a Charlton Heston movie!" Dick said with excitement. "Hell, we must be booked on the wrong flight."

"Doubt if we' d be that lucky."

Quiet settled. Many for a brief moment forgot their destination and watched the movie. After an intermission for the stewardesses to serve food, the movie continued. It ended just before the pilot announced they would be landing shortly to refuel at Kadena Air Force Base, Okinawa, where they could stretch before they began their last leg.

The plane was once again airborne, on an almost westerly course. Inside, an apparent change had transformed the travelers back to their behavior at the start of the journey. There was little talking or reading; some tried sleeping, most merely sat back and stared into space.

The plane glided above fluffy white clouds. The cloud cover broke into white patches and blue appeared below.

After a few hours, the blue disappeared, and dark splotches of land came underneath. The pilot's deep, resonant voice sliced the tense air. "We are now approximately twenty minutes outside Bien Hoa Air Base, Republic of Vietnam." Bits of nervous laughter rang out only to be swallowed by an awesome silence.

A clammy sweat filtered to the surface of Hank's palms as he fastened his seat belt.

The aircraft descended.

It banked left to make its final approach and dipped smoothly as the hot pavement seemed to rise up in welcome.

CHAPTER 2

S TAGGERING SLIGHTLY, FRED Sadler negotiated the one step to his front door. His legs throbbed with a sharp arthritic pain. Twelve brutal hours of solid standing, sorting mail at the local post office had set his legs on fire. The overtime was hardly worth the money and agony; though it was worth the excuse it gave him to go to Bernie's Bar and Grill afterward to eat some supper, wind down, and shoot the shit with some of his cronies. Besides, a few brews would help ease his pain. He had tried to relieve more than a little pain. *He had closed the place down!* And now he suffered no pain except for the conflagration that still raged in the joints of his knees and ankles, which now had spread down to his toes and up to his groin. Thank God he had tomorrow off; getting up at 5:00 a.m. with only about three hours sleep would kill him.

He exhaled a long sigh of relief at finally being home, fumbled a little inserting the key, opened the door, and entered his three-bedroom, two-bath, Florida block home.

Anybody awake?" He called out, surprised to see a light on.

"I am, Daddy. Mom's sleeping." Pam Sadler answered, the sound of her voice coming from the direction of the source of light.

He limped across the living room, stopping by the kitchen to get a little more pain reliever, a bottle of Pabst Blue Ribbon, and then headed for the small den. As he entered, he observed his only offspring curled up on a small sofa illuminated by the solitary end table lamp. She wore a beige terrycloth robe and her bare legs were tucked up beside her. Her head was bent forward, spilling a fall of shiny hair down her shoulders. She was engrossed in writing a letter. Five handwritten pages lay next to her feet, and her lap held a piece of powder blue stationery, supported by the latest issue of *Glamour* magazine.

He dropped heavily into a rocking chair and faced her. She acknowledged him with a smile, but kept her head down as she busily scrawled. While she did, he let himself admire his daughter. She was the most beautiful thing alive. Instead of having his squat frame, beak nose, and drooping jowls, she had her mother's lithe frame, cute nose with a little upturn, and high cheek bones. Her hair was hers alone, though. Her mother had not been that perfect. His daughter was. She was meant to have the world at her feet. She deserved the very best. Something he had never attained for her mother.

"You're home late," Pam said as she continued to write.

"Couldn't get out of Bernie's. Every time I got up to leave, someone would order me another round or start tellin' some joke I didn't want to miss."

Pam didn't comment. She kept on moving her ballpoint pen across the page.

"And how 'bout you?" he questioned. "It's way past midnight and here you are by yourself, doing something that looks like work."

"I couldn't sleep. Had to do this."

"And what's this? Are you writing a letter or a novel?" he asked and smiled at his humor.

"It's a letter. I don't think I'm the Margaret Mitchell type," Pam chuckled softly and didn't miss a stroke of her pen.

"To who?"

"It's to Hank."

"Hank!" He raised his voice and his eyebrows. His jaw fell. The smile faded. His joints in his legs throbbed, his breathing became faster. "What the hell for? He just left the other day. You can't even have an address."

Pam now looked up from her writing. Her expression turned from thoughtful to drawn. She didn't feel as if she had to explain. "I don't," she said softly, "I'll have to wait until he sends me one before I can mail it."

"Swell, I can't see why you're writing him already. Seems like you've said everything you could possibly say while he was here."

Her first impulse was to take refuge in her bedroom, away from the impending conversation. But she thought better of it and decided to weather it once more. "I miss him. I've got to do something and this makes me feel close to him. Like…like I'm talking to him. Like my thoughts are with him in some sort of spiritual way."

Fred Sadler pushed back in his rocker, took a long swallow of beer, and then stared up at the pool of light on the ceiling. "Uh-huh," he belched as he seemed to be inspecting the plaster. "Seems to me you ought to be spending time with Dave Watson, not thinking about Hank. You know Dave's reporting soon to the Miami Dolphins rookie camp. He's a third-round draft choice. He's gotta good shot at making the team. Especially with the Dolphins. They need all the help they can get."

"We've been through it before, Daddy." Pam tried to keep her voice steady. Why couldn't her father understand her feelings? "Dave and I are through," she told him. "He knows how I feel about Hank."

"Then why does he still call?"

"Dave isn't the type that can take no for an answer. He's always had his own way; so he keeps buggin' me, thinking I'll come around and see the so-called 'light.'"

"I keep thinkin' that, too," he sighed remorsefully. "You've got a football star, who'll make a ton of lettuce as a pro, he's nuts about you, and you can't give 'em the time of day. Instead, you think you're hooked on a guy that studied to be a garbage man. Christ! Hasn't my daughter learned anything?"

"Hank's not a garbage man!" Pam protested. "Can't you realize that? He specialized in sanitary engineering. He's an engineer, not a garbage man. Why can't you like him? Why do you have to cut him down?"

Her tone upset him. He gulped down a sizable portion of Blue Ribbon, gasped, then sucked in a lungful of air, and exhaled a reply. "I've tried, Pam. He's not what I want for a son-in-law. He hates to hunt. Fishin's not his bag. I don't even think the guy likes football, if you can believe that. That's almost un-American. We got nothin' in common."

Pam grew irritable. "How about what I want, what your daughter wants? Hank's a very sensitive person. He's extremely intelligent, too. He doesn't like hunting and that sort of thing because he's the conservationist type. He'd rather see an animal alive than dead. And believe me, the world needs more of his kind."

"Uh-huh," he grunted. "If that's the case, he should've burned his draft card with the other slimy cowards instead of ending up on his way to Vietnam."

"He didn't want to go in the Army," she said, disregarding the remark about coward. "His father pushed him into ROTC and he got obligated. He tried to transfer to the Medical Service but they wouldn't let him."

Fred Sadler's lips curled maliciously. "His old man probably made him take Rotcee to make a man out of him. That I can see. Too bad he's not going to a real war like your dad was in. Don't forget, Pam, I was in the Marines and served on Guadalcanal. Now, that was a Goddamn war," he stated proudly.

"I thought you were in a support unit that didn't get in the fighting." Pam shot back. Her words frosted.

The remark caught him off guard. His jowls started quivering slightly and his eyes narrowed into slits. Pam looked away. She had seen this expression too many times before and hated it.

"There was fighting! It was ten times worse than those guys fightin' them VC," he said defensively. "We had it rough like everyone else. Your Hank will have it easy compared to the stuff most of us leathernecks went through. If he gets a Purple Heart, it'll be from some VD he'll pick up in a Saigon bar."

"That's not true!" she shouted back. Tears filled her eyes and she trembled noticeably. "Everything you've said is not true. People are dying over there. Can't you understand that? I may never see him again!"

At this outbreak, he stormed up from his chair, setting it madly in motion. He couldn't reason with her. She didn't know what a real war was all about. Hank wouldn't either. *At least he was out of the picture for a year,* Fred thought as he stomped from the room. That would be time enough to get Pam to "see the light," as Dave termed it.

Alone in the room, an empty chair rocking slowly back and forth, Pam held her tear streaked cheeks in her hands. She felt overwhelmed with loneliness. The gap between Pam and her father was tearing wider. She wiped the wetness from her palms on her robe and picked up the pen. She stared at the stationery in her lap, and saw Hank's face among her words.

His physical features were handsome. His brown hair, a shade darker than her own, was parted neatly on the left and he wore it shorter than what the students were now wearing in Gainesville. Still, it was a longer length than what was Army regulation. His complexion tanned a deep brown in the summer sun and the contrast highlighted straight white teeth when he favored her with his broad smile. Then there were his dark eyes. That was his real beauty, because they transcended his physical features. His eyes showed his true self, the inside of him, the warmth, the friendliness, the humor, the compassion, and the love. His eyes also betrayed the fear that she shared with him of the year ahead. "A year is such a long time," she said to herself.

CHAPTER 3

THE BOEING 707, a tiny moving speck amidst a massive system of runways, access aprons, helipads, and hangars of all shapes and sizes, taxied to its final destination. Inside there was much commotion as heads jockeyed for position to catch their first glimpse of their new environs.

The honey-haired stewardess with the "follow me" hips hurried to the fore section and spoke into a microphone. "Gentlemen, please remain in your seats until you are instructed to leave the airplane," she instructed them over the intercom.

Slowly, reluctantly, the middle and aisle seat passengers withdrew their faces from the windows and settled down. Then their attention was diverted to the fore section. Honey-hair was opening the forward door. Someone was on the outside, waiting. They watched the door with curiosity.

A young man strode in wearing clean, starched jungle fatigues with a black, first lieutenant's bar on the right collar and a black wheel, the insignia of the transportation branch, on the left. On the back of his head perched an Army-green baseball cap with a black bar on its raised crown. A Colt .45 automatic hung from his right hip in a black leather flap holster. The edge of a clipboard was on the other hip, held fast by the crook of his arm. He looked like a too-young baseball manager in a funny green uniform with ample pockets. His clipboard was the starting lineup for the day's game; the pistol suggested there would be no argument over who was playing.

Honey-hair handed him the mic. "Gentlemen," his voice was soft and steady over the intercom, "I am Lieutenant Blake of the Ninetieth Replacement Battalion in Long Binh. Welcome to Vietnam." His face lacked the emotion of a warm welcome.

Scattered boos followed. Blake ignored them. Two hundred and eleven days ago he had replied the same. He began to rattle off his patented spiel, his eyes hitting a foot above their heads. "When you leave the plane, you'll form six ranks and move to the baggage platform near the terminal. You'll claim your bags and then place them on four trucks to the right of the platform. Officers' bags on the leading truck, enlisted on the other three. From there you'll proceed to the terminal to do initial in-country processing. Then you'll board buses to Long Binh where you'll await assignment to your unit. Officers will board the first bus. Enlisted the last three." His gaze moved to their faces. "OK, gentlemen, you may now depart the plane."

A blast of hot, moist air smacked into Hank as he stepped outside on the platform of the gangway. His cotton khaki uniform fastened to his body like a piece of gauze sticking to a congealing wound. A blinding glare from a merciless tropical sun reflecting off white concrete caused his eyes to squint as he tried to look around before descending. The great air base before him was only hot, white light, as if from an interrogation lamp. He couldn't answer. He didn't know why he was here.

He followed Dick down and into the third rank which had started to form.

Once in ranks Dick began spewing sarcasm out of the side of his mouth. "All through Benning they kept shittin' on us about bunching together and here we are, lined up like rows of corn waitin' to get plowed under by some VC rocket." He paused to spit, nearly connecting on the heels of a major in the second rank. He wasn't fazed at the near hit and went back to fuming. "Now I know why this place is hell. It's so Goddamn hot! Makes the Canal Zone feel like New Hampshire. Bet I could fry an egg on this concrete."

"It might not always be this hot," was Hank's only reply. He knew Dick was rambling from nervousness just as he was reticent for the same reason. His eyes were adjusting to his environment and he was able to look straight ahead with half-closed eyes between the evenly spaced heads of the front ranks. There were about a hundred meters of open airfield and then a huge corrugated roof supported by tall four-by-fours; it looked like part of an old farmers market. It was the passenger terminal, teeming with khaki clad bodies.

Finally, the ranks were full. Lieutenant Blake nodded to his master sergeant nearby, who marched to the front and faced the contingent. He said, "Gentlemen," to first acknowledge his deference to the commissioned officers in the group, then in perfect parade ground resonance issued a "Right face."

There was a sliding of soles and clicking of heels and then a "Forward march." Then after fifty meters a "Column left."

It was not necessary that they keep in step and there was no cadence to help, but for the most part they did.

Hank belonged to the minority that didn't. And he was a minority within a minority as he purposely avoided being in step and even had to skip a few times to avoid accidentally falling in with the majority.

Drawing near the terminal he watched the bodies under the tin roof materialize into faces. Smiling, ebullient faces. Faces going home.

Scattered shouting broke out at the marching incumbents. "Going home! Short! Short! Short!" the faces yelled. A short NCO leaped from the mass, raised his right arm horizontally and began pumping it like a West Point cheerleader at an Army-Navy game. "Three-sixty-five! Come back alive! Three-sixty-five! Come back alive!" he chanted. In unison his chant was picked up and blurted out across the expanse of concrete at the arrivals. "Three-sixty-five! Come back alive…"

"They really make you feel welcome," Dick muttered behind Hank.

Hank swallowed hard, hoping to dislodge the lump clogging his throat. His eyes glanced down to the moving heels before him. His thoughts strayed to Pam.

A half hour later he and Dick sat perspiring in the lead bus. Casually, like a Greyhound tour guide, Blake stood in the front stairwell waiting for the other buses to fill. The steel gratings on the windows contrasted with his casualness.

Stooping his tall frame, Dick walked down the aisle to Blake and began talking. After a minute he finished and returned to his seat beside Hank.

"What was that all about?" Hank asked.

"Nothing much. I asked him how long we'd be at the 90th before going on to our unit."

"What did he say?"

"Said he didn't know. Could vary between a day to two weeks, depending on the backlog they gotta push through."

"I hope it's two weeks."

The bus jerked forward.

The convoy of olive drab buses and deuce-and-a-half trucks steamed out of the air base, leaving in its wake large reefs of barbed concertina wire and grottoes formed by sandbags. In the town of Bien Hoa the convoy mingled with a conglomeration of trudging water buffaloes pulling ox carts, honking beat up trucks, sputtering lambrettas, and weaving motor bikes. Brownish yellow tinged pedestrians in conical hats and simple clothes moved all about in seemingly helter-skelter patterns. The convoy passed a gutted block of stucco ruins, further evidence that all was not right in this strange world.

A block farther, amidst one-story stucco shops in faded pastels, was more evidence; a Vietnamese army compound surrounded by a red brick wall garnished on top with plenty of barbed wire. At its corners, sandbagged .50 caliber machine guns glared flagrantly at passersby. Through rusted iron gates could be seen Vietnamese soldiers, the ARVNS, lazily lounging around inside, outfitted in green T-shirts and fatigue pants. Some slept in hammocks hung from posts or truck bumpers or anything else convenient. Pigs and chickens mingled freely and seemed as much a part of the compound as the ARVNS.

After a short while the convoy turned into a wide entrance road guarded by two MPs. Over the gateway, arched in pieced, wood letters were the words "90th Replacement Bn." Behind it was more than a replacement battalion. There was also the huge military installation of Long Binh with sprawling subdivisions of A-framed dwellings, built by the Corps of Engineers and affectionately labeled "hooches" by their residents.

CHAPTER 4

HERE IS EVERYBODY? Hank wondered, as his eyes wearily surveyed the empty hooch. On either side, he saw ten double bunks shrouded by brown mosquito netting. He dropped his duffel bag as his eyes went around one more time. Then he caught a glimpse of a duffel bag with the big black letters of **LT. RICHARD H. KISTLER** stenciled on its side. It was on a top bunk on the left, about half way down.

He half carried, half dragged his own bag over. He let go of it, pushed the brown netting on the bottom bunk aside and, on bending knees, sank down on a faded, naked mattress. The initial in-country processing at Bien Hoa had been only a warm-up, a form of mental stretching exercise to prepare for the paper work marathon he had just completed. He had finished dead last. By at least four DA—Department of Army—forms.

He rested his head in his palms, supported by elbows on his thighs. The last few hours played in his mind and his thoughts kept coming back to a particular form he had stumbled upon which had caused him to lose momentum.

The form had dealt with the disposition of his Army pay should he be reported MIA, missing in action. It had given him two choices: his pay could continue on a monthly basis to go to either a dependent or his parents; or his pay could accumulate in an interest-bearing account until such time as he was declared legally dead, and then to either a dependent or his parents. At first, he had been afraid to fill in the form, thinking it would be some kind of jinx, the thought of being declared legally dead was too much to think about. He set it aside for a while and went on to other forms, wishing a breeze would sweep it away. But it was still there waiting for him after all the other forms were completed.

He had no dependent. His parents had separate lives now and neither needed his money. If he was MIA he really couldn't give a shit about his bank account and the same would be true if he were legally dead.

There was only Pam. Whatever he could do for her was all he cared about. He got up from his table, looked around the mess hall that now looked like a classroom emptying after holding a final exam, and walked over to a captain in charge of getting the forms filled out. He looked the part, the stern face of an assistant principal, a little older than most captains, probably having been passed over in promotion a few times. Surprisingly, the Army might have fit the right man in the right slot.

He asked this old captain how to fix the form to give his money to his girlfriend. The old captain said he couldn't do that; it was either a dependent or parents; or he could hedge his bet by putting it in an interest-bearing account with the possibility of him being found alive, before it going to either a dependent or parent. He told the captain he was going to marry his girlfriend. The captain said not if you're MIA.

Hank returned to his table, which had emptied. He decided to marry Pam. Now. Today. This minute. He listed Pam Sadler Kirby, his wife, to receive his pay. He didn't know if the Army would really give it to her, but if he were legally dead, he wouldn't be worrying about it.

"Come on Hank!" Dick's booming voice jolted his mind back to the present. "You're running behind. Blake's giving an orientation briefing." Dick's towering silhouette filled the doorway and started coming toward him. He cut an imposing figure in his khaki uniform, from his spit-shined shoes slightly scuffed from the long travel, to his overseas cap angled cockily on the right side of his head. "Cunt cap," soldiers called it, and he had told Hank the Army had fucked up and should have had the cap worn on the face rather than the head. Hank was now thinking Dick would not look so dashing if it were over his face.

As Dick drew near, his second lieutenant's gold bars, one on the front right of his cap, the other on his collar, glinted at Hank. He suddenly wondered. Why did a second lieutenant have gold bars, when a first lieutenant had silver? A first lieutenant outranked a second lieutenant, but did the Army give less value to a "first"? Weren't most lieutenants in Vietnam "first"? Wasn't Hank due to be promoted soon to a "first"? And this promotion was not due to his service record to date for if it were he'd stay a second looie. No, thanks to Vietnam, all seconds made first. It was sort of a backhanded gift, just for being there.

Dick did not like to repeat himself and Hank felt those big, brown eyes boring into him. He looked up.

"Let 'em wait. I've gotta take a dump. It's been two days." Hank grimaced as if he'd swallowed a sour ball.

"Plug it another hour. Let's go. All the officers are there. Maybe we'll hear something important." Dick sounded eager, his spirits better now than they had been at the air terminal.

"I doubt that. But all right," Hank grudgingly consented. "After two days I can plug it a little longer. If not, it'll be a short orientation." He stood up slowly and grunted as he shoved his bag under the bunk with his foot. He followed Dick outside.

They walked along a sparsely graveled path, flanked by a series of wooden A-framed hooches that served as billets. Between the hooches stretched long, tunnel-like bunkers covered by half sections of corrugated metal culverts with layers of sandbags on top. Hank mentally measured which bunker was nearest in case the VC somehow decided to interrupt his walk. They were supposed to be very innovative little bastards, according to Benning.

The path ended at a square, screened-in hut. They went inside, removing their caps. A small audience, the officer contingent of the new arrivals, sat in metal folding chairs, their backs to the door. Above them a lone paddle fan futilely stirred the hot air. Standing in front of the contingent, right arm supported by a podium beside him, left hand grasping a long cue stick-like pointer, was Lieutenant Blake. Behind him loomed a large map of Vietnam. His eyes coldly followed the two late lieutenants to a pair of vacant seats in the last row. More than a few heads turned to see what was happening.

Blake waited for the heads to work back around; then he began. "Gentlemen, my purpose here is three-fold. One, give you a geographical orientation to Vietnam. Two, provide a brief historical overview as to why you're here. And three, provide needed information about the 90th Replacement Battalion."

He looked around the room to make eye contact. "Now, to the geographical orientation. Militarily speaking, the Republic of Vietnam is broken down into four corps. The First Corps is located in the north at the DMZ and the others to the south. The Fourth Corps is the southernmost and is located in the Mekong Delta." He tapped the map with his pointer. "At present, you are here in an area approximately six miles northeast of Saigon in the Third Corps sector…"

As Blake began discussing the history of Vietnam leading to U.S. involvement, Hank's powers of concentration broke down. He'd heard this old song many times before. Sung with the same banal, unimaginative lyrics typical of the Army, to the tune of the KISS principle: Keep It Simple, Stupid. Every Army lesson plan had to have this theme, and every lesson had to be given in three parts, always in three parts: tell them what you're going to say; say it; tell them what you said.

He yawned. He gazed down at his watch. It was 1630 hours. His sphincter was barely holding off a rebellion by his bowels. He told himself to think of something to divert his attention. Think a good thought, a favorite poem… of Pam's secret places he had recently explored. He squirmed in his chair and adjusted his pants. A tent began to rise from his lap. At least a part of him showed some life, though that part might as well stay dead for a year. Smiling grimly, the chant he heard back at the airfield started in his head and grew louder and louder and louder. "Three-sixty-five, come back alive; three-sixty-five, COME BACK ALIVE; THREE-SIXTY-FIVE, COME BACK ALIVE."

"…As for the latrine, it's located fifty meters behind here." The word "latrine" snapped Hank back to Blake's presentation. "The officer's mess," Blake continued, "is across the road behind the officer's club."

"When your orders have been processed, your assignment will be posted on the bulletin board outside the orderly room. Some of you have orders that have been cut for a specific unit. Be advised that you may not get that unit. Uncle Sam has the right to change his mind. If for whatever reason other units have higher priorities for replacements, you may be reassigned."

The two lieutenants in the rear of the audience exchanged glances. Could the general be wrong? Could they have been screwed twice? First by the general, second by the Army itself? Would he be going to I Corps and Dick to IV Corps? Inexplicably, Hank now wanted to go to the Big Red One. With Dick.

"In closing, I would like to define what is meant by the alert signs posted throughout the area. Gray alert means enemy situation not critical and the possibility of enemy attack not likely. Yellow alert is cautionary and signifies that an enemy attack, either rocket, mortar, or ground, may happen. Red alert means that an enemy attack is either imminent or in progress. If a Red alert occurs, go to the nearest bunker and remain there until the all clear is given. Are there any questions?"

Blake looked around at a patchwork of faces. Seeing no raised hands, he cleared his throat. In the gravely tone of military authority he remarked: "Gentlemen, it's chow time."

There was a sliding of chairs and shuffling of feet as the men broke up and began to file out. Two lieutenants in the rear watched the procession go by before standing.

The two moved near the door and faced each other. "Don't worry, Hank," Dick said, "The general said the Big Red One. He got us this far, didn't he?" Dick laughed.

Hank didn't. The general *had* gotten them this far.

Dick slapped his flat belly with both hands and started rubbing vigorously. "I'm due for a good feed. Let's head for the mess hall."

"I'll meet you there. I've got to find that latrine. Save me a seat, OK?" Hank replied.

"Sure, just don't get lost."

Hank followed a narrow dirt path down a slight incline between a hooch and a long, narrow bunker. The path wound behind the bunker. The heavy, humid air became putrid. He had found the latrine.

Hank sat on his bunk, his face once again in his hands. He was alone in the dim light; outside the sun was dying. The others were somewhere else, looking for any sort of activity, waiting for a movie to start, or browsing through the small PX, or playing pool in the rec room. Or at the Officers' Club, awash in drink and talk. That was where Dick was. And where he would be going once he wrote Pam a letter.

He wore his Stateside fatigues, the decree dictating they change out of khakis being disseminated during their supper. No longer was he dressed as an arrival. Nor was he dressed as a native in comfortable, loose fitting, multi-pocketed jungle fatigues. Rather he wore his stifling, sticky, stateside fatigues.

He reached under his bunk, head between his legs, and extracted some wrinkled, plain stationery and a ballpoint pen from his duffel bag. He stood up, rifled Dick's duffel bag until he found the *Playboy*, and sat back down. He lay on his stomach on his bunk, bunched a pillow under his chest, and angled the paper to catch the little natural light still available, the magazine underneath for support.

His mind searched for words.

My darling Pam,

Just a brief letter to let you know I've arrived safely. I miss you very, very, much. Right now, I'm at Long Binh awaiting orders.

The living conditions aren't the best and the climate is the worst. But I'm safe. You wouldn't even know there was a war going on if it weren't for the sandbags and bunkers everywhere.

I love you more than ever. Please keep on loving me. Without your love, I couldn't make it. You are the carrot, the golden ring, the prize at the end of all this.

As yet I don't have a return address, but as soon as I'm permanently assigned to a unit, I'll let you know.

All my love,

Hank

He knew the words were grossly inadequate. If only he had an ounce of Shakespeare's eloquence.

He followed Dick's directions to the mail drop outside the orderly room. Having listened attentively to Lieutenant Blake's orientation briefing, Dick was his fountain of knowledge.

The letter mailed, he set off on the bearings Dick had given him for the Officer's Club. As he walked in the dark of early evening, a warm, gentle breeze brushed his face. On the distant horizon above the dark shapes of tin roofs, yellow flashes pulsated, followed seconds later by low, clipped rumbles. He first mistook them for heat lightning, but of a form unfamiliar to him. Then he realized it must be salvos from a far away Artillery Battery.

His skin bristled. Somewhere out there something was happening. Those shells weren't landing on a firing range at Fort Benning with keep-out, no tres-passing signs. Those shells could be killing someone, or saving someone, or both. It didn't seem to make a lot of sense. Especially right now, on his way to partake of a few brews after sending a poor excuse for a love letter to Pam.

He shrugged off his jitters and entered the club.

It was air-conditioned, offering a refreshing respite from the heat outside. And was dark, with thick clouds of tobacco smoke, and filled with blaring noise from a juke box. A din of voices shouted to be heard above the Stones', who couldn't "get no satisfaction." He squinted, and finally his eyes adjusted. Dick was gesturing to him from an occupied table in a far corner.

He made his way over, zigzagging past packed tables littered with beer bottles and overflowing ashtrays.

"Here, Hank. Have a seat," Dick invited, as he grappled with a chair beside him. From the look in his eyes, Hank calculated Dick's current consumption to be about four or five beers. His eyes were like a barometer when he drank, getting wider and wider, and he was capable of much more consumption before the barometer registered gale force.

Hank sat down, straddling a table leg, and looked around at the three other lieutenants at the square table. Two wore stateside fatigues, like himself; the other was weighted with combat decorations above the left breast pocket on his khaki shirt.

"Hank, this is Sam Johnson. Sam, the lucky ass, is going home tomorrow."

Hank reached across Dick and shook hands with a redheaded, freckled-face artillery officer.

"Hell," Dick rambled on in his usual beer-induced loquacious manner, "Sam's so short, it's a wonder he can reach his beer without standing on his chair." This brought a few chuckles from the other two lieutenants. Their collar insignias said one was a quartermaster and the other, transportation. Dick was in a gregarious mood. One would think he was surrounded by old drinking buddies, instead of men he just met.

Hank stretched his arm across the table to shake hands with the quartermaster, then turned to his right for transportation. His eyes then turned back to Lieutenant Johnson. "You must feel pretty good about going home," he said, trying to sound friendly, hoping to disguise his envy.

As Johnson grinned, the freckles on his cheeks pushed together and it looked like he had two big birth marks. "Damn right. Feels great," he answered emphatically with a Jersey accent. He pounded a half-filled bottle of beer on the table as if beating a drum. Then his smile faded, his eyes narrowed, his drum beat stopped. Somberly he said, "This past year was the longest, fucking year of my life. I feel thirty-four instead of twenty-four."

"See much action?" the transportation officer asked, eying Johnson's two rows of ribbons through the bottle top lenses of his drab standard Army issue glasses. Hank identified one ribbon as a Bronze Star with "V" for valor, another as a Purple Heart.

"Enough. I was an FO with the First Cav in I Corps…during Tet."

"How was Tet? Heard it was pretty shitty," the quartermaster eagerly joined the interrogation.

Johnson sucked deep on a cigarette. He stared at the center of the table and blew out a long stream of smoke. Not wanting to miss a word, the others leaned in. "It was a fucking nightmare. Nobody was safe, not even the remfs." He looked up and around at his audience, their faces showing puzzlement. "Know what a remf is?" They shook their heads in unison. He shifted penetrating eyes to the quartermaster, then to the transportation lieutenant, and then back to the table. "It's a rear echelon motherfucker." He paused, gulped some beer, and let his definition sink in, letting the two in question know who and what they were before continuing.

"The VC attacked about every town and city of significance. One of my OCS classmates with the Ninth said they leveled city blocks in Saigon to root them out. The VC would go into buildings, drag the poor people out, and shoot them point blank in the street. Up in Hue, it was the same. Fortunately, my company didn't have to fight in the cities but we kept plenty busy screwin' with the NVA in the boonies. We messed with so many NVA, it was like being outside of Hanoi."

"Lootenant want drink?" Johnson's narrative was broken by a high-pitched, singsong voice over Hank's right shoulder. He twisted in his chair and looked up at a lean, amber-skinned girl with long, thin black hair and a pretty face. A split purple tunic hung down her front and back to about mid-thigh and black silk pajama bottoms showed between the splits. She was looking at Hank. He returned the look, staring into dark, slanted eyes.

"Uh…yeah, I'll… I'll have a beer… a Bud," Hank stammered nervously as he spoke to his first Vietnamese.

"Hey, Girl-San! Get all my friends another round," Johnson yelled across the table. He noticed Hank's uneasiness and when she left he leaned over and said, "Don't worry, buddy. You'll get used to them."

"I'd like to get used to that one," Dick bellowed with a huge lascivious grin and banged his beer bottle on the table. "She's not bad, not bad at all. Say Sam, what's a GI's sex life like over here? I've heard all kinds of wild stories about the ladies of Saigon."

Lieutenant Johnson smiled crookedly. "Don't know nothin' about Saigon, but enlisted men don't have much trouble gettin' it most any place. I've seen men manning listening posts at a fire support base banging a few from a nearby village. 'Course the EM's don't have much trouble catchin' the bull-headed clap either. Officers generally are more discrete, but in most cities you can find a mama-san madam with a bevy of choice ass and sometimes you find a nice set of tits too. Vung Tau's your best bet. That's the in-country R and R center."

The bargirl returned with their drinks. Johnson leaned to one side and pulled out his wallet from a back pocket. "I need to get rid of this MPC. Every time I fool with this military script, I think I'm playing Monopoly. Thank God tomorrow I'll cash in this stuff for some crispy new U S of A greenbacks." He stuffed some bills into her hand and waved her off with a flick of his wrist.

The juke box went from fast rock to a slow ballad, "Unchained Melody." The Righteous Brothers, complaining that "Time goes by so slowly…" pre-cipitated a momentary lull in the conversation. The lyrics mesmerized Hank, carrying him like light through a lens, arriving at a focal point thousands of miles away…Pam.

The song ended and the spell broke. Hank took a few long swallows of his beer. He wiped his upper lip with the back of his hand and renewed the questioning. "Did you get the Purple Heart during Tet?"

"Yeah. But let's leave it at that," was Johnson's terse response. Hank looked away; he could barely see the lights of the juke box through the thick smoke. His question had been too personal.

Johnson softened a bit, and continued. "I feel sorry for you infantry guys." His eyes shifted between Hank and Dick just as they had done to the two remfs earlier. "An artillery spotter like me is bad enough but an infantry pla-toon leader over here is about the worst you can be. You're the top of the bottom and the bottom of the top. You get shit from both directions. Not to mention Mr. Victor Charlie tryin' to zap your ass. Platoon leaders are on the VC's most wanted list."

Johnson noticed the lieutenant who had asked about the Purple Heart was starting to turn as gray as the swirling tobacco smoke. "Don't let me scare you, though," he added, looking at the pale lieutenant. "Not all infantry looies are platoon leaders. I knew a few who got good, safe remf jobs."

Hank was feeling queasy. He asked, "What do you think our chances are of landing a safe assignment?" He gulped more beer to wet his throat.

"Christ, that's impossible to answer. Depends on where the goddamn Army needs you, or thinks they need you. On the average, an infantry looie will spend about six months in the field and the other six months somewhere else not as bad." Johnson chugged down his beer and wiped the overflow with his forearm. "You guys ready for another?" It was a challenge more than a request. He was tired of talking about the Army and Vietnam. It was time for some serious drinking.

The newcomers met the challenge and they closed the club. Johnson was stone-drunk and puked as soon as he stepped outside. The quartermaster and transportation lieutenants volunteered to get him safely to his bunk.

Hank and Dick helped each other back to their hooch with a fair amount of staggering, but with no falls, no pukes and only three pisses, two by Dick in the middle of the gravel path.

The two friends collapsed in their bunks fully clothed, Hank on the bottom. He lay on his back, eyes closed, the inside of his head spinning. His bunk shook as above him Dick rolled his large bulk from one position to another. He opened his eyes and stared in the dark at the springs and mattress above him. Eventually, the turntable slowed. He heard a loud rumble. Was it the artillery again? Raindrops began pelting the tin roof. Inwardly, he gave a sigh of relief.

Hey Dick," he whispered to the upper bunk, "you asleep?"

"No," Dick groaned, "Why?"

"Is this the monsoon season?"

"Yeah. Didn't you hear Blake?"

"No…I… Dick…do…do you ever wonder if you might become… legally dead?" Hank's words came haltingly, knowing they were tacitly verboten.

"Wha…what's that?"

"You know…those forms we filled out today. The one about being legally dead."

"Shit, Hank, I didn't read those fucking forms. Just closed my eyes, checked the boxes, and where I had to write something just put N/A," Dick answered, a little too loudly for Hank, who worried about them waking up their fellow hoochmates. "But I'll tell you one thing. I'm not going to worry my ass about being legally dead, and you better stop that shit, too. I'm going to be legally drunk right here in this same goddamn bunk one year from now. Just wait, you'll see. We're going to blow it out our ass in the O'club just like Johnson did. But we're not even going to make it outside to puke." Dick stared bleary-eyed at the rafters where the rushing sound of a heavy downpour reverberated.

"You'd better be fuckin' right, Kistler. If not, I'll be real pissed. But even so, you've got an advantage over me. You don't have a girl back home. Thinking about Pam is making me a mental case. I keep thinking I might not see her again." He wanted to add *might not ever make love to her*. "Maybe I can hedge my bets a little. Maybe I can get a remf job like Johnson said. What do you think?"

Hank waited a good two minutes for Dick to reply. There was none. Only the rain. He dropped the conversation and let his thoughts become captured by the downpour. It had an antiseptic, mind-draining effect that soon produced sleep.

CHAPTER 5

D ICK HADN'T DOZED off. He lay in a semi-foggy state. Thoughts rolling around in his head like a loose pinball, banging against painful memories, lighting up the scoreboard with Hank's words "you don't have a girl back home."

It was true. He had no particular girl. Though he had at one time, while a cadet at VMI. Her name was Francine and she went to Sweet Briar and she was from Richmond, Windsor Farms area, the right side of town. She was FFV, First Family of Virginia, and had successfully entered into Richmond's elite society via the debutante status her parents bestowed upon her during her senior year in high school. She never failed to bring up this gala, prestigious event at least once every time they were together.

It wasn't that he was from the wrong side of town. It was just the wrong town. Covington, Virginia, a pulp and paper mill town in the western part of the state where there was always a sick stench, a low, clinging cloud of smog, and a black river filled with dead trout. It was a place where his old man wore a blue shirt and carried a lunch box. It was also place which had a high school football team that he played on, and which, thank God, got him an athletic scholarship to VMI. It wasn't that he'd been inclined towards attending a military school. Rather he had just wanted to get the hell out of Covington. And VMI had been the only college to offer him a full ticket out.

Francine came into his life in the form of a blind date during the spring of his sophomore year. A Brother Rat fixed him up for a Hop weekend. She was blonde, blue-eyed, and beautiful; and he was tall, at once handsome and imposing in his tailored cadet uniform and spit-shined shoes. They fell in love, of course. They were too striking together not to.

That summer he took a job in Richmond to be near Francine. He boarded at the home of a Brother Rat and by day worked as a chain man on a survey crew for the Virginia Highway Department. By night, he courted Francine, usually winding up in the back seat of her father's caddy, parked in a secluded spot along the James River. Then one weekend he invited her to his home in Covington, and with no uniform to hide in, she discovered who and what he really was. And from there they started sliding.

In the early Fall back at VMI, after a losing football effort against William and Mary, the relationship hit bottom. It was in her room at the Mayport Inn, a withered and weathered hotel of dark, ancient brick and threadbare décor, located across the street from the cemetery where Stonewall Jackson was a permanent resident. Dick lay there, battered and bruised, a fallen gladiator from the afternoon's dismal contest, while she stood in a far corner of the room glaring at him. It was while he was lying on that iron-posted bed of broken springs and a sagging mattress, that she told him, with venomous sarcasm, that she'd rather be with Stonewall in his grave than in this room with him.

He merely grunted in reply and exhaled a long sigh at the ceiling. This set her off and she launched into a shrill tirade on how they were different people, how they had nothing in common, how they were going nowhere together, and that this was The End. He said nothing, didn't move, just kept staring at the ceiling. All week long he had imagined this moment together in her room, getting all horned up in the process, waiting with bated breath and a hard dick for this moment.

Now his dick was probably so shriveled it would look like a wet noodle if he pulled it out. Francine was dead wrong. They had something in common. Something very strong and very important. They both liked to fuck. They particularly liked to fuck each other. He wanted to remind her of this mutual interest, but he just wasn't up for it at the moment. All he could muster was a glazed look at the ceiling.

She yelled at him to get out. He didn't move. She called him a blue collared bumpkin. He didn't move. She said she didn't want to see him again and to get out. He still didn't move. She grabbed her pocketbook in a huff and stomped out of the room, slamming the door.

The shadows grew longer and slowly swallowed the room in darkness. Street lights came on outside. All around, faucets were running, toilets flush-

ing, doors closing, footsteps echoing. Then silence. Hours passed, then footsteps again, toilets flushing, faucets running. Midnight approached, curfew
for cadets. The clock in his head hit 11:45 p.m.; time for him to finally
move.

Back in his own room, with his three sleeping roommates, he lay on his
hayrack and looked up at the ceiling, so dark it looked like a flat, homoge-
neous storm cloud. His dick slowly, but methodically, began to unshrivel.

He wanted to fuck Francine one more time.

He heard the door creak open. Someone was moving around inside, bumping into things in the dark, trying to steer clear of the scattered hayracks.

A dark face got in the way of the ceiling. It matched Larry Fetherford's, a
Brother Rat.

"Kistler," he whispered, "you awake?"

"Yeah."

"I'm running the block."

No answer.

"I'm headed for the Mayport Inn; I know your girl's staying there.
Thought you might want to have a little visit. I got a taxi waiting in back of
the barracks for us."

"Why me?"

"Because you got a girl there. And I want some company."

"Why?"

"My girl's staying there too. Supposed to be anyway. I want to check. Holt
says she's late-dating. I wanna find out."

VMI was unique, not just for its military status, or its rigid, archaic code
of discipline that prevented cadets from drinking, even if they were of age,
and from staying out past midnight on Saturday night, even though they
were also college men. It was also unique in that another college was adjacent
to it. Washington and Lee University, also an all male school, but from there
the similarity disappeared. From there, it was like a saloon next to a semi-
nary. At W&L booze was plentiful and there was no curfew and quite often
the minks, as the students of W&L were called, would date a cadet's girl
after midnight when the cadet had to be tucked away in his barrack. It was
called late-dating.

Kistler lay in bed, looking up at Fetherford, mulling over his offer. He
had mistakenly taken Francine's room key with him when he left earlier. He

could use it now to sneak in while she was asleep. He would take her in his arms, soothing her initial fright and shock of an intruder, and whisper that this time was for old time's sake. One more time they would make love. One more time she would be his girl…And maybe there would be other one more times…

"Let me get dressed," he said to Fetherford.

Silently he opened the door of Francine's hotel room and peeked inside, surprised to see a light still on. He was jolted by what he saw. It was as if his expectations and his balls were dropped simultaneously into a vat of concentrated sulfuric acid. Before him it was all too clear from the burning bedside lamp as a big hairy ass humped away inside two heels that dug into the cheeks. The humping continued unabated, the two copulating figures oblivious to the onlooker. He fought off his urge to pound the fuckers to bloody pulps, and silently closed the door.

It was the last he ever saw of Francine. It was the last time he had a girl. From then on he just had lays. Fuck 'em and forget 'em. Hump 'em and dump 'em. Those were his mottos. And it worked out well that way. After all, nothing was better than a strange piece of ass.

Dick Kistler's memories faded into a restless sleep as the rushing rain continued to drum on the tin roof.

CHAPTER 6

I N A CLOUDLESS blue sky, the hot sun sent its burning rays onto the beach at Canaveral Pier, erupting tiny perspiration beads all over Pam's deeply tanned body. She welcomed the feel of it, the pulsing heat. For a moment she imagined herself lying on her towel without her bathing suit. She pictured herself naked and reclining, with two snow-white bands where her two-piece had covered her body. She laughed without mirth at this image of a naked virgin on a blanket. A twenty-one-year-old, naked virgin. A silly prude. What was the matter with her?

She spread her legs slightly, inviting the warmth between her thighs. She wished it were Hank. Maybe if he had been more persistent during their last night, she mused. But why was she blaming him? One of the reasons she loved him was that he *hadn't* pushed himself on her.

So here she was, still a virgin, and wishing she wasn't. But wishing she had given her virginity only to Hank. Certainly not to Dave, who had always turned their dates into perpetual wrestling matches. And worse, she had almost given in to him. But why hadn't she given in to Hank? She still wondered. She loved Hank, not Dave.

So why not?

Maybe it was the thought of disappointing her mother, kind and gentle…and a devout Catholic. Or maybe it was the fear of her father's wrath. Ever since junior high he had warned her not to get 'knocked up'. She once overheard him tell a neighbor that he should be glad he had a son since he only had one dick to worry about, rather than a daughter and worry about every damn dick in the neighborhood. Maybe it was because of her best and dearest girlfriend who, as a sophomore in high school, did get "knocked up." Maybe it was all of these maybes.

Maybe.

But now, none of these reasons mattered. Only Hank mattered. She and Hank together mattered. Why did she have to realize this now? Why not before, when she'd had the chance to show him how much she cared?

The sun was directly overhead and the tiny perspiration beads felt like they were starting to boil. She propped herself on her elbows, hoping the soft onshore breeze would cool her off. Her hair, streaked with gold, spilled over her shoulders, down to the top of her two-piece bathing suit, where a thin line of milk white contrasted sharply with her bronze tan. The coconut smell of suntan lotion mixed with the salt air and the pleasing scent surrounded her.

She perched her horn-rimmed sunglasses on top of her head, glanced around the uncrowded beach, and then gazed outward at the calm ocean. A few surfers, lying passively on their boards, bobbed lightly in slight swells, waiting hopelessly for a wave large enough to end their boredom. She had noticed the same surfers yesterday, an even calmer day, waiting and hoping.

Spiritually, she seemed to be in communion with them. But her wave would be a long time coming. And she could only wait. And hope. At least in another month and a half, when she started teaching junior high, she'd be able to keep busy, to keep her mind occupied by something new and different.

Hank's first letter was so short. If only it had been pages upon pages to read and reread again and again, long passages she could cherish. But at least it was something. And he was safe. With no address yet, her letter to him was still growing.

Her father took every opportunity to scoff at her letter writing. Endlessly, he harped about Dave Watson. He made Dave sound like the coming savior of the Miami Dolphins. And he said soon to be a rich savior.

Unbearably hot and totally frustrated, Pam rolled to her feet in one fluid motion and broke into a run. Her feet kicked back sand as she raced for the inviting water. She dove in, and with strong strokes swam out near the surfers. Just as she reached them, an unexpected swell seemed to rise from the ocean's depths. It grew larger and larger until it reached the surfers, where it crested and took them for their long-awaited ride. Leaving Pam behind. Alone. And still waiting.

CHAPTER 7

"SHIT, WE'RE WALKING right up a duck's asshole," Dick loudly blurted out.

Too loud, Hank felt. He followed Dick up the tail ramp of the Caribou, a small two-toned troop plane, the top half a deep Army green, the underside a creamy white, and with the tail ramp down, looking much like a duck's asshole. To his surprise, the EMs in the file laughed and nodded their appreciation of such humor and Hank realized that Dick's remark had let some tension out of the air, forming a camaraderie of sorts. And once again Hank admired Dick for his leadership. Whether leaders are born or made he didn't know, nor did he care. He knew, either way, he had missed out.

There were two lines filing into the Caribou under a hot midday sun. They wore new jungle fatigues and unscuffed jungle boots. Green soft caps, looking like poorly contoured baseball hats, covered their heads. Each man carried a bulging duffel bag over one shoulder. Each left shoulder sleeve had a shoulder patch with a number simply displayed. The number one. A red one. A big, red one.

The general had been right. They were both assigned to the First Infantry Division. But that was as far as the general had gone. It was Dick who got them to the same Battalion.

Their stay at Long Binh had ended after three days. From there they were based north in a more remote suburb of Saigon: Di An, a base camp of the First Infantry Division, and home of its Second Brigade and the in-country processing center for the Big Red One. Here there were even more DA forms, most seeming like the ones at Long Binh. And here the assignments were made to the units; "the end of the line" Dick called it. And here Dick had lobbied heavily to a major in charge of seeing that the new troops got to the "end of the line."

The major had a narrow, expressionless face, a thin moustache, and round wire-rimmed glasses. A descendent of Himmler, Dick had said while they killed time in an O'club drinking beer. But his looks had been deceiving. The major had listened patiently and quietly to Dick's rambling of how he and Hank had been together ever since entering this man's Army, how a general in the Pentagon had specially arranged for their assignment to the same division, and how now it was time for that final stroke of the pen on the right DA form to get them to the same Battalion.

And for some reason the major did it.

And now they were on a Caribou sitting side by side, facing inboard, on faded orange canvas benches that ran nearly the length of the fuselage. Going to Quan Loi, home of the First Brigade.

Dick sat in a slouch, his big legs stretched out in front of him, using his duffel bag as a hassock. His arms were folded, forearms bulging out, laid bare by neatly rolled up sleeves, standard dress for jungle fatigues. He had not bothered with a seat belt. He was the picture of cool nonchalance.

Not so for the remaining thirty-two raw replacements.

Hank looked across at his fellow travelers, all EMs. They looked back at him and the others on the bench with him, particularly at Dick, sitting calmly in his semi-reclined position. Every minute or so a pair of eyes would make contact with a pair on the other side and carom up or down or sideways. All were quiet and most looked nervous. And in their brand-new jungle fatigues and boots, they could have passed for paratroopers on their first training jump.

The Caribou's propellers gathered momentum and churned into an invisible blur. A shrill, high pitched ringing reverberated painfully in their ears.

They were airborne. Hank tried thinking of Pam, but, for once, his mind couldn't focus long enough. The loud ringing drove off any rational thought.

Less than thirty minutes passed. Then like a lumbering albatross, the plane banked to the left and commenced a landing approach toward a narrow airstrip. Dick finally moved, stretching his neck and shoulders around for a look out the porthole between him and Hank. An Air Force sergeant, the flight's load master, stood up in the rear and shouted in competition with the plane's noisy vibration, "This stop is Lai Khe! Those going to Quan Loi, stay on board!"

Hank twisted around and joined Dick staring out the window.

The plane touched down and sped by a half dozen Cobra gunships, immobile, looking like a school of sleeping man-eating sharks.

Bouncing roughly on an uneven access apron the plane taxied around near where it first touched down. It stopped. The tail ramp dropped, and Hank stared out the "duck's asshole." He saw a square, wooden building at the edge of a sparse wood line. Next to the building was a huge sign with big dark red letters on a blue background:

LAI KHE
HEADQUARTERS OF THE FIRST INFANTRY DIVISION
NO MISSION TOO DIFFICULT, NO SACRIFICE TOO GREAT,
DUTY FIRST —MAJOR GENERAL KEITH L. WARE COMMANDING

Hank swallowed hard. He hoped this Major General Ware didn't take those inspiring words too seriously.

Fifteen new fatigues disembarked. Then the asshole closed. The engines revved, and the propellers became a blur again. The Caribou moved onto the runway and sprang forward.

"Brace yourself, Hank, this damn duck'll make us stone deaf," Dick shouted above the shrill sound.

They leveled off on a northerly course and followed a ribbon of dirt road where each side was brown and sterile for seventy-five meters, the Rome plows, those large, specially modified, armored bulldozers, having obliterated the terrain. At the edge of the sterile area, thick green vegetation snarled the earth in great tangles. Farther north the jungle gave way to low hills of huge groves of rubber trees, and eventually the dark gray rectangular shape of an asphalt airfield appeared.

As the plane descended, tents materialized beneath the rubber trees. For a short moment there was a glimpse of an eight-inch and 175mm Artillery Battery. A distinctive red soil, the foundation for the entire base camp, filled the voids between the trees and tents.

The Caribou came to a halt just off the runway. The asshole dropped open and its feces slowly filed out.

They were met by a glaring sun and two waiting trucks, a deuce-and-a-half and a three-quarter ton. A short, squatty spec-four wearing thick glasses, reddish soiled fatigue pants and a green T-shirt, waddled forward. He called in an out-of-character commanding voice. "Replacements for the Third of the Thirteenth. Get your butts over here." His tone became less authoritative when he saw Dick and Hank. "You must be the lieutenants we're expecting," he said almost deferentially.

They nodded and stood before the spec-four with their duffel bags on their shoulders.

"That three-quarter's mine," he told them. "Stow your stuff in back and hop in the front seat while I square away the others."

Minutes later, the small truck contained four EMs seated in the rear, and Hank and Dick crowded in the front with the spec-four.

"I'm McKenzie, Headquarters Company," he introduced himself and turned the ignition. He let the clutch out too fast and the truck leaped forward, generating a wake of bronzed dust.

"How's the enemy situation around here, McKenzie?" Hank enquired while maneuvering for comfort between McKenzie and Dick. He had to ask. It was all that was on his mind.

"Ain't been nuthin'. Charlie dropped a few rockets couple weeks past, but that's it. 'Course there's the usual report of movement on the perimeter, but that's just some remf's imagination."

A few rockets were not nuthin', Hank thought to himself.

The road ran alongside the airstrip. On their right, rows of olive-drab tents, stained by the red clay, stood out uniformly; behind them was a whole subdivision of tents.

Spec-four McKenzie applied a heavy foot to the brakes, abruptly halting the truck in front of a sign bearing the inscription, S-1. Behind the sign was a large tent. Its sides were rolled up to allow for a porch-type enclosure with plywood sheeting and metal screen.

"That's it, sirs," McKenzie said. "Point your bags out to the guys in back so they can toss them off." He motioned behind him with his thumb.

They did so, and their bags came flying down unceremoniously. Dick looked pissed, but McKenzie stepped hard on the accelerator before he could say anything.

"I guess this ain't the Waldorf," Dick mumbled as they dragged their bags to the front step and dropped them.

Inside, three metal desks, supported by a wood pallet floor, lined each side. Clerks inhabited each desk and were busily punching the keyboards of big, black manual typewriters with their index fingers. Three paddle fans over the aisle between the desks kept the hot air circulating.

One clerk stopped typing, looked at the two lieutenants in their brand-new jungle fatigues, and pointed behind him to a plywood wall.

Behind long strings of blue and beige beads, in a tiny, plywood cubicle, they met the Battalion's adjutant, Captain Lawson.

The usual pleasantries and handshakes were exchanged and then everyone sat down, the adjutant behind his desk. Sitting on folding chairs, the two lieutenants squeezed into the tiny space between the front of Lawson's desk and the plywood wall that cut the clerks out of his office. A small black fan on a side bookcase rustled the adjutant's short, dark hair and contributed, together with his starched jungle fatigues, to his cool crisp manner.

The two lieutenants, not receiving any of the air flow, sat sweltering as Lawson shuffled papers on his desk.

"You'll be here for the next week or so before you're assigned to a company in the field," Lawson finally said, his face thick whiskered and friendly despite not sharing his fan. "Our Battalion is known as 'Demon.' Helluva name, ain't it?" He laughed at his remark. "Demon is currently operating from NDPs east of Phu Loi." Hank and Dick traded side glances. They didn't know what an NDP was. "Enemy activity down there has been at a lull so we haven't had a body count for a while. That's unfortunate, but we hope it'll pick up."

Fuck it's unfortunate, Hank screamed silently.

Lawson paused to offer them cigarettes. When they declined, he lit one for himself, carefully palming the match to shield the flame from the fan's stiff artificial breeze. "As you know, you're now at Quan Loi, the provincial capital of Binh Long. The Division's AO is in Three Corps and starts just north of Saigon, up Highway Thirteen. This highway passes through all the Division's base camps Di An, Phu Loi, Lai Khe, and here at Quan Loi. It continues north through An Loc and then Loc Ninh on the Cambodian border. We call the various stretches, 'Thunders.'"

He took a long drag and set his cigarette in a nearby overflowing ash tray. "Starting Monday, you'll attend Jungle Devil School from 0800 to 1700 hours. It's a three-day orientation designed to bring you up to speed on the way Brigade's fighting this war." He reached for his handkerchief and blew his nose. Maybe he had a problem with the draft, Hank thought cynically, feeling the wet perspiration on his back.

"Today's Thursday. What do we do between now and Monday?" Dick interjected a question during the pause.

"Get settled. You'll have to draw additional gear. Go to Headquarters Company and see Lieutenant Voight. After you finish JD School you'll join Demon in Phu Loi, where Colonel West, our Battalion commander, will personally assign you to a company."

"Any chance of us getting the same company?" Hank said as Lawson began to stand. "We've been together ever since IOBC."

"I doubt it. All companies urgently need platoon leaders," he said and walked two steps to the beaded doorway. Hank and Dick followed. "Leave three copies of your orders with my clerk at the end of the hooch on the left as you go out. And good luck, men."

They found Lieutenant Voight in the supply tent. He and McKenzie, both bare-chested, and beer-bellied, were rooting like two hogs at a garbage dump through the gas masks, M-16s, and ammunition that were strewn all over the floor.

Voight issued them helmets and M-16s with one magazine sans ammo. He slipped a fatigue shirt over his hairy, heavyset frame and guided them to their temporary quarters. It was a small tent hooch with six twin-size beds and two paddle fans. The head of each bed was separated by metal lockers along the wall.

"Take those two there," Voight pointed to the near corner. He spoke rapidly in Brooklynese but clearly enough for them to understand. "This hooch is for junior officers of headquarters, but since we have two vacant beds at the moment you can join us. That's my bed and locker next to yours. You can use my wash basin until you guys get your own. A water buffalo is three tents down toward my supply hooch. PX is behind us across the road next to the four deuce mortars. Can get about anything you want there. Shower's right next door, and if I can get that damn immersion heater working, we might have hot water tonight."

A loud boom overhead followed Voight's words. The three men froze as they nervously glanced at one another. There was another boom, only not as loud, which tapered out into a low rumble. It was then that they noticed the darkness outside and felt a cool gust of moist air through the screen door and recognized what had been a precipitous clap of thunder.

Their tension evaporated. Voight laughed heartily. "That reminds me. Our bunker's just outside." He pointed. They looked through the screen at the far side of the hooch, through rain that was starting to fall, at three layers of dry-rotted sandbags stacked on half sections of metal culverts over a narrow thirty-foot long trench. He laughed again. "You'd think I'd get used to loud bangs after ten months."

"Getting short," Hank stated.

"Yep, fifty-nine more days and I'm back in the World."

"Seems like a good job you got here," Hank said, subconsciously wishing it for himself.

"It's all right. After eight months on line they had to give me something close to being a remf," Voight replied. He moved to the near entrance and took up a miler's crouch. Outside the raindrops had turned to opaque sheets. "If you need anything let me know. Oh, and one more thing, chow's served in Demon's officer's club at 1730 hours," he said. Then he dashed out.

"This is perfect sleeping weather. I'm taking a nap till suppertime. How about you, Hank?" Dick looked at their canvas ceiling. The rain was the sound of drummer sticks beating a long monotone roll.

"No, not me, you go ahead. I'm gonna write Pam and give her my address so I can start getting mail."

Searching for the O'club gave them a quick tour of the Battalion area. To Hank, it partly resembled a south Florida subdivision, houses all alike and close-together. Only there were a lot of trees, rubber trees, the tall latex-producing variety. They had a fairly slender trunk and a high, thick canopy of green leaves that provided an abundance of shade, having filtered out most of the sunlight. And, thus, there was no grass, just sticky red mud, the residue from the now departed downpour. The tent hooches were essentially of the same structure: rectangular frames of skeletal wood draped with olive drab canvas. There were two basic sizes, small and medium. Some were customized by plywood walls sectioning off individual rooms. Others, mostly the barracks variety for the field troops, had no walls and their canvass sides were rolled up to afford maximum ventilation and minimum privacy. Most of these were deserted, their tenants in the field.

A sign pointed out the O'club. Next to the words "Demon, 3rd Bn/13th Inf, Officers Club" was the picture of a grotesque black devil with dark red eyes and a pitchfork. It was about 1700 hours when the two lieutenants stepped inside this one room hooch with four square tables and a varnished plywood bar, with five bar stools. A spec-five stood behind the bar and waved hello to his only customers.

They drank beer at the bar until other officers began to saunter in at which time they sat at a table and were soon joined by Voight. By 1730, the tables were nearly filled.

The officers were mostly lieutenants, with a sprinkling of captains. Some wore silk scarves around their necks like boy scouts. The scarves were a light green camouflage pattern. In the middle of the scarves' triangle was a smaller version of Demon's devil logo.

Captain Lawson entered wearing his scarf and was greeted with the respect granted a senior-ranking captain. All acknowledged with smiles, nods, and hellos the presence of the two new lieutenants, but none filled the remaining vacant seat at their table. When Lawson was seated, two giggly Vietnamese girls carried out large trays of generous portions of veal cutlet, peas and carrots, mashed potatoes, and huge piping-hot rolls.

The meal was the best the two new lieutenants had tasted since arriving in-country. After supper, most officers sat around drinking beer and giving their opinions on a montage of subjects from Ho Chi Minh to the miniskirts being worn back in the states. Some watched a small TV behind the bar broadcasting the Armed Forces news from Saigon.

As the sun faded, Voight shepherded his two new charges outside. Cautiously stepping to avoid slipping on the slimy red mud that stuck to their boots like glue, they walked a few hooches down to a small square where they found a crowd of thirty or so, mostly EMs, sitting on boxes, barrels, benches, and a few chairs. There was a little talking and a lot of beer drinking. A large blank white sign mounted high between 4x4 posts loomed at the far end. Voight ducked into a nearby hooch and emerged carrying a long bench. Dick helped him place it and they sat down.

Five minutes later, the sign was splashed with light and then the title of a movie *The Sound of Music*. In Hank's mind, the movie conjured up the image of Pam and the longing for home, but then he became absorbed by the story and he let the girl he loved, the country he missed, and even the country he was in, escape from his mind.

Then the rains came. Before Julie Andrews had made her exodus from Nazi occupation, the viewers made their own exodus, scrambling in all directions.

The three lieutenants reassembled at the O'club where they drank beer until midnight.

Later, inside their hooch a light drizzle pattered softly on the canvas roof. The air was rain-cooled. Hank wrapped himself in his poncho liner. He was tired, dizzy, a common nightly occurrence since arriving in-country, and he was asleep shortly before the rain stopped.

In the wee hours he stirred. Something was hammering inside his head. His eyes opened a little, then popped wide. There was no mistake. This was not a thunderstorm.

He bolted from his bed, flung himself to the floor, covered his head with his arms, and screamed, "Incoming, incoming!"

The hooch came alive like a fire station with a five-alarm. Bodies leaped up. Arms, elbows, legs, feet flailed away in a wild scramble for the bunker. Hank managed to look up through a crook in his arm at Voight's nude body and helmeted head running away. Dick was last, clad in his GI jungle green boxer shorts. He stopped and turned at the exit and looked at Hank cringing on the floor in the dark.

"Come on! Get up, Hank! We gotta get to the bunker!" he hollered and hurriedly waved for Hank to move his ass.

Hank grabbed his helmet near his bed. He pushed up and sprinted in his boxer shorts, pumping his arms, forcing his legs to move as fast as possible.

Five feet from the bunker's entrance Hank went into a Ty Cobb slide, feet out straight, body horizontal, and canted to the left. He went down the steep incline, hit the slick mud, and kept sliding as if on a frictionless plane. Until he smacked into Dick, sending him reeling in the dark, crashing him into the others who went down like bowling pins.

There were grunts and moans and curses. There was heavy, hyper breathing. All in near total darkness.

"Where they hit?" A voice gasped among the six scared souls, muddied and shivering, crouching down in the slimy, mud-oozing bunker. It was Lieutenant Voight. He was addressing the human bowling ball.

"Soun…sounded like a hundred meters…north of our hooch," Hank answered. He mopped mud from around his eyes with a trembling forearm.

"How many?" It was Voight again.

"Four."

As if on cue, four big booms shattered the night air.

Hank cringed; his knees dropped into the mud, his mind expecting a direct hit, disintegrating them all into jagged bits of bone and flesh. "That's as close as the first four!" he yelled up at Voight.

"Fuck if it was, Kirby. That's outgoing! That's one-five-fives firing counter-battery at the gooks' incoming. A good half klick away," Voight corrected.

"No, it couldn't be. That's the incoming. That's what I heard."

"Are you shittin' me?" Voight shot back angrily. "That wasn't any goddamn incoming! That's our own one-five-five's firing H and I's!" he snorted disgustedly. "Well, there goes a good night's sleep blown to hell!"

A soft "Oh" was all that was audible from Hank.

The others, minus Dick, trudged silently by him. As they fought the steep, slick incline like spawning salmon, they muttered "Asshole…shithead… fuckstick motherfucker" and other epithets under their breath.

"Sorry!" Hank called miserably after them.

Dick worked his way out of the bunker. He turned and planted his feet and braced himself on a sandbag with one hand. He extended the other to Hank and pulled him out.

"Don't worry about it, Hank," he murmured. "It was an honest mistake. Sounded like incoming to me."

"Yeah…sure," Hank replied, his tone flat and unconvincing.

They followed the others to the outdoor showers, now filling with brilliant stars as the rain had ended. A magnificent sight in another time, another place. The immersion heaters had been off. The water was cold. There was more muttering and cursing. In a far corner, Hank observed their grumblings. Dick was beside him, hyperventilating as the water cascaded off his head.

Hank faced his own set of valves, turned one, felt the cold stream smack his forehead. He felt claustrophobic, trapped in a small, black manhole called Vietnam. There was no escape. He had heard rumors about those refusing the field. Six months in LBJ, Long Binh Jail, then back for a full year tour of duty. The Army had him by the balls.

Too bad the Army didn't realize he didn't have any.

CHAPTER 8

WARM SUNLIGHT CREPT slowly into the hooch. It was halfway out when Hank woke up. He was hot and clammy; his quarters an oven of moist, stagnant air. He kicked his poncho liner blanket off and propped himself on his elbows. He surveyed the room and found all beds empty but Dick's. Everyone else was gone. Dick was sleeping coverless on his stomach in his undershorts.

Hank looked up and saw the paddle fan motionless. So that was the problem. One of his roommates must have switched it off before leaving, knowing they would soon bake. Revenge for last night, he reasoned. And it was deserved, he knew. But only for him. Not Dick.

He kicked his blanket away, slid out of bed, and pulled the chain of the paddle fan. He lay back down, the churning air cooling his clammy body. He closed his eyes. He would force himself to fall back to sleep. He didn't want to face Vietnam alone. Not without Dick.

A little after midmorning, they stepped into the Battalion's small O'club. Yesterday's waitresses chattered in Vietnamese at each other from behind the bar. Paddle fans stirred slowly. A captain sat alone at a table sipping a Bloody Mary. A celery stalk stabbed his cheek.

The captain put his drink down and greeted them jovially. "Hello. I'm Captain Unser." His head wore white walls that reached to a short, reddish flat-top in stark contrast to a big, bushy moustache. His complexion was ruddy, his cheeks plump and his smile gargantuan. His left collar said he was medical service.

They introduced themselves and sat down at his table. He shouted to the girls to hustle out two more Bloody Marys.

"That's all that's left for breakfast," he said, taking a sip of his own. "The mess sergeant stops serving regular chow at eight thirty." His eyes looked them over. "So you're the new lieutenants waiting for JD school. Lieutenant Voight spoke about your escapade last night." He chuckled loudly.

"Yeah, I'm the one," Hank confessed, "I must be quite popular in the Battalion."

"Hell, that's all right, Kirby. I'm sure Voight doesn't mind some bogus drills once in a while. Anything to keep him alive." Unser's smiling face was forgiving, then became serious, his voice softer. "Back in Tet he led an eleven-man patrol that was ambushed. He was the only survivor. Killed a VC with his bare hands while hiding in some undergrowth. Leastwise that's what I heard from the adjutant, Captain Lawson. I'm kind of new here, too. Been with Demon only a month."

The drinks arrived, each with a leafy celery stalk. To Hank, they looked like bleeding potted plants. His belly begged for bacon and eggs. He calculated his alcohol consumption since in-country and wondered when he would become a full-fledged alcoholic. It seemed it was going to be difficult to dodge both the VC and the booze. He picked up his celery stalk and bit into it with a loud crunch. His other hand picked up his drink and he chased his chewings. If he was going to be hit by one or the other, he'd rather it be the booze.

There was a moment of silent table gazing, as if giving reverence to Voight's survival and his men that didn't, until Unser's face turned one hundred and eighty and lit up like a jack o' lantern. He raised his glass for a toast. "Here's to you infantry types. The noble knights of Vietnam who joust face to face with the enemy."

Smiling, Dick clinked glasses with the Captain. Their eyes fell on Hank. He clinked their glasses and gazed suspiciously at Dick's happy expression. Did Dick really want to be here? Could it be the VMI influence? No, he decided, Dick was merely being the Virginia gentleman in humoring the captain.

Unser raised his glass again. "And here's to my medics, faithful squires of the noble Knights, responsible for repairing their mantle at the risk of endangering their own."

Three glasses clinked again.

Unser took a long swallow and set his three-quarters empty glass on the table. His mood suddenly became morose. "My job is pure drudgery, pushing papers, administering support and supplies to my medics in the field. I'm kind of like their den mother and I never get out of the den. Yet I'm as qualified in first aid as they are. Sometimes I wish I could change these captain's railroad tracks for a spec-four's patch."

Hank slowly shook his head in outward commiseration with Unser. Inwardly, he was experiencing twinges of resentment. He would give anything to swap places.

Hank sipped heavily from his Bloody Mary.

Unser's grin reappeared, and he asked, "Have you hit the steam baths yet?"

His question brought Hank back from his reverie."

Dick stirred, his eyebrows arched up. "Steam baths! What steam baths?"

"I thought you guys might have heard about it. The brigade uses an old French villa as an officer's club. Right next to it is a steam bath for the officers. Of course," Unser's lips twisted slyly, "the bath also comes with little Vietnamese beauties that give massages."

"Well, I'll be damned. Sounds awesome. Sounds like just what we need to get loose." Dick looked over at his friend. "What do you think, Hank?"

"I still got last night's mud plastered to me. Least it feels that way. Let's give it a shot after lunch." Hank patted his stomach. He was getting dizzy from hunger. Or was it the Bloody Mary?

"You haven't heard the whole story," Captain Unser interrupted eagerly, his exuberance frothing in his voice as well as his face. "The steam bath plus massage costs three hundred piasters, or about two and a half bucks in script. But for an extra thousand P you get extras. About anything you want. Just name it," he chuckled. "That's one aspect of this Army life I don't write my old lady about."

"You're kidding," Dick said, his face unbelieving, his voice ecstatic. "You mean to say the Brigade is operating a cat house for officers?"

"Fuckin' A," Unser replied with a wide grin that tried to reach his ears. "In fact, the girls are examined once a week to make sure they're safe. I can guarantee that. I'm the one that does it. Call me the resident beaver inspector. I look first, then probe with my instrument." He chuckled some more, this time throaty and lascivious.

"Goddamn, Hank! What the hell we waitin' for?" Dick boomed authoritatively. "Let's get some piasters and be on our way."

"After lunch," Hank protested. "And I don't intend to spend any more than two-fifty."

"Okay, okay, but I plan to enjoy this godforsaken war, if I can, and while I can."

"Go ahead. I would too, under other circumstances. But you know how things stand with me and Pam."

"Yeah. I know. You've got too many old-fashioned principles."

"Sometimes you've got to 'rise' above principles," Unser interceded and laughed at his pun.

CHAPTER 9

THE SUN AT midday had changed from oppressive to unmerciful. Going to a steam bath at the moment seemed to Hank as crazy as going to an ice cream shop during a snow storm. Yet he walked with Dick along the airfield's perimeter road, its dirt baked hard by the sun like thick pottery clay from a kiln.

They noticed the same inactivity of yesterday. Occasionally, a truck or jeep would pass them by, or a lone chopper would land across the airfield. But nothing much else. Most of the tents lay vacant, waiting for their troopers to come home for a quick respite before venturing out on another mission.

The road turned left, bending around the landing strip. The rubber trees faded away into a large wedge of open space. They stood at the point of the wedge.

In the distance, across two helipads and a large field of weeds and wild flowers cut in half by tire ruts, loomed a mansion of white stucco and orange, barrel-roof shingles. Palm and fruit trees surrounded it. They had turned a corner and stumbled into a Palm Beach residence.

They crossed the field and entered the foyer. They peeked around at large rooms on either side, one with a ping-pong table, the other a pool table. Beyond the foyer was a grand mahogany staircase. There was an apparent absence of life.

Dick challenged Hank to ping-pong and lost. They crossed to the other room where he won at eight ball. Then they started up the staircase.

At the top was a hallway. To the right a closed door, to the left a curtain of red beads. They took the path of least resistance and turned left. Behind the beads they found a comfortable lounge of rattan and wicker. There was a small, highly polished bar near the right wall. Behind the bar a staff sergeant swabbed out glasses with a dish towel.

The staff sergeant greeted them with a peevish, sidelong glance, as if their entrance was going to divert him from his enjoyment of drying glasses. They ignored him and sat down in cushion wicker chairs under a speedy paddle fan. They faced a small knee-high table also of wicker.

"Two gin and tonics, Sergeant," Dick called over, his voice gravelly and cold, taking on the tone of the sergeant's facial expression.

Hank grimaced at the thought of more alcohol. At least his stomach was content, he consoled himself. The meatloaf lunch had been served with huge piping-hot rolls. He had devoured four of them. He now knew why Lieutenant Voight and his spec-four assistant, McKenzie, had such big bellies.

The drinks came, and Dick told the sour-faced sergeant to run a tab. They toasted and sipped. Then Hank started grinning at Dick.

"What's so funny?" Dick answered the grin.

"You are. You're not really the hot pokered, horny toad I thought you were."

"Oh? Why's that?" Dick sounded slightly offended.

"You don't seem so anxious about all this. Before lunch you acted like it was going to kill you to wait. Now, with the ping-pong, the pool, and these gin and tonics with an open tab, looks like you're stalling. But that's fine with me. I'm only getting the massage. Maybe that's all we both should get."

Dick began to laugh. Hank was puzzled at this reaction. He had actually suggested there was evidence that Dick was not a complete sex maniac. That he had some redeeming value, such as not partaking of prostitutes. Dick had once proudly told him he had never paid for it. So Hank had expected a strong defensive reaction. Instead, the laughter got louder and louder.

It was his turn to ask. "What's so damn funny?"

"Hell, Hank, don't you know why I'm 'stalling?'" Dick's voice gave that last word a special emphasis. "I'm dwelling on the expectation. It's a type of foreplay. I figure these brigade sanctioned Vietnamese ladies will just give a wham-bam-thank-you-ma'am. So the foreplay is in the expectation. Right now I'm as hard as a cue stick. My mouth is getting watery. But that's all right. I like a lot of foreplay."

Hank merely shook his head. Dick *was* a sex maniac.

He sat back in his chair and gazed past Dick, looking out opened French doors and beyond a small balcony. He saw the perimeter: bunkers and plenty of barbed wire and a tall observation/sniper tower. Away from the wire, the ground tapered down to a narrow grassy valley. A good distance beyond there stretched endless rows of thriving rubber trees. They were not the small variety used for landscaping in Florida. But tall trees with thick canopy that made a dark, deep forest beneath.

It was a great view of the perimeter, much like a choice fifty yardline seat. He pondered morosely what the scene had held several months ago. According to Captain Unser, there had been a heavy ground attack, supported by rockets and mortars. It was hard to believe now, as he comfortably sipped his gin and tonic across from Dick who was smiling lewdly at him as the advanced stages of his mental foreplay began to set in.

They ordered another round. Then they asked the staff sergeant directions to the steam bath. With a pained look of reluctance, as if his sisters were the masseuses, he told them. Dick, his imaginary foreplay ending, gulped his drink down and urged Hank to do likewise.

It was behind the villa, connected by an awning-covered walkway. At one time it could have been a huge ice house. On a pink, chipped wall next to a narrow open doorway hung a yellow sign with bold black letters reading STEAM BATH & MASSAGE, 300 PIASTERS.

They entered cautiously, their movement hesitant. It was dark and dank and smelly like an old high school locker room after gym class. Their eyes adjusted, and they discovered they were not alone. Three Vietnamese girls in their late teens or early twenties sat on a narrow bench, watching the two prospective customers and emitting high-pitched giggles. They wore skin-tight slacks and loose-fitting blouses that offered many opportunities for the nervous glancing eyes that hovered over them. Next to the bench was a three-sided counter that surrounded a more moderately attired middle-aged mama-san. She smiled matronly from her stool perch.

"Geeice want steam-bath-massage?" the mama-san asked pleasantly as they approached. They nodded and fumbled around in their wallets for the necessary piasters received in exchange for their MPC at the S-1 hooch. They handed her their money and her smile broadened. In return, she placed two sets of towels, flip-flop sandals, and plastic bags on the counter. She pointed left to the far side of the room. "Change there, round corner." She pointed behind them at a plain, plywood door. "Steam bath there." She pointed at two side-by-side doorways with bead curtains next to her. "Massage there."

Dick picked up his set of accouterments. Hank looked at his, puzzling over the plastic bag. "That wallet," the mama-san answered his questioning stare.

Around the corner, they found a cubbyhole with rusted metal lockers and a wooden bench. The floor was damp cement conducive to athlete's foot. They quickly stripped and covered themselves with small towels whose ends failed to meet around their waists.

Clutching towels in one hand and plastic bags with their wallets in the other, they moved briskly to the steam bath, passing once again through the main room amidst the smiling mama-san and a chorus of silly giggles. Hank followed Dick into a hot and steamy blinding white vapor. When he filled his lungs for air he thought he would drown.

They groped about in the hot, white cloud, finding one shower and on the opposite wall a small bench.

Damn, I can't believe this shit. This heat is killing me," Hank complained.

"Relax, Hank. Sit down and get your pores cleaned out," Dick replied.

They sat down together. Though only a foot apart, they could barely see each other in the impossibly hot, thick foggy mist. Hank leaned forward, elbows on knees, and believed he now knew what it was like on the inside of an autoclave. He had used one many times during his sanitary chemistry course to sterilize lab ware. Now it was tit-for-tat, and he wondered if *he* was being sterilized.

He stood and shuffled blindly away, leaving his towel and wallet behind.

"Where you going?"

"To find that shower. It's my only hope." Though he knew he could simply end this torture by stepping outside, he didn't dare. Not without Dick. Not to face mama-san and her three hyenas alone.

He found the shower head at eye level. Below was a large, ceramic spoke handle. He turned it, not knowing if it was hot or cold, sticking his hand out to test it. The water came out in a light sprinkle and was refreshingly cool. He sighed loudly and stuck his head under, the water cascading slowly down his neck and back like a cool mountain brook, a white mist swirling around.

"How is it?" he heard Dick ask.

"Delicious, simply delicious."

"Well hurry it up. My dong's about to shrivel up," Dick responded impatiently.

"Is that what happens with too much foreplay?" Hank kidded, his eyes closed, enjoying the cool sensation of the shower.

A big arm butted his back. "Bite my ass, Kirby, and move yours."

"Fuck you, Kistler. I'll share it, but I'm not giving it away. I've got my riparian rights."

They stood together, shoulder-to-shoulder, until the cool water recharged their steam-sapped energy. Then Dick led them to their towels. They clutched them once again around their waists, and with short choppy strides went out the door dripping wet into a room with three giggling girls and a smiling mama-san.

The mama-san motioned with her outstretched hand for the GI lieutenants to make their selection. Dick wasted no time, choosing the one in the middle with the leering smile and good-sized breasts, amply displayed as she leaned forward, letting her blouse fall open. She took his proffered arm and they disappeared behind one of the two beaded curtains beside mama-san's enclosed counter.

The two remaining girls looked up at Hank like puppy dogs at a pet store. He looked down at his bare feet, dreading his decision, already feeling some of the hurt the rejected girl would feel. One was a little less pretty, and with a little less cleavage, and her eyes reflected a little less confidence. She was probably most often the last one selected, and with only two beaded curtains, she probably spent a lot of time warming the bench.

Hank nodded for her to come with him.

The hand with his wallet sliced through the curtain, pushing half of it aside. Stopping at the threshold, he peered inside at a small windowless room starkly furnished with a wooden massage table set up in the middle and a tiny square table in the far-left corner. A naked sixty-watt bulb overhead illuminated a white sheet draped over the massage table.

He gripped the towel with white knuckles. His pulse beat frantically as he felt small hands on his hips nudging him inside. His movements were nervous jerks, as if he thought he was getting an autopsy rather than a massage.

"Me Lin," she introduced herself. "You, on table. Lie down," she commanded gently, the store window puppy now in charge of its master. She took his wallet away and placed it on the table in the corner.

He obeyed. Staring straight ahead at the back wall, he climbed aboard, still grasping the towel around him with his left hand. He lay on his stomach.

She moved behind his head, leaned forward, and put both hands on his back. She started massaging, her fingers sweeping in circles of deep strokes followed by gentle tickles. The hands worked their way from the small of the back to the shoulders. It felt good. He began to relax.

Her fingers moved to his neck. His eyes closed and he signaled his pleasure with a soft moan. He relaxed even more. She moved around beside him and started on his back again, first with the kneading, then with her hands lightly pressed together, gently slapping in a clippity-clop rhythm before coming back to kneading in the small of his back.

If he were a cat, he'd be purring. He let both arms fall loosely toward the floor like pliable rubber hoses.

His mind floated in a near semiconscious state, like a big gator wrestled to sleep. And then his eyes popped open again. He *had* been struck hard. Or more like pushed hard, right at the base of the spine, the pressure severe, followed by more pressure between his shoulder blades, causing a gale to rush from his lungs. Reflexively, he bucked and turned just in time to hear his masseuse cry out and to see her feet slip off his back. Her hands caught the right-side wall and prevented her head from striking before she half fell and half jumped. There was a loud "oof" as she landed on the floor, her feet hitting the floor first, her shoulder the wall, and then she was on her rear end.

But only for a moment.

She sprang quickly to her feet and gazed wild-eyed at Hank, trying to decide whether to run or attack.

She did neither, seeing that this GI looked as frightened as she felt, and hearing his pleading words, not knowing their exact meaning, but knowing what was implied.

"I'm sorry…It was an accident…You startled me," Hank apologized profusely. "Look, I'll be still. I promise." He lay back on his belly and his face motioned with contrite innocence for her to remount.

Her eyes softened. Cautiously, she climbed back on the table and hesitantly put her foot on his back as if testing a pool for cold water. She balanced with one hand on the side wall, a partition between their room and the other massage room. She began her walk, pinching his skin with her toes.

"Hey, Lootenant," he heard Dick cat-calling through the wall, "What you do—GI, rape and pillage?" Dick guffawed, which was accompanied by tiny giggles from his girl.

"A little misunderstanding. That's all," Hank called back gruffly. He grunted and groaned and gritted his teeth as she literally walked all over him.

CHAPTER 10

THE INTERIOR WAS dark. Soft, red running lights cast an eerie glow. There were fifteen in number, replacements for companies of the Third of the Thirteenth. Their laps held helmets wrapped with green-camouflage canvas, their legs cradled M-16s, and their feet rested on bulging rucksacks.

Hank peered down beyond his boots through a large square cavity. He watched the fading twilight spread a gray blanket over the quickly passing rice paddies. After a short while, the blanket grew black and he stared into a void. Slowly, the landscape having vanished, his eyes shifted to the short, thick beam that cut the cavity in two and from which dangled a huge iron hook, like the kind on crane cables. He reflected on it, thinking it must be what gave this gigantic Chinook helicopter its Army moniker. "Hook," it was affectionately called. Or, un-affectionately, the "shithook." Either way his air travel was still in regression. First, it had been a crowded Boeing 707 to Vietnam; second, a noisy, rattling Caribou to Quan Loi. And now a green mechanical monster with a gaping hole in its belly was ferrying him and Dick and the other thirteen poor souls back south near Di An to a place called Phu Loi.

They bedded down in Phu Loi. An hour after first light, they were motoring out to the NDP (night defensive perimeter) of the Battalion's HQ. The two new lieutenants led the way, chauffeured by jeep. The enlisted replacements trailed in a deuce and a half.

The morning air was fresh and, with the rush of dew laden air that hit their faces and fluttered their clothing, it was surprisingly cool. The black-topped stretch of Highway 13 was sparse with traffic, a few trucks and some ox carts. On either side were vacant fields, orchards, some rice paddies, and small isolated farm hooches.

Hank's pulse raced excitedly at this unescorted excursion beyond the protecting tangles of barbed wire. He sat by himself in the back seat, a tight hold on the front handguard of his M-16. He locked his gaze between the driver and Dick at the road ahead, as if shifting his eyes to the left or right would invite sniper fire from a distant tree line or the doorway of a hooch. He hoped the troops in the truck were maintaining the needed vigilance. He wished the formation was reversed, with the jeep in the rear.

He tried to convince himself he was overreacting. The driver, a lanky specfour, seemed calm. And after all, would the Army send them out like this, if unsafe? He tried to swallow his fear. Not all of it went down.

The jeep turned onto a dirt road. "We've got another mile. It's down this way. We're about five miles from Phu Loi," he heard the driver tell Dick.

The NDP emerged, alien from its environs. It sat in an open field adjacent to the east side of the road and filled the void between two little Vietnamese hamlets. The small outpost was no more than fifty meters in diameter. It was confined by stacked rolls of concertina wire, as if it were a special stockade, only here the guards were inside and the prisoners outside. Low-silhouetted firing bunkers ringed the inside in a star formation. From each bunker protruded two firing apertures that looked like sculptured, evil eyes. Behind each bunker, and connected at the sides, was a square pit formed by three layers of sandbags. These were the sleeping positions. Over them, tied to nearby engineer stakes, were stretched ponchos and camouflage-patterned poncho liners, providing shelter from both sun and rain. Beyond the sleeping pits stood a small, squalid community; four tents, three sprouting slender radio antennas, and two circular 81mm mortar pits. There was a small labor force of shirtless, sweaty bodies; some were filling sandbags, some were digging, some were cleaning weapons, and some were milling around, waiting their turn at the work.

It was a slummy stockade. Its guards sentenced to hard labor.

A sergeant met their vehicle. They climbed out and he ushered them through a maze of barbed wire until they were finally inside the perimeter and had become new members of this strange community.

The sergeant deposited the two lieutenants amidst empty 81mm mortar boxes, between a mortar pit and a dangling Lyster Bag sweating with water. He informed them that they were to see the Battalion CO, Lieutenant Col-

onel West, after lunch, and then he departed to deal with the enlisted replacements.

They spent the next four hours milling around the NDP, observing the
hive-like activity from a distance, cautious not to highlight their lack of involvement. Back at the ammo boxes they lunched on C-rations left by the
dutiful sergeant. Hank was stuck with the canned ham and eggs which he
threw into a discarded ammo box. He kept the side dish of fruit cocktail,
and the hunger pangs that were left unsatisfied.

At 1307 hours, the sergeant showed them into a small round tent and
left them standing alone. The sides were rolled up to provide ventilation at
the expense of privacy. Even so, their heads were baking under the hot canvas
top. Stacked sandbags formed a two-and-a-half-foot circular wall around
the tent's base. Next to this wall were three canvas cots with air mattresses.
The legs of the cots were set into holes for the obvious purpose of keeping
prone asses from being ripped apart by flying shrapnel and assorted missiles.
Near the center post stood a beat up wooden easel that held a map streaked
by grease pencils. A faded red beach chair with no legs faced the easel.

Their eyes had just enough time to take in the full scene when Lieutenant
Colonel Samuel C. West strode into the tent. He was of medium height, forty-
ish, with a hard, chiseled face, a granite jaw, and graying temples showing just
below his helmet. His fatigues had been recently starched and looked squeaky
clean, despite a fine brown mantle of dust. His sleeves looked like he had spent
the better half of the morning rolling them. Their final roll was over muscular
biceps that led down into powerful Popeye forearms, sun-burned to the color
of a hearty red wine. One collar had a black oak leaf, the other the crossed
rifles of the infantry. The Big Red One patch just above the immaculate sleeve
role on his left arm seemed to have an especially shiny luster.

The colonel removed his helmet and set it on a cot, revealing close cropped
dark hair. Then he faced the two lieutenants. "Hello, gentlemen, I'm Colonel
West," he introduced himself with a low, gravelly voice. He held out his hand
and issued overly tight handshakes. The lieutenants exchanged their names.
Colonel West motioned for them to be seated on one of the cots. He adjusted
his beach chair to face them and then situated himself in it.

Hank and Dick sat down awkwardly on a low cot, its canvas no more
than six inches off the ground. There was a brief moment of quiet and spastic
shifting as they tried to manage the best placement of their legs. Even in the

low beach chair, the colonel's eyes looked down at them, emphasizing the relationship of superior to subordinate.

Colonel West began, his voice low, yet rock hard, "The Third of the Thirteenth is the best damn Battalion in the Division. You're fortunate to join us and I'm sure we're fortunate to have you. It seems we're always short of platoon leaders. Every company is short at least one."

Why were they always short? Hank wanted to ask, though he knew the answer. He wasn't feeling particularly fortunate at the moment.

"You'll find our company commanders are very capable, professional soldiers. And there's one thing I stress above all else," he paused, giving a lingering emphasis, "and that's unswerving allegiance to your CO. A good officer is one who makes his commanders look good. Remember that." His eyes glanced to Dick, then to Hank, holding their gaze for a brief moment as he let his point sink in.

"There are a few things I want to caution you about before you take command of your own platoon." There was another pause for effect. "One is always carrying at least four smoke grenades during all operations, and make sure that your men do likewise." Again a pause. "The second is map reading. I'm sure you've both had adequate training in maps back in the world. You'd better have. Over here it's essential that you know your location at all times.

"The third is that you never allow your men to carry the AK-47 instead of the M-16. The AK is the standard assault rifle of the VC and NVA. It has a very distinct cracking pop when fired, much different from that of the M-16. In a firefight when that cracking sound is heard, soldiers tend to cut loose in that direction. Shooting first, looking later. So you can see what might happen. Not to mention the problem of ammo re-supply and the fact the M-16 is a superior weapon."

The colonel had a point, thought Hank, though he'd heard barracks talk contrary to the colonel's opinion of the M-16. Some vets had criticized the M-16 as too sensitive to dirt, needing constant cleaning to prevent stoppages. Others said the 5.56mm round and high velocity deflected too easily and lacked stopping power. He had used M-14s in the States at Benning, though he had to qualify with an M-16 before shipping overseas. Nevertheless, he agreed with the colonel, preferring the M-16. For one reason; it was lighter, thus easier to lug.

"The fourth and final thing you should be familiar with is the construction

of a good bunker with proper firing ports and firing lanes. We pride ourselves in our bunkers, even though we borrowed the design from the NVA.
Did they show you how to build one in JD school?"

"Yes, sir," Dick spoke up quickly. "We spent the better part of a day digging those damn things."

"Digging is a common chore over here, Lieutenant Kistler. You'll find the
rifle companies are continuously moving to other areas, setting up fire support bases and NDPs. Did your JD school orientation include the enemy
units that are our usual adversary?" the colonel inquired, changing tack.

"Negative, sir," Dick answered crisply.

The colonel's dark eyebrows came close together, perturbed at this ped-
agogical omission. "Most of our fighting is against two primary units: the
Dong Nai Regiment consisting mostly of hardcore Viet Cong; and the Seventh NVA Division, a well supplied and well organized unit. Both are tough.
But then so are we," he added.

He reached over and picked the map off the easel. He positioned the map
to face the two junior officers, leaned over it, and pointed his right index
finger. "This is where we are now," he said as he pointed to a black grease
penciled dot. "Besides my command post, Bravo Company is also located
here. To the northeast, two klicks, is Charlie Company. Directly to the east,
four klicks, is Delta. Alpha is currently operating outside of the Di An base
camp, opcon temporarily to another unit."

He looked at Hank. "Lieutenant Kirby."

Hank stirred uneasily

"I'm assigning you to Bravo." His eyes shifted to Dick. "And lieutenant
Kistler, you'll go to Charlie Company."

"Yes, sir."

Before I send a platoon leader to his company, I send him to another company for an overnight stay. That way he can see first hand how platoon
leaders perform in the field. This will give you further insight before taking
over your own platoon in your assigned company. Consider it your final
part of JD school.

"Kirby, I'm sending you to Delta. Tomorrow you'll return here to join
your company. Kistler, you'll remain here with Bravo for the night before
going to Charlie. Any questions?"

Hank had one. "Sir, when can we expect mail?"

"Anytime now, I suppose, depending when you informed your family of the Battalion's address and APO number." The colonel waited for other questions. None came. "Get your gear ready, Lieutenant Kirby. A loach will be here in about a half hour to fly you to Delta. Both of you see Sergeant Andrews about arrangements." The colonel rose, and the two lieutenants scrambled to beat him to his feet.

They saw Andrews who advised Hank to take just the necessities that would get him through the night. This totaled only his rifle and equipment harness with its accouterments of magazine ammo pouches, canteens, and snap links.

The two friends stood around the mortar boxes, realizing their time had come.

"Hey, Hank, take it easy," Dick said, offering forth his big paw, seeing the melancholy in his friend's eyes. "We're in the same Battalion. We'll stay in touch."

Hank took Dick's hand with his two hands. "Yeah, sure," he replied without conviction. Being with Dick had made things bearable. "Let's make sure we get our R and R together."

"You bet," Dick grinned. "We'll tear up Australia. They got some nice long-legged babes there, I heard."

Hank smiled wryly. He'd abandon his friend in a second for an R and R in Hawaii with Pam. They had discussed that possibility their last night together, but had decided it was not in the realm of possibility. Simply because of money, or rather lack of it. It was important to build a nest egg before their marriage, they had decided, though it had been mostly Pam. She would live at home and pinch pennies and he would put most of his $518 per month paycheck in a special investment fund for Vietnam service personnel that earned ten percent tax free. You couldn't beat that, they had decided. Though now, standing around ammo boxes in the midst of the NDP, he knew he could. He'd give every damn cent for one week in Hawaii with Pam.

"Now, Hank," Dick was saying with a facetious grin, "don't be too much of a hero. Save some of the medals for us other guys."

"Yeah," Hank laughed halfheartedly. "I'll try."

CHAPTER 11

OUTSIDE THE WIRE, a shirtless, helmeted soldier pulled the pin on a smoke grenade and tossed it to the ground. A thick violet cloud streamed forth. Almost immediately the loach, a small, green, light observation helicopter, dropped down into the smoke, swirling it in all directions. The soldier motioned Hank to move. Crouching low in fear of the spinning rotor blades and tightly gripping his M-16, Hank rushed, eyes squinting, to the cockpit. He climbed in and strapped himself into the seat beside the warrant officer pilot. The loach rose slowly in the air, pivoted ninety degrees, and headed east.

Like a large gnat, the chopper buzzed over huge fields of rice paddies and two narrow muddy streams. Hank was apprehensive about the low altitude. He mentally braced himself for the likelihood of AK rounds peppering his behind.

Shortly, another NDP came into view. Bright yellow smoke billowed from an open area just beyond the perimeter. The loach sank into it, its skids touching down. The pilot gestured for Hank to get out.

He gladly obliged and stepped down and scurried in a bent position away from the beating blades.

At the edge of the wire a tall, ebony-skinned sergeant greeted him. "I'm First Sergeant Williams. Welcome to Delta Company, Lieutenant Kirby," he said as they wove through one of the wire maze entrances standard with NDPs and fire support bases.

The sergeant led him past the mortar pits and into the command tent. The sides were down and it felt like a sauna. "Captain Harding, this is Lieutenant Kirby," the sergeant introduced Hank to the company commander who was standing next to the center pole, lazily scratching a bare, pinkish chest matted over with curly red stubbles. He wore gold rimmed glasses rather than the drab gray frames the Army issued. A smoldering cigarette protruded between the scratching fingers.

Formalities were exchanged and the three men seated themselves on air mattresses. Hank guessed only the colonel had the luxury of cots.

"So you're with us for tonight, eh?" Harding said more as a statement than a question.

"Yes, sir."

"What company you gonna be assigned to?" Harding inhaled deeply on his cigarette.

"Bravo Company, sir."

"Bravo, huh? That's Captain Connors' outfit. Good soldier. West Point." Harding took another drag and exhaled the smoke slowly through nose and mouth. He scratched his chest some more. "I've got my First Platoon going out tonight on ambush. How'd you like to go along? You might learn something. And who knows, maybe we'll bag a few Charlies." He smiled sardonically. His eyes probed Hank's.

"Well…I guess so," mumbled Hank. He knew he had little choice. What else could he say? Fuck no; he wanted to stay here on the air mattress until the chopper came for him tomorrow?

Captain Harding picked up the handset to a nearby PRC-25 radio set affectionately nicknamed "prick twenty-five."

"Lima Six, this is Delta Six, over."

"This is Lima Six," a voice came from the squawk box next to the radio.

"This is Delta Six. I have a guest for you tonight. Come by my CP ASAP."

"Wilco, out," came the reply.

Moments later a short man with a dark, bushy moustache entered the tent. His unbuttoned fatigue shirt was a patchwork of dirt and sweat. A lieutenant's bar was penciled in on his right collar.

"Lieutenant Kirby, this is Lieutenant John Simpson. John has the First Platoon."

Hank came to his feet and the two men shook hands. "John, I want you to take Kirby with you on AP tonight. Show him how we do it over here. Give him all the know-how you can."

"Wilco, sir," Simpson replied.

"Kirby, go along with John now as he prepares for tonight's program."

Hank nodded.

The two lieutenants emerged into a glaring sun. Simpson led him to the platoon area. Along the way he learned Hank's first name and enquired about how things were back in the World.

"How long you been in-country?" Hank asked, as he seated himself on the edge of a firing bunker.

"Not too long. I've only been in the field a little more than a month."

"Much action?"

"Nope!" Disappointment showed all over Simpson's face. "Been sniped at a few times. That's about it. We haven't had a body count since I've been here. Shit, there just ain't any VC around."

"I wouldn't be too upset about that," Hank said and laughed weakly.

Simpson ignored his remark and turned to a wiry man sitting on a nearby bunker. "Hey, Brown?" he barked. "Go tell Lima Five and the squad leaders that I want to see them in ten minutes."

Brown put down the M-16 he was cleaning, checked the volume of the PRC-25 next to him, and trotted away from the bunker.

Simpson turned back to Hank. "See those three lone palm trees about six-hundred meters from here?" He pointed west across an expanse of open rice paddies.

"Yeah."

"Right behind them, in that narrow string of woods, is our ambush site."

Squinting into the sun, Hank studied the area closely. The idea of traveling across open paddies didn't appeal to him.

He busied himself while waiting for supper. He cleaned his rifle, checked his ammo, and was issued four smoke grenades, one Claymore mine, and two fragmentation grenades which he carefully put in a canteen pouch attached to his pistol belt. This was Battalion SOP he learned from Simpson. For safety sake. Months ago, a soldier in Alpha carrying grenades hooked to his harness had had the pin removed by a jungle vine. They never found his head. So said Simpson.

After filling his three canteens from the water buffalo, Hank moved through the platoon of twenty-five men and observed them getting ready. They appeared calm. It seemed routine to them. He wondered if they could tell that their guest lieutenant was close to cardiac arrest.

At 1800 hours hot chow was served from mermite cans that had been prepared in Phu Loi and shipped out to the NDP by Chinook. Following supper, the platoon made final preparations.

At 1845 hours Simpson picked up the handset of the PRC-25. "Delta Six, Lima Six. We're getting ready to depart," he radioed Harding.

"This is Delta Six. Roger. Let's get a body count tonight."

"Will try. Out." Lieutenant Simpson gave the handset to Brown, his RTO.

"Lima Five," Simpson shouted to his platoon sergeant. "Have them saddle up and move out."

Hank picked up his equipment harness by its straps. It was heavy, weighted by a pistol belt to which were attached two ammo pouches, each containing four magazines, two canteen covers, one holding a full canteen, the other the frag grenades, two smoke grenades, their levers set in loop holes on the outside of the ammo pouches, a bayonet, and M-16 cleaning gear. Two canteens dangled from snap links where the back harness straps held the pistol belt. On the front straps were two more smoke grenades and a first aid packet, which was the Army's grandiose name for a big bandage.

He staggered slightly under his load and added to it, as he placed a bandoleer of seven magazines, eighteen rounds per, over his left shoulder and under his right arm.

Then the crowning weight, the Claymore satchel, came over the other shoulder to counterbalance the bandoleer. This bothered him the most, not just with the added weight, but with the thought of it resting just above his left hip. The Claymore was a gray-blue, arc-shaped mine, electrically detonated through one hundred feet of wire. Small and innocuous in appearance, it could obliterate most anything within a fan-shaped radius of fifty meters with its multitude of flying tiny steel balls. Even the back blast reached fifteen meters.

With the bandoleer and rifle he looked like a modern day Pancho Villa. Though with all the weight he carried, he could have been Villa's jackass. This thought ran through his mind as he started moving with the flow of the platoon.

The platoon passed in a long, snaking file through the maze at the perimeter wire. Once on the other side they became two files, about fifty meters apart. Hank followed in the first half of the right file about fifteen meters behind Simpson's RTO.

They headed toward a falling sun.

When they reached the rice paddies, each file climbed on a dike and followed a straight, symmetrical path. When the dike ended they turned ninety degrees onto another dike. As each dike ran out another one would meet, and so on, as they proceeded in zigzag fashion towards the three palms and the thin wood-line beyond.

Hank winced inwardly. Walking on dikes was not according to Benning. They were totally exposed, like moving ducks in a shooting gallery. Well, he wasn't going to follow the leader. Not when his life was at stake.

He slid down two feet to the base of the paddy amidst the sparse green rice stalks, and quickly found his boot adsorbed in soft, sloppy mud. Suddenly, in a feeling of panic he understood why they were walking on the dikes as he struggled to set his legs free from the sucking mire. Managing to get one foot free, he became unbalanced and in order not to fall, slipped his free foot back into the black ooze, now deeper than before. Then he fell back and sunk up to his waist. The rice paddy had become a quagmire. The weight of his equipment pushed him further into the mud. He hissed a curse.

The PFC following him saw his predicament. In a hushed voice he called forward to the platoon leader's RTO who, in turn, trotted up to Simpson, tapped him on the back, and then radioed the left file to hold up. The platoon halted. They all turned and watched the new lieutenant, his ass stuck in the mud.

Hank felt the knowing weight of their eyes. He wanted to scream back at them, admitting that, yes, they were right. He didn't belong over here. He was a bozo. He'd get someone killed, probably himself.

Two PFCs hurried up the file and tossed ropes to Hank's waving arms. He could detect faint smiles that wanted to burst forth into loud snickers as they observed his helpless plight. Chuckles hid behind their wide eyes of fake concern. He slung his rifle over a shoulder, grabbed the ropes tightly, and pulled hard with his arms, kicking his legs, his upper torso leaning forward in the mud. Finally, he freed himself and crawled, gasping, up on the dike.

As he got to his feet, one of the men pointed to the inside of his left forearm and whispered calmly to him, "Sir, you got a leech."

Hank looked down and saw a dark, hideous creature attached to his skin, hungrily sucking his blood out. He started to reach a shaky hand over and pluck it away when the PFC's hand stopped him.

"Hold it. I'll get it." The informer plucked a white plastic bottle of bug juice from the rubber band around his helmet. He squeezed a few drops on the voracious intruder and it instantly dropped off.

"Thanks, trooper," Hank smiled weakly. He felt faint, as if the leech had gotten a few pints rather than just drops.

Seeing that Hank was ready to continue, Lieutenant Simpson shook his head in disgust before signaling for the platoon to start moving again by swirling his hand around in the air. The two files rose slowly from their kneeling positions and resumed their mission.

Muck and grit bit uncomfortably into Hank's legs as he squished along in soaked boots. His fears flamed his already over-active imagination. What if more leeches were on his body? He imagined legions attached to his legs, and groin area, trying to devour him, taking particular delight in munching on his balls. If only he could stop the platoon once more, take down his pants, and thoroughly check himself over.

Maybe get one of those snickering PFCs to look up his ass. That would keep him from laughing, he thought cynically.

Darkness was accelerating as they neared their ambush site. The platoon stopped and set up in a temporary over-watch position where they waited for complete darkness. Then in blackness, they sneaked into a thin wood-line with open fields on either side.

Now they broke up into six groups of at least four men each, and with minimal confusion, strung themselves out in a long line. They became part of the woods. Every other group faced in the same direction. Hank kept close to Simpson's side as they settled next to a small tree.

After each group was in position, they stripped off their equipment and began putting out their Claymores.

"Where do you want mine?" Hank asked as Simpson arranged his equipment neatly on the ground. He wondered if Simpson would get the pun. He was playing his own mind game to escape reality.

Simpson swept his arm toward a sector of the open field they were facing. "Out there about sixty feet."

Hank crouched low and crept stealthily with a racing heart into the knee-high grass, his Claymore in one hand, his rifle in the other. He adjusted the legs of the mine at an angle to give maximum range, inserted the blasting cap, and quickly unrolled the wire back to his position where he fastened the end to the electrical detonator called a "clacker" and checked its safety mechanism. *Shit*, he swore silently. He should have checked the safety first before fastening the wire.

Hank was aghast at the way this ambush was shaping up. The men seemed too complacent, and the groups were watching for their quarry in the open fields. More than likely, he thought the VC would come down the tree-line they were hiding in, not from out in the open. To make matters worse, their flanks were guarded by groups with no radio commo, the only ones without any, though they needed it most. The two M-60 machine guns, the best he could tell when he tried to observe them setting up, had no fields of fire to cover likely enemy approaches.

"Hank," Simpson whispered. "At twenty-two hundred hours we begin taking our turns on watch. One man up per group. You've got the fourth watch from two-thirty to four. Wake me at zero four hundred for mine."

Hank nodded nervously. It would be a long, lonely hour and a half.

Most everyone settled into a prone position. A few sat up, their backs against trees. Some wrapped themselves in poncho liners like cocoons, their heads barely exposed. Was this an ambush or a Boy Scout overnight? Hank sought escape in his silent sarcasm. He tried not to think about how long it would take for them to unwind themselves from their cocoons.

When he saw Simpson's head go completely under his blanket, he figured it to be around 2200 hours. He searched to find some degree of comfort and rest. But it was impossible. His bulky gear poked him in the ribs and back, and though it seemed ill-advised from the standpoint of readiness, he, too, quietly slipped out of his magazine bandoleer and harness straps and placed his equipment to his front. This helped some, but the worst was his wet, muddy pants which kept him cold, clammy, and gritty from the waist down. The mental torture of the ambush was excruciating enough without this constant reminder of his stupidity.

The night was alive with insect noises. Crickets droned incessantly in the distance. More disturbing was the maddening buzz of mosquitoes. But there was little biting as faces and appendages were saturated with the oily bug juice from the white squeeze bottles.

Hank managed a half slumber as he lay in the fetal position with one side of his head partly tucked into his helmet and his right hand resting gently on the handgrip of his rifle.

"Sir." Someone tapped him lightly on the shoulder.

Instantly awake, he twisted around and tightened his grip on his rifle. The dark shadowy face of the RTO was peering down at him.

"It's your watch," Brown said in a hushed tone.

Hank pushed himself up to a sitting position as Brown handed him the handset. "The company calls sitreps every half hour. Just answer 'unchanged' or 'negative.' Our AP call sign is Dapper One," Brown whispered. Not waiting for a reply, he crawled a few meters away and silently plopped down in the grass.

A half moon had come out, emitting a dull, milky light that cast a ghostly hue over the fields of mostly interlocking rice paddies that Hank now observed while on his stomach. His elbows supported his head, the handset flush against his right ear. He let his eyes stray cautiously around the ambush site at the dark lumps of sleeping bodies scattered around. One soldier in the adjacent group was sitting up, slowly swiveling his head back and forth like a lighthouse beacon in the opposite direction of Hank's vigil.

Minutes dragged by. He sought to escape the lonely watch by taking refuge in a daydream. In his mind's eye, he'd just returned to Travis Air Force Base. He was off the plane. Pam had surprised him, had flown to California, unable to bear the waiting for him any longer. She ran to him, crying tears of happiness…

The sound of loud snoring transported him back to Vietnam. It wasn't the low muffled variety that had blended with and become part of the myriad of night noises. The sitting sentry at the position to his right had fallen asleep. A power failure in the lighthouse. "Goddamn him," Hank cursed under his breath. His only recourse was to crawl over and wake him. And though it was but ten meters, it looked a hundred.

Half anticipating being shot accidentally by some trigger-happy ambusher awakened suddenly, he stealthily crawled on all fours with his M-16 gripped tightly in his right hand toward the sleeping sentry. Once there, his left hand clutched the slumbered body with a vice-like grip. "Wake up, damn you!" he admonished in a vicious whisper.

The sentry sat up instantly, looking alert, as if nothing had happened, as if the visiting lieutenant had imagined his nodding off. Hank was tempted to say more, but then thought better. He was only an observer, a guest so to speak.

Hank returned to his spot. The moon had vanished, and a chilling downpour had begun. He regretted not having a towel or poncho liner.

"Dapper One, Dapper One. This is Delta Kilo. sitrep?" The voice came into his ear from the handset.

He pressed the push-to-talk button. "This is Dapper One. Sitrep unchanged."

"Dapper One, Dapper One. This is Delta Kilo, Delta Kilo. What is your SITREP???"

"This is Dapper One, I say again. Sitrep unchanged." This time Hank's voice was a shade louder.

Again the same transmission persisted and Hank checked the radio for a malfunction. After adjusting the squelch and placing the whip antenna to a more upright position, he repeated the answer. "This is Dapper One. Sitrep unchanged. Over."

"This is Delta Kilo. Roger. Keep awake out there. Out."

"Bite my ass," Hank muttered angrily to himself.

The rain had slackened by the time he aroused Simpson to take over the watch. Finished with the transfer of responsibilities, simply symbolized by handing over the radio's handset, Hank lay back down and huddled into a ball to conserve what warmth he could in the miserable dampness.

No VC intruded during the wee morning hours. At 0530 he was awakened by a firm hand shaking his shoulder. The platoon gathered in their Claymores, folded their poncho liners, and suited up in their battle gear in preparation for their hike back to the NDP. A half hour later, they were secured within the perimeter.

Hank immediately rid himself of his wet fatigues. While washing away the caked mud and grit under a cold field shower, he thoroughly inspected himself all over three times for signs of any lingering leeches. He found none and felt a huge sense of relief.

After the shower, the First Sergeant Williams rewarded him with a clean, wrinkled pair of fatigues and dry socks. He shaved with Simpson's razor and ate a hot breakfast of eggs, sausage, and toast served from mermite cans, courtesy of a Chinook from Phu Loi.

Shortly before noon, he was waiting near the perimeter wire for his loach. His spirits were surprisingly high. He had survived his first test.

He saw the loach approaching from a distance, a small, growing speck in the sky. He closed his eyes and silently prayed Pam's letter would be waiting for him.

CHAPTER 12

"SIR, BRAVO'S CP is over there. They should be expecting you." A staff sergeant directed him past the two mortar pits.

"Thank you, Sarge," Hank replied. He was wearing his combat gear and toting his rucksack which he had just picked up by the colonel's tent.

He trekked over to a round tent with its sides down. He was about to poke his head in, when a bronze skinned, bare-chested man in his mid-thirties stepped out and faced him.

"I'm First Sergeant Mendez. You must be Lieutenant Kirby." There was a trace of a curious blend of Mexican-Spanish with south Texas. His droopy eyes glinted warmly and were recessed in a leather-lined face that looked older than his years.

"That's right," Hank answered as they shook hands.

"Take your stuff off and come inside. Bravo Six ain't here right now. Went to Phu Loi."

Inside, it was another canvas oven. It was cluttered with combat gear; poncho liners, ammo boxes, air mattresses, and one large prone body. A half naked fellow lay belly down on an air mattress. He twisted his head and peered up. His face was a contrast of baby fat jowls covered by thick, steel wool whiskers.

"Lieutenant Kirby, this is Lieutenant Sawyer, our FO."

The artillery forward observer sat up to shake hands. "Glad to meet you; what's your first name?"

"Hank."

"I'm Jack. Kind of new myself. Ain't that right, Top?"

Right, sir," Mendez smiled slyly. "You've been here two weeks but it seems like two years the way you've taken over our CP. I can't find nothin' in here with all your junk scattered around. Sir."

The FO tilted his head back and emitted a long, gurgling chuckle. "That's the price you pay, Top, for my expertise in laying those rounds just where you want 'em. Remember, it's the artillery that has the balls and the infantry that gets fucked," he chuckled again and looked back at Hank. "Where you from back in the World?"

"Florida. Vero Beach."

"Never heard of it. But you should feel right at home in this beautiful tropical paradise," Sawyer laughed. "And that reminds me. It's God-awful hot in here. When you going to get the sides up, Top? You trying to get me to sweat off my fat ass?"

"No, sir. I didn't want to interrupt your beauty nap."

It was obvious there was an affable camaraderie between the two.

"Have you had lunch, sir?" Mendez asked Hank.

"No, I haven't."

"Well, we'll fix that," Mendez said and then exited.

Hank's posterior sunk down in a nearby air mattress. "Where you from, Jack?" Hank returned the question, guessing that the FO expected it.

"California. San Diego."

"I've heard of it."

There was a moment of silence. The geographic distance in their lives too great to sustain the conversation.

"How do you like being with Bravo?" Hank asked, getting back to common ground.

"Damn good company. Even if it hasn't had a body count since I've been here."

Mendez returned with a box of C-rations and a cold can of Coke. "All I could find was ham and eggs," he said apologetically.

"That's all right, Top. I'll wash it down with the soda." *Why me?* he asked himself. He was convinced that canned ham and eggs was dog's puke.

Mendez seated himself on an empty mortar box. "When you finish, I'll take you to meet the other platoon leaders. I'm told that Bravo Six might not be back before supper."

Reluctantly, Hank plucked the can of ham and eggs from the box and with the little Army-issued can opener, complimentary with each box and better for slicing fingers than can tops, he started opening it. He would have avoided this torture and foregone this main course had he not wanted to waste the Top's benign efforts in securing him a meal.

Not having to carry the conversation as he ate, the first sergeant and FO filled this role, discussing the company. The Third Platoon and Mortars didn't have lieutenants. It was their guess he would probably be assigned to the Third Platoon.

As they chatted there was a rumble of thunder that preceded a heavy rain shower which momentarily cooled the air. The beating rain drops gave Hank a strange, cozy feeling. After the rain had passed, the first sergeant guided him through fresh, slippery mud to the Second Platoon's bunker positions. Here he met Lieutenant Frank Cronin, a skinny, friendly fellow, soaked from the rain and his own perspiration. The exchange of pleasantries was brief, since he was busy overhauling a portion of the perimeter defenses.

Even so, Hank liked him immediately. Saying that they would get together later, Lieutenant Cronin continued with his chores. After next meeting Sergeant Bird, the Mortar Platoon leader, the pair trod carefully over the slick mud to the First Platoon.

"Lieutenant Brussels, this is Lieutenant Kirby, our new platoon leader," Mendez performed the introductions.

Shirtless, Lieutenant Brussels had been throwing a large hunting knife into a wooden post. He paused and stuck out his throwing hand. "Call me Ed," he said, and with the other hand brushed his thick, dirty blonde hair back from his forehead.

"I'm Hank."

"Lieutenant Kirby," the first sergeant interjected, "I've got a few things to do before the CO gets back. I'll leave you here with Lieutenant Brussels."

"OK, Top, I'll see you later."

Mendez strode away.

Brussels went back to his knife throwing, apparently not wanting to indulge in idle conversation. Hank perched himself on a bunker and watched him. A cigarette dangled loosely from Brussels' lips as he intensely focused his concentration on the 8x8 post standing five feet high. The post seemed to have no purpose except as a scabbard for Brussels' knife. He would slowly wind up until his right arm was reaching far behind him like a tennis server, his lips biting the cigarette, becoming rigid. Then with a grunt he'd send the blade flying, rotating through a single loop and then thudding a good inch into the post. Not once did he miss. If he had, it would have carried through the perimeter wire.

And it was fortunate he had a deadeye because outside the wire Vietnamese children from one of the nearby villages had gathered. The youngsters shouted at Hank whom they had figured from his idleness had little purpose and who was, therefore, a good mark for their banter. "GI give baby-sans chop-chop? GI number one, give chop-chop?"

Hank shrugged and held his palms outward to show he was helpless to help them. He looked over at Brussels for assistance who responded by letting go a mighty heave that penetrated the post almost two inches.

Brussels left the knife embedded. He tossed away his cigarette, reached down into the sleeping position behind the bunker, and picked up a C-ration.

"Sir!" One of his men saw what he was about to do. "Don't let Bravo Six see you."

"Fuck it!" barked Brussels. "He ain't around. Neither's the colonel."

He then sailed the can high over the razor-edged concertina wire and into a large mudhole. The children scampered for the can. They pushed and shoved one another. Finally, one muddied lad emerged victorious. He ran from the others, holding his prize high above his head, his gloating face filled with smiling dirty teeth.

Brussels laughed aloud at this newest sport and gleefully said to Hank, "Now watch them this time." He picked up an empty C-ration can. Using a sidearm motion, he hurled it into the middle of the mudhole. Once again, the children fought one another in the mud.

The winner's elated expression swiftly changed to one of bitter disgust when he discovered the ruse. With open animosity he ran toward the wire and threw the empty can back over at Brussels. "GI number ten!" he yelled at the top of his lungs. Soon his playmates joined the chant in unison until Brussels pulled his knife from the post and flipped it menacingly in his hand. They quickly scattered like a frightened school of shark-chased fish.

Brussels doubled over with laughter.

Hank decided he didn't like Brussels. He got off the bunker, wanting to go elsewhere. But where? Mendez approached and made the decision for him.

"Bravo Six came back early. He's ready for you," Mendez informed him.

Hank returned to the CP tent, now with its sides rolled up. Inside he found a broad-shouldered man sitting cross-legged on an air mattress, twisting a large unlit cigar in his mouth. His face was rugged, his eyes discerning and gray. "Lieutenant Kirby, I presume," he said in a thick, whispery voice. "I'm Captain Connors, your CO," he said, extending his hand.

"Hank Kirby, sir," said Hank as he bent over and shook hands. He guessed the CO to be in his mid-twenties.

"Have a seat, Hank," Captain Connors gestured with his cigar to a flat wooden ammo box opposite him. "How was your stay with Delta last night?"

Hank hesitated before answering. Finally, he said, "I thought it a little hairy."

"Hairy?" Connors' eyebrows flew up. "What happened? You see a few Charlies?"

"No, sir. It was the way the ambush was conducted." Hank paused, wanting his remarks to end there. But his CO's cold, questioning stare and active lips rolling the soggy tip of the cigar forced him to continue. "The site selection seemed poor. We should've been ambushing where we were sleeping…" The stare stayed on him. "And the fields of fire were not carefully selected. And there was too much noise…and too much indifference…." Connors' eyes felt like hot lasers. "At least it seemed so. Maybe I'm wrong, though. I just got over here. I'm too inexperienced. I…"

"The whole damn Battalion is too inexperienced!" Connors cut him off. "That's our problem. After Tet we've had a big turnover. And you're right about Delta. They can't ambush worth a shit. They just go out and sleep till dawn. Don't even adjust defcons." He referred to Defensive Concentrations, the act of registering artillery or mortar rounds around the ambush site.

"Let's get down to business, Hank. I'm assigning you to the Third Platoon. Its call sign is November. Staff Sergeant Gomez is your platoon sergeant. He's been the platoon leader for about a month now. Done a fine job fillin' in. The lieutenant who had the platoon got an early ticket to the World. Got into a pit of *punji* stakes. He'll be all right but, by God, he should've been more careful."

Hank grimaced. He wondered if the razor-sharp tips of the bamboo *punji* stakes had been dipped in water buffalo dung. According to Benning, that was the usual SOP to cause infection in the victim.

"Tonight, your platoon will secure the NDP. You've got to take charge right away. By the way, have you had much air assault training?"

"No, sir, not really. At Benning we rode out in trucks and hopped out to the side of the road. That was our air assault training. I really don't know much about it." Hank feigned a look of regret.

"That figures. The shitty infantry school teaches you just enough to get your balls shot off, and JD school specializes in digging holes," the captain grunted in disgust, and Hank nodded his head in complete agreement. His CO was sounding like he knew his stuff. "But that being the case, we'll go over the particulars of air assault tomorrow. I want your platoon to rehearse it because in the past they've never done one right. It won't be with trucks, but it won't be with choppers either. It'll be with your feet. And you'll still learn more than at Benning. OK, Hank, let's go meet your platoon.

"Oh, by the way, something came for you." He reached back between the air mattress and low wall of sandbags. When he turned back around his hand held a thick, pink envelope from which emanated the strong, sweet fragrance of Shalimar.

Hank's face filled with ecstatic, boyish delight as he snatched the letter. "Thank you, sir," he nearly shouted. "I've been waitin' for this."

"You'll have to wait a little longer. Let's get going. That smell should hold you over for a while."

They were about ten meters from a supplementary bunker, one behind the front-line bunkers, with firing ports having fields of fire that covered two front line bunkers, when Connors stopped and motioned to a short, stocky man with a small, black moustache. He wore a floppy jungle hat and looked to be in his early thirties. He had been huddled with three men, appearing to give them instructions. When he saw the CO, he immediately ended the meeting and walked over.

Captain Connors' introduction was simple and brief: "Sergeant Gomez, you got a new platoon leader. This is Lieutenant Kirby. I'll let you two get acquainted. I'm going to check the perimeter before chow." He turned and strode away, leaving Hank with Gomez.

"I hear we got a good platoon, Sarge." Hank hadn't heard it but thought starting with a little honey was a good way to begin.

"Yes, sir. I think so. But I'm glad you're here," said Gomez whose English was flavored with a slight Puerto Rican accent. Gomez kept a big smile on his face.

"Really?" Hank was somewhat surprised. "I was thinking you might be a little upset having someone new take over. Especially someone with no actual combat experience," he said candidly. If Gomez was going to have resentment he might as well flush it out now.

"Oh no, sir. On the contrary. I'm a platoon sergeant, not a platoon leader. Captain Connors is very good company commander, but he loves to chew my ass. Now with you here, it will be your ass, not mine." He grinned at Hank.

"You don't sound encouraging," said Hank wryly.

"Don't worry, you'll manage. As for the combat part, that's something I can't teach. You learn for yourself. In fact, we all learn together. The Third Platoon has many newcomers. I am one of the few veterans. I been here since March, and seen little action. I guess the Third Platoon might be considered blessed. For that matter, so are the other platoons. The most Bravo seen of a firefight or popped ambush since Tet is what we read in the *Stars and Stripes*. And there's hardly anyone in the platoon, the company, and for that matter the Battalion left over from Tet. Those that weren't killed or wounded or derosed got remf jobs."

Hank thought of Lieutenant Voight as one that had earned remf status. He would try to maintain the platoon's blessed stature. "Captain Connors said things had been quiet, but I didn't know that quiet," he said, and for the first time he wondered if things were quiet because the war could be winding down. Maybe after Tet, the VC didn't have much punch left.

The platoon sergeant's big smile became huge. "Bravo Six always tries to keep us on our toes," he replied.

Hank nodded. It was up to the coach to keep the players fired up. "Tell me more about the platoon. How many men do we have? And weapons?"

"Good question, sir. The T, O, and E here's different than in the field manuals. At present, we have thirty-two men assigned, but only twenty-eight with us. The others are sick except one who's back at Quan Loi awaiting court martial. We don't worry about them. That's XO's job. Our platoon has two rifle squads and one weapons squad with two M-60s. But we generally attach one gun to each rifle squad.

"We have four prick twenty-fives, all working. Each rifle squad leader has one, and of course, you and me." Gomez paused from his recitation and glanced around at the men milling about the sector of bunkers designated to the Third Platoon. "I'll get squad leaders together for you to meet."

"Not just yet, Sergeant Gomez. Let's wait till after supper." Hank gave his first official command as the new November Six.

"Roger that, sir. By the way, take my compass. It's best in the platoon." Gomez took the compass that was hanging from a nylon cord around his neck like a long, pendant necklace and handed it to him.

"Thanks, but won't you need it?"

"Don't worry, I'll get another one. Here, take my map too," he offered, and pulled a clear plastic bag containing a folded map from the leg pocket of his jungle fatigues.

"This is one to twenty-five thousand. That's the scale you need here. Some places where it's hilly, one to fifty-thousand is better."

As he delivered the map to Hank, a scrawny redheaded kid drew near. "Sir," Gomez looked at the sunburned youth, "this is your radioman. Best damn RTO in company."

Hank measured him cautiously, as if this half-emaciated freshman was not the same one to whom Gomez referred.

"November Six, I'm PFC Tucker," he introduced himself with a shy, friendly grin. He then added in a tone of diffidence that cloaked its brashness, "I hope you're not gung-ho like the last one."

Hank was taken back by Tucker's forthrightness, and lack of military courtesy. After an awkward moment, he replied: "I may be a lot of things, but don't worry, I'm not gung-ho." He looked up and down at Tucker and imperceptibly shook his head, wondering why the skinny, frail guys always seemed to lug the heavy radios on their backs. Well at least he and Tucker were tuned to the same non gung-ho frequency. Maybe that should help them function together.

He turned to his platoon sergeant. "Sergeant Gomez, I'm going to sit down and read a letter before chow. Afterwards, I'll get my gear and then meet the squad leaders." He addressed Gomez with some formality, wanting to keep the game going of an officer in command. Later he'd let Gomez know that he would be a mere figurehead, that he would keep his head low and his nose out of Gomez's way. He'd help out with the map reading. He was good at that.

"Roger, sir," Gomez answered crisply and then departed.

"Don't worry about your gear, sir," Tucker said. "Tell me where it is and I'll get it."

"Thanks, Tucker," Hank replied, "it's right in front of the CO's CP."

Hank squatted down on a sandbag and stretched his legs out on the ground. He let out a deep sigh, venting the pressure that had built up from his first contact with members of his new platoon, and making room for the sweet, new pressure of anticipation. His fingers trembled slightly as he fished the letter from his breast pocket. He whiffed the flowery fragrance of Pam and gazed at her handwriting on the envelope. They were bits of her that were here with him and he cherished them. His mind slipped back over the past few weeks and how he had anxiously waited for this moment. The first leg of the journey had ended. He was now, officially, an Infantry Platoon leader, and he now had received his first letter from Pam. Finally.

He slowly read it, pausing long at phrases that proclaimed her love. Re-reading them, memorizing them. He marveled at this biochemical bond between them. It was unique; a whole world of people, yet they felt toward each other a feeling unmatched by others.

Her letter was long and touching and sad, her worrying, his loneliness. There seemed an infinite distance between them. How could he reach out 10,000 miles to her, comfort her, reassure her that he'd be coming back to her?

He thought for a long moment. Then his lips stretched into a thin, contemplative smile. Maybe there was a way; maybe the only way. He would begin at once, tonight, after he met his platoon. He would give her the comfort she needed. The comfort she deserved.

He inhaled her sweet fragrance once more and shoved the letter down into the right-side pocket of his fatigue shirt. He stood and walked slowly toward the mess line. In his thoughts he was a long, long way from this NDP. A very long way.

Hope you're not gung-ho… There, he had said it to his new platoon leader, PFC Tucker thought to himself, feeling somewhat ashamed that he'd spoken out of line, while at the same time relieved he'd done it for Cheryl. "Don't be a hero," she'd beseeched. "You're too accommodating, too helping, too nice. And I know that's why I love you, but this is one time I want you to think of only yourself. And if you can't, think of me and our child I'm carrying." Her words had been soldered to his brain. He appreciated her opinion of him, even though he knew the pedestal was imagined. Still, he always had a strong sense of fairness and duty.

And this duty is what had scared him with the first platoon leader, who had been a crazed bloodhound in search of the VC, the NVA, and their dead bodies he wanted to count. And as his RTO he had followed behind with no leash to pull on.

Thank God for those punji *stakes.* The lieutenant had laughed at them when the point man had found them at the bottom of a water-filled ditch. He wasn't going to go around them like everyone else was doing. He was going to jump over them. And he did. And his feet slipped on the mud bank and he let out a bloodcurdling scream as he fell back and his ass received their sharp points.

And even then he had wanted to feel sorry for his lieutenant who lay on his stomach, sobbing in pain, waiting for the dust-off to arrive. But then the lieutenant had somehow managed a twisted smile and said this would get him a Purple Heart.

Standing near the perimeter wire, Tucker stared outward across rice paddies, his stare traveling as far as Hank's thoughts had been. In a darkening late afternoon sky, light rain began to blur the landscape.

Tucker's mind wandered elsewhere. Back to the first day of his thirty-day leave following completion of AIT, Advanced Infantry Training, and before heading to Nam.

He would never forget it. Would never want to. He still had the letter in his left breast pocket, sealed in a plastic wrapper from a PRC-25 Battery. It was the letter from Cheryl, the one telling him of that night when they had created their first child.

He reached for the letter, as he always did at certain times, when certain things made him want to relive the reality of the past and ponder the future and forget the moment.

Things like when his first platoon leader fell on the *punji* stakes. And like when a new platoon leader took his place.

CHAPTER 13

P AM'S HEART BEAT with elation. Even the electrical storm outside with its brilliant flashes of light and ear-splitting claps of thunder could not dampen her spirits. Nor was she bothered by the loud blare of the *CBS Evening News*, which her father watched intently from his favorite overstuffed chair in the living room. Nor was she disturbed by the continuous, repetitive movement of her mother's needlework, as she sat beside Pam on the sofa, sewing.

Her fingers clutched the letter she had been reading. She simply had to share her exhilaration. "Daddy, do you mind if I turn the TV down a bit? I've got some really good news from Hank. You and Mom might want to hear it." Her voice bubbled like fine Champagne.

Her mother, Marion, an older, gray-haired edition of Pam, looked up from her handiwork. Her daughter's expression was contagious and she smiled, glancing at Fred, eagerly awaiting his consent.

His brow furrowed and veined, puffy jowls quivered slightly with indecision. He seemed immune to his daughter's excitement. Yet he had been the catalyst for Pam's current emotional state. He had come across Kirby's letter at the post office while sorting the incoming mail and had brought it home himself, this evening, not putting it aside for the carrier which would have delayed its delivery an extra day.

Well, he might as well wallow deeper in his good deed and force himself to listen to his daughter. Besides, Cronkite had little to offer at the moment. He already knew what a fucking fiasco the democratic convention in Chicago was. The only candidate worth a damn was Pegasus, the hog nominated by the Yippies. Nixon was his candidate; he'd get the peace, and with honor. But not too soon, he hoped. Otherwise Kirby might come back before his tour was up.

He grudgingly nodded his permission. Swiftly, Pam stretched from the sofa and turned down the volume. The sound of wind driven rain on the jalousie windows filled the room.

Glancing at key passages, Pam enthusiastically narrated the main theme of Hank's letter. "He writes that he really lucked out. For an infantry lieutenant he's got the plushest assignment possible. He's in a headquarters company of a Battalion and…let's see… he's taking over the responsibilities of a supply officer from a Lieutenant Voight. He says Quan Loi, where he's stationed, is a safe place that hasn't discovered there's a war on. He gets three hot meals a day at his Battalion's officers club and there is a full feature movie every night under the stars. The brigade which his Battalion's part of even has a steam bath where he relaxes every other day. He just hopes he doesn't get the gout over there," Pam giggled. "He wishes his buddy, Dick, who got assigned to a rifle platoon, could have things as good." Eyes brimming with tears of joy, she finished.

Her mom patted her hand reassuringly. "Oh that's wonderful, Pam. Hank's going to be just fine. Why that sounds better than his tour at Fort Gordon. From what you told us, he couldn't stand that."

Her dad didn't feel like provoking his perpetual argument about Hank, so he merely commented, "He's got it made," and went over to the TV, and turned the volume up.

He dropped back into his chair and rested his aching feet on the hassock. He thought about what Pam had said. It figured. The Army had sense enough not to put that guy where he could hurt someone. If only Pam could see her Hank the way he did, with both eyes open, not blinded by love, or infatuation, or whatever the hell it was. To make matters worse, it seemed that Dave Watson was giving up on her. He didn't write; he didn't call. Maybe he was too busy with football. That's probably it. A *Miami Herald* sports writer wrote he was a shoe-in to make the Dolphins as a reserve running back and special teamer. Now *he* was some kind of young man…and would be a perfect son-in-law.

"Daddy, will you do me a favor tomorrow?" Pam interrupted his sour thoughts.

Her voice was too sweet for him to refuse. "Certainly, sweetheart. What is it?"

"Mail a letter for me when you get to work so it goes out right away. I'm going to answer Hank's letter tonight." She had been pleasantly surprised that he had personally handed her Hank's letter and that he had not made any nasty comments tonight about him. If he would mail this letter, she might have hope his attitude toward Hank was changing.

Inwardly, Fred Sadler bridled at her request. But his outward composure denied his inner turmoil, except for his fingers digging into the arm rests. Before he answered, lightning from the storm flicked a short pulse of brightness into the room. And with it, like a revelation from a thundering heaven, came an idea. He gave a slow, benevolent smile. "Sure, Pam. Leave it on the table in the foyer and I'll get it on my way out the door in the morning."

Pam felt so happy. So much good was happening; Hank's assignment, her father's agreeable manner.

Fred Sadler gazed at the TV, but saw and heard nothing. He was too absorbed with his new idea. He needed carefully to formulate the plan. The stakes were high, but it could work. He would make it work. Maybe he could start implementing it when Pam started teaching. That might be the best time.

He would first have to make his daughter sad. It would be painful for him as well. But ultimately, she would be happier. And so would he. He was sure of it. Didn't someone once say that the end justified the means?

PART 2
THE CONFLICT

CHAPTER 14

G RIMY, SWEATY, EXHAUSTED, the Third Platoon trudged in double file, lugging all their gear into the Chinook. Its rear ramp closed, the beating rotor blades tilted and lifted the platoon up into the late afternoon sky. Ten minutes later they came down on a helipad in Phu Loi. They crowded into the back of a deuce-and-a-half and were trucked to Demon's forward supply area, a complex of mostly semi-permanent, A-framed structures that had been sublet from an armor unit currently operating outside of Saigon.

An NCO directed them to a hooch of solid construction: a tin roof over a wood truss and concrete floor, starkly furnished with a disorderly array of bunks with bare mattresses. Tired, the platoon dragged themselves and their stuff inside. Some fell into the bunks; others, goaded on by the expectation of a cold brew at a nearby EM club, readied themselves for showers.

Hank brought up the rear and trudged toward an unoccupied bottom bunk in the far corner. He dropped his gear and slid out of his equipment harness. He sat down gingerly, trying not to disturb his aching muscles. After a moment of resting his elbows on his thighs, he reclined on his back and shut his eyes. It would have been nice if his mind could have relaxed along with his body. But his mind stayed active, spinning slightly, replaying the events of the past week from which his body was now so loudly protesting.

The first three mornings his platoon had rehearsed for air assaults. It reminded Hank of his childhood days of playing make believe. The platoon would split into five groups, each pretending to be a helicopter sortie, and they would walk in file formation along the road next to the NDP. At his command, a waving of the hand, they simulated landing: the first, third and fifth group breaking to the right, the second and fourth to the left; everyone hitting the dirt and each group popping a smoke grenade to outline their boundaries. Running through the motions had been simple and they had mastered every detail. He now was very confident in his platoon's ability to conduct an air assault if they would be allowed to do one without helicopters.

The afternoons had been divided between ambush practice and perimeter maintenance. After his initial introduction by Lieutenant Simpson of Delta to the art of ambushing, Hank devised his own technique, much different from Simpson's and unlike any his platoon had used. It consisted of maintaining four groups.

This way, each group would have a PRC-25 radio plus at least a squad leader in command. The two machine guns could always be positioned to any situation and still keep full circle security. Two men were to be awake at all times at each group and sitreps were to be radioed every fifteen minutes from Hank's group to the other three, even though the distances between them would probably never be more than fifteen or twenty meters.

His rationale for this ambush arrangement was not to achieve a maximum kill zone, but to maximize control and security. This reasoning seemed widely accepted among his platoon and the first live ambush had gone smoothly, especially since no VC had ventured by.

On his fourth day, the entire company was Chinooked in four sorties to a small, flat hill overlooking rice paddies and a little Vietnamese village. There they established a new NDP, one and a half miles from the old one. The Battalion's CP had remained behind, secured by its Recon Platoon and the Mortar Platoon from Delta Company.

It was tough manual work constructing an NDP, much like doing hard labor on a chain gang. Only here there was no place to escape. Bunkers were dug, sandbags filled, firing lanes cut and leveled out, sleeping pits made, ponchos stretched into shelters, mortar pits prepared, barbed wire set up, and the company CP and supply tents pitched.

Hank had also spent the first week assiduously taking inventory on the key personnel in his platoon. Gomez was a good soldier, liked by the men, firmly in control.

On average, the squad leaders seemed okay. Sergeant Smith had the first squad. A light complexioned, blonde fellow, about the same age as Hank, he appeared to have a fair knowledge of small unit tactics and handled his squad well. Sergeant Percy, second squad leader, was a powerfully built black man a year younger than Hank. He seemed somewhat inexperienced, but with that Hank could empathize.

Hank had not sufficiently scrutinized the weapons squad leader, Sergeant Bennet, but according to Gomez he was a dud. He was older than Gomez, and with more years of service. Gomez predicted that he would never make staff sergeant and said the fact that he was already a buck sergeant was ample proof of the Army's ability to promote beyond one's capabilities. Something Hank could also empathize with.

Based on Gomez's evaluation, Hank became skeptical of having him as a squad leader; however, Gomez allayed his doubts by saying that since Bennet, as weapons squad leader, would only have charge of the two M-60 machine gun crews, and since each crew was usually attached to one of the rifle squads, he basically would have no field control. He merely tagged along behind one of the guns, his chief responsibility being to assure the guns were clean and functioning. This arrangement, Gomez had stated, would keep Bennet from getting somebody killed and at the same time, by being labeled a squad leader, gave deference to his long time in grade. This also alleviated a Bennet morale problem. Hank accepted this line of reasoning. Gomez was proving to be not only a good soldier but a wise one as well.

In contrast to Gomez's low opinion of Bennet, was his high praise for Spec-four Milton, a coal-black, lean, serious minded person in charge of the point element. Nicknamed, "Beacon," he had the stealth and caution of an Indian scout.

But next to Gomez, Hank's most valuable asset was PFC Tucker, his RTO. He was like an additional appendage, always keeping close to assist Hank with any chore, large or small, deftly manipulating radio traffic with great dispatch and authority, seeing that Hank, when preoccupied with a briefing session with Captain Connors, never got the worst pick of the C-rations or missed any hot meals. The skinny young man had tremendous energy, even when humping the heavy prick twenty-five. More amazing, considering Tucker's years, or in this case, the lack of them, was Gomez's revelation that Tucker was married.

Within the short span of one week, two other individuals stood out in Hank's mind, PFCs Franklin and Nordstrom. They had attended JD School with Hank. They were stateside friends, like he and Dick, only more so, having enlisted together in the Army's buddy program. Gomez had assigned

Franklin to one of the M-60s, the previous gunner having left after completing his tour, and no one else wanting it, since an M-60 was a magnet for enemy fire. Keeping the buddies close together, Gomez made Nordstrom, Franklin's chief ammo bearer. To Franklin, a taciturn twenty-year old, the gun had quickly become his fetish and he doted over it like a stray dog he had found and befriended. Nordstrom, the more outgoing of the two, continually joked and kidded about his friend's strange new relationship with his pet gun, and had even given it the name, Clyde. Both men, like Tucker, labored extremely hard around the NDP, and never had to be told to get off their lazy asses.

While assessing the platoon as a whole, Hank searched himself for some personal quality which would help him assert himself as the platoon leader. His rank would give him authority, not respect. His college degree gave him more education but not necessarily more sense. He had no combat experience, but then neither had the platoon. At least he was on par in that category. Only one thing, flimsy at most, was found, his age. At almost twenty-three, only Bennet and Gomez were older.

Due to the long lull in enemy activity and the battalion's close proximity to Phu Loi, a major base camp, Colonel West had instituted a policy of rotating one Rifle Platoon at a time into Phu Loi for stand-down, a night of rest and relaxation in the midst of clubs and recreation facilities. Bravo's turn to send its platoons began with the construction of their new NDP. The First Platoon, Brussels' unit, went first and missed a large part of the back-breaking NDP work. Then Cronin's platoon. Finally, Hank's platoon was given stand-down.

Hank shook his head, clearing the cobwebs. He decided his first priority was to get clean. He sat up and slowly bent over, sensitive to the painful twinges in the small of his back as he searched for soap in his rucksack. After finding a used, thin dirty bar, he looked up and saw Gomez approach.

"November Six, I told the men to do as they want. But be sure they sleep here tonight," Gomez said. His thin black moustache was flecked with brown grit. He looked pale and weary.

"Very good, Sergeant Gomez."

"Sir, I haven't been feeling so good lately. If it's OK with you, I'll get checked out by a doctor. Fletcher says there's a medical unit nearby."

"Of course it's all right. Probably just too much work and no play." Hank's light tone masked his concern. He couldn't afford to lose Gomez for a minute. "What seems to be the trouble?"

"Oh, a little fever, I think. Nothing serious. I'll be back tonight." He turned slowly and walked away, looking a bit unsteady as he exited.

Hank glanced around for the medic. Sighting him sprawled out just a few bunks away he called over, "Hey, Fletcher."

A small-boned, dark-haired youth looked up from a top bunk. His eyes blinked away his fatigue and he answered after recognizing the caller. "Yes, sir?"

"What's the story with Sergeant Gomez? He says he's not feeling well."

"That's right. Got a slight fever."

"Anything else?"

"Don't know, sir, but the doctor'll find out. I told him to see one. He knows where to go."

"Yeah, well keep me posted. OK?"

"Yes, sir."

Hank looked around for Tucker. Not seeing him he called back to Fletcher. "Also, Doc," Hank addressed him by the moniker given medics. "If anyone wants me, tell 'em I'm taking a shower."

He tugged off his boots and sauntered to the makeshift showers outside, a towel in one hand, a clean set of fatigues in the other. His right leg was about to swing free from his soiled pants, leaving him naked, like most field grunts, he wore no underwear, when Fletcher ran up shouting, "Lieutenant Kirby! Lieutenant Kirby!"

Hank peered over the plywood partition. "What the hell is it?"

"Sir, there's some big baldheaded bastard tellin' us we gotta move out of our hooch."

Fury swept through Hank, recharging his energy. It wasn't right. They had been assigned this billet. "Hell with that!" he replied angrily and stepped back into his fatigue pants. As an afterthought, he slipped on his shirt. It might be necessary to display his rank.

He hurried from the shower in time to see some of his men grudgingly moving their gear outside. "Hold up!" he ordered. "What's going on?" He felt an electric current of command course through him.

As if Simon said, they halted and gladly dropped their belongings in place and stood still. Fletcher pointed to a large bare-chested man rapidly striding toward them like an enraged bull. His razor-shaven head looked like a ruddy bowling ball.

"Who told them to stop?" The bald-headed bull growled.

"I did." Hank, the matador, stood his ground. "This is my platoon. We were told by the S-4 NCO this was our quarters during our stand-down." His eyes narrowed and his face contorted into an ugly scowl, like the bull's. "And who the hell are you, coming over here and ordering my men around?"

The bull sucked in a portion of his ample stomach and the eyes went to the lieutenant's bar penciled on Hank's collar. "I'm Captain Woodson, The battalion S-4. Now get your asses outta here," he snarled.

Hank felt gored in the balls. "Well, sir," he stammered, his voice an octave higher.

"You aren't properly identified." God, that was the wrong thing to say, he chided himself. "Your own NCO gave us these quarters just minutes ago," he said more evenly.

"Lieutenant!" Captain Woodson shouted. "You need a lesson in military courtesy. But right now I want your platoon completely out of these quarters in ten minutes. And clean it up as you leave."

"Are we to sleep under the stars and ambush the officer's club?" Hank injected this little dose of sarcasm before he could catch himself. It was his only weapon.

The S-4 directed a large arm towards a shabby tent hooch a hundred meters away. "That's your quarters!" he hissed before pivoting and stalking off.

There was no clean up. The move was unjust enough; to clean up the dirt they had tracked in after working their butts off was absurd. Hank would not let his men suffer this indignity. He would rather take the abuse from Woodson.

With heads lowered, the third platoon plodded the hundred meters to their new quarters, much smaller, hotter, and dirtier than the other. Only six bunks made up the furnishings, meaning that most would have to bed down on the splintery wooden pallets serving as the floor boards. It was decided that those whose air mattresses had punctures would be eligible for a bunk sweepstakes lottery.

Hank's air mattress was in fine shape and he began laying squatter's rights in a corner until Tucker stopped him, saying that their November Six must have a bunk. Tucker was seconded by others, the whole platoon in agreement. Hank reluctantly consented, embarrassed by his preferential treatment, and selected a nearby top bunk.

As he sauntered again to the showers, he felt an inner satisfaction, derived from an ageless leadership axiom, watch out for your men and they'll watch out for you. He had stood up for his platoon, though in vain, and in turn, they had reciprocated. More than in name only, he was suddenly beginning to feel like their platoon leader.

But that evening his position in the platoon carried a lonely isolation. He wasn't an EM or a sergeant and was excluded from their clubs and activities. Left to stand-down by himself, he found a nearly empty officer's club belonging to an aviation unit. A PFC behind the bar kept the juke box wailing slow, thought-provoking songs and maintained Hank's bourbon and water at a constant level.

Each large, grimacing swallow magnified his loneliness. He missed his friend and drinking partner. He wondered how Dick was doing. He hoped he was safe. And Pam. From the juke box the Bee Gees cried that they had to "get a message to you." Now there was an idea.

He borrowed a ballpoint pen from the PFC bartender and started composing a letter on his wet napkin. It would be a draft; tomorrow, before returning to the NDP, he would rewrite it. What should he say? He was in Quan Loi, dealing with routine supply matters, sitting behind his desk, conversing with his clerks… one time he flew down to Phu Loi to ensure the forward supply area was well stocked…Phu Loi was even safer than Quan Loi…

It was after midnight when he slowly stepped out of the bar. Staggering slightly, he navigated his way to the tent. Inside, at the far end, three tiny orange glows clustered like lightning bugs, among them seven shadowy forms moved surreptitiously. He sniffed a sweet aroma and figured it to be pot. His only reaction was to hoist himself up and flop face down on his privileged bed, not bothering with his boots.

He was asleep instantly.

Something was jerking on his arm. His first thought was that he had caught a fish. He opened his eyes half-way. In the dim light of the dawn shafting between the tent flaps his semi-stupor conjured a fat, puffy pumpkin with evil penetrating eyes and sardonic lips. "Get up, damn you! Get up!" The pumpkin could talk. Hank blinked hard and saw that Captain Woodson was roughly twisting his arm.

The pain convinced him it was not a nightmare. Groggily he sat up to avoid his arm from being wrenched off. "What's the matter?" he mumbled. His mind was clearing. He half expected Woodson to boot them out again and make them clean yesterday's contested quarters.

"Get your men up! A village was hit last night by VC. Your platoon is being used as a ready reaction force. You'll air assault in that area ASAP." Woodson's words bombarded Hank. "Be in my headquarters in five minutes for your op-order." He let go of Hank's arm and rushed out in long, jarring strides.

Hank rubbed his eyes, swung his legs out of bed, and slid off the top bunk. He was surprised to hear the clomp of his boots striking the boards instead of the slap of feet. His eyes scanned the mass of sleeping bodies for Sergeant Gomez. Not spotting him, he rushed over to Fletcher who was curled up peacefully on his air mattress, his head half hidden by his poncho liner blanket.

"Fletcher, wake up!" Hank shook him from his slumber.

The medic opened his eyes. "Yes…sir," he groaned and pulled the poncho liner from his head.

"Where's Gomez?"

"I looked for you, sir. But I couldn't find you last night," Fletcher replied, slowly becoming aware of his platoon leader's urgency.

"Looked for me? For what?"

"About Sergeant Gomez. They think he's got malaria. They sent him to the hospital at Long Binh."

"Shit! Listen Fletcher, get Sergeant Smith up ASAP. Tell him to get the platoon ready for an air assault. Understand?"

"Yes, sir." Fletcher jumped to his feet.

Hank hastened inside the one-room S-4 shack. He found Woodson and a major bent over a dilapidated field table intently studying a map, weathered and wrinkled from many foldings.

"Here he is, sir," Captain Woodson said to the major who wore a helmet and clean, starched fatigues. A .45 automatic was strapped to his hip.

With no introduction, the major spoke to Hank in a cool, efficient manner. "OK, Lieutenant, we've got a mission for your platoon." He motioned with his hand for Hank to look at the map. "A small VC force, probably a reinforced squad of about fifteen men, terrorized a small village last night. Here." His slender index finger tapped a penciled circle west of Bien Hoa near the Dong Nai River. "They killed four militia; then demanded tax money and rice from the villagers. The village chief tried to negotiate and was rewarded by being hacked to death by machetes. His wife and two daughters were shot in the head. Every male over twelve was kidnapped."

Hank shuddered. He couldn't believe he was here hearing this stuff. He couldn't believe he was supposed to do something about it. He stared wide-eyed at the map, then at the major, and then back at the map.

"Now, then," the major continued, "your platoon is to recon that area and search for any sign of the VC. Listen carefully because here's precisely what I want."

"Wait one, sir," Hank interrupted. He wanted to remember everything and nervously patted his breast pockets for his small notebook and pencil. They weren't there. He had left them in his discarded fatigues. Awkwardly, under impatient eyes, he glanced quickly around the room and, without asking, commandeered a piece of paper and a pen from Woodson's desk. Woodson said nothing, but his face, particularly the pulsating vein on the side of his head, vividly displayed his irritation.

The major began again. "In three zero your platoon will be trucked to the airstrip where five lift ships will pick you up and insert you east of the village." He swept his finger along the map. "When you hit this road running through the village, hold up. A platoon of A-CAVs will link with you in that vicinity. You'll work with them for the remainder of the day. At night you'll ambush. During the day, I'll be in a command and control ship much of the time. My call sign is Dragon Three. What's yours?"

"November Six… Bravo November Six," Hank added the prefix designating his company. He could have tacked Demon in front of the Bravo but his call sign was long enough without it. Besides, the major knew his Battalion.

"Very well. Have all your prick twenty-fives set on frequency fifty-three point sixty. Your contact for the A-CAVs is Crazy Acres Four. Captain Woodson will issue C-rations for two days and any necessary equipment you might be lacking. Leave your excess baggage behind. Any questions?"

"When will we rejoin our company?"

"Can't say. Perhaps one day. Maybe a week."

"One more thing…this is my first air assault…and…" Hank's voice deserted him. He flinched slightly, not immediately comprehending the reason for his disclosure.

"If you can't do it, turn the damn platoon over to a sergeant," Captain Woodson acidly interrupted.

"I didn't say I couldn't do it," Hank replied defensively. "We've been rehearsing them. I just thought the major should be informed."

"OK, OK, Lieutenant," the major refereed. He decided more details on the insertion might relax the young lieutenant, who seemed extremely nervous and upset at the suddenness of this operation. "The five choppers will insert in the usual Christmas tree formation. Be sure to have each position pop smoke once you're on the ground. We expect an easy insertion but you'll have two gunships covering nonetheless. As long as the smoke's out the cobras are able to hit anything outside your smoke ring. Also, Lieutenant, as soon as you land give me a sitrep on your LZ. Just say if it's hot or cold."

Hot LZ! The thought made Hank's stomach drop.

"Now get your unit ready. It's now zero-five-thirty. Use this map. I've already marked check points on it." The major refolded the map to leg pocket size, keeping the terrain in question visible, and handed it to Hank.

Back in the hooch the men buzzed with commotion as they fixed their gear and speculated on their mission while griping about an interrupted stand-down.

Sergeant Smith greeted Hank at the entrance. "What's this all about?" he asked, already outfitted in harness and helmet.

"We're a ready reaction force to search for some VC that hit a village last night. Get Percy, Bennet, and Milton over to see me right away and I'll give the whole scoop. I'm making you the platoon sergeant in Gomez's absence. Select one of your fire team leaders to take over your squad. Better get him too."

"Yes, sir. I'll get Martin. He's a good man, and recently made sergeant," Smith replied. "Too bad about Gomez. Fletcher told me about it."

After relating the gist of their mission, Hank eyed the five men that formed a semicircle before him. He started in on the particulars of the air assault. "I want Milton on the first slick, Percy on the second, Bennet on the fourth, and Smith the last. Martin, you go with Bennet. I'll take the third slick." He turned to Bennet. "I want a gun on the second and last. That way we'll have both flanks covered when we jump off." He faced Smith. "Make sure the men are divided evenly and try to keep squad integrity as much as possible." He swept the half-circle with a nervous fleeting gaze. "Got any questions?"

They shook their heads in unison. "OK, let's hurry," Hank concluded.

At 0600 hours, the November Platoon lined the airstrip in five groups, each thirty meters apart, and awaited their transportation. Their outward calmness at first surprised Hank who sat fidgeting beside Tucker in the middle group. Then he guessed why. Though they were going where fifteen Viet Cong had been sighted, no one imagined they would still be around, figuring the operation would be standard no VC, no contact, no danger. Hank wanted to become a believer too. His orders to his platoon so far had been crisp and structured with a facade of confidence. But he alone knew it was only a facade.

Tucker nudged him. "Sir, it's Dragon Three," and handed him the handset.

He grabbed it. "This is November Six," he said into the mouthpiece.

"This is Dragon Three. Have your lead element pop smoke. Slicks should arrive in zero one."

"Roger, break. November Papa, November Six. Pop smoke."

"Wilco, Six," came the reply over the radio from Spec-four Milton.

From the north end a yellow plume of smoke rushed skyward. At the opposite end five UH1 Huey slicks descended, dipping one after the other.

With his right hand, Hank tightly secured his helmet from the turbulent air currents as the first two slicks chattered by. When the third settled its skids on the ground, he arm-signaled them to climb aboard. He entered last and sat on a canvas bench that stretched across the chopper.

He faced the backs of the two pilots. Behind him, on both flanks, the door-gunners leaned casually on their swivel-mounted M-60s. On his left sat Doc Fletcher. Sitting on the floor in front of his feet was Tucker, the handset glued to his ear, one leg dangling outside, above the skid. To his right there was nothing, just outside air.

He frantically searched for a seat belt as the chopper lurched into the air but found none. There was none. The chopper suddenly heeled to the right like a small sloop catching a big gust of wind and his fingers grew white from clutching the edge of the bench. He marveled at Tucker, his leg hanging out, calmly monitoring the radio, holding onto nothing, obviously a staunch believer in the principles of centrifugal force.

The chopper leveled off and played follow-the-leader.

The helicopter procession plunged into a large, golden savanna interspersed with a few tall coconut palms. The second and fourth machines broke from the file to the left and formed an uneven V known as the Christ-mas tree formation. Hovering a foot off the waist high grass, the slicks deposited the GIs who ran a short distance and hit the prone position. Violet, yellow, and green smoke lit the Christmas tree.

Soaked from lying chest down in the tepid ankle-deep water, Hank waited for a sudden burst of gunfire and explosions. None came. He thanked God and grabbed the handset from Tucker's ear. "Dragon Three, this is Bravo November Six. LZ cold. I say again. LZ cold," he relayed through deep breaths to the major circling above in his C&C slick.

There was a short pause and then, "Roger. Cease your smoke. Insertion looked good, out."

The air assault had ended.

Hank rose to his knees. With his arm above the grass he gestured to the fourth group with no radio to stop the smoke. He figured the other three units had monitored the major's transmission. He checked his map and compass and then radioed to his point. "November Papa, November Six."

"This is November Papa."

"Move out."

"Wilco."

The point element of Spec-four Milton, his RTO, and one rifleman started slowly towards the west. As they moved, the rest of the platoon formed in two files. When the point had gone about thirty meters, the flank security, two men, twenty-five meters out on each flank moved out; then after about another twenty meters the main body of two files, thirty meters apart, began to follow. The twenty-seven-man traveling formation took on the shape of a giant, blunted arrow, the arrowhead consisting of the point and flank security.

Hank was second in the right file. First and ten meters ahead of him was his pace man, Spec-four Hector, who carried a nylon cord that knotted every time he estimated 100 meters had been traversed. He also was a grenadier, which meant he carried an M-79 grenade launcher rather than the M-16. The M-79 looked like a sawed-off shotgun with a large diameter barrel and fired a 40mm high explosive round in an arching trajectory which gave it the name "blooper" in addition to its blooping sound when it discharged. The blooper could also discharge a canister round full of steel pellets, giving results similar to a sawed-off shotgun.

Five meters behind Hank, Tucker humped while continuously monitoring the PRC-25 from the handset clipped to his harness strap near his ear. Trailing him, PFC Franklin trudged with his M-60 machine gun, carried and made steady by a sling hung over one shoulder. Nordstrom, his ammo bearer, followed behind him. Sergeant Smith, the acting platoon sergeant, and his RTO brought up the rear in the left file.

Movement was painfully slow. The sun was hot, the wind nil. Soft, black mud swallowed their boots, and, with much pulling effort, regurgitated them, causing loud sucking sounds.

Every man peered through straining, sweat stung eyes for snipers and booby traps.

The waist-high grass became knee-high as they passed by large round pools, water-filled bomb craters, relics from a past battle. Then came a long series of irrigation ditches, about five to six feet wide, quite deep and overflowing. Jumping them became tiresomely annoying, leaping from the ankle-deep water and landing boot deep in the saturated mud on the far side.

First, at Tucker's suggestion, Milton's point would check the crossing points for punji stakes. Then, for the main body, it was hurdle a ditch, slosh seventy-five feet through the glade, hurdle another ditch. Almost everyone committed at least one big splash and Tucker, with his heavy radio strapped to his slight frame, seemed on his way to some sort of platoon record.

Hank's untarnished track record was blemished, when pulling Tucker from a ditch, he slipped and tumbled in up to his navel.

But Tucker's ingenuity failed to dampen as he protected the moisture sensitive handset. He had wrapped it in a plastic bag that had packaged a radio battery. He fastened the end air tight by twisting on his elastic helmet band that was normally used to strap insect repellent to his helmet, rather than using the twigs and leaves called for by Army regulations. Hank thought Dick would have likened it to putting a giant condom on the handset and then knotting it.

The many ditches mesmerized the platoon. No longer did they care to keep a vigilant eye. All their attention was now directed to gaining strength for that necessary spring in their jump to successfully negotiate each ditch. Finally, 800 meters from the LZ, the last was leapt and a narrow tree line appeared.

Hank halted the platoon while he oriented himself with his map. The tree line indicated a canal. He radioed ahead for the point to check it out for a likely crossing, preferably a dry one. Fifteen minutes later, Milton reported a felled palm tree bridging it. The files were brought together and they tight-roped across.

They continued on their westerly azimuth. The ground grew firmer and the going easier. They skirted a pineapple patch and padded quietly by two thatched roof hooches with thin, mud-hardened walls. A few chickens, the only signs of life, ran about and squawked nervously in a dirt yard.

A hot westerly breeze picked up and carried with it a strong, earthy odor. Hank tied the smell and hooches together with his map and deduced that the village was close at hand.

More evidence, as a fat sow, screaming shrilly, charged the point and scattered two-thirds of Milton's unit. But Milton stood firm and delivered a strategically aimed boot to the sow's head as it passed near. In pain, it uttered a squeal and hastily retreated. The point reformed.

Human life took shape as they reached the dirt road bisecting the village. Skinny, wrinkled mama-sans, tired, old papa-sans, and little baby-sans warily eyed the visitors from the doorways of their flimsy, matchbox hooches. The normally playful spirits of the children were noticeably absent. None begged for C-rations. Their mothers wore taut faces and the old men moved list-lessly, their shoulders bent, vitality sapped. Last night's rein of terror had left its scars.

Hank felt uneasy and moved the platoon north along the road to the out-skirts. Here they stopped and set up a defensive posture in shallow drainage swales off both sides of the road.

"Crazy Acres Four, this is Bravo November Six, over," he said into the handset's mouthpiece. Receiving no answer, he repeated the transmission.

A husky voice came over the air, "Bravo November Six, this is Crazy Acres. Send your message."

"This is November Six. We've reached our destination, over."

"Roger that. We'll be by in about three zero. Suggest you chow down while waiting."

"Roger. Will do. Out."

CHAPTER 15

FORTY-FIVE MINUTES LATER a loud rumbling and clanking descended from the north. Soon, an armored personnel carrier rounded a bend, its tracks leaving behind a huge wake of dust. Three more APCs emerged out of a brown cloud. Two passed through before holding up while the third clambered to a stop in the midst of the platoon, now powdered a light brown.

Through the settling dust, the steel-plated machine stood out conspicuously. On top two M-60s flanked a fifty-caliber, and together they menacingly stared outward. This additional firepower gave the APC the moniker A-CAV. Three dust-coated men sat on top with the guns. A solitary head protruded from the driver's hole. A muscular, thick-necked man climbed from the cubicle which rotated the fifty-caliber and removed his command helmet and goggles. "Where's November Six?" he called.

Hank got to his feet and came forward with Tucker. Seeing Hank, the man slapped a floppy jungle hat on his head and jumped to the ground.

"I'm Hank Kirby. Also November Six."

"Bob Fritch, here. How things been going?" he asked and offered his hand. He was brown-faced, except where the goggles had been. The remaining white around his eyes made him look like Mickey Mouse with a bull neck.

"Good so far. And uneventful."

"Yeah, we've had the same," Fritch let out a sigh while his mouse eyes scanned both sides of the road at the rice paddies beyond the swales. "Old Charlie skedaddled without a trace. Have you seen how scared those villagers look?"

Hank nodded.

Fritch spoke in the same husky tone that had come over the radio in the guise of Crazy Acres Four. "While your boys been sweeping toward the village, my A-CAVs been runnin' up and down this road as a blocking force. We were hopin' you'd flush them dinks out for us."

"Where you think they've gone?" Hank questioned. The real question he didn't ask but that kept nagging in his mind was—what happens if we find them?

"Don't have the slightest. We'll just have to keep looking," Fritch said and reached into his leg pocket and pulled out a map. "We're here," he pointed to a place on the map.

Hank studied it a moment and agreed with Fritch as to their location. "What do we do now?" he asked, figuring Fritch would be more abreast of the operation's intricacies.

"We're to take your platoon one and a half klicks south along this road where you'll dismount and sweep east four hundred meters past this canal." Fritch pointed at the map and paused to let Hank survey it. The canal was the same one they had crossed earlier. "After that you head north about a klick. You'll then circle back west to the canal and ambush in that area."

Judging from their morning trek of ditch-hopping, Hank wondered if the most critical part of the ambush would be to keep from drowning.

The platoon clambered aboard. The APC was originally designed to carry troops inside. But the danger from landmines and B-40 rockets made them deathtraps. So instead they were filled with sandbags to buffer explosions from underneath, and soldiers rode on top. After traveling 1500 meters, the four APCs slowed to a stop among open rice paddies and waited as the Rifle Platoon dismounted.

Using the paddy dikes for footpaths, the November Platoon advanced to the edge of a grapefruit grove where shade from the thick green leaves offered momentary relief from the blazing sun. Further on they emerged into a field of tall coconut trees.

A black cloud began an eclipse of the sun. Suddenly, drenching sheets of rain broke loose. Lightning flashed, followed by booming thunder. Wind lashed at the trees, bending the slender trunks and whipping the long palm fronds.

The platoon set up an oblong defense perimeter and hunched low for protection from the cold rain and the lightning. Twenty minutes later, the black cloud faded to the west, the rain and wind mercifully with it.

Hank stretched his six-foot frame, the clammy wetness clinging to every nook and cranny of his body. In the east, the sky became a brilliant blue and he gazed into it, observing a large silver plane penetrating it far away. The plane held his gaze as he realized it was an airliner probably leaving Bien Hoa, probably en route to home, to the World.

"That Freedom Bird's a beautiful sight," he heard Tucker say to him.

"Freedom Bird?" Hank watched it recede into a small silver dot before the sky absorbed it.

"Yes, sir, that's what it's called. The one that takes us home."

Hank looked into the blue void once more. A shiver ran down his spine. Then he looked away, to Tucker. "Get on the horn and tell the squad leaders and Sergeant Smith we're moving out."

After the field of coconut trees, they met a shallow swamp filled with tall, green reeds. They struggled through it only to find a black, stagnant canal barricading them.

Above their knees, the sun had evaporated their soaking wetness to a mere sweaty dampness as Milton's contingent searched for a crossing to maintain this condition. None was found and with rifles held high they slowly entered and forded the tepid, shoulder-high water, one-third irrigation canal, one-third stream, one-third sewer.

On the other side, the patrol's route drew three sides of a rectangle east 400 meters, north a thousand, then west, back toward the canal. About thirty minutes of daylight was left when they pulled up 150 meters short of the tree line, mostly palms, which referenced the canal.

Hank called Smith and the squad leaders together to go over his plans for the night ambush. His map told him they weren't far from the fallen palm tree they had used to cross the canal after their morning ditch hopping. Just north of that tree, about twenty meters from the canal bank, he remembered a sugar cane patch and decided to make it their ambush site.

Considering what the land had to offer, the spot seemed a good one: soggy turf instead of the neighboring six to eighteen inches of water; a small, foot-high dike that rimmed the cane patch affording some protection; and tall stalks of sugar cane for concealment. Hank placed three of the ambush positions on the edge of the patch behind the dike and facing the canal bank. He believed this bank, high and compacted above the water, would be a natural path for anything lurking around.

Of these three positions, he put himself in the middle one along with Tucker, Smith, Hector, Fletcher, and Milton, all good soldiers, all giving him a sense of safety. On his right flank was the position commanded by Bennet and, since he was considered a dud by Gomez, this gave him concern. But Franklin, the new machine gunner that had impressed Hank, and his friend and ammo bearer, Nordstrom, were also there and this would probably offset Bennet's shortcomings, or as Gomez had called it, incompetence.

Sergeant Percy had charge of the third position on the left flank and Sergeant Martin, Smith's short, stocky replacement as squad leader, had the fourth position, behind the three line positions, and provided the rear security, though having no field of vision through the cane stalks. If Martin's position heard anything rustling through the sugar cane they would shoot first and, if given the opportunity, look later.

Each position was no more than twenty meters from another. And even though emphasis was given to the canal bank, the Claymores from all positions were intertwined to achieve nearly a full circle kill zone.

It was after dark when Hank assured himself that the ambush was completely set. He reached over to Tucker, who lay on his back gazing at the stars, and picked the handset from the hollow of his shoulder. "Crazy Acres Four, this is Bravo November Six, over," Hank whispered.

"This is Crazy Acres Four," came the reply. But from where, Hank didn't know. He had forgotten to ask, and wasn't told, where Fritch would be.

"We are now ready for nighttime activities."

"Roger. We'll call sitreps every three zero."

"November Six, Roger out."

At 2100 hours, the night shifts began and the men not on watch tried to find comfort. Hank turned on his side and wrapped his towel around his head to muffle the endless buzzing of mosquitoes. He and Tucker had the midnight watch plus the last watch in the morning. Now, Sergeant Smith and Doc Fletcher sat upright and through the cane field scanned the canal bank.

Hank fell into a fitful sleep.

Fifteen minutes later someone was shaking his shoulder. It was Sergeant Smith. "Sir, Fireball Two-Four's on the horn. Wants to fire some defcons for us."

"Defcons?" Hank repeated as he looked up at the dark silhouette of his newly appointed platoon sergeant.

"Yessir. I think Fireball Two-Four is with a 105 Battery."

Hank swallowed hard, remembering his first and only experience with defcons a few days ago, hearing but not seeing the explosions. They had been loud enough, and had been 81s from his company's mortars. And he'd had Gomez's careful tutelage to direct him. Once again, he cursed Benning for all the useless bleacher training with binoculars when it was the ears that needed the attention.

"Tell Fireball Two-Four thanks, but no thanks. I don't think we need them tonight."

"Sir, I think it would be a good idea to have 'em. It's like insurance. If something happens we'll be thankful we have it. If nothing happens, we ain't lost nothin'."

Unless a 105 round lands on our heads! Hank wanted to shout. He looked up, past Smith, at the stars that were starting to come out. With his peripheral vision he could see the tall reeds of sugar cane all around. He felt like he was in a dark pit. There was no way they'd see the rounds. "OK, Sergeant Smith. Call 'em in."

"Sir, that's something Gomez did…And our old lieutenant…I've never done it."

Neither have I, you fool! Hank thought. He sat up. The cane field seemed to be closing in. Sergeant Smith placed the handset in his hand. He brought it up beside his face. "Fireball Two-Four, November Six. You've got our position, over?"

"Roger, November Six. Got it from Crazy Acres."

Hank briefly wondered if they were in the right spot, clearly it was critical that the Battery knew their location, but then he dismissed his doubts. He was sure he had his men where they were supposed to be. Well, reasonably sure. "OK, Fireball Two-Four. How about giving them to me on my westerly azimuth." Hank relayed. Westerly was to the front of their kill zone. The rounds would be on the other side of the canal—he hoped.

"Wilco. You can adjust from about one thousand meters out." There was a moment of static over the air. Then, "Shot out."

"Roger, shot out," Hank answered. He clenched his teeth and gripped the handset tightly. He began to hear the far-off solitary scream of a 105 high explosive round.

Wham!

"Splash," he heard Fireball Two-Four say as he winced and involuntarily scrunched down for cover. It seemed an awful close 1,000 meters.

"Splash wait," he gave the proper response. He guessed it landed about 200 meters south of the west azimuth. "Right 200," he gave the adjustment.

"You don't want us to drop?" Fireball asked.

"Negative at this time." Drop meant get it closer. It sounded plenty close enough.

"Roger…Shot out."

"Shot out."

Wham!

"Splash wait."

It was now about 100 meters south of the west azimuth. But now closer. At least it sounded that way to Hank. He went through the jargon again with Fireball 24 and moved the target another 100 meters. He relaxed a moment thinking this nerve-wracking task had ended.

Until Smith spoke. "Sir, I think we should drop it some. One thousand meters is kind of far out, don't you think?"

Yeah! If it's 1000 meters. Sounds like it's 100 meters. Do you want to drop it on our asses? Hank wanted to shout. Then he thought, *What the fuck?* In all probability it was 1000 meters out. Benning had just not trained his ears to know the difference. He nodded to Smith and squeezed the talk button. "Fireball Two Four, November Six. Drop it one-zero-zero."

"One hundred meters?"

"That's a Roger."

"You could have dropped it when you shifted," Fireball 24 advised impertinently.

Hank ignored the remark.

The next round landed on a line with the last, but closer. The sound was a little louder, which was loud enough for Hank. But he decided to move it another 100 meters. As a sign to Fireball 24 that he was in charge.

"Drop another hundred," he whispered into the mouthpiece.

"It's taken you five rounds. You could have done it in two," Fireball 24's reply came back at him.

"I'm learning," Hank replied sarcastically. And truthfully.

"Shot."

"Shot out."

"Splash."

Wham!

"Splash wait."

It sounded like it had landed beside him. But there was no flash, so maybe it was 800 meters away.

Hank started to end the transmission when he felt Smith's hand on his shoulder. *What was it now,* he wondered. He hadn't noticed the gathering and whispered gabbing of the men at his position. Now he glanced around and saw dark amorphous faces that seemed to be staring at him. All except his RTO Tucker who quietly lay beside him propped on one elbow.

"What is it?" Hank asked Smith's amorphous face.

"Sir. We got a good down payment. Let's go for the whole thing."

"What?" Hank shot back a hissing whisper. Did Smith want to drop a 105 round in their lap?

"Go for the Cadillac, sir. No platoon in the Battalion's got one. Least ways we don't know of none."

Hank wondered if it was Smith or he who was cracking up. "What do you mean, Cadillac?" he questioned gruffly. Had Benning neglected something else in his infantry training?

"I guess you don't know about it." Smith was apologetic.

"No, I don't."

"A platoon gets a Cadillac when they fire enough rounds equal to the cost of a Cadillac."

"What?" Hank still didn't understand.

Then he heard from the earpiece. "November Six, this is Fireball Two-Four. Have you concluded your defcons? I'm waiting to cease operations, over."

"…This is November Six. Wait one. Out."

Doc Fletcher spoke. "Sir, each 105 round costs so many dollars. If you call in a number that totals the value of a Cadillac, then we've bought one. The platoon owns it."

Hank started involuntarily shaking his head, amazed at such madness. "I'd think you wouldn't want to be in the position to buy a Cadillac. If we're in a firefight, there'd be plenty of opportunity to buy a Cadillac. My objective is to never have the opportunity to buy one." His remark had no reaction from the dark faces staring at him. He wondered if he'd said too much. What would his platoon think of a lieutenant who would rather avoid then confront the enemy? *Shit,* he thought to himself, *they'd find out sooner or later.*

"A firefight or any type of enemy contact, don't qualify for a Cadillac, sir. Rounds got to be fired only for the sake of wasting them for no particular reason. That's the only way we can legitimately buy a Cadillac," Smith explained.

"It's gotta be our choice," Milton, the point man, added.

"…November Six, Fireball Two-Four. I'm to close down."

"Roger, Fireball Two-Four. Please hold a little longer," Hank stalled. Trying to sort this thing out.

He looked down at Tucker, who in their brief few days together was impressing him as smart, levelheaded, and quiet, and that was why he was his RTO. Tucker would be the arbiter. "What do you think of all this?" Hank asked him in a frustrated whisper.

Tucker sat up slowly. He looked at the shadowed faces around his platoon leader, then at his platoon leader. "It means something to the platoon, sir . They may never afford a real Cadillac. Why not give them one?"

That wasn't the answer Hank expected, or wanted. The financial waste of it all didn't bother him so much as having to call in more artillery rounds.

"Fireball Two-Four. This is November Six. I want to fire another defcon, over."

"This is Fireball Two-Four. OK, November Six, but hurry it up. We ain't got all night."

Hank could sense rather than see the jubilation on the faces of his men. This made him feel a little better. He thought about the next one. A defcon, or defensive concentration, was a means for establishing a registration point for artillery or mortar rounds. An azimuth and a distance were selected and rounds were adjusted on the azimuth and at the distance, thus establishing a registration point. Should a firefight erupt and the artillery was needed, immediate adjustment could be made from the registration point. Ideally, in an ambush position where there was possible exposure from a full 360 degrees, defcons on all four sides were appropriate. Hank had originally chosen only one side, the west azimuth, as tactically the best of four since it was in front of the kill zone.

Now as he thought about another defcon he realized the west was tactically the worst. The kill zone was along the embankment of the canal on the near side. Should the enemy travel in this kill zone and then flee, the only likely routes of escape were north and south, not west because of the canal and not, he hoped, east because of the platoon. He decided on a north defcon. "Fireball Two-Four, November Six; I'll adjust on a north azimuth."

"Roger. Understand north. Wait."

Hank suddenly thought of something. How much did a Cadillac cost? "How many rounds do we need?" He looked at Smith's dark form sitting in front of him. He felt hot; the air was stagnant as the tall cane cut off any air flow.

"Shot," he heard Fireball 24 say.

"Shot out," he answered.

"Splash."

Wham!

"Splash wait."

God, it was loud. And way over to the northwest. He wanted to say right 400 meters but that would be too much if the objective was to maximize the number of rounds. "Right 100," he relayed. He looked at Smith again. "Well?"

"I'm not really sure, sir," Smith's tone had an edge of embarrassment.

Hank groaned.

"Sergeant Percy knows. I'm sure of it." It was Hector, the pace man. "I'll crawl over to his position and ask him. And I'll go to the other positions and let them know we're going for a Cadillac."

Hank didn't like the idea of Hector moving around to other ambush positions. But then he couldn't radio to ask Percy details on buying a Cadillac. Not with Fireball 24 and who knows who else monitoring. He decided to let the other positions know that a messenger was going to be crawling to them through the cane. "All November elements, this is November Six. Someone from my position will be visiting each of you. He has something to give you."

"Shot."

"Shot out."

"Splash."

Wham!

"Splash wait."

"Right 100 meters."

It took Hank five rounds to adjust the north defcon, same as for the west, only this time Fireball 24 was complaining loudly about Hank's inability to make bolder adjustments and therefore use fewer rounds. It wasn't as though Fireball 24 cared about the number of rounds. He just wanted to shut his battery down for the night.

Hank secretly agreed with Fireball 24. He was gaining confidence with each round and would have been bolder if not for the Cadillac. Even so, this time he had estimated the final round at 700 meters. And that sounded close enough.

He was telling the pissed off Fireball 24 that he might want a south defcon when the cane to his right began stirring and Hector crawled into the group again.

"How much?" Smith asked him before he sat down on their bed of trampled cane stalks.

"Six thousand dollars," Hector said. "Three hundred for a 105 round. Sergeant Percy said a remf at an NCO club in Phu Loi last night gave him list prices of all types of artillery."

Another ten rounds, Hank calculated. "Fireball Two-Four, November Six. We need a south defcon…and an east defcon…"

"I haven't shot round the clock defcons for an AP since Tet. Are you surrounded by NVA or something?"

Hank could feel Fireball 24's sarcasm through the radio. "Based on our briefing this morning, an enemy presence is likely. I'm sitting out here with my ass showing. Are you telling me what I need?" he said, trying to be as forceful as Fireball 24 talking from strength. He hoped to hell Fireball 24 was no more than a lieutenant. He also hoped no one but his platoon ever found out about this. But if they did, would it be so bad? Maybe they'd yank his ass out of the field.

"OK, November Six, I'll give you two more defcons, but I'm only giving two rounds each to adjust. You'll just have to rely on your last round for a reference. Here goes the south."

"Shit," Hank muttered under his breath. It would all be for naught.

"Shot," he heard Fireball 24.

"Shot out," he answered weakly.

"Splash."

Wham!

"Splash wait."

"Right 200, drop 100." Hank gave a correction equal to two corrections of the previous defcons.

The process was repeated. Then the same sequence for the east defcon.

"Is that it?" Milton asked when it had ended.

Hank nodded.

"We're short eighteen hundred fucking dollars," Fletcher stated sadly.

"Shit," Smith hissed.

Tucker said nothing. His eyes were closed and the back of his head rested in his helmet. He seemed miles away.

"Sergeant Percy said 105 illuminatin' rounds were six hundred apiece. All we need's three." It was Hector speaking softly.

There was silence for a moment. Then Smith: "Tell 'em we hear movement, lieutenant. That we need some illum to check it out."

Hank felt himself slide further into the quicksand he had created for himself. Or was it just deep shit? "Fireball Two-Four, this is November Six. I think we got some movement to our front. We need some illumination," Hank tried to sound excited. He was starting to hate himself for this. He felt like the boy who cried wolf.

"No shit?" answered Fireball 24 in a tone of real excitement. "We'll get something out soonest. Bet those defcons moved some dinks in."

"November Six, Crazy Acres. I monitored. I'll notify higher."

Hank felt sick. He was heading for the stockade.

CHAPTER 16

THERE WAS A loud pop and the sky broke into a pearly white. Deep shadows moved with the swing of the flare that swayed from its parachute. The platoon slunk down further into their cane patch.

"Whatcha got?" It was Fireball 24.

"Don't know. Give me another right 200 meters."

"Roger."

Another pop. More light.

"Anything?"

"Negative yet. Wait. There may be something. Give me another just like the last."

"Wilco! Let's get them fuckers."

Pop.

Hank relaxed. He could end the charade. The platoon had its Cadillac.

"Fireball Two-Four, November Six. Movement is a stray water buffalo. Thanks for your help."

"Water buffalo! What the shit's going on!"

"Sorry. Out."

"November Six, Crazy Acres. I monitored. Will tell higher."

"Roger. Thanks. Out." Hank put the handset down next to the reclined Tucker and became aware of his trembling fingers. Around him, he sensed a silent charge of jubilation.

"I'll send Hector to tell 'em we got a Cadillac," Smith said, his voice cracking in happy relief. He picked up the handset between Hank and Tucker and notified the other three groups that a messenger was going out.

It wasn't long before Hector was back. "I got some bad news," he said.

Instantly he had their attention. Even Tucker got up on an elbow. "Sergeant Percy says we ain't got a Cadillac. Says we forgot the sales tax."

"Sales tax?" Hank hissed loudly. Forgetting for a brief moment he was on a live ambush patrol. He swallowed at the thought. "Bullshit!" he whispered. "Tell Percy there's no sales tax in Vietnam. It's Army sponsored."

"We told him that. He says but there ain't no Cadillacs over here. We got to buy from the States. Percy says he'll let us have three percent for sales tax. A hundred and eighty bucks we gotta come up with."

Hank's face dripped with sweat. He wanted to scream over to Percy and tell him to get his big fat ass over here. Who the fuck was in charge here anyway?

"Well, if there's sales tax. Let's say there's sales tax. We gotta pay the full price," Doc Fletcher said.

"Why don't we get rid of the power steering and windows?" Milton broke in sarcastically, sounding as pissed as Hank felt.

"That's not a Cadillac," Fletcher countered. "Buying a Cadillac ain't easy. Costs a lot of money."

Hank was about to tell them all to clam up and forget about this stupidity. What a blunder to let this thing get out of hand. Why did he stick his neck out for these ungrateful assholes?

But before he could say anything, Tucker spoke. "We may have already paid sales tax." Suspicious eyes hidden by the dark fell heavily on him. He parried their unseen eyes with a question. "How many men does a 105 battery have?"

The eyes shifted to their platoon leader who shrugged. He didn't know. He was infantry. Not artillery.

"You think about twenty?" Tucker asked.

"Sounds close enough," Hank answered.

"What do you think the average hourly wage is for the battery on a per-soldier basis?" Tucker again posed a question.

No answer.

"Two dollars an hour?" Tucker offered.

"That's three-hundred twenty a month. With combat pay thrown in, that sounds about right," Smith piped in.

"OK. Let's say the battery spent an hour on us. That includes firing the 105s as well as preparation for firing and clean up after firing. So that means the Army spent forty dollars of their labor on us."

"We're still one forty short," Milton interrupted.

"What's the ratio of remfs to field troopers?" Tucker continued.

"About four-to-one, I'd guess," Hank replied. He knew where Tucker was coming from.

"Right, sir. It's at least four-to-one. And that ratio can be compared to the overhead of a business. For every dollar of labor expended to make a widget, four dollars have to be added on to the cost. So that's four times forty which equals one hundred and sixty dollars. Add that to the forty from the battery and we got two-hundred dollars. We need to get twenty dollars back in change."

The darkness disguised Hank's smile, but his voice didn't. "Tucker's right. Men, we got ourselves a Cadillac."

There was a strange commotion of dark forms fidgeting excitedly and slapping one another.

Smith picked up the horn and radioed that a messenger was going on another visit.

Hank squeezed Tucker's shoulder. He understood why this skinny kid was his RTO. He had the brains. Intuitively he knew he had the heart, too.

"Tucker, how'd you figure all that out?"

"Majored in business at Ohio State before I had to leave to help my dad with his lumber yard," Tucker said. He then laid back and settled his head into his helmet, seeming to leave the others as his mind drifted off again to thoughts of his pregnant wife.

Hank was now on the last watch. Impatiently, he waited for the dawn as he stared into the darkness, his imagination forming nightmarish images from the dark, amorphous shadows all about.

Suddenly, Tucker tugged urgently on his arm. "Sir," he murmured with nervous excitement, "Sergeant Percy's position said they've sighted VC."

Hank's stomach twisted as he grabbed the radio's handset from Tucker. "November Two, this is November Six. What's happening?" As he spoke, Tucker moved swiftly to wake the others.

"This is November Two!" a frightened whisper answered. "We've got three VC spotted in our starlight scope heading this way along the far side of the canal. They're about one hundred meters south of the palm tree crossing. Moving slow. We think they're carrying AKs!"

Hank was slow to reply. Panic momentarily dried his mouth. Slowly, with effort, he said: "Roger. Keep me informed, out…break…Crazy Acres Four, November Six, over." He needed to tell Fritch, to share his dilemma.

"This is Crazy Acres Four Kilo, monitored. Will notify Dragon Three, out."

"This is November Two." The frightened whisper was now more pressing. "This point gook is getting ready to cross the canal at the palm tree."

"Roger!" Hank's voice cracked. His mind raced. What if they spot the ambush? What if there's a large force behind them?

The black shroud of darkness was lifting into a hazy gray dawn.

Percy's voice gulped over the radio and into Hank's ear, "The gook crossed and is heading our way, along the bank!"

"Roger," Hank replied weakly. A cold, clammy feeling shot through his body. His left hand clutched his clacker—the Claymore detonating device. His right hand tightened on his M-16.

The sun began spreading a light golden hue over the horizon.

Making the decision was overwhelming. He alone must give the command that would set off the ambush. Fears kept racing around his mind like pinballs caroming off bumpers and ringing imaginary bells. What if the VC manage to throw grenades or spray them with their AKs? Suppose the Claymores are too close and the back blast hits his men? But worst, suppose the Claymores fail to detonate? Why not just let the VC walk by and let everyone see another sunrise?

The sugar cane blocked the other three ambush positions from his vision, but with his head elevated slightly above the low dike, Hank could barely see the palm trees fringing the canal. Then, his eyes straining through the tall stalks, he detected movement. It became clearer. A small figure moved cautiously along the bank, among the palms. He was a young man clothed in a tattered, dirty gray tee shirt, black shorts, and sandals. An AK-47 with a banana clip hung at the ready from his shoulder, the right hand on the pistol grip. On his back was a bulging gunny sack. Ten meters behind him came more movement.

The lead Viet Cong was now directly in front of Hank and a mere twenty-five meters away.

There was the clack-clack of a detonator being depressed, answered instantaneously by an ear shattering explosion. *Wham!* More explosions, responding to the first. *Wham! Wham! Wham!* And still more…

The earth rocked; a volcano had erupted spewing forth a mixture of dark-gray smoke and gritty dirt.

The mixture fell heavily on Hank as his arms covered his helmeted head. His ears rang and he felt dizzy. After a few moments, he looked around at the others beside him. They lay flat, their eyes blinking at the unnatural cloud that was starting to dissolve in the light early-morning breeze.

His hands trembled as he pressed the talk button on the handset. "Crazy Acres Four, this is November Six!" He spoke rapidly, the words all running together, relaying his sense of urgency.

"November Six, this is Dragon Three. Send your message." It was the major's voice, barely audible through his still ringing ears.

"We've just popped our bush on three Victor Charlies."

"Did you get 'em?"

"I…I think so," Hank stammered. There had been no return fire. Only the Claymores had spoken.

"Well check it out ASAP. I want a full sitrep soonest. I'm sending you a hunter-killer team. They'll check in on this net."

"Roger," Hank acknowledged.

"Roger. Out."

No one but Hank moved. On the edge of the slender reeds of cane his eyes peeked furtively over the dike, ready, given the slightest sound or movement, to duck down. The smoke and dust were gone and he saw stumps where he remembered small, graceful swaying palms. Before them, three heaps, not bodies, but heaps of flesh and bone, lay marinating in the early morning sun. He quickly dropped his head and nodded to the others who then raised their heads and peered over at the carcasses of their prey.

"November Six, this is Dragon Three. What the hell is happening?" The major's impatient voice emanated from the earpiece of the handset.

"This is November Six. We've got three Victor Charlies."

"Three VC KIA?" The voice was enthusiastic.

"That's affirmative."

"Real fine! Real fine! Give me a full sitrep on what they got." The voice was ecstatic.

"Wilco. In a few minutes." Hank's listless response was incongruent with the major's ebullience.

"Also," the major said, "when that hunter-killer team checks in, let's play our cards right and get a few more of those fuckers."

Hank didn't reply and gave the handset to Tucker. He pondered what he

considered the delicate problem of searching the dead Viet Cong and decided to ask for three volunteers, one for each heap. He instructed Tucker
to radio the other positions for volunteers, but then Milton, Fletcher, and
Hector said they'd do it.

Hank forced himself to watch as they went about their task, creeping and
poking into the gruesome remains. Milton inspected the first one and turned
over what appeared to be a torso with arms and a head but nothing more, as
if it had been swallowed feet first by a shark and bitten in two at the abdomen.

Hank had to look away and shifted his gaze to the second heap where
Doc Fletcher milled around, receiving a course in anatomy never found in
medic school. There was a head with a complete leg and hip beside it and
together the combination seemed to perform an amazing double-jointed
gymnast act.

Seeking refuge from what he had witnessed, Hank sunk down into the
sugar cane. His eyes closed, but he couldn't stop seeing. They were the first
dead humans he had ever seen. Yet, they weren't human. Not any longer.
Just mutilated body parts.

The search team returned, their mission completed. An inventory of the
captured booty was conducted: three AK-47 assault rifles, one twelve-inch
CHICOM Claymore mine, twelve magazines full of ball ammunition, bags
of rice, and a few documents.

The results were reported to Dragon Three.

The sun was now beaming in full brilliance as they remained in their ambush positions. Finally, Whitehorse Forty-two, the hunter-killer team, came
on station. The pilot's choppy voice, bounced about by the helicopter's vibrations, instructed Hank to pop smoke for a definite fix. Hank complied and
asked what else he was supposed to do, not really wanting to do anything
else. He got what he wanted as the pilot told him to stay put.

With much interest, the platoon, having cleared away portions of sugar cane
to enhance their view, watched the air show provided by the two helicopters.
Like a hummingbird seeking nectar, the little loach, the hunter, dipped to near
tree level and followed along the dark, quiescent water of the canal, swinging
back and forth from one bank to the other, the boldness of the loach astonishing
its spectators. At a higher altitude, the cobra gunship, the killer, protectively
circled the loach like a mother hawk watching over her nest.

Swish-wham! Swish-wham! The gunship fired two rockets followed immediately by the whine of its miniguns raining down red tracers. This part of the spectacle caused a nervous stir among the watching gallery until Whitehorse Forty-two calmly quieted their concern by explaining he was just re-coning by fire at likely areas.

No trace of anymore VC could be found and Whitehorse Forty-two said goodbye and departed for Phu Loi where his team would stand-down while waiting for another mission. Hank tried to contact Dragon Three to find out what to do next. Failing that, he reached Crazy Acres Four who advised them to come back to the road and wait for his A-CAVs.

Shortly after noon, they were at the road where they set up security details on both sides before resting. The strain of the ambush became lost in its success. There was banter and there was laughter, it had all been so easy.

Hank sat on the shoulder of the road. On the other side, he could hear someone humming the tune of "Three Blind Mice." The hummer stopped and spoke to his buddies, "Hey, listen up, I've composed a little ditty about those gooks we wasted." He then started singing off key:

"Three dead gooks,
Three dead gooks,
See how they bleed,
See how they bleed,
We cut off their heads with a Claymore mine,
We used their arms as a warning sign,
The flies will dine on their eyes tonight,
And we're the ones that made it right,
For three dead gooks,
Three dead gooks."

His audience clapped and then joined in for a sing along.

To Hank it was like squeaky chalk on a blackboard. He was about to send Sergeant Smith over to hush them but the rumbling of steel tracks did the silencing. The lead vehicle jerked to a stop next to Hank and Lieutenant Fritch leapt off. In one breath he congratulated Hank on his body count; in the next, he informed him that the operation was over. The A-CAVS would take his platoon to his company's NDP.

They gratefully mounted their armored transportation.

Hank's A-Cav lurched forward and led the way south. The clanking cacophony of his jostling ride became secondary to the off-key voice from within. He couldn't help it. It kept singing, "Three dead gooks / Three dead gooks." Over and over.

Then the singing inside him abruptly halted, drowned by the clack-clack of a Claymore detonator. The first clack-clack. The one he himself had caused.

CHAPTER 17

CONSTANTLY SHIFTING HIS weight from one leg to another, trying to ease his burning arthritis, Fred Sadler repetitiously stuck letters into the individual slots for the mail carriers. From the mail sack beside him on the floor he pulled a handful and started sorting a new batch. A light blue envelope emerged. He looked at the address, already knowing that it was to Pam. He fingered it thoughtfully as he reviewed the status of his scheme.

Phase One had been operational for over a month, and with Pam now teaching school, he was ready for Phase Two, the most critical stage. His relationship with Pam had never been better. He had her trust. He had feigned interest in Hank's letters, always asking her to read them to him, wanting to know what her soldier boy had been doing.

And she willingly complied.

Not only did he display interest, but help, that was the key. Every letter she wrote he insisted he carry it personally to the post office and place it directly in the outgoing mail to ensure, he had told her, the fastest possible delivery. Pam had been delighted and faithfully put her correspondence on the foyer table for him to pick up. Even on his days off he made special trips to get it out in the early mail.

Kirby's incoming letters were somewhat harder to keep tabs on because they were less frequent and arrived at all hours. He tried to catch them at the post office and bring them home personally, usually a day earlier than by the mail carrier. But sometimes he would miss one and Pam would find it in the morning mail delivery. However, with school just starting and Marion busy until five at her job at the boutique shop, he could get home in plenty of time. He was getting off at two now, a full two hours before Pam. Thus, he would have complete control of all correspondence.

He would wait no longer for the next phase. With butterflies flapping around inside his pot belly, he excused himself from his work under the not-too-false pretense of needing a pain reliever for his legs, to be followed by assuming the reclined position for the remainder of the day.

In his old maroon Corvair convertible he sped off to a nearby office supply center and purchased a small portable typewriter, typing paper, and envelopes. Then he went to the printer where he picked up the rubber stamp he had ordered under the guise of post office business. It had the lettering of a San Francisco APO number, indicating a Vietnam postmark. Then he drove home.

He hurried inside with his purchases. Into the bedroom he went, detouring briefly by the fridge to pluck a Blue Ribbon and pop it with a church key. For safety's sake, he locked the door. He dragged his wife's sewing table next to the bed and placed the typewriter on it. He sat on the edge of the bed, his heavy posterior crushing the springs, his spine uncomfortably bent. He inserted paper in the typewriter.

Finally, he was ready to begin. He would become both Pam and Hank, they the readers, he the composer/sender. He realized he must tread slowly and carefully in the beginning.

Everything had to have the proper transition to be plausible; he mustn't rush it.

He tore open the letter he had intercepted. His eyes scanned it. It contained the usual garbage: pushing supply forms, watching movies at night, pissing away time at the O'club. That guy has it made, Fred thought, his face twisting into a pugnacious grimace.

With his short, stubby fingers he began hunting and pecking the keys, redoing the letter. Changes had to be subtle at first. The intended results would take time. He made the salutation "Dear Pam" rather than Hank's "Dearest." A paragraph was added at the beginning to explain that a supply clerk's typewriter would now be used because it was more convenient. The original letter was long and since he hated all this typing he omitted a few utterly meaningless paragraphs in the bogus version. He closed with "All my love" truncated to "Love."

And that was it.

After finishing his tedious typing, he yanked the paper from the carriage and proudly inspected his composition. It was sloppy, bold X's through some mistakes, others left uncorrected, but this gave the authenticity he desired.

He placed his letter in an envelope, sealed it, typed the address, including the "free" in the upper right-hand corner, and postmarked it with the newly acquired rubber stamp.

The typewriter went into its case, then into his closet. The sewing table returned to its spot and the bedspread smoothed out where his rear-end had been. Hank's true copy, the stamp, and the other items went into his bottom bureau drawer under his underwear. Pam would never look there. It had been forbidden long ago when, as a little girl, he had caught her snooping in his things. He had severely reprimanded her, telling her it wasn't proper for a girl to look at a man's underwear. Actually, his real concern had been that she would find his girlie magazines. And that was why he didn't have to worry about Marion. She never looked below his last layer of underwear for fear of finding one, and he always made sure he never wore that last pair.

Fred finally allowed himself a slow smile. This would be fun, and his little girl would be the better for it. They all would. Next week, in letter form, he would become her. He might even mention Dave Watson; that should get her lieutenant where it hurts.

His legs felt better. He decided to go back to work.

CHAPTER 18

H ANK STARED GLUMLY at his can of Bud. The images of those three mangled heaps of flesh and bone burned like acid, etched forever in his mind. He tried to find an antidote for his misery by concentrating on something else. He did. Pam.

But the thought of Pam and her last letter burned too. It had been stark. The typed words, *even her signature*, were a blazing desert that left his insides withered and parched. And then, amidst the hot sand, a wind storm had swept in, the tiny grains biting into his every pore; she had mentioned Dave Watson. Nothing big, nothing really threatening, but nevertheless there. So what if he had made the Dolphins? Why should she give a rat's ass?

And then there was what she hadn't mentioned. His birthday. September 5. He had turned twenty-three almost a week ago. Maybe it would be in her next letter.

His mind could no longer handle Pam, either, so he returned to the present. His eyes left the beer can and wandered about. The small Battalion O'club at Quan Loi hadn't changed, only its occupants. Cronin, Brussels, and Sawyer sat with him around the table, staring up at the TV, the only customers. In place of Captain Unser salivating about the brigade's whorehouse, the Saigon evening news proudly proclaimed the past week's body count for Vietnam. He knew the Battalion hadn't contributed to this tally. Its only count was over five weeks ago. And had been three. His three.

Now there he was again, thinking about those three heaps.

Again, he forced himself to think of something else.

After the ambush, things hadn't been too bad. Busy, tiring, but not bad. Nothing had happened. Ambushes with nothing to ambush, air assaults with nothing to assault, search and destroy sweeps with nothing to find, much less destroy. The more nothings, the better. The only somethings worthwhile were the stand-downs in Phu Loi and Di An: the PXs, the clubs, the steam baths. But the more he had of that something, the more it began to feel like nothing.

His company was now standing down in Quan Loi, their home base camp. Supposedly, according to the most frequent form of communication—rumor—the entire Battalion was going to stand-down together. Invariably the rumors were wrong, at least the ones one wanted to be right. And he wanted this one, for it would mean seeing Dick.

A platoon leader was isolated from everything and everybody, except the platoon. And his platoon had gotten hold of him. It was now a part of him.

Much to his surprise, he thought most of his men had begun to think him capable. Perhaps it was his specially developed jungle fighting techniques; the ambush position hidden so far into the bushes and off the beaten path that only a stray ant would likely wander by. Or maybe it was the one-thousand meter cloverleaf condensed to just a couple of hundred meters with a long, secure rest stop before heading back to the center of the leaf, the company. His foremost mission he made evident to all: Freedom Bird tickets for everyone.

The evening news had turned into Charlene the weather girl, who espoused the same hot, humid, rainy weather in a husky, deep-throated purr. Charlene gave way to a spec-six with the sports, who thanked Charlene for her informative forecast in a way that seemed to say "I'll be banging you after the show." At least that's how Hank read it.

The spec-six did a rundown on the pennant races and then, in a sneak assault on Hank's feelings, announced the kickoff of the pro-football regular season. But the Spec-six wasn't completely malicious; he picked the Dolphins to finish last in their division.

Now Hank felt guilty. He had always rooted for the Dolphins in their few short years of existence. Always, until now.

He abruptly slid his chair away from the table and stepped over to the bar where he motioned to the EM bartender for another round.

Without warning, a broad slapping hand whacked him hard on the shoulder. He was driven back into a barstool. "Make that two beers," boomed a familiar voice.

A welcome grin lit up Hank's face, despite the sharp pain in his back. The grapevine had, for once, borne fruit. Dick was here; the point man for the rest of Charlie Company's platoon leaders who now filed in and began gathering up chairs around the table occupied by Cronin, Sawyer, and Brussels. The room filled with hearty laughter.

Hank took notice of Dick's Fu Manchu moustache. It intensified his ruggedness. Made him look warlike. And it was against regs. Moustaches were supposed to be neatly trimmed, not drooping. Though most Vietnam army issues were bushy, with walrus styling, Dick's seemed more becoming and more appropriate considering the business they were in.

"Congratulations, First Lieutenant!" Dick roared and laughed wildly after scooping up his beer from the bar. It was obviously not his first. Somewhere he had started the stoking process and now he displayed a warm glow.

"Same to you," Hank replied, trying to display equal emotion. Both had received official notification of their promotions three weeks ago, made retroactive from July. Not as a result of merit, but as an automatic occurrence for second lieutenants after one year of service.

"Well, let's get down to some serious drinking," Dick said and pivoted around toward the group and would have taken a step if not for Hank's hand tugging on his arm.

"What say we sit at the bar first and shoot the shit a while? Just you and me." Hank asked hesitantly as he pulled Dick down on a stool beside him.

"Sure. Why not?" Dick acquiesced and glanced sideways at Hank, eyebrow raised slightly.

Both dug their elbows into the bar counter.

As the other lieutenants momentarily joined them and hovered around the bar waiting for their beers, Hank stayed silent, contemplating what to say and hoping Dick was sober enough to hear it. The ambush and Pam's letter had started pulling hard again at his insides from opposite ends. Each with equal tension. He must be demented. How could a silly letter have equal weight with blowing apart three human beings?

But it did.

A surge of remorse hammered against his temples. Through tight lips, the only words he could utter were: "Something's bothering me."

After this declaration he paused to gauge its effect on Dick.

Dick grew attentive. He waited for the thirsty crowd to retreat back to their seats. The alcohol in his veins had not yet completely clogged his faculties, and he patted Hank's back with his hulking hand where moments ago he had rammed it in welcome. "OK Hank, let's hear it. What's on your mind?"

"Well…you see…I…there was this ambush…and…" Hank started to babble incoherently.

But he wasn't incoherent to Dick. With surprising insight, Dick read the stammering. "You didn't like wasting those gooks, did you? That's what it is, ain't it?"

"Yeah," Hank admitted as sweat broke out on his forehead. "So you heard about it."

Dick couldn't hold back a smile. "Fuckin' A. So did every dog-face in the Battalion. It was outstanding!" Hank's eyes opened wide, startled by Dick's exuberance. "You were the only one killing those sons of bitches. Wish I could've done it. All I've seen on ambush is a big ass field rat, but I let him go figuring he might be on our side."

Hank was unable to absorb Dick's jest. Deflated, his head drooped. "Still," he moped and spun the can with a soft touch of his fingertips. "Didn't even bury them. Just left them rotting in the sun. At least should've buried them."

"Bullshit!" Dick abruptly banged his fist on the bar, causing Hank's head to jerk back. "You can cut the shit! Bury them my ass. You think they would've buried you? Shit no. They'd've sliced your balls off and stuffed 'em in your mouth."

Dick sucked down the remainder of his beer and motioned to the bartender for another. "You just did your goddamn job. Which, face it, Hank, is killing them before they kill you." He placed his hand gently on Hank's shoulder. "What do you say we hit the steam bath tomorrow morning?"

Hank exhaled a light laugh, the tension evaporating. "Steam bath's OK. Just the steam bath though."

"So! This is where I find my lazy lieutenants, boozing again," Captain Connors yelled from the doorway.

All the club's occupants craned their heads around towards Bravo's CO.

"Let me buy you a beer, sir!" Lieutenant Brussels shouted across the room in his best suck-ass manner

Connors stayed in the doorway. "No thanks, not now," he declined. "A beer won't help the news I bring. Since Bravo was the first company in Quan Loi, today, we're the first one with a mission for tomorrow."

"Nothing bad, I hope?" Cronin asked.

Connors shook his head. "Shouldn't be. Just a short RIF outside the wire. Should be back by afternoon. But come by the orderly room now for the op order. Sorry to break it up, but duty first, you know." He waved good-naturedly, turned around and disappeared out the doorway.

"Shit," Hank muttered as he slid off his stool.

"That's life, Hank. Don't worry," Dick consoled, "we'll get together tomorrow night and get shit-eatin' drunk. I heard the whole Battalion will be operating out of here for the next few weeks."

"Yeah, that sounds good. Well…take it easy, my friend."

"Sure thing."

Hank followed the other lieutenants out the door and into a rain cooled darkness filled with the eerie black shadows of rubber trees and tent hooches. He slowly made his way to his company's orderly room, carefully stepping over and ducking under the many tent ropes that tried to booby-trap his way.

After receiving the operation order, he tracked down Sergeant Smith who gathered the squad leaders. When he had them all together, he went over the next day's operation, explaining in minute detail just what was to be done.

It was 2230 hours when he finally retired to his hooch. He was exhausted from trying to be thorough, wanting to cover every possible contingency, if ambushed, if booby-trapped, if, if, if.

Every "if" drained him. What "if" did he forget?

A yellow circle of light flooded a corner of the hooch. Sawyer, the forward observer, lay in his bunk, his knees bent up, a flashlight in one hand, a magazine in the other. Cronin and Brussels were already sacked out.

Hank shed his clothes and wrapped up, naked, in his poncho liner. The bunk springs felt comfortable, even without a mattress and sheets.

Before falling asleep, his hand came out and groped under the bunk. His fingers felt something, closed on it and squeezed it. He wanted to bring it up near him, treat it like a teddy bear.

It was a giant plywood key; the kind cities give to special visitors. Tied to the key was the Battalion's camouflage-patterned silk scarf with its demon patch in one corner. On one side of the key was carved the word "Cadillac", on the other side the word "Platoon".

It had been presented to him this afternoon by his men.

He managed a smile just before falling into a restless sleep.

Something grabbed him and shook violently. He fought it like a bad dream before his eyes popped open. Bright light blinded him.

"Lieutenant Kirby," a loud voice emanated from a dark figure standing over him shining a flashlight.

Hank roughly batted it aside.

Around the room, dark, shadowy outlines were hurriedly dressing.

"Sir!" The voice came again. Hank now recognized it as Sergeant Huff, the company supply sergeant.

He sat up slowly, still groggy.

"Sorry, sir, the CO wants to see you and the other lieutenants right away."

"Okay, Sergeant, I'm awake."

He groped for his fatigue pants.

Hank entered the orderly room. Captain Connors sat erect behind a wooden desk. A taut expression on his face. On the desk a map was spread open. Something was up.

First Sergeant Mendez stood to his right with four rolled maps clapped under his arm. Brussels roosted on the edge of the desk and faced the CO. Sawyer and Cronin sat in canvas director chairs. Unable to find another chair, Hank settled next to Mendez. A curious "what's up?" look showed on their faces.

"Where's Sergeant Bird?" Connors asked about the Mortar Platoon leader.

Mendez shrugged his shoulders. "Shoulda been here by now."

Just then Bird shuffled in, a wide yawn stretching his mouth.

"Okay, now we're all here," Connors began. "There's been a change in tomorrow's plans. As it stands now, the Battalion will move by Chinooks to the airstrip at Loc Ninh. There'll be three to shuttle with and we'll be the first three sorties. The First, Second, and Third Platoons will each be a separate sortie."

He turned to Sergeant Bird. "The mortars aren't going. You'll stay here and work with Huff on getting the company area squared away. No tellin' when you'll join us."

He paused and studied the map on his desk. He then looked up and spoke to the three Rifle Platoon leaders. "We're getting up at zero-five-hundred and awaiting pickup by zero-six hundred. Once we get to Loc Ninh we'll conduct company size RIFs. I don't have Bravo's route yet, but I'll give it to you when we get there."

"Why the big change in plans?" Brussels asked. "I thought our Battalion was supposed to be around here for a while."

"We were," answered Connors grimly. "But now Division G-2 believes there's a large concentration of North Vietnamese in the Loc Ninh area. How large, they're not sure. Maybe a couple of Regiments."

Eyes widened, jaws dropped. *Regiments?!*

He continued: "Being next to the Cambodian border, Loc Ninh is a leading NVA infiltration route to the south. We're supposed to plug that gap and stop whatever forces they have from getting through. Things are already hot up there. A special forces camp and an ARVN compound next to the airstrip have recently received heavy rocket and mortar fire."

"I don't feel like landing on that strip in a shithook. We'll be like sittin' ducks to their mortars," Cronin croaked his unsolicited opinion.

"Landing! That doesn't bother me. *Going* bothers me." Hank tossed in his two cents, unable to contain himself

Brussels' directed a scornful smile at Hank that silently read, *What a stupid ass remark.*

"I don't like landing there either," Connors agreed with Cronin, ignoring Hank. "But higher must see things differently." He stood, stretched, and inserted his hands in his pockets and absentmindedly began scratching the ubiquitous jungle rot growing around his crotch. "I've got to get back to see the colonel now," Connors concluded. "You men look over the maps. Get a feel for the terrain. Then try to get some shut-eye. The first sergeant will get with your platoon sergeants and fill them in."

As they filed out, Sergeant Mendez handed each a 1:50,000 topo map. The scale was twice as small as what they had been working with, meaning they would be operating in hilly terrain.

Grim-faced, the four lieutenants returned in silence to their hooch.

After examining the maps, they tried, but little sleep came during those last few hours before dawn.

CHAPTER 19

THE POWERFUL ENGINES of the Chinooks roared to a deafening high-pitched whine, their rotor blades becoming a blur just before lift-off. Inside their huge bellies blank faces, set rigid by a foreboding tension, stared unseeingly at one another from benches located at opposite sides.

Thirty minutes later, these giant grasshopper-like choppers descended upon the narrow airstrip of Loc Ninh.

Maintaining platoon integrity, the troops disembarked quickly, scurried to the edge of the clay pavement, and stopped just inside a tall stand of rubber trees that surrounded the airfield. A 105 Battery hammered away on the other side of the strip, between the twin sandbagged fortresses of a Special Forces camp and an ARVN compound.

Hank glanced over briefly at the shirtless, sweaty bodies moving busily about, pulling lanyards and reloading in pulsating clouds of gray smoke. The booming artillery pounded painfully against his ear drums. Its loud, rapid firing sprouted beads of nervous sweat. Why were they firing?

Tucker spoke in his ear. He nodded and left his men and headed for the First Platoon to find Captain Connors. As he passed through the Second Platoon someone called his name.

"Hey, Lieutenant Kirby! How you been?"

He craned his neck to look over his left shoulder. Captain Unser, the Battalion medical service officer and self-appointed pimp for the Brigade's massage services, sat perched in the shade on a stack of dry-rotted sandbags twenty feet away.

"Been better," he shouted back and forced a half smile." What the hell you doing here, sir?"

"Thought you grunts might need some help. I can handle an aid bag as well as any medic. Besides, life in Quan Loi was just too damn dull." Unser gave a huge grin.

Hank didn't reply. He waved "so long," and turned away. He thought back to when he first met Unser. How Unser had raved about wanting to be where the action was. As if whoring around with the short-time girls wasn't exciting enough.

He found Captain Connors squatting on a small mound of red dirt between the First and Second Platoons. Sawyer sat cross-legged to his right and the first sergeant stood to his left. Hank also wondered why the first shirt had come. He could have remained back at the base camp if he had wanted.

Cronin and Brussels kneeled on one knee in front of the CO. Behind him, his two RTOs monitored their radios.

Hank dropped to one knee between the two lieutenants.

Connors unfolded a map. From his breast pocket he fished out a grease pencil and used it as a pointer. "This is where we'll sweep," he said. "Look it over. I'll give you the necessary coordinates in a minute."

Eyes followed the grease pencil as it traced a crooked black line on the map. The terrain looked hilly. The route of travel was mostly through rubber plantations, rather than the thick jungles that lay beyond.

"Our RIF measures about fifteen klicks," Connors informed them.

"Fifteen klicks," whistled Brussels, "that's humpin'."

"It's longer than what we've been doing, but the terrain's not bad. 'Cept for the rolling terrain. Some of those hills are on the steep side. But going through the rubber shouldn't be bad. Least ways it's better than the jungle."

"We gonna stay the night?" Cronin asked.

"Don't know yet. There's a road that pretty much follows our route and is wide enough for a PZ. The colonel said we might go back to Quan Loi if we goose-egg it. Evidently, the old man doesn't have much confidence in G-2's work."

"Sounds like the Arty's found something," Hank said and motioned with his head at the 105s blasting away.

"They're prepping the hillsides. Softening our line of march a bit," Connors replied.

Hank sighed. *Maybe if there are any NVA, they'll get the hell out*, he thought. "What about the rest of the Battalion?"

"Charlie Company will be operating three and a half klicks to our right flank and Alpha four klicks to our left. Delta is staying back at Quan Loi as a ready reaction force."

"Lucky bastards," Sergeant Mendez said.

The CO emitted a thin smile and resumed his briefing. "We'll start off in column formation. Order of march; First, Second, and Third Platoon. Keep your two files spread apart and your flank security way out. Any last questions?"

They shook their heads.

"OK, then. As I read the coordinates of the check points, mark them down on your map. Check point one…"

The platoons moved north into the green rubber and down a slope. Rows of tall rubber trees blotted out much of the early morning sunlight casting huge shadows into an eerie darkness.

Soon they were humping up a hill. Half way up, they veered to the right and proceeded laterally. One hundred meters on their right flank, down near a valley, a ribbon of dirt road, the headwaters of Highway 13, paralleled their route. This road, with its origin at the border, wound through the fishhook, through the provincial capital, An Loc, through Quan Loi, Lai Khe, Phu Loi, Di An, and ended in Saigon. Opposite the road lay the gutted carcasses of a few French villas, products of a more stable, civilized time, but now just a pile of stone and stucco rubble, disassembled by the reckless tools of bombs and bullets.

The pace was rapid as Brussels and his lead platoon pulled Bravo along at a fair clip. Perhaps too rapid, Hank thought, his men bringing up the rear.

Under the thick canopy of limbs and leaves, the soil was a reddish clay with a strong adhesive quality that clung to their boots. There was a smattering of low, sparse underbrush which fortunately did not hinder movement.

Hank didn't remain in his usual right file. He and Tucker trekked along between the two files, near the head of the platoon. Fifty meters to his front, he could see the tail end of Cronin's troops.

After four kilometers, the rolling terrain and fast pace began to sap their strength and the CO instructed Brussels to slow down.

Just before noon, Bravo steered east across Highway 13. Another tedious kilometer passed by before they stopped to lunch on tasteless C-rations.

The men were hot and tired and irritable. They drained as much water as they dared from their canteens. Talk was limited mostly to curses and complaints of having to endure this ordeal when only hours ago they had been in the safe, comfortable confines, (by their standards anyway) of their base camp.

After chow, they pushed on, taking an easterly azimuth.

Wham! Wham! Wham! Three bursts of orange-white flame erupted. The Third Platoon belly-flopped to the ground. The violent sound waves of the explosions shook their insides and ripped through their ears.

Wham! Wham! Two more rounds exploded 100 meters left of the two flank men. Scattered bits of metal, innocent remnants of the onslaught, sprinkled down through the leaves like a light rain.

The entire platoon became frozen in their prone position. Tucker passed the radio handset to Hank who took it with a trembling hand.

"Bravo Six, November Six!" he yelled into the mouthpiece.

"Roger!" Captain Connors responded immediately. "What's happening?"

"Five mortar rounds landed to our left flank. I think we have negative casualties." Hank spoke rapidly, his words running one into the other. "I'm going to move one hundred meters to the south."

"Roger. We'll all move."

Hank frantically radioed his squad leaders to confirm they had no wounded and to pull in the flank men. He then jumped up to a crouch, pointed anxiously to the platoon's right and, using his infantry school hand signals, motioned for everyone to get up and move out on the double.

Not only the Third Platoon but the entire company rose up like a wave and ran down the hill. Two long files were still maintained but now in a flanking movement. After covering the prescribed distance, and while still at full throttle, there were scattered shouts of "get down, get down," and they threw themselves down headfirst.

The air immediately filled once again with the sounds of exploding shells. Looking back, they could see dark gray smoke from burst mortar rounds saturating the position they had just vacated.

Hank had little time to reflect on whether it was a timely decision or a survival instinct that had prompted him to run from the sound of battle. Connors' voice boomed over the radio like one of the explosions. "November Six, Bravo Six."

"November Six."

"What were they?"

"Not sure. Maybe eighty-twos."

"Roger. Whatever, we're getting out of here pronto on our east azimuth. Lima Six, did you monitor?"

"Lima Six, monitored." Lieutenant Brussels' voice came through the radio.

"All right then, let's step it out!"

Hank gave the handset back to Tucker and stood up slowly. He waved to the platoon to do likewise and move forward. Most were out of breath from their quick wind sprint and panted heavily as they pulled themselves to their feet.

With nerves taut and hearts pounding, Bravo Company started out hurriedly, still led by First Platoon.

A half hour later, a sudden cloud burst swept in. Captain Connors halted his outfit 1,200 meters from where they had received the incoming. The men dropped heavily to the ground and lay pooped and drenched in the soaking rain. They silently watched the sheets of water cover them and wondered with nervous apprehension about what was behind them.

Hank examined his map, carefully holding it close to his chest to prevent water from seeping into its plastic encasement. He pinpointed their position as being near the bottom of a large, gently sloping hillside. One hundred and fifty meters up the hillside to the north, a dirt road ran east and west. Past the road, the hill slanted gradually upward another three hundred meters. Just three kilometers farther on, across more hills of equal size, was the Cambodian border. Hank shuddered, not so much from the chill of the rain, but from the proximity of the border behind which the NVA purportedly roamed at will.

"Lieutenant Kirby, it's a company call for all platoon leaders," Tucker said and handed the mic to Hank.

"This is Lima Six."

"This is Mike Six."

Hank heard the voices of Brussels and Cronin and then made his transmission: "This is November Six."

"Roger, this is Bravo Six. Got some good news. We're getting air-lifted out of here. Higher says there's nothing around. Those mortars are believed to be eighty-ones from the ARVN compound. The Green Berets were giving the ARVNs a class on mortars and they must have flunked." Hank could hear a throaty chuckle from Connors. "There's a road not far to our north. We'll head there and then west for a hundred meters. Lima will then cross the road to secure the north side of the pickup zone. Mike will stand fast. November will pass Mike on the south and will secure the southwest quadrant. I'll give the order of liftoff when we have the PZ secured. They'll be five slicks per platoon. Roger in turn."

"Lima Six, Roger."

"Mike Six, Roger."

"November Six, Roger." Hank's Roger carried a sigh of relief. He wanted to make the pick-up zone fast. He didn't think those mortar rounds were some amateur fuck-ups.

"This is Bravo Six. Move out!"

The heavy downpour eased to a drizzle. The company swung to the north, twisting like a long, giant caterpillar. Upon finding the road, the two files turned west and followed along the south side for a hundred meters. Then the First Platoon crossed over, the Second stopped, and the Third Platoon swept around.

Hank halted his men after passing the Second Platoon. His point element was at the road and the rest of November had formed an arc to secure their portion of the perimeter.

At that moment, a volcano erupted.

Hank hit the red clay hard, and lay still, his arms tightly gripping his helmet. Behind him the trees were spitting out the sounds of grenade blasts and automatic weapons fire. Bullets whizzed four feet over his head, ripping bark from a rubber tree to his front and starting deep wounds of bleeding rubber sap. He heard the answering pops of M-16s and the staccato drones of M-60s.

"It's Mike Platoon!" shouted Tucker. He hugged the ground next to Hank.

Hank's face paled. He tried holding back tiny bits of vomit. He reached out for the handset. Tucker slapped it into his outstretched hand.

Through the earpiece, he monitored Lieutenant Cronin speaking in a cracked, wavering voice. "We're receivin' heavy RPG and AK fire from the southeast! Tell Sawyer…get that Arty crankin' ASAP! Got some hurt bad… maybe dead! We need to get 'em outta here!"

"Roger! Break! Lima Six! Send five to Mike's position!"

"This is Lima Six," Brussels' voice cracked over the radio. "Can't. We're also receiving fire."

"Any wounded?"

"I sprained my…"

"Break!" Connors cut the transmission. "November Six, are you receiving fire?"

"Not directly! But we're catching stray rounds from behind," Hank blurted into the radio.

"Roger. Keep your boys facing to the southwest! They may try to flank us. Send five to Mike to help out!"

"Wilco!" Hank answered and flung the handset back to Tucker. Not wanting to tie up the radio net, he crawled rapidly to the mid point of his platoon's defensive arc. His men lay prone, rifles at the ready, silently peering outward into a deep, dark, symmetrical forest. His head down low near the dirt, Hank saw mostly a series of boot soles.

"Sergeant Martin!" he yelled over to where he thought was the first squad leader.

"Roger, sir!" Martin lifted his head slightly and shouted back. "I monitored. I'll get 'em and go over ASAP!"

Martin pointed at four from his squad. They assumed a very low, bent over crouch, and without much hesitation, dashed past Hank toward the crippled Second Platoon, leaving him slithering around raising his head as little as possible and hollering for his men to fill in the positions just vacated.

Rounds of 105s began to whistle over and pound out their assistance to Mike. Everywhere Hank crawled, Tucker, lugging the lead-weighted radio on his slight shoulders, fought to keep up. When the gap was finally closed, he and Hank positioned themselves behind the partial ring and Hank again monitored the radio.

"I…I've been hit!" Hank heard a gasping moan that he knew came from Cronin and his stomach turned over again. "That…artillery looks good. Keep it up…"

"Roger!" Connors yelled. "Keep your men returning fire. You've got to try and gain fire superiority. I'm coming to you."

"Willllco!" Cronin's drawn out gasp conveyed severe pain.

The barrage of enemy fire seemed to dry up as the artillery continued slamming 105 high explosive rounds about 100 meters to the east-southeast of the Mike Platoon.

Hank grimaced at the ear-shattering concussions. He looked behind him to try to observe the bombardment through the foliage and saw Sergeant

Martin and two of his men twenty meters away carrying two wounded toward the road. Martin was guiding his men, who ran bent over carrying their load over their shoulders in a fireman's carry. Doc Fletcher, the November medic, left his position near Hank and rushed on all fours to their aid.

Two more wounded were brought near the road. One screamed at the top of his lungs while Fletcher wrestled to steady his thrashing arm before shooting it with morphine. Hank became nauseated when he saw the man's legs. All that remained of the left was a bloody stump just below the kneecap. The right had a grotesque foot, dirty and gray, hanging by thin strips of blood-caked skin.

A sudden burst of automatic weapons fire evident by green tracers and flying bark and leaves sent everyone at the road to the prone position.

Hank ducked his head, tightened one hand around his M-16, the other around the handset. He continued to look behind him at the road and beyond where he thought the new firing had emanated. He saw First Sergeant Mendez emerge over a small crest clawing and side-stroking his way through the red, sticky soil toward the road. A medic's aid bag, its strap a choke chain, was around his neck. Beside him, gripped in a tight bear hug by his left arm, he dragged a lifeless body by the legs. As Mendez drew closer to the road, Hank recognized Captain Unser, the medical service officer.

Hank's stomach turned again.

The new incoming automatic weapons fire died as quickly as it had begun, possibly silenced by the artillery. A lull in the firefight seemed to settle in. There was no more exchange of rifle fire and grenades. Only the welcome pounding of friendly explosions.

Hank now fixed his eyes to the southwest quadrant for the next twenty minutes as he watched over his perimeter and avoided looking back toward the road at the wounded. He then realized there was a gap between his platoon and Lima north of the road. He radioed Sergeant Smith to send a fire team north across the road to provide a link with Lima.

"November Six, Bravo Six."

"November Six," he answered.

"We're ready to bring in a dust-off for the WIAs. Pop smoke on the road and keep it there till the chopper lands."

"Wilco," he answered automatically. He closed his eyes and prayed that this lull was the end of the storm and not the passing of the eye.

Hunching low, he and Tucker raced for the road. Five meters away, he stopped on one knee and hurled a smoke grenade. It burst in the mud into a yellow cloud.

Ten meters to their right five wounded, three moaning and sobbing, were on the ground where they lay bloodied but well attended. Five meters further on two lay alone, sprawled on the road's shoulder, face down as if suffocated by the mud. One was Unser. The other Hank didn't recognize.

One of the WIAs beckoned to Hank with a feeble, bloodstained paw. Fighting the sick feeling in the pit of his stomach, Hank told Tucker to keep the smoke going and hurried to the man's side, conscious that the eye of the storm could pass at any moment.

It was Lieutenant Cronin, his face pockmarked with small fragments of shrapnel, a bandage over one eye. His thighs and groin were drenched with dark, coagulating blood.

"Kirby! Kirby!" he babbled in shock. "My eye! I lost my eye!"

Hank placed a hand on Cronin's shoulder as he knelt beside him. "You're going to be all right, Frank," he encouraged in a calm tone that belied his feeling of wanting to scream. "You're going to make it. There's a dust-off on the way. You're going home." Hank managed a weak smile. "You've made it, Frank!" he comforted, not knowing how badly wounded Cronin was.

"Yeah…." Cronin answered slowly, with obvious effort. "I'm gonna be… back…in the World." He then sighed, coughed, and went silent.

Hank heard the whirl of the medevac. A thin slurry of red mud began kicking up. He yelled over to Martin who had been assisting the medics and First Sergeant with the wounded to help him lift Mike's platoon leader.

Suddenly, Cronin reached out and clutched Hank's fatigue shirt. With his left hand, he slowly reached around and picked a fragmentation grenade out of his canteen pouch. He fingered it a moment, contemplatively, then thrust it at Hank. "Here!" he gasped. "Take it!" and sank back, exhausted.

Speechless, Hank nodded and grabbed it.

He and Martin carefully lifted an arm and leg and carried the shrapnel torn lieutenant to the waiting chopper. With its five WIAs, the chopper climbed above the rubber trees, hesitated a moment, then picked up speed as it headed for safety.

Hank watched it disappear, wanting to be on it, but not in the same condition as its passengers. He ran bent over back to the center of his platoon where Tucker joined him.

The artillery had stopped. An eerie hush filled the void.

Private First Class Franklin's machine gun sliced through the silence! The M-60 spat out a continuous stream of lead, every fourth round a reddish tracer.

"What is it?" Hank yelled over to Franklin's position, where he lay prone behind the gun, his shoulder flush against its butt, his eyes sighting down the barrel.

He stopped firing, but kept sighting. Nordstrom, his ammo bearer, who had been meticulously feeding the ammo belt to the gun, mindful of stoppages should it become twisted, glanced over at Hank. "Gooks! We saw two running down in the gulley!" he shouted.

As Hank was starting to digest this information, Tucker offered him the handset. "It's the CO. He wants to know who's firing."

"Franklin and Nordstrom spotted two gooks!" Hank sang out in a high screech into the mouthpiece.

"Roger. Keep a close eye out. Make sure your men have a good defensive posture. They could be trying to flank us. But with all the 105 shit we poured on, it could be a few were just scattering. Wait about thirty minutes to see if anything develops. If nothing, then come see me. My CPs at the road about dead center between you and Mike."

After thirty palm-sweating minutes, Hank found the CO, Brussels, and Staff Sergeant Daniels, the platoon sergeant of Mike, waiting for him. The CO had bad news. They weren't going to be picked up. They would be staying put for the night. In the morning they would remain in place until Charlie and Alpha linked up with them to form a Battalion minus force. Together the three companies would conduct a recon in force.

As Connors briefed the next day's scenario, Hank studied the face of Sergeant Daniels, who was now Mike's acting platoon leader. It was grim, with glazed, hollow eyes. While appearing to listen to the CO, he stared blankly at the ground. Hank placed his hand on his shoulder and squeezed.

The sky slowly cleared and the sun dwindled to dusk. Another chopper chattered down bringing a re-supply of ammo and drinking water. The two KIAs were loaded aboard and sent back on the return trip.

Connors decided to have the entire company on the south side of the road. The Second and Third Platoons moved a short distance down the hill to make room for the First. The three platoons came together to form a perimeter fifty meters in diameter.

As twilight faded into the trees, the platoons went about preparing their night defenses. Only six entrenching tools existed within the company, causing the soldiers to improvise with such makeshift tools as their steel helmets and bayonets. They were grunts in every sense of the word as they burrowed in like prairie dogs.

Fingernails torn and bleeding, palms hamburger raw, Hank silently cursed Captain Woodson, the big, baldheaded, asshole S-4. First, he had booted his platoon from a comfortable hooch to a slum hooch back in Pho Loi. Responsible for logistical supply for the Battalion, Woodson now had neglected to put the rucksacks they had so carefully packed in Quan Loi on the re-supply sortie. The rucksacks contained personal possessions such as toilet and stationary articles as well as comfort items like ponchos and poncho liners and were, at the start of their mission, to have been delivered upon arrival at their bivouac position. He also had neglected to send additional entrenching tools and shovels, which were now sorely needed, and the reason Hank personally held Woodson accountable for his shredded hands. The re-supply sortie, a Huey slick that was much smaller than the usual Chinook, had contained only an abundance of ammo, water, and boxes of C-rations.

The gluey red clay cloaked him completely, giving him an artificial sun burn to go with the all too real redness of his hands.

Finally, when the hole he and Tucker had been excavating was just big enough for them to wedge in head first with their legs still exposed on the surface, they stopped, their strength sapped.

Hank took the first watch and squeezed on his side partially into the shallow depression with the scrawny Tucker, who was flat on his back, his legs extending upward at an angle, bent at the knees, calves and feet resting outside the hole.

From their night position, situated ten meters behind their platoon's third of the perimeter, Hank peered nervously into thick, ominous blackness. With each minute he expected to see the flimsy perimeter erupt with explosions of incoming mortars and an all-out frontal assault.

There was much speculation and conjecture about the size of the force that had attacked Second Platoon. The initial buzz of rumors that had filtered through to Hank from his platoon was that it had been an NVA company.

Connors had proffered his opinion to Hank when he had checked on November's night defensive position. He said it might have been a hit and run.

Size of force unknown. He theorized the NVA may have been shadowing their RIF, reconnaissance-in-force, and maybe preparing an in-wait ambush. When Bravo had turned west and headed toward the road, maybe they felt they were losing an opportunity for a decisive contact. Then when November had swung around Mike's Platoon, they attacked with small arms fire and RPGs. The artillery from the 105 Battery at Loc Ninh had prevented a much worse outcome.

Connors had high praise for Mike Platoon. When they started receiving fire they assumed an instant defensive position by dropping to the prone, forming a partial perimeter, and quickly returning fire. Connors particularly commented on the courage of Cronin in leading his men in repelling the attack and of Unser scrambling to the wounded at the point of heavy contact. He also said that Hank's men, Sergeant Martin and his four squad members, performed professionally and well in helping with Mike's wounded.

Unfortunately, there was nothing known about casualties they may have inflicted on the attackers.

Hank reflected on these events now. He hoped Cronin would make a full recovery. He refused to think about Unser and Mike's KIA, whom he didn't know. Small arms fire, Connors had called it. What was small about an AK-47 assault rifle? The Army called that small? They just didn't get it.

His mind returned to their vulnerable situation. What if an entire regiment attacked tonight? Hank choked and shivered on the thought. With nothing to do but stare into an inky nothing, he had time to become terribly afraid.

He tried to escape his fear by turning his thoughts homeward, to the World. In doing so he inexplicably began to feel a twinge of dislike for everyone back there. Everyone who was safe; who was now laughing, or partying, or sleeping in a warm bed with sheets. He didn't want Pam to be doing these things—well, he wanted her safe, of course, and would give her the sheets, on the condition Dave Watson wasn't sharing them with her.

About midnight the rain came, biting and cold and windy. He hunched his body close to Tucker's for warmth. He pressed his ear to the handset's earpiece and listened to the transmission of a lonely rushing sound.

CHAPTER 20

H ANK SAT ON the edge of his shallow hole as the early morning sun began warming the day. He stretched his arms over his head and flexed his shoulders. His extremities felt stiff, aching. He scrubbed his gritty teeth with a gray coated tongue.

A red clay-coated mummy resembling Sergeant Smith came over to Hank's tiny foxhole and informed him that everyone was awake.

Hank nodded and rubbed his whiskered face. In a hoarse whisper he said to Smith, "Stay here and keep an eye on things. I've got to get the morning sitrep from the captain," He stood unsteadily, then started slowly over to find the CO.

When he returned, his face was somber. He gruffly instructed Smith to assemble the squad leaders and Spec-four Milton. He tried to get his mind around the missions they had been given.

A few moments later, wearing faces grimy and drawn, fatigues soiled brown-red, his squad leaders and point man knelt before him. He sat facing them on the edge of the shallow foxhole, which resembled more the diggings of a terrier than that of an infantry soldier. Opposite the hole, Tucker sat still and unmoving, like a bronze memorial statue, and monitored the horn.

"Listen up," Hank said softly, his tone pensive. "Around noon Alpha and Charlie will link up. When they do, we're to go up that hill." He pointed north across the road at the gradual incline with its waves of rubber trees. On the topo map, it was denoted as Hill 228. Years ago, it probably would have been a refreshing stroll through the shade, with the breeze wafting the sweet smell of rubber sap all about. "We'll continue to head north until we're told to stop or until we reach the Cambodian border, whichever comes first.

"The companies will move in column, with Bravo in the lead." His eyes jumped around, meeting those that were gathered before him, warning them of ominous words that would follow. "Our platoon will be point."

There was a flood of pale, drowning expressions.

Then they reacted, erupting as he knew they would.

"Shit! The fucking Cambodian border!" Sergeant Martin exploded. "We're the goddamn lead element for the whole damn Battalion…Why us, for Chrissake?"

"Why anybody?" broke in Smith. "Why not pull back about three klicks and B-fifty-two the hell out of everything between here and there?"

"Because some stupid, dick-sucking, glory-hunting general thinks this is World War Two. That's why!" Sergeant Percy burst forth his opinion of the ranking officer corps and their tactics. "Attack, assault, get a good muddah-fuckin' body count. That's what they all want."

All but the usual dissenter, Sergeant Bennet, vehemently nodded agreement.

"For one, I doubt they're around anymore," Bennet commented reasonably. "After those artillery strikes yesterday, the gooks probably *didi-maued* across the border. That's their R and R center. If they were still around, how come we didn't get hit last night?"

Surprisingly, those words made a little sense.

"Maybe he's right," Smith spoke. "Didn't Cronin's platoon get hit from the gully below the hill? Maybe they're not north of here. But maybe they are. So fucking what? We got our orders. Whether we like 'em or not."

There was silence. Hank looked around at each man. Their faces and eyes said they were with Smith. The traditional Army's discipline had held. They didn't like it, but would go up the hill and head north to the Cambodian border as point. There was one consolation, though. Maybe Bennet *was* right.

"Just for good measure, we have another mission this morning. Bravo Six said we got to sweep the perimeter. Out about one hundred meters."

"Ain't point enough? Why that too?" spat Milton, the Beacon. He had a vested interest in the other mission, his element was the platoon's point, the point's point.

"It can't be the Second Platoon," Hank answered quickly. "They got hit yesterday and they're minus a good platoon leader."

"Cronin was good all right," Sergeant Smith concurred in a soft reverent tone.

"Hell, Milton don't mean them," snapped Percy. "He talkin' 'bout the First Platoon, Lima. Since we're gonna be point, they oughta sweep the perimeter." He glanced at Milton for confirmation and was answered with a "that's right" nod.

"I know, I agree," Hank acknowledged, his eyes wide and brow wrinkled in a show of empathy. "I said the same to Captain Connors. He gave me three reasons for his decision: the First Platoon was point yesterday; Lieutenant Brussels has a sprained ankle which slows them up." He hesitated as the group smirked and muttered epithets about Brussels' fortunate fate.

"And the final reason…" There was a short pause as he surveyed their faces and gave a long swallow. "…He said November was the Cadillac Platoon."

Smiles suddenly burst out all around him. Captain Connors had somehow found out about their artillery-wasting shenanigans. And there had been no repercussions. The men before him seemed to grow taller.

"He's right, you know. We proved it. Not just by firing all that Arty, but with that fuckin' ambush," Martin declared, a thin smile on his dirt-caked lips.

"Get your men ready to move out!" Hank ordered.

That fucking ambush, he thought to himself.

Rifles at the ready, the Third Platoon left the perimeter and crept cautiously to the southwest, down the gulley where Franklin had fired at the two NVA.

They hadn't moved. Both lay face down. Both were dead.

Nudging, kicking boots rolled their waxen carcasses over. Their mouths hung open, lips curled up on their teeth like a snarl, hollow eyes stared open to the morning sun. One still gripped his AK-47 with fingers covered in caked, dark red blood. The other had dropped his rocket launcher by his side, probably as his throat was being ripped open from one of Franklin's 7.62mm rounds. New green fatigues gave them the morbidly ironic look of neatness.

The green fatigues puzzled Hank. He had thought the NVA would be wearing khaki brown uniforms.

With careful, delicate movements to avoid contaminating their hands, Sergeant Martin and Spec-four Milton frisked the bodies. Finding nothing, they took their weapons. Milton slung the AK over his shoulder and leaned his own weapon against a nearby tree. With his right hand, he reached across to his left shoulder and tore his "Big Red One" patch off his fatigue shirt. He squatted next to the NVA he had just searched and thrust the patch into the dead man's mouth. As he rose, he kicked the stiff open jaw shut causing the teeth to clinch the patch. Martin followed suit, placing his patch in the mouth of the other and promptly slapping it closed with his rifle butt. The dead gooks were transformed to dead mongrels, the cloth of their intended victims in their fangs.

This humiliating ritual dazed Hank. He immediately waved away the men who had gathered around to admire their bagged quarry.

They headed south of the company perimeter and then around to the southeast where the Second Platoon had made contact. Four more bodies were found. They appeared to have been torn and mutilated by shrapnel from artillery rounds.

Slowly they picked and probed their way through the ugly, stomach turning feast from which big, black flies dined. As if adding spice to the dinner, five members of Martin's squad tore off their patches and sprinkled them on the decaying human meat as though they were salting pork.

Hank stomached it no longer. He abruptly halted others from participating. After all, they had been human beings. Someones sons….

They returned to the company where he reported their findings to Connors. The captured booty—rifles, RPG tubes, B-40 rockets, grenades and some assorted personal items—were stacked beside the road for chopper pick up.

At 1330 hours, Alpha and Charlie Companies had joined Bravo and reinforced the security along the road, setting up a secured LZ. At 1337, Lieutenant Colonel West, the Battalion commander, with his operations officer, and his recon platoon, flew in by five slicks to take part in the RIF. At 1400 hours, the order was given to move out.

CHAPTER 21

HANK'S PLATOON SLID smoothly into the lead as it crossed the road into the forest of tall rubber trees and began the ascent up Hill 228. A light fire team of two Cobra gunships swept in overhead and began circling menacingly above them.

Lima Platoon followed fifty meters behind. Bravo Six and his CP contingent nestled between Lima and Mike. Charlie Company followed Bravo; Alpha trailed. Escorted by the recon platoon, Lieutenant Colonel West and his S-3 provided a link between Charlie and Alpha.

As Hank's platoon advanced, he observed his men from his location at the front of the two main files and twenty meters between them. He particularly noted Milton's three man point team about forty meters ahead creeping slowly forward at turtle pace. Their heads cautiously swept the area like mine detectors, wanting to anticipate the slightest movement on the ground or around the trees. The intent of the point was as an early warning device. They were to step in the shit first.

There was no trace of the enemy as they inched closer to the top. Bennet must be right, Hank considered hopefully. The NVA had gotten the hell out.

Wham! Grapeshot from a CHICOM Claymore tore through the air. Automatic weapons fire spat out green tracers that crisscrossed in the front and on both flanks.

The Third Platoon had made contact!

Hank immediately dropped. Quivering, he strained to press every hair, every bone, every fiber and follicle of his body to the ground, through the ground, wishing it was quicksand.

A stream of bullets passed over his head from three directions, whizzing and snapping over his prone, outstretched frame. A surge of panic spread through him. Incoherent flashes of thought flickered in his mind. What's happening? This can't be happening! He was frozen, totally petrified. He couldn't twitch a muscle. He didn't *want* to twitch a muscle!

Horrible, bone chilling screams of terrible suffering began crying out, mixing with the sounds of battle.

His mind slowly surfaced and he came out of the momentary shock and groped his arm out towards Tucker as if wanting to be pulled from drowning. Immediately, the radio handset was slapped surgeon-like into his open hand. "Bravo Six, November Six! We're into something big!" Hank fumbled the words at a shout into the mouthpiece. "We're receiving heavy concentrated fire from the front and flanks. We got casualties. Get those gunships in here quick!"

He waited an interminable period for the reply. After a few seconds it came, quick and simple. "Roger. Have you marked your point and flanks?"

Overcoming with great effort the tremendous weight of fear, Hank managed to lift his head and glance with straining eyes through the sparse blades of weeds to his front. He wanted to see a bright, colored stream of smoke. Nothing! He craned his neck to look at his right and left. Yellow smoke was starting to billow. At least the squads had monitored.

"Just the flanks! Not the point! Get the Arty cranking. Move it around two hundred meters to our front. We'll get that smoke out. Put the gunships on our flanks. We've got yellow smoke both sides. Break! November Papa, November Six, get that Goddamn smoke out!" he yelled over the radio net at Milton.

There was no answer.

The avalanche of firing slackened a bit.

Hank lay face down, rigid and tense against the buffeting waves of despair. It was a time for decision and he had never felt more indecisive. His first thought was of the old infantry school axiom that had been drilled into him at Benning: When ambushed, do something, even if it's wrong. But his second thought of doing something wrong had no appeal. Nevertheless, being an ostrich after stumbling into a hornet's nest *was* the wrong thing!

The logical course of action, or so it seemed after five seconds of fuzzy cogitation, was to get all the fire support in Vietnam directed to his front and flanks and then run like hell down the hill. The artillery was banging away now but they needed something closer, as close as possible to the front. They needed the rockets and miniguns of gunships. Gunships that needed smoke to mark their position. He contemplated popping his own smoke and throwing it at the point position and letting the gunships do their thing. But what if the point was way beyond the smoke and gunships tore them up? Or what if the point was already dead? Or what if only their radio was dead and they were alive.

Goddamn "what ifs"!

His decision tree had been whittled to a stump. Only one course of action seemed apparent, crawl up to the point and have them pop smoke. At the same time bring in gunships using the smoke from the squads as reference, but allowing sufficient distance from the smoke to protect the point, if that was possible. How far was the point? Surely no more than fifty meters, seventy-five from the smoke on the flanks and close to the fringe of artillery that was hammering away.

Hank began edging slowly forward with Tucker sticking to his side. The handset was like an appendage to his ear as he slid on his belly along the ground, navigating by instinct, unable to see through the sparse grass and unwilling to stick his head up into the spaghetti of green tracers whizzing about. He pressed the push-to-talk button so tight that his knuckles looked as though they would pop from the thinly stretched skin.

"Bravo Six, November Six, we gotta have those gunships now! We'll get the smoke out at the point soonest. Meantime start 'em on their passes to our front. That's where most of the shit seems to be coming from. Tell 'em to keep it at least a hundred meters on a north azimuth from the smoke that's markin' the flanks."

In any given second, Hank expected to be stopped dead. It was at first uncomprehending how the bullets continued to pass over their heads rather than *into* their heads. Perhaps they were firing from low bunkers or from the prone and couldn't get enfilading fire low enough. Whatever the reason, the solution was to stay as low as a gopher and pray like a priest.

From the upper corner of his right eye just past the brim of his helmet he saw through the leaves of the rubber trees one of the Cobras bank wide, preparing to make a pass. The eye widened in abject horror as a flood of green tracers rose from the trees to meet the gunship. The chopper lurched out of control and started angling into a dive, its rotor blade twisting like a wounded duck futilely beating its wings. It limped some six hundred meters past the Third Platoon, then vanished into a fiery swirl.

In haste, the trailing sister ship unleashed her rockets and miniguns from too high an altitude and missed its mark. Taking several hits in return, she staggered uneasily out of sight.

Hank felt he was vomiting his guts out rather than his lunch's canned turkey loaf as he watched the second chopper leave. But at least they still had the artillery, though from its sound it was too far away.

"Bravo Six, November Six! That Arty's too far out. Drop it about one-five-zero and move it back and forth! Put in on the flanks too!" Hank screamed into the mouthpiece while still shoving himself forward. "We lost that light-fire team." For a split second, Hank wondered how the Artillery Battery from Loc Ninh would handle the front and flanks simultaneously. Maybe they'd dedicate certain tubes to certain areas. Could they get it close enough? Does the CO know the coordinates?

"Roger! We know!" Connors answered. "We're expecting fighters on station in about one-five, so get that smoke out at the point. It's more important than ever." There was a short pause in the transmission before the CO asked: "Have you got an estimate of what we're up against?"

"Negative, not yet! But it's big." Hank suddenly swallowed hard, the bits of gritty puke that had remained in his mouth burned his throat. He wanted to kick his own ass. He had been so preoccupied with the point, the smoke, the gunships, the artillery, that he hadn't checked on the rest of the platoon, the main body now located on his rear flanks. He abruptly broke off the transmission with the CO. "Break! Break! November Five, November Six!" he radioed Sergeant Smith. No answer. "November Five, this is November Six! Come in Goddamn it!"

"November Six, this is November Five Kilo. Sergeant Smith's dead."

A block of ice formed in the back of Hank's neck and cart wheeled down his spine leaving a wake of chills. He called Martin who had the right file. "November One, November Six, sitrep?"

"We've been hit bad!" Martin's voice shrieked over the radio. "Our flank men could be dead. I've got dead and wounded in my file. Can't raise my head high enough to see. They seem like they might be in bunkers. Some said they've seen gooks in trees. Whatever, we've received a shitload of AK and RPG fire!"

"Roger." Hank gulped weakly. His hands shook spasmodically. "Do the best you can. When we get TAC air maybe we can get the heat off enough to get out of here."

Hank started to call Sergeant Percy, but remembered Milton's point had the fourth radio.

He called Martin back, "November One, I can't reach the left file. You're the boss for both files while I'm checking on the point. Roger?"

"Roger."

He then tried reaching the point again but to no avail. He wondered if they were still alive. Were they infested with NVA? Still, he and Tucker had to push on. Only a little farther. Maybe ten more meters.

Meanwhile, on the reverse slope of hill 228, Colonel Dao Tri Minh sat tautly in the milky darkness of his command bunker, a slight wry smile on his face. Surrounding him, six North Vietnamese soldiers worked frantically, monitoring and relaying messages received on the mass of field telephones and radios crowded before them.

For a brief moment, Colonel Dao allowed his mind to run from the current conflict to a time one month ago. It had been then since his newly formed regiment of 1100 NVA regulars had left the security of North Vietnam to fight in the South. Armed with the newest and best of weaponry and equipment, they had been convoyed by trucks down the Ho Chi Minh Trail to a little Cambodian village within two thousand meters of the South Vietnamese border.

A week ago, after elaborate final plans and small unit recon patrols, the regiment surreptitiously crept across the border and established an intricate, well fortified base camp in a tangle of rubber trees on Hill 228, not far from the town of Loc Ninh. Their mission was threefold: to harass the American and South Vietnamese forces in the area by rocket and mortar attacks; to conduct a ground attack annihilating the Special Forces camp and ARVN compound that protected the Loc Ninh airstrip; and thirdly, to serve as a link in the chain of NVA base camps that strung south toward Saigon.

The ground attack had been scheduled for tomorrow but now would have to be postponed. Yesterday, an American company had strayed to the base of his hill, and to cope with it he had put in play a hit and run attack using a reinforced platoon. His major objective, besides inflicting maximum casualties, had been to draw the American units away from the airstrip so they could not readily aid the isolated company there, thus putting it in a position where he could easily wipe out the base camp.

Colonel Dao's smile broadened into a contemptuous grin. Leisurely, he lit an American cigarette, took a deep drag, and let the smoke drift from his mouth and nostrils.

Rising from his seat he paced slowly back and forth in the close confines of his command bunker, now and then lightly stomping a foot in a self-satisfied, gleeful manner. His elation knew no bounds. For now a once in a lifetime opportunity presented itself. An entire American battalion stretched critically thin down the hill's south slope, its two columns dangerously exposed.

His hands emanated moisture and turned red from forcefully rubbing them together in nervous anticipation. He eagerly listened to the situation reports coming in from his subordinate command elements which ringed the hill's periphery and the maneuver elements flanking the east side of the enemy battalion. Snug in his CP, the thundering and trembling of artillery shells filtered harmlessly down into his fortified sanctuary.

An overwhelming victory seemed easily within his reach. Only their foe's stinging artillery delayed their futile doom. Their point platoon, which had unwittingly walked right up to the very edge of their bunker complex, was being sealed off and was already badly decimated and ready to fall. But rather than overrunning it in one fell swoop, he would tease it a bit using it like mangled live bait to keep the enemy's main element hanging on. The main element would soon be penetrated in its right column and then rolled up in both directions.

There was no question about the final outcome, and success beamed in Colonel Dao's dark, piercing eyes. His regiment would be the first NVA force ever to destroy decisively an entire American battalion. After its destruction, his forces would simply scamper back across the border to Cambodia, safe from pursuit by other American units. The flush of the coming victory caused all sorts of thoughts to parade through the colonel's mind. The one he dwelled on most was that Ho Chi Minh might give him a promotion to the general staff in Hanoi.

After all, he was a distant relative of Uncle Ho.

CHAPTER 22

THE 105 ROUNDS pounded in precariously close, showering a residue of shrapnel on Hank. But the proximity of the artillery was inversely proportional to the intensity of the cross-fire and offered a protective blanket which slowed Hank's galloping pulse to a moderate canter.

His pulse resumed its breakneck speed when he caught a glimpse of one of his point men a few meters away. He was sprawled flat on his stomach. His fatigue pants were shredded and there appeared to be blood all over his buttocks. Eyes shut, face pallid, his head was twisted and angled toward Hank. His name was Calabrese. His back moved up and down, barely perceptible. He was still breathing.

Hank tossed the radio handset to Tucker. Keeping low, he scrambled toward Calabrese. Upon reaching him, his eyes glimpsed two bodies lying face down, just a couple of meters away. One was Milton, the other Wojic, his RTO. Both looked dead.

With a fumbling motion, Hank hastily jerked a yellow smoke grenade from his equipment harness, pulled the pin, and lobbed it past the two lifeless bodies. He then spun his head back at Tucker and yelled: "Get on the horn! Tell 'em to get those air strikes comin' in! Smoke's out!"

Tucker started relaying the message immediately.

Hank tore out a bandage from his first aid packet, propped himself on his elbows, and prepared to doctor Calabrese's wound. He hesitated briefly, not knowing where to apply the bandage. He swabbed the blood from around the wounded buttocks with his sleeve. There appeared to be a bullet hole through the right cheek, through the crack, and then out the left cheek. Or had the bullet taken the other route? It didn't really matter. What mattered was where he should put the bandage. Finally, he decided to put it in the crack, sealing off two of the holes. He would use Calabrese's and Tucker's bandages for the others.

Calabrese fluttered open his eyes, forced his neck to crane toward Hank, and surveyed the surgery to his posterior. A ghastly questioning look fixed hypnotically on his platoon leader, asking the unanswerable.

Suddenly bullets thudded in rapid succession, ripping into the soldier's back, missing Hank's head by mere inches. In a reflex reaction Hank log-rolled back to a shallow depression where Tucker was frantically yelling into the radio.

Another burst of fire barked out from somewhere about twenty meters to their left front. And then another from twenty-five meters on their right. Tiny missiles snapped overhead, emanating from camouflaged, earth-hardened bunkers.

Two more bursts followed in unison. Tucker dug his nails into Hank's arm and pointed a trembling finger directly ahead. Just fifteen meters away, two small clouds of grayish smoke drifted slowly into the air from out of the ground. They came from a bunker's firing ports, split at forty-five degrees. The angle provided a blind spot to the front which gave Hank and Tucker a flimsy but effective protective barrier from their firing.

Hank's body contoured to the slight indentation of earth where he and Tucker sought refuge. Cautiously he raised his eyes from the ground and peeked warily over at the wounded Calabrese. The bandage lay where he had dropped it. But he knew it wouldn't be needed now. Calabrese lay still.

Perspiration poured in buckets from Hank's pale face, looking as if the blood had been sucked down his neck, his heart a vacuum pump. His hands shook like an old man's as he lobbed another smoke grenade in the direction of the enemy's forward bunker. Perhaps the yellow cloud would help as a smoke screen in addition to marking his position.

A hard, lumpy feeling worked up his gullet and lodged in his throat. His gut contained a set of spinning needles. It was a certain realization that caused these symptoms. The realization he was going to die. And with it came a strange calming sensation. He no longer had to worry about it. Only to accept it.

For some reason he felt better.

Circling like a hawk waiting for its prey to expose itself, Captain Hirsh, the Air Force forward air controller, impatiently watched for the forward friendly position to be marked with smoke. Two F-100 Super Sabres had reported on station from Bien Hoa and he wanted to inform the North Viets of their arrival. Especially since just a minute ago he had spotted the green tracers of a fifty-one-caliber flying by his small, slow, and extremely vulnerable OV-10. He hadn't seen the source but as soon as his fighters started to work he'd find it and waste the son of a bitch.

Finally, a yellow cloud billowed upward from the dark green forest of rubber trees. The other elements had already marked their positions. *So this must be it,* he thought to himself. "Bravo Six, Sidewinder Six. I've sighted yellow smoke. Is that your point?"

"This is Bravo Six. Wait!" Hirsch heard a low, gravely voice. "Roger. Yellow smoke! NVA concentrated to its north. They say bring 'em in close."

"Roger that. We'll start at two-hundred meters and they can adjust from there. Out." Two hundred meters was damn close.

He smoothly banked his ice blue Bronco and nosed it down to get a better look. Zeroing in a few hundred meters north of the smoke he fired a white phosphorous rocket. At the same time, he barked off commands to the fighter pilots, instructing them how to make their pass, using the residue of white phosphorous smoke as his target.

Green tracers streamed in hyphens by his cockpit. "You bastards will get yours!" he muttered to himself.

Wham!

A 500-pounder slammed into the turf, causing it to tremble like an on-coming earthquake. Another fighter zoomed down, raced along the treetops and released its payload.

Wham!

Scattered chunks of half dollar-sized shrapnel sprinkled lightly around Hank and Tucker. But too lightly. It would have to be nearer to be more effective.

"Tell 'em to get it closer!" Hank yelled into Tucker's ear only a foot away.

The bombs came within distances varying from a frightening one hundred and fifty meters to a terrifying one hundred meters. They had the effect of massive quantities of chlordane on ant hills, driving the NVA from their nests in the ground. But instead of driving them away, the enemy moved slowly nearer, crouching and crawling, in an effort to hug the platoon for protection. The closer to the owners of the firepower, the safer they would be.

Through thin blades of grass and freshly strewn foliage, pruned by bullets and shrapnel, Hank caught a brief glimpse of someone crawling about five meters to his right. At first he thought it was one of his men, but a sixth sense warned him otherwise.

Quickly with clawing fingers he tore into his canteen pouch for a grenade. It was too late. Before he could pull the pin a CHICOM potato masher came arching high toward him.

He and Tucker struggled frantically to burrow their heads deep into the ground, bracing themselves against the impact, wondering about death. The grenade sailed long over their heads and exploded, shattering only their ears. Hank neither felt nor noticed the glistening red stream meandering along his fatigue pants; the origin his calf. He was too absorbed with ripping the pin from his fragmentation grenade. Seconds seemed like minutes as he released its safety lever and let it cook-off, preventing the possibility of a toss back. But if the cook-off was too long, the grenade would go off in his hand. His trembling right hand demonstrated his awareness of this scenario.

After three excruciating seconds, he heaved the baseball shaped explosive at the intruder. A following blast tore through the air. A thundercloud of smoke charged with dirt and shrapnel rolled over him, the smoke choking him.

Before the debris cleared, three NVA sprung from spider-holes and charged through the gray-black fog, screaming gook gibberish and blindly firing their AKs in front of their assault. Dirt geysered up everywhere around Hank and Tucker as they countered the onslaught with a steady stream of automatic fire from their M-16s.

Two dropped immediately; dead from the high-velocity impacts of 5.56mm slugs pelting their torsos. The other continued undaunted and unmolested for a few more meters, until the two streams of automatic fire closed to a focal point on the now solitary assailant. Tucker's fire hit him with a long burst to the head, shattering it as if it were a fresh melon. Hank's missiles smacked him in the groin and thudded their way up to his chest. The attacker arched upward and backward, spinning as if caught in the vortex of a miniature tornado, and falling beside a grenade splattered comrade.

Less than twenty meters away, a fire team of NVA clambered out of two bunkers and darted through the rubber, trying to circle behind them to their right.

Tucker's peripheral vision glimpsed the maneuver and he spun toward them, at the same time pushing Hank's shoulder in the same direction and yelling, "More gooks! More gooks!"

A machine gun suddenly coughed out long steady bursts, dropping three attackers. The others plunged to the ground to avoid being caught in the M-60's wake of death.

Hank and Tucker turned their attention around behind them to the sounds of the gun. Through a residue of chopped limbs and scattered bark chunks, they barely made out the helmeted heads of PFC Franklin and his ammo bearer, PFC Nordstrom. They were sheltered in a small swale some twenty-five meters away.

Hank turned to Tucker and hollered in his ear: "Tell Bravo Six the gooks are trying to rush us! Tell him to get some napalm in here and to put it close!" He immediately second guessed himself and wondered if the napalm was a good idea. It would certainly fry any enemy troops in the open. Then again, it could also fry his ass as well. It would have been nice, he morbidly reflected, if Benning had instructed them when to use Napalm. He decided to go with it. If it wasn't a good idea, hopefully Connors or the Air Force FAC would know. He started firing in the general direction of where the gooks were, or where thought them to be. From his vantage point he could see no signs of movement and as long as a wall of lead could be maintained hopefully there wouldn't be any.

Tucker relayed the napalm message and then shouted back the reply. "CO said Wilco, but keep that smoke out!"

The remark caused Hank to look straight ahead into a diffusing yellow vapor. He skittishly groped around his equipment harness for another smoke grenade. It was a fruitless exercise. He was out of smoke. In a frenzy, his eyes frisked Tucker's radio backpack hoping to see a remaining beer-can shaped grenade crimped to its side. Nothing! Not thinking to ask, his hands molested the parts of Tucker's body hidden from his eyes. Tucker reacted by pulling away, shaking his head that he had no more.

Hank screamed what Tucker already knew: "We're out of smoke!" and began shoving himself backwards along the ground toward Franklin's machine-gun. Bullets chewed up the dirt by his feet and he lunged forward. His heart fluttered in an uneven rhythm as he realized they were cut off.

He rolled onto his back, bent this chin down and used the full force of his lungs to yell to Franklin: "We need more smoke!"

Franklin nodded a Roger he understood, but then it was followed by a head shake, a negative, they had none. Hank silently cursed himself. Everyone in the platoon was to carry at least four smoke grenades. It was Battalion SOP. But he had countermanded the order for the M-60 gunners and their ammo bearers. He had decided they were carrying too much so he had allowed them to lighten their load. He thought he was being a nice guy. What a fucking stupid decision, he now realized.

Nordstrom suddenly signaled Hank with a hand flash of the OK sign and started on his belly back toward the platoon's main body where the right and left files had closed to form an elliptical perimeter.

As Nordstrom baby-crawled inside the perimeter among the groans of the wounded, and the glazed eyes of the dead, he gathered up smoke grenades like scattered berries. He collected them at a central point where he found an abandoned rucksack. He filled the rucksack to the brim, slung it over his back, and crawled up to Franklin's position, shifting from all fours to his belly as he approached.

He stopped next to Franklin and lifted his head a few inches to peer over a small protective mound at his platoon leader and RTO. They weren't drawing fire. All the firepower seemed to be their own: sporadic bursts of three reinforced by Franklin's coughing sets of six and the slamming of artillery shells which filled the hiatus left by the departing air strikes. He saw Lieutenant Kirby turn on his side and glance back. With a gesture of the hand, the lieutenant motioned for him to throw him the grenades.

He unquivered one from the rucksack, and lying on his side, keeping his elbow locked, he catapulted a smoke grenade. It fell short, ten feet from the intended receiver. There was another motion from his platoon leader for him to try again. He hesitated, calculating the odds. He gazed out across the twenty-five-meter chasm. But it wasn't a chasm, only twenty-five meters of dirt and a tree-lined tunnel leading directly to his platoon leader. A straight shot.

"Cover me!" he shouted, and slapped Franklin hard on the back. He began madly crawling, reaching out with each arm to pull, bringing his knees to his waist before following through with a powerful kick. He felt himself doing the ground version of the twenty-five-meter freestyle. Ten meters from his starting block, he began to lose his stroke. His lieutenant was vehemently waving him back. He felt alone, naked and scared. He was swimming on a frozen pool from which he climbed out and transitioned into a low crouch which precipitated stereophonic screams of "Get down!" The pool became a cinder track upon which he dashed forward, his legs fighting to keep up with his leaning trunk.

Only fifteen feet from his finish line, an ugly burst of an AK spat out, sending Nordstrom forward on his face.

Hank's mind went numb as he watched Nordstrom fall. Then with no thought, he reacted, wind-milling around 180 degrees, his chest never leaving the earth. On his belly, he sprung like a half-crazed gator toward Nordstrom. Halfway there he used a side roll to add more speed. Bullets churned up a path behind him. He rolled right up beside Nordstrom and pushed his body close, becoming one with him.

Nordstrom's face was buried in the dirt; a round hole now adorned his helmet, two inches from a penciled in peace sign. Muffled murmurs of, "I'm hit…I'm hit…I'm hit…." came out of the ground.

He gently tilted Nordstrom's head to one side and discovered glazed eyes inset in a bluish-milky complexion. Nordstrom's mouth hissed short, irregular breaths.

Hank attempted words of comfort between his own heavy hyperventilating gasps.

"Don't worry, don't worry," he said over and over as he removed the helmet to inspect the wound. There was little flow of blood around a small dark hole above the right ear. He took the bandage from Nordstrom's first aid packet and wrapped it around the wound. His mind rapidly searched other alternatives of assistance, but came up blank. There was nothing else he could think of, except to utter more comfort. "You're gonna be all right," he said, not really believing it.

There was a long groan of reply. It was a groan of hope. Nordstrom believed him!

Gingerly, he slid the arms from the straps and hoisted the rucksack off of Nordstrom's back. He moved meticulously, taking great efforts not to disturb him. Catatonic eyes tried to follow his movements. He pulled the rucksack to his chest which ebbed and flowed with heavy breathing. Slowly, he gathered in his courage like a compressing spring until it was cocked and ready and then he recoiled toward Tucker, rucksack in one arm, rifle in the other, scrambling and throwing himself along the ground. Bullets buzzed like wasps over his head. He lunged into the saucer-shaped depression next to Tucker and immediately plucked a smoke grenade from the rucksack and heaved it out to his front. As the yellow cloud spilled out, Tucker called for napalm.

His cheek pressed hard into the stock of his M-60, Franklin stared unblinkingly through the ammo belt feeding the machinegun at the sprawled Nordstrom, aware from the labored breathing and twitching muscles of a struggle from within the soul. Tears flowed from wide blue eyes and mixed with sweat. The stream spread from his cheeks to the stock before emptying on the ground and pooling on the impermeable clay. They were a team, the three of them—Nordstrom, himself, and Clyde, the gun. Now they were only two. A lonely ammo box from which the belt passed to the gun like an umbilical cord was Nordstrom's legacy. The cord had been severed. Franklin squeezed off a long burst, the red tracers passing over Nordstrom, over Tucker and Lieutenant Kirby, and vanished into the forest.

Nordstrom would know he was watching over him.

From above, Captain Hirsch spotted the smoke. He sat drenched in the cramped cockpit; the strain of his work and the stuffiness of his quarters produced an unbearable sauna effect. He reached under his seat, pulled a barf bag from a hidden pocket, and emptied himself of meatloaf and mashed potatoes.

He felt a little better and immediately ordered two of the four fighters he had on station to make napalm runs from east to west, north of the streaming yellow cloud. The other two would continue their south-north bombing runs a hundred and fifty odd meters off the east file of the Battalion where he had shifted their runs by the frenzied orders of a Battalion CO, known to him only by the call sign of Demon Six. It seemed the Battalion was being flanked.

Through the green canopy below he could make out intermittent whitelight flashes and puffs of smoke. And though he felt like a target in a carnival shooting gallery as he glided around in a bright blue sky, he felt worse for those grunts below.

It was times like these he thought of his brother. He had convinced Danny not to wait to get drafted. Rather play it safe. Enlist in the Navy. See the World. Stay on a ship in the ocean and avoid the ground in Vietnam.

Danny had listened. He was in the Navy. Only he had half-listened. He was a member of Seal Team Two down in the Mekong Delta.

He wondered what special shit Danny was in today. He'd try to kill as many of these fuckers as he could today. For those poor grunts below. For Danny.

Things were becoming very sticky now as he directed the fighters in a right-angle pattern to avoid the danger of longs and shorts while still maintaining heavy fire support for the point element and the right flank of the Battalion.

Two more F-100 Super Sabres came on station with full loads of 500-pounders and napalm. Hirsch pondered where it was needed most, the point or flank. Demon Six had told him not to abandon the point, in spite of the pressure on the flank. But if the flank fell the two files could be knocked down like bowling pins.

Fuck it, he'd split the pair.

It was then he saw something come out of nowhere on his left. At seven o'clock low. It was a Huey slick traveling low and fast, M-60 door guns spitting out steady dashes of red tracers. It was dangerously close to the flight pattern he had for the F-100s.

He radioed headquarters. "Night Hawk three-zero, this is Sidewinder Six. I've got a solitary slick blazing away below me acting like a cowboy gunship. It's interfering with my projected bombing runs. Find out what the fuck is going on."

"Roger that, Sidewinder Six," came a crackling reply through his earphones.

Thirty-five seconds later Night Hawk 30 called back. "Sidewinder Six, Night Hawk three-zero. You ain't going to believe this shit. That slick is Danger Six in his C and C. Copy?"

"I copy!" gasped Captain Hirsch, his eyes as wide as saucers. Danger Six was Major General Ware, the Division Commander of the Big Red One. Hirsch and his fellow FACs knew him. Their squadron was stationed at Lai Khe, the general's base camp. He had met him once at a nightly social function at the general's villa. Youngest lieutenant colonel in WW II. Medal of Honor winner. He knew he couldn't tell Danger Six to stay the hell away. "Tell Danger Six…No, I mean, ask Danger Six to keep southwest of smoke. I repeat. Southwest. I'm going to have napalm runs east to west north of smoke and 500-pounders south to north east of smoke. Copy?"

"Roger, Sidewinder Six. I copy."

CHAPTER 23

WHISH! A HOT blast of napalm engulfed fifty square meters of rubber.

Tucker hollered into the mouthpiece: "Closer! Closer! Drop one-five-zero!"

There was about a minute as his command was relayed from Battalion to Captain Hirsch.

Whish!

"Bring it another two-five…Yeah, goddamn it! I said another two-five meters! We want to roast some fuckin' marshmallows!"

Whish!

"That's good! That's good!" Tucker screamed. "Keep it up!"

A long tongue of fiery orange flame licked within fifty meters of the two men. Coal black smoke swept over them, stinging their faces, burning their eyes, bringing out choking coughs.

Hank popped a violet smoke and yanked at Tucker's arm. The napalm was too damn close. They began edging slowly backward, pushing with their arms, buttocks hunching up and down like two caterpillars moving backward. The napalm was laying a smoking blanket that hid them from direct fire.

When they reached Nordstrom, each grabbed a leg, and with coordinated pulls, slid him on his belly back toward the small rise behind where Franklin's gun droned away. They would have thought Nordstrom dead were it not for every pull on his legs that inched him along there was an opposite push from his arms. The remainder of his body, even his head, was completely limp, only his arms seemed to hold life.

They passed Franklin who started pulling back after them, shoving the M-60 ammo boxes along with him.

Once he was behind Franklin, Hank turned his head and saw his platoon. It was situated on the slight reverse slope and bunched in a tight circle, wounded and dead scattered throughout. It appeared like a twentieth century Custer's last stand as his eyes jumped around at a kaleidoscope of events. Doc Fletcher was working his ass off, his face pale, sweat pouring, helmetless as he lashed a pistol belt tourniquet around the bloody stump of half a leg. Sergeant Martin was crawling around on all fours urging the able ones to keep up their firing even though they could see no enemy and their ammo was getting low. Sergeant Bennet was screaming beside a dead soldier, a state of shock dulling his senses, his capacity to perform extinguished.

A wave of depression overcame Hank as he realized he only had about a dozen fighting men left. As his mind fought to untangle the potpourri of indecision, confusion, and panic sweeping through him, he became aware of a new, different sound. In fact, it was a sudden lack of sound. There were still the pops of M-16s and the swishes of passing napalm to his front and loud explosions of the bombing runs to the east flank and a background noise of firing further down the hill near the company. But conspicuously absent were the sharp cracks of AKs.

There was a lull!

He and Tucker pulled Nordstrom inside the platoon's perimeter and left him. They crawled toward the perimeter's north quadrant. He grabbed the handset from Tucker. "Bravo Six, November Six, over."

"This is Bravo Six! What's happening up there?" The tone was quick and gasping over the crackling static.

"We're no longer receiving fire. Must be the strikes. Keep 'em coming. We're going to be pulling back but we need help with our wounded and... dead. At least another platoon."

Hank was in a prone position facing inward to his platoon, his feet pointing at Franklin. The black cord on the handset stretched taut between him and Tucker who was bending over on his knees, breaking open a fresh ammo can to re-feed Franklin's M-60. Hank almost snapped the cord with a reflexive jerk when he heard the CO's reply.

"Sorry...but can't help at the moment...." Connor's voice cracked. "When you made contact Lima pulled back. We tried to reestablish a link but the NVA got on our flank. We started getting mortared and receiving heavy automatic weapons fire. We had to pull back down to the road. Right now we're pinned down by heavy sniper fire."

Hank could feel his platoon adrift on an iceberg and the surrounding sea was feeling warmer. "You mean we're stuck on this goddamn hill by ourselves?" he hollered with raging incredulity.

"Afraid so," came the CO's answer. "Alpha's been sent to secure the downed gunship, but Charlie is getting ready to try and send a platoon up on your left flank. I've given them your net to make contact."

Hank's mental control lost its elasticity and he fumed with rage. "Tell 'em to get their fat asses up here fast! If our TAC air runs out, get that fucking artillery in here pronto! Roger that?"

"Wilco, we'll get you out…that's a promise."

"Break…Break…November Six, this is Danger Six. I monitored. Hang in there, son. Keep your cool and you'll make it. Danger Six, out." New words of encouragement broke in. They were clipped and filled with static. Words from a chopper.

Hank kept his ear to the handset for a few seconds waiting for anything further from this intruder into the transmission. But there was nothing; the transmission had ended. Hank was in a too confused state to realize the intruder was Major General Ware, commanding general of The Big Red One.

He flung the mic back at Tucker, missing by four feet. Tucker reeled it in, started monitoring, and checked the ammo belt that fed Franklin's gun for kinks.

For a moment Hank was inclined to remain where he was, stretched out on the ground, within the top quadrant of his platoon's defensive circle, until a platoon from Charlie Company, or whomever, picked him up and carried him down the hill. He closed his eyes, but his mind turned up the volume on the dreadful, agonizing moans emanating from the center of the circle.

He opened his eyes and the volume fell off. He started crawling the perimeter. There was a new PFC, Hank had forgotten his name. He was on his side facing outward, his rifle cradled in the crook of his arm, waiting for something to happen, a dressing covered one eye; his upper lip, split in two, was a bloody creek bed winding up to his cheekbone. Hank crawled on, uttering words of encouragement to pale trembling faces that seemed everywhere. He purposely avoided the seriously wounded, knowing his words would sound inadequate.

Martin said nothing as he passed, but merely squeezed his arm. Doc Fletcher, a patchwork of blood and dirt, could only shake his head in doom as he busied himself with the misery of his patients.

Sporadic sniper fire broke out and was immediately answered by M-16s firing in random bursts in the direction of unseen targets. Hank kept crawling. The snipers were ineffective; evidently they were also firing randomly from somewhere behind trees or in bunkers. Now and then dirt would geyser inside the platoon, stopping Hank's breathing as he waited for geysers of blood, his geysers!

He was now back at the top of the small perimeter, beside Tucker. He could feel his wounded calf throbbing as if it were being drum-rolled by a spiked mace. He used a bandage he had picked up somewhere to wrap around his leg. There didn't seem to be a lot of blood. His elbows and knees stung from the sandpapering friction that had generated from his crawling. He became nauseated and puked, his nose clogging with stomach juices. He snorted away the obstruction and lay on his belly and stared at Franklin who peered watchfully from his vantage point. The butt of the M-60, its barrel hot and smoking, at his shoulder.

From high above in his OV-10, maneuvering like a bird of prey, Captain Hirsch couldn't help but admire his aerial display of tactical-air ground support. He was the conductor of a great pyrotechnic symphony. The high-pitched screeching sounds of jet engines, his violins, followed by a cacophony of 500-pound cymbals and deep swishing sounds of spreading flames, the bass horn. One sortie would dive low east to west and let go with a 500-pounder or napalm. Another would do the same from south to north. Then another from east to west, and so forth. He was feeling good about his orchestra.

Then something bad happened.

His eyes had been stealing glances at Danger Six's C&C ship, making sure it didn't stray into his bombing runs. He had just observed it and started to look away when suddenly he saw it explode in mid air. In a fiery ball the chopper dropped from the sky.

"Demon Six, Night Hawk Three Zero, Bravo Six, this is Sidewinder Six," he radioed everyone at once. "I've got some real bad news…"

Hirsch now knew what kind of day it would be. He would stay on station until his fuel became fumes. With luck, and God, he would glide into the airstrip at Loc Ninh.

He took a long pull on his canteen.

CHAPTER 24

THERE WAS A new lull in the cacophony, the blend of high explosives and napalm had stopped. Hank looked over anxiously at Tucker, "What's going on?"

Tucker's eyes found his. "Last fighter dropped its load. CO says more'll be on station shortly. Meantime, he's cranking up that Arty."

Shrieking 105 rounds followed the tail end of Tucker's reply as the Battery at Loc Ninh took up the slack.

Suddenly, new sounds emerged, the throbs and pops of M-60s and M-16s erupting on their left flank; answered, but in unequalled force, by AK-47s and B-40 rockets.

Hank plucked the handset from Tucker's grasp and heard his call sign as he brought the earpiece up. "Bravo November Six, this is Charlie Mike Six, over," came a heavy rasping voice accompanied by the background noises of light weapons fire. The voice was familiar. All at once there was recognition. Jesus! It was Dick Kistler!

"Charlie Mike Six, this is November Six," Hank tried to steady his tone, hiding his emotion.

"Roger, November Six," came back Dick. "Hang on. We've got a few fuckin' dinks sniping out of spider-holes. We need a little time to kick the shit out of 'em. Then we'll be up there to lend a hand."

"Fuckin' A. Get your big ass up here."

Sunlight was shafting at long angles through the rubber trees when Kistler's platoon finally linked up. A tall, burly silhouette crouched its way through deepening shadows, taking in with sweeping movements of the head the decimation of the third platoon, Bravo Company. Two rows of soiled corpses, three per row, some battered and mutilated, others showing no evidence of their demise were in the lower southeast quadrant of the perimeter. In the southwest quadrant, the badly wounded, looking equally battered, groaned and sobbed.

Ten feet from where Hank sat cross-legged at the top of the perimeter the silhouette sunk to all fours and transformed into Dick Kistler.

He propped himself on one knee and searched under Hank's helmet for his eyes. And that was all there seemed, his eyes. Gone was the face he knew. It had been replaced by a bust sculptured from a dark, red clay. The molder had hollowed the cheeks, dropped the chin, and chiseled deep lines that etched the pale, cracked lips. The eyes, glazed and distant, blinked a few times before finding Dick's, taking a brief moment to focus.

"Got hit bad, my friend," Dick said softly, his usual jolly face now a dark somber stone of a shade similar to Hank's. "I lost some, too." There was a stretch of silence. "My men are in place to help with your wounded and KIAs. We'll pick them up all together and run like hell down to the road. If those cocksuckers don't fuck with us much, we'll make it."

Hank gave a barely perceptible nod, twisted his torso around, and pointed over Franklin's gun, beyond the rise to the north. "I've got three dead out there. What about them?"

"Leave 'em," Dick choked the words out. "It's gettin' dark. We can't risk gettin' bogged down out there or we'll never get the shit out of here. We'll get 'em tomorrow."

"We CAN'T do that!" Tucker broke in, totally out of character. He had been sitting next to Hank monitoring the conversation as well as the horn. He clutched Hank's arm and dug his fingernails deep into the bicep. "We can't leave 'em! We don't know for sure they're dead. I think Calabrese is alive."

Both stared at Hank, their eyes boring into his soul. He looked at neither, but closed his eyes and wished for transport to some fourth dimension. It was his decision. God, he hated decisions. He turned his head around to the north and thought of the murderous crossfire. The dead bodies of his point. He knew they were dead. Tucker was wrong. He was irrational. And he thought of Nordstrom rising too high from the ground and taking one in the head. Nordstrom now had a good chance of living, of returning home, of the Freedom Bird. They all did! And the wounded needed to be dusted off or they would be dead too.

"Let's get off this shit-eating hill!" Hank shouted, and then yelled into the handset to whoever was monitoring to pick up the dead and wounded with the help of Dick's platoon and get the hell off the hill ASAP. Then, he immediately hand-motioned to the men near him to move out on the double.

Private First Class Franklin remained in place. He sighted down the long hot barrel, rotating it in a 45 degree arc, watching for any movement, his finger tight and trembling on the trigger. He could hear the platoons grouping together and starting to pull back, but he kept his vigil as the covering force, a force of one. A lump settled in his throat...

He saw his platoon leader toss a smoke grenade and yell into the handset: "Smokes out! Yellow! Hit it!"

His mind strayed to his buddy, Nordstrom. Brave Nordstrom.

He twisted his head around in time to see the two platoons break into a stumbling run, dragging the dead by the legs, carrying the wounded in either fireman fashion or groups of four, each hanging onto an arm or a leg. He fired off two bursts of four, was starting to pick up his gun before joining the race down the hill, when he saw in complete dismay Tucker slide out of the straps of his radio backpack and hurtle himself forward into a mad crawl in the opposite direction— toward the point. He saw the platoon leader of Charlie Company glance quickly at the platoons vacating the hill before charging into a low crawl after Tucker.

Captain Hirsch had been putting in surgical strikes around General Ware's downed chopper when he got the call from Bravo's company commander.

"Sidewinder Six, Bravo Six. Point has popped yellow smoke and is vacating. Go for it!"

"This is Sidewinder Six, Roger that. Break. Wildcat One, Weasel One, green light on yellow, northern smoke. I'll mark." Captain Hirsch turned his attention from providing air cover for Danger Six's downed chopper back to his original mission.

Private First Class Franklin glanced over at November Six. His platoon leader lay motionless on the ground beside him. He saw his head look in the direction of the departing platoons, then his head swiftly swung around at Tucker and Charlie's platoon leader moving rapidly toward the fallen point element. He then turned his head back and looked at him.

Their eyes met. Franklin saw on the dirty, grimy face of his platoon leader a bewilderment of stunned disbelief and indecision. And then his platoon leader lunged forward in a mad crawl, hurriedly following on the heels of Charlie's platoon leader. He noticed that November Six had left his rifle behind. Next to the radio that Tucker had discarded.

His body began to tremble all over with fear. His mind went completely blank for a few seconds. He had heard November Six call in air strikes on their position. His platoon had gone one way and his platoon leader had gone another. He suddenly snapped out of his temporary paralysis. He picked up the radio's handset.

"Bravo Six, November Six Gunner," he shouted into the mouthpiece. He had no official call sign, so he just made one up. Captain Connors would get it. "Stop the airstrike on the smoke! I repeat! Stop it! Hill not completely vacated! I say again! Not vacated!"

He threw the handset down. He looked behind him at the disappearing helmets of the two platoons running down the hill. He looked to his front down the barrel of his M-60 at the soles of his platoon leader's boots moving away.

His mind started fighting demons. Get up and run with the platoons. Wasn't that what his platoon leader ordered? What if Bravo Six couldn't stop the bombing run? What if the NVA closed in on him?

He felt a strange magnetic tug on his right shoulder. He recognized the soft loving hand of his mother gently trying to pull him off the hill. "Don't be a hero, son. I love you. I want you to come safely home," he heard her say. Those same words she had said when he left home. She had tried to persuade him not to enlist in the Army with his buddy, Nordstrom. She was further disappointed when he had trained for the infantry. And the fact he was an M-60 gunner had made her feel worse. It seemed he was always disappointing her. And now he felt the firm pull of her hand on his shoulder.

Tears ran down the shoulder stock of his gun. He fired two bursts of four over the crawling boots. Letting them know he was there for them. He knew they were going to die, but he would try to keep them alive as long as he could. And he knew he would die too. And once again he would disappoint his mom.

He fired another burst from his M-60 as he mouthed the words, "I love you, Mom! I'm sorry!"

CHAPTER 25

CAPTAIN HIRSCH COULD see his two fighters, one behind the other, with the background of a silvery-blue horizon, bank sharply to set up their east to west run. Vicariously he could feel their G forces.

He watched Wildcat One's F-100 streak low toward the intended target. Then he heard an urgent voice in panic piercing through his ear phones. "Sidewinder Six, point has *not* vacated! I repeat, *NOT* vacated! Don't drop ordinance! Do *not* drop!"

Captain Hirsch almost lost control of his aircraft. He yelled into his mouthpiece. "Abort! Abort! Wildcat One, do not drop!"

It was about twenty meters of crawling like a crazed gator in trying to catch up with Dick that Hank realized he had left his rifle behind. It was too late to go back. He could see Dick's boots up ahead about five meters pushing forward at a fair clip. Tucker still had a slight lead to Dick's right.

They didn't seem to be taking any fire. Only the sporadic bursts of Franklin's gun from behind reminded them to keep low. Then came a bright white flame explosion on their left followed by a big puff of white smoke. Hank knew it was a white phosphorous rocket marking a bombing run. Not knowing what else to do, he continued to plow forward.

Dick and Tucker slowed their crawl allowing Hank to gain ground. When Hank was on Dick's heels, they stopped suddenly, catching Hank by surprise. His head rammed into the soles of Dick's boots.

Dick was sighting through his peep-sight ready to fire when Hank's forward momentum hit him. Two shots went skyward.

Hank was now on top of Dick's legs and could see over his right shoulder at the fallen point element. He glimpsed three, scattered bodies in US jungle fatigues, lying at various angles. He could see Calabrese about seven meters away and Milton and Wojic maybe another ten meters further. Only there were others too. And they weren't still. They were NVA in their own set of jungle fatigues. One had been moving on his elbows and knees next to Calabrese, on the side facing Dick, who quickly recovered from the jolt to his legs and lowered his aim. He cut loose with an automatic burst of three. Hank saw two of Dick's rounds smack into the NVA's head and shoulder. The other may have grazed Calabrese's back.

The other NVA immediately went flat to the ground, keeping themselves behind and next to Milton and Wojic's lifeless-looking bodies.

Hank sensed there were between three and six gooks. As he rolled off Dick, he felt the dreaded helplessness of impending doom. Then he heard Dick shouting at him as he continued to sight down his rifle. "Throw your grenades, Hank! Throw your fucking grenades! I'll cover!"

Hank's right hand frantically fingered around in his canteen pouch. There were two. One thanks to Lieutenant Cronin. He quickly grabbed one, pulled the pin and heaved it in the direction of the NVA hiding among his point men. Without hesitation he repeated the process and hurled the other. His arm a human mortar tube.

There had been no cook-off after the pins were pulled. He realized this right after he threw the second. His mistake would allow a chance for a throw back. And sure enough, after the first was tossed an NVA behind Milton's body lunged his body at the grenade. Dick and Tucker both fired, trying to stop him. He hit the ground untouched. Through wide, bulging eyes Hank could see his arm cock for the deadly throw back.

Wildcat One was streaking near tree-top level when he heard the command to abort. It was just at the moment when he released the 500-pounder. Instantly he reacted and pulled back on the joystick, hoping the sudden upward direction would fling the bomb away from its intended target.

There was a terrible blast.

Hank, Dick, Tucker, and everyone else at the point, and even Franklin thirty-five meters behind, were lifted two feet in the air. A wave of blinding smoke swept over them.

Then came two sequential grenade blasts. The sound muted by a loss of hearing from the 500-pound bomb blast.

The smoke diffused slowly. Hank realized he was still alive. The concussion from the bomb had jolted the grenade from the hand of his NVA adversary who in turn had his head blown off by the blast of the grenade. The other grenade seemed to have had a similar deadly effect. There was no more movement around the point. Everyone seemed dead, save for Hank, Dick, and Tucker.

Tucker crawled hurriedly over to Calabrese and shoved aside the NVA soldier Dick had shot.

Under Dick's cover, Hank crawled past Calabrese to within ten feet of where his grenades had landed. He had to see if Milton or Wojic might be alive. Or if his grenades had ensured their demise. His head mere inches off the ground, he peered through the emerging shadows of dusk. He thought he saw them among the mangled clumps of bloodied bodies and parts. He could see their blackened, lifeless faces—at least he thought he could.

Then he heard a moaning sound among the bodies. And then the moaning sound became gibberish crying in a language he guessed to be Vietnamese.

His head snapped around when he heard Dick firing bursts from his rifle. He saw that Dick was firing at the front left flank. That Dick was no longer looking in his direction. No longer providing cover!

Hank's blood filled with more fear. He rapidly turned around to crawl back.

It came as a startling, heart-stopping blur from the corner of his left eye. Instinctively he rolled on his back, his helmet slipping off his head and he became a deer in the headlights as he watched his impending death.

An NVA soldier had seemingly sprung out of the ground. In a hunched over crouch he ran at Hank. His face was hidden under his pith helmet. His arms were extended and his hands held an AK-47 with an extended needle bayonet that was going to be driven through Hank's gut.

Hank was about to close his eyes to accept his fate. A sick, empty feeling sweeping through his body. Then he saw his assailant give three spastic twitches as Franklin's 7.62mm rounds smacked him once in the neck and twice in the rib cage. His would-be killer fell heavily beside him. He pushed him away as if he were a leper and scrambled in a low crawl back to Dick and Tucker.

Tucker had Calabrese by one leg. He motioned for Hank to grab the other. Together they moved the limp body one pull at a time, just like they had done for Nordstrom, back toward the specious safety of Franklin's gun. Dick slid back with them, feet first, his eyes sighting down his rifle, ready to lay a line of covering fire.

When they made it back to Franklin, a blanket of twilight had begun falling on a mangled forest of bent and broken rubber trees. Hank had no idea if Calabrese was dead or alive. If he had to guess, it would be dead.

Dick quickly took over. He shoved Hank aside, and with his greater strength, sped the process of sliding Calabrese along the ground with Tucker struggling to match the rapidity of his pulls. Hank crawled over to Franklin as Dick and Tucker pulled Calabrese another five meters further down to take advantage of the reverse slope. Then Dick jumped to a crouch and hoisted Calabrese to a fireman's carry over both shoulders. Hank and Franklin watched as Tucker and Dick, with his load, broke into a run down Hill 228.

Hank and Franklin stared at each other a split moment. Then Hank yelled, "Franklin, get the hell out of here!"—at which time Franklin grabbed his M-60 and one of his ammo cans, crawled a short way down the reverse slope, and broke into a hunched-over, controlled run.

Hank had started crawling back with Franklin when he noticed in the fading light Tucker's radio set a few meters away.

He crawled forward as Franklin was headed in the opposite direction. He grabbed the radio by the strap and pulled it to him. In the back of his mind a stop watch was ticking toward his demise. His eyes squinted around in the milky darkness and he was about to follow his advice and get the hell off the hill when he glimpsed a smoke grenade. It was near where he had left his rifle. He body-rolled a few revolutions to it. He pulled the pin and tossed it forward to the point and its mangled bodies. He couldn't tell what color. It was too dark. He put the handset next to his ear and pushed the talk button.

"Bravo Six, November Six. Smoke's out. Bring in the shit. Hit the goddamn smoke!" Hank didn't wait for a reply. He was in some kind of a spooky darkness under a canopy of shattered trees and surrounding carnage. He was alone. Fear was coursing through his body.

He picked up the radio by one strap, jumped to his feet, and started running as fast as he could in a hunch-back crouch.

He waited for AK rounds to pepper his back. His wounded leg began to throb. His speed and forward momentum were too much for the hill's slope and he stumbled and fell forward and slid on his face and chest, knocking away his breath. With great effort he managed to suck in some air. He stumbled uneasily back to his feet. There was a moment of hesitation as he tried to orient himself in the darkness. He could feel the slope of the hill with his boots and he started running again down the hill. He wasn't sure where he would end up.

Suddenly he broke free of the forest and he could see a small earthen embankment before him. Someone shouted for him to halt and he heard the metallic sounds of weapons brought to the ready. "Hold your fire!" he shouted, "I'm Kirby!" He slowed his gait as he approached the makeshift berm of a defensive trench that had earlier today been a swale beside the road.

"Kirby! Where's your platoon? What happened to your platoon?" he heard someone yelling from the trench. If he had been in full possession of his faculties he would have recognized Brussels' voice.

There was complete, confused panic on his face that was now a meat of blackened, raw hamburger. "I don't know!" he cried out as he halted helmetless ten meters from the freshly made defensive position. His right hand tightly clutching the radio by one strap, his mind became blank. He turned around.

Then he started running back up the hill.

CHAPTER 26

FROM ABOVE, CAPTAIN Hirsch was acutely aware of the rim of light dying on the horizon. He had been praying Bravo Company's point platoon would pop smoke again. That they had not been annihilated by Wildcat One's bomb. His prayer was answered when the call from Bravo Six came through. Evidently, the point was alive and had vacated the hill. They had again put smoke out to mark for his white phosphorous rocket to be followed by the fighter-bombers.

He could make out a cloud of dark smoke wafting from the trees. It appeared in the enveloping darkness to be a violet color. He asked Bravo Six to confirm and was told he didn't know the color, but if there was smoke, go right at it.

Captain Hirsch abruptly banked his OV-10 to the left before nosing it at the dissipating smoke. He was flying on fumes now and wondered if he'd make it to the Loc Ninh airstrip. But right now all he wanted was to lay down some Willie Peter.

Hank had gone about fifteen meters when there was a loud explosion on top of the hill. The ground shook. Then a hand grabbed him from behind and roughly spun him around.

"Lieutenant Kirby! Lieutenant Kirby!" Hank could hear someone yelling at him. He opened his eyes and could see under a helmet the shadowed face of Bravo Six. "Lieutenant Kirby! Your platoon's down here on the far side of the road. Get your ass down there!"

Bravo Six took the radio from him and placed his hand firmly on his shoulder. He felt himself being pulled down the hill.

Wham! Another explosion.

The tide of victory had somberly flowed away from Colonel Dao. Even his own deep shelter shook violently from the devastating downpour.

Hurriedly he rapped out commands to his communicators. "Tell them to get back into their bunkers! The air strikes have been too much. Tonight, under cover of darkness we shall move back across the border, leaving one company behind as a harassing force."

Panic distorted his face. Incredulity was written in his eyes. It was amazing, he thought, how suddenly the momentum of battle could change. If only he had airpower!

As if telepathy caused Colonel Dao's thoughts to diffuse up into the smoke saturated air, an F-100 swooped low, dropped a tremendous blockbuster, and gracefully sped upward for a darkening sky, leaving behind a clump of motionless bodies, their brains shattered by the concussion.

Colonel Dao Tri Minh's dreams had ended. He would never know that his force had killed the Division Commander of the Big Red One, the highest ranking American Army officer to die in Vietnam.

Darkness had descended. Flashing violet strobe lights, like weird lightning bugs, dotted a seventy-five-meter strip of road secured by Bravo and Charlie companies, marking a pickup zone. The dust-offs came and went one at a time. The wounded first; the dead later.

Standing in the middle of the road, Dick supervised a Medevac, a strobe light held high in one hand, the other directing the operation with traffic cop arm waves, first to the incoming chopper, next to his men who ran out from the wood line scrunched over, hauling the wounded in ponchos.

A detached spectator, Hank sat dazed on the shoulder. His mind fogged. There seemed to be mass confusion: loud night whispers, choppers in and out, men running to and fro, sounds of digging all around. He shook his head to snap away his sluggishness. There was nothing to do here.

He wandered away from the road, into a darkness full of sounds of an army hastily digging in. Like an eerie night shadow, Tucker followed. A faceless soldier in a staggering run, burdened by two arm loads of 7.62 ammo cans, passed by and Hank caught his shoulder, almost flipping him off his feet.

"Hey, watch the fuck out!" Words of protest came from under the helmet. "Where's Bravo's CP?"

"Dunno. But Charlie's near the road on the west end. Might find Bravo's on the opposite end." The faceless form replied and then fled.

Connors sat with his legs straight and crossed out in front, his back supported by a tree, his head helmetless, listening to the noise of his company preparing their defense. He looked up as Hank approached. The night hid his eyes, red and wet with fatigue and emotion.

Hank stood over Connors. "I've got nine men, ten counting me," his tone rang with distraught exhaustion. "I've still got two dead up on the hill," he winced at his words.

Connors nodded slowly and then rested the back of his head on the tree. "Sorry about what happened," he said softly, staring at his soiled jungle boots. "There's a small gap between the First Platoon and Charlie." He pointed south. "Fill your men in there." He looked over at Hank's torn pants leg, picked up a flashlight, and with its dim, red-filtered glow saw a purple stain. "When your men are in place, come back here. We'll have a doctor work on that leg. We've had two choppered in to help us out. We'll try to get you out of here tonight when we evac the KIAs on a re-supply sortie."

Hank turned and was swallowed by the dark, Tucker with him. The last sentence reverberated in his mind like a winning pinball, and with it, the flashing lights of the board lit up. He was getting out of this mess!

Hank's earlier preoccupation on the matters of life and death had pushed away the pain in his wounded leg. Now with the expectation of leaving, the pain came to the forefront and he started limping. He could feel Tucker's cold eyes on his leg, beaming thoughts of "malingerer." But it did hurt. He just had been too busy to notice.

He swung around to face Tucker. But in the dark, under the helmet, was another faceless soldier. His mind conjured up Tucker's face. It was sallow, with sunken, bloodshot eyes.

He smiled weakly, more to himself than to Tucker who he knew was also looking at a faceless soldier, his faceless face. "Sergeant Smith can handle the platoon," he said reassuringly.

"Sir…Sergeant Smith is dead."

The words grabbed Hank and shook him. Of course Smith was dead! So was Sergeant Percy! And Bennet had been dusted off.

"I…I know. I…I meant Martin. He did an outstanding job. He's a good man. He'll…take charge with no problem." Hank garbled his transmission.

He stared at Tucker's amorphous face and saw, guessed he saw, a barely perceptible nod. Tucker was agreeing with him, he thought.

He positioned each man in his squad-size platoon, filling the cavity, carefully locating the two M-60s to achieve an enfilading crossfire.

With the task complete, he limped back alone to the road where the dust-offs had been. He turned left and followed a shallow drainage ditch. He could hear sounds of metal slicing clay, of grunts and groans, bolts sliding back and forth in a fresh film of oil, nervous whispers all about. Adequate preparation had been given a higher priority than silence. And why not… the NVA knew where they were, noise or no noise.

His leg aching, he shuffled along in the sediment of the ditch. Abruptly, he tripped and fell hard, smacking himself into the dirt. Slowly picking himself up, wiping away clinging cakes of clay with forearms equally caked, he squinted to identify the obstacle. Boots! Goddamn boots! The boots of a man lying flat on his back, apparently in a sound sleep. Suddenly all of the tension stored recently in the battery cells of his mind broke loose and unleashed its energy on this lazy, insipid figure that had the gall to sleep peacefully while his colleagues, taking no quarter, worked their tails off with blistered, bloodied hands fixing defensive positions.

"You fucking bastard!" Hank scowled. "Get your fat ass off the ground!" He kicked the boots hard with his good leg.

The figure didn't move and Hank became more enraged. He stepped closer and tightened his fists. He knelt down, bringing himself within inches of a pale, waxen face. The mouth was open; eyes closed, head bandaged. Hank fell to his knees and gave out an inconsolable wail as he recognized the dead body of PFC Nordstrom. Nordstrom, who had battled to live even in his subconscious…but had lost.

Kneeling by his body, Hank welcomed the cold, heavy drops of rain that began falling. The drops diluted the saltiness of his tears that flooded down his cheeks into his mouth and muffled the anguish of his sobs. After a few moments, he wiped his eyes and came to his feet. Instead of continuing on to Bravo's CP, he swung around and limped his way back to his platoon.

Doc Fletcher had had a busy day, but he eagerly treated and dressed Hank's wounded leg. After administering a tetanus shot, all Doc could say was: "Glad you're back!"

Afterwards, Hank got with Tucker. Together, like the night before, they harbored themselves in a shallow hole.

The rain slackened a bit. Hank took the first watch and lay on his back, his helmet tilted over his eyes to shield the rain drops. He monitored the horn in his left hand. He could feel the sting in his raw left elbow that wedged between him and the side of the hole. His face felt on fire and his leg throbbed with pain as it rested in elevated traction out in front of him just outside their poor excuse for a foxhole. He focused on his discomfort and pain; the medication Doc had given him had not yet fully kicked in. It was better than thinking about the worst day of his life.

He thought of Doc treating his leg and reflected on his remark. It had surprised him. Evidently Doc didn't know he had been a complete fuck-up. That it would probably be best for all if he'd gotten on the re-supply hook.

But for some stupid reason that he couldn't understand, he hadn't.

Captain Hirsch sat alone in the Night Hawk's small O'club. He and his fellow FACs had decorated it with wall-to-ceiling camouflaged-patterned parachutes, making the room seem fluffy and comfy and safe. They thought of it as their padded cell with liquor in this insane asylum of Vietnam.

He had retrieved a bottle of Dewar's from behind the bar. He was glad to be there.

He had landed at Loc Ninh with nothing in the tank. There had been no landing lights at the airstrip and so they had used hand-held strobes. Not wanting to spend the night in a Special Forces compound with no booze, he had threatened and cajoled the compound's contingent to give him enough aviation fuel that was available for Chinooks to get him to Lai Khe

It was now 0300 hours and he was on his fourth scotch. His first had been for those poor bastards at Loc Ninh. The Third of the Thirteenth of the First Infantry Division. The second had been for General Ware and his command staff. The third had been for Danny who was who knew where down south in the Delta with Seal Team Two.

The fourth, and it was a double, was for him.

CHAPTER 27

THE EMERGING LIGHT of dawn brought a warming relief as they breakfasted on cold C-rations.

A lumbering Chinook landed and deposited from its rear hatch crates of ammo and Bravo's Mortar Platoon, less their mortars. Wearing clean fatigues and shaven faces, they stood out like church-goers at a garbage dump. Their leader, Sergeant Bird, sought out Hank.

He found him near the perimeter, in the remnants of his Third Platoon, squatting in a small hole under a canopy of rubber trees. He knelt down and gazed into blank eyes on a sick, vacuous face. "Sorry 'bout what happened to your platoon," he said with sympathy. "Decided you might need some help."

There was a stretch of silence.

"We're not used to humpin', but if you'll have us, we'll do our best."

Hank squinted his suspicion. *Why would anybody willingly come out here?* He got to his feet, placed the foot of his good leg up on the hole's rim, and stepped out. He emitted a weak but grateful smile as they shook hands.

Now the Third Platoon was up to twenty-three.

Charlie and Bravo held fast during most of the morning while Hill 228 was repeatedly raked by air strikes. Alpha company returned from yesterday's downed gunship and joined forces. The Battalion Recon Platoon was securing the downed C&C chopper of General Ware. Two other battalions air assaulted three klicks west and north of the hill in a blocking maneuver: a snare for whatever might still be scurrying away.

At 1100 hours, the Third of the Thirteenth, minus Delta, moved cautiously up the gradual sloping ridge of Hill 228 under the cover of volcanic pounding airstrikes. Order of march: Charlie, Bravo, and Alpha.

A burst of AK-47 fire pierced through the din of bombing and was immediately answered by a fusillade of bullets and grenades from Charlie's lead platoon. Dick's platoon. All three companies dropped to the ground and began reflexively to slide backward on their bellies, away from the heated exchange. In a few minutes there was an eerie void as contact had been broken.

Fifteen minutes later, Hank, lying prone, watched four men in Dick's platoon quick-timing down the hill carrying a casualty on a jungle litter, heading for the road to a dust-off. He looked about eighteen. His pallid face filled with shock; a blood-soaked field dressing wrapped around his bare chest.

The ugly reality was that the NVA somehow were still up there, capable of fighting back despite tons and tons of bombs and shells. But even so Hank knew he had to go up, had to get back his dead. They also would need to make it back.

He hated the fact that Dick's platoon was now point. They had chatted about it this morning back at the road. Dick should have received a pass after yesterday's heroic rescue of his platoon.

But Dick had said not to worry. After the pounding of air strikes and artillery, he was sure there would be nothing up there. Hadn't Hank thought the same yesterday when he was the point? But why now, Dick? It was an obvious answer. Because he was the best. His natural leader aptitude, Hank realized, had morphed into that of a real soldier. And this new awakening in his friend bothered him.

Dick's Mike Platoon made a light probe further up the hill, but again, after receiving sniper fire, pulled back. TAC air and then artillery continued to rain on the hill.

Night found the Battalion still on the side of the hill. Instead of retreating down to the road, they had dug in on its side with Dick's platoon about fifty meters from where they hoped would be the remains of Spec-four Milton and PFC Wojic.

This time there were no quickly made makeshift foxholes. Orders came instructing full foxholes, no less than three feet deep, and shovels and picks were distributed up the hill from the road to all units.

From the air, if one could see through the night and the tree canopy, the Battalion's formation would have looked like two long, fairly straight lines stretched up the hill as if let out from two massive spools at the road.

Hank's and Tucker's foxhole was between these lines as were the other command posts of the other units.

And Sergeant Bird and his men again came through for them. They had dug the foxholes for Hank and the other remnants of the Third Platoon. At first Hank had objected, then had decided why not. His men were exhausted; Bird's were fresh.

Hank found himself with Tucker inside a three-foot deep, three-foot square box with ninety degree vertical harden-clay walls. What it lacked in comfort, it made up for it in offering protection.

Inside his box, his back upright and uncomfortable, his feet tangled with Tucker's, Hank considered his defensive position. His men were to his west and to his east, facing outward. All in two, or four-men foxholes. Further out in front of each line were four men LPs—listening posts—the early warning system, and who were most vulnerable. All, save for Hank and Tucker, had their Claymores out.

An assault from either the east or west would be met with the full fire-power of one of the lines. Captain Connors had instructed his platoon leaders how one line should reinforce the other if necessary. Hank had relayed that command to Sergeant Bird and Sergeant Martin who in turn ensured everyone was schooled in this "what if."

But Hank didn't think the NVA would attack at the full fire power of the long lines of the Battalion that extended all the way down to the road. No, they'd likely hit the point straight on, or maybe at the other end, near the road. Hit on one of those flanks and roll the lines right up like Stonewall Jackson did to Hooker at Chancellorsville. He had mentioned this possibility to Connors, who acknowledged this scenario, and in turn notified higher, who then notified Charlie Company to reinforce the point—Dick's platoon.

But Hank thought the most probable scenario was that nothing would happen. There was no way he rationalized that those cocksuckers could mount a coordinated attack. Not after all that pounding from above. And that's why nothing had happened last night when Bravo and Charlie were back at the road, and more vulnerable than now.

But then again what if there were other NVA units—maybe regiments—

operating nearby? That hadn't been part of yesterday's action. Goddamn what ifs again.

At about 0200 hours Hank feared the worst case scenario. Despite his discomfort in the foxhole, he had managed to fall asleep for about thirty minutes when the sound of exploding B-40 rockets shocked him from a shallow slumber. Then he thought he heard what sounded like three popped Claymores up near Dick's platoon. He kept his eyes closed as he hunkered down with Tucker. There was nothing he could see anyway in the dark confines of his hole.

Next came a deafening silence. Nothing. No more explosions. No weapons fire. Nothing. Then he heard the whistling and explosions of 105 rounds landing to the northwest about 300 meters. After ten minutes there was more deafening silence.

The silence stretched until dawn, when, finally, their nerves strained in tension to the edge of the elastic limit, the warm, soft rays of a clear-sky morning filtered through the fractured foliage.

Again, bombs started hammering the hill for a solid thirty minutes. This time no resistance was met as the entire Battalion inched forward unopposed in two long files to the crest.

It was an ugly scar. Trees were strewn about like chewed toothpicks, charred from burning napalm. Those still standing were grotesquely shattered and broken, their lifeless limbs mangled skeletons. A mixture of burnt rubber sap, unburned napalm, and stale human flesh diffused a distinctly putrid-sweet smell into the air.

Found burned beyond recognition were three ravaged torsos believed to be the Third Platoon's point, Milton and Wojic, and one NVA. Because two were believed to be the remains of Hank's men, he had the honor of supervising the placement of this precious human residue on makeshift jungle litters, to be turned over to a loach that had darted down and hovered above a deep bomb crater. His men solemnly placed their remains on the loach. As the small chopper rose carefully to avoid the broken limbs of nearby trees, Hank shouted the command present arms. He and everyone who heard the command saluted and watched its departure diminish into a bright blue sky.

Then he and his platoon joined with the Battalion in scrutinizing their location.

Large craters, some about five meters in diameter and one and a half meters deep, pockmarked the once serene hilltop into the development stage of a moonscape. Bravo and Charlie took up defensive positions on the outer perimeter of these craters. Alpha moved in and began conducting a bomb damage assessment.

Hank's platoon moved into three large craters on the western side courtesy of 500-pounders. Hank reclined on his back on the incline of the crater shared with a third of his men. The original Third—the remnants of the November Platoon.

He stared out over the rim beyond the ruins of what had been a homogenous forest of tall, slim rubber trees and into an ice blue sky. Tucker lay next to him and together they monitored the radio over a squawk box borrowed from one of Captain Connors' RTOs.

The sound from the squawk box was turned all the way up so everyone in the big hole could listen to the reports that flooded from Alpha as they searched.

Twelve dead NVA were found scattered in the open. On the hill's reverse slope, three bomb craters had been covered with a mantle of freshly turned dirt. Entrenching tool diggings discovered NVA corpses stacked within a foot of the top, and in the whispery, excited words delivered by one of the commentators, "gazing stiffly upward like vampires in a mass grave, as though they had just died from exposure to the daylight." All total, Alpha counted one hundred and seven NVA bodies.

Hank had closed his eyes, his head resting in the webbing of his helmet liner, when he heard a commotion stirring before him and felt a hand shaking his left shoulder. He opened his eyes and saw Sergeant Martin on one knee in front of him. Behind Martin the rest of the remnant platoon, save Tucker and Franklin, stood before him in the bomb crater.

He came to his elbows and with concern registering on his face looked back at them.

"Lieutenant Kirby," Martin started, "we've been thinking."

Hank's immediate thought was, *Shit, what now?*

"We want to see. We got to go see."

At first Hank was about to ask Martin what the fuck he was talking about, when he suddenly got it. "Understand. Go ahead."

Only he, Tucker, and Franklin remained behind. He and Tucker continued to lie on the inside slope of the crater and monitor the squawk box.

Franklin had his gun on the crater's rim and maintained a vigil. Over the squawk box the three could hear further sitreps of the findings.

An elaborate bunker complex was discovered. Maze-like tunnels intertwined with sixty bunkers ringed the hill. Each bunker had low firing ports, demon eyes that seemed to stare out of the earth. Two supplementary bunkers supported each frontline position, giving interlocking fields of fire. The same configuration found at an American fire support base or NDP. All bunkers were protected overhead by at least a three-foot layer of sun-hardened clay on eight-inch logs. So cleverly constructed and concealed, one could easily walk over them and never know of their existence.

It was a good half hour when they returned. Martin reported to Hank. He told him they had seen the mass graves and he asked Hank if he wanted details. Hank declined. He noticed the absence of BRO patches from their left shoulders and knew they had substituted for funeral flowers.

Darkness started settling in and any expectations of being airlifted out were badly missed. They had been in the field for four days, they'd suffered heavy casualties, and they'd had practically no sleep and very little to eat. Their morale was frightfully low and they anticipated that this feeling would permeate through to whoever was making the decisions.

Such was not the case.

After a night on the hill and followed by a full morning of further searching of the NVA base camp, the Battalion left Hill 228 and trudged north toward the border of Cambodia. At the border they headed east, staying on the Vietnamese side.

From the massive rubber plantation they burrowed deep into a vine-tangled, triple canopy jungle. Movement became snaillike and punishing as the point elements macheted their way through.

Four more days trudged by. They had received no mail or hot meals since leaving Quan Loi. Not long by other war standards, but interminable in their war.

Finally, morale plunging deeply, the three companies headed straight to the airstrip at Loc Ninh.

Primitive and remote as it was, Loc Ninh nevertheless afforded the Battalion a sense of leisure and security.

Bravo set down at a series of bunkers next to the 105 Battery, between the ARVN and Special Forces compounds. Their mortars had been shipped

in and Bird's Mortar Platoon headed off to set up their 81s. With their departure Hank's platoon came back to near squad size.

Hank's leg throbbed. The wound was puffy and black and ugly pus emanated like a growing mushroom. Fletcher reminded him there was some
metal in there and urged him to see the Battalion surgeon whose aid station
was situated across from the Artillery Battery. Hank consented. It was 1100
hours when he limped his way over.

"Hey, Lieutenant Kirby!" Hank heard a Puerto Rican accent. He raised
his eyebrows in stark surprise at seeing a squat, swarthy man with a pencil
moustache hurrying toward him. It was Sergeant Gomez! "What the hell?"
was all Hank could muster and he shook hands with his old platoon sergeant.

Gomez grinned. "Surprised? Bet you thought I was back in the World.
But my malaria wasn't bad enough. Couldn't even get to Japan." His grin
sunk into a frown. "Heard November got it bad."

Hank nodded, his lips tight. "Yeah…We're down to nine. You coming
back?"

"Yessir."

"Good. November needs you. How about squaring them away." He
pointed over to where his platoon was starting to sprawl out. "I gotta get
over to the doctor."

"Sure thing. Hope it ain't bad."

It was bad for Hank's leg. But for the rest of him it was good. He was getting out. Going to the 93rd Evac Hospital. And then, who knows, perhaps
Japan…*or even the States!* It would be Gomez's platoon now just as it had
been before he arrived. He could leave now.

PART 3
THE BREAK

CHAPTER 28

T O A FIELD TROOPER, that is a field trooper whose stay is short and uncomplicated, the 93rd Evac exists shamefully as a serene heaven. Clean, air-conditioned Quonset hut wards clustered together and attached by hallways safely buried in thick layers of sandbags. Clean white linen with big feather pillows. Three hot squares a day, TV, yes TV, in most every ward, and a featured Hollywood movie every night under the stars.

Hank's first week was, physically, the only uncomfortable week of his stay as he suffered a series of needles to eradicate the severe infection from his calf and an operation to remove a chunk of metal.

The mental part was the worst part. The memories of Loc Ninh that lingered everywhere, during the meals, watching the tube, at night during the outdoor movie. But they were most intense in the ward after the lights were out, when he closed his eyes and watched the horror replay itself, again and again. And he prayed for sleep or morning to hurry and rescue him. Usually it was the morning.

He saw some of his men. Those who were still around and had not yet had the good fortune of being shipped to Japan, or even better, the States, as had PFC Calabrese. Their wounds varied in severity, from the amputated leg of PFC Brown, one of his flank men, to his own shrapneled calf. He didn't see Sergeant Bennett. He heard he was still around, but in a psycho ward.

Near the end of his first week, Brown made the Freedom Bird. There was of course no doubt about him making it. Listening to the others who still remained, Hank began to believe more and more he had a ticket. Until the middle of the second week when he got the news.

He was going back to his unit after his convalescence.

It was shortly after this disappointing revelation, during lunch at the 93rd's cafeteria for the ambulatory, that a dark, fellow patient with a heavily bandaged eye informed him of the "where and how" of calling home. To Hank, home was Pam.

The "where" was a big trailer located on the periphery of the hospital complex. The "how" was the Mars call, an overseas call that bounced a radio transmission off a satellite and into some ham operator's set, which in turn, somehow fed the call into Ma Bell and then into the telephone of your party. According to the fellow patient, half the conversation was filled with "overs" as if you were calling the CO on a prick-25.

That evening found Hank in a rectangular waiting room pancaked on the far side by about thirty bandaged, blue pajama-clad patients. His mending leg throbbing as if the thirteen stitches were slowly being pulled apart one stitch per patient, he was part of the one-third without seats. One hour ago, he had given his name to a freckled-faced spec-five slouched at a card table next to a door Hank believed contained the Mars equipment. He figured he was about five from the bottom since only four had followed him in and stayed. Most prospective callers would enter, eye the crowd, frown, and leave.

As he waited, his mind flashed thoughts of the impending conversation. First he would madly declare his love for her, to be followed by "over." Then what would Pam say? The same, "over"? Or would she be cold and stark, like her letters? Then what would be his reply? Would he ask her about her letters and how they bothered him, "over." And then an argument might entail, filled with terse "overs." And then before he could quell it, a hand would grab his shoulder and pull him away because his time was up. And every ham operator in the States would have heard him and Pam and know they had a problem.

He waited three hours, his leg killing him, his advancement up the list was minute, his chances for a seat marginally improved. Purportedly they were having problems. Either they couldn't find a satellite or couldn't reach a ham operator.

He slowly began squeezing his way out of the hot muggy room, its air stale from the sweating bodies and bad breath breathing of sick and wounded. He would not return.

He would write Pam and tell her he loved her. He would tell her he was in a hospital. Of course, it wasn't combat related since he had a real safe job as a supply officer. Rather, it was some mysterious viral infection. But Pam needn't worry about it. Large doses of penicillin would take care of it.

CHAPTER 29

THE VW BUG sped eastward, its four cylinders beating the whining pitch of an old lawnmower. Behind wide-rimmed Polaroid sunglasses, Pam gripped the steering wheel with white knuckles. So deep in thought her peripheral vision was reduced to nothing, oblivious to the wide stretches of the Banana River flanking the causeway that reached into Cocoa Beach. Her eyes barely focused ahead on the ribbon of road.

She often took these drives to filter out the confusion in her mind. But this late afternoon, with the October sun bright on her rear window, the backwash was malfunctioning; her mind was in a turbid flood.

There was the boredom of her existence. The drag of the weekdays: up at 6:30 a.m., to school at 8:00 a.m., the same tired, dull classes of eighth graders striving for mediocrity. Home at 4:00 p.m., idle conversation with Mom and Dad, the presidential campaigns, the student rioting at Berkley, but not the war in Vietnam, that was taboo, only its debilitating effects on the home front. Then there was the work on her lesson plan, she had her own high standards of teaching, regardless of her sloth-like students, followed by supper at 6:30 p.m., three hours of TV, that addicting idiot box, then without fail, in the blink of an eye, it was 6:30 a.m. again, and the whole damn cycle repeated itself.

The void of the weekends: shopping, brutal crowds, long lines in shops and stores, followed by long lines in traffic. The government was purportedly going to land two men on the moon next year, but before that historical achievement everyone else was landing at Kennedy Space Center and its environs. More…yes more…of the idiot box with Dad, even the endless stream of football games. And the vegetating away of her life alone at the beach or on one of her thought-provoking drives in her VW, such as the one she was now on.

Pam braked at a red light, looked to the left in hopes of turning right on red, but a continuous flow of beach traffic kept her stopped. The light changed and she turned south onto A1A. The congestion of traffic from Cocoa Beach, continuing along the east side of Patrick Air Force Base, through Melbourne, held her thoughts for the next half hour. Finally, she broke loose from her bumper-to-bumper confinement and was on an easy stretch of beach road feeding toward Sebastian Inlet.

A steel-gray cloud, like a huge floating tarp, had sneaked overhead and was now sliding toward the sun, shrouding the now overcast day and turning it even darker. Large random raindrops splattered on the windshield. Pam started the wipers and their slow flapping stirred a blinding concoction of water, road film, and splattered bugs. She let up on the accelerator. Her eyes strained to see the road through a thin, opaque arch that momentarily existed following each thumping sweep of the wiper. The rain finally became pelting and washed away the pasty blur, clearing her vision. The car regained a portion of its original velocity. With the rain beating down on the outside, the small, dry interior of the VW brought a feeling of coziness.

And Pam started thinking about Hank.

He was becoming someone different, transforming from a gentleman Jekyll into a hideous Hyde. She might understand this change if he was in combat, vulnerable to attacks on the psyche. But he was a supply officer, "…safe as a church mouse" had been one of his type-written banal comments.

And then there was his letter yesterday. Its twenty-four-hour gnawing on the gray matter in her head was the reason for this drive. The letter, typed in its usual juvenile form, was fatuous. A farce. Telling of his woeful condition in a hospital at some place called Long Binh. He tried to evoke sympathy at first. But then the *symptoms!* She couldn't believe his symptoms! And his crude, closing remark. Every word of this passage was branded into her brain:

> "Pam, I've got a viral infection. It's manifested itself in a huge sore on the end of a long appendage which I'm quite fond of. Penicillin will hopefully kill it. Unless its one of those Southeast Asia strains that are immune to antibiotics. I'm in the hospital at Long Binh for quarantine. The Army must want to protect all those pretty little Viet girls…"

It was unimaginable; preposterous! He had the gall to tell her he had VD! He was even proud of it!

It hurt. It hurt that she was being slowly pushed out of his life, that he had been unfaithful, that he had told her of the event. It hurt that he would now carry a stigma of disease, one of uncleanliness…of cheating. Most of all it hurt that she had been wrong about Hank.

The rain passed.

The VW U-turned just before the Sebastian Bridge and headed back.

Fred Sadler sat smirking in his big, overstuffed wing chair, his arthritic legs resting on the hassock, his head flush against the backrest. In his mouth he twirled a cigar with his thick lips in between deep, smoking puffs. About every thirty seconds the cigar would come out to make room for huge swallows of Blue Ribbon.

The letter had been a masterpiece and deserved a moment of gloating. He had wanted to wait a little longer before the *coup de grâce*, but Kirby's last letter had given him the opening he needed to close out the relationship. It had all been so subtle. He had seen the effects on Pam of the doctored letters as clearly as if he had been watching a TV serial. Each episode crept toward a final, decisive end. At first, Pam would read Hank's letters out loud to him and her mother, beaming proudly of her gallant soldier boy. Then she started reading bits of the letters that were a synthesis of Kirby's letters and his own editorial license. Recently, he had stopped editing and began producing his own original work. And Pam had stopped reading bits out loud and had started taking long, sulking drives.

But his latest piece, his masterpiece, he couldn't accept full credit. No, that poor, fucking Kirby had taken a turn with the shovel that had dug his grave. Kirby's letter had started the dirt moving. Of course though, Fred Sadler's creative abilities of twisting words, abilities that had been finely honed over the past few months, were the steam shovel that finished the job.

He kicked the hassock away, drained his beer can, and stubbed out his cigar in a large seashell ashtray. He went into the master bedroom; a modestly decorated room of twin beds with floral counterpanes, and sat down on his bed next to the end table that held the telephone. From a drawer he pulled a small piece of paper containing a phone number scrawled in his

own handwriting, the product of a prior phone call to the University of Florida Alumni Association.

He picked up the receiver and with a stubby finger dialed one and then
the phone number in Miami. He could hear the deep purring ring on the
other end of the line. Butterflies swam with the beer in his stomach.

The fourth ring was cut short and an off-key baritone answered, "Hello."
The voice resonated size and strength.

"Hello. Is this Dave Watson?" Fred's nervous tone was unusually high-
pitched and he hoped he didn't sound like a squealing pig in contrast to the
deep voice at the other end.

"That's right."

Silence.

"Dave, we've never met before, but you used to date my daughter in college. Pam…Pam Sadler. I'm Fred…Fred Sadler."

"Yeah?"

"Pam's really been in the dumps lately. I don't know what's wrong. She
talks about you all the time. I told her to give you a call, but she's too proud
for that sort of thing. So I decided to maybe butt-in and let you know how
she's feeling. She's my daughter and I want her to be happy."

"I thought she was going with some Army guy, you know?" Dave knew
exactly who she was going with. That sanitary-shit engineer who had com-
pounded his stupidity by getting into Army Rotcee.

"She was. But now she realizes he was a bad mistake. She wants to forget
him. Sounds like she'd like to start seeing you again."

Barely an inch from the mouthpiece of his red phone, Dave's lips stretched
into the smile of a fox. He had been quite pissed when Pam had stopped
dating him because of that shit engineer. He was far superior in looks and
body and was a third team AP All-American. As for brains, what kind of
brains does it take for someone to want to be a shit engineer.

It had been a jolt when Pam broke off their relationship. Not that they
were serious in any way, but more because of that shit engineer. But the
worst of it, the very worst of the whole damn thing, was that he never got
his prick in her. Only a little nipple and a bit of snatching at pussy hair. It
had been one of those un-reached pinnacles.

Or had it? It appeared that the hunt may not be over.

"Well you know Mr. Sadler, right now I'm pretty busy with football. Being on the Dolphins taxi squad has its demands, you know. I run the dummy plays for practice and I've got to work my tail off for the coaches, you know. Next year I plan to make the regular squad."

"I'm sure you will, Dave. I've been a fan of yours since you've played for the Gators." Fred was not puffing. Ever since he heard that Pam was dating a football star he had become an instant fan, even though he had never before followed college football.

"Well, you know, I tell you what…" There was a pause as Dave sought for words. "Where's Pam now?" he asked.

"In Merritt Island, near Cocoa, living at home with her mother and me. She's got a teaching job," Sadler replied.

"I see. That's a pretty good drive from Miami, you know. About four hours, huh?" Dave calculated the level of effort he'd have to expend.

"More like three and a half," Sadler offered, shaving a little travel time from the commute.

"I see…tell you what. I hate to see Pam in the dumps, so you know, I'll give her a call sometime and maybe get up that way when the season's over. What's your number?"

Fred Sadler couldn't control his beaming lips. He was too excited to pull his number from memory and had to look at the telephone. "Area Code 305…783…" he began to read in slow pauses."

"Okay, I got it," said Dave as he finished writing the number down. "Well, good talkin' to you, Mr. Sadler."

"Uh…one more thing, Dave."

"What's that?"

"When you talk to Pam, I'd appreciate you not mentioning my calling. Don't want her to think her old man was a meddler. You know?"

"Understand. Bye."

Fred heard the line go dead and he hung up. He plucked a big cigar from his front pocket, inserted it in his jowly mouth, and began chewing as he headed for the kitchen. He grabbed a Blue Ribbon from the fridge, popped it with a church key, removed the cigar, and started chugging. Beer had never tasted so good. *He* had never felt so good!

CHAPTER 30

H ANK DREADED THE day of his release. Finally, near the middle of October, it came and he was discharged with orders sending him back to his company. He traveled by Army bus to Bien Hoa. From there, he hopped a Caribou bound for Quan Loi.

The airfield at Quan Loi was different. He noticed it when he stepped down from the tail ramp and his eyes scanned the airfield. Helicopters saturated the strip. A small passenger terminal on the northern edge existed where there was once a huge stand of rubber trees. Beyond the terminal, strolling from the PX, helmeted GIs toted rifles along with their packages. Absent from their shoulders was the Big Red One. In its place was a large yellow shield shaped insignia. The distinctive yellow shield was bisected by a black band running on an angle from top left to lower right like a bandolier, with a black silhouette of a horse head in the upper right. The First Air Cavalry Division. They were out in droves.

Hank gaped at the scene as the passengers, a potpourri of new EMs, noncoms, and second looies passed him by and headed for the terminal. Realizing he was being left behind, he followed, then broke away at an oblique angle that bee-lined across a portion of the airstrip to the road leading to his Battalion area. The road was tire-rutted, pot-holed, and filled with puddles from a recent cloudburst. Upon reaching it, a PFC, head bent down to navigate around the large mud-puddles, rifle at sling arms, tramped by.

"Hey, soldier," Hank called to him.

The PFC gave a startled flinch, saw the black bar of a lieutenant, and whipped on a hasty salute as his left hand reached across his chest to hold the rifle sling.

"Yessuh," he said in a southern drawl.

"What's going on here? I just got back from the 93rd Evac and all I see are First Cav."

"That's right, suh," the PFC said as he carefully traversed a mud hole to face Hank. He eyed Hank's Big Red One on his shoulder. "This here base camp's ours now."

"Your what?"

"Ours," he repeated. "We took it from your First Brigade."

"By any chance, do you know where the First Brigade went?"

The soldier paused thoughtfully. He removed his helmet and ran his fingers through a slurry of sweaty, gritty red hair. "Maybe Lai Khe. That's your division's headquarters, ain't it?"

Hank nodded and thanked him for the info. They departed in opposite directions.

Hank puddle-jumped his way to what used to be First Brigade's officer's club, and its steam bath. Lai Khe could wait. His leg had a dull ache and right now he wanted the therapy of a masseuse with firm, kneading fingers.

His expectations were quickly doused. The once magnificent villa looked like a condemned tenement, boarded up tight with weathered boards. A big padlock was bolted on double doors on which yellow painted letters proclaimed that is was off-limits to all personnel.

Hank went back to the small terminal. The closed O'club was a nostalgic hurt. It had been an island sanctuary, a brief escape into contentment. Now it was gone, and he missed it.

A few hours later, a courier flight landed him in Lai Khe.

"Bravo Company, Third Battalion, Thirteenth Infantry. First Sergeant Mendez speaking." Hank relaxed when he heard the first shirt's Tex-Mex accent over the crackling of the field telephone.

"Hey Top, this is Lieutenant Kirby."

"Lieutenant Kirby!" he heard Mendez shout. The connection made it sound distant, like someone yelling from afar. "Sir, it's about time you got your ass out of the hospital. It's bad enough havin' privates malingerin', but for a first lieutenant it's too much."

"No argument, Top. I'm out at the troop pad. How 'bout sending someone down to pick my malingering ass up." Hank found himself smiling.

"Roger that. I'm on my way."

Five minutes later, Hank was bouncing along in a Bravo Company jeep, Mendez behind the wheel. Lai Khe was flatter than Quan Loi, with more gray dirt and less red clay, more open areas and less rubber, more tin-roofed A-framed wooden hooches on concrete floor slabs and less medium GP tents, more deuce-and-a-halfs, quarter-tons and jeep traffic, and less quiet. The airfield, as in Quan Loi, was the hub of the base camp. Also like Quan Loi, it contained within its confines Lai Khe, a Vietnamese village, sealed off from the base camp by a chain link fence crowned with barbed wire. A compound within a compound.

"What's say we stop by the NCO club?" Mendez proffered while they waited at an intersection for a squadron of tanks and A-CAVs from the 11th ACR to finish parading by in one big dust cloud. "I'll buy you a brew and give a sitrep what's been happening."

"Okay by me. I need to catch up. By mistake, I landed in Quan Loi today. Seemed like the twilight zone without any Big Red Ones walking around."

"Sorry 'bout that. We should've dropped you a line about our change of address."

Two minutes later, they were in a small, boxy NCO club, empty except for a dark-complexioned spec-five wiping the narrow pine bar. The only other activity was the slow revolutions of two low-hanging paddle fans.

Hank sat down at a table in a far corner. The first sergeant came over carrying two mugs. He sat down and slid one mug across the table with his left hand as his right upturned the other to guzzle down a sizable portion. Finished, he wiped his mouth with his sleeve, gave a little belch, lit up a Lucky Strike, and blew smoke through both nostrils. He was ready now, and so he began: "As you learned today, a brigade of the Cav took over Quan Loi. As a result, the Big Red's AO has been cut by a third. Lai Khe's now home for the First and Third Brigades and the Division's headquarters."

"Why the change?"

"Not sure exactly," Mendez paused to consider his answer. The lines in his brown leathery face, plowed by nineteen years of service life and two wars, were deep; crow's feet clawed towards his temples. "Partly maybe because the Cav has better air mobility and so they can cover the border better. And maybe partly because our AO's always been too damn big." Mendez dragged at his cigarette and blew out a stream of smoke. "But that's only one of many changes."

"More? In only a month?" remarked Hank. There was always something ominous about change. Loc Ninh had brought enough change; change that had permanently scarred him. Physically and mentally.

"Our Battalion's no longer under the First Brigade. We swapped with a Mech outfit. Third Brigade had two Mechs and one Rifle. Now both are even with one Mech and two Rifle Battalions."

"Makes sense," Hank broke in. The change didn't seem bad. "What's the Third Brigade like?"

"Damn good. They've treated us real nice 'cept for the pigpen we inherited as our rear area. But that couldn't be helped. It was just one of those things. And I understand we may move to better quarters."

Top drained his mug, snubbed out his Lucky, and told Hank he'd get 'em another round. He headed for the bar. After returning, he lit up again and began again.

"We gotta new company commander," he said offhandedly in a way designed to snare the unsuspecting.

The design worked. Hank was dumbstruck. "What happened to Connors? He didn't get hit?"

"Hell, no. He's in fine shape. He's now the assistant S-3 for the Third Brigade TOC. Good staff job. It'll go good on his record."

"Good," Hank said. *Good for Connors, but would the change be good for him?* "What's the new Bravo Six like?" He asked, expecting to hear a description of a paranoid captain rolling steel balls and looking for strawberries.

"Seems like a fine officer. Name's Torrence. It's his second tour so he probably knows his stuff. Appears to have an interest in his men."

Hank breathed more relief. Not all changes were for the worse. "What's the company doing now?" he asked.

"OPCON to an outfit of the Eleventh ACR. Been riffing from a fire support base north of Bien Hoa in the rocket belt. So far things have been quiet. No action since you've been gone."

Mendez gulped down the remaining draft, excused himself, and set off for a pisser located behind the club. In his absence, Hank drained his first beer and took a sip from the second.

Mendez returned with a third full mug in his hand. As he dropped heavily into his chair, weighted from the effects of two near-chugged brews, Hank queried him on his platoon. "How's November been?"

"They've been all right," he said. "They're back to full strength, so you'll be seeing a shitload of raw faces. And Gomez's bellyaching about the responsibilities of platoon leader."

"I'll feel like a stranger. An old-timer stranger," Hank ruminated out loud.

Mendez tilted his mug and sucked the cold draft in like a huge siphon. When emptied, he set the glass down hard, the clunk reaching the walls of the club. His tongue wiped leftovers from around his lips. His eyes flashed as he remembered something. "I almost forgot to tell you. Your friend, Lieutenant Kistler…" Hank alertly picked up his head like the ears of a dog hearing his name called. *Surely nothing had happened. Not to Dick.* "…he's the Battalion S-3 Air."

"No kidding?"

Mendez nodded.

"That's great…no more humpin' the boonies," Hank exclaimed, or rather he tried to, but his words lacked the necessary resonance. Muffled, he knew, by selfish jealousy. Dick was coming out of the field; he was going back to it, after first tasting the sweet, addicting possibility of going home.

"One more thing," Mendez said, wrapping up the conversation. "Guess who the new exec is?"

Hank furrowed his brow for a moment. "Brussels?"

"That's right."

CHAPTER 31

THE WHIRLY GUSTS from the massive rotor blades kicked up the sand into a dark storm cloud. The flying grit bit painfully into the faces of the men being disgorged from the rear of the huge Chinook helicopter. Once their feet hit the ground, they were pushed by the swirling wind toward Fire Support Base Torch.

Like most fire support bases, Torch was a conglomeration of concentric geometric shapes. Outer and inner circles of three-ply, razor sharp concertina wire were the first lines of defense. Strategically buried along the perimeter wire were fifty-five-gallon drums of foo-gas, a napalm-like, detcord wrapped explosive designed to provide an exceptionally warm reception for the uninvited.

Within these concentric circles over forty bunkers with twin firing ports nearly flush to the ground formed a huge star pattern out of its primary and supplementary positions. The star, when averaged into a circumference, had a diameter of about 100 meters. The star was inlaid with a battery of three 105 howitzers within a protective circle of green sandbags. Three Mortar Platoons, each of their two mortars also sandbagged surrounded, and an assortment of tents, supply, mess, HQs, et al, completed Torch's makeup.

Hank's bad leg throbbed under the weight of full combat gear plus a rucksack of luxury items, air mattress, poncho, poncho liner, toiletries, stationery, Newsweek, Sports Illustrated, four paperback novels, two olive drab towels, and four cans of coke. He limped behind Mendez through a maze in the perimeter's concertina wire and across the fire base to two mortar pits on the far side. He immediately recognized the sweating, shirtless bodies cleaning the tubes of the 81s and stacking teardrop ammo. They belonged to Sergeant Bird's Mortar Platoon.

There were hellos and handshakes all around. Sergeant Bird maintained a friendly smile as he explained the whereabouts of the company to Hank and Mendez. Bravo was booney-hopping about six klicks away; Delta was holding down the fort until tomorrow when Bravo was due in. The Battalion modus operandi was to have one company in for two to three days and the other three out riffing, with the companies rotating every so often back to Torch.

He informed them that the CO's tent was near splitting its seams with everybody's personal gear while they were riffing, but there was a vacant sleeping pit next to the mortars where Hank and Top could sleep, since Delta had about everything else. He promised to get some ponchos and a pup-tent over to them for shelter from the nightly downpours. Mendez then pulled a packet of letters from his rucksack and the Mortar Platoon flocked to him like autograph hounds.

Hank sat on a three-foot wall of sandbags, his feet inside a mortar pit. Freshly showered, he wore only a green towel draped around his midsection. In the west, the late hour sun, filtered by thin, diaphanous white clouds, made the sky a brilliant white. With half-lidded eyes he showed the sun his left cheek. The rays had pulled the beads of water from his body, and he now bathed in the warmth. Around him were the sounds of GIs griping and joking, their bellies filled with Salisbury steak, peas, mashed potatoes, and pound cake. Beyond them was the clanking of serving spoons and banging of mermite cans as Delta Company's mess packed up for Chinook transport to Bien Hoa. They would be back in the morning with cans full of powdered eggs, sausages, pancakes, and hash browns.

Hank felt lethargic, like a big lizard lying on a rock on a hot day. In his marginally comatose state, he reflected on the brilliant white of the sky, and like the ocean, considered its many moods. From the corner of his eye, blurred by the glare, a hulking figure with a familiar gait approached.

"Hell, I thought you'd be in Japan by now," Dick Kistler's voice boomed. He clutched Hank by the shoulder and squeezed as he stepped over the sandbag wall to sit down.

"No such luck," Hank gave a slow, awkward grin. He wanted to show more spontaneity, but he felt too sloth-like.

"How's the leg?"

"Good. But not good enough. It wasn't bad enough to be that good."

Dick nodded. He understood the twisted logic.

There was a silence between them. A Chinook chattered overhead. Life emerged around the 105s as the Battery prepared for its nightly H&Is.

"How were the nurses?"

Hank smiled. "Lot of sourpusses. Too busy shacking up with the doctors."

The sun had left its cloud cover and, before taking refuge for the night, emitted a bright orange glow.

"Patient life a little dull, huh?"

"Not for me. Got a lot of sleep. Watched some movies. Wrote Pam a long letter."

"Think it'll help things?"

"Hope so," he shrugged.

They sat for a long while. Saying little. Just staring beyond the perimeter wire. The sun set, and dark, eerie shadows came out. One of the 105s belched a loud booming yellow flame. Hank listened for a splash. It was a far distance. They were taking random pot shots at any nocturnal VC.

The Mortar Platoon came into the pits to fire a few defcons, evicting Hank and Dick. They went over to Hank's quarters, a six by eight, three layered sandbagged box partially covered by a canvas roof. Sergeant Bird had done more than provide a pup tent shelter. It was more like a full-grown dog. Rather than ponchos serving as two tent shelter halves, Bird had found a large tarp. But instead of pup tent style with two v-shape sloping sides, it resembled a giant postage stamp stretched among four engineer stakes, a good three feet outside of the corners of the sleeping position. This arrangement allowed for maximum airflow since there were no sides, just three feet of open air spacing between the top layer of sandbags and the tarpaulin room.

Top had left clean fatigues and Hank put them on as Dick flopped down on one end of Hank's air mattress. Hank joined him on the other end and they leaned against the sandbags, stretched out their legs and stared out from under their makeshift ceiling at the howitzers.

"Your new CO seems a good one," Dick remarked.

"So I've heard. But I doubt if anyone can replace Connors."

"Yeah. Though I bet Connors is fuckin' happy the Army thinks he can. He's got a good job. Step up. Third Brigade Assistant S-3."

"I know."

"Works in a goddamn air-conditioned bunker."

"Good for him."

"Saw him back in Lai Khe as he was leaving the Battalion. Know what he said? Said first remf job that opens up for a first looie he's gonna make sure Kirby gets it. Guess he knew you were coming back."

Hank's eyebrows arched up. "No shit?"

"Fuckin' A. And when you're a remf I want you to land me a job in that big air-conditioned TOC," Dick grinned, his eyes riveted on the 105s. In the milky dark the guns loomed like some kind of prehistoric dinosaurs.

Dick's revelation of Connors' words was like the kneading fingers of a Quan Loi masseuse. It was the massage he had needed.

He turned his head to look at Dick. "Screw that last transmission, Lieutenant Kistler! You've landed your soft job," he teased. "Battalion S-3 Air does not carry a booney-hopping MOS."

Dick chuckled. "It's not bad," he admitted. "My boss, Major Thornton, is outstanding. But he's short. I'll be getting a new boss soon. And believe it or not this job is still in the field. It's not a remf job, you know. If it were, do you think I'd be out here in this shit-hole?"

"Well, just what the hell does the S-3 air do? Float around like a hot air balloon?" Hank took a shot at some humor. He was getting in better spirits.

Dick sunk further down on the air mattress, hands behind head, eyes now on a forty-five tilt from horizontal, looking out from under the tarp into a night of dim, scattered stars. "Well, I do some hobnobbing with the Battalion aristocracy, the colonel, Major Thornton, and other brass. And then I coordinate air assaults and other tactical air moves. Lay on the number of sorties, select pre-planned targets for strikes, recommend type of ordinance and time of strike, and in general serve as liaison with the air needs of the companies."

"Sounds impressive."

"Anything can sound impressive," Dick philosophized. He glanced at the luminous dial of his gold-plated Seiko watch. "Oh crap!" He abruptly got to his feet. He stooped at about ninety degrees to keep his head from hitting the tarp. "I almost forgot the briefing with Thornton. Listen Hank, I'll see you tomorrow."

"Good enough," Hank replied.

Dick stepped over the sandbags and stretched to full height. He started to walk away but abruptly turned. "I'm glad you didn't make it to Japan, or the World."

This declaration surprised Hank.

"Because it might've interfered with our vacation," Dick said, looking into a black rectangle formed by the ends of the tarp and sandbags. "I've got us two R and R allocations to Australia over Christmas. I thought it would be good for our Yuletide morale." Dick waved a goodbye and walked away.

So, Hank thought, it was going to be Australia. He had asked Pam in one of his letters to forget about the cost, and reconsider a romantic R and R rendezvous in Hawaii. But that was a few letters ago. Now in a letter delivered yesterday by Top, she said she couldn't make it.

So it would be Australia. With Dick.

Around midnight it began to pour. The water trickled over the sandbags and then formed a moat around Hank's air mattress. He huddled in his poncho liner, hoping to stay dry. But a cold, clammy wetness managed to seep through the cloth fabric. At any moment he expected his mattress to start floating. Then he remembered the power of concentration. Forget the water, forget the fucking discomfort, forget the ringworm mushrooming back on his ass, of jungle rot again going after his crotch. Think of those dry, crisp, clean hospital sheets. The nice warm bed. Think of it…

Finally, the morning came. He shaved from his steel pot. Finished, he tossed the water on the ground, put the liner inside the pot, and put it on his head.

With an M-16 slung over his shoulder, he dodged deep puddles on the way to the chow line. Skipping the powdered eggs, he filled his paper plate with sausages and hash browns. At the end of the line, he scooped up an apple, took a half pint of milk from a mess server, and went back to his sleeping area.

After eating, he set to work dismantling his rifle to clean it.

At mid-morning, Hank found Dick near the operations tent. They sat on empty ammo boxes and chatted about politics—Nixon would win the upcoming election and get them home as promised—and sports, and then Dick's theory on the pros and cons of dog-style fucking. At noon, they dined on C-rations.

Afterwards, they separated; Dick to the S-3 and Hank back to his air mattress.

"Lieutenant Kirby. The company's coming in." The first sergeant had reached in and was now shaking Hank's shoulder. Groggily, Hank found his feet and stepped out beside Top. On the far side, past the 105 Battery, a long file of worn out, mud-caked, sweating grunts trudged heavily through the maze in the concertina wire; their once green fatigues soaked a dirty brown.

Hank picked out Captain Torrence from his entourage of two RTOs, one for the company net and the other for Battalion. Behind the entourage, head bent, feet dragging, Lieutenant Sawyer and his RTO followed. Torrence looked compact and solid and, by a trace of bounce still left in his gait, in good shape. Hank tried to locate some familiar faces of his platoon, but he had focused too long on Torrence and once through the wire, the long file had dispersed.

His eyes came back to Torrence and followed him to his tent, where he pitched his helmet to the ground, propped his rifle on the wall of sandbags forming the tent's base, and struggled out of his equipment harness.

Hank and Top headed for him. He saw them coming and nodded hello to the first sergeant. He looked curiously at Hank.

"Sir," Mendez said as he came to a halt. "This is the platoon leader who's been laid up in the hospital."

"Hank Kirby," Hank broke in and offered his hand.

The CO took it with a firm clasp. Hank attempted to measure the man by his grip. It seemed one of confidence and competence. He hoped his intuition was accurate.

"I'm Captain Torrence. Welcome back. I've received a good sitrep about you from Captain Connors," the CO said. He flung sweat from his brow with a swipe of the hand and then raked through the black bristles of his crew cut with his fingernails. He was about thirty-two with a hawk-like nose and sun-beaten, leathery face that looked older. He looked too weathered to be West Point or ROTC, and Hank guessed he had been an NCO before OCS.

An arm grabbed Hank's wrist and spun him around to face the big, friendly smile of Lieutenant Sawyer. "Well shit. I never expected them to get Hank Kirby back to the field," Sawyer said, then looked down. "How's the leg?"

"Pretty good, Jack. How you been?"

"Terrible! Like a piece of buffalo shit!" the forward observer spat with disgust. "Last night I thought I'd either drown or have all my blood sucked out by fuckin' leaches."

As Hank smiled, a young man in wet fatigues and squishing boots joined them. Torrence introduced them. "Lieutenant Kirby, this is Lieutenant Howard, a new platoon leader with our company.

"Hank Kirby," Hank said as they shook hands.

"John Howard. You were the platoon leader of the Third Platoon?"

Hank nodded.

"He still is!" Sawyer chimed in.

"What's your platoon?" Hank asked.

"Lima. Lieutenant Brussels' old platoon."

"What about the Second? Do they have a new Mike Six?" Hank enquired about Cronin's platoon, while briefly wondering how Cronin might be doing. He had not been at the 93rd Evac during Hank's stay.

Sawyer answered, "No, Sergeant Daniels still has it. Been doing a good job too, and…"

"Lieutenant Kirby," Torrence cut in, "I've got to meet Demon Six. Why don't you join your platoon. I've told Gomez what bunkers your platoon will occupy. You'll find a lot of new faces."

"Yes, sir."

Torrence turned to the first sergeant. "Top, get the mail out to the platoon sergeants ASAP." His eyes swept around. "I'll get with you men later." He turned and hastened toward the colonel's CP.

Gomez and Tucker guided Hank around the bunkers secured by their platoon. The men were in groups of three and four: cleaning weapons, rigging ponchos to their sleeping areas recently vacated by Delta, idly smoking, and drinking sodas. There was a certain intimacy, like the sharing of a family secret, in the "hellos" and "how you doin's" with the small remaining contingent of the Loc Ninh veterans. With the majority, the new men, fresh from the World, there were guarded, nervous introductions. Their eyes were like dogs out of obedience school, staring uncertainly at their new master, wondering what would be demanded of them.

The tour over, the three sat on a supplementary bunker Hank had selected for the platoon's CP. He felt in an unusually good mood considering where he was, and where he had hoped to be. He was among people he knew. And liked.

They sat in silence, observing the activity about them.

Having grabbed their rucksacks from the CO's tent, some members of the November Platoon set about unpacking their belongings, made up mostly of an air mattress, stationery, maybe an extra set of clean fatigues, a few squirreled away C-ration cans, probably pound cake or fruit cocktail, pears, or peaches. There was other miscellaneous paraphernalia, such as cigarettes, toiletries, and re-read letters like the one Tucker kept. Except Tucker didn't pack his. He carried it.

Some of those who weren't unpacking, or lying in an exhausted sprawl on a bunker, were inflating their air mattress, their faces drained of color from the effort of blowing and the anxiety of a leak and the possibility of another night on hard ground. Others stood naked in line waiting for their turn under the field shower.

"Sir," Gomez interrupted their quiet. "I'm gettin' short. Two and a half more months till deros." He paused, glancing cautiously at Hank, waiting for some sort of response.

"I didn't know you were so short," Hank said.

"Yessir. I was talkin' to Top and he said when you got back he'd talk to the CO about gettin' me a job back in the rear. That is…" Gomez's voice rose to a nervous pitch of anticipated rejection…"That is, if you ain't got no objection."

Hank read his discomfort and smiled a little. Gomez read the smile and relaxed a little. "Got no objection, Sergeant. I'm a strong believer in field troopers converting to remfs. I hope to convert someday, myself." In his letters to Pam, he was already a remf, he reflected to himself. "I'll talk to Bravo Six and second Top's rec."

"Thank you, sir."

"Don't mention it. What about Sergeant Martin for your replacement?"

"He's my choice. He's been acting platoon sergeant during your absence."

"Good. Now what about those two new NCOs I just met? Sergeant Michael and Sergeant…uh."

"Sergeant Burlop," Tucker helped out.

"Yeah, Burlop. The short one with the long face. Looks something like a mole."

"Funny you should say that, sir. He says he wants to be a tunnel rat."

"Of course, he does, Tucker. That's the Army. He should've volunteered for this outfit and he would've gotten rat duty." Hank couldn't resist throwing in some of his Army cynicism.

"Burlop's just gung-ho. He'll be all right," Gomez commented. "His only problem is he won't keep his head out of the ground."

"He has tunnel vision, you mean," Hank couldn't resist the pun. Gomez and Tucker chuckled out of politeness.

"Burlop's got the first squad," Gomez continued, "Michael the second. He seems like the average sort. Both are wet behind the ears. Instant NCOs out of Benning. That's why they're so young. I feel like their granddaddy," he laughed as he ran a finger across his thin salt and pepper moustache.

Hank laughed with him and then his eyes went down to his watch and then to Gomez. The time, he felt, had come for him to issue his first order as the newly returned November Six.

"It's getting close to chow. How about making sure every man has a clean weapon before going through the chow line."

"Yessir," Gomez answered. He got up with a loud grunt, stretched his weary frame. He gave a waving salute to Hank and left to pass the word on to the squad leaders.

He was right, Hank thought as he watched his platoon sergeant depart; *he was the granddaddy*. And that left him the father. He faced Tucker. It was time for the second order. "Check the other RTOs and see if their radios are working and that they have new batteries." His bottom lip puffed outward to deliberately put on the look of an afterthought. "Oh, one more thing, Jim." With Gomez gone he addressed his RTO by his first name. "Tell Franklin he's now a spec-four. I saw his promotion papers in the company orderly room back in Lai Khe."

"Good. Franklin needs an up."

"You also might like to know, PFC Tucker, or should I now say Specialist Fourth Class Tucker, you've also been promoted." Hank winked at his RTO.

In tandem, Tucker's lips and eyes let out a wide grin. "Good. With the baby on the way we could use the extra cash." He slid off the bunker, a smile still on his lips and while departing, nodded his head at Hank.

Alone, Hank gazed past the perimeter wire. The first two hundred meters out was young undergrowth, the offspring of a recent Rome plow operation. Beyond was the horizon of a sparse tree line. The land was mostly flat giving excellent fields of fire. Charlie Cong would hopefully know that and keep away.

The local folk figured with Hank. They had gathered outside the wire. Mama-sans selling bottled coke and souvenirs, old papa-sans with thin white hair and sparse, threadlike goatees hawking cheap watches and pornographic pictures. Baby-sans played around near the wire next to the foo-gas imploring in broken English, though much better than Hank's three or four words of Vietnamese, for the soldiers to throw them a few cans of C-rations.

Yes, Hank thought, *a fire support base outside of Bien Hoa was quite a social gathering.*

He watched them begin to thin out. It was getting late and they had to be in their hooches before curfew, which began at 1900 hours, at which time anything moving outside a village or compound was fair game. After curfew, it was SOP to shoot first and ask questions later, preferably at 0700 hours the next morning when curfew was lifted.

At midnight, Hank made the rounds of his platoon. Finding everything okay he returned to his CP.

Flashes of heat lightning glimmered in the distance. The three-quarter moon cast a pearlish glint. Hank sat down on a firing port of his bunker and again looked out past the perimeter. This time it didn't look as secure. Maybe the VC could make a go at it. His momentary high at being with his men had evaporated. He was now back on a real downer.

CHAPTER 32

THE BATTALION CAMPED at Torch for a month and a half and operated like a four-tentacle octopus. Three tentacles, in the form of infantry companies, would snake outward, carefully probing, looking for something to latch on to with its suction cups and hold while the other tentacles joined up to devour its catch. The fourth tentacle would stay back to protect the Battalion CP, the brain. Every other day an outside tentacle replaced the one guarding the brain.

But the groping tentacles were not successful. Unfortunately, it was the converse. A tip of one was bitten, severing some flesh. Flesh from Lieutenant Simpson's platoon of Delta. The lieutenant who had indoctrinated Hank with the principles of how not to ambush. Evidently, Simpson had remained a fervent follower of these principles. Five VC boldly wielding flashlights had literally stumbled over Simpson's sleeping ambush. Their AKs quickly sprayed the site like fire hoses before they fled unscathed into the night. Leaving in their wake two dead and one wounded. One of the dead was Simpson.

That was the only significant contact while at Torch, but not the only significant occurrence.

There was news of a significant election. Nixon had won and rumors buzzed about a massive pull-out. Nixon was going to have Vietnamization, a process whereby the Vietnamese were going to start carrying the brunt of the fighting. To Hank, the question was when would the pull-out begin? Nixon would take office in January, six months before his tour was up. Would Nixon be able to get him home sooner?

Then there was a significant change.

Dick's boss, Major Thornton, derosed, and was replaced by Captain Woodson. No more did Hank envy Dick's job.

And a significant addition.

Twenty-four Cambodian mercenaries came into the Battalion fold. Two allotted to each Rifle Platoon. Dubbed Kit Carson scouts, they fit their name. Once they had fought for the Viet Cong, but under a bribe program called the Chieu Hoi, "open arms," program where money, land, and pardons were doled out, they switched their allegiance. Naturally there was a catch. Before collecting the inducements, they had to first fulfill a tour of duty in the military. The attrition by being KIA'd helped to hold down the costs of this program.

Hank counted this addition as a liability rather than the intended asset. They spoke no English and communication was by primitive grunts and hand signals. He couldn't understand or pronounce their names and so resorted to nicknames. One was called "Bundle." Sergeant Martin estimated his height stretched to about five feet. In the field, under the weight of the standard foot soldier load, he became a rolling, waddling bundle.

"Goldie" was almost an inch taller and flashed a gold glimmer when he opened his mouth. Franklin maintained Goldie's smile was worth a small fortune and that he should have sold his mouth rather than signing up for the Chieu Hoi program.

While patrolling, Bundle and Goldie transformed into bloodhounds, scrambling ahead of the point, moving out on the flanks, re-sniffing the ground already traversed. Only the bark was missing. Hank was afraid they might catch a scent, forcing the platoon to pursue. He was sure Custer had similar scouts.

Franklin enjoyed not only his new rank, but his new job as weapons squad leader in charge of the two M-60s. Sergeant Bennet never returned from his crack-up at Loc Ninh and the position had since gone unfilled. Hank anticipated some reservations by Franklin in giving up toting Clyde, his M-60. But he had been wrong. Franklin regarded it as not losing Clyde, but as gaining his brother, even though he would no longer do the trigger pulling. This time the weapons squad leader would have a meaningful role, not just ceremonial when Bennet was in charge and the guns were attached to the two rifle squads.

Gomez converted to a remf, and at age twenty-three Hank reverted to the platoon patriarch, being one of the three or four oldest.

Hank began a countdown to Australia the first week in December when the First of the 28th Infantry swapped places with the Battalion.

The Battalion wound up in Di An, with the companies riffing during the day, standing down at night. He and Dick rendezvoused every night to shoot the shit about Sydney. In his drunken stupor Dick would belch out hoped-for fuck scenarios and in an equally drunk stupor Hank pictured the same scenes but in a vicarious sort of way.

Inside, in his heart if not in his brain, he knew he had to keep faithful. For Pam. Even though the ship was taking on water, perhaps sinking, it was not yet under. Her letters were not patching his morale, but they *were* letters and they had not torpedoed their relationship.

One week before their R and R was to begin, Alpha and Bravo received orders to air assault into an area known as An Son and sweep south toward the muddy north bank of the Saigon River. The operation was to be a joint venture with a Battalion of the 5th ARVN Division.

The specter of this mission interfering with Hank's upcoming plans slightly overshadowed the specter of it interfering with his life.

"Don't worry," Captain Torrence had tried to ease Hank's qualms. "It's a four-day operation. That leaves you three days to get organized and make your R and R flight."

"What if we make contact?" Hank had countered.

"Don't worry." Torrence had comforted. "We'll get you on that R and R flight come hell or high water. Besides, we haven't made contact since I've been CO. Maybe with Nixon coming on board next month, the VC are laying low."

The air insertion was running smoothly. Alpha Company had landed a platoon at a time to secure the LZ. Hank's slick banked sharply to make its run.

He glimpsed the ground below. Various hues of smoke curled upward, outlining a jagged circle in which November's five slicks would enter. Mentally, he snapped a picture of the terrain below. In the bottom of the frame was the wide, dirty-yellow Saigon River. Cutting through the frame in straight geometric lines was an intricate network of irrigation canals and ditches. The surrounding land was mostly grassy marsh glades and fruit orchards. There would be no jungle or rubber, but a lot of water.

Once on the ground, November assembled with a minimum of confusion and as the remaining platoons flew in, struck out on a due east azimuth, through Alpha's perimeter. After 500 meters, the point was halted by a five-foot high earthen berm that rimmed a thirty-foot wide canal. The water looked as deep as it was wide. Its greenish-black cesspool texture offered zero visibility.

Across the canal, on the edge of a hardwood orchard two hundred meters away, faded green fatigues milled around in and out of the trees. The ARVN battalion was sighted. November was at check point one and the joint operation was ready to kick off.

The game plan was to sweep south to the Saigon River, trapping any quarry between them and the river, much like an African hunt with the natives beating the bushes. The canal fed into the Saigon River and the ARVNs were to keep on the east side of the canal and the Americans on the west. November was the pivot point serving as liaison between the two and operated with a degree of independence from the rest of the company.

Because of its role, Hank kept Sergeant Burlop's RTO, PFC Wiley, with him and Tucker to monitor the net of the ARVN's American advisor team, Cloudy Day Forty-One.

Following Hank's calls to Cloudy Day Forty-One and Bravo Six to report the link up, all units started riffing south.

The wind was absent, the sun beating, the air stifling. They hiked feeling they were in a giant steam-bath. Breathing was a heavy form of panting, carefully making sure each breath was drawn through the mouth, or else the stench of the canal would get carried through the nostrils.

The left file walked on the berm on dry, firm footing. Hank kept in the right file, slogging in a wet, brown, grassy glade. He considered switching to the left file, but then it would be a cop out. A creature of habit, in this formation his place was always the right file. He couldn't change simply for convenience.

After a tough hour, Cloudy Day Forty-One, in a thick Bronx brogue, radioed that the ARVNs were going to take one-five. Hank relayed the message to Bravo Six and then hand signaled the platoon to hold up. Their concentration focused ahead, the three-man point didn't see the signal but had monitored the transmission and stopped.

The ARVNs had picked a large, dry shady grove for their rest break. Unfortunately, the opposite bank was sun-beaten and wet. Hank SOB'd them as he sat in the sun with his ass in his helmet to keep dry.

He toweled off the perspiration pouring from his face. Then he rocked out of his helmet, slowly stood up, and looked past his left file lounging dry and lazy on the berm, to the canal's opposite bank.

In cool shade, a platoon of ARVNs gibbered and laughed as they plucked grapefruit from the trees, peeled the skin with long bayonets, and sucked out the juice, their faces wrinkling into grimaces by the sourness. One soldier with half a grapefruit stuffed in his mouth stared back at Hank and then, as if recognizing an old friend, waved his arm madly back and forth. Others looked up and joined in the waving. November's left file came to their feet and reciprocated. Grapefruits began sailing over and C-rations went sailing back. A friendly free trade zone had been established.

Hank was tossed a grapefruit that Tucker had intercepted and squatted back down in his helmet to enjoy the break's last five minutes.

Crack! The sharp sound of a distant AK-47. Followed by exchange of gun-fire. Hank jumped from his helmet as if it were spring loaded and belly-flopped into the ankle-deep water. More shots followed until Hank realized the firing was on the ARVN side. He turned his head and saw Tucker on his elbows giving a sitrep to Bravo Six. Five feet ahead he could see the soles of the boots to PFC Wiley. In a splashing crawl, he moved to the boots, shook one and when Wiley turned around, held out his hand for the horn.

"Cloudy Day Forty-One, this is November Six, over!"

"This is Cloudy Day Forty-One, over."

"Roger, Forty-One, we heard AK fire on your side. Are you in contact?"

An excited Bronx slur replied. "That's affirm. We received it from a small hooch to the south. Got two WIAs."

"Roger! Are you going to call in a light fire team?" Hank wanted to be sure to have his position marked by smoke if they were bringing in gunships.

"Negative. Our captain doesn't want to wait. He's going to assault! Forty-One out!"

There was an eruption of pops of M-16s and deep-throated explosions of fragmentation grenades from the orchard on the other side of the canal.

Eager to do something, Franklin sprang up and rushed to the machinegun in his file to ensure it had a good field of fire. Then, with feet kicking up splashes, he ran to the M-60 in the left file. He slapped the machinegun crew on their backs and led them to a high spot along the berm part way up to the point and pushed them down to the prone and dropped beside them. He raised his head like a long-necked goose and peered over at the orchard but couldn't see any movement. The ARVNs had blended in like chameleons.

The volume of fire subsided to a few sporadic pops of M-16s.

"November Six, this is Cloudy Day Forty-One! We zapped three Charlies!" The ARVN advisor sounded as though the Yankees had just taken the seventh game of the World Series.

"Good going," Hank answered, caught up in Cloudy Day's enthusiasm. His tone surprised him. Three men had just died.

"November Six, Cloudy Day Forty-One, we think a few got away. Better keep an eye out. They might try to cross over."

"Roger. We'll cover it."

Hank jumped up. With Tucker and Wiley dogging his heels he ran over to the berm. Once on top, he settled on his stomach next to Franklin. Two good side rolls to his left and he'd be tumbling down into the long, stagnant cesspool. "They might cross the canal," he shouted in Franklin's ear.

Franklin nodded. Elbowing the machine-gunner out of the way, he slid behind the gun. It was his old gun, Clyde. His cheek on its stock and finger on the trigger felt welcomed. Sixty meters away an old, rotted wooden foot bridge arched shakily over the canal, supported by thin bamboo stilts. Franklin carefully sighted on its flimsy center span.

Suddenly, two scrambling figures dashed out of the tree line on the far side, slid down the embankment, jumped with abandon on the foot bridge, and began to scamper across. A wall of fiery red tracers blocked their path. The lead figure, in torn black pajamas and shouldering a rocket launcher, tried to break through the red stream, but a violent upward twitch of his head told of failure, and he toppled into the water. The second man spastically dropped his AK-47 in the canal and with clumsy balance pivoted in retreat. The red stream fanned to the left. The fugitive lurched forward and fell heavily to the side of the bank. The stream of bullets tore at his body for a full five seconds, as if taking target practice on an old log.

Franklin slowly took his fingers from the hand grip and raised his head triumphantly. A thin ribbon of gray smoke spiraled from the barrel. He turned to Hank and with a wry grin held up two fingers of his right hand, then made a fist and gave a thumbs-up.

Hank swallowed hard. He squeezed his arm in answer.

Tucker started tugging on his pants leg like a nibbling fish. Hank glanced back and saw that he had that pale sour look that portended trouble. "Sir. The point sighted three VC darting inside a hooch."

Bringing the handset up to his ear, Hank felt that dreaded churning sensation inside his stomach. "November Papa, this is November Six." He spoke softly into the mouthpiece, wishing he could control his stomach as well as his voice. "Sitrep!"

"Roger!" the voice came whispering back. "We're in a clump of coconut trees thirty meters away. I'm sure they didn't see us. We didn't engage. Didn't have time to react. Maybe come up for a look? Over."

"Okay," Hank answered reluctantly. "Keep your eyes on it. I'll…I'll come up. Out. Break. Bravo Six, November Six, over."

"This is Bravo Six. We monitored."

"Roger. Might be a good idea to get a light fire team on alert."

"I'll contact higher."

"Roger, out."

Hank motioned for Tucker and Wiley to follow him as he came to his feet and scrambled down the berm. At the toe he got on all fours and crawled. At a cluster of palms, they joined the point and slunk into the ground. Six pairs of eyes nervously strained through the grass and riveted on the upper half of a mud-brick hooch.

It was a weathered blue and had served at least once before as a refuge. A gaping hole opened one fourth of the red barrel tile roof; bullet holes pockmarked the outside walls.

A four-foot wide irrigation ditch only two meters from the onlookers formed a square moat around it.

Hank's chest felt like it contained a used punching bag. If the VC opened up now his only protection was tall thin reeds. "Bravo Six, November Six," he whispered so softly into the mouthpiece he wasn't sure he was making any sound. "I've got the hooch sighted." He picked up the volume a bit. "Negative signs of movement. Get those gunships airborne. We'll try to put a few rockets through the roof."

"This is Bravo Six. No can do. There's a big firefight in which 'higher' has diverted every available light fire team. We can only get a gunship if we're in heavy contact. Over."

"As soon as the VC realize we're right outside their hooch, we'll have a 'heavy' contact!" Hank's whisper increased a few decibels.

"Sorry. Still no dice. Demon Three has ordered your men to assault the hooch."

"Say again?" Hank quickly shot back, hoping the background static had somehow garbled the transmission.

But it was his mind that had garbled it.

"Demon Three says to assault the hooch. And soonest!"

Who the fuck is Demon Three? Hank wondered to himself. "Shit," he muttered under his breath. He was the new Battalion S-3. He was Captain Woodson. That fat ugly bald-headed bastard!

Hank and his two RTOs crawled back to the main body. Tucker radioed Sergeant Martin to round up the squad leaders for a pow-wow. Since one prick-25 was with the point and one on the ARVN's net, there was no radio contact with the squad leaders.

Within thirty seconds they had gathered around, sitting in their helmets or squatting on their haunches. Hank had found a small dry spot of ground for a blackboard and with a waterlogged stick as a pointer, gently outlined, careful not to break the pointer, a rough layout of the hooch and its environs.

"The point thinks three or four gooks are in the hooch. At least that's the way we play it. I asked for a light fire team, but we couldn't get one," Hank said wistfully and then changed his inflection to sound emphatic: "We got orders to assault the hooch."

Martin sucked in air. Franklin and Michael raised eyebrows. And to Hank's dismay, Sergeant Burlop gave a wide grin. But no one said a word.

Hank shut his eyes briefly. His eyes opened, and he continued. "Here's how we'll do it. One squad will slip into the ditch on the north side of the hooch. When I give the word that squad will lay down a covering fire. And I mean heavy. The other squad will take up a position in the ditch running south, perpendicular to the other ditch.

"As soon as I give the word, the squad in the perpendicular ditch will climb out and move forward, assaulting the hooch on a line formation, shooting all the way on rock and roll. But move forward at a walk, if possible. I don't want anybody running ahead and getting shot from behind."

"Sir," Sergeant Burlop said with a formality that belonged at the NCO school. "My squad will be the assault element."

Hank nodded consent, relieved at not having to make the choice. "Sergeant Martin and Franklin, with both M-60s, will be with the covering squad." He paused and looked around at the pale, perspiring faces. He then glanced away. The platoon had formed an elliptical perimeter and the men were either lying down or sitting, some stared at the palms where the point was sequestered. Through the tall slender trunks, the roof of the hooch could be seen. Across the canal he didn't know what the ARVNs were doing. Probably sitting down with a grapefruit in their mouth.

Hank's pause grew. He could feel impatient eyes on him as he gazed down at his dirt carving, the square box for the hooch, the symmetry of the surrounding ditches. What he had here in this mission was a classic case of fire and maneuver. Just like in the classroom at Benning. There was *always* one fundamental principal in fire and maneuver. *Always*. The leader *always* goes with the maneuver element. *Always*.

Fuck shit.

"I'll be with Sergeant Burlop's squad," he said finally. Australia seemed to be in a geographic region known as infinity.

In two long files, the platoon crawled forward. At the ditch, they slid smoothly into the chest deep water. The second squad with Sergeant Martin broke to the right and stretched out and faced the hooch. The first squad, with Hank in the middle, went left for ten meters, took the bend south and formed a line also facing the hooch.

"November Five, November Six. Are you ready?"

"November Five. Affirm."

Hank looked right and left. Rifles were held beside helmeted heads that looked like a string of bobbing coconuts. Short or tall, each man allowed the minimum exposure, preferring the tepid feel of what smelt of liquid buffalo dung to the nakedness of having a portion of their bodies viewed by VC.

Burlop ordered his squad to fix bayonets.

Hank felt queasy. He drew in a long breath through his mouth, nearly carrying water with it. "November Five, November Six. Open fire!"

It was as if all the ammo in the second squad and weapons squad had been collected and thrown at one time into a fiery trash barrel. M-16s, M-60s, and M-79s blasted away in unison.

Hank rose to his full height, bringing his head above the rim of the ditch. Through a tangle of tall grass he saw the hooch. Fist size chunks of kiln dried mud-mortar were flying from about every square foot. Most of the 40mm HE rounds from the M-79s were missing the windows and hole in the roof and exploding off the outside walls, causing a potential hazard to the maneuver unit. "November Five, November Six. Cut the bloopers. We'll bump right into their flak."

"Wilco."

Hank could barely hear Martin's reply through the avalanche of fire. He didn't wait to check compliance. With distant thoughts of Pickett's charge gnawing into his concentration, he waved his men out of the ditch. There was wild scrambling as they clambered out. Hank didn't lead them out; he followed. But that again was Benning. The leader of the maneuver element brings up the rear to better control the maneuver.

And that's what he did as the squad advanced at a rapid walk, firing from the hip with the selector switches on full automatic. Burlop began edging forward, wanting to reach the objective first. But Hank pulled him out of the line and yelled at him to direct his men, not lead them. It was his squad!

As the assault closed within twenty meters, the covering squad shifted their concentration of fire from the front of the hooch to the back. For the first time, Hank noticed that between them and the hooch was another ditch parallel to the one they had climbed out of.

It was about six feet wide. Wide enough to cause them to lose momentum. Should they back off and make a running jump, or jump in and jump out?

Either way, there would be a break in their fire power. Time enough for the gooks to raise their rifles up to the windows and start firing back. That is if there were any gooks in there. Hank was beginning to doubt it.

But there was no let up. When the moving line reached the ditch, there was no hesitation as bodies lunged spread eagle. Some landed hard on their chest, breaking their fall with their elbows as they kept firing, others fell back into the water, but still managed to keep their weapons aimed at the hooch and their finger tight on the trigger.

They were all across except Burlop, Hank, Tucker, and Wiley when something came sailing out a window.

They all dropped to the ground. All save Burlop who plunged helmet first into the ditch.

Nothing happened. Even on the ground the line maintained their fire. Hank glanced up, saw two more somethings fly out, and dropped his head, braced for some explosions. As he stared into the roots of grass growing from the mud-dirt, his mind recognized the flying objects. They were AKs!

Hank took the handset from Tucker and radioed "cease fire" to Martin. He and Tucker then started yelling a duet of "Cease fire! Cease fire!" to Burlop's squad.

In one minute the firing tapered off. Everyone remained down. After another thirty seconds, the hush was snapped by shouts from inside the hooch of "*Chieu Hoi! Chieu Hoi!*" The surrenderers were offering themselves up under the open arms program.

A sun-bleached, bullet riddled door slowly swung open, hinges squeaking. Two trembling Viet Cong, their torn green T-shirts and black shorts splotched with blood, hobbled out, their eyes wide with fear, their hands on their head.

Hank looked into the ditch where Burlop was busy skin diving for his rifle.

" Burlop, send three in the hooch. With extreme caution," Hank ordered.

"Ye…yessir," he sputtered. He jackknifed into one more dive and came up holding his M-16 high in a gesture of accomplishment. He clawed his way out, tapped two men on their shoulders, and the three trotted past the POWs and inside.

"Everything's secured," Burlop yelled. "Better send in Doc Fletcher. Got a wounded girl gook in here." Fletcher was with the support squad and hearing Burlop, came on the run. Hank and Tucker followed him inside.

The girl was in a far corner moaning deliriously. Her black pajamas soaked all over with blood.

It was a one-room hooch. Out the back door, lying face down, cut down by the covering squad was a VC who had not surrendered. Burlop, wearing a gleeful look, turned him over with his boot and wedged his Big Red One patch into the VC's mouth.

"Bravo Six, November Six, over."

"This is Bravo Six. What's your sitrep?"

"We got three POWs and one dead gook. Negative casualties."

"Negative casualties? Good show! We'll get a chopper in there for the POWs."

"Roger. Better make it a dust-off. One's a girl and she looks bad."

"Wilco, out."

Hank gave Tucker back his handset and took Wiley's. "Cloudy Day Forty-One, November Six. One dead gook and three live ones. Negative casualties, over."

"Forty-One here. Fucking' A man. Guess if you're going to be one, be a Big Red One. What'cha say?"

Hank didn't answer. He handed the handset to Wiley.

The platoon bivouacked for the night in a brick kiln under a large tin roof south of the assaulted hooch. A thunderstorm whipped around outside.

At 0200 hours, a series of distant explosions could be heard to the south and north. At 0215 hours, water began creeping up to floor elevation. At 0230 hours, no one slept; the water was up to their knees. The VC had blown holes in strategic dikes and had created a flood.

Morning found the water up to Hank's crotch, but it had leveled out. And there was good news. Alpha and the rest of Bravo had also been inundated and because of the scarcity of snorkel gear, the operation was being shortened. They would make their way to the Saigon River by the quickest, driest route to be picked up by amphibious landing craft.

CHAPTER 33

FOUR CHARTERED BUSES in convoy whisked incoming R and R personnel along toward the processing center at Sydney's Chevron Hotel. They peered curiously out the windows at the passing environs of this populous city. It was a strange relief to watch the hustle and bustle of a westernized atmosphere. Taxis, sedans, convertibles, and trucks passing, sputtering, and honking. Pedestrians rushing in the December Monday morning to their place of work, fretting about their jobs, their spouses, their lovers, the Christmas presents they had to buy. Not having to fret about night ambushes, incoming mortars, or ham and egg C-rations.

The collection of soldiers, sailors, and airmen gave long stares at the Australian birds—females. Shrill wolf whistles demonstrated their amazement and delight at the long, lithe bare thighs exhibited provocatively below their short mini-skirts which had just been emerging into the fashion world when they had set course for Nam.

After in-processing, Hank and Dick rode in a shuttle bus that stopped at different hotels. In the Kings Cross district, the Greenwich Village of Sydney, they hopped off at the Crest Hotel. It loomed straight and tall, and had been recommended by a sales clerk at the R and R clothing rental store where they had rented civvies. It was a moderately lavish hotel with garrulous bellhops in bright green uniforms. They checked in and got adjoining rooms on the fifth floor overlooking the Kings Cross intersection.

Exhausted from his pre-dawn travels, Hank threw his duffel bag in a corner and wearily plopped down on a sofa. A large inviting double bed beckoned from across the room. The old hay monster was calling, but Dick's booming voice chased it away.

"Let's get our bodies clean and jump into our civvies. We gotta see what kind of town this is," he yelled through the open door. "Those Aussie peacocks look like they're ready for a few big roosters. What'd ya say, Hank?"

"I'm all for the shower and town tour. But you can take care of the chicken coop by your lonesome," Hank shouted back.

"Hell, Hank! R and R and women go hand-in-hand. Like ying and yang. It's natural. Relieves the tensions of battle," he joked, then paused and his tone became more serious. "Sometimes you sound like you got shrapnel in the balls instead of the leg."

Dick was getting wound up for one of his dogmatic dissertations, so Hank cut him short. "Stow the lecture, my friend. Let's get cleaned up and hit the streets."

He peeled off his khakis and stepped into the shower. The hot, jetting spray felt good. The warm liquid beat on his head and cascaded over his body and he relished it. This was his first decent shower, even considering the 93rd Evac, in six months. Only the warm feel of Pam next to him could equal such exhilaration.

Regretfully, Hank turned it off and grabbed a towel. Still a little wet, he slowly shuffled over to his duffel, took out some clean underwear and put them on, followed by gray slacks and a blue, pin-striped shirt. As he was tucking in his shirt, Dick sauntered in wearing blue slacks and a white polo shirt that accented his massive chest and bulky shoulders. They had made the transition to civilian.

"Where to first?" Dick enquired.

"I heard Sydney has quite a zoo. Animals from all over the world plus a lot of indigenous types. Let's try there."

"Hmmm…" Dick pursed his lips and placed his hands on his hips. "All right," he exhaled. "We'll go watch the kangaroos hop around. But tonight we'll go nightclubbin' and do a little more than watch."

"Go ahead. That's fine with me."

They took the elevator down, went outside, and walked amidst the King's Cross crowd, wanting to blend in with the natives. Only their black military tie-shoes belied their true identity.

They asked directions from a businessman in a charcoal gray suit carrying a briefcase. He was extremely polite, recognizing them immediately as Americans, and concisely directed them with a refreshing Aussie accent.

They rode a series of buses to a small wharf on the choppy green waters of Sydney Harbor. The zoo lay on the opposite shore. They boarded a fifty-foot passenger ferry and in fifteen minutes were underway.

The old, wooden boat faced into a stiff, salty breeze and bobbed heavily in the white-capped waves. To the left, the massive span of the Sydney Harbor Bridge arched impressively across the harbor. To the right, the fledgling structure of the Sydney Opera House—still unfinished and millions in over-runs—magnificently showed its unique sail-like roofs.

The sound, the smell, the sights filled Hank with bitter-sweet nostalgia. He nearly felt content.

The evening was spent "low-life'n," as Dick called it. Dressed in sport coats and ties, they traveled from night club to night club.

At the Hawaiian Eye, Hank sat in a corner and slowly sipped a gin and tonic as he watched Dick cavorting on the dance floor with what seemed like a new girl with each dance. The loud band blared out songs that brought back memories of college, home—and Pam.

He sucked in a deep breath to get his nerve up and pushed the small table aside and came to his feet. Through squinting eyes, he surveyed the dimly lit room. Two girls sat alone across the floor. He wove his way over and asked what appeared to be the best looking for a dance. She nodded and he pulled back her chair as she bent to rise. They picked their way to the edge of the crowded floor filled with slowly swaying couples in strong embraces.

They two-stepped in stiff silence, the sweet fragrance of her perfume wafting to his nostrils.

The band switched to a rock tempo and they broke apart and began to move with rhythm. A few more dances flew by. The loud quick beats of the music had a sobering effect and when the band stopped he gentlemanly escorted her to her table, said thanks, and left, his heart wanting her name and number, his mind refusing to ask. Or was it the other way around?

He found Dick waiting at their table.

"This place is slowing down. Let's cut out and hit some place else."

"Okay with me," Hand consented.

At the next spot Hank switched to Jack Daniels with a splash. He downed them at a steady clip, one leading into another. He was quickly becoming numb. To his surprise his thoughts were no longer of home, and of Pam. They were of his platoon. Were they all right? There was supposed to be some kind of truce during the holidays. Maybe they would spend Christmas safely in Lai Khe.

The hour was late and they were tired. As they neared their hotel, they found King's Cross still swarming with nighttime activity.

"That sack's going to feel good," Hank let out a long sigh.

"It's also going to be damn lonely," Dick retorted irately.

They came to the wide doors of their hotel. Dick hesitated.

"Hell, Hank. The hour still seems young around here."

"Probably mostly hookers looking to squeeze a few extra bucks."

"Well I sure as hell ain't gonna pay for it. Vietnam, okay, I've got to. But not here. I don't plan to call it quits so soon."

"Soon? It's damn near three in the morning." Hank shook his head and shrugged. "Have it your way. I'm hitting the hay." He opened one of the double doors and entered the lobby, leaving Dick on the sidewalk.

Dick strolled casually along the side of the hotel. A chilling breeze suddenly stirred up behind him. It had the sweet, moist smell of rain. Lightning flashed, followed by a belch of thunder. Big, scattered drops began to plop around him, now and then splatting on his head.

Shit," he muttered under his breath. He quickly spun around, hunched his head between his shoulders, and hurried toward the hotel entrance.

As he started to go in, he glimpsed something flash by him on the wide, wet-splotched sidewalk. It was a pair of long, luscious legs, exposed by a miniskirt that seemed about navel high. He twisted his neck for a better look. He saw the face belonging to the legs glance over her shoulder to exchange looks. She was not alone, but with another girl and a short, bearded fellow. They ran from the rain across the street and into a sleazy looking dive.

Dick wheeled around and broke into a trot, dodging an on-rushing taxi. The rain began to fall in sheets as he reached the other side.

It was pitch dark inside. He could see nothing, but could not miss the loud sound of the band and a conglomeration of feet stomping with what was supposed to be music.

Someone tugged on his arm. "It's a dollar cover." The tugger's effeminate voice spoke up. Dick pulled out his wallet, groped for a bill, hoped it to be a dollar, and gave it to the tugger.

Cautiously he moved in. As if he had triggered an alarm, a purple strobe light began pulsating like a throbbing heart, off—on, off—on. During the flashes he glanced quickly around. He spotted her through gyrating couples who moved in discrete frames from the strobe effect. She sat at the bar watching.

He fought his way across the crowded floor, colliding every so often with moving bodies.

They came face to face. She had a long Aussie nose and big dark eyes. Her hair was parted in the middle and touched her shoulders. "Hello," Dick said and waited for her reply. She didn't. She glanced away toward the couple she was with.

It had been a long night. Dick was tired and frustrated and got to the point.

"Listen," he yelled above the noise. "I just got in to Sydney today and I'm lonely as hell. Why don't we go somewhere and talk and get to know one another?"

She turned back around and gazed into his eyes before taking him all in from head to toe. This scrutiny gave Dick some encouragement. He had half expected her to be insulted, stick up her nose, and stride her bitchy fanny away.

"Well…how about it?" he pressed.

"What did you have in mind?" Her viscous Aussie accent sounded sexy.

"I've gotta fifth of bourbon in my hotel room cross the street. What say we start on that?" His voice was a little shaky.

She pursed her lips and tilted her head in thought. Painfully anxious for her reply, Dick impatiently rubbed his hands tightly together.

Finally, she said, "Okay…but let me tell my friends."

Dick felt wonderfully astounded. In a blur, they were outside running to the hotel in the heavy downpour, going up the elevator, opening the door to his room. Once inside, he threw her a towel to dry her hair and then grabbed the fifth off the dressing table, unscrewed the cap, and poured two glasses. He tossed in some melting ice from the ice bucket he had filled on arrival and handed her a drink.

"Have a seat," he said and motioned to a small couch opposite the bed.

"My—you yanks don't waste time, do you?" she said after taking the glass and sitting down.

He sat down beside her. "Nope. Not when all you have is six days." He put his arm around her and tried to snuggle. She shied away.

"What's your name?" she asked.

So that was it. They had to be introduced first. "Dick. And yours?"

"Margie."

"Hello, Margie." Dick flashed what he hoped was a winning smile. There were a few moments of silence as they stared at each other.

"Are you in the Army?"

"Yeah."

"Vietnam?"

"Yeah."

"Seen any fighting?"

"Some."

"Ever kill anybody?"

"No," he lied.

She moved closer to him. He put both arms around her and hugged her tightly. They kissed one long, wet one. Dick's passion rapidly rose. And then she said something that was akin to spilling ice water on his balls.

"It'll be fifty dollars."

He jumped up in a rage. "You shitty bitch! Get the hell out of here!" He pointed with a trembling finger at the door.

She became frightened and flinched as she stood up. "May I use your bathroom first?" she asked meekly, a mouse up against the pouncing stare of an alley cat.

Dick merely nodded. Disgust and exasperation and disappointment all over his face.

He downed his drink in one gulp while she did her business. All the fervent expectations drained from his body. He was not actually mad, but hurt, beaten, dejected.

She ran out into the room and his jaw nearly unhinged. She was stark naked.

Bright midmorning sunlight slanted through the sliver in the curtains. Hank rolled over on his back and let out a groan of comfort, then swung his feet onto the soft carpet. He picked up his watch. It was 10:00 a.m.

With a sigh he got up, went to the bathroom, took a pleasingly long number one, and then showered and shaved. Despite a hangover headache he felt good. Today was Christmas Eve and tomorrow—tomorrow he would call Pam.

It was now 10:30. Time to pull Dick's hulk out of the sack. Not bothering to knock, he opened the adjoining door and strode in, ready to get Dick up and at 'em.

His forehead corrugated into deep ridges as his eyes widened when he glimpsed two rather large creamy white breasts that couldn't possibly be Dick's. He gave a protracted stare before spinning around and exiting.

Dick woke when the door closed. He crawled carefully over the sleeping girl, put on a pair of under-drawers, and entered Hank's room, easing the door shut.

"Why you sly fox," Hank said with a congratulatory grin as Dick rubbed the sleep from his eyes and shook the grogginess from his head. "I suppose you'll be occupied for the rest of the day and probably for the remainder of R and R."

Dick gave a smirking smile. "It would seem that way, wouldn't it?" But his smile faded and his voice became deep and serious. "However, that won't be the case."

Hank was baffled. "Why's that?"

"Have you ever screwed a wildcat?" Dick asked dourly.

"Can't say I have."

Dick lifted his head up and to the left, exposing an ugly quarter size hickey on his neck. Then he lazy-susaned around and displayed jagged rows of red streaks that were furrowed over his back.

Hank let out a low sympathetic whistle. "She tore you up bad."

"Bad! Hell, she massacred me!" Dick steamed. "After a half-year beating the goddamn bushes, I nearly get clawed to death by some wild beast that's part grizzly and part vampire." His tone then started to soften a bit. "Actually, she's a nice girl, but if I'm going back to Nam in one piece I'll have to send her on her way." He gave Hank a sneaky glance. "That is of course unless you want her."

"No thanks."

"It could be a Christmas present?"

"I don't think so."

"Okay. Have it your way. I'll have to go in there and tactfully tell her to get lost. She's a fine looking girl, though. Wish me luck."

"Roger that," Hank said as his big friend opened the adjoining door and shuffled reluctantly into the other room.

Dick skillfully managed to dump her and they spent the afternoon sightseeing in downtown Sydney: visiting stores, riding double-decker buses, and wistfully eyeing the short-skirted women.

That night it was more low-life'n. But Hank was even less a willing participant as he continuously daydreamed about tomorrow and his phone call.

Hank awoke, looked at the bedside clock. It was 9:30. Dick was probably still asleep and maybe not alone if that skinny girl he brought back to his room last night had decided to make it an all-nighter.

He showered and dressed and skipped down to breakfast. Afterwards he stepped out on the Sydney sidewalks and took in the warm Christmas morning sunshine. He toured the city's blocks till shortly before noon, then briskly strode back to the hotel.

He found Dick finally getting up—alone. "Merry Christmas," he greeted Dick who climbed sloth-like out of bed, letting out a long, exhausting sigh.

Hank grinned. "Get your big ass moving and let's get some lunch." He paused and then added, "Or in your case, breakfast. After which," his tone grew jubilantly loud and high as he spewed out the rest, "I'm going to call Pam."

"Like hell you will," Dick responded bluntly.

"What do you mean?" Hank shot back defensively, shaken by his friend's abruptness.

"Because there's something like fifteen or so hours difference. It's not even Christmas there."

Hank half closed his eyes, compressed his lips, and scratched his head. "Hmmm, maybe you're right. When should I call?"

"Call around one or two a.m. It'll be Christmas morning her time."

"I guess…I…will." Hank sounded like a deflating balloon. It wouldn't be his Christmas, but it would be hers. He'd just have make sure he wasn't low-life'n at that hour with Dick, nor sleeping.

"Hell, Hank. I think it would be better if you don't call."

"What do you mean, 'better?'" Hank gazed up at Dick with cold, suspecting eyes.

"I mean a number of things." There was a pause as Dick organized his thoughts. "Like for instance, how do you know Pam is home? She may be visiting friends. Did you say ahead of time that you would call from Australia?"

Hank sourly shook his head. "But she would probably think so. She's probably home."

"Maybe, maybe not. It's hard to figure about women. But regardless of what *might* be, I don't think you should call at all and I'll tell you why. Long distance phone calls are the worst means of communication, especially for you, Hank, because you're such a chronic worrier. First, you'll worry if she's not home. If she is home you'll worry because her voice will sound too low, or too loud, too sad or too happy, maybe even too normal. All of which will make you miserable because you'll either think that she can't live because of missing you or that she is getting along all right without you.

"In letters, if you forget to say something you can just scratch out another quick note, put it in an envelope and write free in the upper, right hand corner. Not so in a call from Australia.

"What's more, old buddy, you've survived six months without talking to Pam. You've conditioned yourself to it. If you talk to her now, you'll have to start all over again. Just drop her a post card. Tell her you love her. You've said everything that mattered before you left. Let's go out tonight and get dreadfully drunk, and be thankful we're alive."

Twisting his lips up in a weak smile, Hank gave his friend a long stare. He knew he was right. No matter what, if he talked to her now, he would feel more miserable than he did now.

"Goddamnit," he said softly. "Somehow that Kistlerian logic has gotten to me again…I'm going to get obnoxiously drunk tonight."

They both did.

CHAPTER 34

FOLLOWING THEIR RETURN to Vietnam, Hank and Dick decided on taking an extended stay in Camp Alpha, the staging area at Ton Son Nhat for R and R personnel. They spent four days there, drinking at the officer clubs, watching movies at night, welcoming in the year, 1969. Technically, they were AWOL, and so they brainstormed a potpourri of lame excuses for when they reached the Battalion: lack of available transportation, sickness, enemy activity, and of course, the Army bureaucracy.

So Hank and Dick returned to Lai Khe four days after New Year's. Once in the Battalion area, they departed, agreeing to rendezvous later at the Battalion's O'club.

With duffel bag balanced on his shoulder, Hank walked to the A-framed wooden structure that was Bravo's orderly room. Inside, he was met with the unexpected gathering of the company's officers and first sergeant.

Captain Torrance sat in a retread swivel chair, his legs crossed on top of an old gun-metal desk recycled from some government agency. "'Bout time you got back," he said with a stoic face "We were beginning to think you were hiding away in the Australian bush."

Hank answered with a sheepish smile and nodded a hello to the others. Brussels and Howard sat on opposite ends of the desk. Sawyer and Mendez were on folding chairs. The scene was reminiscent of the meeting before Loc Ninh. He hoped this was only a bull session.

He decided not to respond to the CO's mention of his tardiness. All of his concocted excuses now seemed just that…concocted. He asked a question as a tactical diversion. "What's happening? I expected to find only Lieutenant Brussels shacked up with some hooch girl."

"We decided if Lieutenant Kirby can take a vacation, we all can," the first sergeant said.

"That's right," Torrance confirmed. "Bravo has been given stand-down for about a week to work on our rear area. It's dirty from neglect and equipment is strewn all over the place. The colonel wants it ready for the upcoming IG inspection."

"No shit," was all Hank could think to say.

"We wouldn't shit you. You're our favorite turd," Brussels added in his tactless, hackneyed drawl. Others either forced a laugh or a smile, embarrassed at the tension between them.

Torrance turned his smile into a frown. "I'm afraid something serious has come up, Hank."

Hank flinched. "It's about my platoon?"

"No, not that. They're fine. Everyone's fine. No action since you've been gone. This matter concerns only you." Torrance paused to add emphasis to the seriousness. "Tell my jeep driver to take you over to brigade headquarters. Go to the TOC and tell them you're Lieutenant Kirby from Bravo, Third of the Thirteenth."

"What the hell for?" Hank raised his voice and eyebrows. In the back of his mind a worry of the discovery of his AWOL.

"I'm not at liberty to say," Torrance said, his face grim. "My jeep and driver are right outside. Better go and take care of this thing ASAP."

Hank glanced around the room, meeting a barrage of cold stares. He swung around quickly, heaved his duffel bag into a corner, and bounded from the room. Outside, he found the driver and urgently spewed out his destination. As the vehicle scratched away, a roar of laughter blasted from the orderly room.

Third Brigade headquarters was housed in an abandoned French entomological research complex, used long ago for the biological analysis of mosquitoes. The complex consisted of two long, narrow, parallel buildings connected by three short corridors. Each building was of white brick and faded red barrel shingles. One end of the first building contained the Brigade Commander and his S-3 offices. Between them, wooden stairs descended far below the floor, down into an underground installation that was the Brigade's tactical operations center, the TOC.

After great effort of asking directions, Hank arrived and glanced nervously around, shivering slightly from the blast of the air conditioning. He went on a quick abbreviated look-see of the huge bunker complex. Bright fluorescent lighting flooded a busy arena. A long table, set flush against a plywood wall, stretched halfway across the far side of the room. Five radios, some carrying typical commo traffic, others hissing rushing noise, rested heavily on the table. A quarter-inch plywood partition intercepted the end of the table and separated it from another smaller table that held one huge radio operated by an air force NCO. On the opposite side of the room, two offices were partitioned off. Between the offices and long table, a narrow passageway led into another room wallpapered with large maps with multi-colored grease pencil markings and symbols on an acetate overlay.

Men in freshly cleaned jungle fatigues busily worked. The blare of the radios and rapid fluttering of tongues wove together an incoherent rumbling.

Hank returned to the bottom of the stairs, taking it all in, not knowing who to interrupt, not knowing who he was supposed to see. Finally, a familiar figure came out of one of the offices.

It was Captain Connors.

Hank addressed his old company commander, "Sir, it's good to see you." He produced his hand and Connors took it. "Captain Torrance told me to come down here. He said I'm in some kind of trouble. Maybe you might know something about it?"

Connors' smile befuddled Hank. "You're not in trouble. He is!" Connors' voice was loud in trying to compete with the cacophony from the radios.

"Huh?"

"Torrance is going to lose his most experienced platoon leader," Connors said and then asked with a sober face, "Hank, how would you like to spend your remaining tour working down here with me?"

Hank looked as if he had been lashed with a high voltage electrical wire. Then he narrowed his eyes in suspicion, waiting for the catch.

Connors went on, filling the gap that had been reserved for Hank's reply. "I realize the seventy-two degree temperature might be a little uncomfortable for a boonie-stomper. And of course the ten feet of overhead cover, mostly reinforced concrete, might cause a claustrophobic to long for the wide open rice paddies."

Hank was finally able to talk. "Hell! I'd polish boots and kiss ass day and night to stay down here."

"It won't have to come to that, but it won't be any R and R either. Let's sit down and I'll tell you 'bout it." Connors guided Hank into his office and sat behind a paper cluttered desk. He beckoned for Hank to sit down in a chair opposite his desk.

"Okay," Connors began, "here's the sitrep." Hank's ears were like directional antennas tuned in to Connors' net. "As you know, I'm the Brigade Assistant S-3. My boss, the S-3, is Major Duncan, and this TOC is our baby. Three duty officers work down here, each one on an eight-hour shift. That's where you come in, Hank. I've lost a duty officer for reasons I won't get into. I've recommended you to Major Duncan as his replacement. He, in turn, contacted Colonel West, who said we can have you, providing you want the job. I'm sure he doesn't want to lose a platoon leader and I know Torrance has probably got a case of the ass, but one more Third of the Thirteenth man at Brigade level might give them a break now and then. So they'll go along with it." He looked into Hank's eyes. "Well, what do you think?"

Hank rapped his knuckles on the desk. "Sounds too good. Tell me more."

"Your official title will be Liaison Officer, LO. You'll work some with the S-2 section, which has their operation in the connecting bunker. You'll also coordinate operations with the artillery LO, and with the Air Force."

"Air Force?" Hank interrupted. "I saw one of their sergeants working behind an overgrown radio and wondered what the hell he was doing."

"He has radio contact with the FACs. All requests for TAC air come from the Battalions to us. We get the fighters up in the air and an Air Force FAC puts in the strikes. We have a unit of six pilots attached to the Brigade, plus the NCOs who operate the multi-frequency radio down here. But don't worry too much about it, that's mostly our S-3 Air's headache."

Hank nodded as Captain Connors continued. "Now your primary responsibility will be keeping a close watch on our battalions. In effect, you'll be a glorified RTO, always monitoring the nets of the Battalion's and the Division's. The battalions will be asking us for support all the time, dust-offs, light fire teams, hunter-killer teams, scout dogs, artillery, TAC air, you name it. Of course, they can't always get what they want, when they want it. But we try to accommodate them if possible. Sometimes it gets pretty damn hectic down here weighing priorities.

"There's also the daily convoy from Di An to Quan Loi up the Thunders. We have to worry about that while it passes through our TAOR. Also, when there's something big happening, the Division is always nagging us for a si-trep, but don't blow your cool like telling 'em to go to hell, you're too busy. Just give the bastards something to hold them for a while, even if it's vague.

"An important item is keeping the map of the Brigade's TAOR up to date with all friendly locations, B-52 grids, free fire zones, and such. Always keep up to date on every situation. If the colonel or major comes down here or calls on the radio, make sure you have the answer to any questions." Connors glanced at his watch. "Still want the job?"

"You bet I do."

"Real fine, Hank. You report down here day after tomorrow, but you'll move into a Brigade billet late tomorrow evening. The other two duty of-ficers have been doing twelve-hour shifts. You'll be a welcomed addition. That'll continue for a little while as you'll need time with them for OJT in-doctrination. Any questions?"

"Can't think of any at the moment," Hank smiled.

"Okay then, get with the Brigade S-1 tomorrow when you report. He'll get you situated." Connors came out of his chair. Hank followed and they shook hands. "I'd show you around the TOC but I've got to meet with the brass in about zero-one.

"Yessir. Thanks, Captain Connors. See you soon."

Outside the jeep was waiting. While the vehicle sped back to the com-pany, a reflective smile dominated Hank Kirby's face. He was getting out of the field, becoming a remf, a "rear echelon motherfucker." His first impulse was to scratch out a quick letter about his good fortune to Pam. But to Pam, he had always been a remf. He couldn't chance his credibility by now telling her the truth, especially now the way her mood was.

He didn't wait for the jeep to stop before hopping out and dashing into the orderly room. It was empty. They were probably at the O'club. Hell, they could wait. Besides, they already knew. He strode quickly out of the orderly room and over to his platoon's A-framed billet. The Third Platoon's quarters contained only Franklin and Tucker. They were sitting on air mat-tresses. Tucker was concentrating heavily on a letter he was composing. Franklin was meticulously inspecting both M-60s.

Hank stepped inside, banging the screen door behind him. "Where's ev-erybody?" He tried to boom his voice like Kistler and then he grinned.

They looked up, immediately caught Hank's grin, and stood up.

"Welcome back, sir, and Happy New Year," Tucker said.

"How was Australia?" asked Franklin.

"Great! Wonderful people. Wonderful country. Only wish I could have stayed longer. And Happy New Year to my two favorite soldiers," Hank said effusively. He was nearly giddy. He glanced around. "Where's the rest of you guys?"

"Steam baths or clubs," Tucker answered.

"Round them up. I've got some big news. Hank pulled out his wallet and counted out three-fourths of its contents, thirty dollars MPC and his ration card. "I've got a mission for you," he said to Franklin, giving him the money and the card. "Round up a few of the men, go to the PX and buy all the beer this will buy. Then get some ice from the mess sergeant and pack it down. We're going to have a platoon party tonight."

"Party? What for? New Year's over." Franklin was puzzled but excited.

"New Year's, hell! We're celebrating your platoon leader's debut into the world of the remf," Hank winked. "I'm going to Brigade tomorrow to work in the TOC. I'll be working for Captain Connors, soft liaison job," he said elatedly, his face beaming. Then his face suddenly lost its emotion. This was good news for him. Not for them.

"Fuckin' A, man! That's great news, sir," Tucker responded.

"Damn right it is!" Franklin echoed. "I'll get the guys together. We need to party." He scooped up a shirt from his air mattress, and headed out, putting on the shirt as he went.

Hank and Tucker stared at each other. They had been a team, a twosome, through what had been the worst days of their lives. Tucker had been there when Hank arrived. Tucker would be there when he left.

Their exuberance had faded when finally Tucker spoke. Hank knew as he opened his mouth what he'd say. "I ain't lookin' forward to a new platoon leader. Sergeant Martin will do all right for a while, but before long some gung-ho son-of-a-bitch fresh out of Ranger school will come along. I'm gettin' too short for that, sir. Only four more months."

"Don't worry," he said, taking great effort in holding his voice from cracking. "Things will work out. Maybe…maybe I can do something. I don't know." Their conversation seemed rolling toward a precipice. Hank tried to reverse it. "How's your wife getting along?"

"Pretty good. Baby's due anytime now. I may even be a father and not even know it."

"If you are, you'll know real soon. The Red Cross lets people know those kinds of things in a hurry. Well listen, I'm going over to the Battalion O'club now. I'll see you tonight."

"Roger that, sir," Tucker smiled. "But don't get too shit-faced."

Catcalls of "lucky bastard," "remf," and "pansy-ass" were fired on automatic as Hank came through the doorway. All of the officers of Bravo were present and accounted for along with Dick, Captain Lawson, the S-1, and three captains whom Hank didn't recognize.

"Buy us a round!" Brussels shouted over the others.

Hank readily nodded and advanced to the bar to inform the spec-four bartender to put the drinks on his tab, forgetting he gave his money to Franklin. Dick sat casually at the bar and dropped his massive hand on Hank's shoulder.

"I knew it was just a matter of time before Connors grabbed you," he said. "Now you can line me up with a job. The Brigade TOC ain't a bad layout."

"It sure ain't," agreed Hank, climbing on an adjacent stool. "I'll see what I can do. I promise."

"Good enough, fella."

"Say, Dick…speaking of favors, maybe you could help me. You know pretty much what's going on back here in the Battalion rear area," Hank whispered, shielding the conversation from others. "My RTO, Tucker, he's been in the field eight months. He's good, damn good man. Got a wife that's expecting, any day now. He deserves a break. Know what I mean? I was wonderin' if we could find him a job back here."

Dick stared at his beer, rotating the can with both hands. His eyes widened and brow furrowed. "Yeah, come to think of it, we might work something out. One of the mail clerks I know's gettin' short. I might be able to swing Tucker in his slot, but we'll have to have your CO's blessing."

"Captain Torrance, huh? I think he'd do it. I'll go ask him." Hank slid off the stool and faced Dick. "I almost forgot. There's going to be a little celebration tonight with my platoon. How about stopping by for a few? Just don't bring your boss, Captain Woodson."

"Heh, heh," Dick laughed, "I'll be there. And minus Woodson. Only it's Major Woodson, now. I found out when I reported in today. He's supposed to be comin' here tomorrow for a shit, shower, and shave, and then escort me out to the Battalion's new fire support base."

"Hell," snarled Hank, "why can't the bastard shower out there like everybody else?" Then he asked, "Say, where is it anyway? Not that I'll ever see it."

"Somewhere out near the Trapezoid. Alpha worked on it over the holiday's stand-down. Kept them sober and out of trouble. They named it Condor and stocked it with a battery of 105s."

Hank slapped Dick on the back. "Well, I'll catch you later," he said and moved to the table where the officers of Bravo were seated.

Sawyer pulled up a chair for him, but he politely waved it aside and addressed the CO. "Sir, may I have a word with you, alone, for a short moment, please." He pointed to an empty table in a corner.

Torrance gave a puzzled smile, "Sure Hank."

He shifted over to the empty table…Sitting down, he said, "Understand you'll be reporting to the Brigade tomorrow, late afternoon."

"Roger that, sir," Hank answered. His eyes stared off in space as he pondered how best to put his question. He figured Torrance to be in a good mood, perhaps from the beer, perhaps from being able to have a beer. The club was infinitely better than any place else to be. "It's about my RTO, Tucker. As you know, sir, he's a good soldier."

"I know. I know," Torrance nodded, "I plan to have him as one of my own RTOs."

Hank became momentarily rattled. His eyes retreated from space and found Torrance's and held them. "Sir, I'm hoping you'll reconsider that. There's an opening coming up at Battalion for a mail clerk. The S-3 Air thinks Tucker has a shot at it and he needs your okay before he starts lobbying," Hank said. He tried to have the right mixture in his voice, a little pleading, a touch of strength, a bit of reason. "Tucker has only four months left. His wife's nine-months pregnant. He needs a favor. He deserves a favor."

The CO rubbed his chin carefully. "Hmmm," he murmured lightly, "Maybe you're right, Hank. Tell you what. I'll mull it over."

"Thanks, sir. That's all I ask."

"In the meantime, though, I've got one more mission for you."

"What's that?" An ominous feeling sneaked inside Hank's gut.

"Major Woodson has directed our company to serve as a Ready Reaction Force. We need one platoon to be at the helipad all day in case needed by the Brigade. I want your platoon to do it tomorrow. The others will be busy working in the company area and they'll get their chance the next two days. After that, it will be it for your career with Bravo. We'll send you to Brigade right after you return from the helipad"

"But what if something happens? I've got to report to the TOC for duty day after tomorrow," Hank countered.

"Don't worry, Hank. Nine times out of ten an RRF hangs around with its thumb up its ass. Nothing's been happening in the Brigade's AO. All you'll wind up doing will be sitting on your ass recovering from a hangover. Hell, take a good book with you."

CHAPTER 35

P AM FINISHED THE tedious ritual of applying makeup and stared in the mirror, critiquing the results. It was a good job. A mask of beauty. It was the best she had looked since Hank had gone.

The doorbell rang, and she heard her father stirring and then voices of an excited greeting. She pushed up her hair from her shoulders and watched it fall back, bouncing firmly from the invisible springs of a new permanent. Her stomach churned nervously with guilt. But she wouldn't be doing this if it hadn't been for Hank's letters. It was that, but it was something else too, and that was the primary source of the guilt. She was bored!

She slid the chair back and stood up, keeping her eyes on the mirror of her dressing table. She admired her dress, a simple, yet sexy, soft green shift that reached down to mid-thigh. She knew she looked quite attractive and as she started to open her door, she closed her eyes and wished that everything had been some sort of bad dream and that waiting for her in the living room would be Hank.

Dave Watson came to his feet as she walked in. His eyes sparkled with the recognition of her beauty. Her father leaned forward in his overstuffed chair, his face beaming with unrestrained delight. Her mother sat in a rocking chair across the room and smiled warmly. There was a brief exchange of pleasantries all around, and then the commotion of leaving.

Five minutes later, she and Dave were speeding toward Cocoa Beach in his royal blue, Mustang convertible, the top down, exposing the snow-white interior.

It was hard to carry a conversation with the harsh rushing sound created by the jets of wind that swept through the car. Pam regretted not bringing a scarf. She gazed over at Dave. He wore a blue sport shirt and white slacks that blended with the upholstery. The muscle fibers in his forearms stood out like hard ropes. Even the sharp outline of his high cheekbones and the tight, seemingly perennial smile on his lips looked muscular. He had a certain rugged handsomeness, regardless of his crooked nose that had survived so many breaks. She had not recognized this before. Well, maybe she had when they had dated at Gainesville.

Dave could feel her eyes, but pretended not to, and kept his eyes ahead on the stretch of road illuminated by the headlights. His mind was not with his eyes and turned over again, much like the repetitive plays of football practice, his much thought out game plan.

His objective, of course, was to fuck her. The thought of this had lived continuously in his mind since the phone call from her father. It had, he hated to admit, even let it upset his concentration on the practice field. But now the season was over and next year his thoughts would be of this victory, one more notch. And what a good notch. The memory would be an after practice indulgence to help relax his mind as well as his battered body.

His game plan was hatched from a general marketing course he had taken as an elective. He had even made a C+ which was why he felt comfortable in using one of its fundamentals; know your consumer behavior.

He felt he knew the tickings of Pam. He silently went over the data: she would be turned off by a hurry pop-it-to-her approach; she wanted a closer relationship, the boy/girlfriend type that she and Kirby had had; she was smart, and a man's athletic prowess, unlike many women, did not turn her on, rather she liked the more intellectual stuff, like talking about why are we here and how does life fit together with the phases of the moon and all that shit. She was also probably horny and maybe he would have the advantage of a rebounding effect.

He also had had an elective in drama and that was where his plan would really jive. He would act out a scenario, much like having his own screenplay. He would ad lib and all that shit, making up what he didn't know. He also would use patience, now that might be difficult, he thought, though it was now the off-season and he had no plans to do anything much. If she didn't want to fuck tonight, he would take it in stride. He would impress her with his gentlemanliness; he could wait a little while. A strong ground game that moved slowly, but steadily, toward the goal line was needed, and he would be the one carrying the ball for the score. Or should he say balls?

He chuckled to himself.

Five hours later they were heading back along the same highway, away from Cocoa Beach, toward Merritt Island, with top up.

It had been a good evening, reflected Pam, watching the high beams clearing out the road ahead. It started with miniature golf as they bided time for the show to start. Then it was an enjoyable, scary couple of hours with *Rosemary's Baby*, followed by dancing at a crowded club with a loud, no talent band.

Dave had changed. Had he mellowed? No, that wasn't the word. Matured, that was it. He no longer talked incessantly of his own exploits, his ego fueling boasts about his greatness. Professional football had had a good effect on Dave. The Army and Vietnam had acted in an opposite way on Hank. It was paradoxical, and it was too bad.

Her only tense moment tonight came when he had suggested parking at the beach. She had given him a firm no and she had waited, cringed, for his vituperation. But he merely shrugged and said how he respected her wishes. She could hardly believe his tame reaction! What's more he had asked her *first* about parking. Normally he would just do it and then start from there with the wrestling match.

The car coasted to a stop outside her home, differentiated from the other houses by a lighted porch light. Dave cut the engine, opened his door, and swept around the other side to help her out. They held hands, their first physical contact of the night, as he walked her to the front door.

"I hope you had a good time?" Dave asked, his voice a whisper of sincerity.

"It was a lovely time, Dave."

"Say, how would you like to be my date at the Super Bowl, two weeks from Sunday?"

"The Super Bowl?"

"Yeah, the Jets and the Colts in the Orange Bowl. I got tickets through the Dolphins front office. I don't care what nobody says, the Jets are gonna take 'em, you know. Joe Willie will be too much. Just wait."

"But won't the drive be too much? From Miami to Merritt Island to get me and then back to Miami and back to Merritt Island. You'll spend the entire time on the road."

He stared at her for a moment and Pam's suspicions resurfaced. He would probably want her to spend the night with her in Miami.

"Well actually, Pam. I'm going to be living in Cocoa Beach during the off-season…"

"You are?"

"Yeah, at the apartment of a fraternity brother of mine. So that will knock off two legs back and forth to Miami. You know, we can leave in the morning and be back late in the evening."

"That…that sounds like it might be fun."

"It will. Believe me it will. I'll even introduce you to a few of my teammates. We've got a second-year quarterback who's going to be damn good, you know, Bob Griese."

"Yes. I know. Dad says he's going to be all pro someday."

They stood by the front door facing each other, their eyes searching. She felt the firm pressure of his thumb as it rubbed feverishly back and forth over the back of her hand. He came down to her and kissed her hard. His tongue fought to penetrate her lips. There was a moment of resistance and then none, as it broke through and found the wet cavity of her mouth and rubbed against inside, just as his thumb rubbed her hand.

He swallowed her with his arms, pressing his body into hers, ensuring that she felt his hardness on her pelvis. Pam experienced a moment of panic, pushed back, and somehow squeezed out of his arms.

"Please Dave…don't. This is too much…I can't get into this kind of thing. At least not now."

"Sorry, Pam. I got carried away with a beautiful girl in my arms. We're still on for the Super Bowl, huh? I'll be good. I promise."

"We're still on," Pam said and rocked forward on her toes and pulled Dave down to peck his cheek.

CHAPTER 36

T HE THIRD PLATOON languidly stretched themselves among weapons and battle gear underneath the shade of rubber trees and beside a long strip of gray asphalt serving as a helipad. They were quiet and moved sloth-like from last night's celebration. It had been a good, drunken party.

Hank was sprawled out in shade at the base of a rubber tree. His back was propped against the bundle of his equipment harness with its attached web belt and all its bulky accouterments: two ammo pouches crammed with eighteen-round magazines, four smoke grenades, three filled water canteens, one canteen cover with three hand grenades, and one first aid packet containing a square compress with gauze bandage strips. A set of field glasses in its tan shoulder strap carrying case was next to him. His M-16 was behind him up against the tree.

Surprisingly, he felt no discomfort from this masochistic mattress. The pain was all directed to his forehead where a ball pein hammer of a hangover pounded unmercifully.

A deuce-and-a-half brought them a hot lunch. Hank's head and sensitized stomach prevented him from partaking, save for a half pint of milk. God, he felt bad. Even so, he fished out a small notepad from his breast pocket and began a letter to Pam. It was the usual, telling her he still loved her and hoping she would write him the same.

After finishing, he started thinking about the end of the day. He would return with his platoon to the company area, turn in his rifle and field gear, use the landline in the orderly room to call the office of the First Brigade S-1, who would send a jeep to shuttle him over to the S-1 office. He'd do some paperwork, be assigned quarters, eat in the Brigade's mess and show up for duty in the TOC at 0700.

His thoughts were interrupted by two jeeps that suddenly appeared as if in a stock car race, one tailgating the other, kicking up a cloud of dust as they barreled along the road opposite the helipad. The dust was a fine grayish-white, dirt talcum, a sign the dry season had set in. The lead vehicle cut sharply to the right, across the pad and toward the platoon. The second vehicle stayed on its rear bumper.

Despite his debilitated state, Hank jumped to his feet as he noticed the man in the front passenger seat. It was Woodson! Behind him in the rear seat was Dick with rolled maps locked in the V of his armpit, his lips drawn and cheeks taut. The second jeep had Torrance and Sawyer.

The lead jeep skidded to a halt. The trailing vehicle swerved to avoid colliding and braked heavily. Woodson grabbed the top of the windshield and hoisted himself from the seat.

"Where's the platoon leader?" Major Woodson shouted as he put on his helmet. Someone pointed to Hank who was now walking slowly forward so as to minimize the vibration to his head. "Get your ass over here, Kirby!" Woodson barked. "Your lift ships will be here in one-five."

Everything was happening too fast. Hank needed time to get his mind straight. Dick shoved a map under his arm. Torrance and Sawyer scampered over to Woodson's jeep. Snatching a map from Dick, Woodson unfolded it on the hood in front of Hank.

"Right here," said Woodson, pointing with his right index finger to a grid square. Hank gazed blankly at the map, a dizziness spinning inside him. "That's where you'll be inserted. You've got five slicks coming."

"What happened?" Hank reacted gruffly, upset by the urgency.

The major spoke in a harsh, low tone. "A re-supply hook heading back from a fire base briefly sighted what they think was an NVA company. We've put in gunships and air strikes on the suspected location. Now Bravo is to be inserted for a BDA."

Hank's lips formed a wry smile and he turned toward his commanding officer. Surely the CO wouldn't let him go on this mission. He was leaving the company, going to Brigade as a liaison officer.

Torrance's next words dispelled any optimism. "Hank, your platoon will secure the LZ. The rest of the company is getting packed up and will be trucked over here. I'll be in the second wave with the First Platoon. The landing zone is marked on your map. Get your platoon ready ASAP for your birds."

Hank's mind started to race, to oil the alcohol corrosion of his brain cells, to search for something he could say to get him out of this. He found nothing.

Tucker rounded up Sergeant Martin and the squad leaders and then Hank issued the order to immediately prepare for the arrival of the lift ships. With much griping and cursing, the platoon gathered in five groups, thirty meters apart, to wait.

Dick monitored the radio in the jeep for the five sorties to come on station. As he heard the voice of the flight commander, he signaled Hank, who, in turn, waved for the lead group to pop smoke. Like pelicans in a trail formation, the five dull green helicopters swooped down.

CHAPTER 37

ARTILLERY SHELLS PREPPED the LZ, numbing it like multiple shots of Novocain. As the choppers circled the northern edge, Hank searched through the dark gray puffs to compare the terrain with the map that he pressed tightly against his lap. The map said a meadow. Hank's eyes staring down 500 feet put knee-high grass into the meadow.

On the map the meadow was branded by a huge Y, the fork of a stream. On the ground the stream was nearly dry. Both map and eyes agreed on thick, brownish-green jungle encroaching on the meadow.

Glancing between map and LZ became too much for Hank. Clutching the bench-seat he stuck his head out the open door and puked. His stomach contents were sprayed back by the air current, hitting the door gunner behind him who immediately started fidgeting all around, shaking his fist, and mouthing obscenities at Hank that were drowned by the loud, staccato drone of the spinning rotor blades.

The vomiting had a benefit, not to the door gunner, but to Hank. It made him feel better.

The choppers dropped down like dipping cars of a roller coaster, broke into their Christmas tree formation and landed. When the skids touched down, Hank hesitated. A strange notion whirled in his head. What if he stayed on board? In a few seconds the chopper would be taking off, heading back to Lai Khe. But he had an end seat, the exit side, and the momentum from the others clambering to disembark carried him out before his strange notion developed into a decision.

He found himself wedged in a small 155 shell crater with Franklin, Doc Fletcher, Tucker, and Romero, his pace man. He heard Tucker speak into the handset. "Demon Six, this is Bravo Six Kilo. LZ cold, LZ cold."

He heard the Battalion Commander's reply coming through the earpiece like a muffled broadcast from a transistor radio. "This is Demon Six. Roger. Cease smoke. Have lead element standby to pop smoke for following sorties."

Tucker wilcoed Demon Six and then notified in turn three groups by radio and the radio-less group by arm signal. Tucker had taken care of everything. A well-oiled soldier, a platoon leader's right arm.

Hank peered from the crater. He could see the west fork of the stream twenty meters away.

The platoon remained dispersed into its five groups and remained motionless, obscured in the grass, waiting for the next five slicks. Only Hank showed life as he folded his map, placed it in his leg pocket, and took the handset from Tucker. As if responding to his touch, the handset emitted the Battalion CO's voice. "Bravo November, this is Demon Six. Pop smoke for lead ship."

"Wilco," Hank replied. "Break. November Papa, November Six, pop smoke."

A belch of flame from a tossed can followed by streaming violet smoke acknowledged Hank's transmission.

Five slicks escalatored down from the north and headed for the LZ in trail formation. Just as their skids grazed the top of the long grass, a thunderstorm of automatic weapons fire burst forth.

"LZ HOT! LZ HOT!" Hank screamed into the radio as he desperately battled the other four occupants of the crater for rights to the bottom of its epicenter.

Without unloading their passengers, the choppers pushed to full throttle and slanted upward. The third ship had taken the brunt of the fire and limped slowly along, tenaciously trying to remain airborne. Eyes of the Third Platoon gazed up at the wounded slick, waiting for it to sputter and fall, praying for it to keep going, get higher, get the hell away. The wait gave way to prayers and the crippled chopper gained altitude and followed the others out of the LZ.

"Bravo Six, this is November Six, over! Bravo Six, November Six, over!" Hank shouted into the mouthpiece with alarm. It had been Bravo Six's ship!

There was a quiet pause; the automatic weapons fire had vanished with the same suddenness as its arrival. Then a break in the rushing noise from the handset.

Someone was keying the net. Then a crackling sound. Someone was going to transmit. A weak voice, its tone laced with pain, came slowly through the receiver. "This…is Bravo Six…we…we caught a few rounds. Should make it… back to Lai Khe…Caught one in the back…Looks like your show…Hank."

"Roger," Hank gulped and was reminded of the sour taste of vomit lingering in his mouth.

"November Six, Demon Six," the Battalion Commander's voice cut in. Pop smoke on your east flank. We're bringing in gunships. Those bastards are somewhere around there."

"This is November Six. Wilco." Hank then called Sergeant Martin over on the east flank. "November Five, November Six. Did you spot the source?"

"We got a rough fix."

"Roger. Pop smoke and when the gunships come on station give them an azimuth and a distance."

"Roger that." Sergeant Martin's voice came through calm and matter of fact.

Two Cobra gunships began working in tandem. One started down in its run, cut loose with two rockets that played out a jagged trail of white smoke until exploding on impact in the jungle, then tracers streaming from a burst of its miniguns followed the rocket trails, pouring out a huge quantity of lead before reaching the bottom of its run and heading up on a reverse slant. When it banked to start its circle for a repeat, the second Cobra came in and did an imitation of the first.

Hank watched the first set of runs, then settled down in the hole, his back against the side, the accouterments of his harness digging into his kidneys. The pungent smell of hot, sweating men stuck in his nostrils. He kept the handset to his ear; the cord stretched three feet from the other side of the hole where Tucker had ended up. He and Tucker stared at each other. Fletcher stared back and forth at both of them. Franklin and Romero kept their heads up, looking out as security.

Wham! Wham!

Hank slid six inches further down. Franklin and Romero dropped their heads back into the hole. Goddamn those fucking rockets sound close, Hank's mind muttered to himself. What the hell those gunships doing? Wham! Wham! Hank shuddered. Those weren't gunship rockets! They were being mortared!

Eighty-two's pelted the LZ. All they could do was huddle in the hole. Hank wondered about the rest of the platoon. How many had shell craters to hide in? What if a mortar shell landed in one? What if one landed in his!

After twenty seconds, a very long twenty seconds, the mortaring stopped. Hank thought he had counted eight rounds, plus or minus.

There was a moment of silence before the handset came screechingly alive in his hand. "November Six, November Two," Sergeant Michael spoke frantically. "Goldie's dead! Foster and Bosa are hurt real bad! Need help fast! Need Doc!"

"Roger! Hang on!" Hank answered with equal frenzy. He put his hand on Fletcher's shoulder, took it off, and pointed to the right, where Michael's group was a little less than sixty meters away. Their eyes met briefly and he nodded, grabbed the strap of his first aid satchel, and crouching low, sprung out of the hole toward Michael's position, thinking that the mortaring would start again when he was running in the open.

"Demon Six, November Six, over."

"Demon Six. I've ordered TAC air. The gunships aren't enough. We couldn't get a fix on their 82s."

Hank waited with the frustrated impatience of a child for the Battalion CO to conclude transmitting. Why was he talking? Hank had initiated the commo. His impatience had drowned out every word the colonel said. All he heard was the rushing noise which meant the airway was finally free.

He pushed the talk button. "We need an urgent dust-off! Two WIAs, critical…one…" His throat constricted. It stopped him from talking. He cleared it with coughing. "One KIA. Get it here ASAP. We can't stay in our LZ much longer. Got to get into the jungle before another barrage."

Colonel West's reply was placid, almost gentle. "Roger. Understand problem. Pop smoke for dust-off."

"Wilco," Hank said and immediately relayed the command to Michael, who had monitored and yellow smoke was bellowing before Hank said his "out."

Hank was astounded that a dust-off was already coming in. Then he saw why. A Huey clattered in fast, descending amidst the smoke. It was minus its red cross. It was the colonel's C&C ship!

Lieutenant Colonel West and newly made Major Woodson and an Artillery liaison captain scurried from the chopper, its skids hovering a few feet from the grass. The smoke diffused rapidly and Hank could clearly witness the rescue.

West and the captain carried a heavily weighted poncho. As they reached the chopper a door gunner hopped out and helped lift the load aboard. Hank saw a blood-soaked arm hanging out. Following them, Fletcher, Michael, and one other struggled with another heavy poncho. Bringing up the rear, with two boots protruding from his armpits, Woodson dragged the KIA like a plow horse. The toes of the boots pointed down. Woodson was dragging Goldie, the dead Kit Carson scout, face down.

Hank was pissed. His mind pictured Goldie's nose furrowing the soil, the nostrils clogged with dirt. Suppose, just suppose, Hank reasoned, that Michael had been wrong. Suppose he hadn't been dead!

The rotor blades spun into a blur and the chopper rose six feet, then set off at an angle, using the length of the clearing to gain speed and altitude. It passed over Hank who instinctively gave a thumbs-up gesture. Someone must have seen it because a thumbs-up fist was thrust out the open door.

Hank turned his attention from the chopper to the plotting of a strategy to get his platoon quickly and safely into a hoped-for briar patch. He considered having the platoon on a prearranged signal run like hell across the stream's west fork and into the jungle. But then maybe they were surrounded and would run into a company of VC. The alternative was to go one group at a time, the point group securing a parcel for the rest. If there was a VC company, at least only six or less would be in the hornet's nest and not twenty-six.

The group that had been in the first sortie contained the point element and it was logical that they should be first. Hank radioed them their instructions. They sprung from the grass and sprinted from the field, across the stream, and disappeared into a tangle of vines, brush, and gnarled trees.

"November Six, November Papa. Looks okay, over."

"Roger. Break. November Two, November Six. Take off."

What remained of Michael's group with the addition of the Doc scurried away.

"November Six, November Two. We made it."

"November Five, November Six. Go."

Sergeant Martin's group traversed the meadow.

"November Six, November Five. Send the next."

"Roger."

The Christmas tree lost three of its limbs as two groups now remained, Hank's near the west fork and Sergeant Burlop's at the east fork nearest the believed vicinity of the enemy.

Burlop's group having no radio, Hank rose up and shouted, "November One, November Six. Move out!"

Hank held his breath. Of all the units, this one seemed most likely to draw fire. But they ran right by Hank with no mishap, and into the shallow stream before vanishing.

"November Six, November Five," Martin called. He had taken charge. "We're all here."

Hank waved his group out of the hole and they tore out on the same course as the others. He was surprised to find only Tucker behind him. He had always considered himself fairly fast.

The stream was only knee high, but the mud below was deep and grabbed and sucked at the ankles. While he and Tucker were in midstream, automatic weapons' fire came out of seclusion, burping three and four rounds at a time. Reacting, they belly-flopped into the water. Five-foot geysers flew up around them. Hank's head stayed under water as he debated whether to stay in the stream or break for the far bank. He wasn't aware of a streaking F-105 bearing down on the jungle canopy under which there had just been an eruption of spitting bullets. A reddish ball of napalm splashed over a fringe of trees.

Hank's head surfaced for air and he heard a contingent of his men shouting at him to move out. He did. On the double.

They reached the jungle.

The dense foliage forced a single file formation. Hank moved in the front one-fourth. Up at the point, machetes hacked and slashed at the thick tangle of vines and green bamboo. After an hour of heavy panting, as they slogged their way through the hot, stale air, confined by the walls of vegetation and the roof of triple canopy trees, a distance of three hundred and fifty meters was called back over Romero's shoulder to Hank. At this pace, Hank cynically reflected, he would finish his tour and still be aimlessly beating these goddamn bushes. After another fifteen minutes, he ordered a halt. It was no use to keep moving, no sign of VC, and he was moving with no purpose, no objective.

Each man picked a resting spot. Only the rear of the file where Sergeant Martin was in charge thought about security. The abundance of jungle provided what seemed like ample protection from all other directions.

Exhausted, hot, and soaked, Hank dropped first to his knees, then to his haunches and braced his back against the wide smooth-barked trunk of some exotic tree. Tucker slipped out of his PRC-25 and swung it up against the trunk beside Hank. He kneaded and massaged his shoulders. Then he plopped down on the other side of the radio, his back sharing Hank's tree.

The platoon rested amidst the sounds of heavy breathing and the dispersed rustling of bodies shifting and fidgeting in constant search for comfort.

Hank sat with his legs stretched and crossed, feet elevated on his helmet. His bare head tilted back, resting on the trunk, his eyes stared upward at a mass of limbs, branches, leaves, and vines. Just scattered bits of blue sky were visible. He thought about thinking about what to do next. But then he decided not to think about it for a while, to think of nothing and try for five minutes of relaxed oblivion.

"November Six, this is Bravo Five, over." A crisp, familiar voice seemed to come out of the tree trunk. Hank turned his head. It was the radio beside him. It was Lieutenant Brussels.

He reached over and picked the handset off the power pack and brought it slowly to his ear. "This is November Six. Send your message," he said in a monotone.

"Bravo Five. Roger. We've landed at an alternate LZ located from Lion up one-point-five, right one-point-three. What is your location?"

"So Brussels was now in command of the company," Hank whispered to himself. "Roger, wait," he said and held his breath while he took out his map and unfolded it. He exhaled a wind of thanks. Dick had marked the checkpoints on his map. He called Brussels back. "We are from Pelican down one-point-eight, left two-point-six," he guessed. "How copy?" This put them roughly one klick from the company.

"Good copy," answered Brussels. "Tonight, you are to establish an ambush site in vicinity from Pelican down one-point-seven, left two-point-eight. Tomorrow we'll link up, over."

"Roger. Understand ambush site is from Pelican down one-point-seven, left two-point-eight. How's Bravo six and my WIAs?"

"He'll pull through. Probably got a safe ticket to the States. Negative info on others."

"Roger. Anything further?"

"This is Bravo Five. Negative further, out."

Hank studied the map. The ambush site was an oval shaped clearing roughly thirty meters by fifty meters, two hundred and thirty meters farther to their northwest. They should make it right around nightfall.

There was about a half hour of light left when Hank halted the platoon. He sent Burlop with one of his fire teams to cloverleaf with the intent of finding their ambush site. It took only ten minutes to hear over the radio from Burlop. They found it. Hank was too damn nervous, worried, and in self-denial to congratulate himself on his superb performance in land navigation.

He waited, sitting with his back to some sort of big ficus tree, his rear end gorged by gnarly protruding roots. Tucker was beside him with equal use of the tree. Through the jungle leaves he could see moving splotches of Burlop coming toward him.

Burlop dropped to a knee. His right hand stuck his rifle butt to the ground for balance and he tossed his helmet down revealing the full extent of his small ferret features infested everywhere with tiny beads of sweat. He informed Hank that the clearing they were to ambush was an elliptical low spot in the midst of the surrounding jungle. If it were the wet season they would be ambushing a small pond. Now it was a small glade with knee high thick-bladed grass.

The clearing, he said, was a wide spot in what looked like a well-traveled jungle trail that ran east/west. The trail itself was large enough to handle small trucks, and the clearing was made for a classic ambush. His ferret smile and dark beady eyes beamed with this revelation. He advised that they should set up on the south side in the thick vegetation and ambush to the north.

Hank nodded. He didn't like the thought of a well-traveled trail. Not in this jungle. Hiding in thick vegetation would be good. The more hiding, the better.

Then Burlop made a request. He asked permission to convert the Claymores into animals to maximize the killing zone.

To this request Hank merely asked, "What the fuck are animals?"

Animals, Burlop answered eagerly, were the latest in optimizing the killing opportunity of an ambush. The technique of gang-rigging Claymore mines had been taught and demonstrated during his NCO school. Now would be as good a time as any to try it out, Burlop insisted. The procedure involved connecting detcord to a bank of two or more Claymores, ideally about four or it could be as many as twenty. When a clacker popped a Claymore to the bank all would explode instantaneously. At NCO school it had been quite an impressive demo, Burlop informed him, letting out a wide, weaselly grin.

Hank reminded Burlop that as far as he knew they had no detcord, to which Burlop enthusiastically replied, "To the contrary," telling Hank that unbeknownst to him he and two of his men had been carrying enough detcord in their rucksacks to rig three banks of four. Outwardly Hank quietly leveled an icy stare at Burlop. Inwardly he was pissed.

Burlop should have asked his permission.

He could give Burlop a resounding no. He could say that he didn't like spontaneous innovation. Particularly since this was his last ambush—he hoped. And what if the clacker to the animal bank failed to detonate due to some electrical malfunction or other mishap?

But then he re-thought his first instinct. Why not let Burlop have his fun? He'd soon be getting the hell out of this platoon leader business.

And this WAS his last ambush. It had to be. He was going to be a remf. The setting up of these so-called animals was just going to be another long exercise in futility. One more ambush to end his ignominious platoon leader career. One more night. Statistically, the odds were in his favor. One more night of miserable sleepless discomfort hiding in the bushes.

Damn, he wished he were back in Sydney.

If only they hadn't had a hot LZ. If only he hadn't lost Goldie. If only Burlop hadn't found a fucking mini Ho Chi Minh Trail…

The jungle began fading to gray. Inky flittering shadows of the platoon stealthily moved into their ambush positions. Per their leader's SOP, there were the usual four groups. Three faced the clearing along its longest strip on the south, set in about twenty meters and fifteen meters apart. The M-60s were posted at the corners, vines and brush were pushed aside and the tall grass matted down into firing lanes. The middle group, the focal point, was the CP. Claymores from the three frontal positions, each with an animal, were strung out to the edge of the tree line. The fourth group remained another fifteen meters further back in the rear, totally immersed in thickets, their ears their only sentinels.

Passing minutes eased the gray into a deep black. From Hank's nest of prickly briars and itchy grass, he tried surveying the intended kill zone. Mostly his vision was met with frail saplings, leafy twigs, stringy vines, and just plain brush, but there were a few irregular holes of black void remaining, from beating trails to the clearing to set up the Claymores. Even so, in the moonless night, a bright yellow tank could be in the clearing and he'd never see it. The M-60 groups on the flanks would have the best view and they had the starlight scopes.

Not only had the moon abandoned them, but also the wind. The night became one where minute sounds would magnify into crescendos of croaking, buzzing, chirping, and droning of frogs and insects. Hank heard a rushing sound among them and with a long groping arm he reached over and twisted the radio's knob to squelch.

He picked up the handset and whispered to Bravo Five's RTO that he wanted a defcon to the north. In a matter of minutes, the jungle noises became lost, replaced by the dull thunder of far off 105 shells. When the thunder was no longer dull, about 600 meters from the ambush site, Hank stopped his adjusting, called for a sitrep from his other groups, and ended his transmission. The sounds of the night came back in full volume.

As he sat in the darkness listening to the jungle Hank allowed himself some time to reflect on the layout and methodology of the ambush. He had always designed his ambushes with careful detail. This one was no different and it was in accordance with his usual specifications—attain the best damn defensive position possible.

All together the twenty-six-man platoon was protected by a total of twenty-three Claymores. There were twenty Claymores that stretched along the south side of the rim of the dry pond and they essentially covered the entire fifty meters of the long side of the ellipse—the kill zone. His middle group had six of the twenty, one animal and a Claymore on either side. Next to these single Claymores, the flanks (the corner groups) had animals aimed at the kill zone, a Claymore next to the animals, a Claymore at the trail junctures leading to the clearing, and one each on the flanks. The rear group had three Claymores, one to the rear and one each on their flanks.

Maybe one would consider all this overkill, Hank reflected, too absorbed with the situation to appreciate his pun. But then when it came to ambushing, the word overkill had never been part of his lexicon.

He assumed an assault on their position would come across the clearing and not from the flanks or the rear, simply because the jungle was too thick. An attacking force would too easily get hung up in the thick foliage. Nevertheless, he had some Claymores to cover this contingency. The popping of the Claymores would, as always, start with his group. The protocol was for him to pop an animal to be followed by the other two animals from the flank groups. The single Claymores would be held in reserve, initiated on an at will basis. Of course, all of that was subject to change based on what the hell was actually happening.

His biggest concern was the lack of clear fields of fire. His middle position and the rear one had none. The flanks with the M-60s had limited, based only on what they had beaten down during their short setup time. They would essentially have a forty-five- to sixty-degree firing lane into the kill zone that could achieve some overlapping fire. That was it. And throwing hand grenades and firing bloopers was out of the question due to the abundance of vines, leaves, limbs and other assorted vegetative crap.

Everything would depend on the Claymores.

Now here he was getting paranoid. He had to remember the best feature of their ambush. It was a good hiding place. A Brer Rabbit style briar patch. Just had to make it to morning and get the hell of here, out of the field, and out of the platoon.

And become a remf.

CHAPTER 38

AT TWENTY-TWO MINUTES before midnight, with Hank and Tucker sitting watch, a low whisper, edged tightly with subdued panic, came from the earpiece of the handset resting in Tucker's cross-legged lap. "November Six, November Two." It was Sergeant Michael on the left flank. "We're gettin' movement to our left. Lots of it! Lot of rustling and clanking. It's somethin' humongous!"

Hank's first thought was crazy and out of place, that Michael could have a career as a drama actor. The stirring pitch in his voice that started low and traveled upward through higher octaves until ending shrill and cracked would have easily wrung the emotions of moviegoers. It sure wrung his.

He took the handset from Tucker who a second before had picked it up and held it in waiting. Relieved of that task, Tucker began quietly crawling around, waking Sergeant Martin, Franklin, Romero, and Doc with soft nudges from one hand while the other hovered a few inches over their lips to muffle an inadvertent gasp or groan.

Hank now regretted having Sergeant Martin and Franklin with him. Martin was the platoon sergeant and should have been with another group. Similarly, Franklin was the Weapons Squad leader and should have been with one of the M-60s. But this was his last ambush and he had wanted them with him.

In a nervous whisper, he answered Michaels. "November Six, Roger. Which way's the movement?"

"This way! To the east!" Michael's voice sounded stuck on the highest octave.

"Roger. Sit tight. Keep me posted…Break. November One, November Papa, this is November Six. Did you monitor?"

"November One. Affirmative."

"November Papa. Affirm."

Hank battled to suppress the turmoil raging under his skin. He battled well. Only his left hand trembled noticeably. By tightly gripping the front handguard of his M-16, he controlled it.

He radioed the company. "Bravo Five, November Six, over."

An RTO answered. "This is Bravo Five Kilo. Monitored. We're waking Bravo Five."

There was a long pause, then a groggy Brussels said, "This…is Bravo Five. What'cha got?"

Major Woodson had just checked the last perimeter bunker of Fire Support Base Condor. He was heading for his tent and some long-awaited sack time when a spec-four trotted up and panted something about a Bravo ambush platoon hearing heavy movement. He rolled his unlit cigar stub in his mouth, adding to the heavy secretion of his salivary glands that had started when hearing the news.

With long strides that shook his heavy jowls he hurried to the command bunker. Should he inform the Old Man? Negative. The colonel was peacefully sleeping in his field tent, exhausted from a trying day. He was capable of handling this situation for now.

He carried his bulk down into the bunker, a small, stuffy cube dug into the ground and covered with three layers of sandbags and crowded with four large radios, one on the Battalion frequency, one on Brigade, one on an Artillery net, and one standby.

Two spec-fours sat on canvas chairs in front of the radios. The dim light of a naked sixty-watt bulb, energized from a generator outside, offered little definition to their pale, taut faces.

One RTO vacated his chair and selected another away from the radios. As he moved he informed the major that Brigade had already been given a sitrep.

Woodson's broad bottom took over his chair. His beefy hand switched on the standby radio and tuned it to Bravo's net. He was now inside and could light his cigar, and did so. He puffed smelly, eye-stinging smoke and palmed his bald pate as he listened in to Bravo's net.

"Movement's getting louder. I think they're coming through the clearing!" Sergeant Michaels inflections made his soft whispers appear as frantic shouting.

The entire ambush was alert and nervously listening to the light trampling of troops trying to move quietly. The watching ears magnified the sound and converted the sound to visions of an NVA regiment.

"Sit tight!" Hank barely breathed into the mouthpiece. "Let them pass. There's too many!"

Woodson's cigar almost fell out of his mouth. It clung precariously from just inside his upper lip. Too many to engage? Such a thing was not dreamt of in his philosophy. Brigade had already been notified, which meant Division knew. They'd all be wanting action. Fuck them. *He* wanted action!

He twisted uneasily in the overstressed canvas chair and worked the cigar back in his mouth with his lips. He grabbed the radio's handset.

"November Six, this is Demon Three. Why can't you engage?"

Hank instantly recognized the loud shouting of Major Woodson. He was sitting up, as was everybody in his group, and he reached over and turned the volume control knob down before answering.

"This is November Six!" Hank muffled back a nearly inaudible shout. On the receiving end Woodson turned his volume control all the way up. "The situation is unsafe. We estimate at least an NVA company moving in front of us."

Woodson blanched and his teeth clinched down in reflex like a bear trap, severing the ash from the butt. In another reflex action he gagged before spitting the well-chewed cigar to the far side of the bunker. The RTO beside him surreptitiously wiped a mist of spittle from his face with a forearm.

An NVA COMPANY! Right in FRONT of their AMBUSH! Of all the Battalion's platoon leaders it would have to be that smart ass, pissant Kirby. Well he, Major Miles E. Woodson, West Point Class of '57, wasn't going to let a company of NVA *didi mau* from a goddamn ambush. It was hard enough just finding the shits. Once you found them you had to kill 'em! He pushed the mic button. "This is Demon Three. I'm ORDERING your ambush to engage. Repeat ORDERING!"

The words resounded in Hank's ear. He sat there in the dark looking at the shadows of the men around him, sensing their heavy breathing, aware of much movement to their front.

Woodson repeated his order three more times before Hank responded.

"NEGATIVE!" he answered with defiance and finality, and perhaps a little too loudly because it invoked a hand on his shoulder from Tucker.

Tucker, Martin, and Fletcher had stuck their heads in close. Hank sensed they had heard Woodson's order and his reply. He thought he saw barely perceptible nods of agreement.

There was no agreement by the squad leader of the right flank. On propped elbows, handset glued to the right side of this face, Sergeant Burlop had intently been monitoring the transmission. A sweet salivary taste had sloshed in his mouth when he had listened to Sergeant Michael describe the heavy movement to November Six. Now, after hearing Six's negative pronouncement, his saliva had soured. His platoon leader was a eunuch. The whole platoon lacked balls! His platoon leader had castrated them. And now his platoon leader was disobeying an order from a superior officer.

Small pulses of low guttural gibberish flared briefly in the clearing and the dull thudding of many feet, like a giant combat-laden centipede, halted. Hank's stomach seemed to roll up in his esophagus. He kept one hand gripping the handset to his ear and the other clutching a Claymore detonator.

There were sounds of commotion and lots of loud whispering. He guessed they were taking a rest stop. He worried about the Claymores being discovered.

The corner groups had the starlight scopes and a modicum of a field of fire and so he listened intently as Michael and Burlop took turns calling in hushed sitreps. Michael confirmed he saw eight to ten heavily armed, pith-helmeted soldiers, looking every bit like NVA. The heavily armed part included a two-man heavy machine gun team and what appeared to be a mortar squad toting two 82mm mortar tubes.

Burlop reported about a dozen with AKs and RPGs.

Hank radioed them to keep monitoring and to hold tight. To which Michael gave a quick wilco and Burlop urged him to take immediate action.

Major Woodson kept breaking into the radio net with tirades of invectives—ordering, or rather demanding, Hank to initiate contact, to which Hank would answer by breaking squelch three times which in turn further infuriated Woodson even more.

It had been seven minutes since the NVA unit of undetermined strength had taken up residence in the November Platoon's kill zone—hopefully to rest and not to bivouac—when Hank decided to become proactive.

He slowly rose from his sitting position to his knees and peered through the dense, dark jungle. He could only see a black darkness amidst a myriad of vegetative matter. He moved from his knees to his feet. Finally, as he slowly and stealthily swayed his body to varying positions, he came across a foot diameter void space through the jungle where he could make out a few dark silhouettes moving around about twenty-five meters away.

As his men in his group remained immobile, silently sitting, he leaned over in slow motion, careful to keep silent and make no disturbance. He picked the pair of binoculars from its carrying case. He looked through the binoculars and peered through the one-foot diameter void. The images were now magnified. He suddenly saw the upper half of a dark silhouette moving toward him into the wood-line. The pith helmet made the image look like it was wearing a lamp shade. But the AK-47 hanging at sling arms suggested something more menacing.

Hank was close to panic. Was the silhouette looking at him? Before he could react, the image turned around, slid the rifle from his shoulder, and appeared to look down at its feet as it worked on something at his waist. He then relaxed a bit as the soldier dropped from sight to take a dump.

Then he saw the silhouette jump up like he'd been bitten in the ass.

Instinctively Hank knew what had happened. He knew the silhouette had discovered the detcord of a Claymore animal. The silhouette began frantically yelling.

Hank dropped heavily to the ground. He rapidly patted his hands over a small patch of ground like he was swatting a family of scrambling roaches. Until he found it.

There was the clack-clack of Hank's detonator and the deafening wham of four mines exploding simultaneously, their back-blast cutting deep into the wood-line.

Like a chain reaction there were two other clack-clacks on the flanks and terrifying explosions, belching yellow flames into the night, lashing squalls of steel pellets outward across the grassy clearing.

Hank's group was no longer sitting, but instead sprawling, wanting every inch of themselves on the ground. Half of the foliage to their front had been cut down by the backblast and lay in a tangled pile.

There was an eerie few seconds of silence. Then came a dirge of moans, sobs, and groans from the clearing. Then sharp, loud cries of what in Vietnamese must have been the words for "help me."

Rustling sounds of hurried movement were added and then the deep pops of AK gunfire. The firing seemed to be random bursts with little purpose or direction.

Hank could hear sporadic bullets passing through the underbrush. He figured the enemy had been severely hurt. Those who were alive were in a confused state and were firing randomly as they hastily tried to get to their wounded. This was fine with him. Let them get the hell out of here soonest.

Then he had a bad thought. What if there were more? What if they were only the point element of a much larger force? He started to radio this possibility to the others when he heard the sounds of the M-60s opening up.

Now he really felt sick. The corner groups with the starlight scopes must have still had some semblance of a field of fire. And now they were announcing—even showing with their muzzle flashes and tracers—where their positions were.

Hank lay hugging the ground with his men. His head raised a few inches off the ground, he listened and worried to the sounds of his M-60s throbbing madly from either side. He pictured the fiery red tracers criss-crossing hot lead across the kill zone and cutting down the unhurt but stunned. He imagined some escaping and some who had avoided the kill zone regrouping, homing in on the red dashes, vectoring back, locating the M-60s. Shit! Why hadn't he thought to tell his men to hold their fire? The gooks wouldn't have known where they were. At least his group wasn't firing. They couldn't; there were no firing lanes.

His imagination seemed to conjure up reality. A staccato of AK gunfire on fully automatic shouted out defiantly. Hank brought his head up slowly. Bullets mixed with green tracer rounds sporadically shot by overhead. He kept the handset at his ear waiting for some sort of sitrep from the M-60s groups. RPGs began smashing into trees and chunks of metal ripped through layers of vegetation like a heavy storm of coarse grit. Pops from M-16s reinforced the deep throated rat-a-tat-tat sounds of the M-60s. A small section of jungle had erupted into a micro Vesuvius with ears-shattering explosions and spitting red and green ashes. He could hear all around the cracking, snapping noises of vegetative debris ripping apart.

It was time, finally. Time Hank dreaded. Time he did something.

He shouted into the mouthpiece, no longer concerned about whispering, the terrifying sounds of battle forming an acoustical insulation. "Bravo Five, November Six. We've made contact! Give us illumination one hundred meters to our north, ASAP! Drop two hundred meters with HE from defcon! I will adjust! Have the artillery ready to switch to VT!"

The illumination would give the flanks better vision in the kill zone, while hopefully keeping them concealed in the shadows. The HE would create a lot of noise, maybe convince the gooks to retreat, maybe it would get some during the retreat. The drawback was that this might cause them to hug the south edge of the clearing, or worse yet, to penetrate the wood line. But then that was where the Claymores had been and they might be a little leery about that, not to mention bloodied. If they were smart, and if his platoon were lucky, they'd backtrack. That was the only safe course. That's what he'd do. Now the VT—air bursting explosions—why had he mentioned that? His men would be equally exposed. But then again if the gooks retreated and he knew the direction, he could wait until they would be a fair distance and then call a shrapnel downpour. These thoughts justifying his commands passed through his brain in the microseconds of a computer.

"Roger," came a quick reply.

There was a sudden hiatus in the firefight. Hank could feel the silence. Vesuvius had become extinguished.

His tension ebbed some. He took a deep breath, pressed the talk button on the radio's handset, and started to call his three ambush positions for a sitrep.

Then Vesuvius began erupting again. It sounded like a Chinese New Year and this time it was more focused and directed at November's left flank.

Hank picked his head up and looked through the dense thickets over at Sergeant Michael's position. He glimpsed multiple muzzle flashes that appeared to be coming from the left quadrant of the kill zone. It sounded like a rifle squad of AKs assisted by a few RPG launchers.

Then the left flank answered, the M-60 blazing, the four M-16s on full rock and roll, the one blooper spitting out canister. And then came three violent explosions as Sergeant Michael's group detonated their remaining Claymores. Hank followed and hit the clacker of the Claymore that had bridged his animal with Michael's.

The Claymores seemed to give a positive outcome. The assaulting force seemed to wither away. The only firing was now from Michael's position. After a full thirty seconds of holding their triggers down, they stopped.

And the silence took over again, save for the HE artillery rounds that were now hitting about 400 meters to the north.

"Guys give me a sitrep fast!" Hank called into the handset's mouthpiece.

He was meaning Sergeant Michael, but Sergeant Burlop answered first. "November One. We're real fine." His tone was almost gleeful.

"November Papa," the rear security responded, "we're okay. Negative casualties."

A low voice choked and cracked in Hank's ear and he knew it was bad. "November Two Kilo. We…we've got one KIA and three wounded."

Hank gulped in generous helpings of residual smoke and minute vegetative particulates generated from his recently detonated Claymore before asking, "How bad?"

"Manageable fragment wounds. They'll be all right. Nothing urgent. Tell Doc we'll manage."

"Roger…Who got it?"

"Sar…Sergeant Mi…chael."

Hank acknowledged by breaking squelch twice with the push-to-talk button. He allowed a brief moment to reflect on his dead squad leader. Sergeant Michael had been from Harlem. That was about all he knew about him.

Then a too familiar feeling overcame him. A melancholy mixture of numbness, sadness, queasiness…and relief that it wasn't him.

Scattered tortured moans grew out of the clearing and entered the jungle like a cold unwanted wind, bringing a sick feeling to Hank's stomach.

A loud pop in the sky to the north was added to the crying misery of the wounded NVA. A bright magnesium flare swinging like a pendulum from a small parachute washed the environs in a pearly sheen that deepened the shadows, hiding the platoon and accenting the ghostly pall of the kill zone. But the illumination was not sufficient for a visual sitrep, even by the M-60 groups who peered along the narrow firing lanes now clogged with dark clumps of broken limbs, some trees, and other assorted debris.

Major Woodson kept twisting in his chair as if trying to ward off ants that had mistakenly thought his rectum sugarcoated. Impatiently he listened to the impertinent Lieutenant Kirby adjusting artillery around his ambush site. But right now he could overlook the impertinence. The important thing was the bush was blown. Kirby had obeyed orders after all. Now what had they got? That's what was important. He had to know! "November six, this is Demon Three. Give me a full sitrep"

"Negative," an abrupt reply blared from the radio squawk box a few feet in front of his face. "I'm adjusting Arty. Will give it later. Out!"

Woodson seemed to be killing a large roach as he slammed the handset down on the small field table. A chunk of hard black plastic broke off into an airborne missile that narrowly missed the eye of the spec-four who Woodson had showered earlier with his mouth. "That son-of-a-bitch! I'm going to fry that smart bastard's ass!"

The two RTOs nervously observed the beet red, shouting face. The whole head seemed to pulsate like a giant red, light bulb. They cringed with the fear of the Major's vituperations spilling over on them and waited for a coronary to croak him. They also noted that he didn't break into the transmission now being heard from November Six as he called in artillery corrections to Bravo Five who in turn could be heard on an adjacent squawk box relaying info to the 105 Battery. From the booms of the howitzers outside and the reverberating tremors inside they felt the commo's end product.

Woodson was now beating a heavy fist on his thigh.

A few moments later he heard November Six say "out" to Bravo Five. He stopped pounding his thigh into submission. He heard Kirby calling him in a taut voice stretched tight with piano wire tension.

"Demon Three, this is November Six. We engaged large NVA force moving from west to east. They returned fire. Contact was momentarily broken, then reestablished in an assault on our left flank. Assault beaten back. Results: we have one KIA, three WIA, not serious. They can hold till morning."

"What about enemy results?" the Battalion S-3 bellowed like a high-pressure boiler bleeding off great quantities of steam.

"Unknown. We think we hurt 'em pretty bad, but we can't see much of the kill zone. There's movement around us, and lots of groaning sounds."

Christ! Woodson muttered to himself. The NVA must be dragging off the dead bodies. If that fuckin' platoon waited until morning to do anything, they'd only find a few blood trails. Division didn't give a rat's ass about blood trails.

He stared trancelike at the radio as if it were reading his mind and digesting his thoughts, as if it was supposed to make the next move. After a few seconds he blinked a couple of times and then pulled a long, blunt cigar from his breast pocket. He tore the wrapper off with his teeth and stuck the cigar in his mouth. He chewed at it unlit and brought the mic up like a lighter. "This is Demon Three," he said and rose slowly to his feet to issue his dictum with full authority. "You will search the kill zone *now*, and give an accurate body count and list of captured weapons and materiel."

Even with what pale flare light had filtered through the asymmetrical media of vegetation, it was still too dark for one to see the Jekyll to Hyde configuration Hank's face passed through. To search now was crazy, absurd, and perhaps suicidal. Michael was one dead. He wasn't going to add to that number. And he was tired of this shit. He was supposed to be out of the field. "Negative," he replied. "It's too dangerous. We'll search in the morning…if it's safe. OUT."

Woodson went livid. A different color than the coronary red earlier, though looking just as fatal. But then with chameleon-like agility his complexion took on the familiar color of blood supersaturating his head. He raged: "*You* don't tell *me* out! Understand? I'm the one that ends this transmission. I'm fucking tired of your goddamn insubordination! Now listen here. I'm ORDERING your platoon to search the kill zone. NOW!"

The shouting burned into Hank's ear drum, but he kept the handset pressed to his ear, partly to keep the sound muffled, partly out of some inexplicable masochistic delight. He squeezed the push-to-talk button with all his strength. He wished he was squeezing Woodson's throat. Mustering a hidden reserve of restraint, he answered softly. "Negative. We'll take a look in the morning. We have no idea what we're up against."

Major Woodson again slammed the mic down, again chipping off more plastic. His fists followed and beat the field table like a kettle drum. The mic jumped around like a small, boated fish. The RTOs watched with petrified eyes. They couldn't believe the major had gone berserk.

CHAPTER 39

SERGEANT BURLOP SAT beside his M-60 gunner and gazed down the long narrow tunnel of the firing lane. It had lost its relative smoothness. And now with stalactite and stalagmite shadows and the milky flare light at the end, it now appeared as a mystical narrow, leafy cave. But though he gazed, he didn't see. His hearing had blinded his vision as he closely monitored his PRC-25. His platoon leader had finally cracked under the strain.

He had mutinied. Willfully disobeyed an order. From a field grade officer.

He could understand the major. If they waited till morning, they wouldn't get the body count. By searching it now they might even get a prisoner or two. Wait! Burlop flinched when the light bulb in his head popped on. He could do the searching. What an opportunity! The major would see to it he'd get at least a Bronze Star for valor. Maybe even a Silver. Excited anticipation brought a long, closed smile to his lips and he radioed his platoon leader. "November Six, November One. I'll search the kill zone."

"Negative," Hank replied in a nasty whisper. "No one goes until morning and then we'll all go as a unit."

"Break! Break!" Woodson's shouting butted in. "November One, this is Demon Three. I'm overriding November Six and ordering you to conduct the search. Do you Roger?"

"This is November One, I not only Roger that, but I wilco it." Burlop sounded like fine champagne bubbling over.

Hank's bottom teeth knifed into his upper lip. He was pissed. "November One, November Six! I'm in command here and I say no go."

"Sorry November Six, but I'm under orders from a higher-ranking officer. I'm going to crawl out to the clearing right now."

Hank jerked the handset away and stared maliciously at the hard, black object barely outlined amid the dark shadows. It symbolized Burlop's insolence and he wanted to slam it into the ground and suffocate any future sound. His temper briefly overtook his emotions and he felt nothing else until the fear gnawed back to the forefront and he remembered he was afraid. Afraid for himself, and afraid for Burlop too. Deflated, he called Burlop. "All right. Be careful and be quick. You're on your own."

Burlop didn't hear. He crawled in a rough culvert of vegetation cluttered with debris from the claymore storm. He cradled his rifle on his forearms like he'd seen the marines do in the movies when working their way up the beach under a deluge from Jap machine guns. Vines grabbed like gnarled fingers at grenades hanging from his harness in violation of SOP. He stopped, worked the vines off and proceeded again, at a slower pace, giving him time to avoid becoming tangled.

He looked behind him, expecting one or more of his men to be following. There was no one. He was alone, on his own. Was he the only one in this fucking platoon with balls?

Movement came with increasing effort. Fatigue from nervous intensity set in. Large sweat beads condensed under the head band of his helmet liner and saturated the leather; the sweat poured down into the sluice between his eyebrows and down the run of his nose before dripping faucet-like. His heart accelerated as if it wanted out. And it came out, all watery through his glands. And suddenly he realized he was on the edge of the woodline. And he was scared shitless!

He stayed still. The fear in his stomach subsided a little. He sucked in buckets of air coming from a breeze that swept gently over the clearing. He began to feel better. He edged his way into the tall grass blanketed a ghostly white from the Arty illumination. His head came up slowly, and he peered over a limited section of creamy pasture.

Shit! Burlop gasped inaudibly. It was a graveyard, except the corpses weren't buried. No, it was what it was, the aftermath of a battlefield; graveyards didn't have weapons strewn about. With a semicircle rotation of his head he counted nine, maybe ten contorted corpses. It was ghastly and brought new fears flooding into his gut. And then the fears transitioned into excitement and the excitement into a mysterious anticipation of achievement, of a Bronze Star, of war trophies, of the victory. Yes victory. He was alive, they were dead.

Beyond his limited vision he figured many more. He would move around, get an accurate count, frisk a few, maybe find a CHICOM pistol to go with his medal, maybe even find the source of the low, sparse moans he heard scattered before him, and maybe, just maybe, a prisoner, and then, a Silver Star. Or even if no prisoner, he could kill someone with his bare hands, and have the war story of war stories.

He began his mission, slowly edging over to four mangled bodies heaped together, a gaggle that had borne the brunt of a claymore. His stomach, in opposition to his mind, started turning over as he closed on the dark contorted masses. One seemed to be more pieced together than the others. He slithered over to it. With head turned away he blindly began frisking.

The fingers of his right hand nervously flittered and fumbled as it wandered over the unfamiliar terrain of a dead man. The ammo harness vest fastened to the chest brimmed with AK banana clips. A feel of thick warm ooze near the base of the neck made his hand jerk away.

He kept his head turned. He hyperventilated. He wiped the goo off in the dirt. His hand returned to its task. This time along the side. It discovered a rifle sling and then a rifle, and something cloth-like between. His fingers stretched out over his findings and he lifted it. He twisted his head to see. His hand held a shredded arm from elbow down. He saw it and his mind snapped. He first screamed with only his mind hearing the full force of his terror. Then he screamed again, aloud, not able to contain himself. "Eahhhh!"

The platoon jumped. Each man tensed and braced, vicariously experiencing Burlop's anguish.

Tucker hooked Hank's arm and drew him near. "He's in trouble. We gotta help," he said to Hank's ear.

Hank brushed him away with his shoulder. "Sit tight. Nobody's going out there."

"Yessir," Tucker hissed like a punctured tire.

Hank's hand found Tucker's shoulder and squeezed reassuringly to prevent further deflation.

Burlop floundered. He crawled, a crab in a frenzy, its escape holes filled with sand. He bumped off mutilated corpses like a careening billiard ball. His mind froze on *the* arm, the half arm. A soft plump sounded to his left. It thawed his mind. What was it?

Wham! The exploding fragmentation grenade answered his question.

Blood spilled into his eyes, blinding him. He cried out in terror, "Help me! Help me!"

They barely saw him, a distant silhouette on a badly lit fluorescent stage, staggering, weaving, and bobbing drunkenly.

Tucker raised up.

"Get down!" Hank snapped.

Tucker ignored the command, started crawling, kicking Hank's grasp from his pant's leg. The sense of urgency too great, too huge to consider his own fate.

Hank's group watched the shadows take him.

Burlop's right forearm made windshield wiper passes at his eyes, trying to clear the blood away. His forehead felt like it contained a fresh, abundant spring of blood. He suddenly took notice of his action. He was using his right arm. But his left arm? He couldn't feel his left arm! His right clutched something. He could see it out of the corner of his eye. No. It couldn't be. It was an arm! He threw it down, his sanity with it. It was the corpse's half arm.

His eyes rolled back and he spun around, screaming all the while. As Tucker threw himself at his legs, tackling him to the ground, he pulled the pin of a grenade on his harness strap. Tucker lay on top of him, not knowing, whispering sweet nothings to the back of his head. "Don't worry, Sarge. You'll be all right. I'll…"

Wham!

Glassy eyes stared skyward at a false daylight. Tucker lay on his back, conscious of the unreality. Burlop, what remained of him, lay beside him.

God it hurt! He knew there was a cavity in his chest. He could hear it gurgling. Yet he couldn't move. He couldn't help himself. And he couldn't cry out for help. That might make him a target, or lure someone else out just as Burlop had done to him. He would just have to lay here and pray the flare light would turn to sunlight and that he would see it.

God it hurt!

After hearing the grenade blast, Hank sat and stared and waited for some sound, any sound. There was nothing. No moaning, no movement; only an intermittent pop of a new flare just before the old one fizzled and died. He told Tucker to stay. *Why didn't he?*

Hank beat a fist on his knee. He reached far to his left and tapped Martin who was staring into a bush that held his thoughts. "You're in charge."

Martin left his thoughts in the bush. He looked for Hank's eyes, but couldn't find them.

He gave a slow nod and then in a hoarse whisper said, "Good luck, sir. Let us know if you run into trouble."

Yeah, Hank thought sardonically, *sure, why don't you go, and I'll stay. I'm in command. I give the orders.* But he couldn't speak his thoughts; they were too embarrassing. After all, he had ordered Burlop not to go. And Tucker. He could only order himself, and that was a hard order to follow and just as hard to understand.

As he got on all fours, a hand clasped his ankle. He looked behind him and recognized Franklin's outline. "Lieutenant Kirby. I'm going," he said matter of factly. Hank answered by crawling forward.

They reached the edge of the clearing side-by-side just as a flare died and for the first time there was not another in rapid succession. The blackness was total and claustrophobic and blinded them. They waited a moment for their night vision. Before them the ground stretched out like a dark, inky pond.

"Tucker!" Hank tried shouting a low whisper. It was chancy, to be sure, but so was crawling any further. "Tucker!"

There was a moan, maybe it was a grunt, no, more like a baby's coo. A few meters away to his left. He slid slowly toward it on his belly, his rifle pushing ahead, its tip a feeler. After five feet he discovered he was alone. There was no Franklin beside him. Perhaps he was at his heels. He fought back urges to return to the platoon. He heard the groan again, louder, and kept going.

It was a moan. Long and eerie. His ears locked in and then his eyes. A dark, bulky sack-like something. A body.

"Tucker," he whispered a few feet away.

Like a striking snake a needle-sharp bayonet leaped out of the ground at his head. He saw the blur. His body reacted faster than his mind and he instinctively twisted to his side and flattened out. The bayonet hit off center of his helmet and with a sharp clunk deflected to one side. He acted with animal reflexes, his mind no longer trying to diagram decision trees and alternative courses of action. His only human quality the stark terror of believing in imminent death.

He caught the barrel just behind the sights as it started its recoil. He wrestled it with both hands fishing rod style and scrambled to his knees, keeping the end of the jerking, twitching barrel away from him. The AK-47 suddenly went limp in his hands. He straddled the assailant.

There was bucking and writhing. He dug his knees in hard and rode until its spirit was broken and the grunts had turned to short, choppy gasps. He felt a warm viscous fluid seep into the side of his pants. He saw the shape of a head below him and held the AK cocked back beside him. Suddenly a flare popped, ending the dark intermission and washing the surroundings in pale, creamy light.

Hank looked down into wild, bulging eyes. He thought he saw the fear subside, and a plea for mercy emerge as he plunged the rifle's bayonet behind his shifting weight into the center of the throat. There was a sharp gasp, a gurgle, and the plea vanished and became hollow, glassy, and very still. He kept his weight on the stock until the tempered steel needle slowed and was stopped by the crinkly, granular resistance of dirt. He rocked back, leaving the weapon.

"Lieutenant," Franklin's low, sibilant call brought his mind away before he could dwell on what had happened. Feeling vulnerable, he quickly dismounted and became prone. "Tucker's over here. He's…he's alive."

Hank grabbed his M-16 and slithered like a frightened lizard toward a helmeted head above the grass. If he had glanced around he would have seen the graveyard of dead enemy soldiers. If he had looked back he would have seen the silhouette of a rifle slanting into the ground, a leaning soldier's cross.

Hank looked at Tucker in the pearlish sheen of the flare light. He seemed to be conscious; his eyes were open and blinking, but spacey, as if they were someplace else, as if *he* were someplace else. Franklin pointed at his chest where a puddle of dark blood bubbled slowly in a widening diameter. A sucking chest wound.

Crouched on his knees, his fingers shaking from the urgency and seriousness of their work, Hank tore Tucker's shirt away from the wound, took a bandage that Franklin handed him, and pressed it firmly on his chest to stem the flow. He kept the bandage in place as Franklin worked a strip of gauze around his back and to the front where he tied the ends off.

Their meager surgery finished, Hank began thinking about their vulnerability. Why hadn't they been shot dead yet? There was a sudden tug on his fatigue shirt from behind and his heart leaped. He turned quickly, expecting an NVA bayonet, but instead saw a dark shadow that he recognized as Doc Fletcher. Near him were Sergeant Martin and Spec-four Romero.

Before he could acknowledge them, there was a soft thumping sound. It was somewhere out in the middle of the human carnage about ten meters away. They all flattened before the grenade exploded.

Wham!

A potpourri of dirt, shrapnel, and human flesh from a probably dead NVA that was near ground zero crashed over them in a violent shock wave.

Instinctively Hank started log rolling toward the explosion, his rifle tucked into his chest, increasing his spin rate much like a figure skater. As he rolled over a collection of spewed weapons, a body, and apparent body parts, he wondered what he was doing. Was it to create a diversion from the others who had crowded around Tucker and who were now trying to save his life? Or was it because he didn't think lightning struck twice in the same spot if another grenade were to follow? And that maybe what he was doing was the safer course of action.

But now he didn't seem safer as he found himself in the middle of a ghoulish graveyard, in the midst of the living dead. He hoped mostly dead.

He was breathing heavily, smelling shit, and lying uncomfortably on top of an RPG launcher locked and loaded with a B-40 rocket. At least he hoped it was locked as he stared wide-eyed at the cone shaped warhead inches below his face. It was aimed at the rear end of a dead body a mere foot away. And that explained the smell of shit.

The dead NVA was in a semi fetal position and Hank edged a little closer to the right so his bare head—he had lost his helmet during his impulsive body roll—could take refuge in the crook of its knees. He moved slowly, careful to minimize any disturbance to the RPG launcher and have it go off and up the ass of the dead NVA and taking Hank's head with it. He would have to live with the stench. The key word was live.

There was another body sprawled face up only a foot to his right. In a morbid way they provided him with some measure of cover and concealment to his front and right.

To his left from whence he came was another body that boxed him into a human horseshoe. It was a breathing, living body. And it gave Hank a strange twinge of security. Franklin had been stupid enough to have come with him, and was now at his side facing west, at the back of the same dead body that served as a small low curb to hide behind.

The parachute flares from 105s were no longer their friends as they cast a pale, ghostly light over the bloodied open spot in the jungle where in the middle he and Franklin now found themselves. But they were two of what appeared to be many and if they didn't move maybe no one would notice.

Lying on the ground in the slight depression of a dry pond, surrounded by the tall shadows of triple canopy jungle, with the smell of shit and blood from the dead and wafting burnt cordite from the grenade explosion, Hank felt the fear of having fallen into a huge cesspool with no way out and no help in sight. After a long moment he found enough courage to move his head slowly, which felt naked without his helmet.

His head lifted to see to his left, over Franklin and the tall grass. He could barely make out through overhanging branches and leaves a shadowy helmeted figure kneeling very low just inside the wood line. He guessed it was Doc working on Tucker. He couldn't see Sergeant Martin or Romero. They were hopefully somewhere near.

Why hadn't he and Franklin stayed with them? What dumb shits!

Hank now raised his head slightly higher to look over his dead combatant to his front. He peered at what seemed like a black hole maybe thirty meters away. It was the west entrance to the trail from where the NVA had emerged. And from where he thought they had counterattacked Michael's position. And where Hank now thought they were waiting and watching. But then that's what he thought. They could have just as easily scattered north into the thick jungle. Maybe some just retreated, or maybe fled into the east trail entrance—the black hole behind them.

Then again, maybe they were all around on all three sides. Watching and waiting, maybe for reinforcements; maybe planning another counterattack.

Hank thought he could never be as afraid as he was at Loc Ninh. He had been wrong. He was now in a horror movie watching himself drown in a sea of death. But in this case, it was an intermittent pond. Now dry, there was no water to drown in. Which brought no comfort. Drowning might be better than being blown to bits.

He had the feeling Franklin felt the same way since he could feel his finger nails digging into his left arm, letting him know he was there. That he was OK. That he too was scared shitless.

Could they lie here all night and pray for the morning? Should they start edging slowly to what may be a specious safety of the woodline where the others were?

But he knew they couldn't wait things out. They somehow had to get Tucker on a dust-off.

He then suddenly heard a rustling of movement and shifting of equipment and weapons behind him to his left. Worst case scenario! Gooks were behind him!

He and Franklin turned their heads together and glanced over their shoulders behind them. In the pale sheen of flare light they saw a number of turtle shells about eighteen meters away hovering above the grass and hugging the woodline. They weren't pith, but rather of the steel pot variety. They were Burlop's men. They had moved up to the clearing.

Before a level of comfort could sweep over Hank, he heard a soft thump five meters to his front. Evidently lightning could strike twice! The grenade throwing had resumed!

Wham!

The force of the blast with its rain of chunks and bits of metal were absorbed by their dead human shield.

Their minds cried out a question and screamed for the answer. Where were the grenades coming from? Maybe from some last-ditch effort of a dying gook somewhere around them. Maybe coming from the black hole on the west side of the clearing. Maybe even from the east side, which would be really bad if the gooks were over there, behind Burlop's men.

With Burlop's group moved up, they were now beside those claymores which they hadn't yet detonated, rendering them useless except if they wanted to blow themselves up. And now they were vulnerable to an attack on their right flank.

And if that happened, Hank realized, the flank would be rolled over like a runaway lawn mower and they'd soon be dead.

There was another soft thump. This time it was to his right front.

Wham!

The dead body on his right took up most of the blast. Only his and Franklin's ears suffered as the sound deafened their hearing. Except for a razor thin piece of one-inch shrapnel that embedded itself in the right side of Hank's cheek. He flinched as if stung by a wasp. Instinctively his right hand went to his face and his fingers like tweezers yanked the jagged piece of metal that had lodged in his cheek bone. His movement caused his body to shift over the RPG tube and he felt the nub of the belt buckle of his accoutrement harness snag inside the trigger guard of the RPG launcher which brought on a quick form of paralysis.

He knew nothing about the workings of an RPG. He thought it likely the safety catch was on. But he could be wrong. Or it could have been on and his movement dislodged it. The blooper didn't have the safest form of safety, so why expect a simple, cheap Soviet or Chinese made weapon to be any better. A little Ft. Benning bleacher training on the use of various types of enemy weaponry might have lessened his current state of anxiety and apprehension. And it wasn't like he could call time out and slowly figure out how to eradicate his buckle that was somewhere in close proximity to the trigger of the RPG launcher.

His mind began rapidly taking stock of his situation. He was lying on the ground among an undetermined number of dead bodies at the bottom of an open giant, elliptical grassy bowl, his body pressed closely to a deadly explosive in which he was ensnared.

There was one live body on his left with pinching fingers that left no doubt that he wasn't dreaming. He was facing the haunches of a dead gook who had shit in his pants. Another was on his right sprawled lengthwise with him. There were an undetermined number of enemy combatants lurking that could be hidden mostly anywhere, probably planning an assault on his platoon, wanting to recover their dead and wounded, if any. And who probably were pretty pissed off. He had one dead squad leader among the dead enemy combatants. He had another dead squad leader with his men, some wounded, in the left flank ambush position. The finest soldier he had ever served with was dying of a sucking chest wound in the nearby bushes. And somebody was playing toss the hand grenades at him and Franklin.

A state of queasiness swept through him. His stomach felt like a vacuum pump, sucking in organs and blood from everywhere, leaving his body weak and his head spinning.

Wham!

Another metallic shock wave came from the same direction as the last, but not as close. Maybe the grenade thrower's arm was getting tired.

His head suddenly cleared. Flushed clean with the last explosion. The sad, stark realization that he was going to die brought on a certain clarity to his predicament, and with it the motivation and obligation to start doing something. What had Benning said? Do something, even if it's wrong. Clearly it was military bullshit. And hadn't he already done something wrong by winding up in the middle of this living purgatory. But maybe in this instant they had a point.

He turned his head toward Franklin and whispered that he was perilously positioned on top of a loaded RPG launcher, pinned to the trigger housing, with the possibility of any movement blowing their brains out. He instructed him to start chucking his grenades ASAP and when done to get his own grenades from his canteen pouch on his left hip and keep them going.

Franklin immediately turned on his back, picked a grenade from his canteen pouch, pulled the pin, let go of the spoon, and lobbed the baseball shaped explosive far overhead like a catapult in a westerly direction toward the west black hole.

Before it exploded he repeated twice more.

Wham!

Wham!

Wham!

He then fished into his platoon leader's pouch and started extracting grenades and throwing.

Wham!

Wham!

Wham!

Hank nudged Franklin to start moving over to their left, to the woodline where he hoped Tucker, Doc, Martin, and Romero were. Then he heard rushing movement near where Franklin had thrown their grenades. They must have stirred things up. He raised his bare head slightly over the haunches of his protective malodorous dead body and saw what he thought were three or four inky shadows moving inside the jungle trail.

Again, he acted out of instinct as his mind connected with the urgency to point out this movement to Burlop's men whom he hoped were still behind him. Not wanting to think about the consequences, he kept his head down, his body staying in close contact to the steel pipe with a large warhead with a tapered shape looking nicely designed to fit up a dead dink's ass. He propped his right elbow on the ground while lifting his M-16 by its pistol grip and started blindly firing on automatic at the dark, west entrance to the jungle trail.

Franklin immediately joined in.

Tracer rounds, a reddish hue of sporadic hyphens in the night, shot into the black hole in the jungle. A burst of muzzle flashes and green tracers immediately retaliated out of the hole. A bunch of red tracers followed from the four M-16s and one M-60 in Burlop's group. Then to their left, Romero's M-79 started blooping out 40mm rounds.

Hank and Franklin stopped their firing. They kept their heads down and bodies to the ground and listened to the snapping of bullets passing over their heads, as they prayed to God and to Jesus and to anyone else who had an outside chance of saving them.

It must have worked. After ten seconds that seemed like ten hours there were only the dashes of red. Burlop's men with the assistance of Romero had gained what the U.S. Army would consider fire superiority.

Hank gave Franklin a pointed shove with his left elbow. He stayed still as he watched him stealthily crawl away. He wanted him out of harm's way before he unhooked himself from his entanglement with the trigger mechanism. Franklin was the second finest soldier and he didn't want him around if he were going to be blown to bits. If Dave Watson had been next to him it would be different, he reflected morbidly. And he knew this type of thinking meant he was mentally losing it.

His breathing became more labored and his perspiring intensified as he let go of his M-16 with his right hand and started sliding it underneath him. He sucked in his stomach, and with his thighs pressing in the ground for support he created a slit of a passageway for his hand. He used his right so as to approach from the butt end of the hand grip.

His fingers felt their way up to the trigger guard and then touched lightly around the half-inch steel curve of the trigger itself. His finger tips could feel the trigger, its guard, and the tab end of his web belt buckle. He carefully worked the tab against the guard and slid it a few millimeters down where it appeared not to touch the concave portion of the trigger. He didn't know the amount of pull to fire the weapon and so he had to assume it was a hair trigger, especially if the hammer was cocked. The light pressure of his abdomen on his hand contained his trembling.

He slowly pushed the buckle tab out of the trigger housing. Nothing happened. He was still alive. Maybe the safety catch had been on and it was all paranoia. He didn't care. He grabbed his rifle, did a few, quick body rolls, and started crawling with a cautious haste toward the southern woodline.

As he moved, his eyes focused directly ahead on a fence of waist high grass that seemed to hold back a bunch of jungle thickets. His peripheral vision picked up in the flare light blurry images of amorphous, clumpy shapes.

When he was about two meters away from the high grass, someone stuck his head out and waved him in. It was Romero. Franklin was there in the grass beside him.

It was Sergeant Martin crawling on all fours who guided them to a small, open space set in a cluster of reedy bushes. Tucker was on his back. There was enough flare light filtering through the jungle debris to see that he was fighting consciousness. Hank could see his hands trembling. Doc Fletcher lay next to him holding an IV bag two feet off the ground.

"We should get back to our ambush position," Sergeant Martin whispered wildly into Hank's ear. They were on their stomachs staring at Tucker's feeble state. "Not fucking safe here, sir."

Hank looked at Doc. "Can we move him?"

"Got no choice. We got to."

Hank nodded a weak affirm. "OK…let's do it." There was enough flare light for the others to notice a dark patch of blood covering the right side of their platoon leader's face.

They hadn't stood on their feet since first settling into their ambush position for what they had hoped would be a routine, uneventful night. Now they did so almost in unison with a degree of temerity and courage. It was the only way to move Tucker without killing him.

Romero wedged his hands in Tucker's armpits. Franklin grabbed around the knees and in one precision movement they swooped Tucker up. Doc stayed beside him holding the IV bag. They followed their platoon leader who was rushing into a prickly, scratchy haven of briars, brush, and other assorted jungle. Martin brought up the rear carrying the radio. As they trampled through breaking and swishing branches a sudden scenario dawned on Hank. A scenario of his own men mistaking their commotion for an NVA assault element.

Then as he pushed through the interior darkness of the jungle, another scenario came to mind, compounding the first. What if he's lost and can't find where their ambush position was and aimlessly wondered into the rear security unit to be shot dead?

Hank stopped. His heart didn't. It kept racing. He tried to think where their position had been. His mind sprinted to the route he crawled getting to the kill zone. And his memory backtracked. He felt they had drifted too far to the left. He turned right and headed in what he hoped was in a westerly direction. He came to a small trampled down area. He found it.

In the light it would have looked like an abandoned esoteric picnic with strewn poncho blankets, C-ration cans and boxes, left behind claymore bags, smoke grenades and other discarded non-essentials and two rucksacks that Romero and Franklin had humped.

There were spent claymore clackers, and one that was still live. The one between their animal and Burlop's. The one they had been facing while crawling around in ghoulsville.

Franklin and Romero carefully laid Tucker down. They all dropped beside him and sat on their haunches. Doc checked the placement and tightness of the bandage while Romero held the IV bag.

Sergeant Martin set the radio down upright next to Hank. He straightened the antenna. He nudged Hank with his forearm and gently rapped Hank's knuckles with the handset. Hank took it.

"Bravo Five, this is November Six. We need a jungle penetrator." There just wasn't an LZ nearby. The kill zone would have been perfect but there was no telling what shit was still around. "Bravo Five here. I copy. We'll…" The transmission was suddenly cut. The net was keyed.

"Break! Break! This is Demon Three," Woodson intruded. "The tactical situation is too dangerous. A hovering chopper would be a sitting duck."

Regrettably, Hank had to admit the major was right. It wouldn't be safe, to Tucker or the chopper. He considered the kill zone again, but again discarded it as fool hardy. "All right," he finally said, "we'll move to yesterday's LZ."

"Negative! Can't do that. Not at night with a possible NVA company out there. It's stupid, asinine. That LZ is too far. No. You'll have to sit it out till daylight. I'm not going to have you gamble your platoon's safety for one man. Do you copy?"

Hank hyperventilated, rapidly sucking in and out short bursts of air, trying to blow off some of the tremendous pressure steaming up deep inside, fueled by his frustration and nerves. Finally, his thin shell could no longer accept all the crap being stuffed inside him and he exploded.

"Listen you bastard!" his voice raged over the radio as well as around his men. He felt a quieting hand clamp on his shoulder and he dropped his volume but kept the venom. "This is your goddamn mess. Now I'm getting Tucker to that LZ ASAP. And you better have that fuckin' dust-off on station when we get there. Understand? Because if you don't…I'll shove my rifle so far up your ass you'll be spitting bullets!"

CHAPTER 40

LIEUTENANT COLONEL WEST had been in deep, exhaustion inspired sleep. A foggy dream of a violent thunderstorm pelted somewhere in his brain as the 105 battery hammered away in support of Bravo's Third Platoon. The storm slackened to a drizzle as all the howitzers save the one firing illumination halted their salvos. The drizzle stopped momentarily as the gun jammed, then started again as the rhythmic firing resumed from another gun.

West woke up. He rubbed his eyes, raised his head up from the cot, and listened to a solitary howitzer booming every minute or so. He swung into his boots, didn't waste time tying and lacing, and trotted to the TOC bunker in a funny gait, carefully avoiding tripping over loose laces and bunching his toes to keep from losing a boot. He stepped down into clinging cigar smoke and overheard Hank's threat.

"What the hell's going on, Major?"

After waiting a few precious seconds for the major to answer, time in which Tucker's heart pumped a few more milliliters of blood up against his bandage, some being absorbed by the compact layers of gauze, some oozing out the seams, and only a portion going back into his system, Hank threw down the handset, muttering, "Screw it."

It would be pure hell beating a new path back to the LZ and there was the strong possibility of getting lost. He thought about backtracking over the same ground they had stomped down in coming from the LZ. It was a big risk. In the dark they might not be able to keep on the same path. Their beaten down trail wouldn't be that prominent. It wasn't as though they had cut a symmetrical swath. It had been a lot of bending branches, and stepping over and around things, and so they could lose time by cutting some new stuff. And though they wouldn't be blazing a new trail, it would be a rough carry for Tucker

And than there was the LZ. Yesterday it had been hot. But the TAC air had probably uprooted them. Who knows, maybe their attackers were now just meters away, and all dead. But *all* wouldn't be dead, not an entire NVA company, if that's what it had been.

And then there was the fastest route to the LZ. Maybe....There was the wide, well-traveled NVA jungle trail heading east from the clearing. The one where the gooks were headed before their journey was tragically cut short.

What were the odds that trail continued due east straight to the LZ? Even if it veered about twenty degrees either way it would probably intersect a portion.

They could make good time. If it started veering more than twenty degrees off the east azimuth they could then start plowing through the jungle.

And then what if the NVA were on the trail? What if they set up their own retaliatory ambush?

But he thought that unlikely. All the movement after popping the ambush—the counterattack, the shadowy movement, the grenades—had been near the west trail.

He had to quickly come to a decision if Tucker were going to live.

He first radioed Burlop's men to ensure they had returned to their ambush position. He then radioed all three remote positions telling to get down to the prone. He then went back to Burlop's men and told them to pop their three live claymores. The ones that pointed in the general direction of the east NVA trail.

There were three explosions, followed by one more as he hit the clacker on his position's remaining Claymore.

He ordered his group to saddle up, picked the handset up, brushed dirt from the earpiece, and echoed his saddle up to the remainder of the platoon.

Hank noticed Franklin's shadow reach down to pick up Tucker's radio. He grabbed his wrist and stopped him. "I'll carry it," he said.

"I can do it. You're the platoon leader."

Hank answered by picking it up, hoisting it over his back, and letting the shoulder straps slip through his arms. "Stay by me," he told Franklin. He suddenly realized he was without his helmet, having lost it somewhere in the graveyard.

Somehow Sergeant Martin assembled everyone together in a single file with a minimum of confusion and noise. Hank was the fourth man back, Franklin behind him, and Tucker in the middle of the file on a makeshift jungle litter carried by four volunteers. Others carried Sergeant Michael's body. The wounded were ambulatory. Burlop's body was out in the kill zone with maybe a dozen other mutilated corpses. And there were probably some that weren't corpses. It was too dangerous to retrieve his body. And there was no time. Burlop would have to wait.

As they started to move out, a call came in over the radio. "November Six, this is Demon Six. Get to the LZ. We'll have a ship on station, over."

The Battalion CO's transmission jabbed Hank like a hypodermic full of adrenalin. "Roger, thank you, sir," he answered, breaking regulations by using "sir." Benning said it was never to be used over the radio. But now it seemed the only quick way of expressing gratitude. "We're beginning to move. Have the artillery out the illumination. And have it prep our LZ."

Hopefully the 105 rounds would deter the NVA from lingering around their landing zone, which would now be the pick-up zone for Tucker's dust-off. And the sounds of the exploding rounds would be an addition to the azimuth in helping to vector them.

"Demon Six, Wilco. Good luck."

Hank broke squelch twice.

He had made his decision on the route. They were going to go with what offered to be the fastest. They were going to use the NVA trail.

It turned into a long, black tunnel of the type youthful nightmares are made.

The swiftness by which the point man moved reminded Hank of some sort of ass dragging snail as he inched along, moving his head slowly side to side before taking another step. Hank sensed Tucker's life winding down. There was only one way to move faster. He quickened his pace, and with Franklin at his heels, just where Tucker had always been, he passed the three snails and took over the point.

Now they moved in and out of a walk and a run. A brisk walk until someone stumbled and fell and then a run to catch up before the dark figure ahead disappeared into the black overgrown mineshaft they were trying to get through. The four carrying Tucker acted as shock absorbers, when one tripped the others took up the slack to dampen the jolt. Of all, they sweated and grunted the loudest. Hank kept glancing at the luminous dial of his compass as he advanced into the lesser blackness of the trail guarded on either side by the total blackness of the jungle's walls. Occasionally he would drift too far to one side and the brush of branches and vines deflected him back along the centerline. He could hear the sounds of exploding artillery shells getting louder.

They were getting closer. Another fifty meters he guessed until the stream that ran next to their LZ. He started seeing lightning like flashes beyond what he hoped was the exit from this surreal nightmare. He radioed for the artillery to stop the HE and switch to illumination.

A star shell popped its flare and an eerie, milky light penetrated the triple canopy. Then he came upon an intersection to the jungle trail. Another even wider trail heading north/south. He passed it swiftly, glancing right and left, expecting something bad. Then ahead he could make out the exit to the stream, and beyond it, the tree line that was the western edge of their LZ. And he started thinking something good.

And then he stumbled and fell.

A large root that snaked across the trail after he passed the intersection had caught his foot, bringing him down hard. Briars streaked thin blood lines across the left side of his face as he fell and landed heavily on his chest taking in the radio's extra weight. He let out a big grunt as the ground whacked him. He started to rise slowly to clear a few cobwebs and allow his system to recharge. And then his hand brushed something steel and thin and out of place and he jerked his hand back as if electrocuted. His brain circuitry rifled through data files pulling together memory with feel. It was a wire, a taut wire. But it couldn't be. His hand sought to confirm his suspicions. It was a wire. A tripwire!

He froze. Slowly his eyes lifted upward with all the vision he could muster. Franklin reacted immediately when he saw, mostly heard, his platoon leader nose dive. He pivoted around and hissed a halt to prevent a pile up. The file accordioned together but kept its integrity. He turned back around and knew something was wrong when he noticed November Six's bare head rise slowly and then start to scan like an animal sniffing for predators. He quickly went to the prone and waved a frantic hand for the man behind him to do likewise. A chain reaction rippled and in a few seconds no one was standing.

Where was it? What was it? Were they almost in a kill zone of an ambush? Was there really nothing at all but his paranoia? Hank's mind rummaged around and could only find questions. Suddenly his eyes provided the answer as they glimpsed the dark outline of a giant plumb bob dangling over the trail from the limb of a tree a few meters behind him near the intersection. He had passed right under it. A 105mm high explosive plumb bob. A boobytrap! It had probably been set up to trip by coming in the other direction. Yesterday, if his platoon had found this trail to escape their hot LZ they would likely have detonated it.

Shivers ran up his spine. His gut felt like ice cubes in a blender. With an unsteady hand he unclipped the handset from his harness. "November Five, November Six. We've got a one-oh-five round connected to a tripwire. We got to blow it. Send up all the rope you can get."

"Bravo Five. We ain't got no rope. Burlop was gonna bring some, but I told him to forget it. I didn't think we were going anywhere but back to our hooches." Martin's tone reeked with apology.

Shit. Hank bit his lip. "Okay, how about claymore wire? See if anybody's got any left and get it up here ASAP."

"Roger that."

A full minute and a half went by. The spring in Tucker's life unwound some more. Hank could feel it around his neck choking him. He heard the soft trot of footsteps and then Martin was beside him on the ground thrusting two coils of claymore wire in his face. Thank God the rear ambush position had not blown their Claymores.

"Two hundred feet enough?"

"Let's hope so," Hank answered.

"Why can't we bypass it?" Martin asked urgently.

"Not sure we'll locate where the trip wire ends and can't waste time looking."

Martin's head nodded his understanding, his face lost in its shadows.

"You and Franklin get everybody back."

Again the helmet nodded.

Somehow Hank willed his hands to stop shaking like a jackhammer and he looped the claymore wire around the tripwire using a bush for support to insure the wires didn't touch and the weight set it off. As he tied a knot to close the loop, perspiration poured from a spillway between his eyes and down his nose. Finishing, he carefully unraveled the coil of claymore wire as he backed away. As he moved back, so did the platoon. When he reached the end, he tied the next wire to the end. He moved back thirty more feet then thought, *Fuck it. A hundred thirty feet should be enough.* He didn't have time to retreat further. The casualty radius for a 105 he guessed was about thirty meters.

He glanced around and his eyes fixed on the huddled shadowy shapes of Franklin and Martin on the ground behind a tree just off the trail. Deductively, he concluded everyone was down. He went to the prone into thick jungle foliage. He slowly pulled in the slack, wrapped a few feet of wire around his right hand, and gave a sharp, powerful tug.

Wham!

The blast was deafening. Shrapnel shot out in all directions, cutting through the jungle with the sound of a violent hail storm.

Hank jumped to his feet and waved Franklin and Martin up and he bounded into a slowly dissipating fog of smoke, dirt, and cinders of pulverized foliage.

He ran. The platoon ran with him. He emerged choking out of the smoke. He panted and gasped. His lungs couldn't suck air in fast enough.

He stumbled and fell out of the jungle and into the west fork of the shallow stream flanking the landing zone. He struggled to his feet and splashed across. He turned and saw Franklin in the water and others behind him.

He took refuge in a thin tree line next to the wide meadow where he observed his men fording the stream. He put the headset to his ear and leap-frogged the protocol of chain of command and radioed Colonel West. "Demon…Six… this is…November…Six," his heaving chest vied with his voice, stammering his words, "We…are at the…LZ. Dust-off…not on station."

"Demon Six, Roger. It should be checking in in zero-five."

Hank remained standing in one spot as he watched a perimeter form in the clearing like circling wagons. He ran over and positioned himself in the middle, dropping to one knee. Tucker and Sergeant Michael's lifeless body were laid down a few meters away. The slightly wounded sat down nearby and gazed skyward for their chopper.

Hank wasn't able to look in Tucker's vicinity. He got up and busied himself by checking the perimeter. It didn't seem the securest of LZs. It was too large to post men in the tree line at the corners. Instead, they were all in the open, sitting ducks to enemy fire from the vast blind surrounding them. Maybe they should have stayed together hiding in the tree line.

He wished the goddamn chopper would come on station.

He had been around full circle and was staring at one of the M-60 positions when he felt strong, pinching fingers in his left bicep. He swung around. It was Doc Fletcher, his face cold and dark in the flare light. His eye sockets hollow.

"What is it?"

"Tucker's dead."

He heard a voice near his heart where the handset hung. "November Six, this is Red Hawk Forty-seven. I'm a dust-off. Understand you have an urgent WIA. If your PZs secure, mark by strobe."

"This is…November Six. Dustoff…no longer urgent. Two…KIAs… Three ambulatory."

"Roger, November Six. We are only required to pick up urgents at night. We'll send out another dust-off at first light. Do you Roger?"

"Roger."

"This is Red Hawk Forty-seven, out."

Hank could hear the helicopter in the distance. It gained altitude as it turned around.

At dawn the dead and wounded were choppered off. November plowed through more jungle to a second LZ, secured by Lima and Mike Platoons under overall command of Lieutenant Brussels. From there they were air extracted. They set down at the Battalion's fire support base and were winding through the concertina wire as Lima's point was reaching the clearing that had served as their night's kill zone.

Sixteen mostly mangled, fly-infested, dead NVA soldiers and assorted weaponry, along with the remains of Sergeant Burlop, were found. Half of an NVA platoon had been annihilated.

Hank stood at rigid attention, heels locked, back ramrod straight, in front of a small wooden field desk inside the Battalion CP tent. His disheveled hair, grizzled whiskered face—left side looking like a cat had attacked him, the other with a bandage that covered his right cheek—mud and blood caked fatigues, and unbloused boots parodied his strict military bearing. A stocky man sat behind the desk, face of brown leather with deep creases, narrow eyes void of emotion, lips tight. Hank waited for him to speak in a harsh, clipped voice. He wasn't disappointed.

"Major Woodson wants me to bring court martial proceedings against you," Colonel West said in a flat, weary tone. He didn't seem to look at Hank, but rather through him. "Do you have anything to say?"

"No, sir."

While West's eyes held no emotion, Hank trumped it with a face that had stopped caring.

West's eyes continued to X-ray as he methodically tapped a pencil on his desk like a small hammer.

"You're not getting one," he said.

"Sir?"

"A court martial. It's a pain in the ass court martialing an officer." Some life, not much, but a little, came into his dark stare. "Besides, you're on your way to the Brigade. That should get you out of our hair. This afternoon you'll take a re-supply Chinook back to Lai Khe and process the hell out of the Battalion. Any questions?"

"No, sir."

The pencil stopped tapping. "You blew your cool, Kirby. You goddamn blew your cool with Woodson. No one, I repeat, no one talks to a superior officer the way you did, regardless of the situation." The eyes had reached their limit. They weren't going to let in any more warmth.

"Yes, sir."

"Did you know your platoon has stepped on more gooks than any in the Battalion?"

"Sir?"

"It's a fact. We keep records, just like professional baseball. Your men have batted in the most runs. You've made me look like a good manager. Too bad you had to blow it. I'd like to have given you a medal on your departure; now, just be lucky I'm not burning your tail."

"Yes, sir."

"By the way, this Red Cross letter is for someone in your platoon." Colonel West reached out over the desk and handed an envelope to Hank.

Hank took one step backward, held a salute until the colonel returned it, then about faced and walked out.

In bright sunlight he examined the envelope with squinting eyes. It was addressed to a Specialist 4th Class James E. Tucker. He tore it open and read the typed message:

THE AMERICAN RED CROSS IS HAPPY TO INFORM YOU THAT YOU ARE THE FATHER OF A 7-POUND, 8-OUNCE BOY BORN JANUARY 4, 1969. BOTH WIFE AND SON ARE IN EXCELLENT HEALTH. CONGRATULATIONS!

PART 4
THE REMFS

CHAPTER 41

FRED SADLER WAS goddamn happy. Elated. The commercial afforded him the opportunity to struggle out of his favorite chair for a piss stop and beer run. Though it didn't matter there was a commercial. The game was over and yes, by God, he had seen the greatest upset of modern day football, the Jets had beaten the purportedly mighty Colts.

He gloated over the game while watching a strong white stream of urine splash loudly in the toilet water.

And Pam, she had had the best view of the game. She wasn't limited to the narrow field of camera vision, of only the quarterback, his line, one fullback, and one half of the tailback that just couldn't seem to fit all of himself into the TV screen. It seemed his tail was always missing. Maybe that's why the commentators called him a tailback. Fred smiled broadly at his own little private joke, shook off a few remaining drops, poked his tool back in, and zipped up.

He headed for the fridge, the grin a permanent fixture on his face. Pam had seen it all. She and Dave together. He had intently studied the screen every time it briefly switched from the field to the spectators in hopes of seeing them. But no luck. He could hardly wait until late this evening when they'd be getting back. He and Dave would have a long rap and laugh and gloat over the NFL's demise and the AFL's emerging dominance.

He had no trouble finding another brew from the many cold bottles that stood before him on the top shelf. He interrupted the perfect formation as he grabbed one, popped the cap with a church key and took a long tug, inhaling nearly one fourth of the contents. He felt himself stagger slightly as he retreated to his chair, tired from his activity, and fell back into his place of domicile.

There was some post game commentary, but his head was swimming a little and he had trouble understanding what was being said. So what, the screen was now so blurry it really didn't matter.

He tugged another fourth and belched and tilted his head to stare at the ceiling. Now that seemed sharp and clear. He sighed as he began to reflect. He was nearly content. He knew that. Only one thing had to be done to feel really good and have peace of mind.

He had to stop the damn letter-writing business. It was time to Dear John that worthless shithead and Dear Jane Pam.

Sure, things had run fairly smoothly. The only real incident had been that time he had pressured Pam to finish the letter so he would be sure to mail it. It had started innocently enough. He just suggested it, pointing out the benefit of him taking it personally to the post office. But she said no, almost friendly, but he detected a little mental tightness, maybe because of that letter she had just received from Kirby, or rather from him. God it was getting bad when he thought of his letters as actually being Kirby's.

Anyway, he got a little firmer, telling her to go ahead and finish it, that he wanted to mail it. Pam exploded, getting all worked up and livid and frown-mouthed. And he had gotten all hot and sweaty worrying about that letter getting by him and Vietnam bound.

But then he rapidly changed tactics and out of character got all apologetic and wet-eyed and poured out his emotions saying that all he wanted was to help his daughter, that he knew things were rough with her boyfriend and though he didn't like him, if getting her letter to him any faster and safer would help, he wanted to do it.

To his much-relieved mind she had kissed him, spent an extra half hour to wrap-up the letter and gave it to him to personally see that it got the right kind of send off.

And it did. It sure damn did.

But it was all getting too damn much he thought as he continued focusing on the grainy texture of the ceiling. Only he didn't see the grainy texture. It looked smooth right now.

He'd have to end this thing now. Even so he'd still have to post a vigil against a possible stray getting through. But when he saw one he'd just deep six it. His literary days would be ending shortly.

He sucked in air with a long heavy snore. The bottle dropped to the floor and lost the other half of its contents.

CHAPTER 42

THE LOUD RUSHING noise from the bank of four radios staring at Hank sounded like a bleak beach wind whipping surf. Trembling slightly, the imagined wind biting frostily into his skin, Hank stood staring back at them, his nerves pushed on edge. Suddenly there was a lull as three of the radios keyed simultaneously; the prelude to receiving transmissions, and Hank dreaded this superficial quietude even more.

He looked frantically to his right for assistance from his NCO, Sergeant Durgin, a portly, jowly, balding SFC, sitting on a folding chair, his back to Hank, writing on a pad of paper while casually conversing as if in pleasant conversation with a good buddy on the fourth radio, a secure net with a special scrambler for sending secrets. But Hank knew it wasn't a buddy, that it was a Battalion RTO calling in platoon AP coordinates for posting with those of other ambushing platoons that made up the nighttime activities in the Third Brigade AO. And Hank also knew that Durgin was adroitly attuned to avoiding crises, his conversation a cocoon insulating himself from involvement with Hank's problems, the other three radios. Durgin had isolated himself for most of the afternoon, ever since the first crisis began.

Resigning himself to the sergeant's non-support, Hank glanced up from Durgin's Friar Tuck bald spot, which seemed to watch him coolly like a cycloptic eye. He looked past him down near the far end of a dead-end hallway of plywood at the artillery spec-four who manned two more radios sitting next to the Air Force liason NCO. The dark-skinned spec-four sat with his chair on its back legs, facing Hank, his large droopy dog's eyes, like golf balls with tiny black dots in the center, seeming to offer Hank some sympathy. Or was it puzzlement, Hank saw, for not knocking Durgin aside the head?

But Durgin would soon get his. For Hank had discussed his ineptness with Captain Connors, and Connors had agreed to ship him out to MAC-V to join an advisor team to an ARVN unit. Hank couldn't help but wonder how Durgin had managed to survive with Hank's predecessor. But then again, his predecessor had been relieved of duty after going berserk and shooting one of the radios with a forty-five. Maybe his predecessor had chosen shooting the radio to shooting Durgin. If so, he had been even crazier than they had thought. No wonder Captain Connors didn't want to give reasons for his predecessor's departure.

Connors had been supportive of Hank during these trying first two weeks. And why not, after luring Hank into this dead-end hallway of a duty station he called with glorifying hyperbole "the heart of the TOC." A heart of white fluorescent lights; of a long blue counter top laden with bulky radios and covered with acetate adorned with grease penciled hen scratchings, products of hurried and harried notes, messages, and coordinates, all in combinations of individual shorthand systems embossed in glare from the fluorescents. A glare Hank gave partial credit for his recurring headaches.

And there was more glare reflected off more acetate that stretched across the chess board of the Third Brigade, a huge topo map encompassing the entire wall opposite the long counter. In lieu of hen scratchings, this acetate was grease penciled with a form of hieroglyphic graffiti, the chess pieces— military symbols—for types and sizes of units, for ambush positions, for boundaries of other friendlies not part of the Brigade, for suspected enemy locations, and for various artillery and air fire zones including football field like rectangles, denoting the next day's B-52 strikes, heavy artillery they called it, as if it were some sort of lethal weather pattern. The enemy location chess pieces were placed on the board using guestimates, greatly complicating the game.

So this little dead-end hallway, one wall of radios, the other wallpapered in a funny, crazy mosaic pattern, was the lifeblood of the TOC.

To Hank it wasn't the heart. Connors had mixed up the anatomy, confusing it with a giant sphincter. With Hank at the opening catching all the shit. Even so, no matter how much he hated it, he would take all of this to be free from the field. Despite of it all, he couldn't fault Connors. Not at all. And when he was off duty, away from here, he realized this. But not now. Not when the three radios in near garbled unison became a case of diarrhea.

His mind fielded their transmissions, getting their gist. He had been listening and responding to their diatribes for some time now. And it was the same old thing. Each radio had taken on a familiar personality.

Radio One's latest transmission was more panic wailing from a young Lurp (LRRP-Long Range Reconnaissance Patrol) whose five-man recon patrol had fled from a squad of VC at the expense of one casualty, the patrol leader, who took an AK round in the shoulder and who, in the prognosis of the young Lurp, would be dead if a chopper didn't get there soonest to get their asses out. The young Lurp's wail proclaimed Hank the one accountable for getting the chopper, and thus for the life of his patrol leader.

Maybe the Lurp was now designating Hank as God. But why not? For them it was now that time to believe.

Such was Radio One.

Radio Two was a platoon of A-CAVs that had been waylaid by a land mine and a hit and run onslaught of RPGs. The bush had been popped when the lead A-CAV disintegrated in a gigantic explosion. Radio Two's first report suggested a new, terrible weapon in the employ of the enemy: one of immense and frightening power. Almost a miniature nuke. Hank guessed it less exotic. Maybe more like an ex-dud 500-pounder the gooks had salvaged from an air strike and replanted it for their own use. Just like the 500-pounder an engineer's outfit discovered four days ago during a morning sweep ten klicks further up the road.

There was little trace of the unfortunate armored vehicle. There was no trace of its four men. Two of the other three vehicles had taken RPG hits on their thin metal skins above the tracks. Another MECH platoon immediately rumbled in a blind cavalry charge to their rescue, to be greeted with their own quota of RPG rounds, all four taking hits. A small stretch of Highway 13 between Lai Khe and Quan Loi had become a scrap iron junk heap peppered with screaming bodies and stray arms and legs. Just now Radio Two screeched that people were dying because Hank hadn't sent out the dust-offs.

But Hank had. A bevy of dustoffs. Everyone in the Brigade. Plus the colonel's C&C ship with the colonel, S-3, and Connors, and a second Command and Control chopper under the command of the Battalion CO whose MECH units had just been decimated. And then there were the light fire teams, Hunter/Killer teams, and Ready Reaction Forces barreling ass out there. All intent upon getting even.

All but two of the light choppers were headed to that carnage. One of the other two was being used by a Battalion CO for a VR of a future RIF route for one of his companies.

The other second chopper was being demanded by an impatient, shrill voice: Radio Three. A Captain Macy. The tall, black, one-time wide receiver at Morgan State, recently made company commander of the Lurps, paced back and forth at the helipad, anxiously waiting for a slick to take him to rescue his patrol, now hiding in the Hobo Woods from a VC squad.

Hank liked Macy, though he had only met him briefly one night in Looie's Lounge. It distressed him that he couldn't magically materialize that chopper for him and his Lurps, especially since he had promised him a chopper in one-zero and it was now two-zero. By all rights, Macy should have had it by now. But how did Hank know that Lieutenant Burns, the Brigade S-3 Air, would once again give an unauthorized slick to Nadine and the other Red Cross Donut Dollies for transportation out to a fire support base to play "Simon says," "seven up," and "why don't you drool over our sweet little asses" with the field troopers. They'd then come back to Lai Khe and spend the evenings with the remfs.

And to Hank, one of the biggest remfs and biggest pricks was Burns. Maybe that's what big-titted, tight-assed Nadine saw in him, a big prick. Hank saw someone else, someone too manicured, too smooth, too snotty, too smug. Someone with a nose up so high that he looked you in the eye with his nostrils.

Hank knew Burns was at the opposite far end of the massive TOC bunker in his cubbyhole next to Connors'. He was on the horn radioing Nadine's pilot to instruct him to head back, drop the dollies and swing by for Macy. Hank also knew that Burns didn't really give a shit if the pilot turned around, or whether Macy rescued his Lurps. Burns was too damn short; too much of an asshole. Tomorrow he'd be gone, derosing, leaving Hank, who had been his roommate for the past two weeks. This thought offered Hank the only thing good out of all the wailing, screeching, garbled sounds that blew like a gale at him at the same time.

He sucked in a breath, held it, and answered each radio in turn the same way. "This is Duty Five-Five. Will be on station shortly. Hang on."

His stomach churned, the knots pulled tighter.

He wished he was God.

He put the handset down on the long grease-penciled, acetate coated table and sunk down heavily in a metal folding chair. He stared unseeingly at the bank of radios as he subconsciously traced the scar on his right cheek with the tip of his right index finger

Doc Fletcher had volunteered to stitch it up after Hank had had his ass chewed by the colonel and before taking a re-supply Chinook back to Lai Khe to officially transfer to Brigade HQ. But he had declined, not wanting to chance the Doc's field handiwork turning half his face into a Frankenstein monster. Doc was OK with the turn down, but urged the now former November Six to get a proper stitching by a doctor at Lai Khe. A piece of advice Hank failed to follow for one simple reason: he didn't care.

The Doc's advice for stitches, however, proved sage since the wound kept pulling and tearing when he ate and talked. As such, instead of having a razor thin line on his face, he now had a line that looked drawn by a blunt No. 2 pencil.

He looked at his watch. It was 1515. Finsley was late as usual. Hank had the 0700 to 1500 hours shift, though he always, in his two weeks as a TOC duty officer, worked to 1530 hours, or longer, in transitioning the duties over to his relief, Lieutenant Finsley. It was usually longer. Finsley was usually late.

Hank recognized that Finsley was a turd of a similar feces as Burns. Only Burns was a cool shit in a sly, quiet, devious way. Finsley was more of the hot shit specimen. He was a unique person: he knew everything, he was always right, and evidently, he wanted the world aware of his genius because he was always shouting, which revved up into a roar if someone proffered the slightest disagreement.

As his mind badmouthed him, Finsley entered the sphincter. Hank was standing and staring at the radios; Durgin was sitting and talking on the secure net, back and bald spot to Hank; the spec-four was now sitting and conversing on his radios with a 155 SP Battery firing on behalf of the A-CAVs and a 105 Battery attempting comfort for the Lurps.

"What's going on, Kirby?" Finsley yelled effortlessly. Hank turned and looked at him. His expression was neutral, masking his feelings. "Things have gotten hot, Spence. Two MECH platoons have been ambushed and got a slew of casualties. They're no longer in contact but they're sweating about the status of the dust-offs."

"Well, how about the dust-offs? What are you doing about it? How come they don't have any yet?"

"The whole fucking Medevac was scrambled ASAP. They should be on station any minute. They can't fly the speed of sound you know."

"Don't be a smart-ass Kirby," Finsley now put a slight effort into his yell. "What else?"

"A Lurp patrol had a short contact with a VC squad. They're hiding in the Hobo Woods with a patrol leader that took one in the shoulder. Macy's been waiting at the helipad for a slick. He's pissed because it hasn't showed. He wants it to go out for the rescue."

"Well, where's his chopper?"

Hank's lips turned into a frown. He tilted his head toward the entry way aiming across the hall at Burns' cubby hole. "The S-3 Air gave it to the Donut Dollies. Right now he's trying to save his ass and get the pilot to come back and pick up Macy."

"Heh, heh," Finsley chuckled and his voice came down to normal, a whisper for him. "Floyd's something else. Keeping Nadine satisfied to the last," he said smiling and shrugged his shoulders. "Shit, so what, those choppers are his until tomorrow. If he thinks the Dollies should have a higher priority than the fucking Lurps and a new CO, that's his business. Besides, if those jerk Lurps are stupid enough to hop off in the middle of the VC infested Hobo Woods by their lonesome, the gung-ho bastards deserve a little grief."

Hank tightened his fists. He mustered every ounce of restraint to keep from grabbing Finsley around the throat and choking with all his might until those big brown blotches of freckles turned red, then purple, then white. He looked him in the eyes, a stare of disgust and dislike. Finsley returned it with equal force. A Mexican standoff.

Hank released his stare. "Durgin's still posting AP coordinates. Not much else to report," he said calmly, as if there had been no confrontation of eyeballs.

He picked his fatigue cap off Radio One and moved past Finsley and out of the TOC's heart, sphincter or whatever it was. Before he could turn the corner and head down the plywood partitioned hall to the TOC's exit, Finsley called out. "Can't wait to get back to the hooch and try to get some pussy off Wan, huh Kirby? Well forget it. I'm going to be the first to tap that gook cunt. Just wait!"

Hank caught his last words as he was driving the stairs, two at a time, hurrying to get out of the claustrophobic air-conditioned bunker, weighted with its tons of concrete overhead cover that now felt as if it were pressing down, squashing his head into a pulpy, throbbing migraine.

Wan was their hooch girl, which in Wan's own description was "same, same maid." Which she was. She cleaned their quarters, washed their fatigues, made their bunks, and polished their boots. In return, the six lieutenants in the hooch each paid her ten dollars a month.

But to Hank, Wan was more than "same, same maid." She was the most unique Vietnamese girl he had met. A mixture of Vietnamese and French, and one of the most beautiful girls—Vietnamese, American, Australian, or whatever—he had ever seen. Just as her blood was a mixture, so was her beauty. Part was physical: an exquisitely shaped face with high cheekbones, surprisingly large eyes, dark yet light with much expression, lips not too fat or too thin, and they easily worked into a smile and then a wide grin of flashing white teeth that an orthodontist could not have made straighter. Her hair was silky black and flowed down her back past her shoulder blades. She even had nice boobs and a round ass that her white tunic, gray with the dirt of her job, and black pajama bottoms couldn't hide.

And then there was her personality. Very warm and genuinely friendly. She possessed also a shy sense of humor that, together with her unusually good, but still fragmented English, was most becoming.

And then there was her virtue. He couldn't prove it, yet he knew she hadn't fucked any of the lieutenants. He had heard rumors of her refusing fifty dollars for a quickie during her daily chores.

The sun was hot but reassuring. His migraine lessened the further he got from the TOC. He walked across a dirt parking area next to the mess and glanced to his right at an OV-10 racing down the airstrip on takeoff. His legs maintained their forward strides as his eyes followed until it was airborne. Then his eyes came back in his line of march. Fifty meters ahead he saw his hooch, a long A-frame on a cement slab. Behind it was a high chainlink fence that was the limits of the Vietnamese Village of Lai Khe. The fence was dual purpose. It kept the Vietnamese in at night, and the horny GIs sniffing for short-time girls, out. He was apprehensive about sleeping beside a Vietnamese village. A chain-link fence did not a stone wall make.

He would have preferred a stone wall. Though he recognized that a stone wall did not safety make. It was still better than a chain-link fence.

On the Vietnamese side of the fence were the back sides of lean-tos, constructed of wood, tin, and cardboard, that served as market stores for the village. Garbage and other refuse were usually stacked up high behind these stores making for a sorry view. Sometimes when the wind was wrong a rotting smell would waft through Hank's hooch, mingled with loud snorts from rooting pigs working hard at their task of disposing of the waste.

Take away the closeness of the fence, with its representation of unforeseen danger and its occasional stench, the location of his hooch wasn't in a particularly bad spot of the subdivision of billets of the Third Brigade Headquarters. It was isolated from other hooches. Its long side ran east-west. Twenty meters to the east was Highway 13 which cut south-north through the base camp, then into the hinterlands that preceded Quan Loi, Hank's first base camp home and now property of the First CAV. Just a klick up the road was the helipad where Hank now imagined Captain Macy pacing frantically back and forth, cursing his name, seething at the delay of the chopper. Hank prayed he wouldn't be pacing much longer.

Many klicks further up there were the wasted A-CAVs and unimaginable horrors.

Immediately west of his hooch, only a short distance away, was Looie's Lounge, a self-service barroom for junior officers. In his two long weeks with Brigade, he had familiarized himself quite well with Looie's Lounge. South of it were a latrine and showers, then an air force FAC hooch, and then, to Hank's dislike, a big radio antenna looming tall, stark, and foreboding, the perfect registration point for incoming mortar rounds. South again was the eastern edge of one of two long rectangular buildings that were connected by short, open corridors and that reminded Hank somewhat of his high school, and that housed the Brigade headquarters which blanketed the underground complex where Hank worked. East of this at an oblique angle, was the mess hall and then Highway 13. And in the middle of it all, the open space where Hank now walked, heading to his hooch.

All around, looking like an infestation of giant mole tunnels, were the long bunkers of half sections of corrugated pipe, upon which were stacked brown, dry-rotted sandbags.

West of all this was a low-income area of EM hooches before giving way to the upper income of high ranking captains and field grades. Connors lived there. South of the upper incomes and west of the entomological complex, now Brigade headquarters, was the terminus of the subdivision, the colonel's quarters, or villa as it was called. And it was.

And north of it all, there was the Vietnamese village fence.

And now to Hank's left about a hundred feet away in the open-air showers between Looie's Lounge and the FAC hooch was Wan. She was squatting on her haunches in a spreading pool of water delivered by a cascade fed from a shower head tapped into a fifty-five-gallon drum supported overhead by four-by-four beams. Her hair seemed to glisten like black satin as she busily scrubbed a fatigue shirt on an old washboard. Feeling Hank's eyes, she glanced up from her chore. She smiled warmly and waved a soapy wet hand, then went back to her scrubbing.

Hank waved back, his eyes staying on her, caught by her innocent beauty. Suddenly a blurry line came into his peripheral vision and he quickly ducked to avoid possible decapitation by a clothesline strung between a corner edge of his hooch and a rubber tree not far from his door. He swore silently at the near mishap. It hadn't been the first. He glanced at Wan furtively to see if she had witnessed his spasticity. She hadn't, and he felt relieved as he entered his hooch.

The screen door banged shut.

His was a tidy room. Containing two bunks carefully made up a la Wan, along opposite walls, as far apart as physically possible. His on the right, Burns' on the left. Tomorrow Burns' would be stripped to the bare mattress, just as he had found his two weeks ago. The room was sectioned off from the other two-thirds of the hooch by a wall of plywood sheets nailed to studs.

The room would have been clean if it weren't for the tiny bits of sand and dirt that lay concealed in the pores of the cement, safe from Wan's waist-high broom. They only came out on Hank's feet when he traipsed around barefooted.

And then there was the hole.

It had a semi-symmetrical opening about two and a half feet in diameter and was five or so feet deep, set into the floor next to the plywood wall and in the neutral zone between Hank's and Burns's bunks. Burns had told him the hole was there before him, probably made when Lai Khe was noted throughout III Corps as rocket city. The almost nightly shelling must have driven some poor, and either energetic or frenzied, soul to burst through eight inches of concrete and shovel big gobs of dirt. Maybe he had gotten tired of scurrying to a bunker every night.

Burns, in his resourceful way, had discovered it made a good trash dump and the bottom two feet were filled with cups and discarded envelopes. Wan had told Hank, as if she thought he expected her to clean it out, that the hole was too deep for her to get into and get out. He said he agreed and that it didn't really matter.

He dropped wearily on his bunk, unlaced his boots, and pulled them off. He swung his legs up and stretched out. He was drained.

On the plywood wall at a vertical seam he found a focal point for his concentration. He began staring at it, and he let his mind loose. He thought about how he hated his job and how the TOC bunker seemed to be collapsing on him. And he had only started. There were over five more months.

He relinquished the focal point and closed his eyes. He felt ill and began to wish he was back in the TOC, preferring its suffocation to the loneliness that was now slowly choking him.

And the memories.

He wondered how his platoon was getting along. Missing them, but mostly Franklin, Fletcher, and Martin. He missed Tucker most of all. He would never see him again. It was final, permanent, and yet there was so much he wanted to tell him. He missed him dearly. He had failed him.

Tucker slowly faded.

Dim memories of Pam now flickered in and out of his thoughts like an old sixty-watt bulb fighting to stay alive. It had been a while since her last letter and that letter was as usual far from the heel clicking type he so badly needed.

Abruptly, he sat up and put his boots back on. In seconds, he was out the door, long legs striding towards Looie's Lounge.

There was a padlock on the door, but he had a key and opened it and went inside.

Behind a small bar that looked out on some bar stools and four, square tables with chairs, he picked up the lid of a large ice chest, reached in and from the depths of ice cubes plucked out an icy can of Miller's. He set his catch on the bar; then fished out his wallet, took out some of the monopoly-like MPC, and threw it down on the counter. It was enough to cover him for more than a few brews. Looie's Lounge operated on the honor system, though the drinks were priced to cover the pilferers. Or at least so said Lieutenant Grosser, who had been appointed the Lounge's manager by the S-1. Maybe Grosser was the pilferer, Hank thought cynically as he rounded the bar and mounted a stool. Hank then regretted his unfounded accusation. After all, he liked Grosser. He was a good man.

Dark shadows of dusk gradually crept upon him. A potpourri of empty beer cans stood before him. He heard the door open and slam. Boots clomped behind him.

"How's your dong doin', Hank?" He heard Lieutenant Grosser's greeting in his deep Texas drawl and returned it by slowly raising his hand.

Grosser rounded the bar, moving quickly on light feet. He was short and barrel-chested, his skin textured a dark red, perennial sunburn. And his look now was not entirely trusting as he took a suspiciously sideways glance at the money and cans on the bar, his eyes squinting to overcome the darkness, to mentally check the goods Hank had received matched the purchase price. They checked, and he then pulled a string, snapping on a white flood of 75 watts, to take inventory of the contents in the ice chest and along the shelves. Everything seemed in order and he nodded his satisfaction to himself.

"You goin' to eat at the colonel's tonight?" he asked Hank who was now busily shielding the sudden intrusion of light with his right hand, squinting to see in the unwanted brightness.

Hank lowered his hand, eyes adjusting. If he had not been a little more than fuzzy-headed, he would have given a firm no. However, he was buzzed and he waffled.

"Maybe," he answered.

Grosser looked disappointed. "Make that maybe into a yes in five seconds and I'll give you a lift."

Hank gazed down at his can collection as he considered the offer. Grosser's jeep was better than walking, especially when there was some doubt in his mind if he actually could walk. "Ok. I'll go." he responded, then burped.

The officers of Brigade Headquarters had two choices for their supper meals. They could eat in the mess with the troops or they could dine in semi-opulence at the colonel's villa. His first night at Brigade, Hank had broken bread at the latter. For the other thirteen nights, he had opted for the former.

Tonight, his senses were too dull for him to realize he'd have a shitty time. And he had forgotten that during the supper there would be a little farewell ceremony for Burns upon whose chest the colonel would pin a Bronze Star for what would be proclaimed a meritorious service during his tenure with the Brigade.

CHAPTER 43

THE COLONEL'S VILLA was French, and had actually been one. It was a big white stucco structure with a red barrel tile roof.

Hank stepped unsteadily into the large foyer. It was like passing through a space warp, from a desolate planet to a Riviera-like nirvana. The size of the foyer was typical. All of the rooms were large and were furnished in an incongruous blend of oriental wicker and pseudo early American.

The hour was early for dinner, so Grosser challenged Hank to a game of pool. But the game room was filled to capacity with chaplains and Donut Dollies. They detoured to the bar.

The colonel's bar had a supply of Coors, which Looie's Lounge lacked, and Grosser highly recommended one to Hank. A middle-aged Vietnamese man with an identification badge conspicuously dangling from his white coat served them. The badge allowed him to remain outside the village's chain-link fence after the 1900 hours curfew, but under no circumstances after 2300.

Hank paid for the first round. He took a sip, letting the liquid slosh around in his mouth.

A half hour later, he followed Grosser into a spacious dining room. It had one long dining table and smaller tables for four around its periphery. He sat down in a corner seat of the long table, Grosser opposite him. His head floated and swam and he greeted others sitting down.

Connors moved in next to him, squeezed his shoulder, and sat down beside him. If Hank had been a cat, he would have purred. He knew he was Connors' boy. He knew everyone knew it. He knew that Finsley had been more than pissed when Connors had booted him off the 0700 to 1500 shift into the evening slot, banishing him from the festivities they were now enjoying. But Connors knew Finsley was an asshole and that's where he belonged.

And Hank knew why he was Connors' boy. It was Loc Ninh. They had been through it together. Hank had been his point. Together they had entered into an exclusive fraternity. The initiation would always be etched indelibly in their minds and their thoughts would turn to it at least once every day for the rest of their lives.

Hank's swimming head bobbed to the surface. He willed his senses to clear. It helped a little. He turned his head to the right, past Connors, and looked down the table. At its head, sitting tall, back erect as if in the West Point mess hall, was Colonel Carter, Brigade commander.

The colonel had a stern, lined face, but not overbearing. His hair was white and dignified and his eyes had a certain versatility, as if running through a matrix of emotions. Right now they showed a reserved friendliness. Hank's two-week judgment of him was that he was a good CO, but while around him it was best to stay unobtrusive and unnoticed.

On the colonel's right was a small, dwarfish lieutenant colonel. He had a gray flattop that he must have picked up from the fifties. Hank had never seen him before.

Burns occupied the colonel's left. His lips maintained a perpetual kiss-ass smirk as they moved easily in making conversation with the colonel. Now and then when the Old Man glanced away, Burns snuck glances at one of the other tables where Nadine batted her eyes back at him.

Next to Burns sat Major Duncan, the S-3, Connors' boss, Hank's boss once removed. He was a short, stocky, leather-faced man in his late thirties or early forties and probably had been passed over at least once in pursuit of the silver oak leaf. It figures, Hank reflected, because he was extremely competent. Carter knew it and that's why Duncan had the prestigious S-3 job, involved with fighting the war instead with the bootlicking major types that pushed and shuffled papers all day.

The composition of the rest of the table was made up of the other staff officers, and Warrant Officer Bono, who, surprisingly, had not been relegated to the outlying tables with the chaplains, Donut Dollies, and others of lesser status or lesser rank, or lesser importance.

But then Bono was not of lesser importance. The steaks two Vietnamese servants with dangling identity badges placed in front of those dining at the villa were complements of Warrant Officer Bono. So were half of the plywood sheets used as partitions in Brigade, and the ample portions of ice cream that would follow the steaks, and the colonel's Coors, and a fine stock of first-rate movies every evening after dinner, and the twenty-five-inch cabinet TV in the villa's TV room. Bono was the Brigade trader and Army black marketer, bartering with remf units in Bien Hoa, Long Binh, and Ton Son Nhut, exchanging some of the Brigade's rich reserves of SKS rifles, AK-47s, and other war memorabilia for a comfortable supply of the basic luxury items.

Hank participated little in the constant buzz of three or four discussions around the table. He had nothing to say and if he had, he would have slurred it. Instead, he screened the conversations of others and if one appeared interesting, he tuned in as if finding the right radio station.

The ambush of the MECH platoons and the Lurp CO were number one on the charts. It was agreed the ambush of the MECH unit was a tragic affair and worse yet was that there was not one dead gook in return. On a positive note, Macy finally got a chopper and managed to recover his Lurps and the WIA pulled through.

Hank pushed his half-eaten steak aside, then his chair away, excused himself to Connors, walked to the bar with only a little sway, collected another Coors, and returned. This time he didn't tune in.

He was working on still another Coors as the strawberry jubilee faded from sight. The colonel started dinging his water glass with a butter knife, cutting the buzz of conversation.

The Old Man rose slowly, the corner of his lips pulling a thin smile. He flipped his fingers up and Burns came to. The colonel then heaped banal accolades on Burns, and then the S-1, Major Rutkins, came forward with a small dark blue case and handed it to the colonel. The colonel took the Bronze Star Medal from it and pinned the medal to Burns's starched fatigue shirt. There was applause, during which Hank prostituted himself by joining in. Before he sat down, Burns said a few words more banal than the accolades.

The colonel's other hand flipped up the small lieutenant colonel on his right. He looked even more dwarfish standing next to the colonel's six-one frame. Hank wagered he had barely met the minimum height requirements at the Point. He knew he was a Pointer because his black onyx ring matched the colonel's. His eyes were narrow and beady and Hank could tell he was uncomfortable in front of his audience.

The colonel introduced him as Colonel Higbee, the new Brigade XO, and he added, a West Point classmate. Higbee tried smiling at this last bit of info, but to Hank the smile appeared more a scowl of embarrassed resentment since Carter's bird outranked his silver oak leaf. The alcohol in Hank's system made him conclude that Lieutenant Colonel Higbee was a latent asshole. The portent of him as XO made Hank shudder.

Passing up *Rosemary's Baby* in the movie room, Hank staggered back to Looie's Lounge, had a beer alone at the bar, then somehow found himself in his bunk, staring up at the darkness through the fine mesh of his mosquito netting, knowing that somewhere up there was a tin roof.

The darkness was spinning like a wild carnival ride when he looked into its vortex and conjured up Dick's face. A surge of well-being swept through his veins, brought on by what Connors had told him just before he left the villa. Dick Kistler was to be Burns's replacement as S-3 Air. He felt himself smiling and glanced over to see Burns's sleeping form that would soon be Dick's. Only Burns wasn't there. He usually wasn't. As he was usually somewhere with Nadine.

He gazed back into the spinning vortex. Dick's face was gone. There was a moment of complete blackness. Then the usual night faces paraded. He had been hoping tonight would be different. That they would be AWOL. Even Tucker.

But it wasn't so. And he started to cry.

CHAPTER 44

DICK KISTLER'S BOOTS clunked in hollow echoes on the pine stairs leading down into the TOC. He felt like he was descending into one of the caverns of Luray, Virginia where he had often visited during his boyhood. The turned-up air-conditioning offered that same coolness of damp limestone. He stopped at the bottom of the stairs, the echoes vanishing, and looked around at the maze-like plywood walls which compartmentalized the huge room. He followed the widest corridor and after six steps took in the scene that Hank had to face every day. There were four men sitting down, watching the radios as if they were TVs. The man nearest was his friend.

Hank saw something big form in the corner of his eye. He turned his head and looked up and his face immediately changed from serious to ebullient. He pushed his chair away and sprang to his feet.

A bear's paw intercepted his hand and started pumping. "What's your sitrep, Hank?" Dick asked, grinning.

Hank's right hand tried to match Dick's power. "Sitrep's negative, big fella. What's yours?"

"Negative. Fine. Fine and negative."

Hank expanded his smile. He motioned Dick to a nearby folding chair; the one Connors used when he visited Hank's duty station, and then dropped himself back into his own. "We're going to go out the same as we came in—roommates," he happily stated. He glanced over at his three radio companions: Sergeant Durgin, the artillery spec-four, and Air Force NCO. He had felt their eyes watching this soapy reunion. His face turned serious, signaling them to finish their eavesdropping. Begrudgingly they returned their focus to their respective radios.

Dick waited until Hank was again all smiles, and then replied, "Yeah, I already dropped my gear off at the hooch. It's not the Ritz, but then the Ritz ain't in Nam. No, I think it's fine. Except for that fuckin' hole. What you tryin' to do, Hank, escape?" His head tilted back in laughter.

His laughter was contagious, infecting Hank, who had not laughed since the celebration with his platoon and Dick prior to his leaving the Battalion. "That's affirmative," Hank said between howling gasps. "I'm digging a hole back to the World. Can't wait five more months."

They laughed a few minutes in unison then Dick's face transformed to a lower key. In a lowered voice, he confided, "I saw the most beautiful gook babe exiting your hooch. She gave me this smile that made my heart melt and my prick hard as a diamond. What's her sitrep?"

"Nothing. She's our hooch girl. That's all. Very nice. Does real good work. But you'll have to pay her twelve hundred piasters per month for her services."

Hank saw Dick's lips twist into that sly, womanizer half smile. The dark, full moustache flecked with yellow bits of dust camouflaged a leer. He didn't like it. Nor Dick's next remark, though he expected it. "And what *are* her services?"

"Not what you're thinking."

"What if the ante's raised on her monthly rate?"

Hank shook his head with gospel authority. "Nothing. Most everyone's tried."

Dick's eyes glinted mischievously. "Except me, of course."

"She's untouchable. Completely."

"Married?"

"No. I don't think so. Just a good kid."

"Hell, Hank. That's no kid," Dick burst out, his head rocking back in a raucous laugh.

Again, Hank made it a duet, but this time more subdued.

Their laughter died, killed for a moment by a radio coming to life. Calling for someone called Duty Five-Five. That someone was Hank. He pushed out his chair, stood up, turned toward the radio, and picked up the handset.

Dick observed Hank standing before him in his clean fatigues with his name sewn over one front pocket and a black bar sewn on one collar and black cross rifles on the other. Hank's flesh was paper white, as if it were drained nightly by a vampire. But instead of a vampire, Dick concluded it was this fluorescent lit, cold, drafty hole where most of Hank's daylight hours were spent. His face was gaunt, his eyes hollow. His face said he was skinny, but as Dick gazed at his right profile, he could see the outline of a small paunch, the early stage of a developing beer belly, where before there had been a flat gut.

He was staring at a field trooper gone remf and he didn't like it. Now that he knew what this disease looked like, he would take the proper precautions to inoculate himself with plenty of exercise and as much sun as he could squeeze-in during escapes from this subterranean meat locker. He'd get Hank exercising and healthy too.

There was one more thing he couldn't help notice—the new feature on Hank's face. A one-inch purplish pink hyphen etched across his right cheek, a permanent addition, which over time would probably transform to a whitish pale. He knew it was from his ambush. He wondered if Hank knew that contact had made him a legendary figure in his old Battalion, both from the body count, and his telling off the Battalion's S-3 and getting away with it. He guessed Hank probably didn't know, and that he probably wouldn't want to.

He heard Hank say "out" and watched him sit back down. His eyes went back to the scar.

Hank saw where Dick was looking, and his right hand reflexively touched his healed wound.

"You're lucky," Dick stated matter-of-factly.

"Yeah…guess so. A little higher, I'd be a one-eyed monster."

"No. Not that. You're lucky to have that scar. Makes you look rugged. Babes love that shit."

"Kistler, stop your fucking bullshit."

"No. I'm dead serious. They have these dueling clubs in Germany, or somewhere, where members long for a facial scar from an opponent's saber. It's some sort of symbol of honor. And it actually enhances their looks with the women. And yours looks cool. Wish I had it."

Hank had to smile. Thank god Dick Kistler was back in his life. And now maybe he could get back to having a life.

They continued chattering away.

Lieutenant Colonel Higbee liked the sound of his boots on the wooden stairs going down into the TOC. It was as it should be, a sharp, resonant sound of authority. He needed that sound where he was going. He had been everywhere but the TOC for the past two days. Poking around, inspecting, and asking loads of hard-ass questions, locking more than a few heels when necessary.

Colonel Carter was a capable field commander, but his rear area, the life-blood of any army, was a totally undisciplined, poorly-led shambles. Soldiers strutted around outside like slobs, their boots unbloused, faces unshaven, fatigues dusty and dirty, sleeves rolled down or rolled up or half up or only one up, half with heads uncovered, those covered wearing anything they wanted, flop hats, soft caps, helmets, berets, anything. A total lack of uni-formity. So what if there were different units. At a base camp, a soldier strol-ling to the PX should look like a soldier, and all base camp soldiers should look alike.

The worst thing about the discipline, he reflected, was the absence of sa-luting. Hardly anyone saluted him. Well, Carter was purportedly a good field man, but he certainly didn't know the cardinal rule of command; take care of the little things and the big things will take care of themselves. That rule had served him faithfully at the Point and throughout his Army career. Vietnam would be no different.

And now he was entering the labyrinth of the TOC, the bridge between the field and the rear. Because of its mission it was likely to be here that he'd find the prima donnas, and they would be the hardest ones to convince to accept his authority. He suspected that Major Duncan, next to Carter, was the one wielding power in the Brigade. That was going to change, he vowed to himself as he descended from the last step.

The sound of his authority stopped as his boots fell silent. He heard radios and talking coming from the walls that seemed to run everywhere at right angles. The cold crept up his arm and he considered rolling down his sleeves for only a second before abandoning the thought. Proper uniform was sleeves rolled in neat, straight folds half way up the bicep.

He followed what appeared to be the main passageway. After ten steps, he saw the lieutenant that Connors had introduced him to at his welcoming supper at the colonel's villa. His name was…Kirby. He looked pallid and sickly sitting and glibly talking to a big, tanned, muscled lieutenant with a sloppy moustache. The big lieutenant was casually leaning back in his chair. They were obviously goofing off. Major Duncan would hear about this.

He went over to them. Hank looked up and offered a polite, hello smile. He didn't smile back. He stood between them, rotating his head back and forth, eyeing each through cold, narrow eyes. There was a long quiet among the three. Higbee looking from one to the other. Hank and Dick catching his look with wide innocent eyes, and then glancing at each other in puzzlement.

"Good afternoon, sir," Hank politely ended the uneasy quiet. He tried another smile, a little more cautiously this time.

Higbee yelled. At least *he* thought it was a yell. To the other two, it sounded more like the high-pitched yelp. "Don't you lieutenants know enough military courtesy to get to your feet when a ranking officer, particularly a field grade, comes into a room?"

They came to their feet. Their manner in doing so surprised him. They didn't blast off like rockets the way he had intended. Instead, Lieutenant Kirby rose at a normal speed to his full height, a head over him, and gazed down with upset eyes and a pale face that was beginning to color a little from the embarrassment he was experiencing in front of the EMs who covertly watched the scene from the corner of their eyes with nervous amazement. He noticed the lieutenant's menacing fresh scar on the side of his face.

The other lieutenant moved with deliberate slowness. He brought the front legs of his chair down very carefully, as if eggs were underneath and he was concerned with crushing them. He put his hands on his knees and pushed up in slow motion to straighten himself. Higbee knew he was big, but it shocked him to see him towering over him with dart-throwing eyes.

Higbee grew nervous. His position had become tenuous at best as he became sandwiched by their height. He felt their cold eyes mocking his stature, and the EMs looking on, amused at the pickle he had walked into.

"That's better," he lied. It was actually much worse. His voice became a little lower. "Things are too lax around here. As Brigade Exec it's my job to maintain proper discipline and restore some military courtesy."

He then looked up, way up, at Lieutenant Kistler. "What's your business here, Lieutenant?"

Dick was opening his mouth when Hank cut in. "This is Lieutenant Dick Kistler, sir. He's the new S-3 Air. Burns's replacement."

"I see, Lieutenant Kirby. Are you his spokesman?" His head had turned to Hank and his eyes had dopped a few inches.

"No, sir. But I thought I should introduce you."

"I see," Higbee said sharply. He twisted around slowly like a swiveling owl's neck, glancing again at Dick and winding up back to Hank. He had to get out of here. They were making a fool of him and he couldn't think how to counter it. "As I said, I'm going to shape things up around here." He then pivoted smartly and retreated. He felt all eyes on him, watching his tail between his legs. He hated it.

Dick looked at Hank, waited a few moments until he was sure Higbee was gone. Then blew off some steam. "What a miserable little squat butt."

"He's new. The asshole's got a lot to learn," Hank added.

"It'll never happen."

Hank nodded in agreement.

It was 1535 hours when Hank finished turning the duty reins over to Finsley. He emerged from the TOC bunker, squinting at the white brightness of a clear, brilliant afternoon, having left Dick to his new duties. They were similar duties, though on a larger scale, to what he had done at Battalion and under tutelage from Captain Connors, Dick would quickly get the hang of it.

He walked briskly toward his hooch. The tension of an hour ago was now replaced by tension of a different sort. Tension from an unopened letter now clutched in his left hand that had been delivered two hours ago by a bespectacled spec-four. It had remained unopened those two hours, burning a hole in the long table of radios as well as his brain as he tried clairvoyantly to imagine its contents. He had neither the time nor the privacy to open the letter in the TOC.

And he had a funny feeling about this letter.

As he often saw her, Wan was again on her haunches. She was in his hooch putting his second pair of boots, all shined and nice, under his bunk. She smiled as he stepped inside, halted, and let the screen door slap his rump.

She stood up. Her head motioned to two scattered duffel bags opposite her. "You got new lootenant," she said, her face a picture of new, interesting information. Her eyes rolled upward. "Big lootenant. Beaucoup tall."

"Yes. I know, Wan. He and I old friends."

"That good," she said. She picked up her straw broom with a short, straw-woven handle and walked past him, smiling and nodding her goodbye.

His eyes followed her as she went by. He didn't like it particularly, but he couldn't help but stare at her black pajama clad rear-end as she pushed the door open, leaving him, the door slamming.

He flopped down on his bunk amidst the sound of stretching springs, and elevated his legs by resting his boots on the tubular metal railing at the foot of the bunk. He felt queasy and his fingers shook imperceptibly.

He definitely had a funny feeling about this letter. Maybe it was the trend he had identified. Each one was getting worse. How bad would this one be?

His finger broke into a corner and slit the envelope open in a jagged tear. He took out Pam's letter and read it.

Dear Hank…

He didn't bother reading it a second time as he often did, even when they had started getting worse. His head rested on his pillow, his hands folded on his belly, the letter beneath his limp palms. His exterior lay without emotion, but inside his stomach churned, his heart pounded, and his head hurt. Suddenly, his hands moved together like striking snakes, crushing the letter, hurting it as it had hurt him.

He gazed past the rafters at the tin roof, a sky of a gray, immobile storm hanging over him. Only his future moved, a gentle white cumulus full of warm, sunny rays, it had skittered away to some unknown point. All of his tomorrows had inexplicably been blown away, by some strange, unforeseen, enigmatic wind.

Was it enigmatic? Or did it have a certain smell…like maybe Dave Watson?

It was dusk when Dick entered. The room was casting long, dark shadows. On the right side in one dark form, Hank lay on his bunk, emitting small sobs.

Dick pulled the chain of a naked light bulb suspended from a thin cord in the middle of the room. The light burned Hank's raw eyes. Was he some kind of prisoner to be interrogated? He draped a forearm over his face to protect the raw nerve endings in his pupils, and to hide his wet, red eyes from Dick.

"What's a matter?" Dick said, looking down, his dark figure towering over him. His voice edged with concern.

Keeping his face covered, Hank's free hand thrust the crumpled letter toward Dick. "It's this fucking letter."

Dick grabbed the letter, back-shuffled to his bunk, and sat down heavily.

The springs shrieked from the sudden overload. He opened the wad of paper, spread it flat against his thigh, and read it. He read it again. His eyes lifted and gazed over at Hank who remained motionless. "You were kind of figuring this, weren't you?" He said with deliberate softness. He detected a slight nod from under the crook of Hank's left elbow. "There's only one thing to do." He paused, waiting for some reaction. There was none. Finally, he said in a loud, commanding voice, "Write her."

There was movement. Hank's arm slid slowly over his eyes, soaking up any residue of wetness. His head craned toward his big friend, revealing red, hollow eyes. They were wide eyes. Dick's advice had surprised him. It was the last thing he expected him to say.

Dick read the dismay in his face. "Write her, Hank. Only one letter. Keep it short. Just one theme. Ask her to meet you for a face-to-face talk when you get back. Face-to-face, to get everything out, hash it all over, and if that's it, then that's it. You'll simply accept it. For whatever the stupid reason is."

"You think it'll do any good?" Hank asked timidly, a ground hog now peeking from his hole, searching for a shadow.

"Maybe. Maybe not. But as I've told you before, letter writing is shit. So is telephone. Remember my advice in Australia? The only way to settle matters, to get the feel of things, the back and forth, give and take, is a sit down, hash it out confrontation. Yeah, Hank. Just one time. No more. Tell her your exact schedule. The ETA of the Freedom Bird. You can't forget that date. You've come too far. June twenty-seven. The day we'll all remember. Include the processing time at Oakland. Probable ETA to Cocoa Beach. Set up a rendezvous date."

"What if she says no?"

"Don't let her. Say you don't expect an answer. Only that she be there. If she's not? Well, so what, you're right where you are now."

"Hmm," a dull moan of contemplation came from Hank's tight lips.

"Tell her if she wants she could even meet you in San Francisco. That you'll pick up the reimbursables. A kind of TDY for her." Dick kept the pressure on. "Let her know when and where you'll be in Oakland so she can link up. Get the info from the S-1, he should know all about how you get out of this Army. But tell her if she's not there, you at least plan to see her in Cocoa Beach."

"I don't...don't know," Hank's tone was riddled with indecision.

"Look, Hank. Your alternative is just to worry yourself sick over here. Your letter will give you something to look forward to. If you get stateside and things bomb out, well, so what, why give a duck's turd? At least you'll be home and can put this thing into some kind of perspective. We can get together after a little while, say in Augusta, and blow the smell of this one year out of our asses at the Pheasant Inn."

His friend's logic, however unsound and illogical, seemed his only alternative. "OK," Hank grunted and he turned his head away and resumed his earlier state of gazing up at the gray metal ceiling. Dick balled up the letter and tossed it into the jagged hole in the concrete-slab floor where it landed among Burns' trash, the only thing of his he had not taken with him. He glanced at his watch. "Let's get cleaned up, Hank. Major Duncan says the colonel's going to introduce me to the other Brigade officers at supper tonight at the colonel's villa, wherever that is."

Letting out a deep sigh, Hank pushed up with his elbows. He swung his legs over and sat facing Dick. "It's one of the four-star eateries around here. Funny how I can't stand it. But tonight, you're guest of honor." He paused and looked into the big, brown eyes of his friend. "And Dick?"

"Yeah?"

"Let's blow some of that smell out of our asses tonight."

CHAPTER 45

I T WAS ANOTHER evening at the colonel's villa. For Hank, it was the usual uncomfortable feeling that came with elbowing with the brass, and listening to the day's war stories while cutting into a thick, medium rare side of beef and chasing it with a cold beer. Dick's presence muted his discomfort somewhat. And if it wasn't for the vice-like pressure on his temples every half minute when a vision of Pam, naked in Dave Watson's arms, flashed inside his head, the villa would have been almost bearable.

For Dick, the villa was a huge candy store with delicious treats of good food, plenty of booze, and Donut Dollies. After supper, he made moves on Nadine. But she had made a quick recovery from the heartbreak of Burns's departure and now seemed enraptured with an Air Force FAC captain. Dick gracefully retreated, but in a corner, stocking up on Jack Daniels, he gleefully plotted, explaining to Hank how this FAC competition would get the first mission devised by him in his role of Brigade S-3 Air.

"Too bad OV-10s don't carry enough gas to get back from Hanoi," he laughed and grabbed Hank behind his neck, squeezing with such force that Hank finally had to knock his arm away.

Still, Hank's mind was able to become tuned to the moment, rather than wandering back to the nostalgic past, or to a smashed future.

They entered Looie's Lounge with a heavy glow on their faces. There were three lieutenants at the bar watching "Star Trek" on the small black and white TV located beyond the bar, and there was Lieutenant Grosser and a very young-looking captain playing darts.

Hank motioned to Dick to take his choice of tables and went behind the bar, ducking as he passed in front of the TV, to take an unopened fifth of Jack Daniels from the shelf. From the corner of his eye, he saw Grosser eyeing him. He took out a five note and threw it in the kitty and noticed that Grosser was now carefully aiming a dart at a hoped-for bull's eye. Filling two plastic cups to the brim with ice, he completed his mission and rejoined Dick with the night's final ration.

Dick broke the seal and poured a generous portion. He looked up in surprise as Hank exited, saying over his shoulder that he'd be right back. He was doubly perplexed when Hank returned carrying a pad of paper and a pen.

"What's that?" he asked; puzzlement wrinkled into his face. "You gonna write my biography?"

Hank smiled. "Nope. More important. I'm going to write that letter right now. Get it off tomorrow morning. I talked a little with the S-1 tonight, as you were sniffing around Nadine. Told him our deros dates and he figured our ETA in Oakland and out of the fucking Army, so now I'm ready to write."

"Some drinking buddy," Dick slurred and frowned, though he had a glint in his eyes. He sipped his JD, leaned back in his chair, and started watching Star Trek between two shoulders at the bar.

It was a good-ways past midnight when the bottle became past half-empty. The letter had been finished; Saigon network had signed off the air; everybody had gone but the two of them.

They were shit-faced. Hank pleaded with Dick not to throw the Jack Daniel's bottle at the dartboard.

After three stabs at it, Hank finally managed to set the padlock on the O'club's door, and they helped each other to their hooch. As they drew near, Hank halted Dick with one hand and with the other stuck it out straight in front of their path and groped it around as a clothesline detector to avoid their decapitation. His wrist hit the rope and he pushed down on Dick's head to get him safely under, then he ducked and followed him the remaining few steps to the door.

Inside, they stripped to the raw. Hank snapped the light out. Unfamiliar with the particulars of the room, Dick fumbled and wrestled with the mosquito netting before finally turning on his stomach and stretching out full length on his bunk. Hank had an easier time slipping into his bunk and settling on his back.

He floated a long while in a funny, semiconscious state, waiting for the faces. They came now. He heard them rushing through the air, their swiftness sounding like a speeding train.

Wham! Wham! Wham!

Hank bolted upright like a whip cracking. "Incoming! We got incoming!" he yelled across the room before scrambling naked from his bunk and into Burns's five-foot deep trash pit.

Dick rolled off his bunk and landed with a heavy splat on the hard floor. He twisted his head toward where Hank had vanished. "I don't hear anything," he called to the black hole that appeared like an incongruous ink blot on the dark floor.

Hank's voice climbed out of the ink blot. "There were three rounds. I think they splashed down near the south end of the perimeter."

Dick was now supporting himself on one elbow, his eyes straining at the hole, trying to catch a glance at the top of Hank's head. He didn't see it. It was eerie, this verbal intercourse, like talking to a void. "Hank, you sure this ain't one of your sky is falling revelations, like that time in Quan Loi? Isn't there some kind of Arty Battery at the south end?"

He now saw half a head rise up in the void with large, self-doubting eyes.

The train came boring down again in two loud screaming swishes.

Wham! Wham!

Two 107mm rockets slammed into the airstrip not more than 400 meters away.

Hank's half of head ducked back in and Dick barrel-rolled to the hole. First two big feet brushed the side of Hank's face, slid to his shoulders, and then off. Next a big ass and dangling balls bore down on him. He pushed to one side of the hole to avoid them, his back against rough, cool dirt.

Now Dick's elbow was trying to impale his chest. "Move a little, will you? I can't breathe," Hank grunted. It was like being strapped in a straight jacket with a naked gorilla.

"Shit, I don't know if I can. I nearly got castrated on the edge of this fuckin' hole," Dick groaned.

Wham! Wham!

Another two rockets hit the airstrip.

"Don't get a hard on, Hank. We'll be squeezed to death."

Hank laughed. It was impossible to suppress it. It was a natural function;

it just had to come out. Such a melding of unlikely circumstances. Even the pain in his chest from Dick's elbow couldn't stop it. Even the danger of death. "We're…" it hurt to talk, his chest couldn't expand. "…We're in a goddamn two-man black hole of Calcutta."

Dick started chuckling. Hank could feel it in the tremor of Dick's body as much as he could hear it. "Fuckin' A. We'd have been safer staying in our bunks," Dick said, and would have roared with knee slapping laughter if he could've moved.

Suddenly there was a rustling in the trash below them. "What's that?" Dick asked in a muffled voice, his face wedged into the seam between the jagged cut of concrete and the earth.

"You're moving your toes."

"No I'm not. I can't move shit."

"You're not?"

"No."

There was more rustling and fidgeting in the trash. And then a squeak, not high-pitched, but a deep throated, mature squeak.

"Rat!" Hank screamed.

There was pushing and shoving and wild and confused commotion. They used a varied version of the LIFO inventory method for exiting the hole, last in, everyone first out. In what must have been a split second, they were out, sitting naked around the hole, bruised and battered, their bodies a patina of brown, gritty, itchy sand.

Wham! Wham!

Two rockets screeched in and hit 300 meters away, the closest yet. The base camp was now alive with counter fire of 155, 105, and 4-deuce mortars.

And they sat back and bellowed hysterical, tear-inducing laughter.

Finally, after a short period in which no more incoming freight trains could be heard, Dick said, "Let's get a shower. I feel like a sand crab."

They grabbed towels and strode naked to the outdoor shower amid the sounds of artillery and mortars firing madly. Their bright flashes lit the sky like fierce lightning.

Hank was astonished at his feeling of safety. He was with Dick, and next to him nothing could get him.

The counter-firing had stopped when Hank got back into his bunk.

On the verge of sleep, the faces came.

CHAPTER 46

DAVE FLOORED THE accelerator of his Mustang, enjoying the burst of speed as it started up the bridge over the Indian River, on a westerly course toward Cocoa. It was late, and his car, flashing a wide arc of bright high-beams before its path, had the bridge to itself. The top was down, creating a cool rush of air over his body. A moonless but starry sky seemed to blanket him, a welcomed passenger. He felt good.

This enjoyment behind the wheel was his most fulfilling moment yet tonight. Maybe his only fulfilling moment. Ten minutes ago he had dropped Pam off after their usual Saturday night date. They had kissed goodnight, also as usual, her tight lips a barrier to his aggressive tongue, as usual. And also, as usual, that had been the sexual highlight of their evening.

His ground game was becoming stymied. He had punted often, unable to gain against her tough defense. His attempts at hand holding at the movies were always adroitly thwarted by her hand quickly darting away protectively into her lap as soon as he touched her. When his arm would pull an end run around her shoulders, she would sit up straight and ignore it. If he tried to rest it on her and use it to cuddle her near, she would overtly resist, and grab his wrist and return it to him as if it had wandered off by itself like some lost vagrant. His suggestions of heading for the beach for a little parking and philosophizing and whatever else they wanted to do were always quickly rebuffed with "Let's don't. Maybe I should go home now."

Bitch!

His patience waning, he had started contemplating a passing game, going deep for the long bomb: driving her to the beach, even under her protestations, brushing aside resisting arms, and putting the make on her where she would finally succumb to his charms and manliness. She would melt slowly and compliantly in his arms like hot wax. And she would love it.

He braked at a traffic light at the intersection of U.S.1. He grinned at the tent pole that had just been set up in his pants and which now was brushing the steering wheel. One hell of a horny bastard he chuckled silently to himself. The light flashed green. He pulled a scratch, crossing U.S.1, and staying on his westerly course.

There had been a reason, though, why he hadn't yet used the long bomb and tonight Pam had given him another reason to be patient and stick to his ground game. This reason was her somewhat sobbing comment that Hank had officially given her the shaft in a recent Dear Jane letter. That in so many words she was given the "get lost I never want to see or hear from you again" walking papers.

That Kirby had to be a fucking jerk. Thanks, pal, I'll fuck your ex-babe on the rebound.

Then there was another reason not to hurry and play catch-up. It was Thelma Jackson, his Saturday midnight relief from his throbbing cock and aching balls that Pam cursed him with every time they were together.

He had met Thelma a month ago at a rodeo in Indiantown. He had a fetish for cowboys and horses. A local rancher who often invited Dick out to his ranch to ride and talk football, had given him two tickets to the annual cattlemen's association rodeo. Pam had declined an invitation to join him; so he went alone, scalping the extra ticket outside the gate. Unfortunately, he had to accept less than par value. But so what? He didn't pay for it anyway.

In the bleachers, he had sat behind one of the tightest ass cunts he had ever seen. When she got up to go for a coke she had turned around to face him and his eyes nearly exploded from his sockets as he stared at the crotch of her extra-tight britches. It almost smacked him between the eyes. It was apparent she wore nothing underneath and she wanted him to know it! It wasn't until she had returned with her coke that he noticed her face, with its receding chin and chronic case of acne, looked as if she had played chicken with a Mack truck and lost.

After her return, and after he had managed to overcome what was above her shoulders, he let loose a barrage of his charms, manliness, humor, and, naturally, informed her he was a pro-footballer for the Dolphins. He had said it just like that: *footballer* with the emphasis on *baller*.

She responded the way he had wanted. Her voice was a deep hillbilly drawl and he knew straight away she was a full-blooded, nympho redneck.

Everything in their conversation was going great guns, despite her face, until she mentioned her husband was one of the Brahma bull riders. His tire was immediately punctured, but soon inflated again when she mentioned she lived outside of Cocoa. He said how about them coincidences because he lived in the same area and he casually, though not real casually, suggested that maybe they could get together sometime. She didn't say yes and she didn't say no. She said that every Thursday afternoon she did her grocery shopping at a Winn Dixie west of town.

The next Thursday he met her outside double automatic doors. She was pushing a full cart load of beer and groceries, and to his chagrin, she carried an infant in the crook of her arm. He had helped her with the cart, deciding not to let the infant interfere with his plans, and tried to coax her into stopping by his apartment for a drink and some fun. He emphasized the 'fun' part of the invitation.

She said she couldn't. Then opening her car door, she turned to him, the baby wedged in her left arm, asleep and sucking a thumb, and she grinned. It was a wide-angle grin that absorbed what little chin she had. He wanted to slam a thick fist into her tobacco-stained teeth, to let off the steam that her cock-teasing had stoked, and hopefully to improve her looks.

But then she told him her husband had been laid off as a ranch hand, and was working at odd jobs, one of which was being a night watchman at a tomato packing plant during the graveyard hours on the weekends.

Dave's mind continued to revel in the past, as his Mustang charged forward into the lonely country night, trying to shake the unending strands of barbed wire, half hidden by palmettos, that seemed to race along beside him.

The Saturday night after that Thursday afternoon, after dropping Pam off from their weekly date, he had raced the same barbed wire. The race had ended in one of the best fucks of his life. Thelma's body could do miracles, her pussy had the muscular moves of an Olympic gymnast, and it was tight, which was all the more surprising, considering she had probably been plugged by half the rednecks in Brevard County. And afterwards, as he lay back spent and content, the infant quietly sucking a thumb in its bassinet across the small room, she had gone down on him, bringing his tool back to the playing field for another quarter.

Dave turned onto a narrow dirt road and headed north three miles before turning again, this time onto a long, rutted driveway. He was aware that his tent was still up. Among a tall stand of pine trees was a small trailer with an antenna sticking up from behind it that competed with the height of the pines. Out front, taking up half of the sand-spurred yard, was the rusted hulk of a white '63 Ford Galaxy set on concrete blocks. The old Ford looked not much smaller than the trailer.

He killed the engine, bringing to life the assorted sounds of frogs, crickets, and other insects. A light in the trailer came on. The door of the trailer swung open just as he was about to step on the concrete block leading up to the door. Thelma greeted him with open arms wearing a sheer negligee top.

CHAPTER 47

A STRIDENT METALLIC buzzing swarmed around in the back of Hank's head. It was irritating. After about ten seconds it forced open his eyes. The room was dark. The luminous dial on his watch indicated 5:15. He groaned. The last two weeks had been filled with too many 5:15s. He had Dick to thank for that.

Angry at its neglect, the field telephone erupted again in a long whirring sound.

Groggy and hung over as always, Hank managed to get out of his bunk and slide his feet to the wall where the field telephone rested on a long, narrow chest-high shelf.

The land line was beginning another cycle of protest as he picked up the receiver.

"I'm awake," he said.

As he was putting the receiver down, he heard a voice say, "Yes, sir. Good morn…."

He looked through the darkness at Dick. He could barely see his large ass sticking through the slit in the mosquito netting. The dense fog that was compressed inside Hank's head was slowly starting to burn off, relieving the discomfort in his brain. He shuffled over, reached for Dick's shoulder, carefully avoiding the huge ass, and shook him.

Dick sat up right away, wide awake, just like every morning. His metabolism still reacted as it did in the field on ambush, as Hank's had reacted. A soft touch and one was immediately awake, all of the faculties and senses churning at peak efficiency from a dead start only a millisecond before. A soft touch, but not a blaring field phone.

They slipped into cutoffs self-tailored from fatigue pants and shoved their feet into their jungle boots. The still early morning air felt cool on their bare chests as they stepped outside and began their daily jog.

They trotted on the edge of Highway 13 past the mess hall, took a right at the intersecting road, ran along side the long facade of brigade headquarters, past the colonel's villa, and five minutes later they took another right onto perimeter road. The shade of darkness was now being pulled up by an emerging sun whose light orange glare could be seen above a tangle of jungle far beyond the rows of barbed wire.

With the advance of the sun, the perimeter began coming alive. Sleepy-eyed soldiers, hair tousled and face stubbled with whiskers, crawled out of bunkers or climbed down the ladders of the watch towers, tall, stolid sentinels, spaced every 200 meters.

They took another right, and then another, as they headed back on Highway 13 with the airstrip to their left.

The sun had now fully established itself, turning the air hot, leaving no question that the night had vanished without a trace, except for its remnants of tired soldiers who had stood their watch.

They showered and dressed in clean fatigues, compliments of Wan. Their own names, first lieutenant bars, and infantry cross rifles were sewn neatly onto their fatigue shirts, also compliments of Wan. They walked to the mess hall feeling refreshed, ready for another day, though dreading it.

After breakfast, they parted. Hank to the TOC to begin his shift, Dick to the hooch to relax a little before joining Hank in the TOC a half-hour later.

It was a little after 1300 hours when Dick, squinting against the bright sunlight, emerged from the TOC. His stomach grumbled a bit. Once more he had missed lunch. Some stupid ass gunship from the 25th Division had been firing rockets within their AO and near one of their Battalions. He and Hank had worked frantically to prevent getting someone killed. Hank had battled out the communications with the distressed Battalion. It's CO chewing Hank's ass, blaming him for the stray gunship, threatening to shoot it down.

While Hank was busy with the Battalion CO, he was making a painstaking search to find out who the hell the chopper belonged to. He knew it wasn't one of the Brigade's and had called the Division accusing them. They said it wasn't one of theirs and then there was a lot of name calling and accusations and further commo all over III Corps before it was discovered that somehow the 25th Division, or at least one chopper of the 25th, had taken a particular interest in the adjoining AO of the First Division. But, finally, after struggling through the quagmire of military echelons, the problem had been resolved and luckily with no casualties.

Dick breathed deeply, glad the ordeal was over and glad he was out of the TOC and on a direct course to his hooch. But sorry that Hank was still underground, a prisoner to those goddamn, mother-fucking radios. Hank's duties, though similar to his, were more hectic. But like a hospital nurse, he only had to carry shit around for a fixed duration until the shift was over. While Hank was the nurse, he was the doctor, less shit to handle but on call 24 hours. And right now he was on a well deserved, self-imposed break, and he was relishing getting to the hooch and back to his new found project.

He swung open the screen door and pushed through blue and yellow plastic beads he and Hank had put up two days before. The door banged behind him. Glancing around the room, he saw its tidiness with neatly made bunks and two straw scatter rugs, one just inside the room that he was standing on and the other across the room, near the partition wall and over the hole, or the "pit," as they had dubbed it, minus the rat which they had beaten to death with a two-by-four the day after the incoming. Their second pair of boots was missing, probably being shined by Wan.

His eyes left the floor and stared at the far wall above the "pit." He smiled proudly at his project.

There was a fad going around Brigade. A nude pin-up fad. The wall lockers of EM remfs were full of them, as he had noticed last week when strolling through an EM hooch searching for one of the mess cooks to ask him to fix him a snack. Not only did he get his stomach full, but a damn good eye full.

And then he had begun his project. And in one short week, thanks largely to the assistance of his old Battalion, especially members from his old company, Charlie, and Hank's Bravo, he had amassed and tacked on the sheets of plywood that represented the far wall, what he believed to be the greatest collection of monthly centerfold playmates that existed in Brigade. Eleven months worth, nearly one third of the wall, now stared back at him, exhibiting in all their glory, big, jutting tits and firm, round asses. In his footlocker, delivered yesterday evening by Bravo's first shirt, Sergeant Mendez, were six more months. Eagerly awaiting their spot on the wall.

Miss February of a year ago smiled coyly at him as he held her high on the wall with one hand while carefully maneuvering his feet to avoid stepping on the rug concealing the "pit." He plucked a tack from his lips and finished nailing Miss February as his mind contemplated more pleasurable methods of nailing her.

He sensed the door open and heard the beaded streamers rustle. He turned around, stepping in front of the rug, and saw Wan standing there with a pair of polished boots in each hand. There was a trace of a blush on her face, which she tried to hide by staring down at the concrete slab floor.

He was pleased with her reaction. He knew she had been seeing them every day, but this was the first time she had seen them in his presence. He let out a chuckle, "What's wrong, Wan? You no like wallpaper?"

He wondered if she understood. Hank said her English was surprisingly good.

Her eyes lifted slowly. Her face followed. She smiled as coyly as Miss February. "You big lootenant. Got beaucoup girlfriends."

Dick's loud laugh kicked his head back. "These girlfriends of all GIs. Only GIs never get to see real girls. Just pictures. Pictures, and not real thing, can upset GIs." He wondered if she knew where he was coming from, or where he was heading.

She must have figured something because she sheepishly dropped her eyes to the floor again and hurried over to each bunk to place the boots underneath. Before she had finished, he had crossed the room and his big bulk was blocking the beads in the doorway.

Her eyes became wide and he noticed they registered concern as they stared past him at the exit he was blocking. A funny thing happened to him. Her big, black eyes, her finely shaped, angular face, filled with nervous tension, touched him somewhere inside. Somewhere he wasn't familiar.

He stepped aside, freeing the doorway. "Heh, heh," he forced a laugh, "I've startled you." He was now looking sheepish.

Her fear seemed to subside. Her eyes came back to their normal size. And she smiled. This situation was not new. A few weeks ago Lieutenant Finsley had trapped her in his room, grappled his arms around her, locking her arms to her sides. He had tried kissing her as he pressed and rubbed his hardness over her hip and abdomen. Her squirming had made him press harder. Only when she started sobbing uncontrollably did he ease up.

And then he shook her hard as if he wanted her insides to come out through her throat. Finally, his grip had lessened and she had run out, hearing him scream that she was a shitty gook slut.

She shuddered now at the memory. No, the situation was not new. Though this one was better than the last one.

She walked out of the hooch, thankful she didn't have to run. Dick followed. They stopped outside beside the tall rubber tree that held one end of the low-hanging clothesline. The tree also now held Dick as he leaned a shoulder against it and gazed down at Wan.

At her eyes.

Goddamn he liked those eyes.

"Where you go now, Wan?"

"I go polish other lootenant boots. Got beaucoup work," she answered, looking up at him.

She stared curiously at his full moustache and he thought he saw a mischievous glint in her eyes. "You like my moustache?"

"It nice. Vietnamese men no have like that."

"Speaking of Vietnamese men, do you have boyfriend, Wan?"

Her eyes went cold. She gazed across the road at the airstrip at an OV-10 revving up for takeoff. A deuce-and-a-half passed by, interrupting her view. She looked up at Dick, who was now regretting his question. There was a slight quivering of her soft lips. "I had boyfriend. ARVN soldier. He die last year. Tet. VC kill him."

"I'm sorry," Dick said. It was all he said. He couldn't think of anything else.

"I go now, lootenant."

"Call me Dick. That's my name."

She blushed. "Me call you Dick? That not right. Not for lootenant."

He smiled. "Sure it is. Consider it an order from lootenant."

Her face lit up like a warm sunrise. "OK," she said, laughing. "I go now… Dick." She turned and started walking away.

"Tomorrow, Wan, we talk more?"

"Why?" she said, stopping and glancing over her shoulder.

"Because…" Dick paused, searching for the answer, not only for her, but for him. "Because…I'd rather talk to you than look at those girls on my wall," he said and pointed at his hooch.

CHAPTER 48

LIEUTENANT COLONEL HIGBEE walked purposefully to the next hooch, intoxicated by the importance of the mission. Last week he had inspected one of the Brigade's Battalions, going through every goddamn thing tied down and some that weren't. Living quarters, supply rooms, mess halls, arms rooms, orderly rooms, showers, even the Battalion CO's quarters. Of course, he performed the inspection when he knew the CO was out in the field at a fire support base with his Battalion. This avoided possible confrontation of equal rank officers, and the Battalion CO, having a field slot, might have the advantage if Colonel Carter got into any ensuing fray.

So the only ones around were the area lice, as he liked to think of them. And as typical of lice they lived in filth and squalor, which of course made his inspection much easier and enjoyable.

By the time he had finished with his inspection, the Battalion XO, a young major, was sweating blood, begging forgiveness for his incompetence in policing the Battalion area, and promising that the next inspection would be different. Higbee had been generous; he gave him a next time.

Today, he was concentrating a little closer to home, the enlisted quarters of Brigade's headquarters company. Holding his big clipboard snugly against his hip, he stepped inside a hooch with the company CO, Captain Sanders, dogging his heels. Higbee smiled inwardly, knowing that Sanders was in awe of his rapid strides. A foot taller, Sanders was almost trotting to stay with him.

To Higbee's disappointment, the hooch was in near pristine condition. The rows of bunks in straight dress right dress alignment, made with poncho liners smooth and tight. The extra pair of boots placed neatly under them.

The graininess of the concrete floor contained the bare minimum of dirt and grit. Either these soldiers had top notch hooch girls or they were specially prepared for him, probably having been tipped off by the Battalion he had recently ripped.

He believed the latter. He walked to the center and did a sharp right turn reminiscent of his many marching days on the Point's parade ground. Watching with a dumbfounded look, Sanders remained standing in place near the doorway with his hands held tightly behind his back, his fingers fidgeting nervously.

Higbee stopped at a wall locker between two bunks. He opened it and his eyes popped wide before narrowing into cold, penetrating little slits. There they were, just like in nearly every other wall locker he had spot checked today. *Pictures.* Pictures of naked women, plastered all over the inside. Some hooches even had these pictures taped on the outside of the wall lockers.

No wonder these enlisted men were always chasing after short-time girls and coming down with the bullheaded clap. They had created an erotic, immoral environment within their quarters. And this led them, no, it drove them, to these sluts. And compounding the problem there was no lack of these prostitutes. Lai Khe was infected with them and they in turn were infecting the soldiers. He wouldn't be surprised if the VC were somehow behind this.

He slammed the locker shut. The loud metallic bang caused Sanders to jump. The locker was still quivering as he exited the hooch. An idea to solve this rampant problem began to form.

The Saigon news ended, giving way to "Wild, Wild West," Lieutenant Grosser's favorite show. He sat at the small bar of Looies Lounge, looking up at the TV, a most incongruous sight in his fatigue cutoffs, bright Hawaiian plaid, R and R souvenir shirt, and creamy felt cowboy hat. A big, foul-smelling cigar protruded from one side of his mouth. He puffed in short, rapid draws, keeping a locomotive-like stream of smoke spewing forth. His mind was totally absorbed by the black and white twelve-inch screen.

Lieutenant Finsley sat a stool away, head down, concentrating on a can of Schlitz that he twirled by his flicking fingers, spinning it in quarter turns. He didn't quite know whether to be happy or depressed, so in compromise he felt in between, with a big case of the blahs.

Connors had booted him off the TOC team, handing his job, which he hated terribly, over to a West Point lieutenant fresh from Benning's Ranger school. The new lieutenant had at first been surprisingly outspoken about his disappointment in landing a staff job rather than leading a rifle platoon in combat, and of course at the same time racking up valuable career points. But Connors, a fellow Pointer and, Finsley knew, an avid practitioner of military incest, subdued the new lieutenant by avuncularly explaining the tremendous benefits to his 201-file that staff experience of working in a Brigade Tactical Operations Center, the "lifeblood" of the war effort, would bring. And so the new lieutenant was pacified.

And that's why he, Lieutenant Spencer R. Finsley, OCS Class of 1967 B, was really irked. His 201-file would contain a lemon: removal from a key staff position.

Then there was the upside. He was rid of a job he detested and into a job he really liked: Indigenous Personnel Officer, reporting to Captain Sanders of Headquarters Company. He was now the man in charge of all the gook civilians that worked at the many sundry jobs for Brigade. It was a prime slot for plenty of short-time action. And it would be free stuff. He might even have some of the papa-sans deal him some dope and then retail it to the EMs.

He stopped twirling his beer can and took a long swig. His fingers then resumed their flicking at the can. The .45 caliber pistol holstered at his side pulled heavily at his hip. Its weight conveyed a satisfying feeling of power and authority. Its presence provided a harbinger of a future, superior OER, Officer's Efficiency Report, from Captain Sanders, which would sweeten the sourness of the lemon in his 201.

Sanders had been duly impressed at his suggestion of a security officer for the Brigade area. Not to safeguard them from an attack of gook sappers, that's what the perimeter security was for, but to stop the pilfering from the thieves that called themselves supply sergeants and who, together with their cohorts, pulled night raids on other units for supplies to make up for shortages in their own inventory. Not that Brigade Headquarters had a problem with this. But the battalions did.

And so wasn't a security officer good preventive maintenance that was worth a pound of cure, and all that good shit? And he, Lieutenant Finsley, had volunteered for this additional duty, which meant spot-checking the area in the evening and once at some odd early morning hour to ensure no marauders from other units. Sanders had been overwhelmed at his volunteering his free evening time and loss of precious sleep for the after-midnight round. Little did Sanders know that his security officer very rarely made the early morning round. The old rack was just a little too comfy. But after all, wasn't it the thought that counted?

The idea to carry a pistol had been Finsley's. Sanders had reluctantly agreed, succumbing to Finsley's argument that a security officer most certainly had to be secured, especially since they were in a war zone.

As Finsley meditated over his revolving can of beer, behind him Hank and Dick rounded out the night's Looie Lounge contingent by enjoying a game of darts.

Finsley snapped out of his reflections. He looked up, then over at Grosser, then craned his neck around to catch a glimpse of the dart action. His eyes swung back to their starting place, his beer can. He let out a long belch, fouler than Grosser's cigar, and loudly proclaimed to anybody who would listen, "Goddamn I'm horny!"

He again glanced around and discovered nobody had listened so he rapped his beer can heavily on the bar, sending vibrations through the varnished plywood that rippled Grosser's scotch. "How about it, Barry? Had any short-time action lately?" he asked in his usual loud voice as if Grosser was hard of hearing.

Grosser shook his head. "Negative, not lately." He kept his eyes on the tube, intent on the outlaws pursuing James West and Artemus Gordon.

Realizing Grosser's poor gab potential, Finsley rotated his ass around on his stool to observe the dart match. Kistler was meticulously sighting down a feathered dart. He slowly drew back his forearm in a cocked position and in a swift jabbing motion uncorked the missile. It blurred across Finsley's vision, and with a sharp pop, stuck deep into the board. Bull's-eye.

With a long sigh of another defeat, Hank dropped to his seat beside a table stacked with empties. The board was looking slightly out of focus and so now he at least had an excuse for losing.

Dick came over, face lit by another victory. He found a can with a pinch of beer, and inhaled it. It tasted flat.

"Shit, Kistler, how come your dart's the only one around here getting bull's-eyes?" Finsley slobbered his words, his butt hanging half off his stool like a drunken seagull on an old rusted piling.

Dick shrugged a shoulder and turned his palms up. "Don't know," he grinned in mock modesty. "Guess it's simply a steady hand and a good eye." He sat down and winked at Hank sitting across the table.

"I don't mean those darts," Finsley grunted. "I mean your prick dart. I know you've been jabbin' the hooch maid as regularly as I take my morning shit."

Dick's grin reversed into the troughs of a deep frown. He glared up at Finsley. "That's not your concern," he said coldly. His eyes two round ice cubes.

Hank's eyes were not as frigid and were larger with shock. He stared at Dick, who now stared at the edge of the table, his eyes having fallen from Finsley. Hank's shock was not so much from Finsley's remarks, but from its revelation. Even Grosser had found something more interesting than James West and had turned on his stool to face Finsley and Dick.

Finsley refused to stop, especially now that he had a captive audience. "You must be payin' that whore a helluva lot. I offered her beaucoup piasters the other day and she turned it down. You on the family plan with the gook bitch?"

Dick shot out of his chair, knocking it to the floor with a sharp crack. He stood tall…and still. His movement ended abruptly as it had started. "Finsley, shut your fucking mouth," he said evenly through clenched teeth. "You mention Wan one more time, or proposition her again, I'll flatten your head like a squashed melon. Even though it would improve your looks."

Finsley hopped off his stool like a bird kicked off his roost and faced Dick. Two big roosters in the prelude of a cock fight. He gave way to two-plus inches and about twenty pounds, but his sneer carried a certain cocky confidence that came from the experience of past barroom fights.

"What's wrong, *stud*?" Finsley's sneer grew more intense. "You gettin' too fond of gook pussy? You want to take one back to the World and spread the clap?" He thought his remark so funny he relaxed for a moment, tilted his head back and gave a stained, toothy laugh.

He kept laughing as his head rocked forward and this was what Dick was waiting for. A charged bolt of lightning that a millisecond before had been Dick's arm lashed out. Dick moved his weight behind the bolt and his fist smashed into Finsley's mouth. Finsley reeled backward, his legs making choppy backward steps trying to stay with him. His back smashed into the wall, toppling the dart board on his head. He dropped heavily to the floor, landing on his rear with a thud.

His mind focused first on the blood and two teeth that filled his mouth. He spit the mess on his shirt to avoid choking. Dazed, he looked up, vision blurred, and saw Kistler in duplicate standing over him and poised for another blast should he rise. He considered reaching for his pistol, but discarded it, not for its absurdity, but because he knew he couldn't do it fast enough to prevent Kistler from teeing off on him again.

He stayed on his ass, back against the wall, glazed eyes glaring hate up at his attacker. He spit again on his shirt, the blood and spittle soaking into the cloth. His mouth ached miserably, especially the left side where moments before two teeth had been firmly in place. His tongue worked its way tenderly around the gaping holes.

He knew it was going to be painful to talk. His jaw could very well be broken. Still, he had to do it. "You'll…pay for this…Kistler," he choked the words out. "I'm going to the adjutant and press charges…for assault and battery." He looked slowly over at Kirby standing with mouth agape and astonished, bulging eyes, and then moved his head like a stunned, de-treed sloth to Grosser who calmly stared down from his stool. "You…you guys saw what happened."

Hank looked away from Finsley's wounded face. He stood slowly, wanting to compose himself. He placed his hand lightly on Dick's shoulder. He spoke softly to Grosser. "I didn't see anything. What about you, Barry?"

"Yep, I saw it. Saw it all," Grosser stated emphatically. His words caused Finsley to relax with the comfort of a witness. Dick tensed and turned to gaze at Grosser with somber eyes and stoic face. Grosser met Kistler's eyes head on. He inhaled his cigar and blew smoke rings at the ceiling. Kistler's roundhouse right had impressed him. James West couldn't have done better. "I saw that some drunken cowpoke can't sit on a bar stool any too well. Lieutenant Finsley's stool started bucking and he just couldn't hang on. He fell off and banged his jaw against the edge of the bar and look what it done to his po' face." Grosser paused and glanced down at Dick's bleeding knuckle. "I saw Lieutenant Kistler try to catch the po' cowpoke before he hit the floor, but instead he caught his knuckles on the same edge. Damn bar edges, they're an awful hazard to a boozer." He puffed and blew more smoke rings and smiled wryly at Dick. "Yep, I saw it all."

"You're an ass, Grosser," Finsley hissed, spitting out more blood.

"Mebbe, but I'm not sitting on mine now," Grosser countered. He slid off his stool and walked for the door, flicking a long ash on Finsley's head as he passed. He stopped at the door, turned to look at Dick, and then tipped his cowboy hat.

His body quivering, Finsley struggled to find his feet. He did with Hank's help. On rubbery legs, he stumbled out the door, his mind set on figuring where he could get immediate medical assistance.

Hank stood beside the fallen dart board. He watched Finsley's pitiful retreat and then his eyes followed Dick, who went behind the bar, switched off the TV, grabbed a towel from under the bar, wiped his bloodied knuckles clean and moved to the ice chest.

With a bayonet, he chopped on a block of ice using his left hand and wrapped a few chunks in the towel. He wrapped the towel tightly around the wound. His good left hand reached crossways behind him to his back pocket and took out his wallet from which he extracted a wad of MPC. He threw the funny money in a cigar box, then plucked a can of beer from the ice chest and tossed it with just a little arch to Hank. He repeated his tosses until Hank had his leg pockets and arms full. He scooped up four more cans, cradled them in his left arm, and with his right elbow closed the lid.

Not one word had been uttered since Finsley's departure. Nor was any spoken as Hank trailed Dick out the door, cutting the lights out on the way, and fumbling with a handful of beer cans while securing the padlock.

Inside their hooch, they sat on their bunks and dropped their liquid rations beside them. The room was milky dark, shared with deep shadows. No one had bothered to turn a light on. The silence continued as they faced the dark form of one another from across the room. Each in the same poses slinking down on the bunk, chin on chest, feet up on a footlocker.

Hank noticed Dick's outline rummaging around. There was a pop and a slow hiss. With the cream of moonlight that spilled in through the long, narrow screen windows above his head Hank saw a sliver glint of a metallic object fly toward him like an attacking minnow. The church key hit him noiselessly on his stomach. He picked it up and there was another pop and slow hiss.

Still more silence.

Dick finally spoke. "I shouldn't have hit the bastard," he admitted.

"He had it coming," Hank replied, uncertain as to whether he believed himself. All those early afternoons Dick had disappeared from the TOC for some "rest," or some "search" for new material to add to their collection of wallpaper. No wonder there hadn't been any new editions lately. Dick had been fucking Wan. Sweet, innocent, beautiful Wan. Why did he have to fuck her? Why had she let him?

"Maybe so. Maybe not. Finsley sounded like…reminded me…of me. Wanting to get his rocks off. Frustrated because he hadn't."

"And you're not frustrated," Hank said softly, his tone flat, though trying to disguise the resentment he felt. And the guilt too. Because of the resentment.

"I'm frustrated, Hank. Have been ever since I started seeing her."

"Huh? You mean you haven't screwed Wan?"

"No."

"No you have or no you haven't?"

"No, I have not screwed her."

"But those long afternoon breaks? And what Finsley said? And your reaction to it?"

"I've been seeing her, Hank. Every damn day. Every damn day I've been seeing her, talking to her, joking with her. It's the zenith of my fucking day." Dick took a long, slurping tug of his liquid ration, during which Hank felt strange pangs of jealousy. Jealous of Dick's time spent with Wan. Jealous that Wan seemed more important to Dick than their nighttime drinking and bullshitting.

"I haven't even kissed her. Not even a little peck," Dick continued. "I'm afraid to make an approach shot. Afraid it will be blocked. Don't know if I could handle it. One rejection in life is enough."

"One rejection? That's part of the fucking game, isn't it? No pun intended. You score a lot, Dick, but surely you've had your share of rejects."

"Those I can take. It's when the woman I care about does it that bothers me. You know what I mean?"

"Yeah, I guess so," Hank replied, beginning to feel a little sick inside. He thought of Pam. He knew rejection.

"I dated a girl at VMI that really shafted me, or should I say spread her legs for more than just my shaft. Anyway, since then I lived under the philosophy that women had only four things to offer: Two tits, an ass, and a cunt."

"I know," Hank interrupted. He couldn't believe what he was hearing. Dick was pouring his heart out. It was way out of character.

"In Wan, I could see my philosophy had chinks. It doesn't matter. Not that stuff. But her beauty does, her expressions do, her laughter does. It means a lot to me and I'm afraid to upset it. Do you know what I mean, Hank?"

"Yes," he answered.

He was about to ask Dick if all this meant that he loved Wan. But asking would sound too soapish. "Where are you going with all this? With you and Wan," he questioned, paraphrasing his thoughts, editing out all references to that embarrassing word, love.

"I don't know. I don't know if she feels anything about me. Maybe our afternoon talks are just a diversion for her to get through the day. Sometimes I feel as though we're from different galaxies and that we've met on some intermediary planet and we can't stay on it forever. Someday we'll go back to our own galaxies and that will be that."

"Like the end of June?"

"Yeah, June. Which means I'm a realist. She's Vietnamese and I'm a southern redneck." Dick threw an empty can into the hole. In the dark it set in the floor like the opening to some kind of space warp.

Hank looked at it and then tossed in his empty. He wished he could throw himself in with it and disappear back to the World, to Pam, not the present Pam , but the old one. Life was too dynamic, the changes too sudden and radical. Dick had changed before his eyes. Not physical, but in spirit. He was now a little, confused boy. Damn if they weren't alike.

The dull sheen of moonlight began to disappear across the room. The shadows united in darkness. There was a pop and a slow hiss. Silence. A second pop and hiss. Silence. A flicker of light revealed two slumped bodies staring blindly at each other. Thunder rumbled and pelting rain rushed on the tin roof. It was still the dry season. The rain was out of place. Yet the night was out of place and so the rain and night were in harmony.

A surge of realization flowed through Hank's body and caused him to shudder. He loved Dick, as he loved Tucker. The surge flowed out, leaving him weak. The usual feeling when he thought of Tucker. But that's all right; it's late at night. Sleep was not far away.

It was now time to think of Tucker…and the others.

Dick could be heard snoring loudly. The rain droned on the roof.

Then the faces came.

CHAPTER 49

HAVING BEEN STOKED by the burdens of an S-3 Air, the pressure eased off Dick's shoulders as he walked from the TOC and across the wide, dirt open space between the mess hut and his hooch. His right hand clenched a fist, testing the degree of pain caused by a deep gash that ran lengthwise on his middle knuckle. For a moment he considered having a medic check his wound, maybe stitch it up, but only for a moment. First, he had to see Wan.

He pulled the screen door open. Parting the beads, he entered and saw she wasn't there. Though someone had been. The spare boots were shined and in straight alignment under each neatly made bunk. The straw-matted rugs were set geometrically on the floor, one under his feet, the other just before the hole, as if waiting for someone to kneel down and conjure up some black magic from the dark cavity. It was all very nice and tidy and clean and proper. Someone had done good work. But he knew that someone wasn't Wan.

He became nervous and backed out the door, his eyes still scanning the interior. He hurried around to the middle of the long A-frame and entered the door of the quarters which had the common wall with his. It was larger and had four bunks. A black pajama clad mama-san, with a lean forty-year-old body and a deeply wrinkled sixty-year-old face, sat on her haunches buffing a boot. It should have been Wan. The entire A-frame was her domain.

The mama-san glanced up. She stopped buffing. Dick walked over. She stood up. Apprehension covered her face as though she expected a reprimand. Dick noticed it and realized that his expression must be matching the queasy, upset feeling in his gut.

"Mama-san, what you do here?"

Her eyes nearly rolled up into her head as she looked way up at the towering lieutenant. She shrugged her shoulders and flashed a cautious, tense smile from which gleamed a gold front tooth.

"Where is Wan?" Dick came right to the point.

Again, she shrugged her shoulders, her golden smile growing and vacuous. And more tense.

Shit, Dick thought, she doesn't speak English. He would have to try some body English. He pointed a long finger at her and shrugged. She damn well ought to know what a shrug meant since that had, so far, been her only vocabulary.

Her smile became less tense as recognition and meaning of this latest form of communication sunk in. "Lootanant Finee," she said and pointed to herself and then to the floor.

Dick understood. He began fuming inside. That fucking prick, Finsley, had found a way to counterpunch from a distance. In his new position as head honcho of civilian workers, he had replaced Wan with this mama-san.

Dick stared down at her. She gazed up blankly, wondering what he would do next. The scales in his mind began carefully weighing certain alternatives. He could stomp into Finsley's office at Headquarters Company orderly room, smash his face in again, and break his fingers one-by-one until he told him where Wan was. This alternative had merit, but he would probably eventually wind up in the stockade. And without Wan.

Or he could get Captain Connors and Major Duncan into this thing. But he didn't want Connors and Duncan to know about Wan.

Or he could find Wan himself.

He played a hunch. With his hand he motioned the mama-san to follow him to the door. She did and followed him outside into the bright sunlight. To their left, across the road, was the airfield, to the front across the open space, the mess hall, to the right, A-framed hooches and Looie's Lounge.

His right arm stretched out horizontally and swept a wide arc, then retracted and pointed at her. She blinked incomprehension. He then pointed at her, then his arm swept another arc, and he opened the door and stepped inside. He stepped out again. More blinks. He felt himself getting agitated.

He grabbed her arm. Her eyes grew wide and her jaw dropped in a spreading sense of alarm. He raised his free hand in a signal to stifle it, that she would be all right.

In a compromise she closed her mouth. He pointed her own finger at her, then stuck her arm out and swept an arc similar to what he had done. He repeated the pointing ceremony again before letting her arm go.

Their eyes locked, then broke off. This time her arm moved by itself and her bony finger stopped on the FAC hooch. He sighed. They had finally communicated. Now he had to check his hunch.

With long strides, he made his way to the FAC hooch. Not bothering to knock he flung open the door and went inside.

The Air Force OV-10 flyers knew how to make the best of it. Their quarters consisted of a small combination living room and bar that greeted visitors as they entered. Beyond, running the length of the A-frame, was a hallway with spaced doorways that represented individual sleeping quarters.

He stood in the middle of the living room/bar. It was quaintly decorated with old rattan and shell casing ashtrays and crossed SKS rifles and other war knick-knacks. A parachute was spread across the ceiling and so became the ceiling. He half expected it to drop over him followed by Finsley coming out from behind the bar to start beating him with a baseball bat.

But nobody was around, at least around where he was standing. He debated whether to call out 'anybody home' or start walking down the hallway and checking rooms. He was no stranger to the FACs. In fact, he knew them well. He was their liaison man. He was their link between Army and Air Force, the provider of tactical targets for their white phosphorus spotter rockets, from which the F-4s and F-100s could tee off with 500-pounders and napalm.

As he stood under the parachute, hesitant about his next move, he saw a pair of eyes poke out from a doorway. They were dark, slightly slanted, and they hypnotically held his attention. She came out, smiling shyly, keeping her eyes locked on his as she shuffled slowly toward him.

His hunch had been right. That stupid, unimaginative fart, Finsley, had merely switched Wan with the old mama-san.

He shuddered with emotion as Wan came to him. There was a feeling long dormant and forgotten, a time when he swooned over a girl because of her beauty, rather than her ass.

She was upon him. Looking up at him with soft probing eyes, face smooth and angular, lips slightly parted, her long, silky raven hair between her shoulders. Instinct begged him to swallow her with his arms, squeeze her tight, smother her face with his mouth. Reason, assisted by the fear of spooking her, restrained him. With his arms forced to his sides, a hint of a smile etching his lips, he said in a slow deliberate voice, "Hello, Wan."

The timid look on her face vanished and her smile spread into a grin before disappearing into a frown. "Lootenant Finley make me work here. He say no to talk to you or I lose job."

His hands tightened into fists. His right one answered with a stab of pain. "I'll take care of Finsley. Don't worry. He won't bother us." His mind raced around for a cure to the Finsley plague that had infected him and Wan. Kicking the rest of Finsley's teeth out was the best he could come up with.

Her left hand gripped his right sleeve. Her face twisted with worry. "No. There be big trouble for you…for me," she told him as if she had read his mind through the fluid in his eyes.

Her eyes escaped from his and she gazed deep in thought at the door. The shock of her hand holding his sleeve deprived him of a quick reply to refute her words. Her eyes returned, sharper than before, more penetrating, powered by energy cells of determination. "We still see you and me. At night. I come to you."

His fists unclenched. The spell cast from her eyes and her words left him dumbfounded.

"I sneak out village. Like short-time girls sneak out…like GIs sneak in. Under fence."

The boldness of her plan disintegrated her spell. "It's too dangerous," he heard himself say. Yet he wanted more than anything for her to do it.

She let go of him. "Not dangerous. I know where short-time girls sneak."

"Yeah, and so maybe do the MPs or some GI waiting outside for some action."

She glanced down at his boots, her eyes taking refuge in them. His fingers touched lightly under her chin and brought her back to him.

"OK," he said softly. "I have a plan."

And then he kissed her.

CHAPTER 50

"YOU'RE CRAZY!" HANK yelled, flabbergasted at Dick's hare-brained scheme. They were in their hooch, toweling off from a shower before grooming and dressing for supper at the colonel's.

"It's a simple matter, Hank. Just digging a hole under a fence for Wan to slip under," Dick said reassuringly. He tossed his towel on his bunk, picked his pants up, stepped in one leg at a time, and pulled them up. Neither wore underwear. It was a field habit and a comfortable one and in this respect, they were not conforming to the norms of their fellow remfs.

Not reassured, Hank disgustedly threw his towel into a corner. He stood naked beside his bunk watching Dick buttoning his pants. "It's against regulations and it's dangerous. What if we're mistaken for VC?" Hank questioned with the serious, sibilant tone of a trial attorney.

Dick slipped on his shirt and started on more buttons. His eyes urgently inspected Hank's nakedness up and down, silently telling him that he was lagging behind. "Hell, Hank, where we're going to dig this hole is only fifty feet from this hooch, behind that bunker with the dry-rotted sandbags. Nobody's going to see us. Nobody goes back there. We live as close to the fence there than anyone and have you ever been back there?"

Hank shook his head. His pants were finally on and now he rummaged through his foot locker for a clean pair of socks. The new hooch maid had gotten his laundry in disarray.

Taking Hank's lack of response as maybe having agreed on one point, Dick continued. "OK, fine. If anyone does wander back there it would more likely be some lieutenant from Looie's Lounge in search of a spot to piss. And assuming someone did catch us, so what? Why would they turn us in?

We'd just tell them we're trying to get in the village for a little short-time action. And don't worry about my buddy, Finsley. He's on so many pain pills, according to Grosser, that he'll be in bed in a drugged stupor the whole night. His only activity today was getting Wan switched and the way he did it showed he's not playing with a full deck."

"OK, OK. Suppose I accept the irrefutable Kistlerian logic on this point. What if there's some kind of ARVN sentry inside the village we don't know about?" Dick's mouth moved to reply but was stopped by Hank waving a finger in the air. "Let me add something else. Suppose we successfully dig a hole under the fence. Now Wan will be sneaking out at night. How are we going to hide the hole from discovery during the day?"

He plopped on his bunk and leaned his back against the wall. He looked up at Dick standing in front of the wall of nudes, peering into a shaving mirror set on the long shelf spanning the length of the wall and brushing his hair.

Dick spoke into the mirror. "The answer to your first question is I don't know. I have no idea what goes on inside the fence. Maybe there are sentries. Maybe not. But I just can't believe they'd mistake us for VC. We're too big, especially me. I just don't see it. Besides, they probably see a lot of GIs sneaking in. This is nothing new for them. And if they think they're going to catch us and embarrass us to our unit, they've got a surprise because though we dig the hole, we don't go under."

Dick moved from the mirror and sat down on his bunk causing the springs connecting the wire supports to twang in agony. He leaned forward, elbows on knees, hands folded, the nasty swollen purplish incision on his knuckle aimed toward Hank.

"As for your second question, Hank, I've picked up the cover of a mortar ammo box from our old Battalion today. We'll slide it in over the hole and cover it with dirt." Dick's face was set and rigid. His voice whispering and conspiratorial. He had thought this thing out.

Hank's stomach churned uneasily. He was going to go along with this madness.

Though the sky was cloudless, brilliantly lit with a myriad of stars like some kind of planetarium showing, the night could've been worse; there could've been a moon.

From his bent-over position holding a sandbag to which Dick kept adding shovels-full of dirt, Hank methodically mulled over in his mind the likelihood of discovery.

The bunker with the dry-rotted sandbags was of the long trench type with half of a corrugated culvert for the cover base supporting the bags. It ran parallel to the fence ten feet away and provided an adequate barrier for hiding behind. The high chain link fence was topped with barbed wire that leaned out toward the village on the other side, meaning it was more important keeping the villagers in than the GIs out. Thirty feet further away was the rear of small shanties that served as market stalls for the selling of vegetables and produce. This back area was landscaped by scattered garbage and trash which drew the rooting pigs and afforded a visual screen from the north end.

Only their flanks were exposed. Hank's eyes kept in constant motion, first darting down the lane formed by the bunker and the fence to where he could see one corner of Looie's Lounge and then his head swiveling and his eyes shifting to the same lane heading opposite, out 100 feet to the road that rimmed the west side of the air field.

The sandbag became filled and Hank sidestepped six feet and swung it at the base of the bunker. He returned and picked up a new bag. Dick's shovel, powered by his right foot, sliced deep into surprisingly porous sand, its metallic crunch too loud for Hank's comfort. But they had known there would be some sound; hence, the chosen hour of 2200 hours. Too early, Dick had said, to be too quiet, yet too late to be too busy.

Fifteen minutes later the two lieutenants were looking down into a dark hole, a two-and-a-half-foot cube, split by a strip of chain link fence extending into the hole about ten inches. They were breathing hard and were covered with a gritty patina of sweat.

"She should be able to make that, don't you think?" Dick questioned. His hands on the tip of the shovel handle that supported his frame; his eyes fixed on the blackness in the hole.

Hank's eyes came together with Dick's in the void. His hands rested on his knees, his torso bent at the waist as though he still held a sandbag. "Yeah, even your big ass might make it."

Dick shook his head, seriously considering the remark. "No. I don't think so. The fence is too rigid. It would scrape my cock off."

"So…I doubt if it would be a great loss." Hank couldn't resist the barb. It was a way to vent his displeasure with this whole stupid scheme.

Dick chuckled. He pushed the shovel away from his body. "Let's finish up, wash up, and have a few cool ones at the Lounge."

It was a good idea; unfortunately, they had a problem. They discovered that the wooden ammo box lid that was to cover the hole just below the bottom of the fence was too small, or as Hank allowed with an admonishing tone, the hole was too fucking big. They pondered the matter. Dick deep in thought searching for a solution; Hank deep in frustration over this complication, their eyes deep in the hole, as if it contained the solution.

After a few moments, Dick's eyes came out and looked at Hank. "I've got it!" Dick whispered excitedly. "Wait here."

Before Hank could protest, Dick was hurrying away with long strides, heading toward their hooch.

Hank waited, sitting down, legs in the hole that kept his eyes captive. Suddenly, a mechanical sound awakened his senses.

His pulse accelerated rapidly. He glanced to his right and saw what at first blink seemed to be a rumbling animal coming toward him parallel to the fence on the Vietnamese side. At second blink, it was a jeep.

He had no time to think, only to react. But as he reacted there was room somewhere in his mind to place a few coarse epithets on Dick's name.

He squeezed into the hole, his knees painfully scraping the steel wire endings as his legs crossed over to the Vietnamese side. His hand managed to grab the too small ammo box lid and he slid it over the top of him. He was stuffed into the hole, doubled up in a tight fetal position. Crisscrossing wire strands stabbed his thighs. One third of his body was in the village, the remainder in the base camp. His crotch was somewhere around no man's land.

CHAPTER 51

T HE PURR OF an engine matured in Hank's ears. The exchange of
gook gibberish joined in. Instinctively he closed his eyes, finding little
difference in the darkness.

The sounds receded. His breathing returned to near normal, just before
stopping completely from utter shock. The lid was being removed! His shield
was being taken away, exposing himself. He gasped in futile fright as a dark
face thrust itself upon him.

"Hank, what are you doing, trying it out for size?" Dick looked down at
him, face upside down.

"Kistler, you fucking asshole! What took you so long?"

"It took longer than I expected. I didn't think you'd wait for me in the
hole."

"I'm not waiting. It's called hiding. A jeep with two ARVNs happened by.
Your screwball scheme nearly went down the toilet. Flushing me with it."

Dick's upside-down mouth let out a low whistle. "We almost bought it,
huh? Thank God you got a quick mind."

"Flattery's not going to get you shit," Hank said, though he wondered if
it had been Kistlerian sarcasm. "Help me out of here." He stuck out his
hands. Dick pulled him while he pushed awkwardly with his legs and twisted
and wiggled. It had been easier getting in.

He was out of the hole, standing, looking down where he'd been, his
breathing controlled and rhythmic, the air flowing in his nostrils sweet and
fresh. Dick was beside him with the shovel, fooling around with the hole
some more. Behind him at his feet was the top of a foot locker. Hank tapped
him on the shoulder. "It's going to be too big," he stated.

"Not after I widen the hole, it won't. Don't worry. We won't be much longer; I'm going down ten inches, just enough so it'll fit under the fence."

"Good idea. What are you going to do about a top to your foot locker?"

"Nothing. Mine had corroded hinges that were frozen. Couldn't get 'em off. Had to use yours."

Hank merely shook his head.

It took longer than Dick thought. The problem was layering the dirt on the portion of the foot locker top on the opposite side of the fence. They had to push and throw the dirt through the openings in the links and then spread it with the end of the handle of the shovel.

Finally they were done. Dick's long arm grabbed Hank around the head and squeezed an affectionate thanks.

"Tomorrow night all systems are go," Dick said as they walked away.

All systems were going. Hank reflected on Dick's words of the night before. He lay in his bed on his back and brought his left wrist up and looked at his watch. The luminous hands glowed at twelve past one. He turned on his left side and stared through the dark at Dick's empty bunk. He had offered Dick the use of the hooch tonight, but Dick had declined. Instead, Dick had scrounged a spare cot from a neighboring hooch and set it up in the bunker beside the fence.

Hank turned on his stomach, felt uncomfortable, and twisted around on his back again. He was worrying. Right now, it was about Dick and Wan getting caught. When that worry became stale he would go back to worrying about himself and Pam. His worrying would then soon end, he knew, and then the guilt and remorse. Then the faces would come. First Tucker, then Nordstrom, then Milton, then the others…

Dick paced nervously back and forth, making a worn trail between the bunker and the fence, wringing his hands. She was late. Maybe she wasn't coming. Maybe she couldn't come. Maybe she didn't want to come. Maybe…

He stopped. Something was moving beyond the fence. A small darting silhouette. Ten feet away the silhouette became Wan. He pointed at the hole. She jumped in, crouched low on elbows and knees, and went under the fence, carefully ducking her head low to avoid being snagged by the protruding wires. Dick grabbed her arms and plucked her body from the hole and into his arms. He embraced her, keeping her suspended in the night air. Pointed, sandaled toes dangled over a foot off the ground.

After a moment he gently put her down. Together they hurriedly re-camouflaged the hole.

Their task done, he led her down to the bunker on steps of sandbags, her petite hand lost in his, and pulled aside a poncho curtain. His heart fluttered as he swept his hand out in an expansive gesture indicating the decor to Wan.

It was like a narrow mine shaft with a small cot blocking the entrance. The glow of a battery lantern underneath the cot provided a soft, almost romantic, illumination. An air mattress rested on the cot made neatly with a poncho liner on which was an alarm clock set for 0400 and whose round face now informed Dick it was 0218.

As he sat on the end of the cot, the air mattress made a squishing sound that brought nervous laughter from Wan. She was afforded the rare opportunity of looking down into Dick's eyes in a soft light crafted by reflections off the lower walls of the bunker and the underside of the cot. His fluttering heart developed a hitch, caused by the uncertainty of the moment. They had talked about a clandestine rendezvous at night. They had not talked about what would happen at the rendezvous.

She placed her hands on his cheeks; her thumbs gently rubbed below his eyes. Her eyes filled with a caring contentment. Her lips produced a small smile of sweet satisfaction. "I miss you," she said softly.

"I missed you, Wan."

She withdrew her hands, but not her eyes. Her hands reached slowly down, crossed, and gripped the bottom of her dark tunic, then pulled it up and over her head.

Dick lay awake. His eyes gazed into near total darkness at the blackness of the back of her head just inches away. From the muffled ticks of a sock-covered alarm clock to absorb the inevitable ring, he sensed their time ending. His left arm around her naked chest pressed her even closer. She groaned the groan of a deep sleeper subconsciously begging not to be disturbed. It was a pleasant sound of intimacy.

He was thankful she was comfortable. Better one sleeping than none. Better one comfortable than none. He ached excruciatingly from his back which was suspended in the air, supported by a shoulder flush against the crease of two sandbags that were two of the many lining the inside of the bunker, and from a shoulder blade that bent with surprising deformity on the edge of the cot. It seemed to hurt all the way down to his ankles that hung off the end.

The physical discomfort was accompanied by the mental as he thought about the nocturnal return of the dozen or so spiders he had evicted during the afternoon. Worse than the spiders would be a dose of incoming that would drive a bunch of the guys out of their hooches and into his and Wan's bedroom. But that was remote—not the incoming—but the uninvited visitors. The bunker was only convenient to the hooch at the east end of the adjacent A-frame, his and Hank's hooch. And Hank had explicit instructions to tough it out in the "pit." The occupants of the other two-thirds of their hooch slept with bunk cocoons of sandbags that eliminated the need to seek shelter outside.

The physical and mental discomfort was softened by being next to Wan. He would put up with most anything to keep her at his side.

CHAPTER 52

DICK YAWNED AS he looked down at Miss June, a girl of extraordinary breasts with a seductive smile who had just been separated from her magazine. The yawn told him two things.

One: The lack of sleep from the stream of nights with Wan was making him chronically tired. Not even the mid-afternoon catnaps helped him to catch up. Two: Because of these many nights, adding to his pin-up collection had become boring.

He did so now because Miss June completed his collection which would now cover the entire upper half of the wall from above the knick-knack shelf that ran from end to end. And because Miss June represented the last *Playboy* issue he would see while in Vietnam. And also, he decided, because he and Hank had to defy that fuckin' directive by that lunatic Napoleon-complexed Colonel Higbee limiting nude pin-ups to one per person.

He set Miss June beside him on his bunk and picked up the magazine. He would post her after examining the other pictures one more time and maybe after reading the "advisor," and letters, and maybe even an article.

Things were slow in the TOC. Another half hour or so wouldn't matter.

Leaning back in his folding chair, Hank gazed lazily at the bank of radios, silent but for their conch shell rushing static. A few feet away his duty sergeant doodled psychiatric ink blots on a yellow pad. The usually heavy smog of cigarette and cigar smoke was only a thin mist. He had never known it so quiet, and he felt this changed atmosphere to be perfect. His mood was abnormally bright, due some to this lull of activity, but mostly to the vision of a big 'onc' in a gilded frame at the forefront of his mind. It was *not* a Big

Red One; he hadn't been brainwashed. It was the "one" representing one month. The one month left of his tour. The one month before he'd be gone, back to the World, facing the riddle of Pam's behavior. She owed an answer. He refused to think about what that answer could be and the possibility of once having it, having nothing.

At least he tried not to think about it.

Short, choppy steps pounded heavily on the timber floor. The sound grew louder behind him. He didn't turn; he didn't return the two front legs of the chair to the floor.

He knew it was Colonel Higbee on his daily visit to the TOC, goose stepping toward him to enquire brusquely about the day's tactical situation and trying to act like he needed to know.

"Lieutenant Kirby."

Now Hank turned, the front chair legs touched down, and he reluctantly stood up.

"Yes, sir."

With Hank now on his feet, Higbee ignored him and stuck his nose six inches from the large shiny acetate covered wall map. He read the grease penciled symbols that spoke of the many ongoing operations in the Third Brigade's AO. For much of the story, the diminutive colonel had to read with his head cocked back awkwardly, his beak nose nostrils seeming to have its own eyes.

His head finally leveled out, then gradually turned down and stopped. His eyes froze on a spot on the map even with his navel.

"Beaucoup VC. Beaucoup VC," Higbee chanted in his French version of Vietnamese. He tapped the map with two fingers that had become an enemy-finding witching stick. He tapped the same spot everyday. It was called the Iron Triangle, an area one and a half years ago that had been an extremely dangerous and highly publicized Viet Cong stronghold. Since then it had been bombed, strafed, defoliated, and Rome-plowed and nothing dared live there. But just to keep Charlie honest, every so often it was B-52'd.

Higbee turned, looked up at Hank, and flashed a smirking smile that indicated his intuitive grasp of the enemy situation greatly surpassed the intelligence culled by Brigade S-2. His right hand patted the flap holster of his .45. It was the same hardware Colonel Carter and Major Duncan wore when they went airborne in the colonel's C&C ship. Higbee had not been airborne since he'd been in Brigade. He wore it, according to rumor, to shoot EMs found with more than one pin-up in their locker.

"Seems quiet around here," Higbee commented.

"Yessir. Not much happening."

"Have you seen Finsley around?"

"No, sir. He hasn't been down here since he changed jobs."

"Too bad."

"Why, sir?"

"I was hoping he'd accompany me on a tour of the junior officer billets. I think it's time I start seeing how you lieutenants live. Captain Sanders told me he's made Finsley responsible for the junior officers' quarters, in addition to his other duties. That young man has taken on a lot since he moved out of the TOC. He's a good young officer. Can't understand why he didn't get along with Connors." Higbee's black beady eyes jumped out at Hank to capitalize his remarks and imply that Hank was not of Finsley's class.

But Hank missed the dry meaning of the beady eyes. He stared instead at the Iron Triangle. His countenance paled. The life fluids drained from his face as he reflected on all those unauthorized naked women in his hooch.

Hank did not have the emotions for a good poker player. Higbee immediately picked up on Hank's complexion change. At first, he thought his praises of Finsley was the cause. But then that was a rather trivial matter and was unlikely to bring on such a visible reaction. His beady eyes clung to Hank.

Suddenly Higbee's mind grasped Kirby's changed composure. Kirby was worried that his hooch was going to be inspected. And Higbee knew why. Rumor around headquarters was that some officer was supplying certain EMs with marijuana and other dope. Kirby was that man. Kistler was probably in on it too. The dope was in their hooch.

With satisfaction he watched Kirby searching for refuge in the rushing sounds of the radios. He casually reached into a pocket at the bottom of his fatigue shirt and pulled out a pipe and tobacco pouch. He tamped tobacco in the bowl with his finger as his eyes stayed on a jittery, sick-looking Kirby. One hand brought the pipe stem to his lips; the other exchanged the tobacco pouch for a book of matches. He lit the pipe and stoked it with short, rapid puffs.

"Where's Kistler?" he asked. He thought he detected Kirby stiffen.

"I don't know. Why?" Hank lied with a straight face. He wasn't sure why; it just seemed the thing to do.

"He's not down here?"

"No, sir. Why?"

"Lieutenant Kirby, I'll ask the questions. I was hoping Kistler could come with me as I inspect your hooch. You two are roommates, is that not right?"

A lump blocked Hank's throat. He forced a swallow through it. "Yes, sir."

"Well, rather than Kistler, I want you to accompany me," Higbee said through tight, thin lips, the pipe stem wedged in his teeth. "Right now, Lieutenant Kirby."

"I'm sorry, sir. I'm on duty now. I can't leave my post." Hank's eyes now took on Higbee's and his had the advantage of the high ground which helped in turning Higbee's frail complexion a deep beet red.

"Where's Connors?" Higbee demanded.

"On a thirty-day leave, he left yesterday; his compensation for extending six months over here."

"Major Duncan?"

"Don't know."

Higbee's eyes broke away and swept the long table with its many radios and the faces of the NCO and two EMs who were staring up at him with mouths ajar. His teeth bit down on the pipe's plastic stem.

"Well, Lieutenant Kirby. It seems that in the absence of your immediate superior, and since *I* am your *superior* officer, and since the only thing you're doing down here is collecting moss on your ass, I'm ordering you to accompany me!"

For a brief moment Hank considered shoving the pipe down Higbee's throat. His ears started ringing with another order five months ago. Search the kill zone…search the kill zone…that's an order. His equilibrium fading, he felt faint and sunk into his chair.

Higbee, face livid, hovered over him. This action of defiance was incomprehensible.

"Are you disobeying my direct order, Lieutenant?" He shouted down at Hank who slowly shook his head. His eyes on the floor, he looked like a dazed sloth fallen from a high tree.

"No, sir. I'll come with you. Just feel a little ill. Don't know why."

Higbee knew why! He had this dope pusher nailed.

"Sir, I don't know why you need to inspect the lieutenants' hooches. We all have hooch maids who keep everything clean and neat." Hank gave a last line of defense as they briskly walked across the wide-open area toward his hooch. Higbee's little legs a near blur beside Hank's long strides.

Higbee didn't answer; didn't even acknowledge Hank had spoken. He just kept on with his own short, choppy strides that seemed like pistons stoking his pipe, sending out small gray balls of smoke from one side of his mouth. Twenty meters from his hooch Hank halted abruptly, allowing Higbee to continue on unimpeded for about five feet before realizing he was walking by himself.

He pivoted with an awkward to-the-rear-march and came back a few feet to stare up at Hank. "What's the matter, Lieutenant? Why did you stop?" He questioned, his beady eyes joining the interrogation, his pipe still puffing.

"Sir, I just remembered that Lieutenant Kistler is racked out in our hooch. He was up very late last night working on a number of air missions. I don't think we should disturb him," Hank said slowly with effort, fighting to restrain a high-pitched crack in his voice.

He watched Higbee's face become a red, overheated boiler. "Get your ass moving, Lieutenant! I don't care if a regiment of NVA is assaulting the TOC. We're going to look at your hooch."

Hank shrugged, conceding the matter, and they started walking again. As they approached the hooch, the clothesline that extended from the hooch came in front of their path. Hank quickened his pace, darting a few feet ahead.

"Watch out for your head, Colonel Higbee, sir!" he shouted a warning for Dick to somehow get those pin-ups down. No sooner had he shouted than he realized what a stupid thing he had done. No way could Colonel Higbee's head scrape the clothesline.

His mouth pulsing out smoke clouds, the colonel replied with one more beady-eyed stare as he passed Hank and walked under the rope. Now having negotiated it, he turned around slowly and glanced back at Hank. His eyes commanded the lieutenant to move forward.

Dick got the warning just as he was about to post Miss June. His mind fought with alternatives measured against the severe restriction of time to accomplish them. He couldn't sweep the wall completely clean. He couldn't simply disappear. Or could he? Hadn't Hank done just that the night when the jeep came along as he was guarding the hole?

Dick made his decision and quickly lowered himself into the "pit." One supporting fist clutched a now wrinkled Miss June, the other a box of tacks. As he pulled the straw scatter mat over the top, a twinge of guilt gnawed at his gut. He was leaving Hank alone at the mercy of Colonel Higbee.

The screen door swung open with the pitched whine from its rusted spring. Pushing the beads aside, Higbee stepped in, a spring in his step, put there by the purpose and merit of his mission. His head stayed down; his eyes swept the concrete floor for clues. They locked on something out of the ordinary in front of the bunk on the right side of the room. It was a foot-locker with no top.

As Higbee moved over to the footlocker, swooping down to examine its contents, Hank glanced around. The legion of pin-ups on the far wall glared at him. He wondered where Dick was. Maybe back in the TOC wondering where he was.

He also wondered what Higbee was doing. He had removed the shallow liftout drawer of his footlocker and was throwing his socks and fatigues on the floor with the eagerness of a dog sniffing for a bone.

It wasn't until the footlocker was completely empty and he had run his hand all around the bare inside when Higbee looked up and then came to his feet. His eyes briefly touched on the far wall, glanced over to the other side at Dick's footlocker, then, in a double take, back to the wall.

Higbee stared in a shocked trance at a mass of naked flesh plastered to the large sheets of plywood that partitioned the room. Over two score of eyes, some half-slitted in ecstasy, others wide and alluring, fell on him, causing him to recoil unwittingly. He removed his pipe and gasped before finding his voice. "What's the meaning of this?" he screamed, turning his face an unhealthy red.

"Well…uh…you see…sir," Hank stammered and squirmed. He could feel his cold sweat. He was bathing in it.

A strange magnetic force was drawing not only Higbee's eyes but the rest of him as he slowly shuffled, oblivious to Hank's disjointed mumblings, over to get a closer look, perhaps to confirm the unbelievable disrespect to his formal directive that now mocked him in an array of breasts and buttocks and luring eyes and smiles of naughtiness.

Hank's eyes were focused so intently on Higbee's almost hypnotic state that he failed to notice the "pit" had vanished, replaced by the straw mat that normally welcomed one to it. Perhaps if he had noticed he would have warned Higbee. Perhaps not. What he did do was stand frozen in the center of his room and with mouth agape watch Higbee's left foot step in the middle of the mat and sink down six inches below the top of the floor before landing on something solid. That something solid jerked up quickly upon contact. That something solid also let out a wild "aaahhhh" howl.

Higbee howled too which ended upon the impact of his right cheek and side of his beak nose with the lower third of the centerfold wall. The something solid's howl ended when the mat flew up exposing a large pair of bewildered eyes.

Dick clambered and clawed his way out of the hole. He rushed over to Hank and stood beside him. Both stared down at Higbee who was bent over on his knees. His right hand, having dropped his pipe, gingerly cupped the right side of his face. A long deep moan of pain spewed from his mouth.

The deep moan soon turned into a shrill shriek. "You'll pay for this! You'll pay for this booby-trap!"

Shaken, Higbee slowly rose to his feet. His right hand stayed over the right side of his face. A flow of blood seeped through the fingers. He swayed unsteadily and took a long step away from the hole.

His movements became a little more fluid and gathered momentum. "Stand at attention!" he yelped. The left side of his face was a deep scarlet providing a subtle contrast to the brighter scarlet of the blood oozing through his fingers on the other side of his face. Careful to avoid the hole he leaned over and picked up his pipe.

The two lieutenants locked their heels and stared bewilderedly at Higbee as he stumbled around tearing out the contents of their footlockers, wall lockers, and shaving kits, then shredding the bunks of their poncho liners. He even looked in the "pit" but looked away when all he saw was a box of tacks, a crumpled Miss June and beer cans.

He squared off at the lieutenants. His hand couldn't conceal the red swelling of his nose. "I don't know where you stashed it!" he ranted. "But it doesn't matter. I've got you both for assaulting a field grade officer. You're restricted to your quarters as of this second. Right now I'm going to report your conduct to Colonel Carter." He pivoted to his left and marched out of the hooch with a quick, victorious, though unsteady, jaunt.

It was a good minute after he left that they dared unlock their heels. They looked at each other and blinked questioningly.

CHAPTER 53

AT THE FAR end of a wing that had been part of a giant, entomological research center for the French, and which was now part of the Third Brigade Headquarters, Colonel Carter gazed out of his window. In thought, he looked across the open area between the mess and a cluster of A-frames at a solitary loach descending on its helipad at the far side of the airfield. The chopper appeared as a dark silhouette in the fading light. His stomach grumbled. He wished he was in his villa enjoying a good meal.

The colonel's eyes shifted left from the chopper to the far A-frame near the airfield's perimeter road. He reflected on Colonel Higbee's tirade relating to events that occurred in the far end of that A-frame five hours ago. He reflected, too, on Higbee's red, swollen nose.

He took a long, final drag on his cigarette, giving the granules of ash a light orange glow. He blew out a long stream of smoke at the window, turned around, and sat down in his swivel chair. He stubbed out his cigarette in a sawed-off 105 shell casing that served as his desk's ash tray and paper weight. His eyes now took on Major Duncan sitting with one knee on his desk and rolling a long cigar contemplatively around his mouth.

Major Duncan considered the colonel's eyes as his cue. He extracted his cigar and flicked the ash in the shell casing before speaking. "Let me handle this, sir. They're my men. I'll give 'em a good dressing down. It'll give 'em something to think about while they're waiting deros." He reinserted the cigar and started it rolling again.

"No, Frank. It's my ball game. I told Higbee that I would personally deal with this matter."

Duncan stopped his cigar in one side of his mouth while he spoke out of the other. "I'd bet my life they've got nothing to do with selling dope. If Connors were here he'd second that, unequivocally. Not only do I think it's against their character, but they just wouldn't have a logical source. They're not in the right slots to broker it. And to boot, Colonel Higbee has no evidence at all. None. Only his suspicions."

"I know."

"So what's going to be the verdict?"

"The verdict, Frank, is that I've got to get Higbee out of our Brigade before he destroys its morale. I had no idea about his one pin-up-per-person order. It's one of many little things he's done that, considered together, tells me he must go." Colonel Carter leaned back in his chair as he lit another cigarette. He tossed the match in the shell casing as he exhaled smoke through his nose. "Higbee doesn't belong over here. He'd be best back in the States with a basic training battalion. I'm meeting with General Talbot tomorrow to discuss this matter. It'll take some weeks before there's some place to dump him. In the meantime, I've got something planned to keep him busy while also out of my hair."

"Since Higbee's guilty, why this meeting?" Major Duncan asked and motioned his head at the two folding chairs in front of the colonel's desk. They appeared stark and ominous awaiting their occupants.

"Because no matter how you cut it, Kirby and Kistler fucked up. They defied a written order, regardless of what that order was. They also got a hole in their floor which is a destruction of Army quarters, not to mention, as Higbee can attest, a safety hazard. Who knows, Frank, maybe they set Higbee up to fall on his ass. Or should I say nose."

Carter laughed at his own remark. Duncan removed his cigar with two scissored fingers and joined in. Then he reinserted.

"And there's another reason for speaking to Kirby and Kistler," the colonel continued. "They're involved with my plan to keep Higbee out of my hair."

Duncan's cigar tilted down as his jaw dropped slightly in puzzlement. "How's that, sir?"

"As you know, Operation Geronimo kicks off in less than two weeks from Fire Base Stork. I want a quasi forward brigade TOC at Stork. It'll be a communication relay between the task force and our TOC here."

"Is that necessary? I thought the Battalion TOC at Stork would be the relay."

"I don't want to burden the Battalion with a lot of task force radio traffic and tie up commo with its companies. And there's another reason. It affords the opportunity of discreetly moving Higbee out without outright relieving him.

"As I said, I believe Higbee has his place in this man's Army. His place is just not here in this Brigade. So, while his transfer to somewhere else is being worked out with the general, I'm putting him in command of this 'forward' TOC."

"I see," Duncan said and nodded thoughtfully. "You could make this duty sound important to Colonel Higbee. If he fucks up, we'll switch over to the Battalion. When he gets back, you'll inform him there's a more pressing need for his 'particular abilities,'" Duncan high-pitched his voice in a ring of irony, "and that he's regretfully, though your tongue will be in your cheek, being transferred."

Colonel Carter smiled thinly. "It won't be entirely tongue-in-cheek. I will apprise him of his deficiencies. The problem is that those things I point to individually are small. As I said earlier, it's their collective sum that take on significance and that will be hard for him to understand."

"You said Kirby and Kistler fit into the plan?"

"Yep. Higbee will need some men under him and since it's a forward TOC they'll come from your staff. I figure one lieutenant and three EMs should do it." Carter looked up into Duncan's eyes. "I want Kirby as that lieutenant." He saw Duncan's thick eyebrows flicker up. "While Kirby's at Stork, Kistler will assume his duties as well as his own. At least I suggest Kistler fill in. He's the most likely choice. But just consider it a suggestion. I don't want to butt in on your running the TOC. I know you planned for Kistler to help take up the slack in the assistant S-3 duties during Connors' leave."

Duncan was now chewing hungrily on his cigar. He slid off the colonel's desk and started pacing the width of the office. Two fingers plucked the cigar from his mouth. "With Kirby at Stork, it's logical to have Kistler become the day shift duty officer." Smoke ran out of his mouth as he talked. "I've taken over the bulk of Connors' tasks, but Kistler will still assist in some areas when I'm in the field with you. Kistler will be working his goddamn ass off in triplicate though."

"We'll make it sound like it's punishment for this Higbee incident," Carter interrupted.

Duncan glanced at the colonel and nodded concurrence. "But it's Kirby at Stork, sir, that I can't see."

Carter's chair complained with a squeak as it swiveled a quarter turn and he leaned back and propped one shiny boot on his desk. "I expected you to say that. I appreciate you being candid with me, Frank." Carter reached way over, awkwardly keeping his foot up, and stubbed out his cigarette. "But my reasoning is simple. Kirby has had more field experience than the other duty officers, and with Lieutenant Maxwell having derosed two months ago, more duty officer experience as well. I think it's extremely important that we have someone we can be certain will understand reports from the task force and accurately relay the information. I don't want any confusion or misunderstandings because someone on the horn doesn't know what the task force really needs or means.

"You know how commo can break down when intermediaries relay. I think Kirby is our key man. Otherwise I can foresee us using the Battalion very early on." Carter put his finger tips together. "OK, Frank, now tell me why Kirby's not our man and I'll see if I can counter."

Duncan kept pacing, his eyes on the floor, his arguments formulating in his mind, being inventoried before they became spoken. "Chemistry, sir. It's bad chemistry after what's happened. Higbee will be on Kirby's back with track shoes and Kirby could well try to undermine Higbee's authority. The matching won't make sense to either one."

"We're not casting a movie, Frank. Chemistry means little in this man's Army. They're soldiers first. They'll adapt. Kirby can consider this his punishment for the incident. That should make sense to them both."

"Kirby's short, sir, less than a month. He'll be in the field shortly before derosing."

"I know. I don't particularly like sending soldiers back to the field when they're short. But we're not sending him on patrol. It's a fire support base. And he'll only be there until Operation Geronimo concludes, which should be just over a week."

"The Battalion in charge of Stork is the Third of the Thirteenth, Kirby's old Battalion. As you may remember his departure from there was not under very auspicious circumstances."

"I don't see that as much of a factor. Kirby's interfacing with the Battalion should be minimal. Besides, there's been quite a turnover in Demon recently. A lot have derosed, including Colonel West. Major Woodson extended six months and may be the only officer who's still there that remembers Kirby."

"Wasn't he the one that wanted Kirby court-martialed?"

Colonel Carter swallowed hard. "Yeah," he admitted. "Let's just hope they stay away from one another. I don't see them having to interact. No plan's perfect, Frank."

Major Duncan stopped his pacing and returned to his seat on the colonel's desk. "I surrender." He puffed on his cigar and smiled wanly. "After we tell them about all this so-called punishment, I wonder how they'll react when I ask them to extend six months."

"They'll think you're crazy."

"Perhaps. But I'll ask anyway. I like to keep experienced officers if I can."

Carter pushed an intercom button. "Send them in."

Hank followed Dick into the colonel's office. It was his first visit and he hoped his last. Two lonely chairs were positioned in front of a large gunmetal desk. Dick marched quickly to the front of the one on the left and smartly raised his arm in salute. "Sir, Lieutenant Kistler reporting as ordered," he said and held his salute.

Hank came up beside him and raised his arm. "Sir, Lieutenant Kirby reporting as ordered."

Carter gave a curt salute and their arms dropped in unison. "Please be seated, gentlemen," he said flatly, his tone void of emotion.

A cold silence followed. The colonel sat straight, drawn close to his desk, his face stoic, his eyes shifting back and forth to the two lieutenants in front of him, his close-cropped, thin white hair and starched fatigues giving him a senatorial air. The two flags flanking him, one the American, the other the Brigade's blue with Viking crossed swords, reinforced his stately manner.

His stocky, leather-faced S-3 leaned against a far corner between a wall map of the AO and a window. His thick, short arms were folded, and a cigar rolled around his mouth.

A soft, somber voice disturbed the silence. "Colonel Higbee has stated you deliberately assaulted him with a booby trap in your quarters."

Hank shifted uneasily in his chair. He wasn't sure if the colonel had asked a question or merely was reciting fact. He glanced over at Dick who was also fidgeting. It had been agreed earlier that Dick would answer all questions unless personally directed at him.

"That's not so, sir," Dick's voice was soft like Carter's, though weaker. "It wasn't intentional. I was hiding in a hole in the floor of our hooch. I was hanging a pin-up and was afraid of Colonel Higbee catching me in the act. I hopped in the hole and covered it with a scatter rug. I didn't think he'd step on it."

"I see," Carter said. He picked a package of Camels off his desk and tapped one out in his hand. He lit it, drawing hard before exhaling. "Your collection of pin-ups is in violation of Colonel Higbee's written directive."

"Yes, sir. It is. The collection is solely mine. Lieutenant Kirby had nothing to do with it."

Carter's eyes locked on Hank's. "As far as I'm concerned, both of you have equal responsibility for your quarters. Colonel Higbee says you covertly tried to steer him away and that you yelled a secret warning to Lieutenant Kistler before entering your hooch."

"I…guess I did, sir." Hank answered.

"Why is there a hole in your floor?" Carter abruptly changed course.

"It was there when we moved in," Dick stated.

"I see. Well I want it sandbagged and topped off with cement."

"Yes, sir," said Dick.

"Are you two in anyway involved with the buying and selling of marijuana or other illicit drugs?"

"No, sir," they chorused together, taken back by the unexpected question.

Carter's eyes started shifting back and forth between the two lieutenants. They knew their sentencing was not far. "I could add a nasty tidbit to your 201 files. But you're reserve officers and too short to give a damn. So I won't. On the other hand, I feel I must take some action." Carter paused long enough to start a couple of pulses racing. "Lieutenant Kirby, I'm assigning you to a special S-3 unit that will serve as a forward TOC for Operation Geronimo. This unit's mission will be to relay communications from the task force riffing into the Michelin Plantation back to our TOC. The Michelin is too distant for a direct radio link. Colonel Higbee will be in charge. The forward TOC will be located at Fire Support Base Stork. I anticipate this operation to begin in twelve days and last about ten days.

Hank said nothing. He closed his eyes and rocked back slightly in his chair. He briefly contemplated rocking all the way back and letting his head crash on the floor. Only an extension of his tour would have been worse.

"Lieutenant Kistler, you'll take over Kirby's duties during his absence, as well as some of the duties of Captain Connors that Major Duncan sees fit. At the same time, I expect your performance as S-3 Air to be of the highest standards. In short, to paraphrase Major Duncan, your ass will be working in triplicate." Carter blew out smoke. "Major Duncan now has something he wants to ask you," he added with a cryptic smile.

The major unfolded his arms and came out of his corner. A trace of a smile etched a few more deep wrinkles on his leather face. "Don't consider your sentences entirely as punishment," he said as he sat on the left side of the colonel's desk. "Consider it also as a complement to your abilities as seasoned professional soldiers. Not all officers could do what you'll be doing. That's the advantage of experience." His cigar bobbed around in the side of his mouth as he talked. "What I'm driving at, and despite what inferences you might think we've drawn from this incident today, I'd like you both to consider extending for six months. We could use you. We need you. Connors will be here, and so the team will have the same nucleus.

"What about it? On the first day of your extension, you'll make captain. I guarantee it. You'll also be entitled to a thirty-day leave such as the one Captain Connors is now on. You can take it upon extending or tack it on at the end of your tour for a month's pay by Uncle Sam before discharge."

Resisting the urge to spring out of his chair and thrust a long middle finger protruding outward like a small artillery piece, Hank merely replied immediately with a very definitive, "No, sir. I don't care to."

He looked over at Dick expecting to find a sarcastic smirk on his face like he knew he wore on his. He was stunned to see instead lips pursed pensively and eyes narrowed in thought that gazed down at his boots. He was dumbstruck as he heard Dick say slowly, methodically, "I don't know, sir. Let me think it over."

"Very well. Outstanding. Think it over," Duncan beamed, having dangled the bait and hoping to hook at least one. "Take your time."

He came off the desk as Carter pushed his chair away. "That's it," Carter said.

The two lieutenants rose on cue and stood at attention. They held a salute until Carter returned it with a wave of his hand.

PART 5
THE FREEDOM BIRD

CHAPTER 54

I T WAS LATE. Looie's Lounge contained the last two remnants of the night. They sat at a square table and gazed blankly off into space. Every so often their eyes would meet over a sea of beer cans drained empty from a long evening of sedentary drinking.

Dick's eyes dropped down to his watch. The hands were blurry but still managed to tell him he had fifteen minutes before meeting Wan at the fence. He looked over the empties at Hank and waited until his eyes had made the cycle and were looking at him. "Sorry about all this shit," he said for the umpteenth time.

"Knock it off, Dick. It's that fucking Higbee," Hank replied with a thick tongue. He hated hearing Dick's apology. It was too out of character. But then so was his pronouncement to the major that he'd consider extending.

"You really thinking about another six months?" Hank added audio to his thoughts.

Dick fixed his eyes on the table for a good minute. To Hank, his face seemed dolefully blank, but then Hank was not seeing clearly at the moment. "Man…I don't know what the fuck I want. I hate this shit hole as much as you. But still, since we've been out of the field it ain't been all that bad. And it might not be so bad wearing railroad tracks on my collar and pulling in a little more dough. Remember, I was liberal arts. Don't have a profession to go into as soon as I get out of here. Maybe I should have studied to be a shit engineer. Heh, heh," Dick forced a weak chuckle on a poor stab at levity.

Hank wasn't so drunk to see through Dick. He was drunk enough to tell him so.

"Bullshit," he said. He tilted his head back and drained the can and threw it against the dart board. It fell to the floor and flopped and clattered. He picked a fresh can from a soggy cardboard box that had been filled with ice. They had loaded the box to cut down on trips to the ice chest behind the bar. "Bullshit," he said again after sipping the new brew.

Dick slammed a fist on the table, toppling cans like an earthquake. With a broad sweep of his arm he brushed them off the table then stood up and rifled a half-full can at the already abused dartboard. The can fizzed, sending a rooster tail of foam all over the place. He fell back into his seat and put his head in his hands. "You're right. I'm full of shit," he moaned into his hands. "I want to stay over here because of Wan. What a fucking ass dolt."

"Nothing wrong with that, big fellow." Prickly needles of compassion stabbed Hank all over as he gazed past the big, strong exterior of Dick Kistler to see someone vulnerable and sensitive. Someone he knew about, someone like himself. "If Pam was over here, I wouldn't leave."

Dick raised his head and through his hands looked at Hank. "You left her in the States to come over here."

That fucking Kistlerian logic, Hank thought to himself. "I mean I wouldn't want to leave her. I *had* to leave Pam. I didn't *want* to."

"I have to leave Wan. I don't want to. But I have to. I'm not sure why I want to prolong this thing."

"Maybe you can get her out. Maybe you could…" Hank's voice trailed off. He couldn't say it.

Dick could. "You mean marry her? She's a goo—Vietnamese, Hank. I know that. I ain't a complete moron."

"She makes you feel good. You want to be with her. You…love her."

"I'm fucked up. I know that. Maybe I love her…I don't know. But I've made up my mind. Know what it is?"

"No, what?"

"This month, we're getting on that Freedom Bird. That's a promise." Dick stood up, straddling his chair. He reached over and slapped a big hand on Hank's shoulder. He dropped back in his seat and bent over and plucked another can from the soggy box.

"Good," Hank responded softly, a weak smile set on his face. He wanted to feel good because he and Dick were going home together. He wanted to feel bad because he knew there was tremendous hurt waiting for Dick and Wan. Averaged together he felt a big blah.

Dick chugged his beer and swayed a little as he got up and said he had to get going. He had to meet Wan. He kicked a few cans out of his way as he staggered out.

The door slammed shut. A deep loneliness entered and replaced Dick at the table. Hank tried to ignore welcoming his new visitors by contemplating the task of cleaning up the mess that had been created. But then he decided to fuck it. Let Finsley get a few of his civilian laborers in here to clean up.

He drank his beer. All around him he could hear the base camp snoring. This moment in time he seemed all that was awake. He and his visitors, that is. Soon their faces would come. He would tell them he was going back to the field.

CHAPTER 55

SURROUNDED BY THICK, green vegetation and buffered by a 100-meter Rome-plowed swath, Fire Support Base Stork looked from the air to be a giant star-shaped space ship embedded in a jungle clearing. Instead of deadly ray guns, Stork was armed with a battery of three 105mm howitzers at its epicenter. Fanning out from the 105s were mortar pits of two platoons. Then there was the star itself that provided the final protective fringe—the firing bunkers. Amidst this weaponry and scattered throughout were command and support bunkers and tents, the brains and the brawn and the supply stores of this grounded star ship.

The crew of this immobile war machine would have welcomed one additional feature more than any other. That would be air-conditioning. For it was hot, the sun firing its unrelenting lasers from millions of miles away, focused so it seemed this sunny June day, entirely on Fire Support Base Stork.

And so it seemed focused even further on Hank. His fatigues were grimy and soaked with sweat. His steel helmet acted like a magnifying glass through which the sun's rays passed in their efforts to broil his brain. He realized he had become wholly de-acclimated to the rigors of the field. And with this realization came a truth. He had become in his five plus months as a brigade duty officer a bona fide remf.

He felt his head fry and he cringed at the gritty dirt seeping into his pores as he stood before Lieutenant Colonel Higbee and addressed him. "Sir," he said as he slowly wiped perspiration from his brow with a dirty sleeve that left behind a gray streak of sand on his nose, "a Chinook just delivered the radio shack, trailer and all. Where do you want it?"

His small, butch-cut head covered by a helmet, his nose and cheek still swollen and discolored, Higbee looked like an old tortoise whose face had ventured too far from his shell and had gotten the shit kicked in. He wore on his right hip a .45 pistol in a black flap holster. Peering out from his shell, his eyes silently informed Hank that he was intensely disliked. He then glanced away and took on a thoughtful decision-making demeanor as he searched for the right spot to set up. Finally, he pointed at a vacant piece of land about twenty meters from the Battalion's TOC bunker and fifteen meters behind a supplementary support bunker. "Put it over there. I want the radio shack left inside the trailer. Dig the wheels in and then sandbag both the trailer and shack. I want our commo center to be as good as a bunker."

"We can't sandbag the roof. It won't support it. It's just thin plywood."

"OK, don't."

"Can't sandbag the back because of the door. Won't be able to get in and out."

"OK, don't."

"Then why sandbag it at all? It'll only be as good as its weakest link, which isn't much. If there's incoming we'd have to get out anyway and get in a bunker."

"No you won't. You'll stay in there. That's an order. We'll need to keep commo with brigade."

"In that case, I guess we'll sandbag as much as possible."

"That's what I've been telling you to do."

"Besides you and me, we only have three others on our team. We've…" Hank's inflection of his voice sarcastically emphasized the *we* part, since Higbee had contributed nothing, "…already dug a bunker big enough for all of us," again an inflection, on *us*, "with five layers of sandbags." The fourth and fifth layers were at the direction of Higbee. There was so much weight on the supporting engineering stakes bridging the extra-large hole, again according to Higbee's specification, that the roof of the bunker was close to buckling under its own weight.

Hank continued, "We're pooped. We should try to get help from the Battalion, or at least wait for the sun to go down."

"You'll do it now. And I'm not going to bother the Battalion with this. We can handle things ourselves. I don't, I repeat, I don't want you to request help from Battalion."

"Yes, sir," Hank answered, inflecting heavily on the *sir*. He turned to walk away.

"One more thing, Lieutenant Kirby." Hank stopped, his back to the colonel. He waited for the other shoe to fall. "After you finish with the commo center, set up my tent near it and stack four layers of sandbags around it."

Hank stood stock still. He was short, real short. So why get riled? "Yes, sir," he said with his back still to Higbee as he strode off.

He made his way between two 105 parapets. The 105s were the small easily air transportable M102 model. Their barrels were being swabbed out by two-man teams. Elsewhere inside the parapets others stacked ammo at a slow, even pace. Their sunburned backs and methodical pace showed they had been at Stork for awhile.

There were other signs of activity that showed that Stork was not a new fire base. The perimeter defenses, with its tangle of barbed wire and drums of foo-gas, were well established. All that was left was the little on-going things such as cleaning weapons, writing letters, playing cards, and being bored or homesick.

The life at Stork touched Hank with some sort of strange wave of nostal-gia. He knew Bravo was out riffing around and so he didn't expect to see anyone, though maybe supply and mess and mortar people were probably around. But then was there really anybody with Bravo that he still knew? After all, it was over five months ago. No telling what had become of his old company—and most importantly, his old platoon.

He wanted to see some familiar faces.

He was among a section of firing bunkers when he saw a familiar face. It was coming at him from the row of shitters—sawed-off fifty-five gallon drums capped with plywood with round holes—that were out beyond the bunkers and just inside the first roll of concertina wire. It was a large, beet-red fleshy face, with a bald, reddish-brown dome.

It was Major Woodson.

They passed beside each other, coming as close as four feet. Major Wood-son sought not to acknowledge the meeting and his eyes stayed straight ahead. Hank whipped his arm up in a smart salute.

No one ever saluted at fire bases and this military courtesy served its pur-pose and made Woodson react. His eyes shifted to the smart-assed lieutenant and his face glowered and after passing he grunted. With the grunt Hank snapped his arm down.

He continued walking toward the perimeter wire in a marching rhythm. He was elated at Woodson's grunt greeting. It helped confirm that Woodson was a pig.

He was now among the wire, zigzagging through a mazelike passage that led to the outside of the perimeter. Just beyond the wire, resting on a helipad of horizontal sheet piling, was the commo shack. It was a black box with an area about the size of a jeep, set inside a small two-wheeled open bed trailer, about the size a jeep would pull. His three-man team, shirtless and white-chested, sat in a row, their backs to the trailer, legs out straight, on the side with maximum shade, which with the sun an hour past noon was not a great advantage.

The ranking member of this outfit sat in the middle against the hub of the wheel. He got up when Hank halted and started looking over the main-stay of their mission. Buck Sergeant Morgan was a young man with a flashy brown moustache grossly contaminated by massive bits of gray dust. His white remf body was morphing to a hint of pinkness. So, too, the two young privates. And as with the sergeant, it was their first experience at a fire sup-port base. "What's the word, sir?" Sergeant Morgan addressed Hank, who glanced at him and then down at the other two, who seemed, after digging out their bunker and sandbagging it, desirous of having their asses glued to the ground.

"The word is, Sergeant, that we've orders to set this black box here, trailer and all, up near the Battalion CP. Then we decorate it with a coating of sandbags, after first entrenching the wheels. Then we pitch the colonel's tent and surround it with a nice wall of sandbags."

Sergeant Morgan became bug-eyed. "We'll have to work into the middle of the night! I already think I got a hernia from that fuckin' bunker. I…"

Hank's raised hand cut him off. They couldn't waste time talking. They needed their remaining strength.

It was awkward going back through the wire with, as Morgan aptly put it, "a fuckin' shack." Hank strained and pulled beside Sgt. Morgan at the heavy iron tongue of the trailer, the rank at the helm, the privates bringing up the rear, pushing. But once it was Hank's rear in jeopardy as he missed a turn in the maze, and razors welded in a continuous wire string sliced his fatigue pants, the technology of barbed wire having progressed exponentially since the start of the Vietnam War.

It was not until they were inside the wire, standing around taking a little break before advancing through the ring of firing bunkers, that the reason for this crazy business dawned on Hank. He was staring along the perimeter when he remembered that at the far end of the fire base was another helipad where he had seen a Huey land. Inside the wire…

So, it was premeditated. Colonel Higbee's not so subtle revenge, unfortunately at the expense of an innocent buck sergeant and two PFCs. The maxi bunker with enough overhead cover to cave it in, the sandbagging of a radio shack, which would still be a deathtrap, and the colonel's tent. And then having to drag the fuckin' shack in through the wire…

Hank bet that Woodson was in on this. A conspiracy aimed at their most hated lieutenant. Well Hank had a trump card. He was goddamn short!

CHAPTER 55

AMID CURIOUS LOOKS, they pulled and pushed their black object past the firing bunkers, between the 105 pits, and over to where a half hour ago Hank's tortoise head nemesis had pointed his dainty, diminutive finger.

Unbuttoning his filthy fatigue shirt, Hank walked to the back of the trailer to the door of the shack. He slipped off his shirt, opened the small door that was two-thirds the size of a ship's door hatch, and tossed in his shirt. He slammed the door shut, paying little attention to the commo hardware he glimpsed inside.

He picked up a long shovel. In front of the wheel where the others had gathered he stomped the blade deep into the ground. "Let's start digging these wheels in, then we'll sandbag it," he said grunting. The others groaned to their feet.

The wheels firmly embedded, the stature of the shack became shorter by about two feet. It was now easier to gain entry, easier to sandbag, but a real bitch when, or if, they had to pull it out.

They had just started on the sandbags—Hank holding and Morgan filling—when Hank saw from the corner of his eye another familiar face, fuller than he'd ever seen it, and grinning more widely, though the eyes contained a hollow glint. He dropped the half-filled sandbag and stood up from his squat.

There was a strong clasping of hands. "Lieutenant Kirby, what the hell you doing out here? You're supposed to be getting short."

"About as short as you are, Franklin, my friend," Hank replied. He emphasized *my friend*, as he gazed at his ex-machine-gunner and ex-Weapons Squad leader.

An awkward silence took over.

Hank snipped the pregnant pause. "I'm out here as a radio ham and chief lieutenant flunky for a crazy Colonel Bligh. Brigade doesn't seem to care if I'm derosing end of month. Now what's your excuse?"

Franklin's smile grew wider. "About the same as you, I guess. The new supply sergeant's at the 93rd Evac with some mysterious case of the runs. The old one," Franklin jabbed his thumb at himself, "has to take over and get everything shaped up out here, even though his deros date is first week in July."

"How long you been supply sergeant?"

"Over four months. After the am…after you left. Sergeant Martin was elevated to Battalion staff and I was promoted to sergeant, and Lieutenant Toch, the new November Six, made me the platoon sergeant."

"Pretty damn good," Hank interjected. "From spec-four to buck sergeant straight to platoon sergeant. Lieutenant Toch made a good decision. For once competence triumphed time in grade."

"Well, you might say that. Or you could say I was the only sergeant left in the platoon."

Hank nodded weakly, mindful that Sergeant Michael and Sergeant Burlop had been killed.

"Anyway," he continued, "after almost a month as platoon sergeant I realized that I'd had it and requested to get out of the field. It just wasn't the same anymore. Just wasn't the Cadillac platoon. And with all that had happened, I couldn't push it anymore. Just didn't have the stomach for it. Or maybe the guts. Who fucking knows? The supply sergeant slot opened up. I asked for it and it was granted. Thanks, I believe, to some lobbying from the first sergeant."

Hank opened his mouth to speak, but nothing came out. Franklin had been given a well-deserved promotion to sergeant and he hadn't known about it. He hadn't even seen him since the ambush; hadn't even been over to his old company area. And it wasn't that he was too busy and it wasn't that he didn't care. He often wondered how and what Franklin was doing. More than any other.

His face reddened, embarrassed by the verbal gap he created, and he asked with a forced chuckle to disguise his sudden inward loss of composure. "You thinking of re-upping?"

"No way. I'm getting out soon as I can. But, I'm RA, so it may be another year and a half. There may be a possibility of an early out though. We'll see."

"I'm out soon as I deros." Hank stated, wishing the same could be for Franklin.

There was more silence.

Franklin looked around. Sergeant Morgan was filling the sandbag by himself. The two PFCs had started the first layer of sandbags around the trailer. "What's going on?"

"This is our commo center. Colonel Bligh says we got to sandbag it."

Sergeant Morgan approached them. His face pallid. "Sir," he addressed Hank in a weak tone. "I'm feelin' a little dizzy. Sun's gettin' to me. I don't even want to think about the colonel's tent. Can't that sucker…" He stopped, suddenly aware of Hank's officer status. "Uh…what I mean, sir, is we've got a lot of work to do."

"I know, I know. We'll work at our own pace. Find some shade around here and lie down."

The two PFCs, seeing the discussion, came over, giving themselves a needed break.

"No, sir. Not yet. I'll hang in for awhile longer," Morgan said and sucked up his gut.

Franklin broke in, his voice excited. "Lieutenant Kirby, I can help, And Bravo's Mortar Platoon is here, and they can help. We'll pitch in and have everything done by dark."

"Can't ask you to do that, Franklin. You guys worked hard enough at your own emplacements."

"But we're all set up. Have been for some time."

Hank shook his head. "No. I'm sure there's no one in Mortars who knows me anymore. I can't ask them to work their asses off. I don't want you too either." He glanced down at his boots with their thick coating of dirt. He thought of Loc Ninh. He thought of the Mortar Platoon. They had willingly joined him. Hank owed the Mortar Platoon, despite its turnover into new names and faces. Why increase his debt?

Franklin's mouth filled with protest. "Sir, they'd want to do it. You might not know 'em now, but they know you. Believe me, you're not a stranger. You're…you're a legend to them. To all of Bravo."

With the word "legend", Hank's shoulders rocked back.

"What do you mean legend?" he scoffed harshly.

Franklin became a little sheepish. "Well…you might say I became the company's historian. Thought the replacements should know about the shit November went through while you were platoon leader."

"Then they must know I'm no fucking legend."

"Just told them things that happened. That's all."

"Ok, then. Don't want you fabricating absurdities," Hank said in a softer tone.

He felt three pair of eyes burning into him like blow torches. The task for the four of them was immense and maybe one could get heatstroke or other serious ailments. Raw blistered hands were, at a minimum, a certainty. Then again would the mortar platoon really help them, or would they tell Franklin to stick it.

He decided to see. "OK." He glanced around at the three pairs of eyes, then back to Franklin. "Ask them." He felt the white-hot flames being withdrawn from his body. "But," he gazed seriously into Franklin's eyes, "don't order them. It has to be volunteers."

Not only the entire Mortar Platoon, but also Bravo's supply personnel and stray field troopers waiting to be hooked into Lai Khe on the evening re-supply Chinook, pitched in. With such a massive influx of labor resources they constructed in rapid fashion the sandbags around the radio shack and erected the colonel's tent and its wall of sandbags.

None of this manpower, save Franklin, was familiar to Hank. No one was left from the Mortar Platoon of Loc Ninh, having derosed or remf jobbed or taken sick, or…whatever.

Everything was in place as the sun began to touch the jungle in the west. Everyone had scattered. Putting his fatigue shirt on, Hank watched Franklin's back receding in the distance, past the 105 parapets. They would get back together after chow. The camaraderie of joint purpose and effort absorbing them into the soldiers of Bravo's clique, Morgan and the two PFCs had checked in with Hank before checking out with their new buddies.

Hank felt alone as he stood in the center of the triangle formed by the radio shack, the multilayered sandbagged roof of the huge, ridiculous bunker built to Higbee's specifications, and Higbee's tent. He turned around. Twelve meters beyond the humongous bunker were the sandbags of another bunker. It was just as big, but sturdier, more professionally built. It was the Battalion

TOC, Woodson's bailiwick, as well as the Battalion CO, Lieutenant Colonel Hart, whom he had not met.

Beyond the TOC bunker were two more tents like Higbee's. They probably housed Woodson and the CO. After the tents were more bunkers, supplementary firing bunkers, then front line bunkers. Then the wire and the foo-gas and the plowed clearing and the jungle, now inflamed by the last wash of the sun's diminishing rays. Hank stared past it all, as if trying to see home, to see Pam.

He was absorbed in thought when he noticed Colonel Higbee emerge from one of the tents. Its sides were rolled up for ventilation and it was filled half with slanting sunlight and half with deep shadow in which the burly silhouette of Major Woodson could be seen. The sight of Higbee and Woodson brought Hank's mind back in focus with the moment.

The light was fading rapidly now, the sun slipping into dense jungle. It was an eerie gray in which Higbee approached Hank and twisted his head all around, inspecting the site, his helmet tilting about like a gyroscope. There was still enough light for Hank to note beneath the helmet the cold fire in his eyes.

Those eyes turned on Hank. "Lieutenant Kirby, I want to know what this is all about," Higbee demanded.

"Sir?"

Higbee's arm swung an arc before him. "I mean all this, it's…it's completed. Everything's done."

"Yes ,sir. That's what you told us to do. We did what you told us."

"But you had help. You had to have help."

"Yes, sir."

"But you were told you couldn't have help."

"No, sir."

"What? Didn't you hear my order?" Higbee was shouting now. Any minute Hank expected his helmet to fly off like an erupting volcano blowing its crown.

"You said not to request help. I didn't. But men from my old unit said they wanted to help. I didn't *request* their help." Hank couldn't help the venomous sarcasm in his voice. He was short. Goddamn, he was short!

Higbee tore off his helmet and threw it to the ground. He kicked it a good five meters. "You FUCKOFF, Lieutenant!" His hands gripped his hips and his face poked up and out from his shoulders. His neck distended, as if sprung from a jack-in-the-box. "You pusillanimous shit stick! Let's get something straight. I'll decide if we need help. Got that, Jack?!"

Hank nodded slightly, with a certain composed defiance. His head bent upward. It looked as though he was avoiding Higbee's searing eyes. But he was really trying to get away from Higbee's foul breath.

"Don't look away from me while I'm talking to you, Lieutenant." Hank lowered his head to look down at the small man in a tirade and held his breath. "Now get this, get it good, get it straight, and don't forget it. I want you on your toes out here, walking on egg shells. And if you break one, or crack it just a little, I'm going to be all over your ass like elephant shit on a pissant. And I'm not the only one. Major Woodson knows you're a fuck stick too. That should've gotten your ass court-martialed. It's still not too late, Lieutenant. You may find yourself in a stockade in Long Binh instead of Stateside in a few weeks. Think about that one awhile."

Hank felt himself weaken. The little fucker could probably swing something like that. He exhaled slowly through pursed lips, gasped another breath and held it. Thank God it was almost dark now. The hatred in Higbee's eyes was being dampened by the oncoming darkness.

As Higbee was berating Hank about the requirement to be on his toes, his own toes were being stretched to their maximum as he tried to minimize Hank's height advantage. But it was not much of an advantage and he rocked back down to his heels, allowing Hank to start breathing with timid caution.

Higbee snorted, venting his anger through his nose and shaking his head like an old plow horse. "Have you had a commo check with brigade?"

"No, sir. Not yet. I figured to do it after chow."

"Do it now. Understand?"

"Yes, sir."

"And get this, Kirby. I want you in that commo center all night, every night we're out here. Make sure you got Sergeant Morgan or one of the PFCs in there with you to keep you awake. Got that?"

"Yes, sir."

"And during the day, I want you to make sure the other men are properly monitoring the radios. I want you to personally check them every two hours. I want you also to keep an operational map of the task force's movements and contacts updated. The map will be easel-mounted in my tent and you'll brief me every three hours. Got that?"

Hank wanted to scream out in Higbee's face, splattering him with spittle and with the question: *When am I supposed to sleep, you asshole?* But he knew he couldn't. But what he decided he could do, when he was comfortably aboard the Freedom Bird with Dick, watching through the portal the tarmac of the runway speed-by, was give a finger bird, aimed toward Lai Khe, directed primarily at this squat-butted colonel. And besides, he knew the answer to the question. He wasn't supposed to sleep.

Higbee released Hank from his stare. His eyes fell to the ground. "After your commo check, get this place cleaned up. And I want it to stay clean, always, every minute, every hour, twenty-four hours a day. Got that?"

Hank strained his eyes, peering through the dark, around the colonel's tent, around the radio shack, around the bunker. There were a few stray shovels leaning on the shack and some unused sandbags on the ground by the wall around the colonel's tent. "Yes sir, I'll take care of it right now."

"Take care of what?"

"The shovels and sandbags." Hank pointed in one direction and then the other.

"I'm not talking about that," Higbee whispered in a harsh, belittling tone. And then he commanded, "Look at the ground!"

Hank looked at the ground. Through the darkness it wasn't easy to see, especially where the shack and tent cast black ink pools. Seeing little, he shrugged his shoulders and shook his head.

Higbee became annoyed at Hank's baffled, uncomprehending mind. "Footprints!" he snapped sourly. "Look at all the footprints!" He glared at Hank who stared back dumbfounded.

"This area is a mess with all those footprints everywhere. Just because you can't see them doesn't mean they're not there. I want them all covered up tonight. And call brigade and have some rakes sent out on tomorrow morning's re-supply. We're going to keep our little sector of this fire base immaculate. A showcase for everyone. Hear that, Lieutenant Kirby?"

"Roger…sir," Hank mumbled as his mind mulled over the niceties of planting a footprint on Lieutenant Colonel Higbee's diminutive, but dangerous mouth.

The late-night hour found the "Black Hole of Calcutta," so the radio shack had been dubbed, crowded and nearly black. There were a few dull lights illuminating the radio panels and soft starlight filtering over and around Franklin's silhouette that blocked much of the small entry-way. He sat on the floor, back against the edge of the doorway's frame, one leg inside bent to his chest, the other hanging out, dangling a foot off the ground. Hank sat on a small plywood bench along one wall. Franklin's silhouette was to his left, the radios on his right. Across from him, leaning against the junction of the radios and far wall, was the amorphous shape of PFC Glombowski, a squatty, swarthy, thick-whiskered teenager.

Hank hoped Glombowski was comfortable, for if he was in a position like Hank's, leaning forward with forearms on thighs, they would be banging heads. As it was, their legs were nearly entwined, and when one moved, the other noticed.

The only conversation was the rushing noise from two squawk boxes beside two handsets on a small knick-knack shelf cantilevered from the radios. One radio was set on the task force net, the other on the Brigade's. A minute ago, there had been more conversation than the squawk boxes. It had been a long monologue by the usually taciturn Franklin giving a sitrep of Bravo Company after Hank's ignominious departure.

After the ambush, so Franklin had just related, Sergeant Martin took over as interim platoon leader and Lieutenant Brussels had remained as CO. Lieutenant Colonel West derosed three weeks later. The new Battalion CO, with no field experience during his entire lackluster Army career, so trooper rumor had it, was indecisive and timid. Consequently, Major Woodson became his Rasputin, assuming powers normally belonging solely to the domain of the Battalion Commander.

Woodson exercised one of these powers a week after West left by relieving Brussels of his command and shipping him off to MAC-V. The boot was brought about after a night's ambush debacle. The episode started after a bunch of A-CAVs dropped off the company in a field of scrub brush. The platoons separated. The First and Second Platoons headed east and west 500 meters for ambushing. The third—November Platoon— remained in place with Brussels essentially in command of the platoon and the company, not entrusting the leadership of the platoon to Sergeant Martin. Franklin was there, too, and made it a point to let Hank know this story was not second hand.

Brussels decided on a perimeter ambush formation, forsaking November's four element combination instituted, Franklin proudly reminded, by the old November Six. While claymores were being set out in a 360-degree circle, a dozen VC, one a big gook lugging an 82mm mortar tube on his back, happened through. Not by, Franklin explained, but through. Right through. Bisecting even the fuckin' ambush site, Franklin said.

They were caught completely unaware, many with their claymores in their hands, having taken the blasting caps out in case some dumb son-of-a-bitch decided to hit a clacker with them on the wrong end. It was pull a grenade pin, hold the lever down, hold your breath, pray they didn't see you.

And they didn't. It was so fuckin' dark, as Franklin aptly put it, the VC passed right through unaccosted. Even when they were out the other side, things were so disorganized and discombobulated, they still weren't accosted. The men were too caught up with looking for pins to stick back in their grenades, or getting the hell away from their claymores, or just forcing air back into their lungs. Brussels didn't even call in mortar fire in the direction the gooks were headed. An hour later he did, however, radio in a sitrep of what happened, and the next morning at first light Woodson choppered in and went out with Brussels' ass on his boot.

For about a week after that, the company stood down in Lai Khe while waiting for a new CO, Woodson having no confidence with existing platoon leaders. First Sergeant Mendez became the power while in the rear and made Franklin the supply sergeant before he himself derosed. The company got a new CO and first sergeant the same day. Both have been OK, Franklin had concluded.

Sergeant Martin derosed. All the others that had been in November with Hank were no longer in the field, some no longer in Vietnam, having derosed or become ill or some-such, such as Doc Fletcher. Mendez had gotten Doc a rear job with the Battalion medical service. He had access to some drugs and had become hooked on morphine. He was now in Japan getting cleaned up before his court martial.

"How about you, sir?" Franklin interrupted the rushing sounds from the squawk boxes. "What's been going on at your end?"

The question intruded unexpectedly. Hank shifted his feet, causing PFC Glombowski to shift his. He straightened his back, pressing it flush against the thin sheet of wood that made up a wall. His hands gripped the bench as he glanced over at Glombowski, thinking his movement had awakened him. He didn't know Glombowski's ears—the raw, tender ones of a remf with only one month in-country—had been acutely tuned to Franklin's discourse.

"Can't complain. I've been spending eight hours in the Brigade TOC. Then do whatever I want. Read, eat, drink, play darts, watch the "Saigon News," "Wild, Wild West." Pretty good existence, actually. My old buddy, Dick Kistler, is my roommate."

"I heard. That's lucky."

There was a period of more rushing noise, until Franklin said, "I'm glad things worked out this way. Us getting together one more time. Must be fate. Funny…but I think about you…and the others…from time to time."

Hank said nothing. But his skin flushed. His head tilted back and bumped against the wall.

More squawk box.

And then their dark, tiny domain was penetrated with loud sounds of explosions. *Wham! Wham! Wham!*

"Incoming!"

Franklin's immediate reaction was quickly to pull in his dangling leg, sit upright, and look at the dark outline of Hank's face where he knew his eyes were. Hank stared back at him as he considered some sort of action. Should they try for a bunker, or just wait and hope? His fingernails busily clawed out small chunks of plywood from his narrow seat. Glombowski glanced back and forth at the two, waiting for a command.

More rushing noise.

Then static crackling on one of the radios as it was keyed. Then mortars firing from the fire base. Then artillery joining in the cacophony. Then Major Woodson's monotone coming out of the squawk box. "Duty five-five, this is Demon Three, we've received three rounds of incoming. Believed to be eighty-two mike-mike. Landing about two hundred meters outside of wire. Negative casualties, negative damage. We are answering with counter fire on suspected grids."

"This is Duty five-five. Roger," came the acknowledgment of the Brigade's graveyard duty officer.

Suddenly Glombowski began laughing. Loud, high-pitched and semi-forced. The laugh of a soldier finally, safely, and briefly, meeting the enemy. A war story to write home about. "Wow!" he exclaimed, "That was somethin'. Good thing those fuckin' gooks can't hit the broad side of a barn." He looked back and forth for a reply from someone.

Hank and Franklin continued to stare at one another. They were too short for this sort of thing.

CHAPTER 56

T HOSE THREE ROUNDS of incoming seemed the only direct enemy activity that Task Force Geronimo and its supporting fire base, Stork, would encounter. Nevertheless, Brigade S-2 kept insisting a couple of NVA regiments were wandering around somewhere in the rubber and jungles that made up the real estate of the task force. Two reinforced Battalions of infantry and armor cut zigzags all over the landscape, trying to either plow into these mystical enemy forces to kick ass and take names, or chase the horde into the blocking positions set up by more infantry and armor to entrap the bastards. As it was, at least so it appeared, the chasers were plowing into the blockers.

Hank was elated at this lack of an enemy; elated they had received no more incoming; elated at being with Franklin one more time; elated at being short enough to consider counting the days until the Freedom Bird rather than the weeks.

There was little else to be elated about.

His daily routine mandated by Higbee, in writing no less, following the verbal directive at dusk of the first day, was to pull radio watch in tandem with one of Sergeant Morgan's two PFCs. He'd been mandated to maintain a fully awake status in the Black Hole from 2000 hours to 0600 hours the following morning. At precisely 1000 and 1600 hours, Hank had to stick his head in the Black Hole for a sitrep from Morgan, who pulled the single watch during the day. At precisely 1100 and 1700 hours Hank had to report to Higbee's tent where he scrubbed off the old grease penciled positions of the units of the meandering task force and drew the updated positions on the acetate overlay of the area's 1:25000 topo map.

Hank's routine was now well into its fifth day and though he was growing more tired every day, he refused defeat; too much had happened in a year for some twerp lieutenant colonel to best him. Every time he reported to Higbee, though he felt weaker, he looked stronger, thanks to Franklin's makeup and supply assistance: a close shave, drops for the bloodshot eyes, clean fatigues, and dusted-off boots.

It was in this made up condition on the evening of the fifth day, following a 1930 hours "mad minute" when the company securing the fire base gets down into their low profiled firing bunkers and cuts loose a flood of tracers, that Hank found himself outside Higbee's tent flap five minutes after receiving his summons. His hand slapped three times on the thick canvass and he heard a stern, "Come in." Pushing the flap back he stepped inside and saw Higbee in the pale, ethereal light of a Coleman, standing between the center pole and the easel on which was the situation map Hank was charged with keeping current.

He approached Higbee smartly, purposely putting a bounce in his bedraggled step. "Yes, sir. I'm reporting as ordered, sir," he said, clicking his heels as he stopped three feet away, his helmet under his left arm.

Higbee's beady eyes shot out a menacing stare and his crew cut seemed to bristle. Hank expected he would launch a tirade about errors he had discovered in the location of the task force's evening ambush patrols. Whatever it was, Higbee wanted to keep him in suspense, since the only conversation for the first few minutes was with his eyes. Finally, his voice joined in and Hank soon learned that it wasn't the situation map.

"Lieutenant Kirby," he said and clasped his hands behind his back, then started slowly rocking back and forth between his heels and toes. "As you know, Task Force Geronimo has turned up considerably little enemy activity," he cleared his voice, "actually the only action of consequence was the three mortar rounds our first night." Hank wanted to correct him, to tell the dummy that the fire base wasn't really part of the task force, only a support and commo element, and hence the task force had turned up a zip. Instead, he merely nodded. "As a result of this fact, I would say the probability is increasing substantially that the task force will find the enemy soon and in considerable numbers. Wouldn't you say, Lieutenant Kirby?"

Hank wanted to ask if this brilliant calculation was a result of some probability and statistic course given at the Point. He merely answered, "Could be, sir."

"Could be! Could Be! It's damn well more likely than that, Lieutenant." Higbee's rocking picked up in tempo. "And because of this likelihood and this major enemy action I am anticipating, I've decided to take added precautionary methods. Methods you may think somewhat extreme, but I assure you, Lieutenant Kirby, are quite necessary in these circumstances." He took a deep breath and let it out slowly, dramatically pausing for effect.

Hank swallowed hard, waiting for the other boot to fall, or rather stomp.

Higbee started in again. "I've decided the commo center needs a full-time officer to be ready to handle this likely enemy action. Sergeant Morgan is not capable of monitoring the confused and copious radio traffic that will result and there would be valuable time lost in his getting an officer to handle the situation."

Hank turned his head slightly at an angle to cast a wary eye at this barrage of bullshit. There were only two officers in Higbee's command, Higbee and himself, and Higbee had yet to say even an "over" on the radio. The only part of him to enter the Black Hole was his small turtle head.

Higbee droned on. "To guard against this contingency, I'm changing your routine." Hank braced himself. "From now on, for the next seven or so days we are to remain at this duty station, you are to continuously monitor the radios in the commo center. You will only be allowed outside for the purpose of my bi-hourly briefing, for taking care of necessary bodily functions and grooming, and for sleeping, which, I'm afraid, must be staggered during what I consider to be the low probability hours of a major contact, which are from 0600 to 0800 hours and from 1800 to 2000 hours. And remember, you must not jeopardize the mission of this task force by sleeping while on duty. Do you follow me, Lieutenant Kirby?"

Yes, he followed him completely. Higbee had perceived that he was losing, and now drastic action was needed. Seven or so days a hostage in the Black Hole.

Staring at Higbee in stunned amazement, Hank's mind rolled over his options. Tell Major Duncan of Higbee's insane vendetta against him? No, Duncan would probably think he was fabricating things to get out of the field. Tell Higbee he may be a little man, but he was sure a big prick? Or, gut it out. Even if turtle head catches him asleep, though things could be sticky, there probably wouldn't be a court martial. In fact, he could probably prove cruel and unusual harassment. But even so he could miss his scheduled Freedom Bird flight.

There were no good options.

He straightened to a rigid attention. "Yes, sir. I follow you." He took one step back. "Is there anything further?"

Higbee had the audacity to grin avuncularly. "No, I think that's about it. Your new routine starts immediately. Better get ready for your radio watch."

"Yes, sir. Is PFC Glombowski still going to be with me on the night shift?"

"Why yes. I would think so. You'll need someone to help you keep awake at night. Though I think you should manage all right by yourself during the day, with the briefings stretching your legs. Don't you?" Higbee added a chuckle.

"Yes, sir. I don't see a problem," Hank responded with a surprising burst of enthusiasm, and noticed with satisfaction that Higbee's grin lost some of its intensity.

"That's all, Lieutenant. You're dismissed."

Though out of character at a fire support base, Hank saluted, then about faced, marched a few short steps, opened the flap, and disappeared from Higbee's sight. He crossed in the dark to the Black Hole.

Hank placed one foot on the edge of the trailer bed, grabbed the inside edge of the small doorway, and hoisted himself inside. The outside starlight cast a pale glimmer of PFC Glombowski hunched over with his elbows on his knees and his hands holding up his face. He straightened his back, letting his face go as Hank stepped crouching through the rectangular opening. "Evening, sir," he greeted his lieutenant, only to be acknowledged by a loud, gruff grunt.

Hank took his place opposite Glombowski and stared obliquely out the opening at a distant, shadowy outline of a 105 howitzer.

He remained staring, with little departure, only an occasional bang of the back of his head against the wall. In about an hour, the howitzer became displaced by Franklin as he took up his usual place in the doorway.

There was nothing said by anyone for a full five minutes, Franklin having assumed his typically tacit self, content with the proximity of his former platoon leader and ready to carry a conversation if pressed. Finally, Hank spoke, "Higbee's put the screws to me. I was winning, Franklin. Now he's started a new tactic."

Glombowski glanced from Hank to Franklin. "What happened?" Franklin asked.

A tennis match of words started; Glombowski looked back at Hank. He enjoyed listening to their conversations. There was a certain aura about these two. They had been through hell together.

"Higbee says the impending enemy situation dictates that I spend every waking hour in this fuckin' Black Hole. For sleeping I get two hours out in the morning and two in the evening. The only other times I'm allowed out of my cage is to brief him on the locations of the task force and for bodily functions."

"That fuckin' son-of-a-bitch!"

"That sums it up exactly. He knows I can't make it without falling asleep in this hell hole. I can maybe stand it in here for the remaining week, but not without sleep."

"He'll be watching your ass like a hawk. That little alarm clock of his will go off all hours of the night, getting him up to check you out."

"Yeah. Though I don't think he'll get up too much, as lazy as he is. Maybe twice in a night. If I had some kind of early warning, I could sleep in here and wake up the same time he does. Glombowski could monitor the radio traffic while I'm sleeping." Glombowski nodded enthusiastically at Hank, excited to be a part of this team.

"Maybe we could post a sentry next to Higbee's tent. When the alarm clock rings he'll hear it and wake you up before Higbee gets out of his tent."

"Suppose the sentry doesn't hear it. Suppose Higbee's got it muffled under his pillow. Suppose the sentry falls asleep. And again, how can I ask someone to stay awake all night for me?"

"I'll do it, sir," Franklin rushed to volunteer.

"No you won't. And that's final."

"I'll get some of the guys from Mortars and we'll establish a watch, two per, just like we did on ambush."

"No. I'd be causing everybody problems they don't need. And even so, we still don't know about hearing the alarm clock. If that's what he's got. Maybe he'll have a runner wake him up. Who knows? Higbee catches someone trying to warn me; he'd be in hot water with me."

"We got to do something, sir. We can't let him win."

"I don't want him to. Though all that would probably happen is I'll miss my deros date while I'm countering his charges of my neglect of duty. I'm certain I'd get exonerated."

A thoughtful silence ensued as minds searched for ideas.

"Sir?" Glombowski said, entering the conversation timidly. "I…I think I've got a way for you to be warned when Higbee is about to drop in."

Eyes peered in the direction of Glombowski's dark bulky figure. Without words, they asked him his plan.

Glombowski sensed their question. "Sergeant Morgan's responsible for these radios," Glombowski hit his left forearm against the bank of two radios and related power packs that bridged the short distance between Hank and him. "He also has some commo wire and other accessories."

Hank impatiently shifted around. He wondered what the solution to his predicament had to do with the commo equipment.

"Sergeant Morgan and I can rig a set up where when Higbee pulls back his tent flap and steps outside, a wire will disengage from a contact, sort of like turning off a switch, and a flashlight bulb hooked up in here will go off. When it does, I'll wake you up, sir. You'll be ready for his pop inspection and he won't see the light because it will have gone off. After he goes back to his tent I'll sneak out and reconnect the wire."

The two heads moved again, this time back to each other, acknowledging the potential of Glombowski's scheme.

To Hank, it sounded plausible, but with some pitfalls. It seemed a simple application of a basic electrical engineering principal. Being a civil engineering major specializing entirely in the sanitary field, he had taken only one semester of electrical engineering and it wasn't until near the end of the course when he discovered that the "wee ways" his Chinese professor so often spoke of was really "three phase." But he *had* learned enough to know that copper wire attached to a battery would turn a light on and a break in the wire would turn it off. But still there were the pitfalls that needed to be addressed.

"What about the wire being exposed?" he asked.

"We'll bury it. There are plenty of times Colonel Higbee's away, usually over in that major's tent. What's his name?"

"Woodson."

"And Renta can be a lookout for us and also rake away any signs of digging. It'll be just a small trench."

"What if someone sees us? There's plenty of activity during the day around here and at night Higbee would hear us," Franklin interjected.

"We'll tell them we're rigging a land line from the tent to the Black Hole."

Hank nodded. It was plausible. It would be something stupid enough for Higbee to want. Then it was his turn for a question. "How about the flap? Suppose he leaves it open?"

"He never leaves it open at night," Franklin helped Glombowski out.

Hank nodded. That was a very near certainty.

There were no more questions for a moment as each considered the possibilities for failure. After a minute Hank asked, "What about the battery? Are we talking a radio battery? And where do we put it so it's not discovered?"

"Yeah, just like we use in these babies," Glombowski's forearm bumped a radio out to his side. Twenty seconds passed before he answered part two. He did so with two words. "In here."

"It won't work," Franklin interjected. "Higbee might spot the battery when he shines his light in here."

"I could hide it next to me," Glombowski countered.

"Maybe, but the more things out of the ordinary, the more chance of a screw-up."

"You have a better idea, Sergeant?" Glombowski's voice challenged.

"Could be. What if we hide the battery in a sandbag and place it among those surrounding Higbee's tent?"

It was too dark in the Black Hole to see Glombowski's smile, but his tone of voice gave it away. "That's it. That's a good idea. And that solves the problem I was trying to work out."

"What problem?" Hank enquired.

"How to set it up so as to provide the disconnect. We'll put the battery disguised in a sandbag on the bottom of the stack right next to the flap. With hook fasteners we'll fasten a small length of wire to the bottom of the flap and when it opens it'll pull away from one of the battery terminals, cutting the circuit. Fuckin' A man. We got it whipped."

Glombowski stomped his feet loudly on the thin plywood floor.

Franklin leaned toward Hank, put his hand on his knee, and squeezed, an endorsement of Glombowski's scheme.

Hank was equally enthused. It was a plot to match Dick's crazy hole-under-the-fence caper. Only with Dick it was hatched from insanity. This one was of necessity.

The following night Hank slept in the Black Hole. A little yellow bulb in the corner by a radio lit the interior. At 0150 hours the light goes out and

Glombowski gently touches his shoulder. Ten seconds later, a bright white light shoots Hank in the face. Hank smiles and says "Good evening, sir." There's a gruff response and the flashlight is turned off. Five minutes go by. Glombowski leaves and then returns after reconnecting the wire. Hank falls asleep. At 0500 hours, the light dies again and the scene repeats. At 0600 hours, Hank is free of the Black Hole and feeling fairly fit, though cramped.

CHAPTER 57

HIS TOWELING OFF complete, Dave Watson turned to face the long mirror that took up the length of the bathroom door. The steam from his shower had hidden his image but he found it by making use of the towel and wiping in ever widening circles. He found all of it and beamed with pride, admiring his broad shoulders, his protruding pectorals, his washboard stomach, all of which were dark brown, as if molasses had been poured evenly over most of his body, save for the snow-white band that seemed to cut him in half.

He was a goddamn Greek god! His face beamed. Then immediately changed expressions. His mask ripped away by the miserable, depressing thought that Pam didn't know it.

He opened the door, vanishing his image, and entered his bedroom. He fell back on his bed, subconsciously taking note of where his member flopped. He became conscious of the soreness in his muscles, put there by a grueling session with barbells and a universal. He needed the weight training to get ready for the start of football camp next month. But he didn't just lift for the added strength and power the coaches said he needed, but also for his physique.

His body was magnificent.

And Pam didn't know it.

He languidly placed his hands in back of his head and cogitated over how his game plan had gone sour. A fucking fiasco. For over five months he had held off.

Sure, he made hints to go park at the beach or perhaps a weekend in Nassau. But that's all. Nothing more. It had been a goddamn ritual. Every Saturday night a movie and drinks with Pam. His hard prick bursting in his britches. Then slight overtures to go somewhere countered by polite rebuffs. Then out to see Thelma and get laid. Even that had become a GD ritual. His game plan, the slow but effective running game, had bogged down, every play and every move defended.

Two weeks ago he went for the bomb.

It had begun with the usual start. Once they'd finished the after-movie drinks he said he knew a real nice parking spot north of Canaveral Pier. A side street leading to the beach where they could park and watch through a clear night with full moon and bright stars, as the tide rolled in, or out, whichever. She had responded with her usual polite rebuffs, though they had become more heated as he drove there anyway.

When he pulled up, stopped, and cut the engine it was as though some Ford motor monkey had welded her to the side of the door. She couldn't get any closer to it or she'd have been outside. Actually, that's where she wanted to be as she tried opening the door when he grabbed her broadside, the goddamn stick shift sticking in his ribs. She let out with a million no, no, no's and would definitely have slapped him had it not been for his hands around her wrists. He tried kissing her but found nothing exciting about the top of her head as she had hunched it down to butt him in the jaw. It had hurt. His long bomb was failing.

He made one last attempt, a great spread-eagle dive for the ball. He took both of her wrists into his one right hand. His left went down her blouse, into her tight bra, and grabbed at a firm boob. No nipple, but he goddamn knew he was close. Jesus, it felt good. Too bad she went bananas. Screaming, yelling, crying. It was one helluva banana scene. He had to let her go. She still didn't stop. He started his Mustang.

She still didn't stop. On the main drag she had reduced her tempo to steady sobs.

He of course apologized all the way. How else was he ever going to get her in a similar situation? Though she'd have to be a bit more willing. Maybe pump her with drinks. But she said she never wanted to see him again. Thank God Thelma had fucked the hell out of him an hour later.

Dave lifted his head and looked down his body at a gigantic erection. If only Pam had seen that maybe she would have changed her mind. If only she knew what a gorgeous hunk he was. What a gorgeous cock he had. Clothes just didn't show the whole story.

He sat up and swung his legs off the bed. An idea was forming. He had it. He had a way. He reached over at the phone, picked up the receiver, and dialed Pam's number. He looked down at his cock basking in self-aggrandizement.

"Hello."

"Hello. This is Dave Watson."

"Hello, Dave. How you doin'? Gettin' ready for training camp?" Fred Sadler's voice was the purr of a gentle cat having its neck rubbed.

"Yeah. That's right. I've been running on the beach and pumping a lot of iron."

"Iron?"

"Weights."

"Yeah, that's right. Heh, heh."

"Is Pam there?"

"She is. Just a moment, Dave."

Fred cupped the phone with his hand and looked over at Pam on the sofa. Her eyes were watching television, but he knew her thoughts were absorbed by some other medium. He'd seen that distant stare too often. "Pam, honey, it's Dave on the phone."

She turned her head and glanced glumly at her father. She considered telling him she didn't want to talk to Dave. Then again, if she said that, her father would wonder why and there might be a scene. She nodded slowly as if drugged, got up, and went to the phone. Her father eagerly handed her the receiver.

"Hello."

"Hello, Pam," Dave said, his voice high-pitched and contrite.

"Speaking," she said frostily.

"Listen, Pam, I'm sorry as I can be about what happened. I don't know what got into me. Maybe it was the full moon." Dave laughed.

"Or maybe you should see a doctor and find out."

Outwardly he ignored her remark. Inside his mind called her a bitch. "Listen, I've got to make it up to you. Please let me," he cajoled.

"No way."

"Listen. I owe you for that night. I want us to stop seeing each other with something else to remember besides that night. Please let me do that. Then we can go our separate ways. Listen. I know you can't trust me at night on a date. I've proved that. And I'm sorry for it. Listen. What I'm asking is to take you on a beach picnic Saturday, all very innocent. I'll get some Kentucky fried; we'll go to the beach; then that's it. No more will I ask you out again. But at least we'll part in civilized style. Please, Pam."

There was a long silence. She didn't want to see him again.

But then why not again? The night maybe could've been worse. And Dave had stopped, though more from fright, then respect. Still he was asking, in his own heavy-footed way, for forgiveness, and to part friends. Maybe he deserved at least that.

She had dated him, regardless of her confused, convoluted reasons for doing it. And she loved the beach. And she needed a diversion from her constant thoughts about the scenarios that would be played if, or when, she and Hank saw each other on his return.

She had both his mother's and father's addresses. Somehow, she'd see him and they would talk and discover why he'd changed. He owed her that. And maybe she owed Dave one final time. But this time, for Dave, it would be final.

"OK. What time?"

"What?" Dave couldn't believe what he'd heard, or thought he heard.

"I said OK. What time?"

"How about eleven thirty? It'll give me time to get the chicken and ice down some beer."

"OK."

"I really appreciate this, Pam. You won't be disappointed. I promise you."

"OK. Bye."

The line went dead. Dave grinned. His cock throbbed. She wasn't going to be disappointed. And neither was he.

CHAPTER 58

A S ONE DAY went into the next and Hank's schedule became more routine, the Black Hole became more like Brer Rabbit's briar patch, a place of refuge and, surprisingly, save for the cramped muscles and joints, of comfort. Each night he seemed to sleep better, and in the mornings, he felt stronger. But at Franklin's urging, so as not to have Higbee set fire to the briar patch, Hank feigned tiredness, exhaustion. His change of fatigues became wrinkled and soiled, his hair unkempt, his military bearing slow and bent.

Franklin became his constant companion, sitting with him in the 'black hole' during the day and half the night. It was three days of this companionship before Hank realized that Franklin had no duties to perform at the fire support base.

He pointed this out to Franklin who replied that, yes, this was correct, that after completion of Operation Geronimo and the disbandment of the Task Force, Bravo would be choppered back to Lai Khe, not stopping at the fire base. All that remained for him to do was to strike the company CP tent and coordinate its removal along with their belongings. Actually, he admitted, the Mortar Platoon could do that for him. And since Bravo's new supply sergeant would be taking care of things in the rear, there was really nothing left for him to do except await deros.

Though there was one reason why he remained at Stork. It was Hank. They had begun their tour together; Franklin wanted to end it that way. Hank argued hopelessly that they had already essentially ended, with less than a week left for himself and just a little more for Franklin. Franklin made no rebuttal, just a flat, final, preemptory statement. He wasn't leaving Stork until Hank left.

CHAPTER 59

I T WAS A hot June day. It was close to noon and the wind was from the west.

With an unusual air of formality Dave politely held the door open for Pam. Her hands were loaded with towels and a big blue beach bag. She wore beach sandals and a white blouse with a hibiscus floral pattern that covered most of her two-piece bathing suit. Dave was in a form fitting aquamarine T-shirt with bright orange "Miami Dolphins' printed boldly across his chest, and a small, tight red boxer swimsuit. Beach thongs were wedged between his toes.

While Dave was all happy smiles, Pam countered with a half-smile that was cautious and wary, and cold. The heat had not thawed it. She put the stuff in the back seat, climbed in, and waited for Dave to go around and slide behind the wheel of his top-down mustang.

"Where we going?" she asked him

"How about Sebastian Inlet? It's a good beach and won't be as crowded as the ones around here."

"OK," Pam nodded. She liked the Inlet, though it was a long drive. Over the past year of her life it had been her destination on many of her thought-provoking, solitary excursions in her VW bug.

It was going to be an even longer drive since A1A from Cocoa Beach to Patrick Air Force Base and parts further south would be jammed tight with traffic. It was always crowded during the various stages of the Apollo program. Now with Apollo 11 ready to go next month, the bustle of activity of NASA, associated suppliers, vendors, and manufacturers, and tourist space buffs was at its zenith all up and down the Cape.

CHAPTER 60

T HE RAIN SHOWER had passed. A stiff night wind came out of the surrounding jungle and mixed with perspiration to chill lightly the confines of the 'black hole'. It was the only time during Hank's long ordeal at Stork that the atmosphere actually felt pleasant. The atmosphere, Hank reflected, might also have something to do with this night being his last one in the Black Hole, and third from the last in Vietnam.

He looked over at the slumped, snoring Glombowski. The faint yellow glow of the little flashlight bulb beside him displayed tightly closed eyes set over a rhythmic, heaving chest. Tonight, it was now Glombowski's turn to sleep and Hank's to watch and wait to see if the yellow glow went out. Though he doubted it would. Higbee would surely be snoozing, getting ready for the morning task of drilling his small contingent on the art of dismantling what had been their contribution to Stork's urban development: the Black Hole and trailer, the 292 antenna, the cavernous bunker, and Higbee's tent, or rather suite, as it was known by the occupants of the Black Hole.

The whole fire support base seemed to sleep, save him and Franklin, whose silhouette was filling most of the opening. His head rested on the edge of one side, his stare on the other as the wind buffeted loose strands of his hair. Despite the late hour, neither wanted to say good night. Without speaking it, they were pulling the night watch together to welcome the crisp early light of the next day, their last together in Vietnam. But there would be other days in the States, they had said, and so had promised.

The driving rain had silenced them, and the lull of conversation carried on as the wind had replaced the rain, blowing with it thoughts of other days, future days, of home. For Hank, they were bittersweet thoughts, tangled with questions and imagined scenarios.

He tried to imagine Pam as she was this very minute, occupying her own special space on the other side of the world. Was she asleep or awake? Maybe Pam was at the beach, thinking about him and his coming home, considering the possibility of mending their rift and fulfilling their dreams of a year ago.

And maybe she was with Dave Watson…

The back of his mind picked up a familiar sound. One of a freight train whistling and rushing into the station, funny how the train was hurtling onto the beach with Pam. It just didn't belong among his thoughts. It…

Wham!

The lead round of a barrage of 82mm mortars crashed into the perimeter wire.

Wham!

CHAPTER 61

ICK BROKE FROM Wan's arms, rolled off her bunk—hers until Hank returned tomorrow—and onto his own which had been pulled over to Hank's side and set flush aside the other. She turned on her side, facing him, and wiggled her naked body to the edge of the bed. She was swallowed by Dick's massive arms and legs as they wrapped themselves together for the few hours of sleep before she would have to sneak out in the night and slip under the fence that had become the symbol of their frustration, the barrier between East and West, the wall of sadness blocking two people of different civilizations.

"I love you," Dick whispered.

"I love you," Wan softly reaffirmed into his chest.

There was silence. It was sleep time. Though Dick could not shut his eyes. He stared past Wan at the dark wall as his shoulder became soaked with her tears. No sobs, no sound at all, only silent and wet tears.

His eyes became watery. It was their last night in the hooch and their second to the last night together forever. Forever was so fucking final, he said to himself. So fucking final. Well he wasn't going to let it happen, for forever to beat them, to win out, to cause them suffering at least for now. Maybe later it would be forever. But not now. Not this time. He'd beat it. At least for now, maybe even forever, who knows?

Tomorrow, he would tell Major Duncan he wanted to extend for six months. That would keep them together; maybe give them time to work something out permanently. To write his senator on whatever one did when one wanted to marry a Vietnamese.

His eyes dried and he smiled at the wall, his decision made. His mind mulled over telling Wan, thereby stopping her tears from pooling in the hollow of his shoulder. But why not wait until he had talked to the major? It would be cleaner with everything officially settled.

CHAPTER 62

WHAM! WHAM! WHAM! A new downpour had arrived at Stork. Each drop ear-shattering, white-flamed, and spitting forth steel chunks and slivers at enormous velocities.

Franklin threw himself inside on the floor of the commo shack amidst the booted feet occupying the same space. Glombowski's head leaped from his chest and his eyelids snapped up.

While they reacted, Hank was immobilized by the extreme sudden change in well being. A sick feeling started in his stomach and spread rapidly like an electric shock throughout his body, deadening his limbs.

As the barrage continued its intensity, Hank reacted and quickly dropped down to the floor. Glombowski followed and squeezed in with him and Franklin.

Their Achilles heel was the opening and the thin plywood skin overhead. The other three sides were sandbagged. They could minimize their exposure to flying shrapnel by lying as close to the floor as possible. As for above, they could only pray there wouldn't be a direct hit. There was spastic shifting around as they located their helmets and put them on in a meager attempt to find additional protection.

There was a particularly loud explosion. A missile of jagged metal whizzed through the opening at an oblique angle, smashed a baseball-sized hole in the plywood wall just above the radios, and bit deeply into a sandbag. Sand spilled through the hole like an hour glass measuring the time left in their lives.

"Lieutenant Kirby, should we get out of here and make for the bunker?" Glombowski shouted into Hank's ear.

A few seconds and a lot of incoming went by as Hank thought about Glombowski's request. Some of the incoming rounds had a sharper, different intensity, unfamiliar to Hank than the sounds of 82s. Maybe they were 107mm rockets. "No," he answered with a shout aimed at Glombowski's ear. "There's too much shit. Too risky."

His head rested on Franklin's boot as he listened to the sounds of explosions. There were only the 82s now. Nowhere were there sounds of outgoing as there should have been. No thumps of friendly mortars or crisp cracks of howitzers. He couldn't blame the Mortar Platoons or the howitzer battery for not following SOP. It would be crazy to step out in such inclement conditions. It would be best to have Brigade crank up other artillery, spookies, gunships, and TAC air, the works, to silence those fucking 82s.

Wham!

One mortar round hit beside the commo shack. The force of the concussion was full against one sandbagged wall. The commo shack moved violently upward off the trailer bed and a few feet horizontally before falling over three-quarters upside down, on the seam of the ceiling and left wall. Inside, it felt like a washing machine beginning the spin cycle as heads, arms, and legs flailed wildly about. When the top of the shack touched down, the radios broke loose from their mounts and toppled down, one smacking against Franklin's face.

He groaned and cursed more than the other two.

"You all right, Franklin?" Hank yelled toward his feet, made heavy from the weight of one of the radios.

"Yeah. Bloody nose. Everything else in order."

"Good. We better get the fuck outta here. This hole's upside down, sandbags have been stripped. We're naked on all sides."

"Roger that," Franklin agreed.

"We'll go to the bunker. Glombowski, you first. Crawl on your belly, keep your head down."

"Yessir."

"Move out, damnit!"

Glombowski scrambled out through the opening. A knee caught Hank in the groin and he grunted.

"You okay, sir?" Franklin asked after Glombowski departed.

"Yeah, now you move."

"Negative, it'd be better if you go first."

"Don't negative me, Franklin. Get the hell out of here," Hank barked. Then added, "You and a radio are on my feet. Believe me, it'll be easier."

"Roger that, sir," came Franklin's reply from the opposite end.

There was a shifting and floundering of movement. Briefly the radio pressed heavily on Hank's feet, painfully bending his ankles. Then Franklin's face was beside his, then his chest, then his waist, then his knees, and finally his boots, until he was gone. Hank adjusted his helmet while telling himself it would be just as safe outside with his body pressed to the ground.

Grabbing the edges of the opening with his hands, he launched himself outside. His last thought before landing on his chest and knocking his wind out was that of the rushing sound from the radios. They were still working.

He hit the damp ground crawling alligator style, chest scraping the ground, legs kicking, running on hands beside him. His lungs heaved like runaway bellows trying to suck in much needed air. The bunker was in the opposite direction and he swung around into a U-turn.

The eight meters to the bunker seemed surreal and allegoric. His peripheral vision picked up flashes of explosions. The sky was black with an ugly blend of smoke and dirt particulate. To his left he could see out toward the perimeter where hundreds of green dashes flew in from the jungle and passed red dashes flying out.

It wasn't until he had crawled through the slot in the bunker and dropped head first that the significance of what he had witnessed dawned on him. It was a ground attack! The green tracers had looked like a mad minute in reverse, a gook mad minute!

Four pairs of hands caught Hank in mid air and kept him from falling five feet and landing on his head. In their haste to complete the bunker to Higbee's specifications they had failed to add a step to facilitate ingress and egress.

"You all right, sir?" Hank heard Franklin ask as he was lowered on all fours to the ground which was under about six inches of water. They had not landscaped around the bunker for drainage. In a corner a flashlight with a dark red filter lens hung from the roof by boot laces and cast an eerie reddish darkness on the six occupants.

"Yeah. How about you and Glombowski?" he asked. He looked around in the dark as he got his feet underneath him. He groped for his helmet in the muddy water while trying to recognize the dark forms of the bunkers' inhabitants.

"We're OK," Franklin said.

Hank slowly stood up only to bump his head on the engineering stakes that sagged dangerously close to buckling due to the roof's extra long span and the heavy weight of the layers of sandbags. Only one dark form was able to stand without awkwardly hunching forward. Hank knew Higbee was present.

"It's a full-scale attack! The gooks are attacking!" Higbee yelled at him.

"I know," Hank grimaced.

"We've got to do something! Do you realize that, Lieutenant Kirby? We've got to do something!"

"There's nothing we can do," Hank countered. "This bunker has no firing ports. We've got to sit tight and wait for the attack to be beaten back…And hope we don't have a direct hit," Hank added, aware of what little it would take for the roof to buckle. "As soon as Brigade gives us air support, those gooks won't be getting near the wire. Things will turn around." He hoped he sounded confident. He hoped he knew what he was talking about.

"But doesn't Brigade need to know what's going on here?" It was Sergeant Morgan's dark form that asked the question in a funny high-pitched tone.

"Yeah. But that's Battalion's job; not ours. We should just sit tight." Hank repeated his earlier advice as the violent storm of incoming continued outside keeping the bunker in a constant state of vibration and adding drizzles of sand that fell on their heads. *Was this enough to collapse the bunke*r, Hank wondered worriedly.

"You don't understand, Kirby! You don't understand, you fool!" Higbee ranted. "The Battalion TOC's been knocked out by sappers. I saw three with satchel charges blow the TOC."

Hank wanted to take up the fetal position in one corner and wait and just let whatever would happen, happen. He now remembered the rushing noise of the abandoned radios. There had always been a rushing noise since the start of the incoming. There had been no radio traffic. Battalion had not notified brigade. And now sappers had gotten inside the wire. And were blowing up bunkers. And they were inside a bunker!

The only other source of notifying Brigade aside from the recently vacated Black Hole was through the artillery channels. But those 105s were silent. They should be counter firing: HE, star shells, beehives, the works. But they were silent. Maybe the Battery CP was knocked out! Maybe Brigade didn't know what was happening!

Hank realized that Higbee was right. They had to do something!

"What's the plan? You're the field man! You and your friend here," Higbee's helmet bobbed toward Franklin. "Yes, I know about your friend, too. It pays to know everything." He babbled on and Hank understood. Higbee's mind had exceeded its elastic limit.

Hank felt the cold fingers of responsibility pressing heavily on his bent back, mixed with grains of sand cascading down his neck from the trembling, sagging roof of sandbags. Any minute a round could land square overhead, relieving him of this heavy burden. And he almost hoped it would happen. But he didn't. He had come too far in one year to do nothing now.

He hated this moment. Fate had tricked him, leading him to believe he would be going home. He knew now he would not be making the Freedom Bird.

He took charge, but first in mind only as he quickly sought alternatives from a brain that began feeling the effects of a circuit overload. Only two alternatives flashed with any sort of clarity: make their way to the TOC, what may have remained of it, or head back to the now upside down Black Hole.

The TOC might be completely destroyed, radios with it. On the other hand, if the radios were working, he'd have radio contact with the company defending the perimeter; he didn't have that frequency in the 'black hole'. Also, with the TOC bunker already blown it wouldn't be attractive to sappers. After all, lightning wasn't supposed to strike twice. And then again, maybe the Black Hole had already been blown since they vacated.

But had the TOC really been blown up? Maybe Higbee in his panicked state had just assumed it had been destroyed after seeing gooks nearby. Maybe the reason there had been no traffic to Brigade was the result of all traffic initially being taken up with the defending company, Delta.

"Did you see the TOC explode, or just the sappers?" Hank asked, forcing his tone to a moderate pitch.

Higbee shook his head. "No…no. But I saw sappers. They had charges. I heard the explosion after diving in here. Didn't you hear the explosion? You should have heard it!" Higbee screamed into Hank's ear.

Hank had heard explosions aside from the 82s. Maybe they hadn't been rockets. Maybe they were the satchel charges. Decision time had come, for any second now a sapper team could make any decision moot.

He started with a question. "How many rifles do we have?"

"I have one. And so does Renta," Sergeant Morgan nervously responded.

Hank shook his head. It wasn't much. "Okay," he said, "give one to Franklin. You, Glombowski, and Renta head for the perimeter bunkers and help out best you can. Be careful. Watch out for gooks."

"Wilco, sir!"

"Get moving," Hank said in reply and then turned to Franklin as Morgan provided a stirrup with his hands for Glombowski's boot to get him out of the bunker. Aware of Glombowski's exiting, Hank kept some attention directed outside for possible AK fire. With the rest of his attention he spoke to Franklin. "We're going to the TOC and try to get some commo established with Delta and Brigade."

"You're on, sir. I've got the M-16. I'll go point."

"What about me?" Higbee demanded. "Am I to stay here?"

Hank looked hard at a small, dark helmeted silhouette. With a straight drop from the bunker's slit opening to its bottom and Higbee's shortness, he'd maybe not be able to climb out and would thus sit out this battle waiting for its end, or his end, depending on sappers dropping by or an 82 smashing in.

"You're coming with us, sir," he said and swung his head to Franklin as he bent down and cupped his hands for a boot.

"OK, Tom, let's move," he urged, using Franklin's first name.

Franklin was catapulted out of the bunker and scrambled to take up a position next to the opening. Higbee came flying out. When he landed his head bobbed in an obvious display of disorientation. Franklin let go of his M-16, grabbed him by the pants leg, and roughly jerked him aside from the exit. He then assisted Hank out by pulling hard on his forearms. With Hank clear, he picked up his M-16 and started crawling hurriedly for the TOC, or whatever was there. Higbee followed at his heels, with Hank in the rear.

The frightening sounds of battle were everywhere: crashes of incoming 82s, decreasing slightly in their former intensity, sharp cracks of AKs, increasing in intensity, pops of M-16s, level in intensity. There was no illumination. Surely there had been enough time to get their firepower cranked up. Unless something was drastically wrong!

As he crawled, metal fragments rained lightly on his back and tinkled off his helmet. He sensed a massing of the enemy outside the perimeter, a gathering electrical storm, swirling its dark, heavy clouds, readying itself to send a huge lightning bolt of crazed bodies charging in and overrunning positions, overrunning the whole damn fire support base!

CHAPTER 63

LIEUTENANT FINSLEY INHALED deeply on his cigarette. Its tip turned into a bright orange ball, appearing suspended in a black pool of darkness in the corner of Looie's Lounge. His hand slid along the table to his scotch on the rocks. The cigarette in his mouth was replaced by a cold liquid that burned his throat. He glanced at his watch; the luminous dial showed the late hour. He looked out the window. He could see better in the darkness outside than in the blackness inside.

He looked along the high chain link fence until the visibility ended, but not before the spot where the secret escape hole was. The one he had discovered two days ago while making a pre-dawn security check.

He had been ecstatic over his find, with the uncovering of a secret infiltration route into the Brigade headquarters area. Surely, it was from where a carefully planned sapper attack would spring, or at least so he had thought. And late last night, with the possibility of a Silver Star, or at the least a Bronze, waiting in the wings from his heroism, he had staked out the infiltration route from the same vantage point where he now sat. Only then he had more than his .45 and scotch. He had had two M-16s, five frags, beaucoup ammo, steel helmet, flak vest, M-79, and a PRC-25 to call in support at the instant he dropped the first gook climbing out of that hole under the fence.

He had gotten a late start, what with rounding up his small arsenal. Wanting every ounce of glory, credit, and acclaim, he told no one. Of course, he considered the negative side, the danger. But with the advantage of surprise, and killing the lead man, and spraying the others on fully automatic, he could beat it out of the Lounge and radio for help at the same time. The odds therefore seemed good. He wouldn't have chanced it otherwise.

He had waited a helluva long time before something happened. When it did, he was so pissed off he could've killed them both. He had sure wanted to. Instead of sappers coming from the village and out the secret hiding place, that shit-head Kistler and the whore hooch maid came to the fence from the Brigade side; Kistler uncovered the secret, and the gook bitch went under the fence to the village side.

He should've killed them both.

He had been too stunned to react, to think.

And now, a night later, he knew what to do. Put them under arrest. It was that simple.

He had observed their rendezvous tonight, a sorry spectacle of adolescent kissing and hugging. He had pondered the possibility of taking them then, but decided no. He next had thought about kicking their door in and taking them while Kistler was getting his rocks off. But he'd decided no again. Rather he'd decided to get them during Wan's exit at the fence, when they had almost made it, but just not quite.

Finsley dragged on his cigarette, the tip glowing bright again, then he sipped on his scotch. Briefly he thought about breaking out one of the ten reefers in his breast pocket and have a toke. But no, the scotch would do, and it was free since there was no one else around to know of his pilfering. Smoking one reefer would cut into his profits. And he'd rather have the bucks and the free scotch than a pothead high right now.

He swigged some more scotch. His hands, he noticed, had started to sweat.

CHAPTER 64

TO HIS SURPRISE, Hank reached the TOC alive. He slid up beside a violently trembling Higbee to peer down into a dark, square abyss that only moments ago had been the Battalion TOC bunker.

Hank could barely see Franklin's dark figure rummaging around inside. He watched for a few seconds, questioning his command decision to get to the TOC. There seemed nothing down there anymore. Suddenly he was splashed with a mixed wave of self-pity and vulnerability. He had no platoon to help fight the battle, only Franklin and an old colonel in shock. And he had no weapon.

And he had no girl back home.

So what the fuck really mattered?

A star flare suddenly shot up from the vicinity of the southern perimeter, burst open and began floating over the fire base.

A pale light spilled into the bunker, bringing Franklin into sharper focus along with the rubble of shredded sandbags, broken engineer stakes, six-inch timbers, and other assorted unidentifiable debris. Franklin motioned frantically for Hank to join him.

Hank shifted his body around and slid down an incline of sandbags feet first. Little crooks and crannies were everywhere. He trod carefully, ducking under clutter supported by other clutter and stepping over other clutter. A shell landed not far from the rim where he had been observing Franklin. The blast was loud and cloaked his progress in smoke and dirt particulate.

In seconds he was beside Franklin. The air began clearing. A new flare was passing over. Higbee, somehow, had already reached Franklin.

They crouched low and wedged themselves into a small cave-like shelter formed by a collapsed section of roof that had maintained its integrity of latticed sandbags and was now supported by what Hank recognized to be the bank of radios of the TOC. Franklin fiddled with the radios, taking the handsets and placing them to his ear. At one he wiped away the dirt on the glass of the frequency indicator, which then let out a dull yellow glow.

He stuck his face in the glow, then turned and stuck his face into Hank's ear. "Only one's working. It's on the Battalion net," he screamed a whisper above the din of crashing mortars.

Then suddenly the sounds of incoming seemed to recede like a passing thunderstorm, only to stall over the opposite half of the fire base.

The emotional relief Hank felt from the shifting of the barrage was immediately followed by a stabbing sense of terror, the gooks had lifted their mortar fire because they were going to charge in force. He took the handset from Franklin, pushed the talk button, while looking out from their cubbyhole, expecting at any moment to see a horde of screaming NVA pouring over the edge of the demolished TOC.

Before he could speak, massive rolling balls of orange flame erupted with a swoosh. Even at the distance of about 100 meters he felt the warmth. "Delta Six, this is Demon," he called in a creaked voice the call sign of the CO of Delta company, which now had the unfortunate duty of defending the perimeter. Hank had taken the call sign of the Battalion Headquarters.

There was a seemingly infinite pause, time enough for the huge fireballs to be absorbed by the night, before a shrill voice bit into his ear. "This is Mike Six! Where the fuck you been? We've been trying like shit to get you on the horn. We need Arty, TAC air, the works, ASAP! We've got some gooks inside the wire and a slew outside. We just shot our wad of foo-gas in the south sector on what looked like a fuckin' platoon rushing the wire. We fixed those fuckers and plugged the hole, but I don't know how long it's gonna hold. Read me? Over."

As Hank started to return the transmission, a cluster of 82s burst nearby. The loud explosions caused the three in the collapsed bunker to huddle down into individual balls like frightened armadillos. The incoming quickly spread again over the entire fire base, giving the irony of comfort in the thought that the first wave had been beaten back, thanks to the foo-gas and a bunch of brave guys in forward bunkers.

But what of another wave?

"Roger, Mike Six, we'll contact higher for support," Hank spoke loudly, forcing a tone of authority that belied his panic. "But we're going to need your mortars to start hitting around the perimeter and popping illumination. And more importantly we need Arty to spit out some beehives. Right where you popped the foo-gas. That's where they'll be coming. That's our soft spot."

"This is Mike Six. Can't help with mortars. Our Oscar's helping out in the firing bunkers. It's fuckin' suicide having them in the pits. And Arty's your bag. You get those fuckers to get those fuckin' beehives bangin'."

Exasperation seemed to blow up inside Hank and ripple through his body. The pressure was building exponentially in his temples. It was going to be suicide for all of them if they didn't get mortars cranking and the 105 beehives firing. Why was he speaking with this recalcitrant platoon leader anyway?

"Mike Six, this is Demon. Let me speak to Delta Six. ASAP," Hank demanded to speak to the company's CO.

"Delta Six and everyone in his CP are dead." The recalcitrant Mike Six intoned that seemed to imply that he wanted Hank to fuck off. "Sappers bangalored his CP bunker when the incoming started. It was our Oscars that wasted the suckers," he added with the tone of another hidden *fuck off.* "Like it or not Demon, I'm in charge of Delta. I suggest you get the Arty, and if you want mortars, get Bravo's. We've got our own mess. Over!"

Franklin's ear was pressed flushed against the handset held fast by Hank. He had heard the conversation and now listened to the off-squelch rushing noise as he waited for Hank's reply.

Hank was motionless and watched wide-eyed at the spot of light emitting the radio's frequency indicator. So absorbed in thought his eyes saw nothing as he assessed the situation. Sappers had knocked out the Battalion command, the command of the company defending the perimeter, and in all probability the command of the Artillery Battery. That would explain why no action from artillery. They might all be huddled in bunkers waiting for the infantry to beat back the attack. This would also mean that Brigade had probably not been informed of their plight through the artillery channels. As the link now between Brigade and the fire base, the one working radio in the blown apart, open grave bunker had appointed him in command. And that SOB Mike Six knew that. Arty was Hank's, so was Bravo's mortars, and so was Mike Six.

What were the priorities? His mind asked and then instantly answered, setting them out sequentially. First priority: keep that gap plugged. Get 105s firing beehives at the gap. The beehive round was the modern version of grape shot, only more geometric with its steel fléchettes, and more deadly. He remembered the SOP procedure before beehives started blasting, a red star cluster to warn everyone to get their head down within thirty seconds, or have it taken off.

Second priority was to get mortar flares up and mortar rounds ringing the perimeter as close as possible. His third priority was to get Brigade to bring in the world all around them. Fourth priority, provided the first three had worked, get the dust-offs in.

Now for the first priority, the beehives; they had to get that Arty Battery out of their rat holes. How to do that? Someone had to personally kick, threaten, cajole, plead or whatever, to get them out, after first crawling over to their positions. Who was that someone? Why didn't Mike Six have the balls to send someone? But Hank knew why—Mike Six and his men were fighting for their lives on the perimeter. And his.

He turned his head and looked into the blackness of Franklin's eyes. Silently they conversed and then their silence ended, and Franklin said out loud, "I'll get them cranking. I know where their bunkers are. I'll get Bravo's mortars, too. You need to stay here with the radio. You're in command of this shitty mess."

Hank merely nodded. Deep inside his emotions became twisted and stretched, forcefully pulled in every direction by varying degrees of sadness, regret, guilt, and anger. For he knew Franklin's choice was the right one. For he *was* in command and *should* stay at the radio in touch with Brigade and Delta Company, which did not have sufficient radio power to have direct contact with Brigade. Yet, he wanted someone besides Franklin to go, someone with Delta Company, or…he wished *he* had the balls to go himself.

His hand squeezed Franklin's shoulder. Suddenly an idea hit him, and he pulled Franklin's head near so he would be able to once again hear the transmission. "Mike Six, Demon. We're going to get the Arty. They'll be firing beehives at the south section of the perimeter without, I repeat, without a red star cluster warning. Roger?"

"This is Mike Six, Roger. I'll inform my men," Mike Six answered in a tone a shade more civil, understanding the portent of Demon's message. A red star cluster would warn the gooks to get their heads down as well as the friendlies. Demon's way would hit 'em with no warning and too bad for anyone caught in the line of fire.

"This is Demon. Good. Get your men to put out their claymores in front of their bunkers ASAP. They should have time before the beehives. We need every bit of available firepower aimed outward."

"Mike Six. Claymores are a good idea. We'll get them out ASAP." Mike Six obliged, apparently now responding to what he believed made good sense—provided they did it before the beehives cut loose.

"One more thing," Hank added, "after this transmission, change to Duty's net. Do you have it?"

There was a long pause that filled Hank's ears with rushing sounds from the handset's earpiece and crashing sounds of incoming that now seemed to have taken on an even greater intensity than before. Hank wondered why Mike Six wasn't answering. His first guess was that the platoon leader, now CO, was having his RTO looking for Brigade's frequency. His second guess lingered uncomfortably in the back of his mind: that Mike Six was dead.

He started to give Franklin the go when he heard a voice in his ear. "Demon, Mike Six." Hank breathed relief. "We've got the net, but our radios can't reach that far."

"Roger. I know. But we have only one working radio. I'll be switching to duty's net and I want you to monitor me and not be without commo between us."

"Mike Six. I roger that. We'll switch…and good luck on those beehives."

"Roger, out." Hank terminated the transmission and glanced at Franklin, again his hand fell on his shoulder and squeezed.

"I'll be back, sir. You can count on it," Franklin stated with conviction, and squeezed Hank's arm in return. He then crouched low, turned away, and with one hand holding his M-16 by the carrying handle and the other holding down his helmet, he scrambled from their enclosure and up the steep incline of the collapsed bunker.

And then he was over the rim, gone into the din of exploding mortar rounds and flying metal.

Hank felt alone despite Higbee behind his right shoulder. As his eyes strained at the weak light from the frequency indicator while he twisted knobs to the Brigade net, his mind considered the rubble of this bunker and what it contained. Somewhere was the Battalion CO and somewhere was Major Woodson; and somewhere others. Maybe someone somewhere was still alive. Before he pushed the talk button, he swung his shoulders around to face Higbee.

Sunken, sullen eyes recessed in a face sucked dry of all color stared at him. Higbee was helmetless, his helmet now worn by his ass; it had become a stool for his sitting comfort. The eyes blinked twice, and Hank wondered if Higbee was aware what had been going on.

"Colonel Higbee, sir," Hank's tone was authoritative, but respectful. "Franklin has gone to get the artillery cranking. I'm going to radio Brigade for help. There may be some men around here still alive." His arm swung an arc indicating their immediate surroundings. "If so, they'll need help. Look for them, sir, while I'm on the horn with Brigade."

The eyes blinked twice again. Then twice more as they registered recognition. "You stay on the radio, Lieutenant Kirby. I'll take care of looking for survivors," Higbee said in a voice that rang faintly of command and... courage.

The initial shock of the attack seemed to be wearing off Higbee and he was beginning to emerge from his catatonic cocoon. Hank wasn't sure if the new Higbee being his old self would be a benefit or a liability.

As Hank returned his attention to the radio Higbee pulled out his .45, shifted to his knees, slid the helmet from under his buttocks and placed it on his head. He patted Hank on the back as he moved past and emerged from their cubbyhole. He started rooting among the broken timbers, engineering stakes, sandbags, and other assorted debris, including human bodies.

Hank glanced over and saw him moving in the rubble, pistol in one hand, the other moving debris in an effort to uncover a certain item of Higbee's apparent interest.

"Duty Five-five, this is Demon, over," Hank spoke rapidly into the mouthpiece. His senses became aware of the incoming receding slowly away, to the north half of the perimeter, creating a lull like before. A vacuum to be filled by charging NVA?

After a few very long seconds came a reply from the radio. "This is Duty Five-five, over."

"This is Demon. We are under a heavy mortar attack. Have beaten back one ground assault. A second appears imminent. Sappers are inside wire.

Our situation is critical. Repeat, critical. Get spookies, gunships, TAC air, Arty, and every other goddamn thing out here immediately." There was a short pause as Hank started to say over, but didn't, keeping his fingers pressed on the handset's talk button. There was one other request, one person he needed immediately, one person who on the other end of the horn would know the situation, would know exactly what he was saying; the one person whose platoon had rescued him at Loc Ninh. The one person he had started his sojourn with, and, he prayed, would be leaving with. He needed Dick Kistler. "Get Duty Three-zero. Get him ASAP. Do you hear me? Get Duty-Three-zero now!"

"Wilco, Demon. Hang tight. We'll get everything. Out." Duty Five-five abruptly ended the transmission.

Hank dropped the handset from his ear to his lap. He saw Higbee pulling at some limp arms grotesquely stretching from the rubble as he worried about the portent of the shifted mortar fire and the absence, so far, of the beehives. It was then that he heard a new, muffled sound. He froze, concentrating all his senses, like directional radar, on this new bleep on his mind's scope. But with the blended cacophony of bursting mortar rounds and automatic weapons firing causing too much background interference, the bleep did not reappear. Hank guessed at what it might be and hoped he guessed wrong.

Hoped it wasn't gook gibberish!

A star shell burst in the sky, too bright for a hand fired flare, too dim for a howitzer. A mortar illumination round, Hank concluded before wondering why the illumination before the beehives. Was the illumination compliments of Victor Charlie? Had things gotten that bad?

With fear in his eyes, Hank watched Higbee in a pale milky darkness drag the lifeless body of the Battalion commander from the bunker's ruins. He watched Higbee stand to his full height and peer down at his find. He watched as a pith helmeted figure came into the milky light in a half crouch above the rim of the bunker. And he screamed at Higbee.

"Look out! Gook!"

Higbee instinctively spun toward Hank and pulled his pistol out. He never saw his killer as bullets from an AK-47 thudded into his back and through the nape of his neck.

Hank lunged for cover. Bullets ripped after him, tearing into the radio he had been operating, slamming into the debris on which he had sat.

He huddled in a ball against a wall of sandbags, his heart pounding a drum roll. Through a small opening in a pile of rubble he could see his pursuer, still on the rim, still half-crouched, his eyes below the helmet staring into the darkness of the overhang, the muzzle of the rifle following his eyes, the butt to his shoulder. He must know, Hank knew, that his quarry was defenseless, otherwise his fire would have been answered. Maybe he thought his quarry dead or wounded, or planning a counterattack. There were a lot of things he must be considering, for he just stayed frozen in his position, allowing Hank to live a few seconds longer.

Finally, the time had come, his time, and Hank's time, for he made a decision. He dropped his rifle to his right hand, crouched lower, and sprang upward and outward, catapulting himself, aiming his jump in front of the mouth of the overhang, Hank's cubbyhole, his ledge. A new star shell popped while the old one still contained life and together they brought a greater clarity and sharpness. Hank saw him start his jump and knew his fate, resigning himself and feeling very sorry for himself.

As the NVA soldier reached the apex of his jump, a violent force swept him away.

Simultaneously, a blast so loud that the splashes of mortar rounds in the northern half of the perimeter and the chattering of automatic weapons fire predominately in the southern half faded into the background and pierced Hank's ear drums with painful shock waves.

More blasts followed, becoming to Hank a delightful sort of masochistic music.

Beehives!

Hank sucked in smoky, gritty air, feeling a tremendous relief as he scrambled in a crawl back to the radio. He picked up the handset, anxious to regain contact with brigade.

"Duty Five-five, this is Demon, over," he shouted a whisper, wanting to be heard above the din by the receiving party but not by anyone nearby.

He waited.

No answer.

"Duty Five-five, this is Demon, over," he repeated.

No answer.

"Duty Five-five, this is Demon, over," he pleaded.

Still no answer. No sound at all. Nothing. No sound! Not even a rushing sound! Hank suddenly realized the radio was dead and in the murky light of his den noticed a set of holes diagonally punched across the face of the radio. The gook had nailed both Higbee and the radio.

The light went out as the last star shell fizzled and died and was not replaced. His hole became black. Outside grew into a dirty gray as his night vision took over. He gazed at the radio. Not seeing it clearly, the finger tips of his left hand brushed over it, feeling the new holes as if it were brail. For a brief moment his mind became vacant of thought, and it was at this time a piston-shaped object cart-wheeled through the air and passed over him, landing at the backside of the collapsed bunker.

The CHICOM concussion grenade exploded. The lattice work of sandbags which provided Hank with overhead and some side cover buckled inward, slamming Hank hard against the radio. His left wrist bent funny and bone snapped. His helmet clunked against the radio. His body was pushed under the table supporting the bank of radios, which collapsed on top of him.

Seconds passed as he lay stunned and half buried under the smoke, dust, and detritus. His head slowly cleared. His ears rang. His wrist had a stabbing pain. The table with the radios lay on his lap and legs. Sandbags covered his chest and jabbed with broken metal stakes in his sides.

His face was free and looked skyward. He shook his body, vibrating the articles of his entrapment to loosen their bonds. He also kicked his legs and moved his right arm in the sweep of an inverted breast stroke. His left wrist was jarred and he wanted to scream. In thirty seconds he was out of bondage, sitting on the rubble, his helmet back on, his wrist on fire.

The last forty-five seconds had so occupied him that his fear had taken a short break, but now it resumed its place with a renewed vigor accompanied by the pain of a broken wrist.

There was no radio contact with Brigade; therefore no one to direct the fire support that was, hopefully, now being massed. He had no weapon. And any minute he expected a squad of NVA, led by the grenade tosser, to jump into this shell of a bunker.

The beehives were only a short-term solution. If enough gooks got inside the perimeter they could knock out the howitzers with a crawling assault under the blanket of the flying fléchettes. Delta Company and the beehives and Bravo's Mortar Platoon couldn't keep them out. Not without outside fire support.

For the fire support to be effective there had to be contact with Brigade, and for contact, there had to be a radio of sufficient power to reach Lai Khe. And there was only one place where a radio like that existed, provided that one place still existed. The Black Hole. The radios there had been working when they had abandoned it.

He began crawling around the bunker, his good arm supporting him one moment and the next tossing aside wreckage that interfered with his movement. He needed a weapon before venturing out and heading for the fallen Black Hole, a pseudo hole. He explored where Higbee had gone down, looking for the .45 as his imagination created images of NVA jumping on top of him, of another grenade tossed in, of a mortar round landing on the small of his back.

He found Higbee sprawled face down. He looked and groped around the lifeless body for the pistol.

Suddenly an illumination round popped, glowing overhead like a giant light bulb. The light helped. He saw the pistol grip in a narrow hole, wedged between a sandbag and a big ball-like object, smaller than a basketball, bigger than a soft ball. His good hand scooped up the object to toss aside so he could pick up the pistol. But it looked funny in the diffused pearly light. And it felt funny. And somehow his curiosity had the best of him, so he wasted important seconds as he rolled the object to the crook of his arm and turned it over to examine it more closely.

He glanced down and recognized what it was, or rather, what it had been. He gasped in terror and while on his knees spun his body and flung it away as far as he could, wishing also that he could fling the image of what he had seen from his mind, the feel of the image on his arm. Even in death, even bodiless, Woodson had haunted him. His eyes had stared coldly at Hank; his mouth had smiled grotesquely.

Hank grabbed the pistol, his mind swirling in turmoil. Woodson's decapitated head, the pain in his wrist, the battle around him, the need to regain commo, all became a cauldron of images boiling within him.

He crawled up a rip-rap-like incline on a section of collapsed roof. Once out of the destroyed bunker, he slithered snake-like along the ground. The loud bark of the howitzers firing beehives was deafening. He could feel the rush of a swarm of steel darts passing only about a meter over his head. Their rate of firing seemed to have slowed. Why, he had no idea. Maybe fatigue of the gun crews, or maybe conserving ammo. Maybe a howitzer had been taken out!

He headed straight for the Black Hole. His right hand held the pistol out as point. His left wrist was limp and tucked protectively by his shoulder. His elbows awkwardly walked along pushed by determined leg thrusts.

He moved below a deadly, colorful storm of red and green tracers searching for one another, yellow and orange flashes of howitzer fire and mortar bursts, soft white illumination rounds and flares. Scattered clumps of dead bodies landscaped his way. His eyes focused mostly on the gun barrel that seemed to break through the night like the prow of a ship cutting through troubled water.

A dreaded old acquaintance, the knowledge of impending death, dropped in on his thoughts. It had made other visits during the night. A very long stay just before the gook jumped into the fléchettes. It had made other visits before this night. As he crawled he felt cheated. To know about your demise and think about it so many times, only to pass through it, live through it, and feel good about it, and then to know about it, think about it again, so soon after the last time, and to do it so often, was not fair. It was almost that he wanted to die just to let it finally happen.

Then again, he really didn't want to die, but wanted to think he did so he wouldn't worry about it.

He was three-quarters of the way there and had not yet seen a living being when his mind asked a silly question: *Was there a round in the chamber?* Surely Higbee would have locked one in. Or would he have?

Hank stopped. He tried to grab the pistol with his left hand to pull back the slide with his right, but the pain was too great. He swore at himself and at the worthlessness of an Army-issued weapon that couldn't be cocked without two working hands. He balled up and put the .45 in a vice-like grip between his legs and pulled the slide back with his right hand; no cartridge flew out. He had been carrying a useless weapon. He let the slide go and it slammed a round into the chamber.

CHAPTER 65

WAN'S EYES FLUTTERED open as her subconscious escaped from a bad dream. There had been a swirling mist around her and her lover. His kisses smothering her before he broke off and let her go and stepped back, their eyes now holding each other as he moved further back into the mist until even their eyes had to let go and he was gone.

Now awake, she knew she still had Dick for a few more nights.

She placed her head on his hairy chest and let it rise and fall with his deep breathing. His exhaustion was obvious, caused by many factors. Working late in the evening with the two jobs he was holding down, his and his friend's job. Meeting her late at night. Making beautiful love, followed by soft talk about each other. Whispering sweet words of caring, and then awaking in the predawn to escort her under the fence. And thinking of what their heartbreak would be like when he left.

She wanted to stay beside him, her head riding his chest for the longest time, until the alarm went off and they dressed and they went outside, and crying, she kissed him good night and climbed down into that horrible pit and under that despicable fence and furtively fled into the soon fading darkness into the village of her parents. She also wanted Dick to get the rest he needed. It wasn't easy fighting a war, and her demands on him didn't help. And it would be selfish of her to have the alarm disturb him and have him put his clothes on and take her to the fence.

She made her mind up. Tonight, she would give Dick one of the few gifts she could offer. The gift of a few hours more sleep.

Carefully, stealthily, she picked up his heavy arm, ducked under it, and crawled to the sound of complaining springs to the foot of the bunk where she slid off. There was no sound as she dressed, her eyes staying on Dick, observing his heavy slumber. Finished, she came around beside him, bent down, and lightly placed her lips on his. And then with rekindled tears, she moved quickly to the door, opened it very slowly so as not to squeak the spring, stepped across the threshold and slowly closed the door.

Lieutenant Finsley's visibility along the fence had decreased markedly. Not from any increase in the darkness, but from the consumption of a huge quantity of Johnny Walker Red. Still his vision could reach where it had to. So he thought. It was just a little blurry now. And his eyes were a little tired and a little heavy. And it would be nice to get some sleep and who really gave a shit about what that pussy-eater and cocksucker were doing. And anyway, he could just as well catch and fry their butts tomorrow night. So why not let those eyelids come down. Why not….

Finsley's eyes popped open. He sat rigid and alert, an animal catching the scent of its prey. Something, someone was beside the fence, bending down, doing something. His eyes tried focusing, to identify the who, and the what, that was happening.

He jumped to his feet, ran out of the club, and fumbled in getting his pistol extricated from its holster as he drew near the who and what.

Wan had removed Hank's footlocker top covering the hole and was ready to scoot in when she heard the pounding of running boots. Startled, she turned; she gasped; she cowered. Her back pressed into the chain links of the fence. Above her a mere five feet away Lieutenant Finsley hovered and swayed unsteadily. A large ugly gun trembled at her. Glazed, crazy eyes cut through the darkness and pinned her to the fence with an authority equal to the gun.

"Halt!" Finsley slurringly commanded. It was a needless order since Wan had frozen. Her image appeared blurry, like some sort of hazy apparition cringing on its haunches. "Git up!"

Wan straightened. Her body shook like a cornered fawn feeling the hunter's sights. Her teeth chattered.

Finsley's mind finally registered that he had captured Kistler's whore. He looked around slowly, so as to keep the ground from listing and making him lose his balance. No Kistler.

Finsley smiled.

She saw him leer. The barrel bobbing before her was frightening. "What… what you do with me?" she asked, her voice as weak as her knees.

Finsley kept leering as he pondered her question. It was a fair question. And she had a right to know. And because of that he would think of the answer.

He knew what it was. The opportunity came around probably once in a lifetime.

His eyes narrowed into ugly slits. His leer transformed into a scowl. The pistol became still.

Wan knew the answer too and cried out just as the gun exploded. The bullet smacked into her chest and knocked her flat against the fence. Her eyes were wide and questioning as she slid slowly to the ground next to the hole.

A fraction of a second after the blended sounds of scream and gunshot, Dick flinched and abruptly sat up and looked at the empty bunk beside him. He scrambled out of bed and ran naked from the hooch, around the bunker to the fence. His churning legs suddenly halted, braked by the unbelievable horror before his eyes. Wan lay motionless on her side on the ground against the fence. Finsley was waving a gun back and forth, his frightened glazed eyes gazing down at her. The eyes glanced over at Dick. The gun followed and pointed.

Dick ignored the weapon; he ignored Finsley. He ran to Wan. The gun following.

He fell to his knees. His powerful arms gently turned and lifted her head into his lap.

Vacant eyes set wide with horror looked past him. "Wan?" Dick uttered. "Wan…Oh my God, what's happened?" he cried out, his question rhetorical. He knew she couldn't answer, would never answer. He swallowed her up in his arms, his cheek to hers, his tears for both of them. He rocked backwards and forwards as he wept, unaware of Finsley and of the pistol aimed between his shoulder blades and of Finsley's tightening grip.

"Jesus Christ, man! What's going on here?" Lieutenant Grosser gasped in amazement as he ran in his underwear onto the scene. There were other excited rumblings of bewilderment as Grosser was joined by others who had been rousted out of their bunks by the gunshot.

A semicircle formed around the scene of the tragedy.

Finsley dropped his arm and let the pistol hang toward the ground. He looked about him at the gathering crowd with the quick, jerky movements of a caged animal. "It looked like a sapper coming through the fence…I ordered the gook to stop but then she started to run. It looked like she had a grenade or something in her hand. I had no idea it was one of the hooch maids shacking up with Kistler." Finsley rambled and stammered at what he perceived as a board of enquiry.

He then pointed the pistol again at Dick's back, only this time his finger was not on the trigger. "It's his fault. He killed her as much as I did. He was paying her to fuck him and made her sneak out of the village," Finsley accused, changing his defense to an offense and putting his trigger finger on alert in case Kistler stopped his incessant rocking of the dead gook bitch and came after him with flailing fists.

Dick did nothing, except to continue holding Wan.

There was a bit of silence as no one knew what to do. A nervous spec-four weaved his way politely through the crowd of mostly lieutenants, saying "Excuse me, sir," and "Sir, I need to get through, this is official business."

At the forefront, he looked at the scene: Finsley standing and pointing his pistol at the back of a kneeling Lieutenant Kistler who was stark naked and was slowly swaying to and fro on his knees. Two black pajama clad legs moving slightly with his movement protruded from his lap.

Sweating profusely, the spec-four swallowed hard before clearing his throat and then speaking. "Lieutenant Kistler, sir," he said to Dick's back. "I...I'm sorry to bother you..."

Grosser roughly grabbed his shoulder. "Whatever you want, this ain't the fucking time."

"But the TOC sent me to get Lieutenant Kistler. Says it's an emergency. Fire Base Stork has been attacked. Gooks're inside the wire. The Battalion's command's dead. Lieutenant Kirby's taken over its commo and he's yelling for help. It's like the only one left in charge of the Battalion's a lieutenant." The spec-four shot the words out in a rapid staccato clip.

"Oh shit," Grosser replied.

All eyes were on Dick, curious as to his next move. He leaned over and gently laid Wan down. His fingers closed her eyes. He sprang up and started running. The onlookers parted to let him by. They stared at his face, wanting to know his emotions. There were none. As he ran he shouted back at the spec-four, his tone as cold and distant as his face. "Let me get my pants."

CHAPTER 66

T HE BLACK HOLE was still there, at least a good part of it, the part that counted, the radios. The top, which had been the bottom until the Hole had keeled over, was blown off, probably by a beehive. Hank scrunched down inside, keeping as low as possible, facing out, the .45 in his lap, an illumination round serving as a lamp overhead. He put the handset to his ear and sighed when he heard the reassuring rushing noise.

"Duty Five-five, this is Demon, over," he transmitted.

"This is Duty Three-zero," came the reply from Dick Kistler. "We've got everything cranking—TAC air, light fire teams, spooky. They're all airborne. A one-five-five Battery is ready. Where do you want it all?"

His voice was medicine to Hank, though the low, distant, throaty, almost strange, tone was a little unsettling. "Put some napalm near the southern perimeter! We've had a lot of activity there! Let me contact Delta on this net for further, over!"

"Roger, we'll get it, out."

"Mike Six, Demon, over."

"This is Mike Five. I monitored. Napalm should be on perimeter, not near it. Eastern sector outside wire also needs napalm. Over."

"Roger, break. Duty Three-zero, Demon. Napalm needs to be on, I repeat, *on* the southern perimeter wire. Also put it on the east side outside of wire. Put spooky and gunships on other half from wire out. Bring one-five-fives into surrounding woods; cover as much area as you can. Also give us some one-five-five illumination. Break. Sound good, Mike-five?"

"Roger. Real good. Just get it fast, over."

"Roger. Duty Three-zero, Demon. Copy stands, over."

"Good copy. We may have some problems making simultaneous napalm runs on south and east sectors. If so, we'll hit south first, then east. After napalm we'll put in 500-pounders. Roger that?"

"Roger. Sounds good! Just do it fast!" Hank echoed Mike-five.

His work done for the moment, until Mike Five, Mike Six, or somebody, wanted adjustments, he let the fear back in. He lay on his back and pressed all of his body along the lowest part of the Black Hole, in the V of the wall and what had been the roof. His right upper torso rested uncomfortably on one radio bank. His left wrist set limply on his lap next to his .45 and felt on fire. His eyes glanced anxiously around from the jagged entrance opening to the myriad of bullet and fragment holes that pockmarked the top half of his plywood cubicle, to the sky with its shining flare dangling from a parachute. A varying pattern of colors—orange and green tracers, spitting yellow flames and flashes, black and white smoke—kaleidoscoped before him, accompanied by a wide assortment and intensity of sounds. Once every ten seconds or so a bullet or chunk of metal would pass through his quarters a few feet above him and he would cringe and wonder when one or the other would pass through him.

CHAPTER 67

THE SNAIL-LIKE TRAFFIC thinned drastically past Melbourne. Now they were speeding with top down along a ribbon of road flanked by thick palmettos, through which there were glimpses of small dunes and the ocean on their left.

The turbulent air jetting around the car forced Pam's eyes into narrow squints and turned her hair into a golden-brown streamer. She regretted not bringing a scarf. She closed her eyes and slunk down. Her head rested on the back of her seat. She tried to ease her impatience of what had become too long of a drive. Dave had said very little, mostly a few profanities at rear bumpers that had prevented him from giving his Mustang full rein. She was not disappointed at this lack of conversation.

A new, swooshing sound broke into the discordant symphony and fiery shadows danced off the walls joining the magnificent pyrotechnic display. The napalm had arrived, landing about 150 meters behind Hank as he faced inward of the fire support base. More swooshes and more dancing shadows.

His wrist hurt. His head felt dizzy. His stomach churned.

A face suddenly appeared in the opening above him. He quickly grabbed the .45 from his lap and came close to firing, until the dirtied and bloodied face took definition. He had almost blown away a trusted friend. The thought made him shake nervously and smile weakly at Franklin as he climbed inside and lay down beside him on the bank of radios.

Hank moved his bad wrist next to the wall to keep Franklin from bumping it. "You hurt bad?" Hank asked, noticing that Franklin's left shoulder was hunched awkwardly. His shirt was torn and drenched with blood. His helmet was missing.

"Not bad. Took some shrapnel, but I'm all right. The Arty boys patched it up. The bleeding's stopped." He twisted his shoulder up toward Hank who now saw the bandage.

"How about your head?"

"OK. Blood's from my shoulder."

They lay side-by-side on their backs on a steep incline amid battered radios that had been jostled loose from their mounts. Their heads were at the low end and they could feel the rush of blood to their heads. They bent their legs in to keep them from sticking out of the opening.

"You got those beehives cranking," Hank stated.

"Sappers had taken out the Arty's CP. When Arty fired the beehives, they took out a howitzer. The Arty boys fought them off and saved the other guns. I caught a chunk of shrapnel helping out."

"I noticed that you got the mortar illum going first. I thought when that first shell popped that we weren't going to have beehives."

"I didn't get it first. That was Charlie's illumination."

"Shit," Hank whistled through his teeth. "They must have been ready to run us over."

"Yeah. We could see 'em hittin' the south perimeter. Those beehives stung 'em bad. Stacked 'em up like pancakes. Your idea of no red star cluster did it. A sergeant was getting ready to fire one, yelling at the Battery to standby, when I started shouting that their orders were not to pop it."

"Then you got Bravo's mortars?"

"Yeah. That was no problem. They weren't firing simply because the Arty and Delta's mortars weren't."

"Those beehives saved my life. A gook was about to pack me away when a beehive blew him away, but not before he got Higbee."

"Yeah, I saw Higbee in the TOC, but you weren't there and so I figured you were over here."

"Why...why'd you come back? Why didn't you stay put somewhere in some bunker?" Hank asked, confused that anyone would crawl around out there, especially when wounded, and for no good reason.

"I thought you might need me."

There was a short silence between them. Outside their thin plywood shell the sounds of a battle still raged. Skyward, just above the edge of the portion of the Black Hole that had been blown away, red raindrops began and developed into a heavy downpour. Spookie was on station.

"You did well. Real well," Hank said as his eyes watched a portion of space where the red rain emanated and dropped just a short distance before vanishing into a jagged horizon of ripped wood.

"Thank you, sir."

"Don't ever call me 'sir' again," Hank rebuked gently. "Don't ever call me anything but Hank."

"Yes…Hank."

"That's better." Leaving the .45 in his lap, Hank picked up the handset. "I better check in with Mike Five to see what's happening."

He pushed the talk button. "Mike Five, Demon. Sitrep."

"This is Mike Five. Napalm pretty much on target. Spookie and light fire teams looking OK. Still need one-five-five illumination. Looks like Charlie's lost the mo'. But there's still some bad shit inside wire. They know they're dead and they're fighting like kamikazes. Over."

Hank was about to Roger when in his ear he heard, "Break, break. Demon, this is Duty Six. We monitored and Duty Three is relaying to Duty Three-zero." Colonel Carter's booming, authoritative voice, dampened slightly by the background vibration noise of his C&C chopper, came through. "I gather that Demon Six and Three are inoperable, over?"

"That's affirm," Hank answered. "Neither are Delta Six and Arty's CP."

"Who's in charge?"

"Delta Mike Six. I'm Tango Foxtrot Geronimo Kilo acting for Demon."

"Roger. I know. I'll take over now and get on Delta's net. You stay on yours and we'll get back when needed, over."

"Roger that," Hank replied, his tone one of thankful appreciation. His part was ending.

"This is Duty Six. One more thing. I see that two mortar tubes are firing. One illumination and one HE. Have it stopped; it may hit us. We're not going with one-five-five illum. Instead we'll drop flares around perimeter from the air, over."

"Wilco," Hank answered unwillingly, thinking of the risk of getting to Bravo's mortars. Not wanting to ask Franklin to make another run. Not wanting to do it himself.

CHAPTER 68

THE MUSTANG SLOWED and turned right onto a bumpy white shell-rock road. Surprised, Pam immediately sat up and glanced over at Dave. "Where we going? The inlet's about six more miles. And we're heading west." She questioned in an uneasy voice.

Dave smiled and kept his eyes on the winding road that wove among the palmettos. "Pam, I know a really great spot for a picnic. This road leads all the way down to the Indian River. There's a lot of Australian pines. We can picnic in the shade on a soft bed of pine needles right on the river's edge," Dave sounded like an enthusiastic travel guide.

Pam flushed red in protest. "You said we were going to Sebastian Inlet. That we were going to be around a lot of people. I want to stick to the original agreement."

"Don't worry, Pam," Dave said reassuringly, "we'll just eat the chicken. You'll really like the spot. Who knows, there may be a slew of picnickers at this place. But it don't matter. We'll go to the inlet. I promise you that, but after we eat that chicken. I'm starving."

Pam didn't reply. She stared straight ahead, hoping this picnic would be short, hoping it would rain, and hoping Dave would get a severe case of indigestion. Were all men deceitful liars? Her empirical data seemed to say so. She knew one thing. If Dave put one hand on her she'd scream her head off.

"Demon, this is Bravo Oscar Six. We monitored and will cease firing." The voice of Bravo's Mortar Platoon leader let Hank breathe easier. Thank God they were monitoring. Franklin must have told them too.

"This is Demon. Good show. Out." Hank terminated and put the handset in his lap beside the .45. He gazed up and saw a row of flares parachuting from the sky like airborne troopers.

The light became brighter from the flares and was in concert with his mood. Responsibility had been lifted from his shoulders and all that remained was for him to stay put in the comfort of Franklin on one side and Dick, in the form of a radio handset on his lap, on the other side, and to hope that his vulnerable quarters did not get in the way of the battle.

"The situation seems to be improving…Hank," Franklin remarked, his tone tinged timorously from his new, privileged first name basis with his former platoon leader.

"Yeah, Tom, it's improving. How's your shoulder?"

"Not bad, Hank. How's your wrist?"

"Not bad."

Dave's description was somewhat right. There were tall Australian pines and a shady bed of needles a few yards from the water's edge. The wind was still from the west and had produced on the half-mile expanse of river a light chop with small waves lapping lazily on the narrow white sand bank.

His supposition about a slew of others was in gross error. There was no slew. Only he and Pam.

Leaving the keys in the car, Dave got out and reached in the back seat for an old faded flowery blanket. Uncertain what to do, Pam remained in the car and watched him carefully spread the blanket on the pine needles, his hand traveling over the cloth to smooth it out. He pulled his shirt off and tossed it on a corner. He came back to the car. Pam wasn't quite sure but because of his rigid movement she thought he had sucked in his stomach to where breathing was restricted. And he was clenching his fists to intentionally flex the muscles in his forearms.

"Come on, Pam. Let's get out and have some food," he encouraged. "You get the chicken, potatoes, and coleslaw, and I'll get the cooler."

There was a moment of hesitation before Pam pulled up on the door lever. She pushed the door open and slowly came out of the car. She said nothing as she slammed the door. She leaned into the back seat for one container of mashed potatoes and a bag containing paper plates and plastic forks. Eyes cold and lips pouting, she purposely avoided Dave's eyes as she walked past him to the blanket.

His eyes followed her, scrutinizing the tightness with which her bathing suit bottom contoured her rear-end. It wasn't a bikini, but it was at least a two piece. He wished she'd take off her blouse as he had done with his shirt.

Pam sat down on one corner of the blanket, her legs to one side, pulled close to her body. On the blanket side she barricaded herself with what she had been carrying. She glanced up as Dave approached. From the looks of the cords of muscle leaping from his arms and neck, she calculated that the cooler weighed over a hundred pounds. She then realized Dave was putting on a private showing of Mr. America. She intentionally yawned in a display of boredom.

They ate at opposite ends, not talking, Pam because she was dreading each minute, Dave because he was gorging himself in great haste with chicken legs, breasts, thighs, and wings, and large portions of mashed potatoes and coleslaw. Now and then he paused from his eating and guzzled huge quantities from a bottle of Michelob. When one bottle became empty, he tossed it over his shoulder and started another.

After much food and drink, he finally became aware of the silence between them. "Nice place, ain't it, Pam?" he stabbed at some conversation over a pile of chicken bones in front of his lap as he sat cross-legged.

"I think we'd better go to the beach now, Dave. Either that or take me home."

"What? What's wrong? This place is great! It's got atmosphere. Shady trees, soft ground, right on the water." He pointed all around, up at the trees, down at the ground, past Pam at the wide Indian River and its light chop coming toward them. "And peaceful. Nobody's around for miles."

Pam's eyes cast a hard glare at Dave. "You knew there wouldn't be anybody around. You lied."

"Heh, Pam. Wait a second. Don't be so uppity. I thought we needed to be alone. To talk things over. Look, we're having fun."

"Maybe you are. I'm not. I want to leave," she protested, using her words as a springboard as she shot to her feet, jumped over the now empty boxes, bottles, and chicken bones, and briskly and coldly took off for the car.

Halfway, a large, powerful hand grabbed her shoulder and spun her around. "Wait a second. Don't be so bitchy," Dave protested, his foul breath of alcohol and recent belch on her. "I'm not so bad."

His arms enveloped her. He pressed her close, despite her pushing away, resisting. "Stop it! Get away from me!" She yelled.

She dug her nails deep into his biceps to let him know she was serious. But so was Dave, and she felt her gut leap up her esophagus as he hooked his leg behind her and threw her to the ground judo style.

The carpet of pine needles cushioned her fall and her body cushioned his. His weight jolted out a short gasp of air from her mouth. He distributed his weight heavily and evenly on her like a wrestler to minimize her squirming. His arms pinned her wrists to the ground above her head. His tongue completely mopped her face as she shook her head back and forth to avoid it.

"No! No! No!" she screamed at the top of her lungs.

Her screams had no effect. He raised his head. His elbows clamped on her head, immobilizing it, and he looked into her eyes. "Pam, Pam, Pam," he cooed, oblivious to her screaming and struggling, "It'll be all right. Just relax." His mouth attached to hers like a wet suction cup. His tongue shot out, ramming her lips, fighting to gain entrance. With jaws locked and lips mashed shut, she repelled the battering.

Dave raised his head again. His expression was puzzled at being so effectively stymied.

Pam tried kicking but her legs were shackled by their entanglement. She felt embedded in concrete. She began screaming again for him to stop.

Until now Pam had been filled with anger, resentment, and helplessness. But when Dave locked both her wrists in one powerful hand above her head, holding them fast to the ground with a circulation-cutting grip, and tore her blouse away with his free left hand which then pushed her top up to her neck and began exploring her snow-white breasts, Pam's emotions changed to panic, fear, and revulsion. Dave was raping her. Her screams became piercing shouts of "Help! Help! Help!" Interspersed with sobs of "Don't. Please don't. Don't."

She screamed and cried, her throat becoming sore and hoarse.

Dave was not completely unaware of her plight. In fact, he was becoming more and more perturbed at her behavior. No fuck had ever been this much trouble. He ran his fingers lightly over a nipple, desiring to make it hard and erect. He wondered how long it would be and what he had to do before he hit the magic button and she became aroused and hungry for his prick, which was protesting to get out of his tight bathing trunks about as much as Pam was protesting.

He decided to double his efforts. His mouth went to a nipple. His free hand pulled his suit down to his thighs. He didn't see Pam's head bobbing frantically, hitting the pine needles then violently shaking from side to side, then back to bobbing, her eyes wide with abject fright, her mind wishing the soft ground was a street of brick her head was pounding.

His trunks down, his prick on her thigh, his hand went after the button, her button, and entered her suit, into her thicket. His fingers massaged, looking for a response, but there was none. His fingers probed. The well was tight, but dry.

Still nothing. He knew her body wasn't ready for it, but once he entered her, she'd become ready. He had to let his prick solve this funny dilemma. Afterwards Pam's face would be filled with a content smile on those now nasty, spitting lips.

He unwrapped his left leg from her right. As if spring loaded her thighs snapped together like a bear trap. With one hand still holding her arms outstretched on the ground, the other worked her suit bottom down to uncover her privates; further movement became restricted by her clamped thighs. He slid his hand under her and massaged her firm ass. His fingers sought further but her tight thighs impeded them. He tried the front but could gain little entry.

Pam was now sobbing deliriously. Tears poured down the sides of her face. Every muscle was taut and rigid. Every ounce of strength was directed at fighting off his fingers that felt like hot coals invading her body.

Dave's stiff member became a battering ram, pounding at the intersection of clamped legs and pubis. It couldn't break through. He knew he must try a new maneuver and untangled his right leg from her left. He would support himself on one knee while the other would be used as a wedge to break between her legs, plowing the way for his throbbing prick.

But immediately after freeing her leg, Pam violently kicked out at him with both legs. Her hips bucked wildly to throw him off.

Before he could counterattack and take advantage of her own vulnerability she had created by opening her legs during this bold offensive, her knee crunched his testicles and he grimaced and his heavy body relaxed a little and allowed her to gain a better defensive position. She shifted herself away from him on her right hip, crossing her legs.

He looked at her dejectedly, his lips twisting in frustration. His balls were feeling the reverberations of a deep aching pain, much like he got from an oncoming linebacker sticking a helmet between his legs for a sure tackle. Pam was on her side, suit rolled down below her nice, white ass, legs crossed so tight that the brown on the tops of her feet were turning white from lack of circulation. Her arms were still shackled above her by his powerful hand. And she was crying uncontrollably.

It was then he became aware of the decline in his erection. For a moment he considered letting her go, accepting defeat. But then it couldn't end this way. What was wrong? What had gone wrong? Why hadn't Pam melted into his arms, instead of igniting into a raging, fiery ball of delirium? The answer hit him like a blind-side tackle. Of course, it was so simple. The obvious always was. She hadn't seen his well-endowed prick. That's what she needed to see for her to know what she was missing.

With a strong forceful pull on her shoulder he turned her on her back. He kicked his suit off by squirming his hips and jumped on top of her. He straddled her chest. His bare ass was on her breasts and her blouse was torn open, her suit top around her neck. He ignored her legs that kicked up and out like a wrestler trying desperately to prevent getting pinned. His shin bones dug into the crook in her elbows, locking her arms to the ground. Her hands grabbed helplessly at the air.

His erection returned to its full proportion mere inches from her eyes. Head bent down, he watched with smug satisfaction as her eyes grew big at the sight of his magnificent tool. He assumed her eyes were filling from wonderment, not aware in the slightest of the stark terror that cried out for him to stop.

His hand reached back, found her fur triangle, then his middle finger started patrolling, and began probing. At his first touch her legs had recoiled and crossed to prevent easy entry. Staring down at his penis hovering over Pam's slobbering, whining, grimacing, contorted face, his balls resting on her neck like a new-fangled erotic necklace, the situation became immensely exciting. He started pumping his mighty stick that pointed into the trees. Faster and faster he pumped, oblivious of Pam, of the trees, of the water, of the chicken bones on the blanket. His mind concentrated completely on the object of pleasure, intense pleasure that began to surge and then erupt.

White lava shot forth, splattering Pam's face, the debasement scorching her skin, burning through to her mind, to her soul. She shook her head crazily and screamed the screams of a woman gone berserk.

Relieved of his load, Dave relaxed and rolled off her, content with his performance, ready to let his power regenerate, ready for Pam to concede he held the big key after all. His mind didn't register on the consequences of her action when she bolted to her feet, pulling up her suit bottom as she ran, her top wrapped awkwardly around her neck. It wasn't until she was in the car starting the engine that he became alarmed. And in the next few seconds he was sprinting naked after his Mustang, until it disappeared down the road and was swallowed by thick palmettos.

Pam didn't slow down when she saw the hardtop of A1A. She took the turn on two wheels, burning black rubber onto the pavement. She wished that a semi would hit her head on and end her misery. But there was no traffic and she accelerated to ninety-five before realizing she might kill someone innocent, rather than just herself. She slowed to sixty.

It was then she became aware of the part of Dave still with her and she reached back between the bucket seats and grabbed a towel from her beach bag. She wiped her face hard, rubbing her skin red as though the towel were sand paper. A small part of him was in her hair and she tore at the contaminated strands until they were gone, leaving behind a dime-sized bald spot on her right temple.

She tried to think, but could only sob and cry a flash flood of tears. When she hit the four lane after Melbourne her mind began functioning. She briefly thought of suicide before realizing she was too much of a coward. And then she realized she was rationalizing. So she rationalized some more. Go to the police? What would she say? "Officer, a professional football player tried to rape me, but instead masturbated on my face." The newspapers would really have something hot to write about. And of course, Dave would say that she had actually seduced him and was now feeling guilty about it and now trying to frame him.

She thought about driving home, but that would mean Dave's car would be there and he'd come there for it and she knew she could never see him again. If she just left the car somewhere, he might say she stole it and then there'd be a scene and then she'd also have to see him again and do some explaining to the police. Her only recourse was to leave his car at his apartment and then get a taxi.

Her decision made, she sighed, her crying ebbed and she began hiccupping. It was then she discovered her top was tangled around her neck and she was driving topless.

CHAPTER 69

LOOKING OUTWARD FROM the demolished Black Hole, Hank observed the Fourth of July display going on around him. There were bright slow falling flares, rain showers of red tracers, gunship rocket smoke trails, and intermittent flashes of light from exploding artillery shells. And then there were the loud accompanying sounds. He noticed with a great sense of relief the absence of green tracers and lack of mortar rounds slamming inside the perimeter.

He was on his back on the left side. His right shoulder rested uncomfortably on a part of one of the bulky radios. His head was in his helmet and his left wrist was protectively positioned on his upper left thigh next to the plywood wall.

He turned his head in his helmet and looked over at Franklin, who was in a similar position on the other side. Franklin had his head cocked forward at an angle to better see past his folded legs and out the commo shack's torn opening.

They said nothing. Hank saw Franklin's profile in the milky light of falling flares. This scrawny kid had served him bravely and loyally as his M-60 gunner, and then as his weapons squad leader. And now as a friend.

Maybe he wouldn't go home right away as planned. Maybe he would hang with Dick awhile and then in a week or so make a visit to Franklin's home and meet his mom he was always talking about. Maybe he wouldn't try to see Pam after all.

He kept looking at Franklin's profile. He could see his left eye blinking every few seconds as it gazed skyward at the nighttime pyrotechnics.

Suddenly his eye went wide. His mouth dropped half open as if he were getting ready to scream; his head started to lean forward as if he were trying to sit up. But before he could, a long needle shaped bayonet shot in like a striking snake, piercing his stomach just below his breast bone, sliding all the way through him, until the point hit forcefully into wood.

Hank went immediately into sheer panic. He sat up abruptly. His right hand fumbled in his lap for the .45 which tangled in the cord of the handset. There was a moment of hesitation as the long blade moved around inside Franklin in an effort to be extracted. Then the blade came out as rapidly as it entered. Hank's eyes followed it and saw above him a face under a pith helmet glaring at him.

The bayonet started forward again just when Hank fired. The bullet smashed through the face, tumbling his attacker backward.

Not waiting to see if the NVA would be replaced by another, Hank focused his attention on Franklin, who was holding his wound with both hands, letting the blood seep out through his fingers. He looked at Hank with frightened eyes and mumbled words through a fit of gasping as he choked on the blood that bubbled from his mouth. "My mom…She…so sad," he managed to say with extreme effort before he died.

Dark purple thunderheads were congregating in the west when Pam pulled into the parking lot that surrounded Dave's two-story, quadrangle-like apartment complex. She had no trouble finding it. Dave had driven her by a few times while killing time before a movie. He had hinted at stopping in after the show. She had ignored his hint. Thank God for that.

She switched the ignition off and thought for a moment about what to do with the keys. She left them in the ignition, opened the door, and got out. Distant rumbling of thunder made her look at the car and consider putting the top up. She didn't and went around to the passenger side to get her bag from the back seat. She left behind the towel she had used to wipe her face.

She saw no phone booth, nor was she looking for one. Her objective was to get as far from his apartment as fast as possible. She began walking on bare feet the mile or so to Canaveral Pier.

The jar of her step loosened the cobwebs of trauma in her mind. No longer did she hiccup or dry heave. The memory of an hour ago was slowly healing over, but the scar, she knew, would be severe.

The sky had darkened over when she walked into a small hamburger stand to get change for the pay phone outside. She called a cab company. They said it would be twenty minutes. She waited on the pier, pacing up and down the first quarter of its length, watching the number of surfers slowly diminish as the lightning flickered in the distance and the sound of thunder became louder. With the first large drops of rain that spotted the sun-bleached planks of the pier, she took refuge in the hamburger shack where she stared out a large front window. The rain came quickly in diagonal sheets.

Inexplicably she wished for a cigarette. She had never smoked before, her friends didn't smoke, and Hank didn't smoke, either.

Hank. She said his name to herself and swallowed hard. He had turned against her and in so doing she had turned to Dave. She had known about Dave, yet he still had lulled her into his demented den. It was her own damn fault, though not entirely; Hank would have to share it.

He had been the one to change, to fool her. He was as bad as Dave. Ten thousand miles away and he had placed a lonely void in her heart. Now that was some feat. She would have to retaliate. She would have to make herself hate him. She would have to convince herself that she never wanted to see him again.

CHAPTER 70

COLONEL CARTER SURVEYED the charred remains of the fire support base. He scrutinized the intense activity now taking place. Two fresh rifle companies with a contingent of doctors and nurses and a unit of graves registration had descended like locusts at first light on Stork and had since been in constant motion for nearly five hours.

"Bad news, Frank," he said to Major Duncan and shook his head sadly, his face grim under his helmet. They wore clean, tailored fatigues and equipment harnesses with holstered .45s hanging from their web belts. Flying in a chopper through the wee hours of the morning had not distracted from their well-groomed military bearing. Beside them, sandbags were strewn about like tossed dominoes around a blown-up 105 howitzer eerily resembling a dead, long-nosed dinosaur.

His left arm in a sling, Hank appeared in his dirty blood-stained jungle fatigues like a crippled homeless person as he stood helmetless behind the crisply dressed field grade officers. He was exhausted and at times felt dizzy, but had refused to be dusted off with the many wounded. Not because of a sense of military duty, but of not wanting to be around their agonizing cries and bloodied conditions.

"How many do you reckon?" Colonel Carter asked.

Major Duncan scratched around the back of his sunburned neck. "Maybe a reinforced Battalion, maybe more," he said. "Too goddamn many, that's for sure."

Carter turned around and faced Hank. "You're too short for this kind of thing," he said, attempting a benign smile. "What do you have left, two more nights?"

Hank wanted to return his smile, but the muscles around his mouth refused. There was no spirit to force them. "Yes, sir," he answered, "One in Lai Khe. One in Long Binh."

"I'm sure they won't be like last night," Carter said, still trying a smile, hoping it would be contagious to this despondent lieutenant with sunken far away eyes, and tight, drawn-in lips. "Major Duncan and I are staying out here awhile. General Talbot is flying in and word has it that General Abrams may drop by. Tell my pilot to get you to Lai Khe when he returns from picking up the S-2 and S-4."

"Yes, sir. Thank you, sir."

"Get that wrist taken care of at the Brigade's infirmary."

"Yes, sir."

Hank turned and started to leave when he was stopped by the colonel. "One more thing, Lieutenant Kirby."

Hank turned around. "Yes, sir?"

"Good luck back in the World. And don't let your tour over here get you down. You did your duty as a soldier. Don't let it leave scars where there're no wounds," Colonel Carter said, then paused thoughtfully and added, "If you weren't headed home, I'd want to keep you on my staff."

"Second that, "Duncan echoed.

"Thank you, sir," Hank said, glancing from the colonel to the major. The colonel's remark was a surprise. But he knew better. He'd witnessed real soldiers and he knew he wasn't one. And now it was too late. And the deep scars inside would never fade.

He sat on a stack of discarded 105 ammo boxes in the northern quadrant of the fire base as he waited for the colonel's chopper. His nostrils filled with a lingering stench of burnt cordite and human flesh. His eyes fixed on a few square feet of ground before him while his mind focused on the scene around him.

Out a few hundred meters to the tree line was a smoldering, pockmarked lunarscape. Outside what had been the perimeter wire, much of which was now twisted or missing, were numerous charred dead bodies from which still emanated curling wisps of gray smoke. He had heard numbers varying anywhere from 100 to 150.

Inside and only fifteen meters from his left were two rows of filled body bags, a baker's dozen each row. Their lingering presence produced a hurting emptiness inside him.

On his right side a stream of passing gawkers collected like a tidal pool to stare at a row of twenty dead mangled NVA not yet deserving of body bags. They had been killed inside the fire base, one by him.

As he searched for solace in his small patch of dirt, a pair of scuffed, dirty boots interrupted his view. He gazed up slowly to see a short man of his own age with recently treated wounds. His head was wrapped by a bloodied bandage. The right side of his face was puffy and swollen and caked with dried blood and dirt. His right hand and forearm were heavily bandaged and in a sling that mirrored Hank's.

"Understand you're that son of a bitch, Demon," he said looking down at Hank.

Hank was taken back. He couldn't believe someone was now messing with him. He came to his feet too quickly as he felt a sharp twinge of pain in his left wrist.

His insulter was a stockier version of Higbee. Hank said nothing as he gazed down into the wounded man's hazel eyes. He saw something. He understood.

"Yeah, that's me," he answered slowly, maintaining eye contact. "And you must be that asshole, Mike Six."

There was a glimmer of a smile. "You got that."

There was an awkward moment as they stared at each other. Then Mike Six said, "You did good, man."

Hank shook his head in disagreement, and then asked, "How was it with you?"

"Fucking bad, man. Real bad. It's like the fuckers knew where our command bunkers were. Thank God they only knocked out one howitzer." He continued to hold Hank's eyes. "Had some hand-to-hand, fixed bayonet shit." He motioned with his bandaged head over at the two long rows of body bags. "I got a lot of heroes over there."

Hank followed his gaze. "I got one, too." Hank's eyes started tearing-up.

He should have said two. Glombowski was among them.

A funny thing happened next. Mike Six moved in and hugged Hank with his left arm, being careful not to nudge Hank's injured wrist. He buried the unhurt side of his face in Hank's shoulder and started crying.

Hank wanted to return the hug but was fearful of increasing the pain in his wrist and maybe inflicting pain on Mike Six's wounds. Here was a hero not in a body bag. Hank had heard the colonel tell Major Duncan he was nominating Mike Six for the MOH. Here was a real soldier. He and the other brave men of Delta Company had saved the day. And Franklin…And Arty.

"You've missed the Medevacs. Come back with me on the colonel's chopper," Hank offered softly.

"Can't, man. Can't," Mike Six sobbed into Hank's shoulder.

Hank nodded. He understood.

CHAPTER 71

O UT OF THE west, the late, daylight savings time sun was still bright. The air was hot and muggy stoked by the evaporation of large puddles. In the east, the dark storm clouds had moved out into the ocean.

Dave noticed nothing of the weather, his eyes interested in only the sight of his car in the parking lot as he climbed out of a sedan barefooted and in a bathing suit. He had left everything, blanket, cooler, beer, everything behind.

He stuck his head into the window of the ' 62 Pontiac and thanked the bony framed, leather-faced driver for the ride and promised someday to buy him a few beers and give him a couple of tickets to a Dolphin game. His name was Roger Clark, an Air Force sergeant stationed at Patrick Air Force Base. On his way back to the base after fishing at Sebastian Inlet, he had spotted Dave along the side of a lonely stretch of A1A, thumbing frantically in only a bathing suit, while the first drops of rain splotched his windshield.

After Dave had jumped in the car, the storm cut loose, and Dave thanked his benefactor for picking him up, explaining that a girl he was dating and who was mentally unbalanced had absconded with his car. Roger Clark offered both sympathy and condolences; he too had known his share of mentally unbalanced women. And then he informed Dave he was only going as far as the air base, to which Dave voiced his regret since he needed to get to his apartment in Cocoa Beach. But to Dave's good fortune, Roger Clark happened to be a football fan and Dave proceeded to weave a few football anecdotes about the Dolphins and of course puffing up his own important role in the team's future, despite Roger admitting he had never heard of Dave. Dave knew the guy obviously wasn't *really* a true fan.

A rapport established, Roger decided to go the fifteen miles, thirty round trip, out of his way and deliver Dave to his doorstep. During the ride, when Dave had finished telling Roger his offensive stats his senior year at UF, Roger immediately started in on himself, explaining that he had recently returned from Vietnam. Dave yawned in anticipation of some boring war stories. But they weren't boring, and they weren't war.

Roger spoke fondly and somewhat excitedly of an NCO club at a base called Ton Son Nhut. It was a club with a long foyer lined with beautiful Vietnamese girls. Walking through to a table in the dimly lit joint was like walking through a gauntlet of reaching, searching, groping hands. Reaching, searching, and groping one's crotch and ass. Making it to a table without one of the girls tagging along was near impossible. And the girl who wound up at your table would unzip your fly and ask you to buy her a drink. She would start stroking and just when you were at your peak, she'd stop and make you agree to buy her another round.

Roger's revelation had caused a big swelling inside Dave's swimsuit. But when he saw his car with its top down his attention was diverted and he was only semi-hard when he waved goodbye as Roger Clark pulled away. When he walked over to his car, sloshing his bare feet through a few puddles, he went completely soft at the sight of the Mustang's interior. It had been redone in a new decor-saturated drench. There were water puddles on the seats and the pile carpeting had become a swamp.

He felt just a little better when he saw the keys.

After putting the top up he wearily climbed the outside stairs to his apartment. Once inside, a hot shower absorbed a little of his depressed mood.

He lay naked on the bed, thinking of the NCO club at Ton Son Nhut, and today's explosion on Pam. He soon regained his hardness and shifted his thinking from the past to the near future, to tonight. He'd go see Thelma and play hide the salami.

The day was going to have a decent ending after all.

The stars were out and there was a breeze. With the top down, cruising west at seventy mph into cattle country on a two-laner, Dave wished for a light jacket over his short sleeves; an unusual request for the end of June. The lingering moisture from the afternoon's downpour had something to do with the coolness, as well as popping along at seventy per.

He forgot about wanting a little warmth by concentrating again on what the night at Thelma's trailer would offer. And it had all started when bumping into Thelma at that rodeo in Indiantown. She was a wild, wonderful whore, a terrific lay. But whores like that were only good for fucking, not marrying.

Now Pam, that's different. He could see himself marrying her. He didn't hold no grudges. Already he was considering forgiving her. She'd probably start thinking and dreaming about his big hog spitting in her face and get all wet and horny. Yeah, there was still a possibility with Pam. He'd give her a few weeks and then give her a call.

He turned right, off the hard top, onto the narrow washboard dirt road that a mile away led past a clump of tall southern pines under which sat Thelma's trailer

As he pulled into the potholed, bump-ridden driveway, the headlights washed the trailer, showing the same old peeling green paint and invasion of rust spots. Only something was different. He pondered what it was as he stopped ten feet from the concrete blocks that were the front door steps and switched off the ignition, then the lights. Then he knew what it was. Its absence was as glaring as its presence. The outside light next to the door was off. Thelma always left it on, always. He hadn't told her he was coming, but he never did. Open invitation, always. If there was any car besides her beat-up two-door Dodge out front, he would back off, figuring her husband was home.

Her car was there, up beside the trailer. The skeleton of a jalopy mounted on concrete blocks was also there as usual. Nothing else. A dull light shone through closed blinds. Maybe the outside light had burned out. Maybe Thelma, for once, had forgotten to turn it on. Then again, maybe it was some sort of signal or warning. Dave laughed at his paranoia.

He slammed the car door. He climbed the concrete blocks and rapped his knuckles on the door. It opened four inches and two long barrels of a shotgun poked out and stared coldly into Dave's wide eyes. He blanched and stood frozen, his mind momentarily blank and uncomprehending. The barrels moved an inch closer, nearly touching his nose.

Instinctively, he stepped back down, retracing his steps on knees of Jello. The barrels followed him, growing longer from behind the door, until the dark figure of a small man emerged at the opposite end and began stepping down, backing Dave away from the trailer.

The outside light came on, the naked bulb casting an eerie brightness, the kind at sleazy county fairs. The dark figure became a wiry man with a gaunt face of hollow, whiskered cheeks and sunken, bloodshot eyes. He wore white T-shirt and jeans. He was in all probability Thelma's husband.

Through glazed eyes, his Jello knees quivering, Dave saw him as a blur. When the man's feet were firmly on the ground, another figure came through the doorway. He was a tall, barrel-chested man wearing jeans and a faded green Army jungle fatigue shirt. Missing from his slanted grin were two front teeth. His butch crew cut contrasted sharply with his companion's greasy long hair. In his hand, a .357 magnum waved at the center of Dave's chest, as if gyroscopically balanced to factor in his movement. The magnum moved beside the shotgun, whose barrels maintained their stare into Dave's eyes.

If it were a movie, Dave might have found the scene ironically comical, a Mutt and Jeff side-by-side with Jeff and Mutt weapons, the little man with big gun and vice versa. Only Dave wasn't thinking about a movie. Nor did he think of the past or the future, nor even the present. His mind searched for loopholes in this moment, suggesting he was in the midst of a bad dream, or a cruel joke. That's it, a cruel joke; they wanted to scare him. They were doing a goddamn good job at it.

Three more rednecks of intermediate proportions came out of the trailer and gathered around Mutt and Jeff. Dave hardly noticed as his mind continued the search for some sort of reality.

From after his knock on the door, everything had unraveled in silence until another figure emerged. The light bulb spilled on Thelma Jackson's face. Though it didn't appear as her face, but a mask of disfigurement, of a broken nose, swelled and bent to her left cheek, of welts on the forehead, as if raised by a seismic tremor on the skull, of black eyes, as if charcoaled to ward off the glare of a day game. It was Thelma's face that brought sound to the scene, brought forth in the form of a terror-stricken shriek through Dave's fully opened mouth.

He hadn't wanted to scream. He had wanted to laugh and say that Thelma wasn't any uglier than before, and offer to buy a round of beer for everybody, Thelma included. He also hadn't wanted to wet his new white, cotton trousers, but he couldn't help that either.

The greasy-haired shrimp holding the shotgun flashed a leering smile of yellow teeth. "Hey Lester, look at that, will you?" he said, his elbow nudging the arm holding the pistol. "This big boy squeals like an old sow pig. Mebbe he ain't got no balls. Mebbe he ain't been fuckin' Thelma."

The big, burly, toothless Lester guffawed and wagged his pistol across Dave's chest, the front sight plowing into his skin. "Don't know about that, Herschel. If he do got balls, mebbe he won't after tonight," Lester said and guffawed again.

The Jello in Dave's knees drained out, losing their remaining support, and he fell to his knees crying, his chin on his chest. "Please...please let me go. I haven't done nothin'."

Herschel's left hand let go of the shotgun's barrel, its weight taken up by the butt wedged into his armpit. He reached behind him and grabbed Thelma by the hair and yanked her through the arc of bodies standing poised before Dave. "Come here, baby. Let this boy see what you look like." He pushed her head toward Dave where it joined the ends of the shotgun.

Dave looked up into two long streams of tears and protruding lower teeth biting an upper lip. "You think that's bad, boy. You should've seen her last week when I gave her that face after I waited outside behind a tree and saw you leave." He bobbed the gun's barrel up and down in front of Dave's nose, then pulled Thelma's head back, and pushed her to the ground where she began a sobbing duet with Dave. "If I'd had my gun, you'd be dead by now."

Herschel glanced around at his buddies. They had all volunteered to help him with this unpleasantness. He looked down the inclined barrel. He poked its end under Dave's chin and lifted his head with it, so that Dave's ashen face was looking up at him. "Thelma told me how you followed her home one night from the Seven Eleven and raped her, and how you continued raping her every Saturday night and how you threatened to kill her if'n she told somebody."

"No, no, no," Dave shook his head violently, as if trying to clear away this bad dream that he knew he must be having but from which he couldn't awake. "That's not true. She invited me. She had to have me. Believe me. She said she'd kill herself if I stopped coming. She said..."

The double barrels struck out like glued cue sticks on a nine-ball break, crunching into Dave's nose which flattened on his face and erupted blood from his nostrils. "Aheeeeeee! Ahhh! Ahhhhh!" he wailed.

"Calling my wife a whore, huh boy? Is that what you're sayin'? Sayin' she some kind of whore nympho?"

"No, no, no. I didn't mean that!" Dave screamed through his palms that were over his face like a mask. The pain was excruciating. His nose had been broken a few times before, but never like this. It was as if a firecracker had exploded inside his nostrils. "Please don't do this to me. I'm begging you, please." His eyes became large, pleading, and at the same time conspiratorial, "Look, I'm a pro football player for the Miami Dolphins. Let me go and I'll get season tickets for all of you. I promise."

Herschel's head reared back with a roaring laugh. Lester guffawed. The others chuckled. Thelma wept and Dave slunk down, his buttocks resting on the back of his lower legs and ankles.

"You play for a shit team, boy. And it's a shit team cause they got sissies like you."

"I'll…I'll give you my car," Dave's eyes shifted to the right, past Thelma who was lying face down, her head in her arms, crying at the ground. "And every cent I've got. I promise. It's the truth." And it was. Dave meant every word. There was nothing he wouldn't do to get safely out of this nightmare. Somehow, he still could not completely accept the reality of the situation, even while his hands were filling with blood and his nose, or whatever it was now, was on fire.

Herschel's head reared back again with another laugh, then straightened up and Dave saw that his eyes had not joined in the laughter. "You tryin' to buy all that ass you got from my old lady? You think I'm some kind of peemp, Boy? You think I'd sell my old lady's tail?"

"Please don't hurt me."

"Can't you say nuthin' sides puhleassssse? Well it don't matter if you can't. Lester here," Herschel's head bent sideways toward the large, butch cut, jungle fatigue shirted, .357 magnum waving, man beside him, "he had a year in Nam. He been tellin' us what they do to them slopes when they catch 'em. And seein' as how you no better than a fuckin' slope, we gonna give you a treatment, boy."

Lester grinned, the toothless gap appearing ominous and vacuous. Dave howled, "Please don't. Please don't."

Herschel shook his head. "I'm fuckin' tired of that puhleassse shit. Now git over there to that tree." He motioned his gun to a tall pine tree.

Dave, head down, palms to his nose, haunches on his legs, didn't move.

"I said git!"

Still Dave didn't move. Not even the threatening stares of the shotgun and pistol could prod him. It wasn't that he was intentionally refusing. He really wanted to do as commanded; only his body wasn't following instructions. His body was on hold; his subconscious had paralyzed it.

Herschel was perceptive enough to recognize Dave's problem. So rather than kicking him in the side of the head to get him moving, he instructed his buddies to drag him over to the tree, leaving Thelma lying and sobbing on the ground by herself.

Under the tree, deep shadows moved about by a cool, moderate breeze.

Dave sat at the base, his back against the trunk. Lester had also diagnosed Dave's paralysis, but also concocted a cure for this mind over matter affliction. Crouching down, he brought his face next to Dave's. He put the end of the pistol under Dave's chin and pressed up. "If yuh big footballer here can't stand up in ten seconds, I'm gonna blow yuh head off. One…two…three…."

Dave got his feet under him and shakenly stood up, the tip of the pistol staying on his chin. His arms were suddenly grabbed and forced behind the tree where his wrists were tied with clothesline rope. Then his legs were tied to the tree. His tears half blinded him. All he saw were dark blurs of moving bodies and heard a lot of incoherent talking.

Lester read the symptoms of shock. To hide in a coma of numbness wasn't sporting so he slapped Dave's cheeks back and forth and motioned the group away from the tree to give him time to revive and be able to experience fully the next round of fear and pain.

They gathered in a semi-circle, about equidistant between the tree where Dave was tied and the spot where Thelma lay.

"What we gonna do with that boy?" Herschel and Lester's young cousin, Johnny, asked uncertainly, his voice quivering. "We never decided before he got here."

They had been waiting for Dave every night for the last week, having a drinking party over it. Herschel had even used his vacation from his night job. But they had not made a decision on the end game.

"Treat' em like a fuckin' slope. Cut his balls off. Put 'em in his mouth. Make 'em chew 'em up and swallow 'em…" Lester paused as an oyster built up in his throat. He gagged slightly, turned his head away and hocked the obstruction from his esophagus, getting good distance, the lack of front teeth offering an open chute for frictionless discharge. The others waited patiently, in awe, as always, of the distance he got on them.

"Then kill 'em. Dress 'em in a ton of iron and concrete and throw 'em in a deep canal."

The oldest, Rupert, the group's uncle, his long face sagging like an old hound, spoke quietly, with a sage aura. "We kill that boy, it could be big trouble, he a football player. Lot of people be lookin' for him. Murder takes a lot of thinkin' and schemin'. We could all get fried, and what fo'? That boy scared shitless. He done larn his lesson."

"But we let 'em go, he's goin' to the sheriff. He'll get us ten to twenty," Dan, Johnny's older brother, pitched in his two cents.

"Not so," Rupert shot back, "not that boy. He's scared shitless. He'll never want to be like this again. We just tell 'em that we got a big family. He rats and he's dead. He don't have guts enough to go to no sheriff."

The talking stopped. They had spoken their piece. Their eyes landed on Herschel. It was his show, his honor; he'd say what they had to do.

Herschel looked at each man, brother, cousins, and uncle. "I know what we gotta do," he said, turned and walked over to Thelma. He knelt down beside her and forcibly grabbed her hair. "Git up, woman. Yuh heah me. Git up." He stood up, pulling her with him, still gripping her hair. His shotgun in the other hand, he led her over to the tree as if she were a stubborn mule.

Having exchanged his .357 magnum for a big blade hunting knife, Lester taunted Dave, who was reviving, the fear coming back in its entirety. "You fuckin' slope. I'm gonna cut yer balls off." The blade swung in his hand like a pendulum, Dave's eyes following like the tick-tock of a clock.

Thelma was shoved into Dave and slid down to her knees. "Take his pants down, woman."

Weakly, her hands climbed Dave's left leg. "No! No! No! Please don't! Please don't! I'll do anything you say. I'll give you anything!" His slacks came down first, then his jockey shorts, stopping at his knees.

"Well, look at that. This big jock's gotta shriveled, old man's dick," Herschel laughed diabolically. Lester guffawed and the uncle and cousins chuckled. Thelma sobbed and Dave wept and pleaded. "Put it in your mouth, Thel. Go ahead. It ain't no stranger."

Thelma stared at Dave's feet and shook her head. Irritated by her defiance, Herschel handed his shotgun to Lester and with both hands grabbed her around the neck, roughly pulling her head to Dave. She took him in her mouth and began sucking.

Herschel became enraged. "I didn't tell you to blow him, you shit slut," he yelled and yanked her head away by her hair. "I said to just put it in your mouth." He kicked her in the buttocks and jerked her by the hair back to Dave. She put him in her mouth, her eyes glancing nervously up at Herschel.

"Now bite it."

Her eyes went wide.

Dave cried louder.

Herschel screamed. "Bite it, I said!"

Getting only defiance, Herschel kicked his left knee up sharply against her chin. Thelma's teeth crunched; Dave wailed, a shrieking cry of pain and shock merging with the lucidity of reality.

Her fright and revulsion overcame the restraining hand of her husband. Thelma broke her head away and spit gobs of blood and then vomited. Dave thrashed his head about like a boated fish as five pair of eyes focused on his groin.

"Why fuck me," said Herschel, "it's still on."

"Bleeding like a sum bitch," commented Dan.

"I'd say it's danglin'," remarked Johnny.

"Not very purty, that's for sure. He ain't gonna git no use out of that for awhile," stated Rupert.

"Let me finish it, Herschel," requested Lester, brandishing his knife.

Herschel mulled it over, amidst Dave's shrieking and Thelma's dry heaving. After a moment he shook his head. "Nope. I guess we made our point." He faced off with Dave, slapped his face four times, then grabbed his hair at the temples to immobilize it. "We gonna turn yuh loose, boy. But don't you go squealin' to the sheriff that we done this to yuh for fuckin' my wife, yuh heah. 'Cause then yuh gonna be dead. Dead for shore. 'Sides we ain't nevah seen yuh before, boy. We all playin' poker tonight over at Rupert's. Y'unnerstand?" Herschel slapped him hard again. "Unnerstand?"

Somewhere Dave found the reserve to nod his head.

"Untie him, Johnny."

The rope went slack and Dave's wrists and legs were freed. Awkwardly, dizzy from shock, loss of blood, and the fear of permanent disfigurement, Dave struggled with his pants, fighting for the speed of his movements to equal his desire to flee. He got his pants three quarters up, enough to run, but just before he could, Lester dropped the knife and picked up the shotgun in both hands by the barrel. As Dave made his first, shaky step, the stock of the shotgun came down heavily and landed squarely on Dave's left instep, dropping him like a sure tackle.

They made no effort to stop him as he crawled squealing and crying to his car.

Thirty seconds later, Dave was speeding toward the main drag. He had to breathe through his mouth as his nose was clogged with blood. He drove with his right hand. His left held his crotch to stanch the bleeding. His mind flooded with thoughts of bleeding to death, of passing out and killing himself in a car wreck, of never playing football again, of never fucking again. To keep his presence of mind, he attacked these thoughts by concentrating on other images. One being the image of his foot, healed and powerful, slamming into that cunt's jaw with the force that went with a fifty-yard punt. Her old man was right, she was a fuckin' slut for getting him into this crazy nightmare.

Then there was that other image that flickered in and out of his mind. It was inexplicable. It was at the last, when that big monkey from Nam smashed his foot. The outside light had illuminated his shoulder, framing some kind of military patch. A simple insignia. A big number one. A red one. A big red one…

CHAPTER 72

THAT NIGHT PAM had shut herself in her room. But before she did she had tried to watch TV. This activity had had a very short life as it allowed uninvited thoughts to eat voraciously away at her concentration, baring her soul to a seemingly multitude of horrors, hatreds, and recriminations. And then she tried drowning them all with the hot, powerful jet of the shower. She had scrubbed and shampooed her hair until her scalp was bleeding from the scratches from her fingernails. Even then she could still feel Dave embedded in her follicles.

Once in her room, the thoughts had remained. Reading was tried, but to no avail. And even if it hadn't been from the thoughts, the tears that the floodgates in her mind had opened up would have continued to prevent her from seeing the pages.

Morning had come as no surprise. She had been awake waiting for it all night.

She had heard her father leave, then her mother. And she had wondered why she should get up. But then she wanted to. To do something. To try and occupy herself and fight back to wanting to live again.

And so it was that at 9:45 a.m. Pam decided to sew. Maybe the symbolism of mending her life was the reason. She would first sew new buttons on her blouse of yesterday. It would mark a new beginning.

And it was this desire to sew that at 10:03 a.m. brought Pam into her parents' bedroom in search of buttons and a spool of thread from her mother's sewing table.

It would have been easier if she had decided on sewing a half hour ago, when her mom was still home; then she could have asked where the buttons were since the small drawer of the sewing table was empty. Disappointed, Pam shoved the drawer back in with the resolve of foregoing the sewing. It was just as well, the blouse probably belonged in the garbage along with the memories of yesterday.

She started to walk away, then stopped near the center of the room between her father's bed and the bureau, her mind thinking: Sometimes Mom leaves sewing stuff around in the drawers.

She moved to the bureau, its mirror capturing the image of a young woman in a pink robe with a face of a certain frail beauty shaped by many consecutive hours of sad introspection.

There was nothing in the two top drawers. Nor in the big drawer below them. Or in the next drawer. Then there was the bottom drawer, her father's where he kept his unmentionables and where he had told her little girls shouldn't go snooping around.

Pam knew there was no sewing material in that drawer, so she didn't open it and she straightened up and glanced in the mirror at herself. She thought about her father's foolish fetish of not wanting her to look at his folded underwear. What difference did it make? The drawer had been like one's thoughts, secret and confined. Well who knows, maybe it contained some thread and buttons besides folded unmentionables.

She bent over and pulled out the bottom drawer, the first time in over a decade she had even touched that drawer. Her mind still vividly contained the memory of her father admonishing her at the age of twelve for intruding into the sanctity of this drawer, his drawer.

It was as before, over ten years ago, two piles of white undershirts, two piles of white boxer shorts, all neatly folded.

The drawer was being slid forward when her eye caught sight of something off-white, tucked down, something foreign at the far-right end between boxer shorts and unvarnished wood of the inside of the drawer. She reversed the movement of her arms and pulled the drawer out. She saw that it was the back of a soiled envelope.

Her curiosity violating such sanctimonious space forced her to look closer. As she reached for it, her hand fell first on the boxer shorts which, rather than giving like a soft cushion from the many stacked pairs, resisted with a slight crunching sound. She lifted up the top pair before her. Stacked in the far corner was a bunch of envelopes, enough to fill a shoe box. They had been opened and she could see they still contained letters.

And they were addressed to her!

And the handwriting—*handwriting*—of the address was…definitely…Hank's!

The room started pitching wildly, upsetting her equilibrium. Pam staggered back, staring hypnotically at a bunch of envelopes in her hand. She lost her balance and fell on her father's bed where she remained motionless, looking up at the spinning sand-finished ceiling. She closed her eyes and felt her body spinning along with the ceiling in ever increasing rpm's.

She tried to keep her mind blank, unable to think, knowing the moment had become too complicated. Her heart thought for her, fluttering out of control, with confusion, with excitement—with hope. She bolted upright, dropped all but one in her lap, and her fingers ripped into the envelope and took out a handwritten letter on plain white bond.

She read slowly, not wanting to miss a word, straining through blurry eyes, occasionally pausing to sweep the letter dry of fallen tears. She finished and started on another. Then another. And so on. They told a story that she had told. Of puzzlement, disappointment, concern, loneliness, hurt, of love.

Finished with what she had taken, she returned to the drawer, taking the rest and sitting again on the end of the bed. When there was nothing left to read Pam lay down and looked again at the ceiling. It had stopped moving. But not her mind, which was running smoothly, bringing the future into view after a long, stark absence.

Hank still had nothing. No reassurances, no future on the horizon. Pam wanted to scream out 10,000 miles and let him know everything was all right, that she would be waiting, just as he longed her to.

She sat up and shook the silly notion from her head. There must be some way to get word to him. Telephone was impossible. Telegram? No, she didn't think so. One letter, his last letter, written months ago, had set down his precise timetable for coming home. It was now only three days away. A letter to him wouldn't arrive in time. Besides he may have already left his unit and gone somewhere to do whatever they had to do to leave that horrible place. But in three days he would be landing at Travis Air Force Base. That was a given. And then going through some kind of processing center in Oakland.

As she nodded to herself, Pam knew what she had to do. Every additional minute that Hank went on thinking he had been forsaken was a minute stabbing at her soul. She would go to California and meet him when he stepped off the plane. And afterwards they would make love and make up for this miserable year lost from their lives.

Suddenly she became aware of her own presence in her parents' bedroom, before a bureau with the bottom drawer pulled out, and on her father's bed. Her father's. She sprang up as if the bed had caught fire, and stood trembling before the mirror.

She looked at herself, then turned around to the electric clock on the nightstand between the twin beds. It was 11:02. She'd better hurry and pack and go to the savings and loan if she was going to catch an afternoon flight from Melbourne to Atlanta where she could then get something cross-country. She had plenty of time, three days. But she had to get out of town as soon as possible.

"Pam… Pam! Pam?" Fred Sadler yelled out as he pushed the door closed behind him. Still not home. Where could she be? Did she already know that Dave had been badly injured? He had telephoned her from work four or five times to tell her, but there had been no answer. Maybe she knew and was now at the hospital. He was afraid of what this thing would do to her, especially after her strange behavior last night when she'd claimed to have a headache before disappearing into her room. He had heard her sobbing. What would she do now? Now that there was this bad news.

And while clutching this bad news in his hand, he cut his usual path to the fridge, plucked out a cold Ballantine, popped the cap with a worn drawer handle, and drank a third of the bottle en route to his favorite, overstuffed chair. He belched and plopped down. His lap contained the local afternoon newspaper with the bad news.

The newspaper had not been his first source, but rather was purchased right after work at a neighboring 7-11 to corroborate the first source, the radio. He had been stuffing envelopes in square holes, his arthritis burning his legs, while listening to the local news on the communal radio, when without warning the local news became too local.

A freak accident, so the radio had called it and the paper had backed up with a few details. For the umpteenth time Fred's mind paraphrased the newspaper article. A young, dedicated football player, striving to move up from the taxi squad, pushing himself in the off season to the bare, raw limits of endurance, straining with heavy barbells into the early Monday morning hours, his arms trembling out of control as he tries for just one more rep. Then collapsing, the bar smashing into his nose, he stumbles back to get out of the way, he falls and heavy weights smash his foot. Results: one broken nose, one severely broken instep, one career in jeopardy.

Fred finished off his beer. Puffing with effort and the pain in his legs he made a round trip for another, leaving the newspaper on the side table. He plopped back down again, took three full swallows, set his beer down near the newspaper as he lit a cigarette, blew out a stream of smoke, and then picked the beer up and took another swallow, gazing at the newspaper from the corner of his eyes. He belched and started thinking again.

And then there was that nasty rumor that began circulating after lunch. That was really frying his ass. Someone wanted to ruin an athlete's reputation when he was already on the verge of a career crippling injury.

And then there were the insinuations that his friends, if he could call his coworkers that, must be making behind his back. They knew his daughter was Dave's girlfriend; they sure ought to; he had told them enough times. And now that rumor was stabbing not only Dave in the back, but also his daughter and himself.

It was that lying wop shit, Tony Martignetti, who started the rumor. An asshole. Didn't know shit about football. Unfortunately, he knew how to spread a filthy rumor. He probably even made it up, though he said he heard it during lunch at Jake's diner from a friend who had a friend who was some kind of orderly or aide, or whatever, in the emergency room of Cocoa Beach General Hospital, who said that Dave's dick had looked like somebody had tried to bite it off. What a fucking liar. And everybody was smirking and looking out of the corner of their eyes, waiting for him to go home so they could all joke about his daughter having steel jaws or something crass like that.

What a fucking lie. He didn't even bother to tell them that his daughter was home last night in her room with her door shut, with some kind of sickness, feeling so bad she was crying. If he had told them, they'd think he was lying and trying to cover up for his little girl. Those fucking bastards. They weren't his goddamn friends. They were all assholes.

He finished his beer and brutally stubbed out his cigarette in a large shell ashtray on the side table. He stood up slowly, his mind momentarily focusing on the pain in his legs. He limped into his bedroom to strip down to his skivvies.

A third of the way across the room he stopped. With wide eyes and open mouth he looked down at his dresser's bottom drawer. His drawer. It was

open. He moved to it, his eyes on it, his limp gone, the pain no longer noticeable. His underwear had been disturbed.

And the letters were gone.

He staggered back and sagged heavily onto his bed, onto an already wrinkled depression formed by his daughter having sat there hours before. His
eyes were caught by the mirror, by the red lipstick which was scrawled a
message, as if penned by a demented mind:

Mom. I'm going to California to meet Hank. Father will explain.

His emotions boiled with a broth of self-recrimination, self-admonish-
ment, of disappointment, and of anger. He had caused his daughter a moment of hurt for which he felt sorry, but his contriteness was diluted as he
cursed his stupidity for keeping the incriminating letters. They had been a
monument to the immense task he had accomplished, a reminder of his
achievement. Of many hours hunting and pecking on that damned typewriter, of forcing creative thoughts from his brain, of his stomach churning
with the worry of a letter getting past his blockade and through to the intended recipient, of the satisfaction of shaping his daughter's future into
something meaningful…

His anger flavored his emotions with a bitter seasoning. Pam had opened
his drawer. Pam had disobeyed. Pam had run off. She was abandoning Dave,
someone who now really needed her.

CHAPTER 73

H ANK SAT AT a round empty table in a large empty O'club at Long Binh. He stared at the faded green table cloth between his right hand that clutched a glass of beer and his left hand which rested heavily on the table, weighted by a plaster cast that covered most of his hand and his entire forearm.

He looked around the dimly lit room. The O'club was as large as Looie's Lounge was small and it hadn't changed much in a year. Except that it was empty but for one attractive long-haired girl-san waitress that watched him from a corner next to the door to the kitchen, and one sour, long-faced spec-four bartender who kept his distance behind the bar.

An hour before lunch was obviously not the peak period. In a way, he reflected, this club had played a certain role in the course of events occurring over the year. It had been his first watering hole in-country. Now it would be his last.

His eyes began darting around impatiently. What was keeping him? It was taking Dick a long time to visit the shitter.

He lifted his glass and sipped at the foamy head. It had not been that long ago when he had downed more than a few such brews as the dull ache in his head and the flat, stale taste in his mouth reminded him.

It had been only last night in Looie's Lounge. On a twenty-four-hour basis it had been the same day Franklin died; the same day Wan died. Only a stretch of daylight separated those events with that of Dick and him gazing at one another across the table in a tiny deserted bar. The absence of the other junior officers had been obvious.

It had been SOP protocol that when officers of the First Brigade derosed they were given a small ceremony at the colonel's villa the night before their departure to pay tribute to their service to the Brigade and to the Big Red One. He and Dick proved to be the exception. The fact that the colonel and Major Duncan were out going hither and yon all over the Brigade's AO after the brutal assault on Fire Base Stork provided an acceptable excuse for fore-going the evening's festivities, at least for the senior grade officers, but not for the junior grades.

The absence of their fellow lieutenant "friends" from stopping by the Lounge to wish the departing officers good luck and farewell was noticeable, at least to him and Dick. Though their "friends" had their excuses. Lai Khe had been put on high alert due to the recent aggressive enemy action at Stork. It was a newly invented alert. Not red, which meant enemy activity was eminent. Nor yellow which said that it was a possibility. It was some sort of burnt orange, which gave officers a lot of discretion on whether to get ready for an attack or go to the nearest bar and think about it. And it appeared that no one, not even Lieutenant Grosser, wanted to think about it, not with him and Dick, anyway. It was as if the two of them had con-tracted a contagious, rotten disease. A type of misery and melancholy that had to be avoided, and in Dick's case, shunned at all costs.

Dick had bared his soul that night, openly grieving for Wan. He had bitterly denounced the MPs cursory investigation and their recommendation to the colonel that disciplinary action should be taken against Dick for al-lowing Wan inside the perimeter, which had purportedly precipitated Fins-ley's action. Their recommendation was based they said, on Finsley's perfectly understandable reaction to seeing an unauthorized Vietnamese in the base camp, and unfortunately mistaking Wan for a VC sapper. Of course, Finsley had been drinking and perhaps this had distorted his perception somewhat. The fact that he was a night-duty officer did require full abstinence, so they suggested a stern reprimand should go in his 201-file referencing his inebri-ation while on duty.

Much to Colonel Carter's credit, he had totally discounted the MP's in-vestigation and instructed the U.S. Army Criminal Investigation Division to convene an Army Board of Inquiry into Finsley's behavior and activities.

Hank had listened to Dick's heartbroken litany, or at least to bits and pieces of it. His mind had been preoccupied. Though he felt badly for his friend and deep sorrow at the news of Wan's death, and had wanted to help

Dick soak up some of his heartache, he had his own grief. Not many hours ago he too had lost someone dear to him. Someone he realized, as he had drunk beer and had listened to Dick's cracking and sobbing profanity, meant as much to him as Wan had to Dick.

And later in the wee hours of the morning, after staggering to their hooch one last time and after separating the bunks on which Dick and Wan had slept, Hank had laid down and closed his eyes. As always, the faces soon came. The first one was new. And with closed eyes he saw Franklin's face and listened to his dying words one more time.

The daylight part of the next morning had been better, starting with the buzz of the field telephone at 0730 hours and answered by a Dick Kistler groan of, "What the fuck do you want?" A flicker of his old self. The caller had been a chopper pilot buddy volunteering to ferry him and Hank to Long Binh, provided they were at the brigade helipad by 0915.

At Long Binh they had checked into the officer in/out processing center from which they were sent to a barracks where they claimed bunk beds for their last night in-country. Then they had headed for the O'club, though Dick had detoured to the latrine.

Now, where was he? Hank allowed his lips to suck in some of the golden liquid. He glanced towards the entrance and his question was answered by the sight of a large silhouette outlined by the white, bright outside light coming through the doorway. A smaller silhouette followed him inside before the door closed. For a few seconds the two silhouettes seemed to fade into the wall until Hank's eyes adjusted back to the dimness of the room.

It was obviously taking longer for Dick's eyes to adjust since he stood on the far side of the room peering around. Hank waved his good arm with the glass of beer, and called, "Over here, Dick."

Dick looked in his direction, saw him, waved, and started across the room, followed by the person behind him.

He pulled out a chair and sat down on Hank's left. His follower, a first lieutenant, did the same on the right. "Hank, this is Larry Fetherford, a VMI classmate," Dick said, handling the introductions. "Believe it or not we bumped into each other in the latrine."

"Neighboring holes of all things," Fetherford laughed. The room had enough light for Hank to catch a glint of genuine friendliness in his eyes, contrasting sharply, Hank regrettably knew, with his and Dick's, which seemed devoid of life. Fetherford's face was round and full with baby fat that made him look younger than Dick, whose face, beset with recent stress and frown lines and absent his moustache, looked almost craggy.

Hank and Fetherford shook hands while Dick motioned to the waitress, holding up two fingers and pointing to Hank's glass. Fetherford took off his fatigue cap and put it on the table, revealing a crew cut. He reached his fingers into a breast pocket and took out a package of cigarettes. He offered the pack to Hank and Dick and after their declines tapped one out. He lit it and waved out the match as the girl-san set them up with two more beers.

As Dick threw down some MPCs on her tray, Fetherford filled his glass, picked it up, and held it over the table. "Here's to two of the shortest guys in Vietnam. Today Long Binh, tomorrow the Freedom Bird, the next day the World."

Hank raised his glass. Dick bypassed the glass and raised his bottle. The three officers clinked and drank in unison. And in unison they set their drinks down.

A lull followed. Dick and Hank broodingly stared down at the table. Fetherford glanced back and forth at the two, wondering about their lack of emotion, especially from Dick who had been a hell-raiser at the Institute.

He decided to pry. "What's with you guys? You don't seem too excited about going home. And you're Infantry, too," he noted, his eyes on the crossed rifles sewn on Hank's collar. "I'm half-way, six more months, with a desk job here at Long Binh. I'm a finance officer, actually a glorified pay-master. I drink and watch movies every night. Steam bath and massages twice a week. Go into Saigon every other afternoon on business at General Abrams's headquarters. And you know something. I'm going to be one happy SOB the day before I leave." As he talked the cigarette bobbed in his mouth.

The lull set back in uncomfortably, until Dick said with a weak smile, "We're fuckin' worn out, Larry. We tied one on last night. Got up early this morning, and flew here from Lai Khe."

"Must have been a wild rip-snorter by the looks of that cast. Brand new, right? Bet that happened while you were tying it on." Fetherford's eyes were at maximum glint as they glanced at Hank.

"Yeah. Good guess, Larry," Hank answered, attempting a smile.

"Why then in hell are you two drinking at this hour?"

Hank looked at Dick. Dick shrugged.

"There's nothing else to do, 'cept drink our way to the Freedom Bird."

"Ever hear of rack time, Brother Rat Kistler?" Fetherford threw his head back with a laugh that snorted smoke through his nostrils. The "Brother Rat" term was not unfamiliar to Hank having heard Dick explain it to him while at Benning. It was somewhat of an affectionate reference to a VMI classmate.

"Say, have you ever been to Saigon?" Fetherford asked Dick, shifting the line of discussion.

Dick shook his head. "No. Been around it. Ton Son Nhut, Bien Hoa, and here at Long Binh. Never really in it."

"How about you, Hank?" Fetherford asked.

"No. Same as Dick."

Fetherford's animated eyes grew large. "I'm heading into Saigon this afternoon. Leaving here at fourteen hundred in my jeep. Why don't you two join me? We'll hit a few bars on the way back." Smiling broadly, he glanced from one to the other, watching them consider his invitation. Dick looked at Hank, Hank looked at his cast. "You can grab a little sack time after chow," he added.

Hank shook his head. "I'll pass, Larry. Thanks anyway. There're some forms we need to fill out before processing out of here."

"That doesn't take long. Fifteen minutes at the most. Majority of the paperwork is at Oakland. You can get over to personnel now and get it all done before lunch."

"Well, I'm too bushed, anyway. Last night wore me out. If I catch some sack time after lunch I'll be out cold until tomorrow morning," Hank said, grabbing another excuse, his eyes half closed, showing fatigue.

"When you get on that Freedom Bird, you'll have nothing else to do for hours but sleep. Pump yourself up with some coffee. Hang in there today until you can't hold your head up. That flight tomorrow will be one long snooze," Fetherford persisted.

No way did Hank want to move out of his chair, much less tour Saigon. He would be quite pleased to sit out the rest of his Vietnam hours in this club with Dick, with each feeling sorry for themselves. But more importantly—feeling sorry for the others.

He was determined to resist. "I don't have a weapon, Larry. I feel naked without one. I can't consider riding in a jeep on an open road to Saigon without something for protection." Hank fabricated another excuse. "Who knows, I may have to carry a gun back home while I'm adjusting to civilian life?" Hank forced a low, guttural laugh, his eyes on the table, avoiding Fetherford's.

"Don't sweat the weapon problem, Hank. I wear a forty-five when I make these trips and I can scrounge up one for you and you too, Dick." Fetherford glanced across the table at Dick, who was sitting sideways, his left boot on his thigh, nearly in his lap, both hands holding the ankle, his eyes on the toe; his mind appearing elsewhere.

But he had heard Fetherford and looked up and shook his head. "I don't need anything," he answered, and his eyes gravitated back to the dull, black shine of the toe of his boot. One hand reached for his bottle of beer.

The mention of a .45 made Hank shift his gaze to his cast as memories poured in of him floundering to cock one as he lay under a blanket of flying shrapnel. Fetherford was apparently a nice guy and a friend of Dick's so he fought back the urge to tell him to take that .45 and shove it. "Not a .45, Larry. Can't stand that weapon. But thanks anyway. I'll just while away my time here."

Some of the brightness dimmed in Fetherford's eyes as Hank's resistance ebbed his patience. But he wasn't about to give up. The drive to Saigon and back was boring and he looked forward to some company and some camaraderie at one or more of the small Vietnamese dives that dotted the way. And he thought that if Hank didn't go, neither would Dick. Hank was the swing vote. "Tell you what, Hank. I can get you an M-16, maybe even an M-60, if you want it. How about it? It's not going to kill you to go. I'm not talking about a fuckin' recon patrol."

There was a pause as Hank drank from his beer, buying time to think about how to put Fetherford down as gently as possible. This crazy bantering had gone on long enough. As the glass left his wet lips, a big, familiar ham-hock of a hand clamped down on his shoulder with a comforting squeeze. Mouth open, glass held in mid air, his eyes followed the bridge that had been constructed, the arm leading from his shoulder to Dick whose torso twisted around in the seat and whose eyes now found Hank's.

"Let's do it, Hank. What the fuck. Might as well see Saigon before we leave," Dick said. His face was sad and droopy. The metamorphous of his features was regressing to the gloomy last night in Looie's Lounge.

"All right. Let's do it," Hank consented, his tone half reluctance, half indifference.

Either not catching Hank's tone, or ignoring it, Fetherford's eyes lit up. "Fuckin A!" He exclaimed. "You won't be disappointed. Believe me. You WON'T be disappointed."

But Hank already was.

The two short-timers wrestled with some DA forms for a solid hour. Fetherford's time estimate had been off by a factor of four.

The mess hall was crowded and fully integrated with the clean, starched khaki uniforms of the newly arrived with the mostly cleaned and mostly over starched base camp laundered fatigues of the soon to be departed to the World. Tomorrow there would be a flip-flop of uniforms as the fledglings changed to fatigues and the old timers to khakis.

Hank and Dick managed to find a table together. They shared it with two bright-eyed, khaki-wearing lieutenants, who were pleased that two veteran first lieutenants, with black CIBs sewn above their left pockets and First ID patches on their left shoulders, had joined them. The newcomers began an animated conversation. They started by asking questions of a tactical nature. How were things with the Big Red One? Had they seen much action? What was it like? And were answered dismissively by Dick with one and two-word sentences of: "OK. Enough. You'll see."

Finding such little response, they shifted to a more strategic topic, asking the veterans their opinion on Nixon's Vietnamization plan whereby the Vietnamese would phase into more of the fighting while the U.S. phased out. Again the spokesman, Dick informed them that neither he nor his buddy knew a fuckin' thing about it.

Still undaunted, the fledglings continued to initiate some kind of conversation. This time they focused on the States, something they felt would be more open to discussion. They asked about what they thought of the riots at People's Park at Berkeley.

Dick admitted they were ignorant of this. What riots? When informed of the details about the violent antiwar demonstrations near the University of California, he decided to partake more fully of the conversation and cynically laid out plans upon his return to the World to catch a rally of marching protestors in an L-shaped ambush using animal claymores and M-60s with enfilade fire.

The newcomers laughed and became more at ease and shared similar feelings before giving their brief, unsolicited biodata: OCS at Benning, Airborne and Ranger. Dick nodded acknowledgment of their credentials before proceeding on a soliloquy of all the pussy he was looking forward to back home and even though it was against his principle to pay for it he might have to rise above it if he couldn't find anything free in the first two hours after touchdown on the old U.S. of A.—*terra firma.*

Hank watched in quiet astonishment at the suddenly voluble Dick Kistler. Then he understood. It was the old Dick Kistler using sex as his life preserver.

After their food trays had been reduced to scraps, the conversation ended. They all stood and issued their farewells and good lucks. The new lieutenants had not enquired about the cast on Hank's arm, and Hank was glad of it.

It was close to 1400 hours and there was no time for a little shut-eye as Fetherford had suggested. Hank felt cheated by this chink in Fetherford's credibility as he walked with Dick along a well compacted dirt road flanked by long A-frames. They stopped in front of the O'club and waited, watching the olive drab traffic of trucks, jeeps, and buses pass by.

It was 1415 hours when Fetherford drove up in a freshly painted jeep, crossed the oncoming lane, and skidded to a halt on the narrow gravel shoulder. Rather than the fatigue cap he wore earlier in the O'club, he now wore a jungle flop hat popular with the remfs. Wearing their baseball fatigue caps, Hank and Dick were set apart from Fetherford in attire, and even further by the .45 holstered around his waist.

He reached around to the back seat and picked up a weapon. "Here you go, Hank. Hope this makes you feel better. It's better than an M-16," Fetherford's smile wanted to be contagious as he held in his right hand a CAR-15, a shorter, lighter carbine style version of the M-16. It had a 30-round banana magazine that was almost as long as the barrel. He thrust it out in front of him. "Why don't you ride shotgun and we'll let Kistler's big ass take up the back seat."

Hank grabbed the weapon by the handguard as Dick vaulted into the back seat. "That's fine with me. I don't mind some fanny room. But let's move it, Fetherford. You're late," Dick complained. He flopped into the rear seat behind Fetherford and stretched his long legs catty corner under the passenger seat where his feet tangled with the support bracing.

"Hey, I got some leg room!" Dick exclaimed. "What's the story with this seat?"

"It's been customized," Fetherford answered. "I chauffeur my colonel and major quite a bit. Major's long legged, sits in back and was always complaining about lack of leg room; so colonel had it customized. Notice seat's elevated. Gives the colonel the high ground, looking down. You know how the brass are."

"Yeah, we know," Dick muttered sarcastically as Hank trotted around the front of the vehicle and hopped in.

Hank pinched the rifle butt with his thighs. The CAR-15 with its long banana clip became a big phallus pointing to the sky. As Fetherford threw the clutch into gear and stepped on the accelerator, Hank drew the slide back with his good hand, released it and let the bolt ram home a 5.56mm round.

Fetherford slammed on the brake, jerking them forward. "You can't do that, Hank. You can't lock a round in the chamber around here. It's against regs," Fetherford frowned reproachfully.

Fetherford's reprimand raised Hank's eyebrows and he glanced back at Dick. Dick lay his big hamhock on Fetherford's neck. "Larry, what the fuck's the matter with you? He doesn't want that weapon for a dildo. He wants it as a weapon. And he wants it locked and loaded. Let's get the fuck moving. And easy on the brakes. You nearly bent my fucking legs in half."

Fetherford gave a disapproving shrug before gunning the engine while dropping his foot off the clutch, throwing them backward into their seats.

They rode past a series of chain link security gates capped with barbed wire, turned onto a smooth black top, and joined the predominantly military traffic, mostly deuce-and-a-half and three-quarter tons. The jeep accelerated to a cruising speed.

Hank sat up straight, rifle butt on his right hip, and kept his fingers closed around the magazine well. His plastered left arm throbbed a code of pain around the wrist. Air turbulence slapped and pulled on his fatigues, fluttering parts of his fatigue shirt as if they were tiny flags. His eyes stared straight ahead through a dusty windshield. Only his peripheral vision caught the road side. The scenery gradually changed from barbed wire, sandbagged bunkers, security gates manned by MPs, and the occasional watch tower to the pastel stucco of Vietnamese one and two-story structures and roadside merchant stands managed by goateed papa-sans and wrinkled faced mama-sans.

Before long, after two right turns and a left, they were edging forward in a cluttered stream of sputtering Lambrettas, pickup trucks overloaded with produce and merchandise, bicycles, carts pulled by plodding water buffaloes, and motor scooters weaving in and out like small darting fish. Horns honked from everywhere. Gaggles of Vietnamese civilians milled around small shops and stores packed together in one long outdoor mall, buying and selling, and waving and jabbering.

Hank became uneasy. The people were so close.

The busy roadside crowd grew sparse as they rolled slowly into another block, one that had seen better days, or perhaps more fortunate ones. Rows of two and three-story peeling stucco buildings with a mixed use of store-fronts with upstairs residences lined the street. Thanks probably to Tet it was ready for urban renewal. Dark gaping holes filled their walls and roofs. Victims, Hank figured, of past rocket attacks—107s and 122s. Swept clean of debris, the sidewalk, a tight compaction of yellowish-brown dirt, was much wider than on the other blocks and its smooth flatness contrasted with the gutted shells of stucco, mortar, and dirty brick.

Hank's eyes surveyed the damaged buildings, then found the sidewalk before focusing on a deep drainage ditch beside the road. It was muddy and a few shades darker than the dirt of the sidewalk. Hank's sanitary engineering instincts, dormant for two years, came back briefly and decided an impervious lining was needed to improve hydraulic efficiency and minimize erosion. He wanted to be amused at the emergence of his analytical, engineering mind, but he wasn't, and his eyes focused ahead on the slowly moving right wheel of an ox-cart.

The wheel stopped moving. Fetherford applied the brakes. Blaring horns started blending with loud high-pitched Vietnamese jabbering. Curious as to the latest tie-up, the conical-hatted ox-cart driver in a dirty T-shirt and brown shorts stood up and looked down the line of traffic.

Hank glanced at Fetherford. "Is it always this kind of mess?"

Fetherford was stretching his neck out sideways in an effort to see around the ox-cart. He looked over at Hank. "Tell the truth. It's not. I usually go another way, but thought I'd try a more scenic route today. You need a little variety now and then, you know," Fetherford said and turned away to resume stretching his neck.

Hank shook his head sadly. His buttocks began to feel tremors as Dick's big feet shifted around under his seat cushion. He turned around expecting a message from Dick, but instead saw him squirming half-way between sitting and prone in search for comfort. When he noticed Hank, he shrugged his big shoulders and leaned his back against Fetherford's side of the jeep. He smiled at Hank and gave him a thumbs-up.

Hank returned it, then glanced past Dick at a large, white Mercedes truck behind them. The truck's Vietnamese driver was doing a Fetherford with his neck as he tried to see around the ox-cart to find the hold up.

Hank faced forward again. The toe of Dick's boot was still annoying him through the cushion. His attention turned right oblique to a square, two-story structure the color of faded Pepto Bismol. Two rectangular, pane-less windows stared down from the upper floor. Between the windows was a large, black jagged hole. The building was dead, shot between the eyes by some type of high explosive weapon.

Hank shuddered inexplicably.

A young, buzz-cut haired Vietnamese man in a white short sleeved shirt and khaki pants emerged pushing a bike from the dark, door-less entrance of the bombed-out relic. He appeared nervous and seemed to purposely avoid glancing in the direction of the jeep. His right hand on the seat was mostly blocked by his body from view, though Hank had glimpsed a tightly held brown bag. Oddly, it seemed that his hand had gripped the contents of the bag rather than merely the top.

The man swung a leg over the bike, still seeming to conceal what he was holding. Perhaps he was pushing some dope, Hank considered, watching closely, a probable witness to something clandestine and illegal. To Hank's surprise, the man pushed off in his direction, left hand on the handle bar, right hand held behind his back. Briefly, as the Vietnamese started pedaling, slowly gathering momentum, their eyes caught, and Hank saw a glazed recognition in his dark eyes.

Their eyes broke off and then the bike was beside Hank. In a flash of terror that ran from his brain to his gut, he understood. And his proof was the brown bag that was tossed and was now arching toward the jeep high over Hank's head. There was no doubt in his mind that the brown bag contained an M-26 hand grenade.

"Grenade!" he shouted as he hurled himself from the jeep, expecting while sailing in mid-air an explosion that would blow him past his objective, the narrow drainage ditch. Instinctively before he landed, his thumb pushed the

CAR-15's selector switch to fully automatic.

He landed hard in the ditch, the jolt absorbed slightly by the thin layer of mud and by equal parts of his body distributing the impact. His body braced subconsciously against the shock wave of the anticipated explosion as he sighted through the tiny aperture of the peep sight. The handguard rested on his plaster cast. Up beyond the edge of the ditch the bicyclist leaned forward and pedaled madly along with pumping legs, past the stalled caravan of vehicles. Subconsciously as his finger squeezed the trigger he thought inwardly at the terrorist's stupidity for not letting the grenade cook off and allowing time for them to escape the jeep and time for the VC to not. Nowhere did Hank's mind allow for the possibility of a prank, of maybe the bag containing a mango.

A burst of three rounds smacked into the fleeing cyclist. The first round hit his lower spine. The second hit a few inches higher below his left shoulder blade, lifting his head up. The third hit the back of his head just behind his left ear. His body made a series of funny flinches and twitches.

Hank had not been the only one to react upon his shout of "grenade." Fetherford fled the driver's seat in a fit of panic, the brown bag and its contents hitting his right ankle as his foot moved from the accelerator pedal. There was no drainage ditch to sprawl in as there was for Hank, so his reaction pointed him with scurrying feet in the direction of the ox-cart where he dived under.

Dick had been bending his neck around looking across the road at a relic of a building that looked like its brick and mortar had been attacked by a wrecker's ball and had not seen the cyclist approach. But he had turned in time to see the brown bag in flight over Hank's head and had heard Hank's shout. As Hank dived to his right and Fetherford jumped to his left, Dick started scrambling, his mind set on a rear exit and then a crawl under the white Mercedes truck whose driver had ducked down on the floor board under the steering column. But Dick's feet which had fought for comfort under Hank's seat had become entangled in the steel springs below the cushion and now as he bucked and fought and strained to free himself he seemed to become more stuck. Until finally there was the shocking realization that he wasn't going to free himself within the precious second or two or maybe hopefully three before the grenade detonated.

He jackknifed his body and started stretching for the brown bag with its suspected contents that had wound up between the brake and clutch pedals. His fingers, his arm, his shoulder, his chest, every inch extended over the driver's seat until his ligaments felt ready to snap. His face broke out in sweat streams. His finger tips almost felt the stark metal of the brake. His nails scratched at the paper of the bag.

The bicycle's front wheel wobbled out of control and the bicycle crashed in the ditch, throwing its rider in a somersault over the handlebars and onto the road.

From the moment Hank had depressed the trigger, to a couple of seconds later as he watched the VC terrorist flip from the bike, and then covered his head with his arms, his mind had been on autopilot, controlled only by reflex, not reason. Now his first thought after bracing the whole while for a violent explosion and a wind storm of metal was that the grenade was a dud. He considered unwrapping his arms and lifting his head high to glance over at the jeep.

And then there was an explosion.

He closed his eyes and felt the blast wave of a flying shower of metal roaring over his head. Other innocuous chunks dropped like a metallic sprinkle around him. A part of the steering column landed nearby.

Though his ears had a painful ring, he suddenly felt good, the mixture of vanquished fear and residual adrenalin manufacturing an instant drug-like high. He had just killed a man, but one who had tried to kill them. Fortunately for them, but not so for him, he had failed to allow the grenade to cook off. He had failed to prevent their escape; and had himself failed to escape.

A dumb, dead shit.

He pushed off the ground with his good right arm, came to his knees, and quickly scanned the pavement for Dick who he expected to see crawling out of somewhere, maybe from under the Mercedes truck, and giving him a thumbs-up and a big Dick Kistler grin. His eyes stopped on the wreckage of the jeep. There was more than just the wreckage. There was a butchered side of beef dangling over the right rear wheel; it had wet and tattered, red color rags, save for one part that had been untouched and now fluttered lightly in the wind—an embroidered name tag in bold letters: Kistler.

Hank quickly dropped his gaze into the ditch; his mind determined to erase the image of what he had seen. His heart sank into his gut and dissolved into a painful emptiness.

Slowly, he came to his feet and started shuffling along the ditch, the rifle held loosely in his good right hand just below the front sights.

If the grenade's explosion had not shut off his hearing, he would have heard the bereaved wailing of Lieutenant Fetherford asking God what had happened, and nervous Vietnamese witnesses jabbering gibberish. If he had lifted his eyes, he would have seen confusion running all about.

Blocking a section of ditch in front of him was a gaggle of papa-sans, mama-sans, and baby-sans and an old master sergeant pointing a trembling .45 pistol at the ground and a young open-mouthed, bug-eyed PFC beside him. Hank used the cast on his arm to cut through the gaggle. It sliced effortlessly.

The master sergeant babbled profusely about Hank's good marksmanship in Hank's deaf ear. He reassuringly added that if Hank had missed he would surely have blown the dink's brains out when he had gotten as far as his three-quarter ton.

The sunken path before Hank became obstructed with a lifeless body sprawled upside down the slope. The head was face up on the bottom next to a slowly spinning rusted bicycle wheel. The face had a pencil mustache and a bloodied missing left cheek. The dark eyes were fixed on the powder blue sky. The half-open mouth smiled sardonically at his fate.

Hank's gaze fastened on the smile as his right hand wedged the rifle between closed legs and then strayed to his left shoulder and started slowly fingering his Big Red One patch. Two fingers griped one corner like the fangs of a viper and broke into the thread. Once loosened the thumb and forefinger took over and ripped the patch from his shoulder.

The Vietnamese gibberish and master sergeant's monologue grew silent as Hank crouched down, the rifle falling into the crook of his plastered arm. He put the upper part of the patch in the half-open mouth. As he stood, he shifted the rifle to his good arm. Holding the rifle by the barrel he swung it in an arc. The butt slapped the corpse's jaw shut. The smile was gone. The patch became set in a mongrel-like bite, the red one fully displayed.

The gibberish picked up its intensity. The master sergeant mumbled, "If you're going to be one, be a Big Red One."

In the background Fetherford continued his wailing.

CHAPTER 74

PAM GAZED OUT at San Francisco, at the tops of buildings, at the trolley cars, the bustle of city life, and beyond at the white-capped bay waters and the Golden Gate and Alcatraz. She laughed at herself as her eyes stayed on the prison island. This morning when she awoke she had glanced out the window only to see in a soupy fog the outline of the biggest ship she had ever seen. As the fog burned away, to her chagrin, the ship turned into an island with a stark fortress, Alcatraz.

She had checked into the Fairmont late last night after spending the first night in a cheap hotel near the airport waiting for a vacancy to materialize in what the airline stewardess had said was the grandest hotel in the bay area. She had called the reservation desk twice every hour until in the evening they said they had a cancellation and she could book it for five nights. Only problem, the room was a $125-a-day suite. She didn't care. She took it. She and Hank would have the best. They deserved it.

Pam slid the sliding glass window open a crack, letting in a raw wind that hit her face full on. She shivered as the cold air stripped away her body heat; and she loved it. The cold was a wonderful change from the stifling humidity on Merritt Island. Her body felt vibrant and alive, just as her mind had been feeling since leaving home, or rather her former home.

She shut the window and crossed the room to a large couch, aware of her racing heart. She idly wondered about the possibility of a heart attack brought on by extended happiness. She knew the great muscle pump would be further taxed when Hank was before her and they embraced. She slumped down on the couch and leaned her head back on the armrest and giggled girlishly. She felt so good. Everything had become wonderful. Or soon would be.

She had been out to Travis Air Force Base to make sure there would be no trouble greeting the airplane and had spoken to an empathetic captain. There would be a number of incoming flights from Vietnam via refueling stops in Japan and Anchorage.

Not knowing Hank's flight—though not from trying to find out—she would put in an all-day vigil, anxiously observing the disembarking passengers, jealously, she knew, watching as wives and girlfriends fell in their men's arms, crying with joy, happiness, and relief.

She could bear it though. Her time would come. She was going to the air base tomorrow to watch and wait one full day ahead of the arrival date Hank had stated in his last letter. At least he said it was his last letter. Maybe another had come later and her father tossed it. But why would he do that after keeping all those other letters? There, she was getting paranoid again. Anyway, she was going out there a day early just in case Hank caught an earlier flight, if such a thing were possible.

She knew Hank hadn't arrived yet. That bit of information was gleaned from her trip out to the Army processing center in Oakland. After convincing the MPs at the gate that she wasn't a spy or militant protestor, she was allowed to search for the answers she wanted. She found a freckled-faced young man called a spec-five, or something like that, who had a roster of everyone who had come through in the last seven days.

Unfortunately, he had nothing on when and who was coming in. But he did say that when they did come in to spend a few days of processing to be reassigned, or even better, to become civilians, they were allowed to stay off post, anywhere they wanted, as long as they were at building H at ten hundred hours each morning.

And that's why she had a suite at the Fairmont Hotel.

Her heart kept up its frantic pace while her mind floated blissfully.

CHAPTER 75

H ANK LOOKED OUT the window of the bus bound for Bien Hoa. It was loaded with jubilant, khaki-uniformed soldiers. It was his last look at Vietnam. The sights differed little from the day before and at times his mind caught himself sitting in a jeep and feeling Dick's feet beneath him and seeing a ruined building that had been shot between the eyes and from which emerged a Vietnamese pushing a bike and carrying a brown bag.

His face was of pale stone. His head loosely bobbed back and forth with the sudden stopping, starting, and turning of the bus reacting to the moderately heavy traffic and to the jigsaw route as it traveled point for three other similar vehicles. The bus moved inside the barbed wire of Bien Hoa, past administrative buildings and barracks, and finally pulled up to a large, tin-roofed pavilion that sheltered rows of long benches on a thick concrete slab. Beyond was the wide sweep of runway aprons.

The bus emptied before Hank found his feet. He stepped slowly down into a bright hot sun, walked to the shade of the pavilion, and watched his fellow passengers look and scramble for their duffle bags being plucked from the underneath luggage compartments by the drivers and tossed haphazardly to the ground. Hank was not part of this activity. He had no duffle bag.

His only belongings were a thin dark brown folder wrapped by a thick brown string and holding a tooth brush, tooth paste, safety razor, and a brief history of his Army career. Clamped between the folder and his plastered left forearm was a large wooden key, its chain a silky, camouflaged patterned scarf. The carved word "Cadillac" was displayed outward.

He had considered packing a change of underwear but had dismissed the thought since it wouldn't fit into his folder. He'd try to purchase some at the Oakland processing center. But if that didn't pan out he'd just have to make it home with dirty underwear. Or none at all. Why not? He'd gone a year without wearing any.

Going home, question was, where was it? Vero, to the house he was raised in, where his mom now lived with her fat-assed attorney husband? Or Tampa, where his father had been exiled after the divorce and where he was probably living with the bimbo of the month.

He'd wanted it to be wherever Pam was. Guess not everyone gets what he wants. But hell, at least he was alive. Dick didn't even get that.

Once they found their duffel bags, a short, thick-necked master sergeant in heavily starched fatigues that made his arms and legs look like they were between thin, green boards directed them to the front of the pavilion. The master sergeant pointed, and they threw their bags in a pile as they filed by.

Hank followed them with his eyes as he leaned against a 4x4 support post. He wore the smile of a cynic as he witnessed the futility of the duffle bags, the strife of locating their own, only to deposit it a score of meters away back into another pile of anonymity.

No one but Hank seemed to care, because they laughed and joked as they filled the long rows of benches under the pavilion's large, heat-radiating roof. Hank kept standing, aware of a certain camaraderie among the passengers, like a winning sports team. Although the feeling hovered all around, Hank stood apart from it, a piece of incongruous flotsam floating away.

As they passed by him searching for a seat he sensed their furtive glances at his strange key, at the cast on his left forearm, the scar on his right cheek, and the conspicuous bareness above his left breast pocket. He felt their eyes. He read their thoughts. A weirdo first lieutenant returning home. All that time, all that service as an infantry officer in-country, and all he had to show for it according to the blank space above his left breast pocket was the National Defensive Ribbon. A ribbon representing a medal awarded after thirty days in the Armed Forces. It was the first medal a soldier receives.

Medals told a brief, abridged story of a soldier's service. Non-combat medals told about his loyalty, his efficiency, his commitment, his training, his longevity. Combat medals were different. They told of the varying degrees of shit he had stepped in and the fact he was still walking around wearing them probably meant that others who had stepped in the same shit had not been so lucky as to be walking around. And because of their unfortunate status it was they who were more deserving.

If Hank had worn his ribbons as the others around him, he would easily be in the top-twenty-fifth percentile. Considering the medal the colonel had recommended after the Stork fiasco, he would probably crack the top ten.

This morning he had gathered all the medals accumulated while in Vietnam. They were contained in their sturdy three-by-six-inch blue cases with the medal, its ribbon, and even a little miniature one that could be worn on the lapel of a civilian blazer. He took them out beyond a latrine and tossed them into a sawed-off 55-gallon drum of burning shit.

He had deliberated as to whether he should wear his CIB—combat infantry badge, awarded for serving with an infantry unit in a combat theater for at least one month. It wasn't really a medal. It was a badge. And by its definition he qualified. But he didn't see it like that. To his way of thinking, his time in real combat, when added together, counting all the skirmishes, popped ambushes, Loc Ninh firefight, and Stork fiasco, likely totaled less than two weeks. It wasn't as if he'd hit Omaha Beach with the Big Red One and slogged his way to Germany. Yet, it had been intense, tragic, life changing…and life ending for too many good young men. The dead were just as dead as they had been at Omaha Beach.

Faces turned toward the airfield and then there was loud cheering. The nose of a silver Boeing 707 glided smoothly toward them and turned broadside thirty meters from the pile of duffle bags. Huge black letters spelled "Airlift International" above the long row of portals.

The Freedom Bird had arrived.

The high-pitched whine of jet engines faded. A stairway was pushed out by four privates under the supervision of the short, starched master sergeant. The door opened and a khaki-uniformed captain stepped out and blinked repeatedly and with uncertainty at the bright sun. He came down the stairs, starting a heavy khaki stream flowing after him. With guidance from the master sergeant the stream turned into a formation of six ranks and eventually the stream had trickled to a stop. The new arrivals did a right face at the bark of the master sergeant, and then they marched away to the sound of more cheering and cat-calls from the pavilion.

Twenty minutes later the master sergeant was back. He motioned to the soldiers on the first row of benches. They stood and filed out toward the Freedom Bird. Then the next row of benches and the procession was in full swing, like an orderly exit from the pews of a church, only the usual solemnity was replaced by exuberance.

The benches beside Hank were now emptying. He followed the wide shoulders of a spec-five with his eyes, his feet not moving, a chasm growing wider. A captain standing in the neighboring waiting row growled abuse at Hank for not moving forward.

Hank glanced at the snarling, thick-whiskered face and started moving, hurrying to close the gap, only to do so and then slow down to a snail's shuffle in the long file boarding the plane.

With each step, he inexplicably became more depressed. He kept his head down, not wanting to look at where he was going. Tears welled in his eyes. He was coming undone. He felt embarrassed. Dick would think he was acting like a baby, and for no reason. He had reached the Freedom Bird.

The first step came into view. After nearly one year, all that was left was a few steps. He stopped in place, the chasm between him and the broad shoulders became wide again. He heard someone from behind ask him to move faster. He started to place one foot on the bottom step. Inexplicably, he stepped out of line, allowing the others to move ahead.

He looked up at the airplane. As men filed by, his eyes scanned from the cockpit past a huge wing with its heavy engines, to the tip of the tail section, and then back to the cockpit, to the head of the Freedom Bird. It was an awesome sight. Such a magnificent creature. What dreams are made of. His dreams.

His body shivered. And then he bolted, sprinting away awkwardly with his wooden key squeezed by his broken arm and his folder clutched next to his right side like a deflated football.

There was a long cylindrical profile of a Quonset hut not far from the pavilion. He ran for the nearest end. He came around the side to a screen door, swung it open with a quick flick of the right hand, and rushed inside, the door slamming behind him.

Four clerks, all PFCs, stopped clacking their typewriters and looked up in bewilderment at a panting first lieutenant with a big wooden key under a plastered arm and a brown folder held by the other. They were thankful for the green Formica countertop separating them from this visitor with panic in his eyes and a scar on his face, who had suddenly barged in as if to report a VC ground attack.

"Do you have a phone? I must have a phone!" The first lieutenant demanded in a gasping voice.

A skinny, boyish-looking PFC with crew-cut red hair glanced nervously around at his colleagues and saw that he was the closest to the strange lieutenant. With a hesitant movement reflecting uncertainty, the PFC meekly stood, grabbed a black telephone off his desk and set it on the counter.

"How do I get the base switch?" Hank barked at the PFC as he dumped his key and folder on the counter beside the phone.

"D…dial…z…zero," the PFC stuttered, wondering if this lieutenant, dressed in khakis and cunt cap like he was either going or coming from home, had just gone bananas. The single ribbon on his chest suggested the latter.

Hank grabbed the receiver from its cradle and with the forefinger of the same hand dialed. As the dial clicked back, he choked the receiver as he brought it to his ear.

The PFC stood frozen as he watched the lieutenant.

"Operator," Hank spoke frantically, "give me the First Infantry Division switch."

He waited, listening to the static crackling in his ear as he gazed out the window behind the PFC. He could see the Freedom Bird, all of it, as big as life, maybe even bigger. The long line of men feeding it was gone. Only the blackness of the hole that swallowed them and the rolling stairs leading to the hole were left.

At the base of the stairway, the PFC contingent of the master sergeant watched their leader walking away, walking as stiffly as his starched fatigues. He wore a scowl on his face that grew worse the closer he came to the Quonset hut.

"First Infantry switch," Hank heard a young man's voice break into the static.

"Switch, get me Duty TOC in Lai Khe," he urgently responded to the voice.

The static resumed its place. The master sergeant, so close Hank could see in his dark, leathered face the deep crevices and crannies of a career of over twenty years, turned to his left and lost his place in Hank's sight, leaving the Freedom Bird and PFC stair contingent who now appeared to be staring through the window at Hank.

Hank looked away as he heard another voice in his ear. "Duty TOC."

"May I speak with Major Duncan?" Hank asked. "This is an urgent matter." The screechy tone in his voice made his latter words redundant.

The voice replied with what Hank thought was "wait one," but he wasn't sure because at the same time the master sergeant charged in behind him. The screen door banged. The PFC clerks jumped.

Hank and the master sergeant glared at one another as if .45s were strapped to their sides. There were more electrical charges around them than the phone's static was putting in Hank's ear.

The master sergeant won the war of eyeballs and Hank dropped his to the master sergeant's embroidered black name tag that said "Jones."

"Sir," Sergeant Jones said with an inflection in his 'Bama drawl that meant shithead. "This Freedom Bird don't wait for nobody. Them boys want to get their asses home. Know what I mean?"

"I've got to make a call first," Hank replied.

"Sorry 'bout that, sir. But better be quick 'cause I'm goin' back to the Bird and tell my boys to yank the chocks and clear the steps. If you're not ahead of me by then, you'll have to get back to Long Binh and get a pass on another Bird. Know what I mean, sir?"

"I've got to make a call first," Hank repeated.

The master sergeant swung his arm in a mock salute, turned around and stalked out, the banging door tolling his departure and final word. Hank watched his march back, hoping it was something up his ass and not his fatigues that made him walk so stiffly.

"Major Duncan speaking," Hank heard in his ear.

"Sir, this is Lieutenant Kirby. I…"

"Kirby!" Duncan broke in. "What the hell you want? Aren't you supposed to be heading home today?"

"Yes, sir. I'm supposed to," Hank began, spewing out his words, their rapidity accelerating with each step the Master Sergeant took toward the Freedom Bird. "You talked to me about extending my tour over here. I'd like to do it now. I'd like to extend for six months. Is it too late? Can I still do it?"

The familiar crackling came over the line for a few long seconds. Hank held his breath and shuffled his feet around as if he were in dire need of a bathroom. Through the window he watched the master sergeant arrive at the Freedom Bird. Then the static receded into the background, replaced by Major Duncan's loud voice of disbelief. "Goddamn, Kirby! You waited til last minute." There was a pause and more static. "Get your ass back here ASAP to fill out the damn forms. How about Kistler? Has he gone off his rocker too? Frankly, after that incident with Finsley and the hooch girl he's not too popular around here."

Now the static was Hank's fault. He gazed down at the dull shine of his black shoes. He had not worn them since Australia. "No," he answered with a soft whisper, "just me."

"Well, OK Kirby. I'll see you when you get back to Lai Khe."

The static died in Hank's ear as the major hung up. He moved closer to the window. The PFC clerks, their mouths open in dismay, silently observed him.

The Freedom Bird was alone now, the stairs having been pulled away and the door closed. It seemed to glint in the bright, hot sun. The whine of its jets came through the window and their hazy, hot waves of heat shimmered, portraying the mighty beast as a huge mirage. It lurched forward, turning, and then accelerated to a taxiing speed as it headed for the runway.

The tears pouring down Hank's cheeks belied his contentment. As the Freedom Bird gathered speed and raced down the runway, he felt a sense of purpose never before experienced. For today he knew who he was, and he was satisfied.

He was what mattered most. He was now a Dick Kistler. He was now a Franklin, a Tucker, a Nordstrom, even a Higbee, and a Woodson. He was all of them and all of the others like them, and they were like him.

And their faces came before his eyes, one-by-one, as the Freedom Bird lifted off and angled up into the blue of the sky.

For he, too, had missed the Freedom Bird.

GLOSSARY

A

A-CAV – Armored cavalry assault vehicle. A modified APC equipped with two M-60s in addition to a .50 cal machine gun.

ACR – Armored Calvary Regiment

AIT – Advanced Individual Training. Specialized hands-on training and field instruction designed to provide a soldier with expertise in a specific career field.

AO – Area of Operations (AO)

APC – Armored Personnel Carrier

APO – Army Post Office

ARTY – Artillery

ARVN – Army of the Republic of Vietnam; the South Vietnamese Regular Army, usually referred to as "arvins."

ASAP – As Soon As Possible

B

BANGALORE TORPEDO – A log-shaped high explosive device.

BATTALION – Basic military organization commanded by a lieutenant colonel. A battalion consists of companies.

BDA – Bomb Damage Assessment

BEEHIVE – Anti-personnel, direct-fire shell carrying several thousand small steel darts or "flechettes."

BERM – A rise in the ground such as a small dike.

BIG RED ONE – Nickname for the 1st Infantry Division, based on the red numeral "1" on the division shoulder patch. "If you're gonna be one, be a Big Red One!"

BLOOPER – M-79 grenade launcher

BOONEY-HOPPING, BOONIES – Term used by US troops in Vietnam to reference the remote countryside as opposed to urban areas.

BRIGADE – Basic military organization commanded by a colonel and belonging to a Division. (See Division)

C

C-4 – Extremely stable plastic explosive carried by infantry soldiers. Since it can be safely burned, soldiers would often break off a small piece of it for heating water or C-rations.

C&C SHIP, also CNC SHIP – Command and Control helicopter used by the commander at the Battalion, Brigade, or Division to direct battle action.

CHICOM – A grenade or other weapon manufactured in Communist China.

CHICOM POTATO MASHER – Chinese Communist manufactured stick-style hand grenade having a distinctive appearance.

CIB – Combat Infantryman Badge

CLACK-CLACK – The sound of a Claymore mine detonator being depressed.

CLACKER – Firing device ("exploder") for triggering Claymore mines and other electrically initiated demolitions.

CLAYMORE – Command-detonated and directional anti-personnel mine that fires a 60-degree fan-shaped pattern of steel balls.

CP / CP BUNKER – Command Post

C-RATIONS – Individual canned, pre-cooked, and prepared wet ration.

CO – Commanding Officer

COMPANY – Organizational unit commanded by a captain and consisting of two or more platoons. An Artillery Company is known as a Battery. A Cavalry Company is called a Troop.

COMMO / RADIO COMMO – Communications

CONCERTINA WIRE – Coiled barbed wire with razor-type ends.

D

DA – Department of the Army

DEFCON – Defensive Concentration. A means for establishing a registration point for artillery or mortar rounds.

DEROS – Date of Expected Return from Overseas

DETCORD – A long, rope-like plastic explosive.

DEUCE-AND-A HALF – Two-and-a-half-ton truck

DIVISION - Military unit usually consisting of a headquarters and two or more Brigades.

DIVISION AO – Area of Operations for a Divsion.

DMZ – Demilitarized Zone

DONUT DOLLY / DONUT DOLLIES – Young women from the Red Cross who were stationed in many of the rear areas. Some were known to visit troops in desolate areas out in the field.

DUST-OFF – A helicopter used for medivacs of wounded soldiers.

E

EM – Enlisted Men

EXEC – Executive Officer

F

FAC – Forward Air Controller

FATIGUES – Combat uniform, green in color. Jungle fatigues were lightweight and multi-pocketed.

FIRST SHIRT – A first sergeant.

FISHHOOK – A geographical area of the border between Vietnam and Cambodia shaped like a fishhook, and called such by the military.

FO – Forward Observer. The FO calls fire missions to Artillery.

FREEDOM BIRD – The airplane on which soldiers left Vietnam.

G

GRUNT – Nickname for infantrymen in Vietnam.

GUNSHIP – Armed helicopter.

GUNG-HO – Overly enthusiastic.

H

HE – High Explosive

H & I – Harassment and Interdiction. Random artillery fire in hopes of interfering with the enemy.

HOOCH – Soldiers living quarters, or a native hut in Vietnam.

HOWITZER – Type of artillery piece.

HQ – Headquarters

HUEY – A utility military helicopter powered by a single turbo-shaft engine, with two-blade main and tail rotors.

HUMPIN'– To slog through rural areas on foot.

HUNTER-KILLER Teams – These were typically two helicopters, a Loach, and a Cobra gun ship operating in tandem. The concept was that the Loach would fly low and in tight circles to find the enemy. When the enemy was spotted, the Cobra gunship would use their miniguns and rockets to attack.

I

ILLUM – Illumination. A parachute flare usually fired by a mortar or artillery piece.

IOBC – Infantry Officer Basic Course

J

JD SCHOOL – Jungle Devil School. For orientation of new replacements to the particulars of the Brigade's operations

K

KIA – Killed in Action

KLICK – Kilometer (.62 miles)

L

LIGHT FIRE TEAM – Two helicopter gunships (usually Cobras) operating in tandem.

LOACH – Small, green, light observation helicopter.

LOOIE – Lieutenant

LRRP – Long-Range Reconnaissance Patrol

LURPS – Name referring to LRRP.

LYSTER BAG – A 36-gallon canvas water bag.

M

M-60 – American-made caliber 7.62mm, belt-fed machine gun. The M-60 gunner is accompanied by an ammo bearer that carries the belted ammo in cans.

MEDEVAC – Medical Evacuation by helicopter (see Dust-off).

MERMITE CAN – Insulated containers used to keep hot food warm in the field.

MORTAR – A muzzle-loading short tube cannon that throws projectiles with low velocity at high angles.

MOS – Military Occupational Specialty

MP – Military Police

MPC – Military Payment Currency. The scrip U.S. soldiers used in Vietnam.

N

NAPALM – Incendiary bomb of a mixture of a gelling agent and gasoline or a similar fuel delivered by fighter-bombers often flying tactical air support.

NCO / NONCOM - Non-Commissioned Officer

NDP – Night Defensive Position

NVA – North Vietnamese Army or a soldier of same.

O

O'CLUB – Officer's Club

OCS – Officer Candidate School

OJT – On the Job Training

OPCON – Operational Control

OSCAR – Military phonetic for the letter "O".

OV-10 BRONCO – American turboprop aircraft. One of its primary missions was forward air control (FAC) to spot targets by white phosphorous rockets for tactical air strikes.

P

PFC – Private First Class

PIASTER – South Vietnamese currency. In 1968, 300 piasters = approx. $2.50 US.

PLATOON – An organizational unit consisting of squads under the command of a platoon leader with the rank of lieutenant. Most times in the First Infantry Division in Vietnam, platoons were under-strength and consisted of two rifle squads and a weapons squad with two M-60s. Total number of men including the platoon leader and platoon sergeant was around 30, plus or minus.

POP SMOKE – Ignite a smoke grenade to signal a ground position to aircraft.

PX – Post Exchange. A military store.

R

R and R – Rest and Recreation. A three- to seven-day vacation from the war for a soldier.

RECONING – Reconnaissance. Going into the jungle for observation purposes attempting to identify enemy activity.

REGS – Army Regulations

REMF – Rear Echelon Motherfucker

RIF – Reconnaissance-In-Force

RIFFING – Conducting a RIF.

ROGER – Message received and understood.

ROTC – Reserve Officer's Training Corps

RPG – Rocket-Propelled Grenade

RTO – Radio Telephone Operator. The soldier who carried his unit's radio on his back in the field.

S

SAPPER – Small enemy commando team used to infiltrate and destroy military positions usually with satchel or bangalore explosives.

SHORT-TIMER – Soldier nearing the end of his tour.

SITREP – Situation Report

SLICK – UH-1 (Huey) helicopter used for transporting troops in tactical air assault operations.

SPEC-4 – Specialist 4th Class; spec-four. An Army rank immediately above private first class.

SPEC-5 – Specialist 5th Class; spec-five. Equivalent to a sergeant, but usually with a specialist rather than a formal leadership role.

SPOOKY / SPOOKIES – AC-47s. A propeller-driven aircraft with 3 miniguns capable of firing 6,000 rounds per minute, per gun. The miniguns were on one side of the plane which would bank to one side to fire.

SQUAD – A small military unit that when combined with other squads makes up a platoon. A rifle squad was often sub-divided into two fireteams. Weapons were mostly M-16s with some carrying M-79 grenade launchers ("bloopers").

STEEL POT – Standard U.S. Army helmet. The steel pot was the outer metal cover.

T

TAC-AIR – Tactical air strikes by fighter bombers.

TAOR – Tactical Area Of Responsibility, geographically.

TET – Tet Offensive: A major uprising of the Viet Cong, VC sympathizers, and NVA characterized by a series of coordinated attacks against military installations and provincial capitals throughout Vietnam. It occurred during the lunar New Year holiday (known by the Vietnamese as *Tet*) on January 31, 1968.

TOC – Tactical Operations Center

TOP – An affectionate term for the first sergeant.

TOPO MAP – Topographical map

TRACERS – Rounds of ammunition chemically treated to glow so that their flight can be followed.

U

V

VC – Viet Cong

VMI – Virginia Military Institute

VT – Variable Time Proximity Fuse

W

WATER BUFFALO – Horizontally mounted tank shaped like an oversize hot water heater, mounted on a two wheel trailer, and containing approximately a 400-gallon supply of potable water.

WEAPONS – **.50 Caliber vs .51 Caliber machine gun**: American and Allied forces had .50 caliber and NVA had Chinese/Russian .51 caliber machine guns, which could use .50 caliber ammunition. **81mm mortars vs 82mm mortars**: Same as with calibers. The NVA used 82mm mortars and mortar tubes which could also fire 81mm mortars.

WHITE PHOSPHORUS – An explosive round emanating white smoke from burning phosphorus. Often used by Air Force FACS flying OV-10s to spot targets for tactical airstrikes.

WILCO – Will Comply, understand.

WILLIE PETER – Slang for white phosphorus.

WORLD, "THE WORLD" – America/Home.

X

XO – Executive Officer. The second in command of a military unit.

www.hellgatepress.com

CPSIA information can be obtained
at www.ICGtesting.com
Printed in the USA
BVHW031924110820
586131BV00003B/9/J

9 781555 719845